DS HUNTER KERR INVESTIGATIONS

Books 1-3

Michael Fowler

Heart of the Demon
Cold Death
Secrets of the Dead

DS HUNTER KERR
INVESTIGATIONS

Published by Sapere Books.

24 Trafalgar Road, Ilkley, LS29 8HH

saperebooks.com

Copyright © Michael Fowler, 2022
Michael Fowler has asserted his right to be identified as the author of this work.
All rights reserved.

No part of this publication may be reproduced, stored in any retrieval system, or transmitted, in any form, or by any means, electronic, mechanical, photocopying, recording, or otherwise, without the prior written permission of the publishers.
This book is a work of fiction. Names, characters, businesses, organisations, places and events, other than those clearly in the public domain, are either the product of the author's imagination, or are used fictitiously.
Any resemblances to actual persons, living or dead, events or locales are purely coincidental.

BOOK ONE: HEART OF THE DEMON

PROLOGUE

25 July 1988

Gripping one shoulder firmly, with a quick sawing movement he began to slice into the first layer of flesh with the curved edge of the blade.

Tough little bastard.

He'd thought it would be easy to separate the head from the body with the Bowie knife he had recently acquired. However, the neck tissues and sinews were far tougher than he expected and he had to drag the blade repeatedly against the leathery skin. As the knife finally tore into the vertebrae, drops of warm, sticky blood splattered his hands and his clothing.

Not such a tough little bastard now, are you?

He had hoped to torture the creature a lot longer but it had brought about its own death much quicker than he'd wanted.

A little earlier, he had chuckled, watching the rabbit's brown eyes almost bulge from its sockets as he twisted the leather leash tighter round its neck. His own heart had pumped so fast he feared it would burst through his chest and it had felt like his head was ready to explode.

The rush had been almost unbelievable and it had made him exert even more pressure on the leash. That's when the *tough little bastard* dug those buck teeth into his clenched fist, drawing blood — his own blood. He'd almost released his grip on the thrashing rabbit, nearly letting it escape. In a flash of anger, which he later cursed himself for, he had grabbed its twitching back legs, swung it around and smashed its fluffy head against a tree stump.

That had put paid to the life of the New Zealand dwarf.

Sarah is going to be really pissed off when she finds her pet gone. Highfalutin' Sarah, with her lisping posh voice who thinks she's a cut above the others on the street. Yes, she's really going to be pissed when she finds her little Bob-Tail gone. Little Bob-Tail, with its posh imitation jewelled collar, the rabbit she walked around her garden — on a leash, of all things.

He had repeatedly listened to her clucking her tongue against the roof of her mouth and shouting for Bob-Tail to come for his 'din-dins'. It really irritated him. Many a time he had wanted to rip that clucking tongue right out of her snooty little mouth. Luckily for her she lived too near. She didn't realise just how fortunate she was.

She won't be acting so highfalutin' when she finds her dear little Bob-Tail in pieces. Spoilt little brat.

12 October 1993

He drew heavily on the cigarette he'd pinched from his mother's packet; the packet which was always tucked between the cushion and arm of 'her' chair. He'd been hiding in the bushes for over half an hour and had a good view of the front door of the block of flats when he spotted the regular visitor lock up and leave his car in the unlit car park.

He took a final drag on his cigarette, flicked the remains to the floor and ground it underfoot. Glancing quickly at his watch, and knowing this guest would be at least another hour and a half, he pulled on a pair of leather gloves and moved slowly from the bushes towards the Ford Fiesta. Taking half a tennis ball from his jacket pocket, he placed it over the lock on the driver's door and with a quick bang forced out the air. The suction made the plastic locking mechanism shoot up and the door opened without a sound. He forced a screwdriver into the ignition barrel, turning the handle like a key. The car's engine fired first time and, taking a final look around, he slid into the driver's seat. As he reversed, he gave a wicked smile. No doubt about it — the CID officer was going to be well and truly pissed off when he came out of that flat.

Head bowed from hunched shoulders, jaw resting between his hands, elbows on desk, Hunter Kerr chewed on the end of his pen and double-checked the contents of his most exciting arrest file to date. This was the most tedious part of the job, but also the most important, and being on the evening shift helped his concentration. It meant a virtually empty office, no incessant chatter or the ringing of phones to distract him.

Closing his eyes, he massaged his eyelids and pushed back in his chair. Wiping away the tiredness, he forced them open again and refocused on the document on his computer screen. Then, clicking back into gear, he started tip-tapping the keyboard, putting the finishing touches to the arrest summary.

Over the past week, he and his partner had cleared up twenty-three burglaries committed by a team of four teenage tearaways who were now on remand in a young offender's institution — and that was only the ones they were admitting. Since their arrest, only two house break-ins had been reported. It was obvious the team were responsible for a lot more, but he would probably only know that when they were sentenced and begged him for a prison visit to clear their slate, so they wouldn't be arrested again when they were released.

Hunter was in the final month of his six-month CID aide period and things had gone very well. The contacts and informants he had built up from his previous two-and-a-half years working the streets in uniform had ensured an impressive number of arrests, which had included a ram-raider who had admitted a string of shop burglaries, and a team of chemist burglars who he'd caught in the act with their haul of stolen drugs. It had already earned him a Chief Superintendents commendation and a leg-up into CID.

The strident ringing of the phone on his desk made Hunter jump. He pulled the pen from his mouth and snatched up the handset from its cradle.

'PC Kerr, CID,' he said.

'Hunter,' said an excited voice. He recognised the high-pitched tones of his working buddy, Paul Goodright. 'Listen, I'm up shit creek, the car's been nicked.'

Hunter clamped the handset between head and shoulder and, with pen poised over a pad of paper, made ready to jot down information.

'What do you mean, nicked?'

'Just get the other car and come and pick me up on Church Street.' For a few seconds there was silence, then Paul added, 'And don't say anything to uniform ... yet.'

The call ended.

Hunter rose quickly and began scanning the desks in the office for the other CID car keys. He moved crime reports and files around in other officer's trays, knowing the keys would be somewhere amid the paperwork. At the same time, his thoughts rolled back to a conversation with Paul an hour earlier. His partner had smiled mischievously when he had mentioned he had an enquiry to do and would be back in an hour or two. Paul really meant was that he was off shagging and needed Hunter to cover. And although deep down he had disapproved, Hunter had chosen not to voice his thoughts. After all, Paul was two years longer in service and an established detective. Besides, Hunter enjoyed having Paul as a partner. The pair had hit it off quickly and already established themselves as a formidable partnership in the department. Despite not having the experience of some of the more seasoned detectives in the office, both had more hunger and enthusiasm when it came to chasing villains.

Finally finding the car keys, Hunter took a deep breath. This reminded him of the time two years ago when his car had been stolen; three shit-holes had nicked it to carry out an armed robbery and then crashed it. It had been written-off in the accident and he had lost his pride and joy. He hoped for Paul's sake they would find the CID car without any damage. This could be his job on the line if anything bad happened.

Hunter found his colleague pacing the footpath outside a block of flats on Church Street. As he pulled up beside him, Paul flung open the car door and dropped into the passenger seat.

'This is my worst fucking nightmare. I can't believe that some little bastard's nicked the car. I'll fucking kill him when I get hold of him. It was in the car park at the side there.' He pointed back towards the flats. 'Before I report it in, we'll run round all the dumping spots — and if we don't find it I need you to back me up with a cover story.'

As Hunter pulled away from the kerbside, he could see Paul anxiously wiping away beads of sweat from his brow.

For half an hour, the man drove furiously around the twisting unlit country roads on the edge of town, roaring past slower cars and cutting them up as he forced the Fiesta back into the correct lane. On several occasions he laughed loudly, even though there was no one else to hear. He wondered if that CID guy had discovered the car had gone yet. As he increased speed, the sensation swelled inside him. He felt wired. His alert eyes were as dark as the night around him, and he focused intently on the surroundings as they flew by. Ahead lay a series of bends and he pushed the car's engine until he could feel it throbbing on its mountings. Then he eased off and decided to head back to Barnwell.

He was approaching the outskirts of town when he noticed her standing at a bus stop. Carol Siddons. She was blowing into her hands and stamping her feet. He slung the car hard left and hit the brakes. The tyres squealed as he skidded to a halt beside her.

She looked up as he leaned across the passenger seat and wound down the window. Bending down, she peered inside, squinting to see who the driver was. 'Oh, it's you,' she said. 'Where did you get this from?'

'Nicked it,' he said. 'And guess what? It's a fed's car.'

'Yeah, all right, spin me another.'

'Don't believe me, eh? Well, look at this then.' He picked up the police radio handset from the dash and thrust it towards her. 'Believe me now?'

She started giggling. 'Bloody hell, you're going be in some serious shit if they catch you.'

'Naw, no chance of that. Fancy a spin?'

'You are joking.'

'No, come on. I'm gonna dump it after this. I'll give you a run round and then drop you off home before I get shut.' He sensed her hesitate. 'It's freezing out there and the bus might not come for ages.' He flipped up the door catch and pushed it open. The glow of the interior light shone on his grinning face. 'Come on, live on the edge.'

Carol Siddons looked around. Nothing stirred. She edged forward apprehensively, took another look around, and then slipped into the passenger seat, slamming the door behind her. 'Let's get out of here fast, you crazy bastard.'

He pressed hard on the accelerator and the Fiesta screeched away.

As he tore around the country roads, he was conscious of Carol's excited jabberings, though he was unable to catch exactly what she was saying as he concentrated on the narrow lane ahead, his focus shooting back and forth between road and rearview mirror. His arms ached as he gripped the steering wheel, and as he checked his speedometer, he realised he was shaking and sweating profusely.

As he threw the car into a sharp bend, far too late he spotted the rear lights of another car. Instinctively, he smashed his foot down on the brake. His effort was in vain and there was a thump as the Fiesta smashed into the back of the other vehicle. In a split-second reaction, he swung the steering wheel to the right and the tyres protested with a concerted squeal. There was a loud scraping noise as metal gouged metal, and the car in front bucked and slewed sideways towards a wall by the side of the road.

He felt the Fiesta's engine surge and almost stall as he fought to disentangle it from the other car. It crabbed sideways for several yards before he managed to bring it under control and point it back in the direction he had been heading. Glancing back, he saw the other car had embedded itself in the stone wall. Suddenly, there was a loud whoosh as the front end of the crashed car exploded in a fireball. Within seconds, searing incandescent gashes of red and yellow flame were licking from beneath the wheel arches and up onto the bonnet and windscreen.

'Fucking hell!' Carol screamed.

He hammered the accelerator and, with a squeal of rubber on tarmac, sped away from the carnage.

Every nerve in his body was straining and he became acutely conscious of each sound as he sped through the countryside.

After ten minutes, he found the unmade track that wound its way towards the old pit coking plant, no longer in production since the demise of the mine five years previously. He braked sharply and the car slid on the rutted and muddy surface before coming to a halt. Throwing open the driver's door, he jerked out his head and threw up violently into a puddle of oily water.

'You crazy bastard!' he heard Carol shout. 'You fucking crazy bastard! You've killed them!'

He glared at her. She was white as a ghost. He studied her features. He had always thought she was pretty, and yet now in a surreal way he found her scared look even more attractive. A tingling sensation erupted in his groin.

Snapping himself out of his thoughts he launched himself out of the Fiesta and listened intently. Every sound was distant. They had not been followed. He could see finger-like wisps of fog drifting over the fields surrounding them and he knew that in an hour or so its blanket would provide cover for him to disappear and for the car to lie undiscovered until at least first light.

Carol joined him. She was shouting, swearing and stabbing his chest with her finger.

'Pipe down, for Christ's sake,' he spat back, wiping his mouth with the sleeve of his sweatshirt.

'You're fucking mad. Did you see what happened to that car you hit? It blew up. Jesus. They're probably fucking dead. I can't believe this. We are in some serious shit now. You know that, don't you?'

He put a finger to his mouth and moved towards her. Then he grabbed her shoulders and fixed her with a stare. There was panic and fear in Carol's eyes. He needed to calm her down. 'Everything's gonna be okay. Don't worry.'

'Don't worry, he says. They're probably dead, for fuck's sake, you stupid bastard.'

'Don't call me stupid, Carol. I'm not stupid.' His features took on a distinct hardness and his dark eyes became glassy.

'No, you are not stupid,' she growled, screwing up her eyes. 'You're fucking crazy.'

He snapped. The punch was swift, smashing into her face. He felt her nose give and heard the crack as the bridge broke. A film of tears flooded her eyes as she sank to her knees.

Gulping back sobs, she glanced up at him, 'Now you've fucking done it. You're fucking mental. I'm going to the cops myself,' she choked.

He unfastened the buckle on his belt, whipped it through the loops of his waistband and gripped both ends. It was around Carol's neck in a second and as he tightened it around her throat, he saw her big brown eyes bulge.

Just like Bob-Tail's.

A malevolent look masked his face as he pulled her close. The corners of his mouth curled upwards as she thrashed and clawed for survival. Less than a minute later he squeezed out her last breath.

Bob-Tail is staring back. Didn't someone once tell him that the image of their killer was captured in their eyes as they died?

Well, mine is the last face she'll ever see and Carol Siddons is not going to identify me to anyone.

DAY ONE

6 July 2008

She bucked and jerked wildly and he had to bear down all of his twelve stone onto her wiry yet well-toned young body as her limbs smacked against his... She was fighting for her life.

Then the air exploded from her chest in a heavy moan and she stopped thrashing.

Gasping for breath and drenched in sweat, he pushed himself up from her limp figure. He'd thought she was never going to die, amazed at the fight she had put up. He took several deep breaths and tried to slow his racing heartbeat, watching with fascination as dark viscous blood belched from her eye sockets, joining other rivulets which were already matting her dark bob of hair and forming a pool around her head.

Bending down, he scraped the mess from his knife into the dusty earth and then dropped it into his coat pocket and set to work.

He couldn't leave her body here.

Dragging the bloodied corpse by the wrists along the flagstone floor, he soon found himself gasping for breath again, and he could feel fresh beads of sweat tickling his ribcage as he hauled her towards the barn entrance.

Then a distant unfamiliar noise caught his attention; a noise which didn't belong to the surroundings. He paused and listened. It was coming nearer. He dropped the girl's arms and dashed to a slit in the barn wall, threw himself against the damp stone and twisted sideways to peer through the gap without being seen. For a split-second the sunlight blurred his vision but as it cleared, he spotted a flat-back lorry bouncing along the uneven farm track, coming his way.

He closed his eyes and held his breath, gritting his teeth. He couldn't believe his bad luck. He had sought out this place especially for its remoteness, visiting it at different times over the past few weeks to finalise his plan. In all that time no one had come near and now, today of all days, he had a visitor. For a few seconds he thought about killing the driver, but then realised he didn't know this adversary.

He looked back along the lane. The truck was only a few hundred yards away and there was no sign of it stopping.

He took one last look at the lifeless form, realising he had no other choice but to make his escape, leaving behind this bloodied mess. He couldn't afford to be caught. Not after all this time.

'Damn,' he cursed, realising he wouldn't be able to finish off what he had set out to do. He slipped the playing card from his trouser pocket and, suit side up, placed it over the gaping wound in the middle of her chest. Now was the time to show them that this was his handiwork.

Dennis O'Brian swung the Bedford lorry through the broken entranceway that led to the tumbledown farm and braked sharply, throwing up a cloud of dust. Surveying the old Yorkshire stone buildings in a bad state of repair, he smiled to himself. Then, making a quick call on his mobile, he shut down the engine, flung open the driver's door and leapt out of the cab. For a good few seconds he scanned the ramshackle buildings, weighing up which portions of stone would reap the most rewards.

Then he froze and his heart skipped a beat as he caught the sound of running feet. He was about to leap back into his truck when he realised the footfalls were growing fainter. *Whoever had been here was legging-it*, he thought. A grin snaked across his mouth and he chuckled to himself. Bet it was another stone thief who thought he was going to be caught.

As he stepped out of the sunlight into the dimness of the barn's interior, he wasn't prepared for what greeted him. Sprawled across the uneven dirt floor was a lifeless and bloody form. Only from the clothing could he tell it was a girl; the injuries inflicted upon her were like nothing he had ever seen before.

He began to retch as he fished in his jeans pocket for his mobile.

As he pushed the CID car door shut with his hip, Detective Sergeant Hunter Kerr paused for a moment and gathered his thoughts while casting his gaze out over the very active crime scene before him. He watched a line of uniformed officers, regular intervals apart, striding slowly through waist-high crops, their white short-sleeved shirts standing out against a backdrop of lush green trees.

Above him the Force helicopter hovered, the drumming noise of its rotor blades disturbing the peace of the surroundings.

He had raced here at breakneck speeds, listening to updates being broadcast over his radio. By the time he arrived, he had enough information to formulate a picture in his mind of what had happened.

Scanning the surroundings with his steel blue eyes, he knew that in one of the dilapidated and derelict farm buildings ahead a young girl's battered body had been found, and that her killer had fled the area only about an hour beforehand. Right now, everything was being done as quickly and thoroughly as possible to track down her murderer and secure the site.

Hunter knew this area well. As an amateur artist, he had visited the location on many occasions and painted the subjects in the vicinity. In fact, the old farm buildings had been captured many times in his oil sketches. It was disconcerting that such atmospheric surroundings, which featured in paintings back home, were now centre-stage in a gruesome discovery.

'Hi Sarge.'

Hunter turned to see his partner DC Grace Marshall tramping towards him at a pace. In her smart, pale grey business suit, Grace looked more the confident professional businesswoman than a hard-working front-line murder detective.

She was corralling her dark hair into an elastic scrunchy. Her face was grim.

'It's bad in there, Hunter. You ought to see what he's done to her.'

'What have we got then, Grace?'

'It looks like it's Rebecca Morris, the fourteen-year-old who was reported missing only a few hours ago. She should have turned up for an exam at her school this morning but didn't.' Grace finished bunching her hair. 'She's in a real mess. Her face is barely recognisable. No one's moved or touched the body. First uniform on site could see from the state of her that she was dead and immediately cordoned off the area. The three nines call came from a guy who had driven here in his lorry. He's now back at the station being interviewed. His story is that he just happened to be driving up the track to the farm for a quick ten minutes rest, but he's got form for theft and it's my guess that he was going to nick some of the stone or slates from here. Anyway, he says he just got out of his cab, heard the sound of someone running from the back of one of the buildings, and then a car starting up and screeching away. When he goes round to look, he finds the girl dead in the barn.'

'And do we believe him?'

Grace shrugged her shoulders. 'No reason not to at the moment. As I say, he is known to us. He's got previous for nicking stone and lead from church roofs. He's also got a couple of convictions for drunk and disorderly, but those are over fifteen years ago, and he's got nothing for violence. And to be fair, he did ring it in and stick around until uniform arrived, and they say he appeared to be genuinely shook up over it. I've had him lodged in a cell and he can stew there for a couple of hours 'til we're clear from here. I'll get a statement from him and then kick him out.'

'Any description of the person he disturbed?' Hunter asked.

'No, unfortunately not. Well gone before he got to the barn. The guy says he heard a car or van driving off up the dirt track over there.' Grace pointed to a small copse of trees several hundred yards away.

It was warmer than he'd anticipated and Hunter tugged at the crisp collar of his blue shirt. Before he had shot away from the station he had slung on a jacket. Now he wished he hadn't and he undid the top button of his shirt and loosened his tie.

'Where does that track go to, Grace?' he asked, pointing at a line of bushes just beyond the old farm buildings.

'It leads up to a B road half a mile away. It takes you past the Ings and eventually brings you out near the village of Harlington. I've got uniform to seal off that area as well.'

'Okay, good job, Grace. Are Scenes of Crime here?'

'Just arrived. The forensic pathologist and the senior investigating officer are also en route. Everything should be in place in the next hour.'

Hunter realised it was an ideal opportunity to slip off his jacket and make the most of the warm breeze drifting across the fields. Going to the rear of his CID car he sprang open the boot and dropped his coat into the back. Then, pulling the sides of his shirt from his sticky and clammy skin, he reached into one of the storage boxes and pulled out a white forensic suit and set of shoe covers. He handed these to Grace and then pulled out another set for himself.

'Come on then, show me what we've got,' he said as he stepped into one leg of the protective suit.

Having satisfied themselves that all the relevant evidence sites were secured, Hunter and Grace made their way back to the murder scene, carefully following the police cordon tape, past the ruined farmhouse building and into a tumbledown barn. Streams of light burst through gaps between the old roof timbers where slates had become dislodged or broken, but despite the sunlight the interior was cool.

The body lay unceremoniously on the dirty stone slab floor, a pool of thick, congealed blood around the head and shoulders. The battered and swollen face was caked in blood. Where the eyes should have been, only two dark sockets crusted in dried blood looked back. At first glance, because of the injuries, if Hunter hadn't already been told he was looking at the face of a young girl, he would never have known. The arms were outstretched above the head and the hands had already been forensically bagged. The girl's T-shirt and padded pink lace bra had been pulled up, exposing her small pale breasts. A huge gash exposed the breastbone, and other less deep cuts covered her abdomen. Her jeans were undone but still around her hips.

In another white forensic suit, bending over the cadaver, he recognised Professor Lizzie McCormack. Slim and petite, in her early sixties, with features not dissimilar to the actress Geraldine McEwan, she had dutifully earned herself the nickname 'Miss Marple'. She was one of the small number of British forensic experts who had been invited to work with American scientists at the Tennessee body farm, studying detection experiments on decomposing murder victims, and had gained national recognition in the location of human remains and the linking of offenders to the scene.

He was pleased Professor McCormack had been called out. Hunter had first seen her at work a year ago when the remains of a young mother had been found in a muddy ditch just outside town. She was one of a handful of forensic botanists in the country and had been able to establish that the pollen found on the shoes of the girl's partner exactly matched the type found in the ditch. Not only had this evidence broken the man's story but also, such was her presence in the witness box, the jury had no difficulty in reaching a guilty verdict and he'd been sentenced to 22 years in jail. It had been a good result.

Her light-grey eyes looked up from the dead girl and, from behind a pair of thin gold-framed spectacles, fixed his. 'Detective Sergeant Kerr, long time no see,' she greeted him in her soft Scottish lilt.

Her welcome surprised him. 'You've remembered me after all this time,' he said.

'With a fine Scottish name like that, how could I forget you?'

'And there's me thinking it was because of my good looks.'

She smiled, tut-tutted, and gave him a quick dismissive shake of her head. 'By the way, before I start my examination, I think you need this.' She handed him a clear plastic exhibit bag. Inside was a playing card, its reverse side facing him.

He turned it over. The seven of hearts. He gave a quizzical frown.

'My sentiments exactly,' the pathologist responded. 'That card was partially covering the gaping wound you can see in the centre of her chest.' She turned her attention back to the cadaver.

Hunter watched her move painstakingly around the body, her every move captured on video. The samples she pointed to were quickly photographed and bagged by the Scenes of Crime officers and forensic team who followed in her wake. Pausing, she lifted her head towards Hunter and Grace. Glancing over her spectacles, which had fallen down her nose, she enquired, 'Has anyone moved the body?'

Hunter gave Grace a questioning look.

She responded with a shrug and shake of head. 'Not that we know of. The man who found the body couldn't get away quick enough before he phoned in. Though he said he heard someone running away from the scene.'

'Well, the body has definitely been moved. There are scuffmarks in the matted blood on the floor; clearly where she has been dragged. And also, we have the arms outstretched above her head which tend to reinforce that theory.' The pathologist rolled the corpse towards her and exposed an ugly pattern of purple beneath the surface of the back's flesh, the result of the muscles and organs no longer pumping blood around the body, and gravity taking over.

'The lividity is just starting to blanch. Hypostasis is in the early stages and body temperature readings would indicate she has been here for only a few hours. By the drag marks through the blood I would say that someone has attempted to move this body after death.'

'We believe it's a fourteen-year-old girl who was reported missing only a few hours ago. Her name's Rebecca Morris,' said Grace.

'Well, my initial findings would suggest she was most probably murdered less than two hours ago. She has multiple stab and incised wounds to her head and as you can see a sharp instrument has penetrated both eyes. There is also the deep wound to the upper chest. Despite the considerable amount of congealed blood, I can't say for sure yet if she was dead before or after the wounds were inflicted because I have also found this.' Professor McCormack pulled down the neckline of the dead girl's T-shirt a few inches below the throat. With a latex gloved hand, she pointed out several red weals around the front of the neck.

'There is petechial haemorrhaging on the skin which is consistent with some type of ligature being placed tightly around the anterior neck. In other words, she has been strangled with something approximately five centimetres wide. And looking at the nip and graze marks on the side of her upper neck my first thoughts are a belt of some type. The post mortem will give us a better indication.' She snapped off her gloves. 'I've finished now if you'd like to bag up this once dear creature and remove her to the mortuary for me.' She eased herself up gently, her hands clasped around her knee joints. 'The arthritis is playing me up today.'

The smell of death was something Hunter Kerr could never get used to. Despite the air conditioning in the white tiled mortuary, the stench was a nauseating mixture of decaying flesh and stale blood, which enveloped him and which he knew would be clinging to every article of clothing he wore for the remainder of the day. He popped an extra strong mint into his mouth in an effort to cover the smell. The mortuary also brought back the memories of when he had dealt with his first cot-death. The baby had been roughly the same age as his own first-born and all he had seen throughout the procedure was the face of Jonathan superimposed on the dead child. For days after, he had lain awake at night watching the movement of the Moses basket at the side of the bed and listening to Jonathan's breathing pattern.

The girl on the metal slab had been cleaned up and he could now clearly see the horrendous wounds inflicted on her head. The dark mushy sockets, devoid of eyes, gave the face an almost surreal appearance. He had never been squeamish when it came to looking at dead bodies, whatever state they were in, though as a young cop he had never liked having to physically handle the cold flesh. That was a job he'd faced with trepidation and, whenever possible, avoided.

Now in her green pathologist's scrubs, Professor McCormack moved gracefully around the body, her dexterous hands measuring and moving limbs, picking up and setting down the many shiny precision instruments, each having its own function to perform, whether it be cracking and cutting bone or slicing through flesh. She probed orifices with swabs and scraped under fingernails, meticulously noting and labelling each sample, all the while speaking with her soft Scottish brogue into a metal microphone hanging from the ceiling, poised above the cadaver.

'The body is that of a normally developed pubescent white female, and appears generally consistent with the stated age of fourteen years,' she began. Moving to the head, she scrutinised, probed and measured the numerous wounds. 'There is evidence of multiple sharp-force injury,' she continued in a steady voice.

After spending some considerable time counting and detailing each of the head wounds, she moved to the neck. She pointed out several marks to the Scenes of Crime officer and stepped back while close-up photographs were taken. Then, taking a small surgical scalpel, she began the process of incising the yellowing flesh at the base of the neck and peeling the scalp and face completely over the head to reveal a glistening white skull.

Inside fifteen minutes the professor had removed the brain, measured and weighed it, and sliced off small samples of the grey tissue for further analysis. She then began moving down the body, examining the many cuts and gashes inflicted on the upper torso. Within a minute she gave out an elongated 'Mmmm', paused, and caught Hunter's gaze. 'You're going to find this very interesting, very interesting indeed.'

Hunter furrowed his brow.

'That's grabbed your attention, hasn't it?' She grinned, and began circling an index finger above the cadaver's abdomen. 'I thought at first these were minor stab wounds,' she continued, pointing to several regular marks gouged into the flesh. 'These cuts are nowhere near as deep as the others. The blade has only penetrated the first subcutaneous layer.'

Hunter moved in closer, bending over Rebecca's body, focusing on the area Professor McCormick indicated. He stared at the series of consistent slashes above the navel, unable at first to make head-nor-tail of them; that was until he followed the slow deliberate movement of the pathologist's finger, then he did. He could quite clearly make out the letters 'I I V' and a number three lined across the stomach. He glanced at the professor. She looked preoccupied.

'This is a first for me,' she said. 'Well, in the flesh anyway, so to speak, but I have seen photographs of similar markings of corpses and read about this some time ago.' She paused again before continuing. 'What you have here, Detective Sergeant, is the killer's signature. What you make of it is the same as me at the moment, a series of letters or Roman numerals, and what appears to be the number three.' She took a step back while the Scenes of Crime officer moved in with his camera and rattled off a sequence of photographs, its flash highlighting the red marks carved into the marble-like flesh.

'Add to this the playing card, which was found lying across her chest, and I can say with some confidence that this is definitely the killer letting you know it's his or her handiwork. Though, given the viciousness of the attack, I am more inclined to favour that a man's hand is responsible.' The pathologist caught Hunter's startled look. 'I would start by contacting other forces, because it's my guess that this young girl is not his first victim.'

She returned to her examination of the body, and just over an hour later she snapped off her latex gloves and turned to Hunter.

'Many of the wounds to the face and head are regular and suggest a knife of at least ten centimetres in length with an angled blade at its point. Many are stab type wounds, which have penetrated both the facial and muscle tissue of the head, and in places the bone beneath has actually been chipped. The most serious of those are to the eye sockets. Here, the knife has actually sliced through into the brain and penetrated to the extent of ten centimetres. The downward slant of these wounds indicate a continued jabbing action. A real frenzied hacking at the face.' The professor emphasised her words by thrusting her arm up and down several times. 'My other findings are death by asphyxia due to ligature strangulation. The hyoid bone and the thyroid and cricoid cartilages are fractured, which would indicate tremendous pressure around the throat. The marks suggest a belt of some type and I reinforce this by a buckle-mark where it's nipped the upper neck. The mark is so clear that if you find the right belt, I will be able to confirm a match.

'This is a particularly vicious and sustained attack. From the lack of defence injuries, I would suggest she was strangled first and then, as she lay dead or dying, she was stabbed numerous times to the face and head. There is no evidence of any sexual interference, though swabs have been taken for more detailed analysis. It never ceases to amaze me just how cruel the human race is,' she finished as she turned towards the shower room.

'Earlier today, the body of a teenage girl was found in old farm buildings close to the town of Barnwell. Police have identified her as fourteen-year-old Rebecca Morris and confirm that she had been brutally murdered.'

The hairs at the back of the man's head bristled and he could feel his face flush. The rest of the news report became a jumble of words as he stared at the TV, which flicked between scenes showing the regional newsroom and a reporter who was broadcasting in front of the derelict buildings — the farm from earlier.

That was the closest yet to being caught.

He screwed up his face and shuddered, feeling a little light-headed. He had held his breath for far too long as he concentrated on the news report. He exhaled sharply and took in a gulp of air.

In the depths of his mind he recalled the events of the past two days. In the early hours of the night before last, and for most of yesterday morning, he could barely contain his excitement. It had increased ten-fold when he had caught sight of her waiting by the bus stop where he had arranged they should meet. As she climbed into his car, he could feel himself getting an erection. He had to pull the hem of his T-shirt over his lap to hide the bulge.

He could recall the conversation as though it had just happened.

'Didn't think you were going to come.'

'I promised I'd be here, didn't I?' she'd smiled back at him. 'Though I don't know what I'm going to say when Mum and Dad find out I've skipped an exam.'

'That's not going to matter once we get this portfolio done. A modelling agency will soon snap you up and the money you're going to earn will take care of any exam marks,' he'd lied.

In the barn he'd watched her change out of her school clothes, blushing with embarrassment, and managed to shoot several frames of her undressing before she stopped him. She'd put a hand over his lens, with the other arm across her chest, covering the pretty pink cotton bra that hid her small, firm breasts.

He'd laughed and tried to pull her arm away but she'd resisted and got angry.

'I want to go home,' she'd said. 'That's it. I've had enough.' And she'd put her blouse back on.

That's when he'd slapped her across the face. He couldn't believe it when she'd slapped him back. The surprise made him drop his camera.

He'd snatched off his belt without thinking and wound it so quickly round her neck that she barely registered what was happening. He pulled it so tight that the veins at the sides of her temples had swollen and he feared they would burst.

The rest was a blur and over as quickly as it had started. All he could remember was standing over her body, staring at the bloodied mess he had created.

As he had surveyed his work, a surge of power shot through him, tightening every sinew in his body.

He tried to recall if the rush was the same as before and decided this time it had felt better. His erection remained, even when she had breathed her last.

The noise in the background brought him back to the present, and as the vision in his mind blurred, he felt his chest fill with a sense of urgency and excitement again. There was movement in his groin. He was getting erect just thinking about what he'd done.

From the kitchen, he could hear the domestic sounds of his mother getting their evening meal ready. He pointed the remote at the TV and switched over to the other local news channel to see if the story was being aired there, too.

DAY TWO

With a spring in his step, Hunter breezed into the office, humming the tune of *Summer of '69*, the last song he'd heard on the radio as he'd parked in the rear yard. The strong, heady aroma of freshly percolated coffee greeted him and as he unbuttoned his jacket, he saw that most of the squad were already in. The Barnwell Major Investigation Team office-cum-incident room, was a hive of activity and there was a hubbub of excited chatter.

Nothing like a murder to get the energy levels flowing, Hunter thought to himself as he shrugged off his suit jacket and made for his desk.

Draping his jacket over the back of his seat, he levelled another look around the room and dropped down into his chair. The case teams would be fired up, because for the past four months the majority of the detectives had been working on two of the district's old undetected crimes — the strangulation of an 81-year-old woman in her bungalow 25 years ago, believed to have happened after she disturbed the burglar who'd broken into her home and stolen a necklace and £200 in cash — and the discovery of human bones belonging to a man aged between 40 and 50 found in a hedge bottom by a farmer 30 years ago, and although they knew he had died from a head injury they still didn't know his identity. The work had been laborious — poring over old witness statements, cross-referencing interviews with suspects and alibis, and finally checking old exhibits for DNA traces — science that wasn't available when the original crime was committed — yet they hadn't been able to progress either case and the case-files had been returned to the basement.

Grace Marshall handed him his Sheffield United mug.

Hunter sniffed at the freshly brewed tea and mouthed a grateful 'thank you'. He couldn't abide coffee first thing in the morning.

Warm sunlight poured through the large double-glazed windows which ran the length of one side of the office, making Grace's tawny complexion glow, while her mop of brown curls glistened wetly in places.

'Running late?' he said, pointing to her damp hair.

'Don't ask. Mad rush. David's started his new job this morning and wanted to get in there early to make an impression, so I've had to sort out

Robyn and Jade's arrangements for when they finish school this afternoon. They're going to my dad's,' she said, turning to a mirror in the office and softly patting at her hair. The damp curls were beginning to cascade onto her shoulders. 'Do I look a mess?'

He smiled, thinking of the similar routine at home, or rather the organisational skills of his wife, Beth, whenever he was working on a murder enquiry. Many times, he had grabbed a quick shower and shave at work while working back-to-back sixteen-hour days, telephoning home often and updating Beth with new timescales. She never complained when he finished the day off with a swift beer at the pub with the rest of the team just to wind down. He was constantly amazed at how placid she was about it all — especially when he got home mentally drained, and just sunk into his armchair, not wanting to talk about his day. He knew how fortunate he was to have someone so understanding and supportive as Beth for a wife. Many police marriages ended in divorce.

'Been there, done that, and no, you look fine,' Hunter smiled.

Overnight, the Home Office Large Major Enquiry System (HOLMES) team had been busy, going through the few reports currently in existence and drawing up the timeline sequence on the whiteboard at the front of the room. A school photograph of Rebecca Morris, fresh-faced and smiling in her school uniform, was positioned near the start of the line at the time when she had been reported missing. A couple of other pen marks showed where there had been reported sightings, and the last indicator showed the time when her stabbed and battered body had been discovered. Alongside that last mark several post mortem images had been affixed and the close-up shots of the curious symbols gouged into her abdomen were particularly gruesome.

A sudden clatter and scraping of chairs caused Hunter to turn his head. Detective Superintendent Michael Robshaw, appointed Senior Investigating Officer for this investigation, was making his way to the incident board at the front of the room.

Hunter had known Michael Robshaw a long time. At an early stage of his CID career he had been his DI, and the one who had first suggested that Hunter apply to join Drugs Squad. He had also supported him for promotion to DS five years ago. Hunter liked and respected his boss and admired how he kept his feet on the ground, despite his elevation in rank.

He had maintained his reputation as a thinking man's policeman. Some officers who climbed up the ranks sold themselves out to Home Office bureaucracy, but Robshaw employed a common-sense and practical approach to today's policing.

Michael Robshaw swelled his broad chest, removed his spectacles, rubbed his handkerchief around the lenses and replaced them on his nose.

'Ladies and gents,' he began in his deep, broad South Yorkshire accent.

The room went quiet.

'Rebecca Morris.' He pointed to the school photograph. 'A fourteen-year-old girl with everything to live for. According to her mother, she left home at a quarter to eight yesterday morning, wearing her school uniform, saying she was going in to school early to hand in some work and to prepare for an exam which she should have sat at ten a.m.'

He pointed to the next timeline sequence.

'At five to eight, she was seen by a school friend at a bus stop on the main road, five hundred yards from her home. She was still in school uniform. The girl who saw her states this was unusual, as Rebecca normally walked to school. She was on the opposite side of the road and shouted across to ask her what she was doing. Rebecca said she had to visit an aunt first to pick up some books for school. From the initial missing-from-home enquiries, we are almost certain this was a lie. She never got to school. The school secretary contacted her mother at ten-fifteen yesterday morning after she failed to turn up for the exam. At eleven, after making several phone calls and finding her daughter's phone switched off, her mother contacted the police.'

He moved along the board.

'The next sighting we have is the discovery of her body at two p.m. yesterday in the barn of a derelict farm between the villages of Harlington and Adwick-on-Dearne, by a local thief who has admitted being there for the purpose of stealing stone. We are as confident as we can be at this time that he had nothing to do with this murder.'

He broke off to lick his dry lips.

'She was found wearing a T-shirt and jeans and there was no sign of her school uniform or the school bag she had left home with. A fresh search for those items is to be carried out later this morning.'

He paused and straightened. At six-foot-five, he had an imposing presence.

'Several avenues have to be gone down today. We need to know if she actually did get on a bus — and if she did, which bus was it and where did it drop her off? Are there any other sightings of her, in or out of uniform, in the lead-up to her body being found? Was she meeting anyone? Did she have a boyfriend? These are all questions I'd like answering by the end of the day's play.'

The superintendent pointed to the post mortem photos of Rebecca.

'And to add a different dimension to this enquiry, the pathologist has highlighted a series of marks cut into the girl's stomach. Professor McCormack has every confidence that these are the killer's calling card.' He tapped the photographs showing the symmetrical incisions 'I I V 3' along Rebecca's abdomen. 'I've never seen or known of anything like this. The professor says she is only aware of similar cases from her past work in America. Quite clearly, we are dealing with someone who is very disturbed — and judging by this calling card, we cannot rule out that they haven't struck before.'

He paused again, scrutinising the faces of the MIT detectives, then continued, 'I want to know what the significance of these marks are. What do they mean? Do they have any links to either religion or the occult? What also is the significance of the seven of hearts playing card found placed on the body? Whoever is given that task, check the internet for anything similar. Nothing is ruled in or out.'

Superintendent Robshaw placed a hand, palm flat, against the whiteboard.

'This is a really vicious murder. The extreme violence and sadistic nature of the attack shows we have someone with a very sick mind. We need this person behind bars as soon as possible. I want no stone unturned. Now let's get out there, ladies and gents, and see if we can bring whoever did this awful crime into custody as soon as possible.'

Hunter Kerr hated these moments. He could handle angry and violent men with no problem, but facing grief-stricken parents, particularly the parents of young children, brought a lump to his throat. Rebecca Morris was the victim of a crime that haunts every mother and father. Hunter and Grace had been given the job of visiting Rebecca's parents to tease out as much background information as possible, while bearing in mind the possibility that one or both of them could be involved in the crime.

Before that, they had driven back towards the scene of the murder. Roadblocks were already in place and groups of uniformed officers, some with sniffer dogs, were combing the area around the derelict farm. Specialists were carrying out fingertip searches, and scythes and rakes were being used to hack back the thick undergrowth in the search for clues. A dirt track running from the rear of the farm into the village of Harlington had diversion signs in place, and a white tent protected the area where Rebecca had been found dead.

Young people had started to arrive with bouquets and small teddy bears. Soon there would be a special school assembly in honour of Rebecca, where pupils and staff would probably be reduced to tears. Hunter felt a shiver run down his spine as he drove away from the scene.

This wouldn't be easy, Hunter thought, as he pressed the doorbell at the Morris's home. It was a typical semi-detached house in one of the many council estates in the area, though looking at the PVC door and modern double glazing, he guessed they had bought their own home during the Thatcher era.

During the next hour or so, both he and Grace would be constantly questioning and cross-questioning the parents, probing long forgotten secrets and opening up old wounds, at a time when they were at their most vulnerable.

DC Caroline Blake, who had been appointed as the Family Liaison Officer, greeted them at the door.

'Anything?' Hunter enquired. It was a typical opening between detectives when visiting the homes of murder victims. What it actually meant was, 'Have they revealed or given anything away?' — until Mr and Mrs Morris were alibied, they were suspects.

Caroline Blake shook her head. 'They're just numb. Still finding it difficult to accept that their daughter is dead.' She showed Hunter and Grace into the front room and went off into the kitchen to make a fresh pot of tea.

Hunter was pleased Caroline had been given the job as the FLO. He had interviewed her for the position only two months ago and guessed this was her first case. Despite her newness to the job he knew she would cope admirably.

As soon as they entered the room, Hunter and Grace could see from the dark rings circling their eyes that Mr and Mrs Morris had suffered a sleepless night, and the redness of their eyes revealed many hours of crying. As the questioning began, it was obvious they were trying to be strong. Mrs Morris broke down repeatedly and tears welled in Jack Morris's eyes as he talked about his happy daughter and showed them cards pushed through their door by well-wishers.

Hunter and Grace talked to them for almost two hours, going over home and school routines and asking about Rebecca's closest friends.

'Any boyfriends?' Grace asked.

'There were boys who were friends,' Mrs Morris replied. 'But she had no boyfriends that we are aware of,' she added, glancing at her husband.

They could not give any explanation for Rebecca changing out of her school clothes into the T-shirt and jeans she had been found in. It was a mystery which was tearing at their heartstrings.

'She was a typical teenage girl, loved her boybands, dressing up and playing around with make-up. She was always so cheerful — the life and soul of the house. Rebecca was a very special person who touched the lives of so many people. We don't know anyone who would want to hurt her like this,' said Mr Morris, a film of tears washing over his eyes, and, as he hooked an arm around his wife's shoulder, she began to sob uncontrollably.

'Can you let us see her room?' Hunter said. 'Just in case there's anything which may give us a lead.'

Mrs Morris led them upstairs and to the left of the landing. There was a plaque on the door — *Rebecca's Room* — more than likely put there when she was a young child. A more up to date one, no doubt added by Rebecca, said KEEP OUT — GENIUS AT WORK.

'Do you regularly check her room?' asked Grace.

'Not exactly check. The odd flick round with a duster and a bit of straightening. Rebecca is a very tidy girl — *was*,' Mrs Morris corrected herself and fresh tears welled into her eyes.

Hunter touched her gently on one shoulder. 'I'm afraid we need to do a thorough search of her room. If you find this upsetting you can wait downstairs.'

'No, I'll be okay.' Mrs Morris sniffed and dabbed at her eyes. 'It still doesn't seem real. I feel as though she'll burst through the door at any second.'

Hunter couldn't find the right response and chose to shrug his shoulders as he pushed open the bedroom door. He paused for a second, surveying the surroundings. It was a bright and airy room, a stream of sunshine warming it. The pink and beige walls matched the bedding. Two large purple cushions lay against a pine headboard, surrounded by a horde of fluffy teddy bears and other creatures. He had already gathered from the Morris's that their daughter was still a child at heart. These things reinforced the innocence of the girl. Posters of several boybands adorned the walls, together with photos of A list celebrities snipped out of magazines. Coloured post-its and paper arrows, with handwritten personal comments, such as 'gorgeous' and 'luv u' covered some of them; she had stamped her own identity on this room.

In the centre of the wall, opposite the foot of the bed, was a pinboard filled with photographs. Many were of Rebecca in different poses and in different periods of her young life. All happy scenes. On the beach. At fun parks. Pulling faces. On rides. With family and with friends. He scanned them for the up to date ones. And they were there. Her brown hair longer and styled, blue glistening eyes, a nose that was a little prominent. The word cute came to mind. These were more serious poses — more grown up. A smiling face in a group of her friends, and he wondered for a second which of those she had confided in. These were the last treasured memories Mr and Mrs Morris would have of their daughter.

Hunter and Grace separated and began to move methodically about the room, checking under the bed, dressing table, wardrobe and bedside cupboard. They opened drawers and rifled through her clothing, then picked up books, CDs, DVDs — opening, shaking them and replacing them. The two detectives had done this many times before and were on autopilot as they went about the task. Hunter caught a glimpse of Mrs Morris, motionless in the doorway, hands clenched together, prayer-like and stifling a sob. He wondered if she could feel the presence of her cherished child as they disturbed Rebecca's things. He fired off several questions about her regular habits and then asked, 'Did she have a computer?'

'No, she shared the one downstairs,' said Mrs Morris, 'so we could keep an eye on her, what with these chat room perverts you read about.' Then she checked herself and her voice faltered.

'Did she keep a diary that you know of?'

'No. Not to my knowledge. If she did it was more than likely in her school bag. She did the odd scribble in her school planner, but I've not checked that for weeks. She recorded most of her stuff on her mobile. Those are with her.' Mrs Morris paused. 'Who could have done this to her?'

Her face looked tired, care-worn, and dark lines were etched around her eyes from lack of sleep. Hunter wished he had an answer for her.

He gave the room a final once-over. It would probably remain untouched for many years to come, the Morris's memorial to Rebecca. A shrine to their beautiful daughter. He felt a cold shudder run down his spine. Someone had walked over his grave.

Hunter closed the bedroom door with a sense of foreboding. He had hoped for an early breakthrough, a discovery. A name, or an indication why such an innocent girl had met such a brutal death. But there had been nothing. If Rebecca had any secrets, they hadn't found them in her room.

There was a deathly silence about the evening, broken only by the soft squelch of the man's rubber soled training shoes on the wet garden path as he moved through the fine drizzle. Despite the rain, it was still warm. He glanced back up the garden where the lounge window was illuminated in a warm yellow glow, and he could see flashes of light from the television. He looked at his watch — his mother would be engrossed in one of her favourite soaps. He wouldn't be disturbed for at least half an hour.

He snapped back the padlock on the old shed and slowly eased open the paint-blistered door. It creaked slightly and the sound prompted a cascade of images from the horror movies he had watched. He stiffened and glanced over his shoulder. The evening was still, the rain keeping everyone indoors. He stepped inside and secured the door after him. The interior was dingy and he had to strain his eyes to survey the muddle of garden equipment and discarded household items. Finally, his sight adjusted and he spotted the pile he wanted. He pulled at the wooden packing crates, garden tools and old blankets he had placed there several days ago, then opened one of the plastic sacks that lay in an ordered heap. A pungent, musty smell hit his nostrils, and images of a girl struggling flashbacked into his mind. He shuddered, then composed himself.

Item by item, he spread out her school shirt, skirt and tie and then pulled books, a pencil case and the mobile phone from the pink bag she used for school. He double-checked the battery and SIM card — they were disconnected. He'd read somewhere that while the battery and SIM were connected a mobile could still be tracked, even if it wasn't in use.

After yesterday's close shave he couldn't afford to take chances. *Not now, after all this time.*

He picked up her school shirt — white cotton, freshly washed — and buried his face in it, sniffing the fragrance of her deodorant. His flesh went goosey and a cold sensation tingled up his spine. The muscles of his face twitched involuntarily as he savoured a final glimpse of her face in his mind. He was getting erect again.

He would have to get rid of all these soon.

Folding the clothing carefully, mentally double-checking each item's return to the bag, he replaced everything and he confidently stepped out into the warm summer rain.

DAY SIX

In a contemplative mood, Hunter Kerr stared into the bathroom mirror, ran a hand around his freshly shaved jawline, dabbed water from the sink onto his head, and then rubbed a wet hand through his brown receding hairline, temples now flecked with grey. He stroked the few mature hairs slowly, for a second thought about colouring them, then caught himself, and smiled at his vanity.

He wandered back into the bedroom, fastened up his shirt and slung a loose tie around his neck. Beth was still snug beneath the duvet. He glanced at the bedside alarm clock and saw that in twenty minutes' time it would be buzzing away. Within five minutes of it ringing, Beth would be into her routine, sorting out their two sons for school and preparing herself for her job at the doctors' surgery where she worked part time as a nurse practitioner. It amazed him how she could juggle managing the house and their boys, and still hold down a professional career. He knew he couldn't do it. Hunter bent down and kissed her forehead. She half opened her eyes and smiled.

'Just off, love. Don't know what time I'll get in. Got a busy day ahead.'

She muttered something incoherent and rolled over.

Hunter crept downstairs, hoping not to wake his two boys, and eased the local weekly newspaper from the letterbox before creeping through to the kitchen at the rear.

He made tea lazily, dunking a teabag directly into a mug, at the same time slotting two slices of bread into the toaster. He made the tea strong, adding a heaped teaspoon of sugar to wake himself up. Waiting for the toast, he stood by the kitchen sink, mug clutched to his chest, staring dreamily through the window, taking in the sights of the morning freshness stirring his garden. Everywhere was still damp from the overnight rain, and a fine mist was rising as the warm sun slowly appeared over the distant treetops. How fortunate he was. His home overlooked farmland that formed part of the old Wentworth estates. A gate at the bottom of his garden opened up onto fields and many a time he had watched his two boys, Jonathan and Daniel, making dens in the bushes, or jumping onto the freshly baled straw.

He recalled his own first home as a child. A terraced house with a shared backyard. It was all his parents could afford, but he could still remember being told by his father that it was far better than the tenement building he and his mother had left behind in Glasgow.

Many times, his parents had reminded him how fortunate he was. They had been born in Scotland and brought up in a time of economic hardship, deciding in the 1970s to move down to Yorkshire to make a better life for themselves. They had never returned north of the border, choosing to settle when he had been born, six months after their arrival.

As he bit into his first slice of fresh toast, Hunter opened up Barnwell's weekly paper. The headline '**BRUTAL MURDER**' shouted back in bold black letters and a cherished family photo of Rebecca Morris, a faint smile across her face, filled a good portion of the page. There had been very little in the nationals, but he knew the local paper would make great play of the macabre discovery. He pored over the article to check if the killer's handiwork had been leaked but there were no surprise revelations. Its column inches had used the original police press statement, a brief update by the senior investigating officer, plus the usual quotes from friends and neighbours to embellish the misery, anguish and cruelty of this human tragedy.

Progress was still in its early stages. Now in the sixth day of the investigation, the finishing touches were just being put around the site of the murder, with exhibit after exhibit being logged and bagged for forensics. So far, they'd not found Rebecca's school clothing, bag or personal mobile. It was painstakingly slow work with no stone being left unturned. And within the next hour, the now twenty-strong Major Investigation Team — two additional teams of detectives from district CID had swelled their ranks — would be ready for another day working against the clock.

Hunter and Grace had been allocated the task of interviewing Rebecca's closest friend, Kirsty Evans, who had just returned from holiday to hear the shocking news. As Hunter entered the Tree estate his mind went back to his childhood years when he had roamed these streets with some of his school pals who lived there. It had once been a model of council planning. Sadly, the estate was now rundown, like many others. A new generation of people with a legacy of problems had moved in, not bothered about their neighbourhood or the people who had lived there for years. Consequently, burglaries had increased to fund drug habits and tenants who had the wherewithal to move had left for more peaceful pastures.

They pulled into Hawthorne Close, a small cul-de-sac, and Hunter could see this was not a street that had fallen prey to the dregs of society. It was how he remembered the estate of many years ago. The Evans had spent money refurbishing their property and a garage and extension had dramatically changed the appearance of the former council house.

Mr Evans greeted them. 'It's been a dreadful shock,' he said. 'Rebecca was such a pleasant, friendly girl. Kirsty is very upset.'

Hunter guessed Mr Evans's comments were a hint that they should adopt a soft and sympathetic approach when they interviewed his daughter. He tried to reassure him. 'Don't worry, Mr Evans, we're just here to get some background about Rebecca.'

Mr Evans showed Hunter and Grace into the lounge, told them Kirsty was with her mother and left, saying he had some work to do out the back.

It was obvious Kirsty had been crying. She was younger than Rebecca by two months, but Hunter thought she looked older. A few years older in fact. She could easily have passed for sixteen. Her hair had been cut and coloured at a good salon and she wore tasteful make-up on her newly-tanned face. Her slender figure already had womanly curves.

Hunter made the introductions, but went no further. They had decided that because Grace's daughter, Robyn, was the same age as Kirsty, she would carry out this sensitive interview.

They settled into armchairs beside the settee where Kirsty sat, her mother alongside her, with a reassuring arm around her daughter's shoulders, and positioned themselves to face her. Hunter, the note-taker, sat back, pen poised over his daily journal, while Grace leant forward, her hands clasped together on her lap.

'Kirsty, this is important,' she began. 'We need to catch Rebecca's killer as soon as possible. We need you to tell us everything you know about her. It's also important that you hold no secrets back, even if you think you might get into trouble.'

Kirsty's bloodshot eyes shot open and fixed on the detective.

'Trouble? But we haven't done anything wrong. We're not like that.'

'I'm not accusing you of anything, Kirsty. It's just that in cases like this we can't afford for anything to be held back. We all have things we want to keep hidden sometimes, especially from parents. I have a daughter exactly the same age as you, so I can say that from experience. Trust me, Kirsty, we're not wanting to get you into any trouble.'

'I'm not hiding anything. We don't have anything to hide...' Kirsty glanced sideways at her mother. 'Honest,' she finished.

'Fine, Kirsty, that's just fine. Now we've got that sorted, tell us about Rebecca.'

For the next ten minutes the girl spoke softly in warm affectionate tones about her friend, Rebecca. Her likes and dislikes. What they did in their rooms and what they did outside and at school. There was nothing untoward.

It was typical fourteen-year-old girl stuff, thought Hunter as he wrote.

Kirsty appeared more relaxed now. Grace said, 'Did she ever fall out with anyone? Have any enemies?'

'Not Rebecca. She was quiet and friendly. We're all like that, our group. We keep away from the girls we know who are going to cause trouble.'

'What about boyfriends?'

'None serious. We knocked about with a couple of lads; walked home with them, saw them at the youth club, that kind of stuff. Just acted around with them.'

The replies flowed but Hunter sensed that the sentences felt false, rehearsed. He tried to catch Grace's attention to indicate for her to change tack.

Grace said, 'Did she ever talk about fancying anyone?'

Hunter smiled to himself. It was like she'd read his mind.

Kirsty paused in mid-thought, and then glanced across at her mother.

Grace picked up on the hesitation. 'Come on, Kirsty, what is it?'

For a few seconds the girl stuttered over the words, until she finally got them out. 'Well, it was the other way round, actually. A couple of weeks ago she blurted out that this guy had been coming on to her, pestering her for her mobile number.'

'Where did she tell you this?' Grace edged further forward, trying to make eye contact with Kirsty.

'She told me at the youth club. She came up to me and said she had something to tell me in secret. Whispered it like. And then we went to a corner and she said this guy had come up to her when she was on a ride at the fair and told her how nice she looked, and asked her if he could take some photos of her. I told her that was weird. She said it wasn't like that. He just wanted to take her picture because she was pretty. Rebecca can be a bit naïve when it comes to lads and all that. I think she thought I was making fun of her. She got the hump and said I was only jealous. I didn't want to row with her so I didn't say anything else, even though I still thought it was freaky. Anyway, I asked her who it was, thinking he was from the youth club or something, or maybe a sixth-former, but she said it wasn't anyone from school or anyone I knew. I tried to get it out of her who it was but she started getting angry with me. She said she thought I didn't believe her and that I was thinking she was making it up. I kept telling her I believed her but she wouldn't tell me any more.'

'You mentioned that she met this guy at the fair. Do you know which fair this was at, and when?'

'I can only think it must have been the Feast fair, which came a couple of weeks ago. It's the one that comes every year on the fields at the back of the youth club.'

'Did she say anything else about him? Mention his name or where he came from?' Grace continued.

'Nope. But there was this one time when we were walking home from school and her mobile rang. She looked at the screen and blushed and wouldn't let me see who it was. She never did that, we always told each other everything. Anyway, she answered it and I heard her say she was with someone. She said it was her friend Kirsty. Then she just said, "okay, speak with you later," and cut off her mobile. I asked if it was her boyfriend, just joking like, and she went bright red. She said if I were taking the mess, she wouldn't tell me anything else. I told her I wasn't and then changed it round a bit to try and find out who it was. She said he was really nice and had his own car. She said he kept telling her how pretty she was, and what a nice figure she had. I didn't say anything but I thought it was really weird to say that to Rebecca. Not that she wasn't pretty or anything like, but I mean she hasn't really developed properly yet. You've seen what she's like. She's stick-thin. You know what I mean?'

Grace nodded. 'Kirsty, you said Rebecca told you he had a car. Which lads do you knock about with who have cars?'

'Well, we don't. I mean, we know some of the sixth formers have cars but we don't talk to them. But it's not what she said about him having a car, it's how she said it. I just got the impression that when she said "guy" she actually meant someone a lot older.'

'A man you mean?' asked Grace, taken aback.

'Well, I suppose so, yes.'

For the next hour, Grace backtracked over everything they had discussed. Kirsty faltered at times, glancing at her mum, and repeating what she'd said previously.

Hunter felt Kirsty was holding something back and wanted to jump in and push her for answers but this was Grace's call.

Grace didn't push. At the end of the talk Grace handed Kirsty one of her business cards. She took a pen and underlined her work mobile number.

'If you can think of anything else, Kirsty…' She pressed the card firmly into the girl's palm, making eye contact. 'If you want to talk to me in confidence, call me on this number.' She nudged Hunter and headed for the door.

DAY SEVEN

Because of the repetitive nature of Dougie Crabtree's work, he often found his mind wandering, reminiscing and throwing up rose-tinted images of how this dark and stark landscape once looked when it was the site of the former Manvers Colliery and he had worked here. He shifted his nineteen-stone bulk from one cheek to the other on the vinyl seat in time to the swaying motion of the cab on the huge Komatsu track excavator. His thick, muscular arms effortlessly and skilfully manoeuvred between transmission and hydraulic gears as the crane surged over deep, rutted tracks, while the eighteen-foot-reach mechanical shovel scooped enormous wedges of cloggy grey earth and slopped them into the waiting Caterpillar dumper truck.

What a coincidence this was! He'd started work at the thriving colliery straight from school, then witnessed its demise and dereliction after the Miner's Strike in 1984. Now he was back on the site and involved in its regeneration. Though he hated to admit it, particularly after the struggle, anger and bitterness he had gone through to fight for his pit, it was refreshing to work in the fresh air on a daily basis. The eighty-four acre former colliery and coking plant site was in the throes of a major transformation. The winding gear, coal preparation plant, site offices and coking unit had gradually gone, and in their place were plush industrial units in a landscaped environment. He was toiling on the final phase, reclaiming the old slurry pits to make way for a £130 million scheme, which would see retail, leisure and residential units woven into the vista.

The engine growled and his cab vibrated as the huge bucket gouged the uneven grey surface, scooping out another lump of the toxic earth. The oily surface water bubbled as pockets of methane gas escaped from beneath the mess and Dougie screwed up his face at the rotten egg smell. He was about to dive the steel fingers of the shovel back into the earth again when he spotted something poking through the scrape he had just dug. He halted the bucket's dip and squinted, peering through the smeared windscreen. He could have sworn that looked like a body. He closed his eyes for a split second, then opened them again and stared, focusing on the object he had unearthed, trying to separate the dirt from the shape.

'It can't be,' he said to himself, as a rush of adrenaline surged through him and his stomach emptied. 'It is though … it's definitely a body.'

Detective Constables Tony Bullars and Mike Sampson, the other half of Hunter's team, had been pulled from the Rebecca Morris murder to join the police and forensic team foraging in the slurry tips on the Manvers site. They took a shortcut to the scene, via a well-used undulating dirt track which bounced them bruisingly around in the CID car, and found their witness, Dougie Crabtree, by the side of a marked police car, talking animatedly to an officer who was attempting to formulate his excited babble into hard facts. A hundred yards away, a half dozen white-suited members of the Forensic Team were on hands and knees, probing around in the solid clods of coal dust. A white tent was in the process of being erected, bright against the stark grey backdrop, reminiscent of a lunar landscape.

'That's where our body must be,' said Tony Bullars, moving to the back of the CID car to collect a forensic suit.

While Tony was tall and slim with a good head of styled hair, Mike was small and podgy, with unruly dark hair and a craggy face badly pockmarked from acne in his adolescence. What they did have in common was a sharpness of mind and a keenness to detect crime, which had elevated them both from uniform into CID relatively early in their careers. Both had joined the Major Investigation Team at its inception eighteen months ago.

Tony skipped across the rutted site while Mike trudged behind him, whingeing and moaning with every step.

'Bloody hell, Bully, just look at the frigging state of me. How come you're not in the same state?' He grimaced, glancing at his mud-splattered shoes.

Tony laughed. 'You've either got it, Mike, or you haven't.' He turned and strode away, leaving Mike to his predicament among the deep ruts.

Professor Lizzie McCormack was in attendance, her latex-gloved hands already clearing soil around the mummified corpse, which was still partly entrenched in the dingy earth. The muddied remains were curled up in the foetal position and in a bit of a mess. Portions of the body were devoid of flesh and the skin which remained on the thin-boned form was shrivelled and hard as rock. The overall colour of the cadaver matched that of the earth around it.

Lizzie looked up, her glistening grey eyes appearing over her designer spectacles. 'Ha, gentlemen, so glad you could join us. Two bodies in less than a week! You are keeping me busy.' She saw Mike Sampson shudder and turn sharply away from the corpse. 'I hope you will have the stomach to see this one out, officer.'

Mike blushed.

'You see this is what sets us woman apart from you men,' she said. 'We spend months changing smelly nappies without thinking about it. But what you don't realise is all those months of shovelling shit gives us a stronger stomach for the messier side of life.'

She winked and gave a wry smile, then continued to move slowly and meticulously around the corpse, picking at it here and there and removing fragments that were quickly bagged by her young female assistant. After three quarters of an hour the professor pushed herself up onto her haunches, snapped off a glove, removed her spectacles and turned her attention to the two detectives.

'Gents, what we have here is the decomposed, yet mummified body of a young female who has obviously been in the ground for some time. There are remains of clothing — what appears to be a shirt or blouse and a pair of jeans. I'm not sure if we are going to be able to get any fingerprints at this time. The body's caked in mud so I'll have to check if we can get into the ridges when the body's back in the mortuary and cleaned. The head also needs some cleaning up but it does have plenty of hair fragments to enable DNA analysis. There is evidence of massive trauma to the nose and lower jaw area, some teeth are missing, and there are incised wounds around the eye sockets.' She bent forward and looked into the dark holes where the eyes should have been, 'I will be able to give firm confirmation of my thoughts after the post mortem, but if I'm not mistaken here, there are some similarities between the injuries inflicted on this corpse and those on Rebecca Morris.'

DAY EIGHT

By the time Tony Bullars and Mike Sampson arrived at the mortuary the next morning, the examination of the mummified corpse was already underway. The dark, shrivelled form lay naked on one of the metallic pathology slabs, having had its clothing cut away. The clothes now lay separately on another table, being photographed by a Scenes of Crime officer.

Professor McCormack was dragging a comb through the dead girl's lank and matted hair, dropping strands, along with soil fragments, into a clear plastic exhibit bag. She was talking rapidly in post mortem legalese into the overhead microphone. She studied the corpse methodically. Pausing from time to time, she pulled at the arms, carefully rotating them, cracking the dried, fragile skin and probed cuts and indentions with a scalpel, before stepping back to allow the SOCO to photograph them.

At times she would take a closer look at patches of the shrivelled skin under a magnifying glass, then instruct the technician following in her wake about where she wanted incisions on the body, and which parts of the body to chop away. Finally, the hand-held circular saw was switched on and the top of the skull was deftly cut and removed, to reveal a murky brown interior that contained the shrivelled remains of a brain.

'Thankfully, because of the toxicity of the soil, very few insects have attacked the body and the internal organs, except one, although badly decomposed, are relatively intact,' the professor said, glancing up.

She continued with the legalese, only halting when she measured and weighed various organs. After the two-hour autopsy she stopped, threw her gloves and mask into a bin, grabbed a paper towel and mopped her moist brow. Then, wiping her spectacles and replacing them on to the tip of her nose, so she could look over them, she turned to Tony and Mike.

'Gentlemen, you have here a girl who is early to late teens. The structure of her pelvis and hips tell me she has not yet reached adulthood. She has collar length brown hair and is five-feet-five-inches tall. She would have been very slender prior to her death. She has multiple stab and incised wounds to the head, neck, trunk and upper extremities. Three stab wounds in particular are very nasty indeed. The blade has penetrated the brain through the eye sockets and part of her upper chest has been sliced open. What is unusual about this is that her heart has been cut out and removed.'

Tony and Mike exchanged startled looks.

'You heard me right, gents. Her heart has been cut out.' She nudged her glasses back into place with her forearm. 'And also, as per Rebecca Morris's examination, I have found similar markings incised into her abdomen.' She paused and studied the corpse's stomach with a critical eye. 'I say similar,' she continued, looking back up. 'In fact, the first mark is slightly different. It looks more like a reversed letter L. The other marks are the same — an I and V and number 3. Could be a combination of Roman numerals; your guess is as good as mine at the moment. I'm going to have to get a scan done of these to confirm this, and I'm also going to re-examine Rebecca Morris to check if I've missed anything.'

Professor McCormick began pulling at the plastic protective apron covering her scrubs.

'She also has minor blunt injuries to the head, especially around the nose, left cheek area and lower jaw. Many of the stab wounds to the head are very irregular and are located mostly to the left-hand side. Her left ear was almost severed. The majority of the wounds to the trunk and upper extremities have penetrated the subcutaneous skin and muscle layers through to the bone. The stab to the sternum has passed into the chest and penetrated the left lung.

'The upper extremities have multiple sharp-force injuries consistent with defensive injuries. Lastly, the hyoid bone, the thyroid, and the cricoid cartilages are fractured. The marks on the neck tissue suggest a wide ligature; most probably a belt.' She paused, as if to gather her thoughts. 'This young lady has suffered a horrendous death. I have moulds to make of the stab wounds, in order to determine both the type of weapon used and confirm they are a match, but I am confident when I say the weapon used has similar curves to that which was used on Rebecca Morris.'

'Do you have any thoughts on the sequence of events?' asked Tony.

'Thoughts, young man. I don't have thoughts. I give out facts based on my forty-two years' experience,' she said abruptly.

Despite her tone, Tony Bullars quite liked being called young man, notwithstanding he was twenty-eight years old — though he guessed to her he must appear quite young and fresh faced. Professor McCormack must be at least retirement age, he thought to himself, and his face creased into a smile.

'Before you arrived, gentlemen, I carefully removed her clothing. Her blouse had several buttons missing — torn off, and was open to the navel. Her bra had been lifted above her breasts and these would have been exposed. Her jeans were still on and fastened and she was still wearing her panties. With that in mind and the nature of her injuries it leads me to believe that she was punched first in the nose and jaw area. Her clothing was either disturbed during this, but more than likely after the assault, which, in my opinion, would have been violent enough to render her unconscious for a short time. She then came to and struggled, during which time she was stabbed repeatedly. Remember, I told you she had defence injuries — like so.' The professor proceeded to raise both her arms and shield her upper body and face. 'The angulations of the incisions and stab wounds lead me to believe he was above her at the time. More than likely sat astride her. Many of these wounds would not have caused immediate death. What would have killed her, without doubt, was the stabbing to either of her eyes, or the slicing through of the chest wall to get to the heart and/or the strangulation. At this stage, I do not know which was first and which was final, though I am inclined to think that the removal of the heart was more a defiling act after she was dead.'

'How long had she been buried, Professor?' Mike Sampson asked as he tugged the zip of his white forensic suit down over his well-fed stomach.

'There are still quite a few tests to do on that front, but my experience tells me she has lain there for some considerable time. Best guess, ten to fifteen years.'

'Anything else I can take back for the briefing, Professor?' said Tony.

'What I am fairly certain about from my examination of both this body and that of Rebecca Morris is that you are now dealing with two murders and one killer.'

DAY NINE

Bright morning sunshine filtered through the blinds, bathing Detective Superintendent Michael Robshaw in a soft, warm light. He leant over the computer keyboard, entered his password and hit the return key. Then, clasping his hands behind his head, he sat back and stared at the screen. Forty-three messages in the two days since he had last logged on. The majority was in-force spam, but a few had to be opened up and responded to before his next command team briefing.

This was another of those bugbears that had crept into the job. Although the computer highway was a very effective vehicle for today's modern police service, much of the system was filled with dross that encroached on time spent better elsewhere. Robshaw's mind drifted to his early days when they had relied on the 'yellow message' system for briefings, notes which were carefully sifted and scrutinised by the morning sergeant before they came across his desk for actioning. He only wished the computer had a similar gatekeeper to save him time and energy. He sighed and stretched his well-muscled shoulders. Despite his forty-six years he still managed to maintain the fifteen-stone physique of his rugby playing days.

Last night Robshaw had spent a restless night fighting the adrenaline rush from the news that the mummified body, murdered more than ten years ago, was linked to the murder of Rebecca Morris. The identical marks gouged into each body's stomach had confirmed it. No one had yet discovered what the marks meant. Especially puzzling was the significance of the playing card placed on Rebecca's chest. He had officers combing the site around the latest find to see if a card had been left there, too.

He'd poured himself a large glass of whisky before retiring to bed, but he had still fidgeted thinking about the latest discovery. He knew he mustn't allow the newest finding to overshadow Rebecca's death and needed to run the two murder enquiries in tandem. Finally, after fighting sleeplessness and seeing the dawn light creep through the fabric of the bedroom curtains he rose early, showered quickly and drove the eight miles to work, hardly noticing what the car radio was playing.

Closing the computer down again, Robshaw scoured the handwritten sheets he had prepared late last night. They contained detailed notes on each murder, featuring relevant discoveries from the enquiries already carried out, together with a list of fresh tasks that required working on today. There was a lot of work to do and he had to be very focused as he scribbled down further notes for the forthcoming briefing. He glanced up for a moment and stared at some of the personal photographs on the wall, in particular the class photograph of his younger self, standing proudly in the middle row at Detective Training School at Wakefield.

Those had been some of the best days of his career. How he wished he could turn the clock back and be more hands-on. He found it difficult not to get personally involved in a case and to accept that his role was no longer operational. He now flew a desk. It was his job to sift and sort the evidence, identify new leads, pick out suspects or break down alibis. The greatest personal satisfaction he could hope for was picking out that crucial bit of information from an action or statement, through his meticulous reading and careful observation, something that others had missed and which would initiate that first step to catching their killer.

Placing the cap back on his fountain pen, Robshaw picked up his notes, pushed himself up from his desk and walked out of his office and down the corridor. He could hear some of his HOLMES team beginning their preparations for the day and the aroma of freshly brewed coffee teased his nostrils. As he entered the MIT office, he saw the new incident whiteboards had been erected. There were timelines for each of the victims and the latest one displayed the rotted face of the Jane Doe. The immediate task was identifying the unidentified, placing a name to that gruesome form which had once been a young girl. Without that, how could they uncover her lifestyle, her habits, where she hung out and who she associated with? That valuable information was the crux of the matter right now. It was important that Jane Doe became a somebody he could give back to her family.

Robshaw reviewed photos of the scene, looked at the dental x-rays and combed through the post mortem report. Behind the scenes attempts would be being made to obtain fingerprints from the corpse and one of the detectives would have the task of making the numerous phone calls to track down the orthodontist who did her dental work. At the same time, forensics would be working with the clothing and other articles found on the body.

Robshaw's mind was finalising the day's assignments as members of the team filtered into the briefing room. He glanced at a few of them and acknowledged their arrival with a smile.

Morning briefing began at eight a.m. He satisfied himself that all who should be here were here, glanced at his watch, and cleared his throat.

'Morning, ladies and gents. You don't need me to tell you that we have a very busy few days ahead.' Referring to his notes, Robshaw began by revisiting all the actions so far relating to the murder of Rebecca Morris. He double-checked with detectives on confirmed sightings, revealed that the reconstruction had not brought in any new leads, and finished by bringing in Hunter and Grace to confirm the work they had done with her parents and revealing what her best friend had stated about the man who had been 'coming on to her' to photograph Rebecca. 'It is vital we find this man. He is our main TIE suspect.'

That was the acronym for trace, interview, eliminate, given to every major player in an investigation.

Robshaw slapped a hand over the blown-up photographs of the symbols gouged into Rebecca's abdomen. 'The pathologist has re-examined these marks and now confirms that the first mark should be a reversed L. She'd originally missed it because it appears the knife had not joined the horizontal to the upright. Therefore, the marks on Rebecca are identical to those found on Jane Doe.' He paused, his hazel eyes peering through his spectacles to survey the room, stopping at Mike Sampson. 'Mike, you had the job of making sense of these. Any joy?'

'Not yet boss.' Mike cleared his throat. 'Visited various websites, talked to the local priest for any religious link, spoken with some occult specialist that I got off the web, and I've also talked to a forensic psychologist recommended to me by the Met. I sent him a fax of the marks and I also sent him info about the playing card. Other than confirming what Professor McCormick has said about it being the killer's signature, he's not been able to help me further.'

Robshaw nodded and thanked Mike for his efforts. 'Okay everyone, back to the job in hand. We are widening the search for Rebecca's school bag and other belongings, and the Press Office is putting out a fresh appeal this lunchtime in case our killer has dumped them. I have got headquarters monitoring her mobile in case it's switched on at any time. There is still a lot of ground to cover on this murder.'

He moved to the second board and placed a hand over the grotesque photo of the mummified head.

'Jane Doe. The only thing we know about her so far is that she was of teenage years when she was murdered. She was discovered yesterday in a slurry pit on the site of the old Manvers coking plant.' He paused and pointed to a large map of the Dearne Valley on another whiteboard. 'This site is only two miles away from where Rebecca Morris was discovered. What concerns me about this is not the fact that we are now dealing with a double murder, but the time span between the two killings. That body has been in that slurry pit at least ten years and more than likely fifteen. Why the gap between both murders? Was our killer in jail? Was he out of the area? Or worse still, has he killed between those years and are there more bodies still waiting to be discovered?'

Without her make-up and now dressed in school uniform, Kirsty Evans looked every inch the fourteen-year-old teenager again, thought Grace, as she stared out through the windscreen of her unmarked CID car, watching Kirsty appear from the school entrance opposite.

Kirsty appeared to look around nervously as she crossed the road and Grace guessed she was trying to avoid drawing attention to herself as she made her way to her car.

Kirsty scanned the line of parked cars she was approaching, spotting Grace, who had her hand raised to grab her attention, and after taking a final glance around, jogged towards the silver CID car parked discreetly in the shadow of one of the trees lining the road.

Grace reached across the front seat and sprang the passenger door open as Kirsty reached the car. She stuck her head inside and Grace could see she looked flushed and nervous. Grace patted the fabric of the front seat.

'Get in, I won't bite,' she invited.

Whipping her school bag off her shoulder, Kirsty slid in.

'You didn't mind me ringing you, did you?' Kirsty asked, staring at the dashboard.

'Course not. I was hoping you would. That's why I gave you my card.'

'Only I don't want to get anyone into trouble, or for anyone to think bad of Rebecca.' Kirsty rattled out her words at pace.

'Kirsty, if what you have to tell me will help catch the person who did this to your best friend then people will thank you.' Grace rested a hand on Kirsty's forearm, causing her to turn and make eye contact. 'I have a daughter your age. I know you don't want your parents and especially the police to know what you get up to, or what you discuss, but this is different. Someone murdered Rebecca and that someone may well have known her. You may well know that person, too.'

Kirsty shuddered and pulled back her arm.

'Rebecca said I didn't know him, and I don't know anyone who could be as cruel as that,' she said.

'Maybe not, Kirsty, but let me be the judge of that. From your phone call yesterday it's obvious that something has been preying on your mind. And, to be honest, I sensed that at your house when we talked the other day.'

Kirsty coloured up again. 'Yes, I suppose so.' She looked sheepish and started twisting a friendship bracelet around her wrist. 'I didn't want my mum and dad to know how Rebecca had changed over the last few months. They might have stopped me knocking about with her if they had.'

'Changed? How do you mean changed?'

'Not in a bad way or anything. She was just rebelling, you know? Because of how her parents were with her.' Kirsty's eyes were uneasy.

'Every teenager goes through a rebellious phase,' said Grace. 'Just because you probably see me as a level-headed police officer now doesn't mean I didn't go through the same thing. God, I caused all kinds of problems for my parents, in fact I've asked myself many a time how I came to join the police. It's something everyone goes through and Rebecca was no exception.' Grace paused to study Kirsty's face. 'What do you mean by rebelling? What form did it take?'

Kirsty looked from the windscreen to the dashboard and back again, carefully considering her choice of words. 'She used to go on about how her mum and dad wouldn't let her grow up. She had asked if she could have her hair streaked like mine but they kept telling her she was too young. Then a couple of months ago, apparently her dad caught her wearing make-up when she was coming to our house and he flipped. Told her to wash that muck off and stood over her in the bathroom while she did it. She was fuming when she came to our house. In fact, she made herself up with my stuff. We went round town and she kept shouting to loads of lads, showing off like. She was a laugh at first but then I got bored and wanted to come back home and listen to some music. She wanted to stay out and we had a bit of a fall-out. I ended up calling her a tart.' Kirsty's voice trailed off with a hint of sadness. 'It was only a joke but I wish I hadn't said it now.'

'What's done is done, Kirsty. Don't beat yourself up.'

Kirsty forced a smile and continued. 'It became regular, the putting on make-up thing and going round town. She'd even spent some of her pocket money on a couple of tops and a pair of skinny jeans like mine and left them in my wardrobe for when she came round.' Kirsty faltered for a second. 'She'd started to smoke as well.'

'That's all part of growing up,' Grace said, but suddenly thought of her eldest daughter, Robyn, hoping this was not an avenue she'd go down. *I must have a talk with her the next time we're alone*, she promised herself. She sensed an unease in Kirsty, the same feeling she'd had during their previous talk. 'There's more, isn't there?'

'Well —' a slight hesitation in Kirsty's voice — 'yes. It was when we went to the skate park once, with some lads.' Her voice tailed off.

'Come on, Kirsty, you're halfway there. It can't be that bad.'

'It's a bit awkward.' Kirsty dropped her head and her cheeks flushed again.

'Please, Kirsty, this could be important.'

'Okay. Well, Rebecca started flirting, really awful like, with these older lads. Fifteen, sixteenish they were. She'd snog a couple of them and then touch them up in the youth shelter, you know what I mean?'

Grace nodded.

'Then when they tried to touch her back, she'd push them away and laugh at them. A few got really angry with her, started calling her a prick-teaser. I warned her. I tried to tell her to stop it and that someone would take it too far if she wasn't careful. She just said it was a bit of fun. But I knew it wasn't. I saw the lads' faces.' Kirsty turned and faced Grace square on. 'Do you think that might have happened; that someone took it too far. That's why she was killed?'

DAY FOURTEEN

Deep below district headquarters, Grace clenched her pen between her teeth and on tiptoes manoeuvred another manila folder from the top row of the steel stacking shelves. She dropped the thick, grubby package onto the table below, throwing up more dust particles to add to the motes already floating around the basement room. She jumped off the metal footstool, glad now that she had chosen her flat ballet pumps that morning, and unfastened the securing ribbon before shuffling out the contents along the wooden surface.

Her conversation with Kirsty Evans had been fed into the system and had sparked much debate that morning in briefing, adding another dimension to the enquiry. As a result, Hunter and Tony Bullars had the job of tracing and interviewing some of the boys from the skate park, while she and Mike Sampson had been given the task of going back over old 'missing from home' reports to determine how many were still outstanding, looking in particular for people who disappeared in unusual circumstances, and especially for teenage girls who loosely fitted the description of their Jane Doe.

Grace had spent the early part of the morning logged onto the UK Police National Missing Persons Bureau computer network, feeding in the details they had of the mummified remains. It had been a frustrating morning with many phone calls to the operators to double-check the information she had entered. The system itself was flawless, providing a cross-matching service by comparing the description of their body, with that of all long-term missing persons. It also held a dental index, which was regularly maintained and allowed liaison with Interpol. Each year 77,000 teenagers went missing, hence the need to double-check everything.

The agitating part was that although the bureau had been operating since 1994, her own force had only joined the network in the past eighteen months. Therefore, anything older than that had to be sought in the files, which the Administration Department had stored away in this grimy basement. It meant she and Mike had to physically check back over every handwritten record — and there were several thousand — in order to identify those marked as still missing. As she began to sift through the latest batch, Grace realised this was a task bigger than she had imagined.

'1996,' she announced, a note of frustration in her voice. 'How many years have we gone back now?'

Mike Sampson glanced down at the pile near his feet. 'Three years,' he said, 'only ten to go.' He gave a wry smile.

Grace scraped back an old wooden chair which, despite its battered and weathered appearance, she had found surprisingly comfortable over the past three hours, and sat at the long table opposite Mike. She gave a long sigh as her eyes roamed around the huge windowless room. It was filled floor to ceiling with metal shelves which appeared to contain just about every paper file that had been generated at the station since it was built in the early 1960s, and at first sight it looked like nothing had ever been thrown away. This was one of many antechambers off the cold windy corridor which connected the station cells to the nearby courtroom, where prisoners could be escorted to their fate without the need to be dragged in handcuffs through the streets. It was a cold and drab room, with paint peeling in places as a result of the damp.

From time to time, Grace or Mike made a welcome cup of tea, not only to stave off the cold but also to clear the dust from the back of their throats. During one of these interludes she had found a large cardboard box containing the Crown Court files relating to 'The Beast of Barnwell', an enquiry which had occurred well before their time as detectives. She had pointed out her find to Mike and the pair had got engrossed as they scoured old black and white photographs and read the yellowing crime files.

During the 1960s, the Barnwell man had indecently assaulted, beaten, and raped several women, before being finally captured in the 70s. Back then it had been one of the country's major enquiries and, remembering what the detective superintendent had said at morning briefing, Grace now wondered if they were also on the verge of something similar.

It was rare that Grace worked with Mike Sampson — Hunter was her regular partner — though she found the experience a refreshing change. He was the character in the department, full of one-liners and jokes and with the ability to come up with a witty punch-line to lighten things. But he had a professional side and he was dedicated, regularly the last person to leave the office at the end of the day. Yet Grace realised she knew very little about Mike's personal life. She knew he was single and spent quite a lot of his time in the pub with mates following a quiz trail around various venues throughout the week, and that he loved to spend his weekends off fishing competitively up and down the country. But that was where her knowledge ended. She had never seen him in a relationship and he had never introduced a love of his life. As she dragged her eyes back to her paperwork, she made it her objective over the next few weeks to get to know Mike better.

First Rebecca Morris's smiling face came into view, fading away and followed quickly by a blurry, distant shot of her in her school uniform standing by the bus stop, the one where the man had picked her up, and it stopped him in his tracks. The hairs in the man's nostrils quivered from a sharp intake of breath and he tried to catch up the two beats his heart missed. A cold clammy sensation swelled inside and the palms of his hands itched from the beads of sweat rolling across his skin. He wavered slightly, but the two cups he was carrying clattered together and a splurge of hot tea splattered his training shoes and the carpet. His heart fluttered as he tuned his hearing to the muted conversation from the television.

'What on earth are you playing at?' screamed his mother, her head whipping round, peering back over her armchair.

He realised what he had seen was a reconstruction of the last sighting of Rebecca Morris being played out on *Crimewatch*, and that, except for her photo, what he had witnessed was someone who had been acting as a body double for Rebecca.

He heaved a sigh of relief and tried to swallow the lump in his throat and answer his mother.

'I don't know,' she spluttered. 'Nearly thirty years old and I can't even trust you to make me a cup of tea without spilling it.'

He plonked the two cups onto the wooden coffee table in front of her, but more tea slopped out.

'Sorry, I'll just fetch a cloth.'

He turned to go back to the kitchen but there was more to the report, which again stopped him in his tracks. He thought he recognised the scene. The colourless grey landscape had changed over the years but there was no mistaking where he was looking at and he tried to hear what the presenter was saying.

'Police say they are not ruling out the possibility that the recent gruesome findings are linked with the murder of fourteen-year-old Rebecca Morris, whose mutilated body was discovered two weeks ago...'

'Oh, just leave it,' his mother snapped. 'I'll fetch it. If you want a job doing, do it yourself.'

She pushed past, slapping at his elbow and trying to move him aside, but he was too strong for her now and she wobbled sideways as he flicked out his arm in reaction to the slap.

His mother, her eyes bulging, glared back at him.

She was getting inside his head again and he could feel the anger welling up. Just like all the other times. Sometimes she really messed with his head. Because of her, he'd missed the remainder of the broadcast. From what had been said, though, he could guess that they had found another one of his girls. He cursed inwardly at his mother's interruptions. Now he would have to go out tomorrow and get the local paper. He'd drive into town and get it from one of the supermarkets. He didn't want to arouse suspicion by going to their usual newsagent.

He heard his mother clattering about in the scullery searching out the floor cloth, clucking her tongue against the roof of her mouth, the way she always did when she was annoyed with him.

One of these days he would fucking do for her.

I feel like a bloody leper, Susan Siddons thought, as she drew on the final remnants of her cigarette before flicking it to the ground and grinding it underfoot. As an uncontrollable shiver moved down her back, she wished she'd put on her cardigan before coming outside. 'I'm going to end up with a cold, thanks to this stupid bloody smoking ban,' she mumbled to herself, looking at her reflection in one of the pub windows. She took the breath freshener from out of her handbag, squirted it into her mouth and then cupped her hand and blew into it, sniffing to see if her breath still smelt of smoke. Then she replenished her lipstick, flicked a hand through her newly cropped hair and made her entrance back into The White Hart, her local bar, just a five-minute walk from her dingy flat. As she entered the snug, she tugged at the seams of her short skirt to cover a little more of her slender legs.

'Another fag break, Sue?' her large-chested, generously proportioned friend Debbie quipped, taking a swig of lager.

'My only vice,' she responded. 'Oh, and the occasional drink,' she added, picking up her own half of beer, before dropping down onto the padded bench beside her best friend.

'And sex,' finished Debbie.

They glanced at each other and laughed.

The television was on, mounted high up on a shelf in one corner of the room and, despite there being no sound on, the pictures on the screen caught Sue's eye. She stopped drinking, resting the rim of the glass on her bottom lip as she stared intently at the screen.

'What's this?' she mumbled, nodding at the TV. Debbie looked blank and shrugged. Susan turned around.

'Terry,' she shouted to the large bellied manager serving behind the bar, 'what's this on the telly?'

He took his eyes off the fresh pint he was pulling and looked at the screen. 'Crimewatch,' he answered and went back to filling the glass.

'Turn it up, Terry,' she said, nervousness in her voice.

'What for? You on it?' he shot back.

'Fuck off and just turn up the sound, you sarky twat.' She slammed down her beer glass onto the round wooden table.

Several heads in the snug turned, but she didn't notice. Her eyes were transfixed by the image on the TV, focusing on the clothing neatly laid out on a table.

'I wouldn't argue with her if I was you, Terry,' Debbie said.

The manager aimed the remote at the television and held his index finger continuously on the volume switch, watching the numbers rise on the screen until it was audible.

Susan strained her ears, just catching the final bits of conversation between the stocky, grey-haired detective and the fair-haired female presenter. She deciphered that the remains of a young girl had been found on the site of the old Manvers pit, wearing clothing similar to that on the table. The rest of the conversation became a jumble as her thoughts began racing. A mist clouded her vision and she clasped a hand to her mouth.

'Oh my god,' she gasped.

Debbie spun sideways and saw how the blood had drained from Sue's face. 'What's the matter?'

Susan didn't respond. She jumped from her seat, banging her legs against the side of the table, causing the drinks to slop out of their glasses. She dashed along the corridor by the toilets, her slim figure bouncing off the doorjamb and she had to catch herself before she stumbled outside into the car park. Her fingers groped around the keypad of her mobile. She hadn't dialled this number for a long time but she could still remember it.

'Come on, come on,' she muttered, as it rang out. Finally, it was answered. The man's voice seemed a lot steadier since the last time they had spoken several years ago.

'Barry, it's Sue,' she blurted out. 'Susan Siddons. I really need to see you. It's about our Carol. I think they've just found her.'

The unexpected phone call from retired detective Barry Newstead later that evening, practically demanding that they meet, took Hunter by surprise. But he knew it was a request he dare not refuse. Barry never rang him out of the blue and therefore it had to be something important.

Hunter told Beth he needed to nip out, jumped into his car, and drove the few miles from his home along the unlit country roads to the tranquil picture-postcard village of Wentworth, where Barry had fixed the meet. He was pondering on the strangeness of the telephone conversation with an old colleague he hadn't seen for over five years.

Hunter replayed his first meeting with the huge, bullish man. It had been on the 1st September 1988 — when Hunter was just sixteen. It was a date locked inside his memory bank, because it was the day the police told him his girlfriend, Polly Hayes, had been murdered. Her battered body had been found in woodland and Barry had been one of the detectives on the case and had interviewed Hunter as a suspect.

They had never found her killer, and a year into the enquiry Barry had broken the news that the case was being closed until further evidence came to light.

Catching his girlfriend's murderer had been Hunter's motive for joining the police. And he'd looked deeply at each murder case since then but still hadn't turned up her killer. This recent case appeared no different.

He'd stayed in touch with Barry to discuss any fresh information about Polly's murder, and they'd caught up again when he had joined the police and been posted to Barry's home-town. Three and a half years later, after gaining Detective status at twenty-two, Hunter had nervously walked into the CID office and Barry was one of the first people to greet him.

He became Hunter's mentor and Hunter quickly learned that Barry was a figurehead of the department and a legend in the office. During the first twelve months, many a time over a pint Barry would regale Hunter with his adventures. He had an incredibly fast and alert mind and could talk the hind-legs off a donkey. Barry had a vast network of informants and when he fingered someone for a job, there was no doubt they had done it.

Along the way, Hunter became familiar with Barry's interview techniques. Occasionally he had seen Barry use violence, out of sight and mind of the custody sergeant, to gain a confession. Hunter became mesmerised by some of his mentor's frighteningly unorthodox methods, which both scared and excited him. Barry was determined to prove that the villains he dealt with were found guilty of their crimes. And, although he didn't approve of his violence, Hunter would listen to him defend his activities by stating, 'I can put my hand on my heart when I say I have never put an innocent man behind bars.' Barry would back this up by revealing how many of his miscreants had written letters from prison for a visit so that they could clear their slate before release. His clear up rate for crime was phenomenal.

When Hunter transferred to Drugs Squad and achieved promotion, they lost touch. In his new post, Hunter had picked up gossip which disturbed him. Barry had brought about his own downfall. Barristers and judges began to challenge his breaches of guidelines, in particular those of the Police and Criminal Evidence Act, and his collars began to walk free from court.

Some of the younger managers labelled him a maverick and a dinosaur and had plotted his downfall. One newly promoted chief inspector had removed Barry from operational CID and sidelined him to a desk job. Hunter had left numerous messages on Barry's voicemail for him to get in touch, but he never had. Then Barry announced his retirement and Hunter caught up with him at his leaving do. It was a big event, and many past and present CID bosses praised Barry's efforts — one retired detective superintendent bemoaning how sad it was that detectives like Barry were no longer allowed to operate to the benefit of the victims.

As he pulled into the rear car park of the village pub, Hunter thought it would be nice to catch up with Barry again, despite the inconvenience and the fact that he was shattered after another gruelling fourteen-hour day.

Built of Yorkshire stone, The George and Dragon was a typical country pub. It had a warming ambience and the décor of an old farmhouse, with heavy stone flagged floors, timbered ceilings and whitewashed plaster walls. Turn-of-the-century sepia photographs of the pub and the village decorated the walls, and the furniture was a mixture of heavy wooden chairs, high backed benches and many different sized tables. It was a pub Hunter visited only occasionally, usually on warm summer evenings, though as he studied the array of good quality real ales, he thought he should pay it more attention in future.

The bar was a hive of activity and he scoured the sea of faces for Barry. Then he spotted him, tucked away in the corner on one of the high back seats, just putting a pint to his mouth. *He hasn't changed one bit*, he thought to himself. The same, dark, rumple of hair and red-flushed face, reminiscent of a hill farmer. Hunter was suspicious of the 'Dorian Gray' appearance; Barry had been retired at least six years and would be in his early fifties. Hunter caught his eye, raised his hand and tipped it towards his face, mouthing 'another beer?' Barry gave the thumbs up and Hunter ordered two pints of Timothy Taylor Landlord, one of his favourite real ales, before squeezing between customers to join his ex-colleague.

Barry still had a bushy moustache, which he stroked frequently and annoyingly and as he got closer Hunter realised why his hair was still so dark — he was dyeing it. As Barry pushed up from his seat and thrust out a hand, Hunter noted he was more beer-bellied and rotund than he remembered, but as Barry gripped and shook his hand there was still strength in those arms, which on more than one occasion had been used to pummel an adversary.

'Looking good, Hunter.'

'You too, Barry.'

'Still as diplomatic as ever I see. That's why you got promoted and I didn't. I've put on a few pounds I know, since I retired —' Barry slapped the side of his girth — 'but I can still give the young 'uns a run for their money.'

Hunter had no doubt that he could.

For a good half hour as they sipped their beers Barry quizzed him about the job, tut-tutting and shaking his head as Hunter described the many changes that the uniform side and CID departments had undergone since Barry's retirement. Hunter wondered if he would be as cynical and critical when it became his time to leave. The chilled, smooth tasting beer went down easily and Barry went to the bar to replenish the glasses.

As he eased himself back into his seat, Hunter decided it was time to get to the crux of why he had driven here. 'Well, I have to say I was intrigued by your call, right out of the blue after all these years.'

Barry took the head off his beer. 'Have you identified your body from the Manvers site yet?' he asked, not looking up.

'Not yet. We're ploughing our way through hundreds of missing-from-home files going back years and the gaffer went on *Crimewatch* tonight, but I don't know if anything's come of that.'

'That's why I rang you. I got a call just like you, right out of the blue. From a woman I haven't seen or spoken to in years. It was the mum of a girl who went missing back in the early nineties. Carol Siddons.'

'Should that name mean anything to me? Like I say, Barry, there are many girls who are still outstanding in our records. What makes her think it's her daughter?'

Barry took another sip of his beer and set his glass down. 'I worked on that case for a short while, as a favour to the mother. Susan Siddons was a girl I knew from my beat days and she became a snout of mine, a very reliable one. Anyway, what I'm getting round to is that she recognised the clothing on the programme tonight. They were the same as the clothes her daughter was wearing on the night she disappeared. Let me just give you a bit of background and then I'll give you Susan's address so that you can go and meet her tomorrow.'

Hunter sat back in his weathered pine chair, nursing his pint, ready to listen. From his early career days, he knew Barry had a flair for recounting the many and varied cases he had been involved in.

'Susan Siddons was a young journalist, in her first job straight out of university when I first came across her. She was a real looker. Could fetch ducks off water, but she always seemed to attract the wrong type of bloke. She came from a middle-class background, both parents were teachers, and I think she just wanted to experience a bit of rough. Anyway, she took up with a guy from a family of villains who was a real bastard to her. She got pregnant and moved in with him. We got called out quite a few times to their house as a result of domestics but she would never press charges, even though he'd slapped her around and blacked her eyes on a couple of occasions.'

Barry took another swig of his beer and wiped droplets from his moustache with one of his shovel-like hands.

'Then one night,' he continued, 'he gave her a real good hiding. Hospitalised her. Broke her nose, an eye socket and a couple of ribs. I was on evenings and got the callout. He was pissed up when I got to his house and spouting off that she'd not complain about him. I gave him a taste of his own medicine and then took him in. I told the custody sergeant he'd resisted arrest and confessed to me about the assault on Sue when we were coming back in the car. He made a complaint, but it was my word against his and the upshot was that he got eighteen months in Armley.

'When he went down, I suggested to Sue to move and get a place for her and her young daughter, Carol. For the first time she took advice from someone in authority. Unfortunately, her lifestyle began affecting her job. She started to drink a little too much and they gave her the push. She carried on drinking even more, and visited some real dives, but she used to give me some real good info and in return I slipped her the odd tenner, or bought her daughter Carol a bit of something from time to time. I later found out she was touting round blokes for beer money, who in return would go home with her at the end of the night. But she wasn't shagging them. She used to give them a large nightcap with some of her sleeping tablets in and they'd go spark out, and then next day she'd spin them a story while they nursed their thick heads.

'That was fine, until one night when one old guy, who'd got angina, took a turn for the worse and was rushed into hospital. Doctors there got suspicious and called in the police. A young sergeant went to the house and recovered a whisky glass, which had the remnants of some of her anti-depressant tablets. I tried to intervene in the case, to make the sergeant see the job for what it was, but he could only see "jobsworth" and she got two years for administering a noxious substance.'

'What happened to her daughter?' asked Hunter, finishing off his second beer.

'Carol got taken into care. She was twelve years old. It changed her. She could already look after herself. Well, she had to because of Sue's lifestyle. But you know how it is. She'd entered a system that was full of young kids who were beyond the control of their parents, who were either on bail from court for violence or thieving, or self-harmers, and she became one of them. A real tearaway. She became promiscuous, regularly went shoplifting, got drunk, fought with kids, fought with staff, even fought with the police. Regularly went missing from home, and so when she went missing in the early 90s no real effort went into looking for her until she had been gone at least ten days. Sue contacted me, and as a favour to her and for old time's sake I put in a fair bit of effort in my own time to try and track her down. But I hit a brick wall. I did have some concerns but the gaffers wouldn't hear any of it. They just thought she'd buggered off to one of the big cities and was working as a teenage prostitute. For years Sue tried to get the police and the papers interested, but because of her history, she got nowhere.'

'A sad story, Barry,' sighed Hunter.

'Very,' agreed Barry. 'When you see Sue tomorrow, a little bit of warning, she'll more than likely be in drink. I contacted you, Hunter, because I can trust you to deal with her sympathetically. But I also have to tell you that during the initial enquiries when Carol was first reported missing, Sue told a few lies and I covered for her.'

DAY SIXTEEN

Before leaving for work that morning, nursing a thumping head, Hunter had telephoned Grace and given her the heads-up of his meeting with Barry. When he gingerly sauntered into the MIT office Grace was already in, searching through a huge pile of missing-from-home files. He wasn't surprised to see her among all that paperwork — she had already told him on the phone that she and Mike Sampson had decided that they could not spend another day in that dump of a store room and had got the van driver to transfer all the remaining folders to the office.

He found her beside her desk, sat crossed-legged on the floor, amid foxed and yellowing folders, sliding report after report into separate piles.

Hunter eyed her carefully. He had known Grace a long time. In fact, they had joined the job on the same day and trained together as new recruits. On their first outing together they had caught a burglar who was wanted by several police forces. Hunter had ended up in a fight with the villain who'd taken a swing at him, Grace ending up on the receiving end when he'd ducked. She had ended up with a black eye and they always joked about it whenever they had caught up. That same outing, they also dealt with an unconscious woman who had been badly assaulted following an attempt rape upon her by a serial rapist and murderer, who Hunter later caught, receiving a commendation and an early attachment to CID.

Grace had also bathed in the limelight in her early years; thanks to her skills in the use of Patois language, down to her Jamaican father, she had been used for undercover work by Drugs Squad and had helped convict a drug dealer who had slipped the police-net on numerous occasions. They had lost touch for a short time because she had taken two career breaks to be with her daughters during their pre-school years, and Hunter had occasionally enquired after her when he had got in CID, and when he had been promoted to DS, he had covertly monitored her performance. Eighteen months ago, when he took one of the sergeant's posts in the newly formed Major Investigation Team, he had called her up and suggested she should apply to join the squad.

She had walked the interview and since then they had been regular partners.

Grace glanced up from her work and fixed her brown eyes on him, grinning widely. Unlike him, she showed no signs of tiredness.

He'd had far too much to drink last night and had to get a taxi home. He'd apologised profusely as his wife Beth had driven him to pick up his car from the pub that morning, but she'd given him a stern look and there was a deathly silence throughout the journey. When he'd tried to kiss her, she turned to offer her cheek. He decided he'd phone up and book a table somewhere nice for them this weekend.

'How are you getting on?' he asked Grace. 'Fancy a brew?'

'I'm sure I've seen Carol Siddons's folder in this lot, it's just a matter of putting my hand on it. Your meeting with Barry has certainly made the job easier. And yes, I will have a coffee as you're offering.'

'I want to keep where I got the info from just between us at the moment. It'll only complicate the enquiry. Just let them think you found the link, okay?'

Hunter poured the boiling water into two cups, adding a teabag to his own and coffee granules to Grace's. He slipped two paracetamols into his mouth.

'Feeling under the weather?' asked Grace.

'I feel absolutely shit. I'd forgotten how much Barry could drink. It was a cracking night and I had a real good laugh with him but I'm paying for it this morning. To add to it, Beth isn't speaking to me. I had to ask her to drop me off for my car this morning, which meant she would be rushing about sorting the boys out before she went into work. I'll have to do some real sucking up for the next few days, but I'll get round her. I always do.'

Grace rolled her eyes and raised her eyebrows at him. That look of hers said a thousand words.

Hunter returned a schoolboy pout. 'Ouch.'

Hunter grappled with his hangover while Grace sifted through the pile of reports from her spell in the basement. Eventually she found a tattered file containing the paperwork relating to a Carol Siddons, who had gone missing in 1993, and just before 9 a.m. they drove out of the police station to meet Susan Siddons at her flat.

Despite wearing a little too much make-up, Susan Siddons was still quite youthful looking for someone pushing fifty. She was slim and petite and both Hunter and Grace had to look down when she opened the door of her first floor flat. Her hair was bleached blonde and in a choppy, modern style, which softened her thin, angular face.

She can't be more than five feet, thought Hunter. He recalled what Barry had told him last night — what type of man would feel the need to batter someone so slight and slender? The prettiness was still there, despite the slight lump on the bridge of her nose, which he guessed was the result of the beating which had put her in hospital. She had an easy, infectious smile and Hunter could see why men fell for her, even though it was always the wrong type of men.

'I'll just pop the kettle on,' Sue said softly and moved towards the kitchen on her left. Her South Yorkshire accent was very broad.

Hunter had mentioned Sue's drink problem to Grace during the journey and he couldn't help but notice the combination of stale beer and fresh mouthwash on her breath.

As Sue disappeared into the kitchen, Grace leaned towards Hunter almost planting her mouth on his ear. 'Her breath smells like yours,' she whispered with a mischievous grin.

'Bollocks,' he retorted in a low voice between gritted teeth.

The flat was tidy and clean, but the furniture was old and worn and Hunter guessed it was the landlord's choice rather than Sue's.

She chattered all the time she prepared the tea, her voice nervous and edgy, making small talk, finding out what Barry had told them of her past.

Hunter responded with a small white lie. He didn't want to bring up the incidents of domestic assault, or anything relating to her term of imprisonment. Instead, he dwelt on the other aspects of her life — her journalistic career, the birth of her daughter and the facts surrounding Carol's disappearance all those years ago.

'You've found my baby now though, haven't you?' Sue said rhetorically, and invited them to sit on a sofa which sank on its springs a little too much. She placed two cups of strong tea onto a stained coffee table before them. She sat opposite them in a mismatched armchair, gripping a steaming mug of tea between her slightly shaky hands.

'I know this will be upsetting for you, Sue, but tell us why you think it's your daughter's body we've found,' said Grace, glancing down at the information on the front sheet of the missing from home folder.

'Is that her file?' Sue said. 'Look, I've got to be straight with you, when all that was written back then I wasn't being entirely honest.' She sniffed, tears forming in the corners of her eyes. 'Now that you've found her, I need to tell you the truth and make things right.'

'But how do you know it's definitely her?' asked Grace again.

'The clothing you showed on *Crimewatch* last night. That was what she was wearing.'

'How do you know?' Grace asked, now scrolling a finger down the report, flicking over pages and speed-reading the handwritten manuscript. 'The last time you saw her was three weeks previous to her going missing, when you visited her at the care home with Social Services.'

'That's just it. That wasn't the last time I saw her.' Susan paused and gulped. 'It was the night she went missing. And there were several other nights before that as well.' She blushed and tried to cover her face by drinking her tea, shuffling uneasily in her chair.

'I think you'd better tell us everything, Sue, don't you?' said Hunter.

Susan Siddons began by recapping some of the background Barry Newstead had already given to Hunter the previous evening. She gave depth and detail to the savage beatings she had suffered at the hands of her partner and they could hear real pain in her voice.

'It wasn't just me he beat. Carol got some real hard slaps from him as well when he was that way out. He bruised her on more than one occasion and I had to keep her off nursery school many a time. One night I came back from bingo and caught him urinating on her while she was in the bath. She was only four years old. Bloody hell, I flipped and went berserk at him, and that's when I got really badly beaten up, which Barry dealt with. You're the only people I've ever told that to. I never even told Barry why Steve gave me that hiding.'

'Steve?' quizzed Hunter.

'Steve Paynton. You most probably will know him.'

Hunter and Grace looked at one another and nodded together. They knew him. There weren't many local police officers who didn't know the Paynton family. Generation after generation of Payntons had been jailed at some time during their lifetime — quite a few had convictions spanning each decade of their existence. Hunter had got involved with Jack and Alice Paynton — Steve Paynton's parents — when he had been in uniform. He had got called to a domestic after Jack and Alice had been fighting and had locked Jack up for assault. After Hunter had handcuffed him, Alice had sought retribution, hitting her husband over the head with a heeled shoe, and Hunter had ended up taking him to hospital to have stitches inserted in the wound. That's how he had met Beth — his wife. She had been a student nurse in A & E.

'When Steve went to prison, Barry found me a place through his contacts and I started afresh. But I got lonely. I was only twenty-four years old. I needed company and I started going out. At first my mum and dad would look after Carol, but when they found out I was seeing different men every few months they lost patience with me and tried to stop me going out by refusing to babysit. I started to feel sorry for myself, and I'm not proud of it, but a few times I tucked Carol up in bed and left her alone when I went to the pub. A neighbour must have phoned up and Social Services got involved. For years I had to put up with their pious interference for fear of losing Carol.'

She took another long sip of her drink.

'Then, as you probably know, I got caught drugging that old guy. I used to get them to pay for my nights out. Many of them were far too old and also married, and I couldn't stand them mauling me at the end of the night, so I'd just slip some of my sleeping pills into a whisky and they'd go spark out. When they woke up on the sofa the next morning many of them couldn't remember what had happened and didn't give me a hard time in case I told their wives.

'Anyway, I went to prison. By this time my parents had disowned me and so Carol was taken into care. When I got out, I was only allowed to see her in the presence of a social worker, so she used to sneak out, or run away and stay with me. A couple of the times, after the police found her at my house, I was served with a notice threatening me with arrest for abduction. Abduction of my own child — I ask you! And so we had to be even more secretive.

'That night she went missing she came to me straight from school. She was wearing that white shirt, which was her school blouse and those jeans you found her in were mine; we were the same size back then. She'd spilt some tomato sauce on her school skirt and she put my jeans on while I washed it. At half nine that night she said she'd better leave so that I didn't get into trouble. The skirt was still wet and she said she'd be back the next day to collect it. That's how I know it's her. Those were my jeans.'

'Why didn't you tell the police all this when she was reported missing?' asked Grace.

'Because I daren't. I thought I'd get done for abduction. I didn't want to go back to prison and lose Carol completely. I just thought she'd had a row at the home because she had got back late and had done a runner. It wasn't until a few days later when she didn't get in touch that I rung Barry. He covered up for me and did some enquiries without his bosses knowing. I started to pester them. I suppose I was a pain at times, but what mother wouldn't be if their daughter went missing?

'Finally, they agreed for me to make an appeal through the media. The press gave me such a hard time. I reacted badly to their questioning, even though I'd been a journalist myself. I came over hard on the telly. They'd edited out much of my emotion and the public slated me. I couldn't win. For weeks if I cried, I was accused of being over dramatic and if I didn't, I was a hard-faced bitch. I suppose my past caught up with me over those awful first few months of her going missing.'

She put down her cup and wiped away a tear.

'Call it a mother's instinct but I just knew something had happened to her. Carol would have contacted me no matter where she was. When I saw on TV last night that a girl's body had been found at the old Manvers site I knew it was her, because you see, I had walked her to the bus stop only a few hundred yards from there.' She paused. 'Can I ask you something?'

'Sure, go ahead,' said Grace.

'Why didn't you show the cardigan she had on? I would have definitely known it was her then.'

'Cardigan?' said Grace, a puzzled frown on her face.

'Yes, a blue and grey striped one, with flowers embroidered on it. I loaned it her because it was so cold that night.'

The description struck a chord in Hunter's memory and he spluttered on his tea.

DAY SEVENTEEN

Linda Morris climbed the stairs to Rebecca's room, carefully draping the freshly ironed T-shirt over her arm. She had found it earlier that morning, still clinging to the insides of the washing machine. She paused for a second at the bedroom door, took in a deep breath, and turned the handle slowly, edging it open like she used to, in case Rebecca was dozing. She would never be able to disturb her daughter again. There was a sickness in the pit of her stomach and she fought back the urge to cry.

The room was exactly as it had been the day Rebecca left for school. Well, except that she'd had to make some minor adjustments, after those detectives hadn't replaced everything correctly. She folded the T-shirt and put it in its rightful place, in the chest of drawers, beside the wardrobe. She opened up the other drawers and checked Rebecca's socks and underwear, closed them slowly and then moved to the jewellery box on top of the unit, placing it back into the right position.

She could hear the sound of children outside, their voices bubbling with excitement and moved towards the window. She spotted her husband below on bended knees, doing something with the borders. He'd hardly spoken since the news had been broken to them. He even averted his eyes when she had tried to catch his vacant stare. It was like the life had been sucked out of him. She knew what he was going through, felt as though her own life had been destroyed since she had lost Rebecca. She lay awake night after night, struggling to come to terms with it.

She turned back to gaze at the room, taking in every nook and cranny, every aspect of Rebecca's life. She spotted her own dog-eared Enid Blyton *Famous Five* books on the small bookshelf beside Rebecca's CDs and DVDs. Mystery stories, which despite being dated, had delighted Rebecca night after night, when they had read them together. White flashes hit the back of her eyes and she felt drained, an unbearable weight pushing down on her shoulders. She flopped onto the bed, falling across the duvet. Reaching across to the bedside cabinet she picked up the framed school photograph of Rebecca and hugged it to her chest. Resting her head on the goose-feather pillow, she breathed in all the smells of Rebecca, curled up in the foetal position and sobbed uncontrollably.

The man stood silently at the bottom of the stairs, holding his breath, gripping the banister, trying to decipher and make some sense of the moaning coming from upstairs. He checked each footfall as he carefully mounted the stairs in his stockinged feet. His parent's bedroom door was ajar, and with his senses heightened, he honed onto the sweaty pungent smell, which was wafting towards him through the gap. It was a new scent to him. Silently, pushing the door open further, he began to edge in to see what was happening. There was the almighty crash behind him, followed by shouting, and he saw his mother grabbing at the sheets, attempting to cover up her nakedness, while a man, whom he recognised as Mr Carson from across the road, scrambled for his clothing. In a flash, his father was pushing past, bundling him against the jamb, causing him to smack his head against the woodwork. He saw his father's lean and powerful arms delivering blow after blow to Mr Carson, but he couldn't make sense of why.

Then his dad was snatching off the broad leather belt he always wore to hold up his work trousers, wrapping the buckle of it into his palm. He watched his father unleash it with such ferociousness across his mother's back, before winding it around her neck. Her eyes were bulging, fingers trying to pull it away from her flesh, mouth gaping, trying to force out words. Instinctively, he launched at his father, pulling at his hair and ears, and clawing at his face. He couldn't understand why his father's once embracing arms turned against him. He was thrown against the wall. The pain was intense, and as the blood trickled down his face, the last thing he could remember were his mother's screams tearing into his eardrums.

He awoke in a sweat, shooting bolt upright. He was wringing wet and there was a damp patch on his sheets. How many times had that dream come back to haunt him? So many nights he had lain awake, scared to go to sleep because he had to relive the nightmares of his past.

He leaned back against the wooden headboard, breathing deeply, rubbing the tension out of his neck and shoulders. Then, as always, he closed his eyes and conjured up the images of his childhood.

For the first ten years of his life he didn't have a care in the world. He had a loving, doting mother and a proud father, who shared his passion for photography. In fact, he had built his son a darkroom and spent many happy hours helping him to develop his photographs. His father worked at the local pit, and he could recall walking down his street with his mother to meet his dad strolling over the pit pony fields, breaking into a jog for his father to sweep him off his feet and throw him over his shoulders for a piggy-back home.

Then she had spoilt it all.

His mother had screwed that fat and ugly Jimmy Carson, and father had left home.

His once so-called mates called his mother a whore, and he had lashed out, venting his anger so deeply on one boy that DC Newstead had told his mother to sort him out, or he'd do it for her.

She had punished him with his father's belt, just as severely as she had been beaten with it herself.

He had been determined not to cry, even as the blood had trickled from the weals on his back.

Father never came back.

He would never forgive her.

He slipped down the bed, curling up, pulling his knees into his chest, and wondering, like he often did, if that was why he kept doing these gruesome things.

Fresh images sprang into his mind. The glint of his knife flashed before him. It was so vivid, as though he was still holding it. Then visions of the girl, throwing up her hands, gasping and screaming in terror entered his head. He was plunging the blade down, again and again, burying it in her chest and head. Her blood was everywhere.

He shot bolt upright again, opening his eyes, struggling for breath. He had drifted off again, dreaming the nightmares, which were becoming more regular. He hadn't had a good night's sleep for years. Why did he keep doing these things? He couldn't answer. He only knew that while he did them, the rush of pleasure and the feeling of supreme power overwhelmed him.

After speaking with Susan Siddons the previous morning, Hunter had set out to trace an old CID buddy, Paul Goodright. A quick telephone enquiry revealed he was now attached to the Task Force Firearms Unit and Hunter tracked him down on his second call.

After a quick catch-up on the phone, and without revealing too much, Hunter asked for an urgent meeting. They arranged to meet that evening in the snooker room of Hickleton Club, a place they'd regularly frequented when they worked together, and where Hunter thought they'd be unlikely to meet another cop, but if they did bump into someone it would look like two old partners having a quiet drink together, chewing the fat over old times.

As Hunter strolled into the club he didn't recognise Paul at first. They were four men at the bar and if it hadn't been for the fact that three of them were elderly Hunter would have walked back out. Paul was completely bald and a lot stockier, virtually all muscle, obviously from intense weight training.

'Long time no see. What's happened to the old barnet?' Hunter said as they shook hands.

'This?' Paul ran a hand over his shiny scalp. 'I've been going thin on top for years, so eighteen months ago I made the decision to shave it off. Makes me look quite macho, don't you think?'

'If you say so.'

Hunter bought them a pint and then, eyeing the empty snooker table at the far end of the room, they decided to play a frame while they talked.

Hunter lost the toss and Paul went up to the table first. Steadying his cue in front of the white ball, Paul followed an invisible path along the green baize to the triangle of red balls at the far end of the table. Taking his shot, there was a loud staccato retort as the frame of balls scattered. The white ball spun quickly away from the side of the table and returned to the bottom cushion.

There was a glint in Hunter's eye as he chalked his cue and strolled towards his first shot. *The perfect plant into the top right-hand corner pocket*, he thought. With cue steady, he smashed white into red, causing it to disappear, as he had expected. During his early CID days, he had played almost daily, and had once been a member of a club. However, promotion into a very busy department and the need to spend family time with his two football-playing sons, Jonathan and Daniel, now ate into the majority of his free time.

Hunter potted the black and then glanced around the table for his next shot.

'Still not lost the old touch, Hunter,' said Paul, swilling the last dregs of his beer around the glass before swallowing it in one gulp. 'Another?' he offered, and when Hunter nodded, he turned to the bar.

Hunter's break of twenty-five ended when the white ball miscued into a pocket, and Paul hurriedly put down the freshly pulled beers and snatched it up.

'Thank Christ for that,' he said, plonking it back in the D at the foot of the table. 'I thought I wasn't going to get a look in.'

Hunter smiled and slid the metal marker along the scoreboard on the wall. 'Sorry about the secrecy yesterday, Paul, but I never trust work phones.'

'Me neither. When you said you needed to speak with me about finding the body of Carol Siddons after she had been missing for fifteen years, and then hanging up so quickly, I confess I was more than a little puzzled. I was going to ring you at home last night but I've deleted your number from my mobile. I spent most of the night racking my brains over what you said about her being reported missing back in 1993. I can't remember that job at all.'

'You won't, because where Carol Siddons was last seen wasn't our area back then. You've heard that we've discovered a mummified body, haven't you?'

Paul nodded. 'I guessed it had something to do with that.'

'Yeah, yesterday morning we found out it was Carol Siddons.'

'So why do you need to talk to me?' Paul said, bending over the green baize, sighting up his shot.

'Remember when the CID car got nicked all those years back?'

'That night ruined my life and my career. Even though you backed up my story about radioing in to check up on a suspicious noise at the back of the shops, and then coming back to find the car had gone, my days in CID were numbered.'

'Well, it's come back to haunt us again,' Hunter responded, a serious note in his tone. 'You more than me.'

Paul stopped his cueing action and turned to face Hunter. 'Why, what's happened?' he asked, frowning.

'From what I've learned yesterday, I'm now certain Carol Siddons was in the CID car on the night she was murdered. Do you recall when we answered the fire brigade shout, because they had found the car on fire on that track that used to run at the back of the old coking plant?'

'Yeah, when we got there they'd put it out. Although it was only partially burnt it was a write-off.' Paul had lost interest in the game now and was leaning against the side of the snooker table.

'And can you remember what you found on the back seat?'

Paul thought for moment. 'A cardigan.'

'That's right — a greyish, blue cardigan. What did you do with it?'

'I bagged it and put it in my desk drawer. I can remember thinking it was strange finding that, because back then we didn't have lasses nicking cars in our neck of the woods.'

Hunter nodded in agreement. 'And do you remember there was front end damage to the car?'

Paul pursed his lips. 'On the same night it was nicked, there was that hit and run accident in which my sister was seriously injured and her boyfriend was killed. I've always believed that it was the CID car involved in that.'

Everything about that night, all those years ago, was now being played out in Hunter's head. He nodded again, sadly.

Paul continued. 'I told traffic what my thoughts were and they got involved in the fatal enquiry. But when I suggested to the DI that I should get involved as well, especially with my sister being one of the victims, he wouldn't have it. All he kept whingeing on about was the loss of the department's car. I had a head to head with him because he said I only had myself to blame. The twat said if I had looked after the car better it wouldn't have got nicked and therefore wouldn't have been involved in the fatal accident. I lost it and one of the lads had to stop me from punching his lights out. That virtually signalled the end of my CID days.'

Paul's face was flushed and Hunter could sense the frustration and anger even after all this time.

'I went on a bit of a crusade for a while and showed the cardigan to every villain I nicked,' continued Paul. 'But no one could place it to any of our female criminals. If you remember, the gaffer went off on one when he found out what I was doing and gave me the shittiest jobs for months. That's when I realised my days were numbered, so I decided to go back into uniform. And that's when I joined Traffic division. To be honest, it gave me some freedom to see if I could track down the bastard who crippled my sister.' He rubbed his shaven head again. 'Do you know, Hunter, every time I see my sister in her wheelchair, I play that night over and over again in my head, wondering if I have missed something or someone — and especially regretting my stopping off for a stupid shag?'

'Don't beat yourself up, Paul. Hindsight is a wonderful thing. We've all done things we regret. Anyway, the murder enquiry I'm involved in now might draw a line under who caused that accident. That's why I called you. I've mentioned the cardigan because yesterday I found out that our murder victim, Carol Siddons, was actually wearing it when she went missing. Apparently her mother gave it to her to wear that night.'

Hunter wondered how to broach the next couple of sentences, but there was no other way around it.

'You know what that means, don't you, Paul?' he started. 'The cardigan belonged to a victim and not the person who nicked the CID car. That's why you didn't get anywhere with your enquiries all those years back. You know we're also investigating the murder of Rebecca Morris, don't you?'

Paul nodded.

'Well, the discovery of Carol Siddons's body is linked to Rebecca Morris. The forensic pathologist has confirmed that the killings are similar. It looks as though the killer picked up Carol Siddons after he'd nicked your CID car that night, drove her around in it, murdered her and then buried her. Her body was found only about fifty yards from the old track where the car was dumped and set on fire. It had been buried in a shallow grave.'

Paul dropped into the chair beside the table where they had left their drinks.

'Fucking hell, I can't believe this,' he mumbled beneath his breath, and snatched up his beer and took a swift gulp.

'Do you still have that cardigan? Because you know what I'm thinking now, don't you?' said Hunter, sitting down next to his colleague.

'DNA.'

Hunter nodded. Things had changed so radically in the past twenty years. Forensic scientists could work with the smallest sample of genetic material, such as sweat or tears on clothing, to enable a match.

'Bloody hell, Hunter — I never actually booked it in as evidence. I've told you what I was doing with it all those years back. It was like treading on eggshells with the gaffer so I kept a low profile with my enquiries. I kept it in my drawer until I needed it.'

'Did you get rid of it then?'

'I'm sure I didn't sling it,' Paul said. 'I can remember taking it with me when I moved. It stayed in my locker for ages.' After a moment's silence, he added, 'I do have it. I put it in my garage. It'll still be there. But if I do get it, how can we get it into the evidence chain without being disciplined for breaching standards? The gaffer back then, Jameson, died of lung cancer a few years back, so there's no one to back up my story as to why I had to suppress it as evidence.'

'Paul, this is something you need to sort out. We need that cardigan for forensic evidence.'

'But how am I going to do that?'

Hunter shrugged his shoulders. 'We need that cardigan.'

'Fuck me, Hunter, this is my job on the line.'

'And it's mine as well.'

For a moment Hunter locked eyes with his former CID colleague. Taking a deep breath, he said, 'Look, Paul, I don't want to fall out over this but I covered up enough for you that night when you were out shagging instead of doing your job, and rightly or wrongly the DI did his best to play down the link of one of his department's cars being involved in a fatal accident, even though it had been stolen. We know your sister's boyfriend died that night in an incident involving the CID car, plus now the murder of Carol Siddons, and the only evidence we've got is that cardigan. You recovered it and it should have been booked in. You know how this job has moved on, especially where it comes to preserving evidence. We really need that cardigan. It could be our best chance of catching this bastard.'

Hunter paused and took on a more sympathetic tone. 'Look, it's like you said, this happened years ago. Things were different back then, and there's no doubt that DI Jameson had some influence on your decision not to book it in. But if you think about this, there must be some way you can turn this around. My guess is that the evidence property books will have been destroyed a long time ago, and you'll be able to come up with something to cover your back.'

Hunter took another sip of his beer, studying Paul, who was wearing a puzzled look.

'Another thing,' Hunter added. 'I need to know where you were that night. Who were you shagging when the car was nicked? She might be a vital witness to all this.'

'I can't do that.'

'She was married, wasn't she?' He sensed Paul hesitate. 'Come on, you've got to be straight with me. I need to know what I was covering up all those years ago.'

'She was married, yes. She still is, to the same guy — and that's why it's so messy.'

'Come on, cough up. You've done the hard part getting this far.'

'He's a local councillor.'

'Why's that so messy?'

'Because he's now a member of the Police Authority.'

'Bloody hell, Paul. You certainly pick 'em, don't you? Now you've told me that you might as well tell me who she is.'

'Karen Gardner.'

'Karen Gardner, married to Jerry Gardner — chair of the Police Authority?'

Paul nodded. 'One and the same. I went to a burglary at their flat and when I caught the kid who'd done it, she sort of rewarded me. After that, I used to visit her every so often when her hubby was at his meetings.'

'A few of the lads used to hint that they thought she was a bit of a warm 'un. You dirty bugger.'

'Yes, she was. In fact, she was red hot. Can you see now why I never said anything? And I know I wasn't the only one doing the rounds with her. I got a whisper she was getting a good seeing to by a local villain and that's when I called it a day.'

Hunter's breath hissed through clenched teeth. 'That puts a different complexion on things. If you knew about him then he might also have known about you being a cop.'

'It's got me thinking now.' Paul screwed up his face, then rubbed a hand across it. 'This is a real fucking mess, Hunter, isn't it?'

Hunter bit down on his lip, and then said, 'You know who the guy is?'

'No idea. It was just a snippet I picked up in the pub, and so, as I say, I stayed well clear of her.'

'You know what I need to do, don't you?'

'Interview her.'

Hunter nodded. 'You and I go back a long way. I promise I'll be as discreet as I can. But it's all fitting into place now. This villain, whoever he is, may well have known about you visiting Mrs Gardner and thought of a really good way to get back at a cop. So, the possibility is he could have either nicked the car that night, or got someone else to do it to set you up. And then somehow or other Carol Siddons got involved and ended up dead.'

Hunter pondered for a second, then added, 'Most probably because she witnessed the accident which killed your sister's boyfriend and was going to blab.'

DAY EIGHTEEN

Hunter felt deflated as he left the club. He slid Bon Jovi's *Crossroad* album into the CD player and tried to lose himself in the music, but as he drove home it slipped into the background and he spent the journey replaying the evening's conversation over and over in his mind and reflecting. Hunter knew that despite everything he and Paul Goodright had done together in the past, things would never be the same between them — that trust they had once shared had ended back there in the club, following their frank exchange of words.

He was restless for the remainder of the night, mulling over his next steps. After several hours of tossing and turning he knew he had to confide in someone. Under normal circumstances he would turn to Beth. But this was a problem within the job and he knew the one person, apart from his wife, who would not pass judgment and who would give him good, balanced advice, was Grace.

Sleep finally caught up with him about four o'clock. When the alarm sounded three hours later, he felt thick-headed and drained and was only able to invigorate himself by staying longer in the shower. Tilting his head backwards, he lingered, feeling the rush of cool water pour over his face.

As he stood on the patio finishing off his toast, taking in all the smells of the fresh morning air and rerunning last night's events, despite having had only a few hours sleep, he somehow felt refreshed and revitalised. He drove to work replaying Bon Jovi, singing along to 'Living on a Prayer' and 'Keep the Faith', before cruising into Barnwell station yard.

When he entered the MIT office Grace had already arrived, face made-up and smartly dressed, looking business-like as usual. She'd scraped her hair back into a tight bunch, accentuating her high cheekbones and showing off summer freckles.

She acknowledged him with a wide smile and as he sidled up he could see she was already adding milk to two cups of tea, one for him.

'We need to talk,' he said quietly.

'We certainly do,' she responded in a formal tone.

Grace's response took him aback and he looked at her quizzically.

'What was the matter with you yesterday? You reacted as though you'd just been shot when Sue Siddons mentioned the cardigan,' she said, stirring in a spoonful of sugar.

Hunter glanced around, making sure no one was in earshot.

'I'll tell you after morning briefing,' he said, picking up the steaming mug and moving to his desk. He set the cup down and began to sift through the pile of papers and files which had accumulated in his tray over the past few days. He hoped he would be able to focus on their content.

The daily briefing centred on the previous day's meeting with Susan Siddons, and Hunter recounted the conversation he and Grace had conducted with her. It had given a new dimension to the investigation. They now had a name for the mummified remains and with this came the task of uncovering Carol Siddons's past, prior to her disappearance all those years ago. It had also thrown up the name of someone who could be considered to be their first major suspect: Steven Paynton, a petty criminal with a hard-man reputation. He and his family had terrorised their community for years and many times the cops had met a wall of silence, or court cases had collapsed, through fear of recriminations. Over the years there had been enough people willing to tell the police about the family's criminal activities, but to get those people to be witnesses and give a formal statement had been damn near impossible.

Therefore, Steve Paynton had very few convictions. Those he had were petty — mainly for theft and burglary — and he had collected those in his early teens and spent several months in a young offenders' institution. More up-to-date police intelligence revealed him to be a minor-league drug dealer who used violence to settle debts. Susan Siddons had also given some personal insight into his brutality towards her and her daughter, now supported by information from Social Services who had their own file on Paynton. A phone call late the previous afternoon from a team leader at Social Services had revealed that one of Paynton's ex-partners had fled the area after numerous beatings.

This was over fifteen years ago, before he had hooked up with Susan Siddons. The paperwork revealed numerous attempts had been made to persuade the woman to formalise a complaint, but she had point-blank refused to speak to the police, choosing instead to change her name and leave. A member of the team stayed in touch for a short time and had helped to rehouse her. The last address in Retford, Nottinghamshire, was now five years old and Hunter and Grace were given the job of tracking her down.

Hunter drove the unmarked CID car out of Barnwell Police station, following the route towards the A1 for the hour-long journey to Retford. Grace, in the passenger seat, shuffled uneasily, scanning the file on Steven Paynton.

'Listen to this,' she said, keeping her eyes on the paperwork, while Hunter negotiated the bustling out-of-town traffic. 'Social Services have written loads of notes on this woman we're going to see. It seems Paynton started to beat her within a month of moving in. He scalded her with hot tea. He beat her with a dog leash and he even pissed on her when she was asleep. And he held a knife several times to her throat and simulated slicing her open. It's making our Mr Paynton seem like a hot prospect in our enquiry. What with this and Sue Siddons's statement, it should give us some leverage to hold him long enough to rattle his cage.'

'We don't know yet if she'll make a complaint. Don't forget this was fifteen years ago. She's got a new identity and a new life now. She probably wants to put all this behind her.'

'I'll do everything I can to nail this bastard,' said Grace.

Hunter knew that was not an idle threat. Although outwardly Grace came across as gentle, he knew there was a sharper and harder edge to her which she could switch on like a lightbulb when she needed to. Back in their uniform days, he'd witnessed Grace standing up to a seasoned detective who had made disparaging remarks about a female witness, and when he'd then turned on her for having the audacity to challenge him she threw a mug of tea all over him.

As he swung the car onto the unmarked country lane that led to the trunk road, Hunter knew Grace was on a mission to get Steve Paynton. And when Grace got something into her head there was no holding her back.

Just before the A1 slip road he pulled the CID car into a lay-by and killed the engine.

'About the other day,' he began, and in the next ten minutes he revealed everything from the discussion with Paul Goodright the previous evening. 'That's why I reacted like I did when Sue Siddons mentioned the cardigan. I realised it was the one Paul recovered from the back of the nicked CID car.'

Grace shook her head. 'Bloody hell, Hunter, what are you going to do?'

'I don't know yet. I'm hoping Paul can come up trumps and find some way of getting that cardigan into the system. If he can, it'll make it easier, but the other problem is Mrs Gardner. At the time she was having her dalliances with Paul she was also seeing someone else — a villain, according to Paul — who likewise could have found out about Paul and was trying to stitch him up. As soon as Paul found out, he didn't stick around to discover who that person was. If we can find out that was the case, it'd make things very interesting.'

'Especially if it was Steven Paynton,' said Grace.

'Great minds think alike. The problem is Mrs Gardner's respectable status now. What she did in her thirties is well behind her and she won't like some hairy-arsed cop stirring up her past. Besides, it's going to go down like a lead balloon if the Police Authority gets whiff of this.'

'What about a hairy-arsed female cop having a word with her?'

'Grace, one thing I don't want to do is get anyone else involved in this mess, especially you.'

'Listen, Hunter, no one is any the wiser yet about Paul and Mrs. Gardner's indiscretion all those years ago, and at this stage we don't even know if they are relevant to this enquiry. If I'm seen going to visit her by a neighbour or a friend it will just look as though I've popped in for coffee, or I'm from one of the charities she's probably involved with. I'll plan it when her hubby is out and also it will be a lot easier coming from another woman.'

'I was worried how I was going to approach this, I'm not exactly renowned for being subtle.'

'Well then, you've answered the question yourself. And if it looks like we're on to something, then we'll worry how we can feed it into the enquiry system after.'

'It would be a help, Grace. Thanks. And I promise if this blows up in our faces, I'll just say this was on my orders.'

'I'll hold you to that.'

'By the way, Grace...'

'Yes?'

'Have you really got a hairy arse?'

'Wouldn't you like to know.'

'What a beautiful house. Victorian by the looks of it,' Grace said as they strode up a black and white decorative tiled path towards the wide-open porch of the semi-detached property. They had tried two other addresses in the terraced rows close to the town centre before being directed to this house on the outskirts of Retford. As they approached the stained-glass front door, Grace snapped open her folder and took a quick look at the photograph pinned inside. It was a dog-eared, discoloured, and dated picture of the woman they were seeking, and she hoped she would be able to recognise her from it. They could hear a woman singing within, and Hunter tried to steal a glance through the front bay window only to find that thick curtains blocked his view. Grace pressed the original brass buttoned bell set in the door frame and the singing stopped, quickly followed by a shout of 'just a minute' from somewhere at the back of the house. Footsteps resounded along the hallway before the front door swung open.

Although there were now crows-feet around the hazel eyes, and a slight greying around the temples of her chestnut brown hair, which was dragged back and tied in a ponytail, Margaret Brown, as she now called herself, had changed very little. She was still the fresh-faced, attractive woman depicted in the photograph, despite now being in her early forties. She glanced from one to the other as she snapped off her yellow marigold gloves. 'Sorry, I only just heard the bell. It's my cleaning day. Can I help you?'

Grace flashed her police warrant card, introduced herself and Hunter and smiled reassuringly. 'Are you Margaret Brown, used to be Mary Bennett?' she continued.

The colour drained from the woman's face.

Her eyes glazed and she went rigid. Then she said, 'This is about Steve, isn't it?'

'Steve? You mean Steve Paynton?' returned Grace.

She began to shake, then clasped a hand to her mouth. 'Oh my God. He's found me, hasn't he?' She looked past them, searching over their shoulders, staring up and down the street.

'Not that we know of. Look, this is about Steve Paynton but it's to do with his past. That's why we've tracked you down after all this time. Please can we come in? We really need to speak with you,' said Hunter.

She hesitated, took another nervous glance along the road, and then stepped back to allow them inside. Then she pushed the front door shut, turned the key and snapped on the safety chain before pointing to the front room.

Hunter and Grace went in first and sat down on a leather settee without waiting to be asked.

'Sorry I reacted like I did,' Margaret said, picking up a pack of cigarettes and a lighter. She shuffled one out quickly and put it to her mouth and then offered the packet to the two detectives. Hunter and Grace declined and she lit up, taking in a long drag, holding her breath for a several seconds before exhaling the smoke from one corner of her mouth.

'If I appear nervous that's because I am. To be frank, I'm shit scared. I've looked over my shoulder for so many years because of that man, and I was just beginning to think I'd got him out of my life before you two showed up.'

'Please calm down, he hasn't found you,' Hunter assured her. 'You've covered your tracks well. In fact, if it weren't for Social Services we would never have found you. And before you go complaining about them, we forced their hands because of a murder enquiry we're involved in.'

'Steve's killed someone,' she said, matter-of-factly. 'That doesn't surprise me. I always knew it was only a matter of time before he killed someone.' Margaret dropped heavily into the only armchair in the room, crossing one slender leg over the other.

'We don't exactly know if he has killed anyone, but he is a suspect,' Hunter clarified.

'Who's been murdered?'

'It's actually two murders we're investigating, both teenage girls, but they're years apart,' Hunter replied. 'In fact, fourteen years apart. Steve Paynton was in a relationship with the mother of one of them — a Carol Siddons. Carol disappeared all those years ago but we've only just discovered her body and as a result of our enquiries we tracked down her mum. She's told us that at the time Carol disappeared Steve was living with her and was violent to both of them. Then yesterday we found out he was with you prior to being with this woman, and that you'd reported to Social Services that he'd assaulted you on a number of occasions. That's why we felt it necessary to speak with you.'

Margaret drew anxiously on the cigarette again. She blew out the smoke. 'Assault is an understatement. He was a real evil bastard.' She sounded nervous.

Hunter sought to dispel her fears by recounting Susan Siddons's story and explaining the measures which were being put in place to protect her from reprisals, now that she had given a statement against Steve Paynton.

'You don't know what he's like. I had to live with him for two years. I've been in constant fear since the night I ran away. He always said he would track me down and kill me if I ever told the police.'

'Things have changed in the last fifteen years,' Grace said reassuringly. 'We've moved on with how we deal with victims, particularly of domestic violence. The magistrates also have a different approach when it comes to punishing offenders. If he's not caught up with you after all these years, then he's not going to do it now. We can and will protect you, but we do need your help to put him away. Susan Siddons has already made a statement and if you also give us a statement about his abuse towards you, it'll give us a real lever and will help us to get him remanded so we can investigate him properly over the murders of the two girls, without him interfering or hindering the enquiry.'

Margaret finished her cigarette and stubbed it out in an ashtray beside her. Then she took another and lit it. She said nothing, just stared towards a photograph on the wall above the fireplace. It was a studio shot of herself flanked by two smiling teenagers — a boy and a girl. Hunter guessed they were her children.

As he waited patiently for Margaret to say something, Hunter was inwardly screaming for her to open up and talk about the battering Steve Paynton had given her.

She seesawed her gaze between Hunter and Grace. A tearful film glazed her eyes.

'Do you know,' she began, 'I've not been able to have a relationship with another man? Since that day I ran for it with both my kids I've not been able to trust another man. Do you know what that's like?' She drew deeply on her cigarette.

Neither Grace nor Hunter responded. In fact, Hunter didn't know how to respond. He'd always been in a loving relationship.

'I've never talked about this. I didn't tell Social Services at the time, and I haven't ever discussed this with Jamie or Samantha — they're my two children. They're twenty and twenty-three now, and I know they wouldn't remember what went on all those years ago, but I'm just so afraid of the damage it would cause them if I brought it all up again. Some might accuse me of burying my head in the sand but that's how I feel I've needed to handle it to get me through all those dark days.' A tear fell from the corner of one eye and trickled down the side of her nose. She dabbed at it with her hand.

'I can't imagine for one minute how painful this is, but don't you feel now that we're here it's time to get rid of your demons?' said Grace quietly.

'What's really hard about all this, is that some would say I brought it all on myself. You see, I knew Steve Paynton from my schooldays. I knew some of the tricks he'd got up to, and yes, I also knew about his violence, but he was different around girls. A real charmer in fact. We bumped into each other several years later when I was going through a bad patch with my first marriage and he still had the same rugged good looks and the charm. We used to meet up in the pubs and my mates tried to warn me when we first went out together, but I thought they were just jealous because he was quite a good-looking guy, a real Jack the lad.

'I'd already got Jamie and Samantha from my first marriage but it wasn't working out. Their dad spent his days at work and his nights at the pub and so I'd already left and moved back in with my parents. Steve was the first bloke after we split up to show me some attention and make me feel wanted, and I fell head over heels for him. Anyway, after we had been seeing each other for the best part of a year he persuaded me to take out my savings and rent a flat with him, and against my mum and dad's wishes I did.' She paused and took another drag of her cigarette. 'Sorry I'm going round the houses with this but I suppose I need you to understand why I ended up with the bastard.'

For the first time, Hunter detected real anger in her words.

'After about six months together he started hitting me,' she continued. 'I kept getting on at him about getting a job. I was out working all day and he was frittering the money I earned down at the pub, so I kept nagging him. They were just slaps at first. But then he would come back from the pub pissed up and wanting sex, and because I said I was tired, he would thump me until I gave in.'

'He raped you,' interrupted Grace. 'You didn't give in.'

'It was easier to deal with it that way. The hidings weren't so bad if I gave in to him and I wouldn't have to cover up the bruises as much.' More tears ran down her cheeks and she stubbed out the half-smoked cigarette so that she could use the backs of both hands to wipe them away. 'Look, what I'm going to tell you now I've never told anyone. Not anyone.' She gripped the sides of the armchair, digging her nails into the leather upholstery. 'He also abused the children really badly. And the reason I've never told anyone this before is because, for a long time, I didn't do anything about it when I should have done.'

'I can see this is hurting you, Margaret, but trust us, we won't pass judgment on you,' Grace said, moving forward to hold her gaze. 'We just want enough to put Steve Paynton behind bars so he can't hurt anyone else.'

For the next hour Margaret Brown told them of the terror with which Steve Paynton had held her and her two children over a nine-month time span.

'He started by beating Jamie, who was eight at the time, with his belt when he wouldn't eat some of the food Steve had cooked. It wasn't that he didn't like the food,' she explained, 'but that Steve had burned it because he'd cooked it when he was in drink. At first, he forced Jamie to eat food coated with curry and chilli sauce, depriving him of his pop. And then when he lost control of his bowels Steve would rub the faeces into his face. Then he began to deprive Jamie of food and would lock him in a cupboard under the stairs. He would keep him there for several days, hungry and thirsty, forced to lie in his own poo.'

She tried to hold back her own sobs when she revealed that she would lie awake listening to the cries of her little boy caged under the stairs.

'The last straw,' she continued, 'was when I came back from shopping one day and found that Steve had stripped Samantha of her clothes and was photographing her. She was only five years old, for God's sake. I just lost it and flew at him, but he was stronger than me and he gave me a right thumping. He took his belt off and strangled me with it. I must have passed out and when I came to he had a knife at my throat, threatening to cut me up if I so much as whispered this to anyone. That's when I came to my senses and realised just how much danger I was in, and was putting my children in. I knew that I had to get away before he killed one of us.

'So, when he went to the pub that night, I gathered together everything I could get in two suitcases and, with the help of Social Services, got into a woman's refuge. Unfortunately, I could only stay for a week because they don't allow males, even though Jamie was only eight. So that's when I changed my name and came to Retford. Somewhere where no one knew me. For over a year I didn't even contact my parents, just in case Steve got to them.'

She sighed, a long sigh, as though a great weight had been lifted off her.

'Can you understand now why I've never brought this up with Jamie and Samantha? I feel so guilty. It holds too many bad memories for me, and I blame myself for allowing this to happen to them.'

Margaret's face was etched with pain, grief and anxiety as she finished recounting the horrors she and her children had endured at the hands of Steve Paynton.

For the next two hours Grace guided Margaret through the anguish of relating everything again into a written statement, and as she put her signature to the pages, Grace touched her gently on the back of the hand.

'I promise you this, Margaret,' she said. 'Steve Paynton will not be causing you any more pain. After this you can put your nightmares behind you.'

DAY NINETEEN

It was early morning when Hunter and Grace, with a small team of uniformed officers from the day shift, sped to Steven Paynton's terraced house, using side streets as cover because they knew how quickly the criminal grapevine worked in this area. They needed surprise on their side.

Before the third knock Hunter put all his force behind a flying kick at the front door. The lock and metal hasp parted company with his first attempt and the door crashed in. He and Grace stormed into the hall, followed by uniformed officers in dark blue search overalls and they were instantly greeted by the strong, pungent stench of cannabis.

The team split up, Hunter and Grace taking the stairs while the uniform team dashed off to secure the ground floor.

Before the pair had got halfway up the narrow stairway they were confronted by a snarling Steve Paynton, who stood on the landing above, wearing only a pair of boxer shorts and wielding a baseball bat.

'What the fuck?' he shouted, glaring down at them.

'Police,' shouted Hunter, halting his jog. 'Drop that now.' He pointed at the wooden bat.

Although Paynton wasn't a big man, his frame was lean and muscular. His well-toned muscles were punctuated here and there by black tattoos of barbed wire and tribal markings. Add a shaved head and he cut a menacing figure.

'I hope you've got a warrant?' he said, lowering the bat to his side.

'Sure have,' Hunter said, continuing up the narrow stairway, though much slower now, wary of how the man might react.

'You could have fucking knocked. You didn't need to kick my bastard door in.'

'I did knock — repeatedly — but no one answered ... did they, Grace?'

She nodded. 'Repeatedly,' she agreed.

'Bollocks.' Paynton backed off to his bedroom. 'I'll get fucking dressed, you fucking morons.'

They followed him into the room. It was a pigsty. Hand rolled cigarette butts, porn magazines, several weight training barbells, and an array of clothing in various states of dirtiness littered the floor. It was hard to determine whether the marks on the carpet were design or stains. This room also had a strong smell of cannabis, mixed with the musty stench of body odour, causing Grace to wrinkle her nose.

'Cleaner's day off I see,' she said, rubbing thumb and forefinger under her nose.

Paynton, who was fastening the last button on his jeans, stepped to within a foot of her.

'You really don't want to be doing this, you black bitch,' he snarled, pushing his shaven head into her face. A large prominent vein from the front of his ear to where his hairline should have started was pulsing angrily.

Grace held his stare. She'd heard this sort of abuse so many times before. 'Roll with it, girl,' her father had told her. 'Never let them see they've got to you. You're better than them. Fight back how you know best.'

'A bit of a racist as well as a wanker,' she said curtly.

'Me? I'm a signed-up member of the Ku Klux Klan,' he shot back.

Hunter rocked onto the balls of his feet, curling his hands into tight fists — ready.

Grace pushed a polished red fingernail at his nose. 'Hey, white boy. You really don't know who your messing with.'

'You stupid bitch,' he snapped. 'I'll sort you out.'

Hunter sprung forward, swinging a punch from the hip. It smacked into Steve's side, catching the bottom two ribs and the breath exploded from his mouth. He sank to his knees clutching his side and for a few seconds his face went bright red, eyes bulging from their sockets as he fought for breath. Then he gasped loudly and fell to one side.

'You bastard. You fucking bastard!' he screamed.

Grace stepped over Paynton's prostrate figure, grabbed the rigid handcuffs from the waistband of her suit trousers and snapped one end onto his right wrist. Then she forced her knee into the small of his back, flattening him to the floor and slammed the jaws of the remaining cuff onto his other wrist.

'Fancy that, Steve Paynton being done over by a little black girl. This is really going to damage your street cred,' she said, twisting the rigid cuffs until he winced. 'You're nicked.'

He tried to force himself up, but Grace was pushing his head into the carpet.

'What the fuck for?' he mumbled, trying to avoid swallowing the fibres from the pile.

'Assaulting Susan Siddons, and assaulting and raping Mary Bennett. Those names ring any bells?'

'Might do, but they wouldn't dare make a statement against me.'

'Oh, believe me when I tell you they have given two very detailed statements about your activities. And we're adding resisting arrest to that, just in case you feel like complaining about police brutality. Now get up and get down those stairs, you insignificant little piece of shit.'

Paynton scrambled to his feet, helped by Hunter's hands under his arms.

Hunter turned to Grace and said, 'My, my, we are somewhat tetchy this morning ma'am.' He helped her guide the prisoner towards the stairs.

As Paynton was led away by the arrest team, Hunter and Grace donned latex gloves and joined the search team who were already busying themselves in the downstairs room.

Much of the house was squalid, despite some very expensive items of furniture and electrical equipment dotted around. They picked their way through dirty crockery strewn across stained seat cushions, which had to be removed so they could search down the sides of the suite. They also checked several large screen televisions and DVD players — no doubt stolen, as the serial numbers and markings had been erased, and removed them to the marked police van outside.

Behind the washing machine in the kitchen they discovered a stash of cannabis, about half a kilo in a plastic bag and hundreds of packets of rolling tobacco, but they knew it wasn't enough for CPS to prosecute for supplying or smuggling so they continued the search. What they really needed was something that could connect him to either of the two murdered girls, so they methodically and painstakingly moved appliance after appliance, household effect after household effect, and even tore up the carpets in the hope of a breakthrough.

And it came — in the bathroom; virtually the last room on the checklist. Working under the dull glow from a bare electric ceiling bulb, probing the nooks and crannies beneath the bathtub, one of the officers spotted a chink of light catching the edge of something metal deep in one corner, and only Grace was small enough to crawl into the space to remove it.

She cursed as she dragged herself back out, her pale grey suit now covered in cobwebs, dirt and other detritus.

The tea caddy she held was probably from the late 1950s and in a poor state. She pulled at the lid and it came off suddenly, spilling some of the contents over the bathroom floor. A collection of black and white and colour photographs of girls, from pre-pubescent children to young teenagers, in various stages of undress, including nude, lay scattered at their feet. Grace dropped to her knees and Hunter joined her as she carefully shook out the remaining contents of the caddy. Using only a forefinger, she separated the photos and began to sift through the images.

'Bingo,' she said as she pulled out four faded colour photographs. They showed a young pubescent girl posing indecently. In two she was wearing a pair of white cotton panties and in the others she was naked.

'Recognise her?' Grace said to Hunter.

'Certainly do,' he replied. 'That's Carol Siddons; a very young Carol Siddons.'

'Do you want to be good cop or bad cop?' said Hunter as he paused at the cell area interview room door, glancing through the folder of paperwork and evidence he was carrying, ensuring it was in correct order for the interrogation.

For a moment Grace looked thoughtful. Then, narrowing her eyes, exposing her laughter lines, she said, 'Bugger it. We'll both be bad cop. We've got enough evidence to send him away for a bloody long time.'

'That's my girl,' said Hunter, opening the door and entering the soundproofed room.

Steve Paynton was already seated behind the table, hands clenched together in front of him. He glanced up, unclenched his fists and tugged at the front of the all-in-one white forensic suit.

'Why the fuck have you put me in this?' he demanded.

'Your clothes have been seized for forensics,' Hunter said.

'What forensics? You've got fuck all on me.'

They sat down and Hunter slid the file across to Grace. Given Steve Paynton's attitude towards women — and people of colour — they had already decided it would rattle him more if she was to lead the interview.

Grace opened up the file, careful not to show the photos they had found, and then switched on the tape recording machine.

She went through the preliminaries; the opening preamble to any police taped interview, the caution and confirmation that he did not wish the services of a solicitor.

'Don't fucking need one,' he said.

Grace chided him with a wagging finger, asking he refrain from swearing for the purposes of the tape and then continued with her questioning, but in a calm, matter-of-fact manner in an effort to throw him off kilter.

'We have a statement from Susan Siddons, whom I believe you were once in a relationship with, Steve?'

'No comment.'

'Susan says that you beat her on a regular basis. Is that correct?'

'No comment.'

'Are you going to sit there all day saying no comment?'

'No comment.' He stared hard into Grace's eyes and smirked.

Grace patiently went through the statement taken from Susan Siddons, outlining each of the beatings Paynton had dealt her. Paynton continued to respond with 'no comment' and then Grace changed tack to discuss the assaults on Carol Siddons, Sue's daughter. His only change in answer came when he was asked about the time he was caught urinating on the girl.

'Look, it's her word against mine. Sue is an alkie. If this gets to court she'll be torn apart in the box by my brief.'

'She wasn't an alcoholic till she met you,' Grace snapped back.

Hunter touched the back of Grace's hand and shot a quick glance at her, raising his eyebrows and willing her to not let Paynton get under her skin.

She took a deep breath and then flicked over to the pages of Margaret Brown's statement.

'Do you remember Mary Bennett?' Grace said, referring to Margaret's name before she changed it.

'Should I?' he replied arrogantly and then leaned back in his seat, clasping his hands behind his head.

'You should do. You were in a relationship with her for two years during the 1980s.'

'A lot of water under the bridge since then, Constable. Refresh my memory.'

Grace again patiently read over Mary's statement, careful to detail every incident of assault and introducing the numerous times he had raped her while she was in fear of being beaten.

'Rape, you say.' He rocked forwards and stroked his chin. 'Definitely not rape. I would say it was consensual sex. She liked it rough if I recall. Don't all women?'

Grace took another deep breath, exhaled slowly.

'Mary says she came home from bingo one night and found you had stripped her five-year-old daughter Samantha and were photographing her,' she said calmly.

Grace saw an immediate change. His face had lost that cockiness.

He said after a long pause, 'No comment.'

Then Grace took out some of the photographs they had recovered from the tin under the bath. They were in two separate evidence bags, each containing a number of images.

She slid out five photos from one of the bags.

'For the tape,' she continued, 'I am now showing the defendant exhibit one — five colour photos of a pre-pubescent girl. She is naked in each one and two of them focus on her genitalia.'

The colour drained from Paynton's face. Grace knew she had him.

She continued. 'These have been identified by Mary Bennett as her daughter Samantha, then aged five, and they corroborate her statement. Can you tell me why we found these hidden in your house?'

He remained silent.

Grace opened up the second exhibit bag and removed four faded photographs. She slid them across the desk directly in front of his face.

'I am showing the defendant four colour photographs of a pre-pubescent girl.' She paused, staring into Steve Paynton's ashen face. 'In two of these she is naked and two show the girl wearing a pair of white panties,' Grace continued. 'This girl has been identified as being the daughter of Susan Siddons — Carol Siddons — whose body was recently discovered buried on the site of the old Manvers Colliery.'

'Whoa. Whoa!' he shouted. 'Just a minute, where's this fucking going? You're trying to pin her murder on me, aren't you?'

'Never mind you shouting the odds saying we're trying to pin the murder of Carol Siddons on you,' Grace said, her own voice a pitch higher. 'We know you lived with Carol and her mum for some time. We also know that you have a history of violence, and now we have found these nude photographs of Carol when she was only a child hidden in your bathroom. Join the dots, Steve.'

He dropped his head into his hands and rubbed his forehead feverishly. After about thirty seconds he stopped, snapped bolt upright and banged his hands on the table.

'All right, you've got me,' he snarled. 'But I ain't done no murder. I had nothing to do with killing Carol or any other girl. Yes, I photographed them, but it was fun like, I'm no pervert. And yes, I'll admit that I slapped Sue and Mary about but that's it. Okay? That's it.'

'Come on now, Steve, you've made a start. That's the hardest part over. Now just get it off your chest and tell us the rest. Shall I make it easier for you?' Grace reached forward fixing his gaze with her own.

A mixture of fear and hate played across Paynton's face.

Grace continued, 'I think as Carol got older, she got the courage to tell you what you had done was wrong and that she was either going to tell her mother or the police. You couldn't afford for that to happen and you realised you had to silence her once and for all.'

'No!' he shouted and banged a fist on the table. 'You're twisting this. Yes, I photographed her, but that's it. I didn't harm her like you're saying. I didn't fucking kill her.'

Hunter high-fived Grace and punched the air as they left the interview room an hour later. The interview hadn't ended entirely as they had wanted, but they had made a pretty good start to the first of what would be many interview sessions conducted over the next thirty-six hours. Steven Paynton had fully confessed to the brutal beatings of both women and went some way to admitting he had forced Mary Bennett to have sex against her will.

That at least would give CPS enough evidence to consider a charge of rape.

Finally, Paynton admitted taking indecent photographs of Samantha Bennett and Carol Siddons when he had been living with their mothers. But no matter how hard they had pressed they couldn't move him on Carol's murder. Hunter hoped it would be only a matter of time.

DAY TWENTY

The headline '**DEARNE MURDERS — SUSPECT HELD**' brought a smile to the man's lips. He'd read the storyline in the *Barnwell Chronicle* several times and the thought that someone else was taking the rap for him only boosted his confidence.

Those around him would be more relaxed and less suspicious, enabling him to go about his activities again without raising an eyebrow.

He rested the compact digital camera on the sill of the open car window, monitoring the crowd through the two-inch screen. The camera had been a marvellous buy for the price. Small and discreet enough to hide in the palm of his hand and yet powerful enough with its 10x zoom to pick out the finest detail at fifty yards.

He checked and double-checked his rearview mirror again, and then scoured the faces of the bustle of parents hovering outside the school, attentive to any suspicious reaction, especially as he had parked in the same spot for the past week while he waited and watched out for her. He glanced at his watch again. She was late today. Or had he already missed her? He hoped not. He liked to see her in school uniform. And this would be his last opportunity for some time; the schools were breaking up today for the annual six-week summer holiday.

At the edge of his peripheral vision he caught sight of her, coming his way from a different part of the school. A shaft of sunlight broke through the clouds as she emerged from a row of trees close to the boundary fence. For a second it cast a halo on her mane of blonde highlighted hair and he snapped off a shot. He wasn't too concerned about the composition because he could play with the image later on his computer to get the effect he wanted. He wondered why she had been so late for him. He zoomed in and caught the frown creasing her pretty face. Something or someone was troubling her. He snapped another shot of her chewing at a finger. She looked particularly attractive today. Was that a hint of mascara around her beautiful brown eyes?

He took another picture of her climbing into her mother's car, catching more thigh than normal as her short, grey school skirt rode up, before she went partially out of his sight as she slammed the passenger door shut. There was a brief exchange of words between her and her mother before they pulled away from the kerb. He wondered what that was about.

Dropping the camera onto the seat beside him, he took another glance around. He let out a long breath, satisfied he hadn't attracted any unwarranted attention, and then he put the car in gear and slowly crept away.

He drove the three miles to his usual quiet spot and veered off the road onto the dirt track to the woods. He edged slowly along the treeline until he was on the long stretch where he would have a good view of anyone approaching from a distance and then he turned off the ignition.

He wound down both front windows to listen and picked up his camera and started to scroll back through the images he had captured. He was particularly interested in the ones he had caught of her two nights ago when he had crawled to the bottom of her garden, waiting for her to go to her room. It had reminded him of his teenage years when he had sneaked around his neighbours' properties with the camera his father had left him, snapping away as they emerged from their bathrooms.

When she had come from the shower, he'd set the camera to video mode, watching her as she gently rubbed the moisture from that long mane of hair. He particularly liked the way the light glistened on her face and neck and shoulders. He had captured her petite, slender form perfectly.

Viewing this was almost as good as being in the room with her.

He was getting excited again and he felt the rush of desire as a burst of testosterone surged through him. He sat the camera on the dashboard of his car, switched to playback mode, cranked back his seat, unbuttoned his jeans and began to masturbate.

'Harder, faster,' barked Jock Kerr, setting all his weight behind the leather punchbag. 'C'mon son, thirty more seconds, put it in.'

Hunter's gloved hands pummelled the sand-filled bag in piston-like fashion. Every muscle in his arms was on fire and beads of sweat ran from his forehead, down the sides of his face and neck, adding to the already soaked patch on the front of his gym vest.

'Okay son, that's it. Good work, call it a day,' ordered his father in his strong Glaswegian lilt.

Hunter punched the bag twice, hard, for luck, then dropped his guard and rested his chin on his upper chest to grab great gulps of air. He was physically drained almost to the point of sickness and yet he was mentally alert, pleased that he had managed an hour of his father's training. Hunter loved his boxing sessions in his father's gym. His passion for them was almost on a par with his painting, but although it was hard to spare enough time for his art, he could usually squeeze in an hour or two at the gym several times a week. It also gave him quality time with his dad, and had the added bonus of sharing a well-earned pint or two with him afterwards in his local working-men's club. Inevitably, conversation revolved around Hunter's job or the distant memories of his father's boxing days.

Repeatedly, Hunter found himself listening to the potted version of his father's life-changing experiences. The same story, over and over again, of how he had boxed since he was a young boy back in his native Scotland. Explaining in detail how he had been introduced to it by his father, Hunter's grandfather, so that he could stand up for himself. He had quickly discovered he had a natural flair for the pugilistic art, and so as a teenager he had been taken on by an ex-professional at one of Glasgow's leading clubs and coached to a high level.

Then he would rerun some of the fights in animated fashion, especially when he had got to the part where he was selected to compete in the Commonwealth Games. And how, at seventeen, he had won a Bronze medal which had carved the way for a professional career. His story tailed off with the bout that ended his career. He'd picked up a nasty cut just above his eye, where the flesh is at its thinnest and, despite several skin grafts, the scar opened with every fight and so at twenty-two his career was over.

Then with immense pride he would pick up the story again. Rather than turn his back on the sport he was good at, he had worked even harder and immersed himself in the training side. His father's story always ended on a note of sadness as he explained how he had soon come up against the seedier side of the fight game, having to ward off undesirables, especially those involved with the Glasgow gangs. When he discovered that he had a child on the way, he decided he'd had enough of Scotland, and moved down to Yorkshire with his pregnant wife. He began a new phase in his life, setting up one of the best boxing gyms in the area, which earned him a very good living. He always ended the tale by putting an arm around Hunter's shoulders and telling Hunter that his birth, six months later, changed his life.

Hunter leaned against the tiled wall of the shower area, rolling his neck slowly while the warm jet of water swept away the sweat from his head, along the curve of his back, and away down his legs. *That felt really good*, he said to himself as he shut off the shower and padded into the changing room. As he dried himself, he switched back into work mode, recalling the previous night's telephone conversation with Barry Newstead.

He had kept in daily touch with Barry since the interview with Susan Siddons, updating him on the latest developments in the investigation into the two murders. He had also shared Paul Goodright's predicament, raising the issue of how he could legitimately introduce the cardigan as evidence without it being subject to too much scrutiny, especially if it proved to be vital to the enquiry. If anyone could resolve this, he told himself, it would be Barry. After all, he had employed some pretty unorthodox methods in the past. The phone call yesterday evening had proved him right.

'I'm your guardian angel,' Barry had said. 'Meet me in the pub after work tomorrow, and bring that young Goodright with you. He can keep me in beer while I reveal all and keep him out of the proverbial shite.'

Hunter dressed hurriedly, slinging on a T-shirt over a pair of jeans, and then stuffed his sweaty training gear into his bag. As he left the gym, he could hear his father turning off the lights and closing doors behind him.

Hunter popped the locks of his car and was about to open the driver's door when there was a shuffle of feet behind him. Before he had time to turn, he felt a sharp blow to his back, directly over his right kidney. The sickening stab of pain made his knees buckle. A sea of stars blurred his vision as he reached out to stop himself falling.

Another blow caught the side of his head, sending him crashing against his car door and throwing him onto his back. He groaned as he slumped to the pavement, but snapped open his eyes to see who his attacker was. There were three men towering over him and he recognised two of them; Steve Paynton's younger brothers; David and Terry. David, the younger of the two, was grinding his fist into the palm of his other hand, a menacing grin on his face.

'Our Steve's asked us to pay you a little visit. He wants you to know that thanks to you and that fucking black tart of yours he's on the nonce's wing at prison and we're here to pass on his regards,' he sneered. 'Oh, and when we've finished with you, we're off to see to that black bitch as well.'

Hunter tried to scramble to his feet but reeled back against his car as a boot caught him mid-chest, knocking the wind from his lungs. The three figures became shadows as a film of tears washed over his eyes, and expecting further blows he pulled his knees into his body.

In that instant, in the distance, he heard raised voices and running feet coming his way. Scuffles broke out around him and as his vision cleared, he saw his father and Barry Newstead grappling with his assailants. Feeling buoyed by their presence, he found an inner strength and sprang to his feet.

He dodged another blow from David, twisted and lashed out with a tightly clenched fist. The punch he swung came from the hip and arced into his foe's head. He knew he had connected well when he felt the crunch of gristle and bone. For a second Hunter stared into the young man's frenzied and distorted face. The eyes were bulging and menacing.

Hunter was hurting but he was also mad. Jumping to boxing stance he let fly again, raining punch after punch on David Paynton. He could hear cries and squeals but he didn't let up until his opponent had slumped to the ground. As he pushed himself upright, Hunter saw that despite their age, neither his dad nor Barry had forgotten how to channel their aggression — nor had they lost their touch. Barry had overcome his foe and was standing over the man Hunter hadn't recognised. The prostrate figure was holding his chest and moaning.

The fate and suffering of Terry Paynton, courtesy of Hunter's dad, was still ongoing. It was only as Hunter took stock of the situation that he realised Terry was out of it. The only thing keeping him upright was the grip his dad had on the front of Terry's sweatshirt, yet the viciousness with which his father still pummelled him was unrelenting.

A knot formed in Hunter's stomach and he lurched forward grabbing his dad's swinging fist.

'Dad, he's had enough.' He caught his father's stare and for a split-second saw something in his dad's eyes which he had only ever seen in drunken street fights attended during his years in uniform. It was a look of sheer hatred and evil.

For a second his father tried to resist his son's grip.

Hunter clenched his dad's wrist tighter. 'Dad, I said he's had enough.'

The look in his father's eyes faded. His command had registered.

Terry Paynton's bloodied head was flopping around like a ragdoll. Jock let go of the sweatshirt and there was a sickening thump as Terry's skull hit the pavement.

The colour drained from his father's face as he registered what he had done.

Hunter reached for his mobile.

'What are you doing?' snapped Barry.

'Ringing for an ambulance,' said Hunter.

'What on earth for?'

'So that we're covered for the mess they're in and they can be nicked later.'

'Don't be so fucking daft. There's no way they're going to complain when they started it. If you were them, with a reputation to keep, would you admit to being beaten up by two old men? We've given them a bloody good hiding. They'll lick their wounds and keep their heads down if they've any sense. Trust me, I used to be a policeman.' Barry gave a wide grin. 'Come on, there's a well-earned cold beer waiting for us.'

'I haven't had so much fun since 1971, when I gave Tam Watson a good thumping for taking my wee dram,' his father added in his broad Scottish brogue. 'I've not lost my touch, have I, son?'

The comment disturbed Hunter and continued to prey on his mind during the journey to the club. He kept glancing across at his dad, who was staring out through the windscreen, eyes fixed, trance-like. It was like he was unmoved by the whole event, yet Hunter had to grip the steering wheel to stop himself shaking.

He swung into the club car park, pulled into a space and killed the engine.

'You seem a little quiet, son.' His dad was still staring out of the windscreen, the gaze nowhere in particular.

Hunter took a deep breath. The image of his father pummelling Terry Paynton flooded his mind, along with the look on his father's face, as if he was enjoying hurting the man. His stomach was churning.

'I've never seen you like that, Dad. I thought you were going to kill him.' He wanted to say more but this was his dad he was talking to.

'Nae chance, son. He's made of stronger stuff than that. Anyway, the little scumbag deserved what he got. Anyone who goes toe-to-toe with my son goes toe-to-toe with me.'

'But, Dad...'

His father held up a hand. 'Listen to me now, son. You need to understand where that came from. I had a hard life in Glasgow. I had to fight for everything I got — literally. I had to learn how to take a punch and come back stronger. That's all I want to say about it. I don't want to talk about it again. And I don't want you saying anything about this to your ma.' Then a smile creased his face. 'Come on, mine's a pint of heavy and a wee dram.'

Before Hunter could say anything further, his dad was pushing open the passenger door.

Whenever a group of policemen gets together, conversation always turns to one thing — the job. It had been a spur of the moment decision for Hunter to take his father to meet Barry and Paul Goodright, especially as he knew what the conversation was about. However, having just dished out a good beating to three nefarious characters with the help of his dad, and then agreeing with Barry to hide the fact, it had not been too difficult a call to make.

Hunter studied his father's smiling face. He was still disturbed by what had happened, and knew at some stage he would have to discuss the events again with him, but this wasn't the time or the place.

Barry was on his soapbox and in full flow, chattering excitedly, recounting the fight. He paused as he finished the story, took a swill of beer, wiped the froth and saliva from his hairy upper lip and leaned forward to Paul Goodright.

'Now then, young Paul, the reason why we're all here.' He glanced sideways at Hunter's dad. 'Jock, we have some quite dodgy business to discuss. Not that we don't like your company but it might be a good time to get the beers in.' Barry tapped his nose.

Hunter saw the disappointment and acceptance on his father's face as he collected the empty glasses and moved from the table.

'Need some help, Dad?'

'No, son. You get your business done. It's okay,' his dad said and winked as he loped off towards the bar.

Barry dragged a bulky supermarket carrier bag from under the table. Hunter had seen him tugging it from the boot of the car when they pulled into the pub car park and had wondered what was in it.

'In my early CID days it was acknowledged that somewhere along the line you were always going to drop a bollock. Whether it was a small one or a big one was not in question, but how you were going to get out of it was another matter,' Barry began. 'So, each office had their own contingency plans. Before the days of numbering pocketbooks or other admin items we kept spares for the inevitable faux pas, usually in a locked drawer or cupboard. I also had my own spares for back up.' He dropped the bag onto the table and pulled it open. 'Ta dah!' He slid out its contents like a poker dealer with a pack of cards. There were two old Police 'property other than found' books, which Hunter and Paul could recall using early on in their careers to record seized items of property required as evidence.

'I forgot I'd kept these, and it's fortunate for you, young Paul, that I did. You'll find one of these books is from the 1980s and the other, which you will need, is from the 90s. All you have to do is fill out one of the carbon exhibit labels, date it the day you seized that cardigan and put it into the bag with it.'

'Barry, you're a Godsend,' Paul said excitedly, then paused. 'Just one thing though, how am I going to get it submitted properly as evidence without having to admit I've kept it in my locker and then my garage for all these years? The last thing we need is for some smart-arsed barrister to knock it back, especially if it has good forensic on it.'

'There's an easy answer to that. These days civilian admin staff have taken over the role of looking after property and my guess is none of them will have been around in the 90s when the cardigan was seized. All you have to do is go to the station with the bagged and labelled cardigan inside your coat. Tell one of the admin staff you need to get some property from one of the stores, and when you go into them, pretend to have a rummage in the shelves, distract the admin person and Bob's your uncle, or in this case Barry's your saviour. When they try to check out the number on the card, they'll just think the relevant property book has been destroyed after all these years.'

Hunter had sat transfixed, and now Barry had finished he leaned back in reflective mood. What he had just been a party to was against every rule in the book, and yet if it would help catch their killer he knew it was something he could live with.

Then, as he slid the books back into the carrier bag, Barry glanced at both of them and spoke slowly. It was as if he had read Hunter's mind.

'Something my old Sergeant once said to me when I was a young CID officer and the words remained with me throughout my service. Sometimes we have to use as much trickery as the villains do. You match lie for lie and make sure yours are better than theirs. At the end of the day you've got to protect the public and pay back the bad guys. Always remember the pen is mightier than the sword. And one last piece of advice. Don't get a conscience about it.'

DAY TWENTY-ONE

Grace arrived early at the tearoom in The Arcade, ordered a strong black coffee and sat down as close to the rear of the shop as she could. She was uneasy and had butterflies in the pit of her stomach. It wasn't every day that a possible main witness had links to the police authority, even if it was only through marriage. This was going to be an uncomfortable meeting and needed a delicate approach. Grace had rehearsed over and over in her head what she was going to say and deep down she wished now she hadn't suggested this to Hunter.

If this goes wrong, she thought to herself, *and the gaffer got to hear of it I'm going to get a right dressing down.* She stared at the glassed front entrance, wondering what Mrs Gardner looked like. It was just after 10.30 a.m. and the thoroughfare outside was bathed in strong sunlight. She tried to recall the woman's soft tones from yesterday afternoon's phone call. The voice had no hint of an accent and was very calming and reassuring, but sounded quite concerned about why there was a need to meet in such secrecy.

While she waited for her coffee, Grace looked around the room. She admired the contemporary décor — something she hadn't noted before, even though she'd used this tearoom many times to meet friends when out shopping. There were only another couple of customers; a young mum with a toddler in a buggy and an older woman, who she guessed was the child's grandmother.

From previous visits, she knew very few people would be in at this time. The other customers were just out of earshot, their conversation a muted jumble of words. That also meant they would not be able to overhear her speaking with Karen Gardner.

Five minutes after ordering, the waitress appeared with her coffee. Grace thanked her with a smile and picked up the cup, holding it with both hands and turning her attention back to the entrance. The coffee was stronger and hotter than she had anticipated. It wasn't the best she'd ever had, but it would do; after all she wasn't here for a coffee morning.

The shop door pinged, and a slim, attractive, faired-haired woman in a dark, well-tailored suit appeared in the entrance. She met Grace's gaze, smiled, raised a hand and came to her table.

'Detective Marshall — Grace?' she asked, standing before her.

Grace nodded and offered the chair opposite.

Within seconds the same young waitress returned, pen poised over a small notepad.

Karen glanced at Grace's drink. 'Another coffee please,' she said softly. 'Cappuccino.'

As the waitress walked away Grace leaned forward. 'Sorry I was so vague on the phone, but I didn't want to give too much away.'

'I gathered that,' Karen said.

Grace had been studying Mrs Gardner ever since she walked through the door and could see why Paul Goodright had visited her all those years ago. At forty-eight, she was still a very attractive woman, tastefully dressed and made-up. This was a woman who could afford to spend lots of time at the gym, judging by her slim figure and sunbed tan. Grace made small talk about the weather and Mrs Gardner's fundraising events, hoping to put her at ease. The coffee soon arrived. Grace waited while Karen took a sip, and then continued.

'Mrs Gardner — do you mind if I call you Karen?'

Karen set down her cup and nodded for her to continue.

'I asked to meet you here away from your home because what I want to talk about is a bit sensitive. I won't beat about the bush. We're trying to tie up some loose ends on one of our enquiries, and well, basically it's about an affair you had with a young detective, Paul Goodright, a few years back.'

'Oh God, is that all this is! I've been fretting ever since you called. I thought it was something more sinister.' Karen started to laugh. 'It wasn't exactly an affair, more a fling and it didn't last that long.'

The response surprised Grace. It looked like this was going to be easier than she had expected.

'How is Paul? He must be early thirties now. Is he married? Kids?' Karen Gardner was now firing off her own questions.

Grace responded with a series of nods.

'About five years ago my husband discovered I was seeing someone, not Paul, another guy, and he confronted me about it. I never denied it. I told him a few home truths about what his position meant for me, leaving me alone at night only to be wheeled out to be the dutiful wife when he needed me at one do or another. We had a big clear-the-air session, and to be honest it was well overdue. I suppose I was a little wild in my late twenties, early thirties. I saw a few guys, just for the attention which I wasn't getting from my marriage, but for the last five years I've been the faithful councillor's wife.' She paused. 'I can see by your expression you're surprised at how forthright I'm being.'

'I am a little taken aback,' Grace admitted. She took another sip of her coffee. It was cold now, and she set it back down on the saucer.

'Look, as I say we sorted our marriage out. My husband forgave me and it's all water under the bridge now. Jerry's not daft. He's a politician at heart and he still sees me as his bit of eye candy, I think the term is. I'm by his side when he needs me, flutter my eyelids and say all the right things to his colleagues, and he allows me my freedom to shop and meet my friends down at the gym, and get my beauty treatments; it's a happy compromise. Now I've bared my soul, Officer Marshall, can you give me a clue what this is about. The investigation?'

'Well, it might not actually have anything to do with our investigation, but as I've said, it is a loose end that we need to tie up. I want you to try and cast your mind back to 1993 when you were seeing Paul.'

'Good God. I can't remember what I did last week without my diary.'

'I think you might remember this, Karen, he had the CID car stolen when he was with you one evening.'

'Oh yes, I do remember that. He was in a right flap. I'm afraid I wasn't too sympathetic when he came back and told me and asked if he could make a call to the office. I'd had half a bottle of wine and I found it quite funny. He got a bit narked and was a bit worried about the compromising position he was in. He said he could lose his job and needed come up with a story to cover up being with me. Wasn't the CID car involved in some kind of accident with another car; ran it off the road or something?'

She stopped for a second, gazed up at the ceiling and tapped her chin.

'Yes, that was it,' she continued. 'I'm sure Paul told me his sister and her boyfriend had been in the other car and that she had been seriously injured and her boyfriend was killed. I think he also mentioned there was some kind of internal enquiry and if I was ever interviewed about Paul being with me, I was to deny everything. That's when he told me he mustn't see me again until things died down. But he never did get in touch again.' Mrs Gardner picked up her cup, took a sip, set it back down again. 'Is that what this is about? Have you found out who took the car?'

'I'm afraid not,' said Grace. 'We're looking into the possibility it was taken out of spite. A revenge sort of thing that went wrong. Paul heard on the grapevine that you were also seeing someone else. Someone with a bit of character shall we say, who wasn't too friendly with cops, and so we're looking into the possibility he found out about Paul visiting you and took the car.'

Karen looked perturbed.

'Hmm, I can see your dilemma. And to be honest, I'm wondering where this is going. How serious is this matter? Is all this going to come out?'

'Not if I have anything to do with it. If you were seeing another guy, and you choose to give us that name, he will have no idea it came from you. We'll make him believe his name cropped up through our informants, because if he did do this as some kind of perverted joke, he will have told someone.'

'I'm going to have to trust you, Grace. Paul isn't wrong. I was seeing another young man at the time. And I suppose he was a bit of a character, as you put it. I met him through my husband's work. Jerry used to be involved in issuing the licence for the local fairground Feast when it came to this area every year. The fairground owner brought his son to our apartment one day and I got chatting to him while they did their business. He was a bit of a rough character but quite a dish and quite a charmer. We met a few times over about a six-month period and then it fizzled out, sadly. He had a hell of a body.' She had a sparkle in her eyes. 'He told me he was some kind of fighter, bare knuckle stuff, illegal. He told me he regularly fought with the gypsies for money.'

'What's his name, Karen?'

'You sure he's not going to find out I told you?'

'Cross my heart.'

'Okay it's Billy. Billy Smith. His family own a plot of land near the canal where they have some static caravans. He's still around, when he's not travelling with the fair.'

'Thank you, Karen, you've been very helpful.'

Karen picked up her coffee cup, wiped the base on the edge of the saucer and took a sip.

'If you haven't already tried it, you should, you know,' she said.

'Try what?'

'Have an affair with a younger man. It does wonders for your self-confidence and it keeps your hubby on his toes. Life's not always Mills and Boon.' Karen gave a mischievous smile as she finished off her drink.

DAY TWENTY-TWO

The intermittent trill of the alarm clock pounded Hunter's ears. Grunting, he rolled over and swung out an arm to smack it off, pulling back quickly as pain registered in his ribs. It was a sharp and tender reminder of the fight with the Payntons.

The strong coruscating early morning sunshine filtering through the curtains should have given him the vigour to leap out of bed, yet he felt drained. He dropped back onto the pillow and shut his eyes as images of the melee flashed inside his head. Especially that look in his father's eyes. Not anger, but pleasure. He opened his eyelids again hoping to dismiss the mental pictures, but they were still haunting him. He eased up into a sitting position and gave a low moan. The movement disturbed Beth, who screwed up her face. He kissed her gently on the forehead, rolled out of bed and made for the bathroom.

As Hunter stepped out of the shower, he delicately dabbed the towel over himself. He hurt like hell this morning. In the mirror he examined his well-defined stomach and ribcage. The bruising had already taken on an intense purple shade. His shirt would cover the bruises and thank God he'd been able to protect his face during the assault. No one would be any the wiser.

It took an eternity to dress and he had to skip breakfast to get to work on time. As he pulled his Audi out of the drive, Simple Minds's 'Alive and Kicking' played out from the radio and he laughed to himself, then winced at the discomfort.

As he turned onto the bypass, he wound down the driver's window to let in the fresh morning air. It was already warm and not yet seven-thirty. The road ahead was clear and ELO's 'Mr Blue Sky' had just started. He turned up the volume and forced down the accelerator.

Half a mile from the station, the wail of two-tone horns approaching from the rear and at speed tore his attention away from the pounding music. Glancing in the rearview mirror, he spotted the ambulance screaming towards him and pulled in and hugged the kerb as it shot past. As he picked up speed, he hoped to God it wasn't going to be another call needing his team's attention. They were fast running out of detectives.

Following morning briefing and the de-camping of the teams from the MIT department to carry out their daily tasks, the detective superintendent had called together Hunter and DS Mark Gamble, the two MIT supervisors, Detective Inspector Gerald Scaife, the office manager who coordinated all the actions, and Isobel Stevens, supervisor of the HOLMES team, to review the investigation.

They had met in the conference room and were now seated around the large table. In front of them they had several A4 computer generated timelines relating to Carol Siddons and Rebecca Morris and a summary of the important issues taken from key statements of witnesses, supplied by Isobel's team.

The detective superintendent wanted to discuss the status of the investigation and, by the end of the meeting, confirm the strategy for the next phase of the enquiry.

'Heard the latest?' said Detective Superintendent Robshaw, leaning forward, resting his chin on cupped hands and looking around the table. 'Seems somebody gave Steve Paynton's two brothers and one of his cousins a good hiding. One of the brothers has got two broken ribs and a punctured lung, another has a broken nose and cheekbone and several teeth missing, and the cousin has a broken jaw and a badly gashed eye. Rumour has it a police officer was involved.'

Hunter saw the SIO look at him. Defensively, he shrugged his shoulders and gave him a noncommittal glare.

'Anyway, it seems none of them want to make a complaint, and we've got too much on our plate to follow up on malicious gossip.'

The superintendent leaned back in his chair, folding his arms, still with his attention fixed on Hunter. Hunter could feel the back of his neck reddening and a long trickle of sweat tickled down his spine. He know that his boss was letting him know he was aware of what had gone on, realised what lay behind it, and that nothing on the shop floor slipped past him and that, given the circumstances, he was not prepared to make a great fuss about it.

A bright shaft of sunshine pierced the gap between the partly closed blinds on one side of the conference room and reflected off the surface of the well-polished table, making the already stuffy room even warmer. Robshaw unfolded his arms and, using a hand-held remote, switched on the air conditioner. A low hum came from the unit high up against the ceiling and in an instant it felt cooler. Hunter was grateful for the drop in temperature.

Robshaw said, 'Okay, I'm going to open things up. Firstly, have we got anywhere yet with the playing card found with Rebecca Morris, or the markings carved into the two bodies?'

Hunter looked up from his papers to the white melamine boards at the front of the room. He focused on the blown-up photos of the killer's signature on Rebecca and Carol Siddons's abdomen. The contrast between the pale, waxen flesh of Rebecca and the wrinkled, parchment-like skin of Carol's mummified body made the marks appear so different. Professor McCormack had done a magnificent job in spotting them.

'I've been thinking,' said Isobel Stevens. She was an experienced detective with twenty-two years' service behind her, who had joined the HOLMES team following the Home Office review arising from the mistakes of the Yorkshire Ripper Enquiry. 'We know from all the enquiries that DC Sampson has made that they are not religious markings or anything to do with the occult. So, could they be a code of some kind?'

Hunter tilted his head and stared at the images, mulling over what Isobel had just said. The puzzle the killer had left behind had been preying on his mind on and off on a daily basis since their discovery.

He moved his head the other way to get a different view. Then it hit him. A flashback to that morning when the ambulance appeared at his rear was the trigger. In his interior mirror, he had been able to pick out the wording on the front of the vehicle because it was written in reverse.

'I've got it!' He made for the feature boards and tapped the shots of Carol Siddons's torso. The marks were clearer on these. 'It's a word, don't you see?' He moved his finger right to left underlining the marks. 'The last digit is not a number three, it's a letter E. It's written facing backwards. And they're not roman numerals they're all letters. Look,' he continued, tapping excitedly. 'He's carved the word EVIL backwards into the girls' stomachs.'

He'd grabbed their attention.

'Bloody hell, Hunter,' Detective Superintendent Robshaw said, 'I think you're right.'

The silence around the table lasted a good ten seconds, then Isobel said, 'So is the killer saying *he's* evil, or the girls are evil?'

Hunter gave it some thought. 'I think he's saying the girls are evil. That's why he did what he did. Think about it, Carol Siddons was taken into care and within a month or two had completely changed character. Her background statement describes her as a drunken, violent and promiscuous girl. She had become known as a girl with a bit of a reputation. And then Rebecca.' He glanced at the school photo. 'We know from her best friend Kirsty Evans that Rebecca wasn't the sweet, innocent girl we have pictured here. She'd become a bit of a rebel in the few weeks prior to her death. In particular she'd started flirting with older lads to an extent she'd get them worked up to expect sex and then she'd push them away and embarrass them. If we surmise that the killer got to know that side of their characters, then maybe in his twisted little mind he saw them as evil and needing to be punished.'

He returned to his seat.

'Okay,' said the detective superintendent, rubbing his hands together. 'Well done, Hunter, you've convinced me with that explanation, unless anyone has another interpretation?'

The detectives around the table looked at one another. A few shrugged.

The SIO scanned their faces. 'So, what's the significance of the playing card? The seven of hearts found on Rebecca Morris's body, none found with Carol Siddons.'

He was met with blank stares.

'We don't actually know there was no card with Carol's body,' said Hunter. 'Quite a lot of earth had been removed around her before the digger uncovered her remains. It could still be among the waste we're sorting through.'

The team nodded in agreement.

There was a further silence, then Detective Superintendent Robshaw said, 'Right, the playing card issue is one we need to think about for future briefings.' He leaned forward, clasping his hands together. 'And I don't need to remind you all that what we discuss here doesn't get to the press. The playing card and the markings on the body we keep to ourselves, okay?'

There were nods from around the table.

The SIO unclasped his hands. 'Right, let's move on. Isobel give us a rundown of what we have so far.'

Isobel dropped her paperwork onto the desk and lifted a pair of reading glasses, hanging from a cord around her neck, onto the bridge of her nose.

She cleared her throat and began to read slowly through the pages of summary, occasionally pausing to cross reference with the two timelines to confirm sightings and evidence. She began with Carol Siddons, affirming that her mother Susan had last seen the fifteen-year-old schoolgirl on the twelfth of October 1993, after making an unofficial visit from school to her mother's house, instead of going back to the residential care home where she had been placed by the courts.

'Carol spilled tomato sauce on her school clothes and so her mum loaned her a pair of jeans and a cardigan and saw her to the bus stop at half past nine. She left her at the bus stop and that is our last sighting until her body is discovered on the old Manvers coking plant site ten days ago. Now, this is where we have had a real breakthrough. PC Paul Goodright, who used to work here in Barnwell CID back in 1993, has come forward following the *Crimewatch* appeal. It appears that on that night he had his CID car nicked while he was out on enquiries, a passing dog walker found it on fire on the dirt track behind the coking plant. The fire brigade put out the blaze and PC Goodright recovered a cardigan from the back seat of the CID car.'

'I remember that,' said Hunter, feigning amazement. 'I was working that night. I went out with Paul after the fire brigade called in with the news. SOCO were called but the car was badly smoke damaged and they didn't manage to lift prints or anything, unfortunately. The car had also got some front-end damage and there had been a fatal hit and run that same night. We were certain it hit a car being driven by the boyfriend of Paul Goodright's sister. The boyfriend was killed and she was badly injured in that crash. In fact, it confined her to a wheelchair. He was trapped inside when it burst into flames. The gaffer at that time, DI Jameson, encouraged the traffic officers, who were investigating the accident, not to make the link with the CID car. I think he was going for promotion at the time and he thought it might affect his chances. Back then, having the embarrassment of one of his department's cars being nicked and linked with a fatal was not a sign of good leadership.'

'Well,' continued Isobel, 'it seems PC Goodright booked the cardigan in as evidence. He's taken the trouble to search through old property at headquarters and found it. It's still sealed in its original bag and labelled and it's been identified by Susan Siddons as the cardigan she loaned her daughter Carol on the night she went missing. It's on its way to forensics as we speak.'

'That is good news,' said the superintendent elatedly. 'This could be the breakthrough we've been looking for.'

Hunter ducked his head and smiled. Paul, and Barry Newstead, had come good.

'Now to Rebecca Morris,' continued Isobel. 'As we know, she was last seen walking towards a bus stop five hundred yards from her home, in school uniform. That sighting was at five to eight on the morning of the sixth of July — three weeks ago. Her body was discovered the next day in the barn of a derelict farm near to Harlington, four miles from her home. There are no sightings during this time and we are as happy as we can be that the man who discovered Rebecca's mutilated body was not involved in her murder. He says he thought he heard someone running from the back of the farm and then a van or car driving away. We have no description of a person or vehicle.'

Isobel ran her finger down the summary, glancing up from time to time as she spoke to see if the others were following.

'When Rebecca's body was discovered she was wearing jeans and a T-shirt. We have not found her school uniform, the school bag she was seen with, or her mobile phone. A close friend of Rebecca's, Kirsty Evans, states that Rebecca hinted someone older had been chatting her up, phoning her and asking if he could photograph her. Kirsty says the impression she got from Rebecca was that this guy was more than likely a young man as opposed to a teenager.'

She paused again and looked over her glasses.

'And finally, our only suspect at this time, Steve Paynton. Steve was the partner of Carol's mother, Susan. He was physically abusing the pair of them and when he was arrested, he had in his possession indecent images of Carol of when she was very young. He also had almost a hundred other indecent photographs of children, none of which were of Rebecca. So, although we can link him to Carol, we cannot link him to Rebecca at this time. As we know, both Carol and Rebecca were killed by the same weapon and the moulding taken from the wounds, which has come back from the forensic team, is pointing us to a Bowie type knife. Extensive searches have now been carried out at all the locations where we know Steve Paynton has lived over the past thirteen years, and we have not found anything similar, or anything relating to Rebecca.'

Isobel paused again, removed her spectacles, and sat back.

'That brings us up to the present,' she said, picking up her paperwork and tapping it neatly together on the tabletop.

The detective superintendent looked up from his copies of the documents and leaned forward.

'Okay, thanks for that, Isobel,' he began. 'Next steps.' He looked up for a second and then focused on the team again. 'The matter playing on my mind is the time gap between the killings. So, while we have teams going over the background stuff of the two girls, we now need to concentrate on some of our old cold casework. Are there any other unsolved murders out there which could be connected to ours? We also need to focus on the killer or killers. What have they been doing, or where have they been during the past fourteen years? We need to make enquiries with prisons and the probation service to see if we can come up with any likely candidates. We have a lot of tasks to be getting on with and limited resources, so headquarters have approved me taking on more staff to help.'

Hunter's ears pricked up and he seized on the opportunity. 'Can I make a suggestion, Boss?'

The superintendent nodded.

'You're probably aware that Barry Newstead, ex-CID, was instrumental in pointing us in the direction of Carol Siddons when her body was discovered.'

Michael Robshaw nodded again.

'Well, what you might not be aware of is that when she was originally reported missing, Barry was the only person who believed what Carol's mum was saying, and worked against the wishes of the then DI to try to trace her. Knowing Barry like I do I'm sure he will still have all his notes, and seeing as we're allowed to take on ex-detectives to help us on these enquiries, he would be a great asset.'

The superintendent pulled a face.

Hunter spotted the look. 'Look, I know what you're thinking. Yes, he was a bit of a maverick in his day, but I've been using his knowledge to good advantage just lately, and I'll vouch for him. I'll supervise his work and if it looks as though he's going out on a limb, I'll draw him back, or get shut. Is that OK?'

Before Michael Robshaw had time to respond they were all taken aback by the hurried opening of the conference room door. A red-faced, perspiring DC Mike Sampson, filled the doorframe.

'Sorry to disturb you, gaffer,' he gasped, 'but another body's been found.'

On their hands and knees, dressed in blue boiler suits, the Task Force search team were working shoulder-to-shoulder, carrying out fingertip searches around the site where Carol Siddons's mummified remains had been unearthed two weeks previously.

Search-grids had been taped off on the old colliery site and white-suited forensic officers, some with metal detectors, were combing the murky topsoil for exhibits. They had also brought in a body-dog.

Police dog handler Peter Broughton and his Springer Spaniel, Lady, were currently outside the roped off area, scrambling around in scrubland at the edge of the old pit site. The undergrowth was thick and dense in places and it was proving difficult for them to keep a straight course. This was a first for Peter and Lady. Generally, they got called out when there had been a disaster, where the likelihood was that someone had been buried alive. But this was what they were trained for. Lady had a nose for finding bodies, even if they had been dead for some time.

On a long rope, the Springer darted in and out of sparse bushes and through the long grass. They had been at it for just under two hours and were due a break when Lady stopped and began sniffing and pawing at a mound of overgrown gorse. Peter increased his pace, taking in the slack of the rope until he was beside his dog.

'What we found here then, girl?' he said, patting the Spaniel's back. He pushed Lady to one side and, on bended knees, delved into the gorse, parting fronds carefully and slowly. Some came away far easier than anticipated and he found himself tugging at a huge clump, taking a good two inches of top soil with it. This looked too overgrown to be a burial site, he thought, and wondered if his dog had found a badger sett instead, and for the next couple of minutes he scraped around an area where the clay was softer.

Six inches beneath the surface Peter's attention was grabbed by an unusual discolouration of the soil, and he was considering calling for a member of the forensic team to join him when he exposed a piece of hemp sacking. Scraping more loose soil away he saw NCB stamped in black lettering across the old, decaying sack and he instantly thought this was the site of where someone had buried their pet. No wonder Lady had reacted like she did.

The dog handler muttered to himself and tugged at a corner, which resisted. He pulled harder and it suddenly came free, sending him rolling backwards. Cursing and disgusted with himself, he pushed up onto his knees, brushing dust from his trousers. He looked into the crevice the sacking had left behind and what faced him rocked him back on his heels. It was time to shout for the forensic team.

With a feeling of déjà vu, Hunter, Grace, Tony Bullars and Mike Sampson pulled up at the cordoned-off area on the Manvers site. They'd been told the second body was a skeleton and what appeared to be girl's school clothing still clung to the defleshed bones.

SOCO, working with the forensic team, were already erecting a second white tent around the site of the latest find.

The foursome stood and watched the activity. At least the majority of the resources they needed were already on site.

Hunter was briefed by the uniformed officer at the entrance to the scene — experts required to scrutinise the skeletal remains were on their way. Professor Lizzie McCormack and the body recovery team would soon be joining them.

For the next few hours very little evidence would be gathered but things would be frantic. The Recovery team would need to excavate and remove the cadaver to a climate-controlled pathology lab as soon as possible, because now the body had been exposed there would be an acceleration in decomposition. At the same time, the body recovery team would be ensuring that the chain of evidence remained intact for the remaining forensic team.

Hunter stood, hands on hips, surveying the scene. His instinct was telling him this was now a serial murder enquiry. Tony, Grace and Mike had already passed through the 'Police line do not cross' tape, and were busy organising and briefing officers about their roles in this investigation.

Within twenty minutes Professor McCormack had arrived. Hunter spotted her by the open boot of her car, stepping into her forensic suit. Within five minutes she was heading towards him, bouncing on the balls of her feet, a perverse grin on her face.

'My, my, we are busy little bees,' she said in her soft Scottish voice.

Soon she was easing herself down over the disturbed earth around the grisly find. The body was devoid of any flesh, a perfect set of white teeth grinned back from the dirty brown skull which still sported hanks of coarse and matted dark brown hair. The skeleton was dressed in a white blouse and dark blue skirt and, although the upper parts were exposed, most of the legs still remained covered in red clay soil.

The professor probed around the body with a scalpel, leaning forward occasionally, lifting the flimsy cotton blouse and skirt and examining some of the bones. She tutted and clucked as she moved around the makeshift grave on her knees. Then she looked up over her spectacles at Hunter.

'This is a difficult one for me,' she said. 'This body, unlike the other one you found a couple of weeks ago, is devoid of any tissue. This is not my skill area, I'm afraid. What I can tell you is that this is the body of a young teenage girl.'

'How's that?' Hunter asked.

The pathologist used her scalpel to indicate the pelvic area of the skeleton. 'These flared bones on the hips are a dead giveaway. This is called the sciatic notch. It spreads as a young woman. Nature's way of accommodating a foetus. Also, look at the forehead.' Still using the scalpel as a pointer, she aimed it at the skull. 'The frontal lobe is flat. In a man's there is more of a slope.' McCormack studied the body a little longer, before releasing a long 'hmm'.

She turned to Hunter. 'What I can also tell you is that injuries to the bones in her neck suggest she has been strangled. Again, just like the others.' She paused. 'And I can also tell you that this looks very much like the handiwork of our killer again.' She pointed to a clear plastic bag poking up through loosened soil, its transparency masked here and there by clinging detritus. 'If I'm not mistaken that's another one of those playing cards. Looks like the three of hearts to me.'

She pushed herself up.

'That's as far as I can take things for you, I'm afraid. I'll put in a call to check how long the forensic anthropologist will be before he can get here. He's a colleague of mine so I can speed things up for you. He'll collect and examine the bones and tell you how long the body has been buried here and hopefully help to identify her for you.'

As the professor left the site, the forensic recovery team had just arrived and were taking out Ground Penetrating Radar, which would determine if there were more bodies buried here.

Josh: Hi Kirsty.
Kirsty: Hi Josh, howa yoo?
Josh: yeah im gud thanx.
Kirsty: wot u doin?
Josh: listenin to sum artic monkeys, jus chillin.
Kirsty: thats cool.

The man had been trawling the social network sites on the internet for weeks, tracking profiles of a number of people, picking up the language and learning how to develop a character. It had been time-consuming but all too easy.

He'd made copious notes at first in his attempt to create a believable character with substance. To step inside the head of a typical seventeen-year-old boy, he had searched the music sites for hours on end, selecting the most popular bands and solo artists and then he had followed up with a little research about each one to enable him to convince his audience. He had done dummy runs to test drive Josh, developing his use of the teenage text language on the websites. It had been a worthwhile exercise and he had hooked several unsuspecting teenage girls in the three weeks he had been socialising across the networks. One thirteen-year-old had even exposed her cute little breasts to him, which he had captured on webcam.

By the time he had hooked up on Kirsty's site he was an accomplished player. She was wary at first and tested him on several occasions, but his research had stood him in good stead and within a week she firmly believed she was conversing with seventeen-year-old 'Josh'.

Josh: saw u at skwl the othr day. u lukd sad.
Kirsty: wot wer u doin nr my skwl.
Josh: jus passin lukin 4 a pretty face.
Kirsty: u r makin me blush. No serious wot wer u doin nr my skwl.
Josh: jus passin. Goin 2 the park for a game of footie. Why wer u sad.
Kirsty: I wantd 2 stay over at my friends wiv sum mates cos of skool brake up but mum wudnt let me cos of wat append to Rebecca. We ad a row she freakd out.
Josh: do u want me 2 cheer u up?
Kirsty: wat do u mean?
Josh: u r cute u no. Do u want to meet up.
Kirsty: r u askin me out?
Josh: Of cors.
Kirsty: but I hardli kno u.
Josh: u do wev talkd for ages on this chat room. Uv seen my foto. Don't u like me.

Selecting the right photograph and then altering it in his Adobe Photoshop programme had been another worthwhile project. He was quite proud of how physically good-looking he had made his character.

Kirsty: u luk nice. u sound nice.
Josh: well then lets meet.
Kirsty: ok but I can't 4 a few days. ive been grounded. in fact im supposed 2 b doin mi bedroom now instead of chattin wiv u. mum wil freak again if she catchs me.
Josh: wen can u get out then?
Kirsty: next satrday evenin. mums out wiv dad wiv frends. Wot about the park?
Josh: souns gud. c u then pretty face.

As he exited the chat room site, he leaned back on his swivel chair, clasped his hands behind his head and grinned widely.
Another lamb to the slaughter.

DAY TWENTY-FOUR

Grace Marshall's desk phone disturbed the unusually concentrated silence in the MIT office. She answered it without looking up from her paperwork, clamping the handset between neck and shoulder. But the nature of the call changed her demeanour. She looked up as she listened intently to the voice on the other end of the line. Picking up a pen, she scribbled notes in her own form of shorthand, answering occasionally with a one-word clipped response. Two minutes later she set down the receiver.

Solemn faced, her eyes swept across four desks that had been recently pushed together into a square.

The opposite two were occupied. Hunter and Barry Newstead were picking through piles of documents spread across their surfaces.

'Do you want the good news or the bad news?' she said.

Hunter looked up and pushed aside notes he had been making on the recent body find. For the past half hour, he had been trying to make sense of it all. He had worked on body count murders before, but it had been where members of the same family had been killed in a single event. He'd never worked on multiple victim deaths, otherwise known as serial killings. His head felt woolly. A mixture of long hours of intense work and a lack of sleep from lying awake night after night, mulling over the recent events, were taking their toll.

'Hit me with the good news first,' Hunter said, sticking an already well-chewed pen into the corner of his mouth.

Barry Newstead dog-eared the page he had been reading and peered over his spectacles at Grace. It was his first day with the case team as a civilian investigator and he had been given the job of sending the profiles of the murdered girls, and the descriptions of how they had met their deaths, to headquarters' Public Protection Unit. In return, they had faxed him the backgrounds and histories of the district's most violent and dangerous sex offenders. He had been shocked at what he read. 'I thought nothing could surprise me anymore, until I ploughed through this lot,' he had told Hunter. 'I'm astonished at just how many paedophiles are living in my area.'

'That was the forensics lab,' said Grace. 'They've found some traces on that grey cardigan belonging to Carol Siddons. But the bad news is none of it is human DNA. All they have are lots of dog hairs and some black woollen fibres which appear to have come from a duffel coat of some type.'

'Dog hairs?' interjected Barry. 'Carol never had a dog, and neither did Susan.'

'Sure about that, Barry?' said Hunter, eyebrows raised, teeth clenching harder on the end of his pen.

'I'm positive. I can give Sue a quick ring, but all the time I was investigating Carol's disappearance there was never any dog around. And I would have definitely known because I hate the bloody things, I've been bitten three times in my career, once by a bloody police dog, would you believe?'

Grace chuckled, then clamped her lips together when she saw Barry's not too impressed reaction.

'And she was living at a children's home, where pets were not allowed. So more than likely those dog hairs will have come from her killer.'

Barry paused, his eyes lighting up.

'Just a minute,' he continued, 'Steve Paynton used to have a couple of dogs; Staffordshire bull terriers if my memory serves me right. He used to keep them in the old outhouse at the bottom of his mum and dad's garden. Rumours were that he trained them for fighting. That was a good few years back, they'll more than likely be dead now. Knowing him though, they'll be buried on his dad's allotment, or somewhere like that. Can they tell the breed of dog if we find them?'

'I asked the same question,' said Grace. 'They can. They'll be able to confirm a match if we find the correct dog. Well done, Barry,' Grace continued excitedly. 'I'll feed in to the HOLMES team what forensics have told me and what you've just said and get a search team round to the Payntons. They are going to be thoroughly pissed off by the time we've finished.'

'That family's had it coming for a long time,' said Hunter. 'You set that in motion and muster up a search team. We've more officers joining us now we have a serial killer on our hands.'

As Grace hurried from the room, Hunter pulled the pen from his mouth and leaned back in his seat, thinking about the sheer volume of ongoing enquiries. They now had three separate crime scenes running, the most recent of which was a hive of activity. Forensic anthropologists were picking over every inch of ground, digging in several areas around the scrubland, following the path of the radar. In addition, Peter Broughton and his dog Lady had identified further hot spots where other human remains might well be hidden. He was thankful there hadn't been any more body finds so far.

Elsewhere, house-to-house enquiries were being conducted around the area where Rebecca Morris was last seen, and the HOLMES team was fully engaged in linking all this together. The work was slow and laborious, but it was necessary.

Thankfully, Barry had already been a big help in the Carol Siddons case and Hunter was hoping that, with his knowledge of villains and their families, together with his previous casework as a detective, he might be able to point them in the direction of their killer. Barry's immediate task was to determine if the modus operandi of the murders fitted the profiles of any of the district's sex attackers. And to add to his workload, he had also picked up where Grace had left off, sifting through the dozens of missing from home case files removed from the basement at police headquarters.

Earlier that morning he had set to work on those and had already been able to dismiss a good number of them. Many of the files still had photographs of the missing girls stapled to the front sheets, and although they were now yellowing with age, by carefully studying the images Barry had found that, either because of hair colour, size of the individual, or clothing description, they could not possibly be the latest victim.

'And how are the missing from home checks going, Barry?' Hunter asked, returning to his own mound of paperwork.

'Painful and tedious,' Barry responded, pushing his spectacles onto the crown of his head. 'I've managed to get a rough height and age of the bones together with colour of hair from the anthropologist, and the exhibits officer has managed to clean up the labels from the clothing to give me their size and original colour for comparison with the reports. What is interesting however, is the exhibit Professor McCormack found. Remember? The playing card inside the plastic bag. I can confirm it's the three of hearts by the way. Well, this was also inside the bag.'

Barry held up a small scrap of paper. It appeared to have been torn from the top heading section of a newspaper and although yellowing and cracked at the edges the black print was still readable.

'Not all the headline is there but it looks like it's from our local weekly paper and it shows the date the sixth of October 1999. On a hunch I went through the misper files and, using that date as guidance, it's helped me separate one girl's folder — a Claire Fisher — but we're slightly out of sync. She was reported missing on the first of October that year — five days before the newspaper cutting. She's roughly the same height as the skeleton and had the same colour hair, but no clothing has been listed on her report.'

'Was the torn newspaper inside that plastic bag with the playing card?' asked Hunter, suddenly on the alert.

Barry nodded.

'This killer is one really twisted evil bastard,' said Hunter. 'He wants us to know this is his work. He placed that with the body so we'd know when she was killed, and I'm guessing that part of the paper will lead us to who she is.'

He pushed aside his notes. This find had his fullest attention.

'We've been making enquiries and wondering why there is such a gap between the murder of Carol Siddons and Rebecca Morris — well, it's my bet that this will go some way to fill in those gaps. Contact the local paper and see what's in the copy, and then get that exhibit to forensics and see if he's left any DNA or prints. Let's just hope he's slipped up somewhere along the line.'

While Grace was organising the warrant and arranging with Task Force to raid Steve Paynton's old family home and allotment, Barry Newstead was at the local history room at Barnwell library.

Following a phone call to the *Barnwell Chronicle*, Barry had learned old archive editions were no longer kept at the newspaper office, but had been put onto microfiche and were held in trust by the local history group.

Within ten minutes of his arrival, Barry was seated at a large microfiche reader, receiving instructions in its use from the female supervisor, who was loading the roll of microfiche containing all 1999 editions of the weekly local newspaper onto the machine's spool. As she leaned over him, he caught the alluring smell of her perfume. Quite an expensive one, he thought, as he sneaked a glance at her face only a few inches from his. It made him realise how much he had missed the smell of a woman since the sudden death of his wife from a stroke three years ago. He guessed she was in her mid-fifties, roughly the same age as him, and he was distracted from the task in hand.

'Right, Mr Newstead,' she said, straightening up.

She had taken him by surprise and he hoped she hadn't caught him staring. He could feel his cheeks flushing.

'You just turn those handles at the side of the machine until you find the edition you want, then when you've found what you want you hit the print button which will copy what you see on the screen. Understand all that?' she checked with him and smiled.

A very attractive smile, he thought.

'If you need anything else, just give me a call.' She turned on low heels and clicked her way back towards her desk.

Barry turned the spool slowly at first, watching the enlarged images of the past editions of his local paper float across the screen. He was soon getting a feel for it, and sped up as he got used to the momentum of the apparatus, soon spinning past the editions until he hit mid-September's pages and then began to slow until he settled on the 6th of October's front sheet. He took out the torn section of the newspaper from its exhibit bag and manoeuvred it around, holding it in front of the reading screen for comparison. Confirming it was from the same paper, he set it down on the desk and began scanning the news sheet. He didn't need to go far. What he had been looking for was contained in the front-page headlines. He began to pore over the story.

POLICE SEARCH FOR MISSING TEENAGER

Detectives leading the enquiry into the surprise disappearance of 15-year-old Claire Louise Fisher from Barnwell are urging the public to help them with information.
  Claire was reported missing five days ago on October 1st.
  The last reported sighting of Claire was by her boyfriend at 9.30 p.m. that night.

There was more to the report. The journalist had filled the remainder of the story with Claire's background, plus interviews with her parents and friends, which he quickly read. And he recognised the photograph of Claire that the paper had used. It was the same as the one on the front of her missing from home file back on his desk.

Barry slapped the table excitedly. He was convinced that Claire Louise Fisher was their latest corpse.

He looked for the print key on the microfiche reader and stabbed a finger on it. Almost instantaneously the copier spurred into action and within seconds a facsimile of the front page had been printed onto an A4 sheet.

Barry sat back in his chair and read the story again. He found himself shaking his head and muttering to himself as he read it a second time, thinking of the ramifications of what he had just uncovered.

Claire Fisher went missing on the first of October 1999, he said to himself, *and the edition of this newspaper didn't go on sale until the sixth. That means the killer didn't bury her straight away. Claire was either alive and held somewhere, or killed and kept somewhere for the best part of a week until the paper came out, and then she was finally buried.*

'This is one twisted bastard,' he said aloud. From the corner of his eye he caught movement and glanced up to see the fair-haired local history supervisor looking his way.

'Sorry about that,' he whispered and apologetically raised a hand. 'Talking to myself. A sign of age, eh?'

She smiled back.

Quite a nice smile; a welcoming smile, he thought. There was something about it which brought to mind Susan Siddons. It seemed perverse that such a painful event as this should bring them back together again after all these years. It made him realise just how much he had missed her. This has to be fate, he thought. And he was a great believer in fate. He wondered about giving her a call.

DAY TWENTY-FIVE

Thunder growled and rumbled overhead, and a split second later the rain fell in streams, pelting the earth like spears. Grace cowered beneath the canopy at the rear entrance of Barnwell Police station. She'd been petrified of thunder since she was a child, would rather tackle a violent man than face it. Her eyes scanned the car park, searching for Hunter who was waiting for her in an unmarked police car. She spotted a dark blue Vauxhall with windscreen wipers working overtime to cope with the sudden downpour, and although she couldn't see who was driving she guessed it was him.

She glanced up at the thick mass of storm clouds, held her clip file over the top of her head and made the decision to dash for it. After a few seconds she jumped into the passenger seat of the CID car, the rain already beginning to soak through her Italian linen trousers. She shook her folder into the footwell and then pulled down the passenger side visor and stared into the mirror. She ran her fingers through her hair in a vain attempt to stop it frizzing and brushed stray droplets of rain from her cheeks.

Hunter stared, shaking his head.

'What?' She turned back to the mirror. 'Image is everything, Hunter, and if you were a woman you'd know that.' She slapped the visor back in place.

'A little rain never did anyone any harm,' he said.

'It does when it takes me half an hour to put my make-up on, and another half an hour to do my hair each morning. Bloody British weather.'

He shook his head again. 'Anyway, I understand you had a good day yesterday.'

'The Payntons, you mean?'

Hunter nodded and turned the demister on top speed to clear the fogged windscreen.

Grace gave a mischievously wicked smile. 'They were really pissed off by the time we'd finished. In fact, old man Paynton almost got locked up for breach of the peace when we dug up his allotment. We found the bodies of the dogs though, just like Barry suggested. Forensic have got those and we should know if we have a match with the hairs on Carol Siddons's cardigan in a day or two. Oh, and by the way, did you know that some of the locals have graffitied Steve's house? *Paedo* sprayed all over the front of it. The family are going ballistic,' she chuckled.

'Serves them all right. That family have plagued that estate for far too long. It's nice to see them get a taste of their own medicine for a change.'

'Anyway, where are we off to today?'

Hunter dropped the Claire Fisher file onto Grace's lap and powered down the misted-over driver's door window to clear it.

The rain had stopped but the skies were still rumbling and threatening overhead.

He pointed at the folder as he drove slowly out of the station car park. 'We're off to see a Mr and Mrs Fisher. Barry also had some success yesterday.'

As he drove, Hunter recounted Barry's newspaper discovery and how he'd managed to confirm his findings with a dental match from Claire Fisher's records.

'It looks as though the killer had Claire for five days at least before she was buried with that newspaper report. Is that sick or what? I find it hard to believe this has been going on in my own district for all these years. Now I know what the detectives were going through when they were dealing with Fred and Rosemary West.' He shook his head.

Grace felt her skin goose-pimple.

'This twisted bastard seems to be taunting us, Grace. He doesn't mind us finding out who his victims are. It's as if he knew we'd eventually find this one and he's helping us to identify her. It's almost as though he thinks he's never going to be caught. That he's cleverer than us. We really are up against it at the moment. I just hope we can get a breakthrough before he kills again.'

Hunter slowed as they met the rush-hour crawl.

'And another thing; Barry did some further digging yesterday, going back across old local newspaper reports and then made a few phone calls to other police stations in the District. As a result, he's uncovered at least another three local teenage girls who have disappeared without trace over the past thirteen years.'

'What?' said Grace, looking up sharply from the Claire Fisher file.

'Yes, Barry's found three other cases of girls missing from this area since 1993 when Carol Siddons was first reported. He's pulled all their files and found that they all disappeared with no apparent reason and more disturbingly, that they all fit the same profile as our present three victims, especially in age and physical appearance.'

The Fisher house was a sumptuous, four-bedroom detached residence on a small, exclusive estate at the edge of Barnwell. The family's engineering business had flourished over recent years and Mr and Mrs Fisher had moved home twice since 1999 when Claire had gone missing.

The woman who answered their knock at the door took Hunter by surprise. She appeared a lot younger than the details on file. In fact, she looked not much older than him.

As if reading his puzzled expression, the slim raven-haired woman responded, 'I'm Julia. Mrs Fisher number two. Derek's new wife. Well, not really his new wife. We've been married for nearly three years now. Beverley, Claire's Mum, died in 2001 from cancer.'

'There's no need to explain,' said Hunter, showing his police badge.

'Derek keeps telling me the same but I could tell by the look on your face that you were surprised I was a lot younger than you were expecting. I'm used to greeting people like this even after three years. I suppose I don't want people to think bad of me. As though I'm jumping into a dead woman's shoes, if you know what I mean. I was his secretary you see, at the firm, and got very close to both Derek and Beverley when Claire went missing. Then when Beverley was diagnosed with breast cancer, I took on a lot of the responsibility of the business and got even closer to Derek, especially when Beverley died. I know there are some people who think I was having an affair with Derek while his wife was dying, but that's so far from the truth.'

'You really don't have to explain all this to us,' Hunter said.

'But I feel better now that I have done. Anyway, Derek's waiting for you. He's in the lounge. Come through.'

Hunter and Grace followed her along a bright and airy hallway into a large, tastefully furnished lounge. The room was filled with sunlight, its brightness enhanced by magnolia painted walls and highly polished oak flooring. Leather furniture and bespoke light oak units containing antique blue pottery added to the expensive look.

Hunter noticed a number of impressionist style paintings hanging around the room. They looked original and under different circumstances he would have loved to have wandered around to view them.

French doors opened up into a large hardwood orangery, which gave a view over a garden festooned with a wide variety of plant colour.

Derek Fisher was waiting to greet them and he energetically offered his hand to shake.

'I've been waiting for this call to come for a long time,' Derek said, pointing to a tan-coloured leather settee, one of three in the large room, inviting Hunter and Grace to sit. 'You're here about Claire, aren't you?'

Grace took over. 'We are, Mr Fisher. We believe we've found her. But I'm sorry to say it's not good news.'

'I guess I knew all along it would come down to this. Is this visit because of the bodies you've dug up on the old pit site? It's been all over the news.'

Grace nodded. 'The dental records point us towards it being your daughter and a simple DNA sample from you would make it conclusive.'

'I'm guessing you won't be allowing me to see her. Although I suppose I won't be able to recognise Claire.'

'I'm afraid not. She's been buried a long time.'

Derek Fisher gave a long sigh. 'I'm not going to torment myself by asking how she died. The one good thing I've got now is closure. It's such a shame her mum's not around to know that you've found her. She grieved right to the end, you know.' He gulped and pursed his lips. 'I'll get the opportunity to lay her to rest?'

'You will, but not just yet. I'm afraid we'll need to hang on to Claire for some time yet until the Coroner gives permission.'

'I hope you don't think that me not being upset about the news reflects on my relationship with my daughter. I can assure you we were very close as a family. But I'm also a realist. I suppose I've known for a long time that Claire was dead. Even though I never said it openly to Beverley when she was alive, I've always felt that Claire was lying somewhere in a grave where she shouldn't be. She's always been in my thoughts. Every time I saw or heard of a body being found, no matter where, I waited for the call. I've been waiting over ten years. The police came back to us on many occasions in the early days, and her disappearance was reinvestigated on a couple of occasions, and both me and Beverley used to get so excited. But then when Beverley died and there was no fresh news, I just accepted the reality of it all.'

Derek Fisher got up from his seat and went to a nearby wall unit. From the cupboard he brought out a bulging photograph album and handed it to Grace. She opened it to find the folder crammed with yellowing newspaper cuttings and scraps of paper covered in copious notes. She leafed through the contents quickly. It had been meticulously maintained, every milestone recorded from day one to the present, interspersed here and there with happy family photographs of the Fishers. Their past was in this book.

'I don't know if that will be of any help to you. It's everything we collected over the years relating to Claire. Every newspaper report. The possible leads. Every glimmer of hope. Keep it as long as you need. I hope it'll help.'

'It'll certainly help us. Thank you. I'll make sure it gets back to you safely.'

'Before we leave you in peace, Mr Fisher,' said Hunter, 'can you just remind us of Claire's movements the evening she went missing?'

Derek Fisher stroked the line of his jaw and chin, cleared his throat and looked from Hunter to Grace.

'Do you know, I don't even need to think about what I'm going to tell you. I've said the same thing so many times over the years. Claire left home at just gone six. She told us she was going to her friend Stacy's and would be back to finish her homework about eight o'clock. At quarter to eight she phoned us from a payphone to say she was at the youth club and asked if she could stay till nine. We were a bit concerned because it was dark, but at the same time we were going through a bit of a rough patch with Claire and we wanted to allow her a bit more freedom, so we told her no later than nine. That was the last time we spoke.

'What we subsequently found out was that she was in fact seeing a fifteen-year-old boy called Gary Martin and that they were at the fair together. She had been dating him for two months without us knowing. Police told us they rowed that night because he found out she had just been stringing him along as cover. It appears she had been seeing someone older. She confessed it to him and he apparently stormed off in a huff and left her. That was about half past nine. You'll see from our own file that Gary was interviewed many times and was a suspect on several occasions but he was alibied by quite a number of people that night. I've spoken with him myself many times over the years and I'm confident he wasn't involved in Claire's disappearance.'

He shifted in his chair and cleared his throat.

'I'm guessing you'll want to speak with him again. Gary's married now with a family of his own. We still keep in touch. He'll tell you things that are not in those folders I've given you.'

He stared at Hunter and then Grace through unblinking eyes.

'In the few months before Claire disappeared, we went through some bad times with her. She seemed to have changed, and it wasn't for the good.' He paused. 'Do you have children?'

Both Hunter and Grace nodded.

'Oh, I know all teenagers go through a phase, but Claire really put us through it. She came in drunk, smashed up her room once when we tried to keep her in, and we even found out from Gary that she was seeing other lads behind his back. She'd become a real rebel in her last days, and that's what's so sad about it. My last memories of Claire are not nice ones.'

Now, where have I heard all this before, Hunter thought. *A pattern's emerging here.*

'Let me just check this with you, Mr Fisher,' said Grace. 'Just backtracking a little. You said Claire was last seen at the fair by her then boyfriend Gary Martin?'

Derek Fisher nodded. 'Yes, that's right. He told me that when he left her, he got the impression she was hanging about to meet up with an older lad.'

'Which fair was that?'

'The local Feast fair that's held on the common field every year. It still is.'

Alarm bells were ringing in Hunter's head. It was the second time the Feast fair had featured in their enquiries.

'I've just had a very interesting conversation with Derek Fisher,' said Hunter, strolling into the office and spotting Barry hunched over a pile of paperwork. He dropped the Claire Fisher file onto his desk jotter, then slipped off his jacket and hooked it over the back of his chair.

Barry looked up from the sheaf of papers he had been reading, pushed himself back into his seat and rubbed the back of his neck. 'Oh yes, and what was that, as if you didn't want me to ask?'

'He told us his daughter Claire was last seen at the local Feast fairground by her then boyfriend Gary Martin on the evening she went missing back in '99. The boyfriend apparently left her in a strop after she told him someone older was fancying her. I don't know if you've managed to get up to date with the investigation yet, Barry, but that's very similar to something Rebecca Morris told her friend Kirsty Evans after they visited the Feast fair a couple of months ago — that someone older was fancying her. Added to that, do you remember what Karen Gardner told us about the guy she was seeing at the same time as Paul Goodright, way back in '93?'

'Crikey, yes,' said Grace, teasing off her jacket stuck to her blouse — a consequence of the muggy heat from the earlier thunderstorm. 'She told me she was being visited by a Billy Smith who travelled with the local fair. I checked his name against the database in the Intelligence Unit and although there was very little on him, an old conviction for drunk and disorderly, I did discover from one of the beat officers that he didn't just travel with the fair but his parents actually own it. He currently lives in a static caravan in a compound next to the canal.'

She paused and her eyes widened.

'Bloody hell. The compound where he lives is only about a mile from the Manvers site, where we found Carol and Claire's bodies.'

'This is just too much of a coincidence,' Hunter said. 'Barry does that name ring any bells with you — Billy Smith?'

Barry pushed his reading glasses up onto his mop of tousled dark hair and fixed his gaze upon the ceiling as though the answer lay somewhere up there. He muttered the name 'Billy Smith' under his breath several times then looked back at Hunter, slamming the flat of his hand on top of his pile of papers.

'Billy Smith — Fairground Billy Smith, of course, I've got him. He's someone I came across way back in my really young CID days. It was from a job in the late 80s. We got a call to a shooting at the Barnwell Hotel — "The Drum" as everyone referred to it. It's been knocked down now but back then it was a real dive. One of our problem pubs. If a fight broke out there you knew you had to go in mob-handed to sort it out. Anyway, I can remember being radioed up one Friday night to attend there. Uniform had responded to an ambulance call and found a man in the back yard of the pub with shotgun wounds to the stomach. He wasn't dead, but half his guts were hanging out and he was in a real bad way.'

Barry paused for a moment, taking in Hunter and Grace's expressions.

'The guy wouldn't say a thing about what had gone on and the place had emptied by the time we arrived. The pub was locked up at first but we eventually managed to rouse the landlord. You could see he didn't want us inside the place, and no wonder. When we got in, the poolroom had been virtually demolished. Chairs, tables, and pool cues smashed up, glass everywhere, and someone had tried to clean up the blood. At first the landlord refused to say anything but after we threatened to lock him up for attempted murder, he spilled the beans. Earlier that night there had been a load of travellers in from a local site and that they had been playing pool for money. After squeezing him a bit more, particularly with the threat of losing his licence for allowing illegal gambling on the premises, he told us that there had been a thousand-pound bet on the pool table and that one Billy Smith from the fairground had won the game, but then the gypsy who he'd been playing wouldn't pay up.

'There'd been a bit of a scrap between him and Billy. Apparently, Billy was very handy. We later found out that Billy was a bare-knuckle fighter who earned quite a bit of money from his illegal activities. Anyway, Billy was getting topside of the gypsy and a few of his pals joined in so Billy had to get away quick. The landlord told us that as he was trying to get the gypsies out of his pub, Billy Smith suddenly reappeared, armed with a shotgun, demanding his winnings. There was a standoff at first and then some of the gypsies started goading Billy that it wasn't loaded. So, Billy shot off one barrel into the ceiling and again demanded his money. The guy who owed him the money responded by mouthing off and that's when Billy shot the gypsy in the guts. He followed that up by smacking another couple of the guy's mates with the butt of the gun and then legged it.'

'Did you get Billy?' Grace asked.

'We did, actually. I was so hyped-up, I can tell you. It was early in my career and the first time I had seen armed police. We surrounded the fairground compound where Billy lived with his parents and he came out meek as anything, telling us he'd been at home all night, and his father backed him up. We arrested him of course and carried out a search as best as we could, but there was no sign of any gun. The gypsy who'd been shot was operated on and they stitched his guts back in and we finally managed to speak to him three days later, but he refused to say anything. He wouldn't even confirm his name. At the travellers' site we couldn't find anyone who wanted to talk to us so, without witnesses and vital evidence, the enquiry went nowhere. We found out later that the elders from the traveller site settled things with Billy's father, whatever that meant.'

He paused and smiled.

'How's that for someone who's supposedly past it?' Then in a hammy *Poirot* accent, he added, 'Hastings, ze little grey cells, zey do not desert me.'

'That was a crap attempt at a French accent. It sounded more Welsh,' said Grace.

'You Philistine,' said Barry. 'Hercule Poirot, the greatest detective in the world — even greater than you — is Belgian, not French.' He gave Grace a quick wink.

Hunter couldn't help but smile. It hadn't taken Barry long to settle in, and he hadn't lost any of his recall. His stash of information on villains, their cohorts and their networks, plus all the jobs he had attended over his thirty years was far better than any local Intelligence Unit computer system.

'Right you two, I'm going to take this to the HOLMES people and then get Tony and Mike. Meanwhile, I think it's time to shake Billy Smith's tree a little. Grace, I want you to sort out the paperwork and get a magistrate's warrant. '

Hunter's team sped into the open entranceway of the Smith's fairground compound in two unmarked cars, only to be greeted by two snapping and snarling Alsatians acting as sentries. The surprise element was long gone. The cars swerved around the slavering animals, churning up the ground of loose shale, and slewed to a halt in front of a thirty-six-foot static caravan where Barry Newstead had earlier indicated Billy Smith should still be living.

Before jumping from the car Hunter looked back at the way they'd just come. The hounds were still frantically jerking and leaping against the chain which was holding them. He only looked away when he realised the dogs couldn't reach him. At that moment, the caravan door shot open, crashing against the aluminium side with a resounding clatter. A tall, stockily-built, man confronted them.

He was well over six-feet tall and, judging by the broad shoulders, expansive chest and bulging arms, which strained the white T-shirt he was wearing, he regularly trained and maintained his physique. His facial features were quite striking and he had a tanned weather-beaten appearance framed by a head of thick, naturally curly, almost black hair. His ice blue eyes, wide and alert, zeroed in on them.

'What the fuck's going on?'

Hunter leapt from the driver's seat. Mike Sampson and Tony Bullars were also pulling themselves out of their car and Hunter signalled to them with a raised hand.

'You and Bully hang back five,' he ordered and turned to the thick-set man framed in the doorway of the caravan. 'Billy Smith?' he shouted, raising his voice over the now hysterical dogs, wishing he could silence them — permanently.

As if reading his mind, the man ordered, 'Quiet! Sit! Sabre, Spike!' Then with a smug grin he turned towards the detectives as the animals stopped barking and settled back on their haunches. 'What do so many cops want me for? You'd think I'd murdered someone.'

'Funny you should say that,' Grace mumbled under her breath.

Hunter caught the comment and nudged her. 'We could do with a word with you Billy. You got a few moments?'

'Sure. Come in, but wipe your feet.' He disappeared back inside the van.

Billy Smith's home was impressive. The plush interior took Hunter by surprise. Thick pile carpets, lush furnishings and soft pine cabinets ran from the entrance into the open lounge. Expensive pieces of Crown Derby were displayed on the windowsills and in glass units. The smell of fresh polish hung in the air. The mobile home was immaculate with everything neatly in place.

'My next question is,' said Billy Smith as he eased himself into an armchair, 'what is so important that it needs two car loads of detectives to turn up at my door?'

Strong sunlight shone through slatted blinds behind him throwing his form into silhouette. Hunter narrowed his eyes to catch a glimpse of Billy's face.

'How did you know we were cops? We haven't introduced ourselves yet,' Hunter responded.

'Dogs can smell you a mile off,' Billy replied. 'Now get to the point and tell me what's going on?'

'We're here making enquiries into the murder of Rebecca Morris,' Hunter told him.

Before they left the station, Hunter had briefed his team and decided against mentioning the murder of Claire Louise Fisher; only he and Grace knew the tenuous link to Carol Siddons through the Billy, Karen Gardner, Paul Goodright ménage a trois.

'I've seen that on the telly. Why do you want to talk to me about that? I don't even know the girl. I've never met her.'

'We believe there's a link to your fair, inasmuch as she was at the Feast fair shortly before she died.' Hunter lied to get a reaction from Billy, which might indicate guilt.

'I hope this is not leading where I think it is. I swear on my mother's death I had nothing to do with that girl. If she was at the fair, I never saw her.'

'In order to satisfy ourselves, is it all right if we do a search of your home?' Grace asked.

Billy thought for a moment. 'What if I say no?'

'Well, we have got a search warrant.' Grace waved the magistrates' document in her hand.

'Looks like I've got no choice, does it? But please don't wreck things. I've heard about police and searches.'

Hunter called in Tony and Mike and the four of them split up to begin a methodical high and low exploration of the caravan.

Hunter made sure Billy was in view throughout his search, keeping an eye on him while chatting generally, endeavouring to relax him, then throw him off guard when it was time for the more probing investigation-based questions.

After about twenty minutes, Mike Sampson shouted from one of the bedrooms at the back of the static.

'Got something!'

He appeared in the doorway holding aloft a small item in his latex gloved hand. He strode purposefully through to the lounge followed by Grace and

Tony. He showed the item to Hunter and then held it in front of Billy Smith.

'Whose is this?' Mike said sharply.

'Mine, why?' Billy said.

'Not with these markings on it,' said Mike. 'This is Rebecca Morris's mobile phone.'

'I've told you a dozen times, I found the damn thing,' Billy Smith said, an agitated note in his voice.

'And so you keep saying,' Grace responded, 'but you're not convincing me.'

Hunter watched Billy's face flush. Grace had pressed him hard, to the extent that sweat was now staining the front of his T-shirt.

'All right, all right, I might well have not been straight with you but I thought you were just trying to pull a fast one on me with that Rebecca Morris business.'

'Believe me, Billy, we do not lie about murder. Especially of a fourteen-year-old girl,' Grace said calmly, giving him a steely glare.

'I thought the phone was nicked — that's why I've not exactly been straight, okay? But I really did find that phone.'

'Tell us where then, and stop messing us about or you're back in that cell and on remand,' Grace said.

Billy dropped his head into his hands for a second. He wiped the beads of sweat from his forehead and pushed himself back in his seat.

'It was partially buried in the woods over by the canal — honest, you've got to believe me. I walk Spike and Sabre there every morning. I go over the canal bridge near the Low Lock and then let them loose in the woods. A couple of days ago they were digging round a hole just above a dyke and when I shouted to them, they wouldn't come away. I thought they'd found a fox hole or something so I went to drag them off. When I got to them, they'd dug out a black bin liner and started to shred it. Inside it there was some clothing, a backpack and that mobile phone. I thought it was gear from a burglary that someone had buried to come back for later. The bag was only filled with what looked like schoolbooks and so I just took the mobile. It was the only thing worth anything.'

Grace turned from Billy and looked at Hunter. If Billy was to be believed, the investigation was taking another twist.

Hunter had been carefully watching Billy during the last half hour of the questioning, studying his body language. Looking for those tell-tale signs that spelt guilt. To put a finger on what those signs were was never easy and certainly not something Hunter could define. It was built on years of experience, gained with every arrest and interview. He'd heard his colleagues refer to it as a sixth sense and he knew he had it. As Hunter observed Billy, he noticed that the man always held Grace's stare. He never shifted nervously, nor gulped when he responded to her probing questions. If he was lying, he was good, thought Hunter, but he sensed Billy was telling the truth.

Hunter said, 'Billy it's getting late now, we're going to terminate this interview, lodge you in the cells overnight and then tomorrow go and see if you're telling us the truth. First thing in the morning, I want you to show us where you found the mobile.'

DAY TWENTY-SIX

As soon as the man made contact with Kirsty over the internet and hooked her with 'Josh', he had begun the same process as with all the others. For over three weeks he had been following, watching and hiding from her, learning her life. And he had collected hundreds of photographs along the way. He put the digital images in an album and brought them out nightly from their hiding place to run his hands over her pretty face, imagining he was touching that smooth, unblemished skin.

Two days ago, after all his hard work, he had finally managed to entice Kirsty into meeting his seventeen-year-old creation, and as he stood very still beside the bushes of Barnwell Countryside Park, he knew that soon he would be meeting and touching the girl who had so far only been a two-dimensional vision in his fantasies.

He took another glance at his watch and surveyed the area around him. There had been a couple of dog walkers earlier but the majority of people who used the park would be at work. It was the perfect meeting place. He knew as soon as he had suggested the venue to Kirsty that it would lure her into a false sense of security. She didn't know the area as well as he did. He had done his homework.

He had tried to disguise his appearance and make himself look old enough to be the father of a seventeen-year-old. He had waxed down his hair, put on a pair of unfashionable spectacles from a charity shop and donned his father's old pit duffel jacket, left behind all those years back. When he looked himself over in the mirror before leaving home, he thought he'd got the effect about right. After all, he didn't want to scare her off because he looked weird. And he had rehearsed his lines so many times.

Spotting movement by the stile, he caught his breath. When he had done an earlier recce of the park, he had identified it as the entrance nearest to the woodland.

He squinted at the moving figure, bringing it into focus. It was her. He double-checked the area was clear, slipped on his gloves and slid out of the bushes.

'Hi, I'm Josh's dad.'

The man suddenly appeared from nowhere and made Kirsty jump.

'I'm sorry, I didn't mean to scare you like that. Josh was delayed at his football training and he asked me if I'd come and meet you and run you back to the house.'

Kirsty's mind was racing. She hadn't expected Josh's dad to turn up. She looked him up and down. He looked silly in that coat — it was too big for him. Although a good eighteen inches taller than her, she could tell he was only slightly built. There were signs that his hair was thinning despite covering it with a layer of wax and he had the kind of facial growth that looks like a perpetual five o'clock shadow. The heavy rimmed glasses hid his eyes, but they seemed to be darting around, not really focused on her.

She thought his face was familiar and yet somehow different. It puzzled her.

'You okay with that?' he asked.

Now where had she had heard that voice before? She hesitated, trying to remember where she had seen this man.

'Well, I'm not too sure,' she said.

Then the man pulled a mobile phone from his pocket. 'You can give him a ring if you want.' He slid the screen up to reveal the keypad, and offered it to her.

This doesn't feel right, Kirsty thought to herself.

'I'll just ring my mum and tell her what's happening.' She could feel her voice burbling nervously, the words almost sticking in her throat. She reached into her pocket for her phone, but the man took hold of her arm gently.

'Josh will be so sad if he doesn't meet you. I can assure you everything's fine, you've no need to worry.'

She tried to act normally and not to freeze. She knew what she should do — what her parents had always told her to do, but her legs wouldn't let her. A panicky fear enveloped her.

Then the man turned sharply. Kirsty saw his eyes in those too big spectacles widen, revealing a look of real evil, and she opened her mouth to scream.

He swung back his hand and she felt a sharp slap which rocked her head sideways. It was less painful than expected; the terror inside was more frightening. She choked back a scream as he grabbed at her jacket.

'I'll kill you if you fucking scream.'

His voice had taken on a deep and menacing tone and she could feel his breath hot on her face. It smelt stale.

'You're coming with me and if you fucking struggle, I'll kill you right here and now.'

For a split-second it entered her head that this must be the killer who had murdered her best friend Rebecca. She made an attempt to pull free from his grip. She never saw the fist, just felt the searing pain around her right eye. There was a crunching noise from the bridge of her nose and a series of flashes and stars clouded her vision. Then came the pain — a sharp and hot pain that made her feel sick.

The man grabbed at her hair, but she twisted away from him and felt strands being ripped from her scalp. Instinct to survive was now taking over and Kirsty was thrashing and kicking out, screaming for all she was worth.

Another blow to her face momentarily stopped her from fighting back. She felt something trickle into the back of her throat and it sent another wave of panic through her. Then something tightened around her neck, closing off her ability to breathe. She clawed at her throat. She felt herself slumping forward and there was a painful thump in between her shoulders. There was the strange sensation, which felt like a warm trickle of fluid running down her spine. Then it was as if someone had thrown a bucket of water onto her back. Darkness seemed to drift over her. The dark became thick, cloying and sticky, throttling and choking her senses. The darkness became black; black as pitch.

'See, I told you I was telling the truth,' Billy Smith said, delving his handcuffed hands into a muddy hole and dragging out a dirtied and battered bin liner which had seen better days.

'You wouldn't believe how many times we've heard that,' Grace said dryly, slipping on latex gloves to preserve the evidence. 'I'll take over now, Billy,' she continued, jumping across the dried-up dyke.

'And I'm guessing you want me to take those cuffs off you now?' Hunter asked, following Grace across the dyke.

Billy offered his encased wrists, prayer like, and Hunter snapped off the police bracelets.

'Thank Christ for that,' Billy said, rubbing the red weal's on his wrists. 'You had me sweating back there in the nick. I really thought you were going to stitch me up for murder, you know. Even when I'd offered to show you where I found that mobile.'

'We don't do things like that, Billy,' Hunter said. 'Anyway, that's for all the times you've got away with it. And you're not exactly in the clear yet — we've still got your alibi to check out.'

Billy coloured up and looked sheepish.

Hunter was disappointed. He had thought finding Rebecca's mobile in Billy's caravan was the breakthrough they had been waiting for. Finding this lot buried as Billy had said took the enquiry into another dimension. It also meant that if Billy's alibi did check out, and Hunter now firmly believed it would, he was also in the clear over the Carol Siddons murder, and therefore his link with Karen Gardner and Paul Goodright wouldn't need to come out. He couldn't wait to ring Paul up later and put his mind at rest.

Grace eased the black bin liner further out of the hole. Looking back over her shoulder, she said, 'Whoever's hidden this certainly didn't want it to be found.' She clawed around the entrance, scooping away debris and depositing it behind her, mole-like.

Slowly she picked out the contents, examining each item carefully before placing them on the ground beside her. Rebecca Morris's pink schoolbag, her school uniform and books were all here.

'Is it that murdered girl's stuff?' Billy asked.

Hunter watched his face. Billy looked fascinated by the events unfolding before him. Hunter guessed that he'd be recounting all this later in the pub, telling his cronies how he had been helping police with their enquiries. It almost brought a smile to his lips.

'It certainly is, Billy. How much of this did you actually handle before you put it back into the black bag?' asked Grace.

'I just opened the bin liner and looked inside. The mobile was virtually on top of everything. I had a quick rummage around inside but didn't pull anything else out. Why? Is that bad for me?' he asked, concern on his face.

'It just means forensics will have to separate your DNA from any other we find on these.' Before Grace could say anything else the ringing of her own mobile disturbed her. She flipped it open and answered. Crooking her head, she trapped the phone between ear and top of her shoulder, listening to the call as she carried on examining the contents of the black plastic sack.

Lines appeared on her forehead, slowly creasing into furrows as she listened intently. Hunter attempted to catch her eye, wondering what was being said over the other end of that phone. He tried to grasp her mumblings but only caught, 'We'll be there inside the hour,' before Grace dropped the phone from her ear and snapped it shut.

'That was Bullars,' she announced. 'He's at the District General hospital. It looks as though our killer's just struck again. And get this; it's Kirsty Evans, Rebecca Morris's best friend. She's in a critical condition but she's alive.'

Hunter and Grace tried to avoid the press who were now swarming all over Barnwell District General, but with every entrance barricaded by a gauntlet of reporters, they'd ended up resorting to storm-trooper tactics to get into the hospital. Hunter had smacked shut the entrance door of the intensive care unit in a cameraman's face. He'd mouthed the word 'sorry,' trying to not break into a grin and jammed his foot against the bottom of the door until a uniformed officer rushed to his aide and took over security.

The surgeon who had operated on Kirsty Evans met Hunter and Grace in the reception area of ICU. He was still in his green surgical scrubs.

'She is one extremely lucky girl,' he began, removing the green cotton cap to reveal a thinning head of ginger hair. 'She's been stabbed repeatedly in the upper back, but none of the knife wounds have penetrated her vital organs. There was also an attempt to strangle her with a leather belt but luckily her attacker was disturbed and the guy who saved her managed to get it off before any serious harm was done. I'm told that the Good Samaritan was an off-duty paramedic who was out jogging. He chased off the girl's attacker and then administered first aid before the ambulance and police arrived. She has lost a lot of blood and we've had to put ten units into her during the operation. There's no doubt she would have died had it not been for him. We've stitched her back together for now and later she will need plastic surgery to some of the wounds. She's not exactly out of the woods just yet but she is off the critical list.'

'That's good to hear,' said Grace. 'Will we able to speak with her at all?'

'Certainly not today, I'm afraid. In fact, it might not even be tomorrow. She has come round since the operation but as you can imagine she is in a lot of pain, so we've had to sedate her with quite a strong dosage.'

Hunter spotted Tony Bullars hovering at the end of the corridor, trying to catch his attention. With a raised hand Hunter acknowledged him, shook hands with the surgeon, thanked him and left Grace to finish off the conversation.

Tony was clutching an abundance of brown forensic evidence bags.

'What have you got for me, Bully?' Hunter asked.

'These are Kirsty's clothes,' Bullars replied, tapping the forensic bags, 'but we've recovered the belt he used. The guy who found her had loosened it but it was still around her neck when uniform got to the scene. I've had a quick word with Mike Sampson who's down at the park and he's bagged it up for forensics. He tells me that from the width of the belt and the buckle shape and size, it looks like the same one our killer used on Rebecca. The surgeon who operated on Kirsty allowed forensics into theatre and they've recovered blood and fibres from underneath her fingernails. She put up a hell of a fight and it means we should be able to get his DNA for the first time.'

Eureka, Hunter thought as Grace sidled up beside him.

He was pleased to see a uniformed officer stationed outside Kirsty's side room. At least for the time being the killer wouldn't be able to get to her.

Hunter flashed his warrant card and he and Grace entered.

The beeping of the heart monitor was the first sound to greet them. Kirsty was hooked up to an IV and a nasogastric tube. Her head was covered in a turban style bandage and the bright fluorescent lighting highlighted the signs of a real battering to her face. Both eyes were heavily bruised and her nose was disjointed and twice the size it should have been. Mr and Mrs Evans were at the bedside, faces creased with anguish, her mother tightly gripping Kirsty's left hand and gently stroking the back of it. They acknowledged the officers' arrival with a solemn nod and Mr Evans rose from his high-backed seat.

'Have you caught him yet?' There was a sharp edge to his voice, his question almost a demand.

They understood the tone. The anger was inevitable.

'Not yet, but don't worry — we will do,' Hunter said.

Grace moved closer to the bed. Kirsty's breathing was laboured; the sedative which had been administered was playing its part in relaxing her system. The girl's eyes fluttered for a second and then stilled.

'The doctor said she's going to be okay.' Mrs Evans caught Grace's gaze.

Grace gave a sympathetic smile. 'She is, Mrs Evans. Kirsty will pull through. You watch — in another couple of weeks she'll be her old self. Young people are extremely resilient.'

'Was she…?' Mr Evans paused and gulped.

Hunter knew what he was trying to say. 'There are no signs she was attacked like that. The man who did this was scared off before he had chance to do anything else. He wouldn't have had time.' Like Mr Evans, Hunter avoided using the word rape.

'Is it the same man who killed Rebecca?' Mr Evans asked.

'We don't know for definite. That's something we're working on. We'll know better when we get Kirsty's clothing and the samples from under her fingernails up to our forensics lab. Your daughter was very brave, she put up a hell of a fight and it saved her life.'

'Do you think Kirsty was hiding something about Rebecca's murder and that's why he's tried to silence her?'

Hunter remembered what Grace had told him after her clandestine meeting with Kirsty, less than a fortnight ago. He decided that no one would benefit by revealing what Kirsty had told Grace. It was something her parents wouldn't want to hear right now.

'That's something we'll have to ask her when she comes round.' Hunter stared down at Kirsty's damaged body. A cold sensation shot down his spine and he shuddered.

'When you catch the bastard who did this, I hope you hang him,' Mr Evans snarled.

DAY TWENTY-NINE

Local and national tabloids, together with the international press, were now following the hunt for the serial killer. They were crawling all over the district, tramping around every cordoned-off crime scene and laying siege to the District General hospital where Kirsty Evans lay sedated. It meant bringing in extra uniform resources just to fend them off. Every witness the police visited received a follow up call from the media. At night, locals shared their stories in exchange for pints from journalists. Every hotel around Barnwell was booked up. It was great for the local economy but not good for allaying the fears of the community. The hacks were making a thorough nuisance of themselves.

The Major Investigation Team had adopted a siege mentality and only Detective Superintendent Michael Robshaw dealt with the daily press conferences.

One good thing had come from the chaos; the high-profile status of the investigation meant that extra staff had been drafted in. Hundreds of actions were now being tasked to detectives and there was a resurgence to the enquiry.

The fresh exhibits from the serial killer's latest attack on Kirsty Evans were being fast-tracked by forensics. The hope was that within days they would have a name for their murderer.

The man had been to six separate newsagents to collect different editions of papers to read what they were saying about him. It had taken him a whole morning to digest the contents, going back over the paragraphs time and time again, picking over the key words, and he was at boiling point.

Speculation about his background and the press's portrayal of him was making him more and more angry. They described him as pure evil and said the victims were innocent.

He wanted to scream. *The stupid bastards have got it so wrong.* It was those girls they should blame for all of this. He was the one ridding society of its evil. After all, what had his mother told him repeatedly when he was young? That he was the Angel sent by God to deliver his message. And the press were liars as well: all of their articles had given details of how close the police were to catching him.

What a load of rubbish, he said to himself. *This crap isn't going to help them catch me.*

What did worry him though were the paragraphs about his latest attack on Kirsty. Sooner or later she was going to come round and give the police a description. Despite the fact he had disguised himself, he couldn't help thinking — remembering that strange look on her face when he'd spoken to her — that she had registered something about him. He hoped what he had already done about that would throw the police off his scent.

In the past few days he had run the attack through and through in his head. How could he have missed that jogger?

I don't make mistakes — not like that anyway.

He'd even had to leave his father's old belt behind on Kirsty's neck.

How could I have been so stupid? I never make mistakes. That's why I've never been caught.

But on reflection he'd realised why that had happened. He'd panicked when he'd heard that guy shouting and running at him.

That was twice in short succession now, when for years he'd gone about his business without being disturbed.

Is someone up there trying to tell me something?

Thank goodness the man had stopped to help Kirsty, instead of chasing after him, otherwise he'd more than likely be in prison now.

As soon as he had got out onto the road, he had checked himself, told himself that this action could get him caught and so he had changed his pace to a gentle stroll and taken stock of who was around. There was no one, so he slipped off his disguise and dropped his coat and glasses in the boot of his car. He'd started the engine and waited, listening for the sound of the police cars and ambulance which he knew would soon be arriving. When he was satisfied they were going in the opposite direction, he had driven slowly away from the parking lay-by.

He took a deep breath, composed himself and continued about his business, carefully snipping out the newspaper articles to place in his files, adding them to the other cuttings and to his own personal photographs of the girls, the ones he'd taken when he'd sneaked around their homes and when he had dealt with them. He smoothed a hand over the images.

He still couldn't believe the thrill he got from tightening the belt around their throats.

Watching the fear in those slags' eyes as I squeezed out their lives.

The identical fear he had seen in his mother's face when his father had done the same.

His mother caught her image in the hallway mirror as she made her way into the kitchen and took a long look at herself. Seeing the large number of deep worry lines etched into her face made her realise that the years had not been kind. Continuing on, picking up pace, she lugged the wicker basket to the washing machine and dumped it in front of the open circular door.

As she bent down to scoop out the dirty clothing, wisps of frizzy grey hair fell across her face. She swept them back over her ears and continued with the chore of separating the colours into piles.

'Dark wash, whites,' she mumbled to herself, like she always did when doing the washing. She stopped abruptly as she caught sight of the stained blue and white striped shirt, stuffed at the bottom of the basket. Using her thumb and forefinger she picked out the shirt slowly, holding it up to the light streaming through the kitchen window.

The dark spots and splashes on the cuffs and sleeves were unmistakeable. She had seen them many times before. Automatically, she reached for the bottle of stain remover kept below the sink. As she gripped the bottle in front of the shirt, ready to spray, a news bulletin from that morning sprang into her mind.

'A fresh plea for witnesses to an assault on a teenage girl three days ago. Links to the murder of Rebecca Morris.' The words from the female newscaster were all coming back to her.

The noise of her son shuffling about in his bedroom above disturbed her thoughts and she looked up at the ceiling.

A vision of her ex-husband surged into her mind. How he'd cursed and berated her over the years. Blaming her for their son's condition.

'You've given birth to a psycho,' he'd blasted at her, the stench of chewing tobacco on his breath inches from her face.

And as he'd grown older her boy had given her as much grief. Saying it was her fault his father had left. If he had only known the truth. He'd never seen the beatings dished out to her. She had taken great care to hide the bruising. She often wondered if the damage had been caused when her husband had kicked her in the stomach when she was carrying her boy.

Her neighbour, Jimmy Carson, had caught her crying many times after arguments and had been the only one to comfort her. She had thought that taking a beating for being caught in bed with him might have been a good thing, might have changed the way her husband had treated her all these years. But it had only made things worse. He had punished her even more by leaving.

Her son had got worse after he'd left.

She hadn't heard of the condition diagnosed by the psychiatrist. Paraphilia, he'd called it. She could see the professor now, leaning towards her, solemn faced, elbows resting on desk, fingers fixed in a pyramid and pointed towards her. He'd spoken so softly, choosing such carefully phrased words.

'The condition means that your son needs to do something extreme or dangerous to get a buzz,' had been the gist of it.

And he'd rightly concluded that it would get worse as he got older.

How ironic that the son she had named after an angel had turned out to be the devil himself. She knew he should be locked up, as much for his own sake as for others, but she couldn't bring herself to betray him any further than she had already done.

She shook herself out of her daydream and glanced back down to the shirt she was holding. Tears welled into her sad grey eyes. She wondered if it was time to bring all this to a halt.

The set of double doors burst open, one of them crashing against the wall. Grace was bristling with excitement as she bounced into the MIT office holding aloft a bundle of papers.

'I've just got off the phone with our Sex Offender Officer in the Public Protection Unit. I've got a cracker of a suspect.'

Grace's sudden arrival made Hunter jump. He was alone in the office, everyone else was out on the ground. Minutes earlier he had looked at his watch, wondering what was taking her so long. First thing after morning briefing, he had given her the task of contacting the forensic lab to see if they had got a result yet from the Kirsty Evans's samples, and he couldn't help wondering why one phone call had taken her the best part of an hour.

Grace almost missed her chair. She spun it out from under her desk with one foot and just managed to catch the edge as she plonked herself down. She adjusted her posture and slid the sheets of foolscap towards Hunter.

'Firstly, we've got a positive result from forensics,' she began, almost out of breath. 'The fibres from under Kirsty's fingernails match the fibres from the cardigan found on Carol Siddons's body. The killer is still wearing the same clothing after all these years. And the belt recovered from Kirsty's neck fits the marks found on Rebecca's neck. That's the good news.'

'What's the bad news?' asked Hunter. 'And take some deep breaths, I don't want you keeling over on me.'

Grace laughed. 'Sorry, but I'm so giddy. I've got loads to tell you.' She took a deep intake of air. 'The bad news is not that bad actually. Although there is a match for the DNA found under Kirsty's nails with that from Rebecca's body and the property Billy Smith found — and it's not his by the way — it's not on the national database. However, all is not lost. Remember you gave Barry the task of going through Rebecca's school stuff? Well, I've just had a cuppa with him in the exhibits room and he's shown me some very interesting snippets from her school journal. I've photocopied them to show you. Look at pages six, seven and eight. There's nearly three weeks between the first entry and the last extract which was written the day before she went missing.'

Hunter shuffled through the sheets and found the ones Grace mentioned. He scoured the excerpts from Rebecca Morris's daily school diary.

Met up with G after school. He showed me the photos he had taken of me. He said I looked very pretty and should consider taking up modelling. He made me blush. We talked for ages. He said I was a lot more mature than my age. Asked if he could meet up again and I agreed.

Went early to the fair today to see G again. I went early because I had arranged to meet Kirsty but G told me he didn't want her to be around. He said she would be jealous of me meeting him, because he said she had been texting him because she fancied him. He took my photograph again and said he was going to make a professional portfolio for me. After G had gone me and Kirsty went to the youth club. I told Kirsty about someone older fancying me and wanting to take modelling photos of me. She just laughed and said it was weird. G is right she is jealous.

Arranged to meet G tomorrow. He told me to miss school for once. He was going to start my portfolio so I could take it to a modelling agency. He told me not to tell anyone just yet as it would be a big surprise. I can't wait to see him again. He treats me just like a grown up.

Hunter whistled through his teeth. 'Bloody hell, Grace, I bet this is how our killer has been luring the girls. He's a groomer.'

'He certainly is, and there's more. I got back on to the technicians at headquarters this morning. Do you remember Tony and Mike were given the job of searching the Evans's house and they seized the computer?'

Hunter nodded.

'Well they've pulled off a number of chat room conversations which Kirsty's been having with someone called Josh, who says he's seventeen. They've managed to trace the IP address and it comes back to one Geoffrey Collins.'

Grace dropped several printed sheets in front of Hunter, adding to the pile already on his desk.

'And get this, Geoffrey Collins is a thirty-seven-year-old man, and Public Protection Unit have confirmed he's on our sex offenders' register. If you look at pages ten and twelve you can see some of his profile that PPU have faxed over to me. His last conviction was over eight years ago and that's probably why he's not on the DNA database. He was done for gross indecency against two girls. One was fifteen and the other fourteen. What do you bet that G in Rebecca's journal is Geoffrey Collins?'

'My, my, we have been busy, haven't we? Looks like you've solved this all on your own. You'll be after promotion and a commendation next,' Hunter said.

'If the cap fits,' Grace smiled back modestly.

'That is really good work, Grace. Now you can help me get an operational plan drawn up with the SIO, so that we can do an early morning knock on this Geoffrey Collins.'

DAY THIRTY

Geoffrey Collins lived in a one-bedroom flat above a charity shop on Barnwell High Street. A decision had been made the night before not to contact his landlord for fear of word leaking out and Collins fleeing before the early morning raid. By 7 a.m., marked and unmarked police cars lined the high street. Overnight, one of the evening shift detectives had secreted himself at the rear of the place to keep a check of Collins's movements, ensuring he didn't leave before he could be arrested.

Hunter and his team were at the back of the queue of police vehicles, watching the Task Force don protective gear and check their firearms. They were taking no chances. Ten minutes later the radios crackled into life, the Task Force inspector had begun coordinating the operation. His instructions were short and precise and in a matter of minutes the immediate area around the flat was cordoned off.

Hunter wound down the car window as the 'Strike ... strike ... strike!' shout went out over the airwaves.

Two dull thuds pierced the stillness of the morning, followed by the shattering of glass and splintering of wood.

Collins's door had succumbed to the Task Force battering ram. Hunter listened intently to the radio chatter as the armed team swept the building, clearing each room, and in less than a minute his name was being called.

'DS Kerr?' the Task Force officer requested.

Hunter responded.

'The flat is empty, Collins is not here.'

Hunter cursed under his breath. Nevertheless, he left the CID car and made his way to the flat, followed by Grace, Tony Bullars and Mike Sampson, already garbed in their forensic suits.

The detectives entered the flat through a door at the rear of the building. The firearms team were just racking their weapons, clearing rounds from the chambers of their Heckler and Koch MP5s.

Hunter gave them a measured glance. He admired the elite team, viewing them as a necessary evil in the fight against crime. It had always been his mindset never to carry a gun — he didn't trust himself with something which could take away someone's life with the slightest touch. He worried that, with a gun in his hand, he might get it so wrong — especially when the red mist came. No, he'd stick with his fists. He had more control over them and the damage he left behind was always repairable. He squeezed past, over the bits and pieces of broken timber and glass which had once been the back door. It had been knocked off its hinges.

Grace, Tony and Mike followed behind.

They screwed up their faces at the rancid smell. The flat was a hovel, filthy and malodorous. A table in the centre of the room was covered in dirty crockery, a half-eaten sandwich, and milk that had curdled in its plastic container.

Hunter wondered if it was normally left in such a state, or had Collins left in a hurry?

A bare electric bulb provided the only illumination, and wallpaper, in a pattern from the seventies, peeled in places from the damp walls.

In the bedroom, a patch of light streamed through a gap in the curtains, picking out objects in the sparsely furnished room. Against one wall was an old-fashioned metal bed covered in an array of yellow stained sheets. It reminded Hunter of Tracey Emin's Turner Prize submission to the Tate Gallery.

On a bedside unit lay a laptop computer which was switched on.

A bundle of newly printed photographs lay scattered on the floor. Grace picked one up, studied it, and turned it to show Hunter. It was a close-up shot of Kirsty Evans — who now lay critically injured in Barnwell General.

He shook his head. 'We need to nail this bastard, and quick, before he attacks again.'

Grace nodded, shook out one of the plastic exhibit bags she had been carrying and dropped in the photo. Pulling the top off her marker pen with her teeth, she timed and dated the exhibit label and bent down to scoop up more of the pictures. They all appeared to be snaps of Kirsty, taken at regular intervals, and she identified the background as the park where Kirsty had been attacked.

Hunter whipped out his police radio. It sparked into life as he pressed the open channel button.

'I want Scenes of Crime and the computer team up here immediately,' he called in.

They wouldn't be long. He had included them in his operational plan the previous evening, briefing the SOCO manager over the phone before leaving work and ensuring that they were in their vans at the end of the street before the start of the morning's raid.

Though his team would be carrying out a thorough search to gather evidence, he still required the full range of specialist skills to process the crime scene and, despite the fact that the firearms unit had trampled through most of the flat, Hunter knew that there would still be some significant clues around.

Within minutes he heard the heavy footfall of several individuals clomping hurriedly up the stairs.

Red-faced and breathing heavily, SOCO manager Duncan Wroe poked his head of straggling hair and unshaven face round the door. As usual the white forensic suit he wore hung limp on his rake-thin frame. He always looked dishevelled; yet despite that appearance Duncan was one of the best SOCOs around. Two years previously he had been selected by the Home Office as a member of a forensic science team to travel to Afghanistan and train up newly appointed Afghan Scenes of Crime officers in modern forensic science methods.

Hunter knew he was going to get a thorough job done. He greeted him eagerly, snapping off a latex glove to shake his hand. His part was over. It was time to update the SOCO manager and hand the crime scene over.

As Hunter briefed Duncan, the computer technician slid past, making straight for the laptop. The pale-faced, bespectacled young man slotted a memory stick into one of the available ports and hit enter. The screen saver flashed on. The desktop image showed another picture of Kirsty Evans, a replica of one of the photos Grace had already recovered as evidence.

The technician pushed his spectacles back over the bridge of his nose, entwined his fingers and bent them back until they clicked. For a few seconds, his elongated digits hovered above the laptop.

It reminded Hunter of a pianist about to play a concerto.

As if reading his thoughts, the technician's fingers dropped onto the keyboard and began their dance upon the keys. After a few seconds he mumbled, more to himself than to anyone else in the room, 'The guy's password-protected his system. This will take me a little time.' The techie began to work the keyboard again.

Around the room, the Scenes of Crime officers were setting up a camera to record the scene and taping the unmade bed for fibre samples.

Hunter knew from experience that finding transferred fibres could link a victim to the scene. He tugged at Grace's elbow.

'There's nothing we can do here for now. Bag up all the photos and we'll get back to the station. We need to get Collins circulated tonight.'

She acknowledged with a nod and finished sealing the exhibit bag.

Barry was the sole occupant of the MIT office. The big man was hunkered over a computer, laboriously plink-plonking the keyboard using his index fingers. Hunter smiled as he watched the seasoned ex-detective thump each key. It was a complete contrast to the typing skills he had recently witnessed being performed by the young computer technician on Collins's laptop.

Hunter scraped back his seat with his leg, slipped off his jacket, dropped it over the chair back and flopped down.

'Shall I get you a bucket of water, Barry? That keyboard's going to be on fire soon,' he said, straight-faced.

'Piss off,' Barry retorted, eyes still focused downwards.

'Now, now, Mr Newstead, show some respect.'

'Piss off, Detective Sergeant.' Barry glanced across at Hunter, pushing his spectacles up onto his head, catching his gaze.

They both grinned.

'Bloody computers, they're more trouble than they're worth,' Barry added, rolling his neck and knuckle-rubbing the tension from around his eyes. 'Anyway, Mr Sarcastic, where's your sidekick?'

'Grace is booking in some evidence we got from Collins's place. We found a whole bunch of recent photos of Kirsty Evans. They look like they were taken in the park just before she was attacked. We've got him bang to rights when we catch him.'

'Any stuff relating to the other girls?'

'When I left SOCO were just starting, and a computer whizz-kid was just going through Collins's laptop. Anyway, I'm surprised to find you in. I thought you'd got a load of statements to get.'

'I heard on the radio that you'd not got Collins and I guessed you'd want all his background stuff to track him down. That's what I was doing, or trying to do, when you came in.'

'Okay, what have you got for me then?'

Barry snatched up a bundle of papers and pointed them towards Hunter.

'I got most of it from the Sex Offender officer in the Public Protection Unit. He told me over the phone what they had got on computer, which wasn't as much as what was held in a paper file they had, so he faxed me that. I've skim-read it and it contains his entire prosecution file. I've also rung Probation and they've given me snippets from his prison intelligence record as well as info from all the meetings they've had with him. They've emailed me everything but I can't seem to pull the bloody stuff off.'

Hunter couldn't help but grin again.

'It's alright for you. This technical crap is all new to me. Give me a phone and a pen any day.'

'You've done a good job anyway, Barry. It's saved us loads of time, but you didn't need to go to all this trouble.'

'Oh, I did, believe me, I did. What I wouldn't give to be part of the team to track him down. Just a couple of minutes with him is all I would need.'

During his detective constable days, Hunter had been with Barry on more than one occasion when he'd meted out his own form of justice on arrest, but it was the way in which he had almost spat out the first part of the sentence which caused Hunter to pause.

'What do you mean?' he probed.

'Nothing, Hunter. I just want to catch Geoffrey Collins like you do. The guy's got a lot to answer for, killing all those innocent girls.' He faltered over his words and that wasn't like Barry.

'There's more to this, isn't there?' Hunter asked.

'No, no. What makes you say that?' Barry was blushing.

'Come on, spill the beans.'

'Nothing to spill. You're reading too much into this.'

It was the guilty look on Barry's face that caused the alarm bells to ring in Hunter's head.

'Barry, I'm not as green as I'm cabbage looking and you, more than anyone, should know that. We go back a long way.' He stopped in mid-sentence. Things were clicking into place. 'This is about Susan Siddons, isn't it? All the work you did off your own bat when her daughter went missing. Susan was more than a snout, wasn't she?'

Barry's face set grim. 'Nail on the head, Hunter. I wanted to tell you ages ago but I knew if I did, you wouldn't allow me onto the team.'

'Damn right I wouldn't, Barry.' Hunter raised his voice. 'Be straight with me now. How long were you and Susan carrying on?'

'On and off for years, Hunter.' Barry paused. 'Carol Siddons was my daughter.'

DAY THIRTY-ONE

Hunter leaned back in his seat, nursing a cup of strong coffee. He didn't normally touch the stuff until mid-afternoon, but he needed a big caffeine hit this morning. He felt so weary after another restless night. What with the images of his crazed father still replaying themselves in his subconscious, coupled with Barry's surprise revelation yesterday, he seemed to be spending more time worrying about people than about this case.

As he replayed Barry's confession, he realised the implication it could have on the investigation. Barry had shouldered this burden for too many years, but what a time to reveal it, thought Hunter. The ex-cop had fathered a child to an old informant. A child who featured centrally in one of the biggest murder cases Hunter had ever been involved in, and the ex-cop was part of the investigation. It could compromise the whole enquiry. If defence counsel got a whiff of this, the case might not even get to court. Hunter knew he had to keep this suppressed, and last night he had warned Barry not to reveal it to anyone else.

Hunter's head was beginning to thump. He reached into his top drawer, took out two paracetamols, popped them into his mouth and swilled them down with the remainder of the coffee.

Around him, the office was beginning to fill up ready for that morning's briefing.

Grace practically fell into the room, bouncing on the balls of her feet. She snatched the cup from Hunter's hands and made for the kettle at the far end of the office. She sniffed at his cup before she set it down.

'What's with you drinking coffee at this time of day?' she said, switching on the kettle and turning to him. Catching sight of the dark rings circling his eyes, she said, 'Jesus, you look shit.'

'Thank you, Grace, for those words of comfort.'

'No, I'm being serious, Hunter. Are you coming down with something?'

'Could do with a good night's sleep, that's all. This case is getting to me.' He wasn't going to expand, not even to Grace.

She rinsed out his cup and dropped in a teabag.

'I'm making you tea, too much coffee's bad for you,' she said, turning back to her task.

'Thank you, Mother.'

'You need mothering,' she said, foot tapping as she impatiently waited for the kettle to boil.

It raised a smile in him. *She's like a breath of fresh air*, he thought to himself, *if only he could tell her why he felt so low this morning.*

She poured steaming water into two cups. 'Anyway, I've had a very interesting half hour with Duncan Wroe. I called in at the SOCO offices on my way to work, just to see if they had got anything.' She stirred the cups, squeezed out the teabags and then added milk. 'He's told me that despite the fact the place was such a shit-hole, most of the surfaces had been wiped clean — and get this — with concentrated bleach.'

She set down Hunter's cup in front of him and sunk into her chair opposite.

Hunter looked puzzled.

'That was my reaction too,' she added. 'Every flat surface; doors, and even the laptop keyboard. The whole place is clean as a whistle of prints. They've found a couple of fresh blood spills in the bathroom, very minute, and they're fast-tracking those to forensics today.'

'That's strange,' Hunter frowned.

'That's what I thought. And also, get this — the computer techie says the images of Kirsty, together with its password protection code were only recently added to Collins's laptop. They think someone else must be involved with Collins, someone who wants to cover up every trace that they were ever there. It's the only explanation they can give to their findings.'

Hunter pursed his lips. 'Someone's testing us to our limits, Grace, and the sooner we get hold of Collins the better.'

A throaty 'gruumph' made them turn to the front of the room, where Detective Superintendent Robshaw was standing in front of the incident boards. This morning another man was in tow, clutching a tumbler of water. He was tall and slim, in his late forties with stylishly cut gelled hair, tailored striped shirt and designer jeans.

Definitely not a cop, thought Hunter.

'Dishy,' whispered Grace in Hunter's ear.

'Gay,' Hunter shot back.

She elbowed him. 'Jealous.'

'Morning, ladies and gents,' Robshaw began. 'Can I firstly introduce Dr Paul Stevens, who is a Home Office criminologist from the Behavioural and Geographical Profiling Unit? Dr Stevens has been reviewing our cases and visited some of the scenes and is here to give us an insight into the type of person we are looking for. It may help us, especially now that we have a chief suspect.'

The criminologist stepped forward and took a swig of the water.

'Good morning, guys,' he began. 'Why am I here? You may well ask. One thing I can assure you of is that I am not here to steal your thunder. Your force has asked me to look at all the stages of your investigation to see if I can give an insight into the profile of the person you will be looking for. I was told this morning that you now have a major suspect in the frame for this, so my arrival might be too late. However, my thoughts on this case may just assist your interview once you catch him.'

He began striding in front of the four whiteboards, one for each of the girls attacked, tapping each as he passed.

'Let me begin by saying that although for many of you, this may well be the first serial killer investigation you've been involved in, it may not be your last. At any one time it is statistically known that there are at least two serial killers operating across Britain. I have only to mention Hindley and Brady, Peter Sutcliffe the Yorkshire Ripper, Fred and Rose West and of course most recently and the most infamous to date, Harold Shipman.'

His hands were becoming more animated as he got into his stride. He had captured Hunter's attention.

'Serial killers fall into two categories — organised and disorganised. I've visited each of the sites where the bodies have been found and also where his last victim was attacked. These are not easy to get to and in the case of the bodies, which have been hidden for a decade, the original tracks to those sites would have only have been known by someone who is local to this area. This is someone who feels confident that they can stop their car and have the time to dig and bury a body. In the most recent case, the attack on Kirsty Evans, that he can secrete himself until she arrives and then have enough time to carry out his attack. The jogger coming along was pure luck.'

Dr Stevens walked past the whiteboards, snatching a quick look at the photographs affixed to their surfaces. His eyes rested on the timelines of each of the murders.

'The intervals are getting shorter.' He settled onto the corner of a desk, dangling one leg for comfort. 'He is killing to fulfil a need and the urge to kill is stronger. The nature of his attacks plays a big part in his psyche as well — the strangulation with the belt and then the viciousness of the stabbings. Its frenzy is almost revengeful, punishing.'

'Do you think that's where the cutting of the word evil into the bodies comes in?' Hunter asked.

'Partly, yes. But my personal feeling is that the marking of the girls is about what he thinks of each of the victims. Looking into the background of all these girls, their rebellious social antics and their activities have made them his victims. Added to that, their physical profiles are similar, and I think that somewhere in his past an abusive woman or girl has featured strongly in his life.'

'We're looking at other girls who are currently outstanding as missing persons. Do you think there is the likelihood he has killed them?' Grace asked.

'Without reading through their files that is difficult to answer. However, a serial killer does not just emerge by chance. He has grown in confidence and is prepared to let you know who are his victims and, as in the case of Claire Fisher, who he abducted and murdered. My guess is there are still victims out there waiting to be found.'

'We know about his signature marks carved into the torsos of each of the girls, but what is the significance of the playing card?' Hunter asked.

'I've given that some thought. In the Rebecca Morris murder, he left the seven of hearts over a gaping wound just above her heart. In the case of the mummified remains of Carol Siddons, although you have not yet found a playing card, the post mortem revealed that her heart had been removed. Finally, with Claire Fisher, she was a skeleton so we don't know if any organs were removed, but he left behind the three of hearts. I think what you have here is the part of the sequence of each of these killings. Claire being his third victim, and Rebecca his seventh. The card suit — hearts, signifies that he has taken their hearts, literally, and physically.'

Dr Stevens took another swig of water, clutched it in both hands and looked around the room.

'You have a pattern here. I am pretty confident when I say this guy is local, and given his most recent attacks on Rebecca Morris and her best friend Kirsty Evans, he still works or lives around here. He knows his victims, either from his past, or he selects them. He carefully finds a place where he can attack them and also has a safe place where he can dispose of them. This is someone who plans meticulously. It was purely by chance that he was disturbed after killing Rebecca, and now this recent attack on Kirsty. It is imperative that you catch him soon — because believe me, he is not going to stop.'

Katherine Winter loved walking her dog at this time of the morning. Except for the wildlife, she had the woods to herself. A fine summer's mist was beginning to drift up from the damp floor, swirling around her legs as she broke into a jog. She whipped out a rubber ball from her fleece pocket and launched it towards a gap between the trees.

'Go get it, Rusty!' she shouted.

The Irish red setter watched the flying ball and then shot after it at breakneck speed. Twenty yards ahead, Rusty darted into the undergrowth out of Katherine's view and for several seconds all she could hear was the scratching of paws in the undergrowth. Her attention was distracted when she became aware of a cacophony of cawing and looked up to see a building of rooks, swirling and swooping, reminiscent of an army of Apache helicopters, an image she had often seen recently on news broadcasts from Iraq. Within seconds Rusty's barking was adding to the discordance. In trepidation, she pushed through the bushes in the direction of her dog.

He was resting on its haunches, staring up, still barking wildly.

Her eyes followed the dog's line of sight. Dangling from a rope, fastened to a large tree bough, was a man's body. The first thing she noticed was the colour of his head. It was purple, and hopping bluebottles covered the bloated flesh. Then the smell hit her, a creeping, cloying mixture of tepid urine and faeces, and her stomach leapt to her throat. Gagging, she pinched her nose and reached for her mobile.

Mike Sampson shifted uncomfortably in his oversized forensic suit, tugging at the sleeves. Because of his body weight to height ratio he had problems finding anything to fasten over his beer-belly — the sleeves were always too long and pulling them back from his hands had become a habit.

He dropped the exhibit bag he had been carrying onto one of the side tables in the sterile room. The clear plastic wrapper contained an A4 printed note recovered by SOCO from the pocket of the hanging Geoffrey Collins. In bold letters it read 'I AM A MONSTER FORGIVE ME.'

Earlier that morning Mike had raced to Barnwell Woods on the orders of Detective Superintendent Robshaw, to take charge of a very active scene. On his arrival he saw that the uniform sergeant and his shift had done a cracking job. The police medical examiner and Scenes of Crime had already been called and were en route and a clear path had been roped off to the location where the woman walking her dog had discovered Collins's body.

Because of the efficiency of the sergeant and his team Mike was merely there to check that everything which needed to be done, was being done. His role at the scene ended when they cut down Collins for removal to the mortuary, ensuring that the loop and knot of the rope remained in situ around his neck.

That had been two and half hours ago and Mike was at the mortuary to observe the post mortem and confirm the suicide, then they could wrap up this investigation and celebrate in the pub.

The post mortem was already underway by the time he had suited and entered the mortuary cutting room. Pathologist Lizzie McCormack, together with a Scenes of Crime officer, were already moving business-like around Geoffrey Collins's naked corpse, which lay on one of the stainless-steel autopsy tables.

The professor was going through the preliminaries for the purpose of the recording tape. Height, weight, state of the body. She hooked a hand behind Collins's head and lifted it from the wooden resting block. Then, carefully, she began to slide the still knotted rope over the bloated, discoloured face. The SOCO officer clicked off several shots of the process with his Nikon camera.

Rolling the head from side to side, she delicately stroked and touched several parts of the neck.

'As a slip-noose was used, the ligature was in contact with the skin right around the full circumference of the neck,' she began.

She moved the head again, pointed to an area of the neck, and the SOCO racked off several more shots.

'Now this is interesting,' she said, pursing her lips, 'although there is evidence of bruising on and around the carotid vessels on the right-hand side of the neck, the ligature marks are faint and deficient on the sides and back.'

Mike took a step towards the body 'What does that mean, Professor?'

McCormack held up a latex-gloved hand, a clear order that she wanted him to say nothing else. With her other hand she took up a scalpel from the tray next to her. Then, pushing her spectacles up onto the bridge of her nose she began slicing into the soft tissue of the throat area of the cadaver. Diving her fingers into the incised front of the neck, she began pulling and probing the larynx.

'There is bone injury in the air passage. There is a fracture of the hyoid.' She gave off a long drawn out 'hmm' before continuing with the remainder of the post mortem. Part way through she scraped under the fingernails, dropped some fibres into sample tubes and held the hands up for the Scenes of Crime officer to photograph. Finally, after two hours, she dropped the last of her instruments back onto a metal tray and snapped off her surgical gloves.

'Suicide by hanging?' Mike asked.

'Oh, indeed dear, this man's demise was caused by strangulation, but this was no suicide.'

Professor McCormack's response took him aback. 'Not suicide?'

'The evidence couldn't be much clearer. This man was murdered. See here?'

McCormack raised Collins's head from the support block and motioned a finger over the incised opening in the throat.

'Contusions to the soft tissue and underlying muscle, and a fractured hyoid, all of which are indicative of manual strangulation. Coupled with the fact that the rope marks around the neck are merely superficial, I conclude that he was already dead when he was strung up.'

She took a long pause.

'When it comes to murder, they can't pull the wool over my eyes. I have a few more tests to carry out but I've also found trauma to the face which leaves me to believe he has suffered significant blows to the mouth and left cheek, which could have rendered him either unconscious or semi-conscious. Finding those injuries caused me to carry out further examinations, particularly of the hands. I found that the majority of his fingernails are intact and there are no fibres beneath the nails. When people hang themselves by means of suicide there always comes a time of panic during which they scramble to release the ligature. In this case there is no evidence of this. I bet if you go back to the tree where you found this man hanging, you will find striation marks on the branch, caused by the rope when his dead weight was hauled up.'

Mike gasped at the magnitude of these findings. His mind was racing. If it hadn't been for Professor McCormack's experience in dealing with murder victims this would never have been spotted. It could only mean one thing — Geoffrey Collins had been set up to look like the murderer.

He pictured the recent bust at Collins's flat. The real serial killer must have somehow got into the place, assaulted and strangled him, used his computer, knowing the police would trace it back to him, left the recently taken photographs of Kirsty and cleaned up any trace of himself before he left. And that's why SOCO found the surfaces wiped with concentrated bleach.

He tumbled everything around in his head. There was only one conclusion. Kirsty Evans's attacker and the slayer of Carol Siddons, Claire Fisher and Rebecca Morris, had tried to throw them off his scent by killing Collins and making it look like suicide.

'The crafty bastard,' Mike said aloud.

'Wash your mouth out with soap, dear,' Professor McCormack said dryly.

'Sorry, Professor, I was just thinking aloud.'

She smiled. 'I know, and you're right, the person who did this is very crafty — and brutal, and if I wasn't so good, he'd have succeeded.'

No pub tonight, Mike thought to himself. *The hunt is back on.*

I don't know why they call this a green room, Detective Superintendent Michael Robshaw thought to himself as he re-read his script, *there's not a drop of alcohol in sight.*

He shuffled uneasily in his seat as the male make-up artist flicked a blusher brush filled with foundation across his face.

'Do I have to wear that stuff?' he had barked earlier, grimacing at the thought of having to wear make-up.

'Despite the fact that you look well for someone who is in their late forties, we all need a little help in front of the cameras,' the make-up artist had replied.

Robshaw made the final notes to the speech he was going to make. His second visit to the *Crimewatch* studios was much sooner than anticipated, but they had to up the ante if they were to catch this killer. He had committed murder at least four times and would have added Kirsty Evans to his list had it not been for the quick reactions of the paramedic out on his evening jog.

Numerous actions were still being processed, and new ones to find a link with Geoffrey Collins were being carried out as Robshaw prepared himself for the evening's live programme.

Detectives had already pulled Collins's prison and probation files and were ploughing through them. The killer must have known Collins was a convicted sex offender and the ideal candidate to throw them off his scent.

There'd been a heated debate during briefing as to whether the use of the leather belt should be disclosed, especially as it was a significant piece of evidence. Robshaw had decided it should be made public. They had to act before someone else was murdered.

'If showing that belt on TV jogs someone's memory and gives us that golden nugget by which we can identify our killer, it will be worth it,' he had told his teams.

The buzzer above the door sounded and the 'three minutes' light flashed on.

The make-up artist pushed the handle of his brush under Michael Robshaw's jaw and moved the superintendent's head from side to side.

'Pretty as a picture,' he whispered. 'Go break a leg.'

Kirsty was following the light along the tunnel. Through the darkness, she could see the trees and fields ahead and the summer breeze on her face brought with it the smell of freshly mown grass. But every stride felt like dragging her feet through treacle and her pounding heart felt as if it was about to burst through her chest.

Though she couldn't see him she could sense he was getting closer, almost hear him breathing down her neck and smell the foul stench of halitosis. Rebecca was shouting to her, waving her to safety. And then he was on her, grabbing at her hair and clawing at her skin. She was tugged forward so hard that her feet left the ground. Then something was tightening around her neck and the air left her lungs with a whoosh.

She tried to fight back, biting and scratching her attacker, but he was on top of her and she couldn't move. She was at his mercy.

He lowered his head and she caught the first glimpse of his face. It was a hazy image but she thought she recognised him. Rebecca was trying to tell her who it was, they'd been together when she had first seen him.

And the voice. It was growling at her, but she had heard it before, when it had been much softer and kinder.

The haziness started to clear. His face was suddenly unobstructed.

Kirsty Evans flicked open her eyes and gasped for breath.

'I know who it is!' she screamed from her hospital bed.

DAY THIRTY-TWO

The persistent ringing of Grace's desk phone was not going to go away. She cursed herself for not putting it onto voicemail, especially as she had so much paperwork to go through.

She snapped it up, gave a curt 'Grace Marshall MIT', and waited for the response.

There was a pause at the other end of the line. 'Grace, is that you?'

She recognised the voice of the desk clerk from downstairs. 'Sorry, Cheryl,' she said pleasantly, 'I've got so much work to do and so very little time to do it.'

'There's a woman just turned up at the front desk. She wants to speak to a policewoman. She says she saw the *Crimewatch* programme last night and she's not sure but she thinks the killer could be her ex-hubby.'

Grace ushered the woman into a side room within the foyer of the police station. Grace pointed to a seat at the table in the room and she took up the offer. Nervous and twitchy, clasping her hands between her knees, she introduced herself as Rachel Beddows, adding that she was twenty-five years old.

With only a little eyeliner on for make-up, Grace thought she looked a lot older.

'The desk clerk says you believe the killer we're after could be your ex-husband,' Grace said, taking out her pen and scribbling onto a sheet of paper to test it was working.

'I'm almost certain it's him,' Rachel said in a raspy, gravelly voice.

'What makes you say that?'

'I've been following all the local news about the murders because a couple of weeks ago I did have a thought it could be him. So when I heard it was going to be on *Crimewatch* I sat down to watch. When I saw that detective — I think he was a superintendent or something — show that belt, I just froze. I heard him say it'd been recovered from the attack on the latest victim and they could link it to at least two of the murders. Was that the exact belt he showed?'

Grace nodded.

'Then I'm certain it was Gabe's. Well, not exactly Gabe's as such, it belonged to his father and Gabe used to play around with it.'

'What do you mean, play around with it?'

'He used to twist it around in his hands while he was watching TV, as though he was getting it ready to throttle someone. It used to scare me.'

'You call him Gabe?'

'Yes, his full name is Gabriel Wild. The last I heard he was still living with his mum.'

'How long have you been divorced from him?'

'Oh, I'm not divorced, but I've been separated from him nearly eight years now. I ran away and haven't seen him since. I've been too scared to go to a solicitor's or anything. He always said if I left him, he'd find me and kill me. I live in Sheffield now and I changed my name.'

'There's obviously some reason why you think it's him besides seeing that belt. Why don't you tell me a bit more?'

'I don't really want to get him into trouble if it isn't him,' she said anxiously.

'Don't worry — we have the attacker's DNA so if it isn't him a quick test will clear him.'

Rachel unclasped her hands and set them on the table. She fiddled with the gold rings which adorned her fingers on both hands.

'I'll start from when we met, that'll give you a picture of what he's like.' She licked her lips. 'Gabe was into photography in a big way and was working as an apprentice at a studio here in Barnwell. He used to come to our school to take all the form's photographs. He was twenty-one when we first met and I was almost sixteen, in my last year at school before college. He chatted up all the girls but I was the one who fell for him. He told me I could be a model with my looks and figure and asked if he could take some private photos for a portfolio for a model agency he freelanced for. Like a jerk I fell for it hook line and sinker.

'I posed for some innocent shots at first and then he persuaded me to have some more sexy ones done. His dad had made him a photo studio in the loft and he used to photograph me there when his mum went out. Then the inevitable happened and we started having sex. Within six months, just after my sixteenth birthday, I left home after a bust up with my mum and moved into his mother's house.'

She paused, her blue-grey eyes focused on Grace. It was a gaze filled with sadness and despair.

'Am I going round the houses too much for you?'

'No, you're absolutely fine.'

'He started to do kinky things when we had sex. It scared me at first but I suppose I just got used to them.'

'What do you mean by kinky?'

'It's a bit embarrassing this.' Rachel wrung her hands. 'Well, he always wanted me to dress up in my schoolgirl stuff, which I could understand. But then he started asking me to resist so he could pretend he was raping me. Then one time he got his father's belt and put it round my neck and started squeezing it. That really freaked me out and we didn't have sex for a good few months after that. After he stopped sulking, we talked about it and he said it was only a bit of fun, that he wouldn't hurt me and it was just bondage.

'Well, after we'd had a good drink one night, he did it again to me. This time he really hurt me. He squeezed the belt so tight that I blacked out. That's when I told him enough was enough. Things soured after that. A couple of weeks after, he started to go out late at night and he would be gone for ages. On a couple of occasions, he didn't get back until the early hours.

'One night he came in absolutely covered in dirt and sweat and I asked him what he had been up to. He said he'd been out for a jog. But I knew he was lying because he'd never jogged in his life; he hated sport. He'd sooner light up a fag than go for a run. Anyway, the next morning I saw he'd put his clothing in the washing machine but when I went to hang them out, I thought there were bloodstains on his T-shirt. I asked him about it but he just said it was some dye from his photography processing.'

'When was this?' asked Grace, as she quickly started scribbling some notes.

'I'm sorry, I can't remember the exact day or even month. It would have been about a year before I left him, so you're talking eight or nine years ago now. Why? Is that significant?'

'I'm not sure at this stage.' Grace thought the timing could coincide with the disappearance of Claire Fisher but there were still a number of other girls outstanding in the missing from home files upstairs in the MIT office.

'Anyway, after the bust-up he asked me to marry him, to show that he still loved me. I said yes, thinking everything would be okay, but within weeks of the marriage he was wanting to use the belt on me again and we just had row after row. I told him he was perverted and I'd had enough and he said if I left him, he'd kill me and bury me where no one would be able to find me.

'A couple of weeks after that I packed what I could, and when his mother was out shopping and he was at work, I left. I never got in touch with him again. I went to a friend's house and didn't even tell my parents where I was for fear he'd find me, and then I got a council flat in Sheffield and I've been there ever since.'

'Besides the incidents you've told me about, Rachel, is there anything else about Gabriel's character which you found to be unusual or different?'

'Weird, you mean?' Rachel paused and ran a hand through her hair.

Grace noted its lack of style and the abundance of split-ends. From her experience of dealing with domestic violence cases, she knew this was a girl who had lost her self-esteem.

'Well, there were the pictures he kept in the briefcase of some of the girls he had photographed at school. And he also kept local newspaper cuttings about girls going missing. I never told him I'd found them. I was too scared. That's what's made me come to you.'

Grace could feel the hairs prickle at the back of her neck. 'Anything else about him?'

'He hates coppers — sorry police — he once told me when he was a kid, he'd been beaten up by a cop who wanted him to confess to killing and cutting up a pet rabbit. He said the cop had been a close neighbour, a Mr Newstead.'

That has to be Barry, Grace thought to herself.

For another half hour Grace back-tracked on everything Rachel had said, testing to see if there was anything that had been missed. She had taken copious notes in preparation for a formal statement, and though she tried her best to stay focused on the important task in hand, from time-to-time her thoughts drifted, imagining what she might be facing within the next hour or so when she finally got home — late again.

DAY THIRTY-THREE

'Does the name Gabriel Wild mean anything to you?' Grace asked Barry the moment he walked through the door. He was first to arrive after her and she could hardly contain her excitement and share with someone what she had learned late yesterday. Everyone was gone by the time she finished talking with Rachel Beddows. She'd tried to get hold of Hunter but his mobile had diverted to voicemail. It had been her intention to ring him later from home, but she thought better of it when her daughters Robyn and Jade sent her on a guilt trip for missing their netball practice. She reminded herself that she had already put her career on hold twice to bring up her daughters. They were old enough to look after themselves, and she needed to do this for her own fulfilment. However, she still found herself apologising all evening and had promised to make it up to them at the weekend.

'Don't I get a "good morning, Barry, how are you this fine day", instead of being quizzed about a little brat who once upon a time used to live near us?'

'Don't be such an old grouch. I got some information last night which could end this enquiry. I hardly slept and look at me — I'm as fresh as a daisy, not a miserable old sod like you.'

'Less of the "old", will you? Anyway, what can't wait long enough for me to even have my morning cuppa?'

'Gabriel Wild's ex-wife came in late last night telling me she thinks he's our killer. She gave me loads of examples and a lot of what she told me could fit the profile of our murderer, but I checked him out on the intelligence system and he's got nothing at all recorded against him. She did mention, however, that he had had a bit of a run in with a Mr Newstead years ago, when he was a teenager.'

'A bit of a run in is an understatement,' Barry said, setting his lunch container down on his desk and removing his coat. 'He was a right little bloody tearaway, and a pervert to boot. He was the bane of my life.'

'Tell me about him and I'll fill you in what his ex-wife told me.'

'It really was a long time ago. I had just gone into CID when he turned up on my radar. He used to live a couple of doors down from us but I hardly noticed him as a youngster because while his dad was around, he was a real polite kid. Then one day his old man came home early from work and found his mother in bed with the guy from across the road. There was a hell of a bust up and he tried to throttle her. I was off duty doing the garden and heard this commotion so I ran to their house and had to pull him off her. I managed to calm things down and I dealt with it there and then — like we used to in those days. I found out that a couple of days after the domestic he'd upped sticks and left. She was left to bring Gabriel up on her own.

'Over the next few years I kept getting complaints about him following girls and playing with himself in front of them and I can remember one neighbour catching him peeping through her ground floor bathroom window. I had words with him in front of his mother and I know she gave him a real good hiding for that.'

He paused and stroked his bushy moustache.

'A few months after, I had to deal with him again. This time for giving a lad a right hammering. I think the lad had slagged off his mum. After that I used to see him hanging around the back of my house and when one day I told him to sling his hook, he put two fingers up at me so I warmed his ear-hole for him.'

His expression hardened.

'About a week later, I heard Sarah screaming from the garden early one morning. I dashed out wondering what on earth was happening and found parts of her pet rabbit had been nailed up on the Wendy house. It had been cut to pieces with a knife or something similar. I knew it was that little bastard Gabriel and I went straight to his house. I tried to get him to cough that he'd done it but his mother just kept covering for him. Anyway, shortly after that they moved. She sold the house and the next thing I discovered was they had gone to a council house on the Tree Estate. I kept a watch out for him but that was the last I saw of him. What does his ex say about him?'

Grace tried to contain her excitement as she related what Rachel Beddows had told her.

'I'm just waiting for Hunter to come in and then I'm going to feed it into morning briefing,' she finished.

'Bloody hell, Grace, that's reminded me of something else involving him.' Barry peeled off his jumper and chucked it over the piled-up paperwork on his desk. 'It must have been about ten years ago now but I'm sure he was interviewed over a girl's body that was discovered in some woods just over the border in West Yorkshire.'

Barry looked thoughtful and Grace could almost hear the cogs turning inside his head. Then he raised a finger.

'I remember the gist of it now. A local Peeping Tom out looking for couples having sex in a well-known lovers' lane heard a girl screaming and from what I can recall he either shouted or dashed towards the sound. Anyway, the next thing he saw was a young man with a small dog sprinting off along the lane. He guessed something had gone off and started looking around and that's when he came across the body of a teenage girl who had been beaten and strangled.'

Barry looked down to his desk, deep in thought.

'I think it was South Kirby way, just outside our force area,' he continued, 'I can remember seeing an e-fit of the suspect, but it wasn't a good one. I know Gabriel Wild was interviewed as part of the enquiry, but I never got the end result. I'm not sure if it was ever detected or not, because it was West Yorks job, but I can make a quick phone call to one of my old buddies from there and get the heads up if you want?'

'Please, if you wouldn't mind, Barry. I'll make you a coffee.'

Five minutes later, sipping at her freshly brewed coffee, Grace heard Hunter's voice outside in the corridor. As he entered the office she pushed herself up from her desk ready to greet him.

'Where were you last night when I needed you? I came back to the office from talking to a witness and it was like the Marie Celeste. I tried to ring you on your mobile but all I kept getting was your voicemail.'

'That's because while you were downstairs in the interview room, Tony and I got called out to the hospital. Kirsty Evans came round yesterday afternoon. She knows who attacked her. It was a guy who took their school photographs. She knows him as Gabe.'

Avoiding the motorway, Hunter took the A61, the less congested route into Wakefield. It was a good few years since he had travelled this road but as he passed certain landmarks the memories gave him a warm feeling. It seemed like yesterday, but it was twelve years since he had made the regular twice-weekly journey to and from Detective Training school. It was in a side road on the edge of the city, and he knew he would have to revisit before returning to Barnwell. He'd had such a great experience there. He had returned to the district bursting with knowledge of the criminal law and, along the learning path, had also made contact with detectives from forces the length and breadth of England, which had proved extremely useful over the years.

As he slowed the car to join the crawling nose-to-tail traffic entering Wakefield he glanced across at Grace, who was studying the notes she had made from her conversation with Gabriel Wild's ex-partner and Barry. Together with the revelation from Kirsty Evans, this was the breakthrough they had been waiting for.

After Barry's phone call to one of his old West Yorkshire colleagues, Hunter had been given the telephone number of his counterpart in MIT in Wakefield. Immediately after morning briefing, he had spoken to Detective Sergeant Glen Deakins and arranged a meet at Wood Street police station in the centre of the city.

Following the detective sergeant's instructions Hunter parked the unmarked police car in a multi-storey car park and he and Grace walked the few hundred yards to the old red-brick police station opposite the law courts.

Despite an attempt to give its foyer a contemporary makeover, the waiting area still had a dark and gloomy feel typical of the Victorian era. After showing their warrant badges to the front-of-entrance clerk, Hunter and Grace took up seats which had been arranged along the front wall below two large sash windows, the bottom section of which held toughened and frosted glass. A pale sunlight had managed to penetrate and was lighting the dimness around them.

While he waited, Hunter eyed the many framed force publicity posters adorning the walls and smiled cynically as he read over the mission statements and modern-day Whitehall spin. *All this bullshit*, he said to himself. What the public really wanted was cops on the streets.

Then his attention was distracted by an electronic buzzer and a side door opened. A tall, slim, steel-grey haired man appeared in the doorway. Wearing a two-piece pinstriped suit and sporting a good tanned complexion, DS Glen Deakins looked more the typical business tycoon than an MIT detective. He greeted them, and Hunter recognised his strong Leeds accent as he rolled his tongue around their names.

'Hi, I'm to give you the full works.' He held out a hand to shake. 'My DCI can't speak highly enough of Barry Newstead.' He glanced behind them. 'Barry not with you?'

Hunter shook his head.

'Pity. The DCI was hoping to catch up with him. They worked together on some secretive joint force investigation into corruption in the Met during the early 80s.'

He held open the door as Grace and Hunter joined him and then pointed an extended arm up the open staircase that connected all three floors of the building.

'We're on the top floor. MIT has the whole of one corridor. Too hot in summer and freezing cold in winter but who's complaining, still get the cheque in the post thirteen times a year, don't we?'

The sergeant grinned. His features were strong and his hazel eyes were friendly.

The top of the stairway opened onto a bright and airy corridor that led to suite after suite of rooms and offices, each bustling with activity. Its airiness took Hunter by surprise.

As if reading his mind, the DS said, 'This place was given a full refurb before we moved in eighteen months ago. Everything we need is here. You ought have seen the place before it got its make-over.' He took them down the corridor. 'I've got us a room at the far end where you can look at the files from the Kelly Johnson murder.'

He stopped at a glass-panelled door and pushed it inwards. They entered an eight-foot-square, carpeted room. It was lit by a pair of fluorescent lights set in chrome for maximum brightness. Along one wall was a framework of metal shelves adorned floor to ceiling with boxed case files. Hunter guessed this was where they stored the cold case work. In the centre, two desks had been pushed together, the light oak surfaces almost covered by an array of paperwork, organised into piles.

'The Kelly Johnson case.' DS Deakins pointed out with an open palm, almost as though he was introducing someone rather than something. 'I know this job like the back of my hand. I worked on this as a young detective back in '96. In fact, it was my first murder case. I spent over six months on it before it was wound down to just a small team. It was filed as undetected after eighteen months and it's one of our review cases now.' He rested his hand on one of the piles. 'Everything is here. The witness statements, crime-scene photos, door-to-door reports and suspect interviews in date and alphabetical order.'

Hunter eyed the paperwork. 'You might be able to shortcut things for us without the need to plough through all this lot, especially as you worked on it for so long.'

'Yeah, no problem. To be honest, when the gaffer asked me to show you the case it gave me the opportunity to skip read back over some of the actions I did on the case. In fact, now it seems like only last week when I was working on it.'

DS Deakins invited Grace and Hunter to sit and lowered himself into a chair. Leaning forward, intertwining his fingers, he rested his chin and gave his guests his full attention, then paused for a few seconds as if gathering his thoughts.

Hunter became conscious of the bustle of activity coming from the rooms further along the corridor. Behind those doors would be similar scenes to those of his own murder team back at Barnwell. Officers busy on telephones or computers following up their leads to crack the case. Working practices the length and breadth of the country were distinctly similar despite each murder being different.

'Kelly Marie Johnson, thirteen years old.'

Deakins unlocked his hands and turned an A5 size photograph of a smiling teenage girl towards them. The colours were still sharp despite the photograph being twelve years old. A picture of a very pretty girl with many similarities to the other victims; dark collar-length hair, glistening hazel eyes and with an air of innocence. The girl was wearing heavy make-up and her pose appeared more confident than the photos they had of the other girls. This shot was more professional altogether.

Grace took the photograph from the DS. 'This is an unusual photo. Was it taken in a studio?'

'It was actually,' Deakins said. 'Kelly had just been taken on by a modelling company. She was doing shoots for catalogues. That photo came from her portfolio. As you can see Kelly was a very pretty girl, looked a lot older than her thirteen years, and because of that she attracted a lot older type of boy. It caused a bit of friction with her dad.'

'What was she like as a person?' Grace continued.

'Well, until she got the modelling contract, just a normal teenage girl, but the six months leading up to her death her parents and her friends said her personality changed. She began to hang out with older teenagers. Putting jealousy to one side, her closest friends painted a picture of a girl who suddenly got very cocky and arrogant and who began picking on girls she considered less attractive than herself, humiliating them and even bullying a couple of them. She began wagging school and we found out she'd been meeting up with a couple of lads, sixteen and seventeen. We questioned them on several occasions and both eventually admitted they had had sex with her, but they insisted she told them she was sixteen. They had unbreakable alibis for the day she was murdered. They were at work, witnessed by dozens of their co-workers.'

He took back the picture and studied it.

'She'd begun drinking as well, cider, and heavily. She rolled in drunk on several occasions and had bust-ups with her parents. She'd also been warned by the modelling agency about her attitude.'

'A girl with everything, pressing the self-destruct button,' said Hunter. 'How many times have we seen that?'

'These characteristics you are describing identically match our victims. All the girls seemed to have been going through a real chaotic phase in the weeks leading up to their deaths,' added Grace. 'What happened on the day she was murdered?'

'She'd come home from school. This was one of the rare occasions she had actually attended recently. She was on a final warning from the modelling agency. A "clean up your act or you're finished" ultimatum. Anyway, she got changed and told her mother she was meeting a couple of friends and would be back for her tea.'

Deakins picked up some typewritten notes, turned over a couple of the pages and continued reading from one of the sheets.

'At four forty-five p.m. on the second of August 1996, Mr William Burridge was in the woods at South Elmsall.' Deakins glanced up. 'Billy was known as a bit of a Peeping Tom in the village. He did admit, under questioning, that he used to visit the woods regularly because they were well known as a rendezvous point for courting couples.'

He looked back to the notes.

'He heard a girl screaming. He could tell from the tone that it was someone in trouble and ran towards the sound and began shouting as he got closer. He described seeing a young man wearing a dark T-shirt and jeans running with a small wiry-haired dog before he disappeared through the trees.'

The DS looked up from his notes again.

'He got a glimpse of his face, just for a split-second glance, but it was enough for him to do an e-fit picture for us. Then Billy found Kelly in some long grass. She had been strangled by a belt of some type and she had been stabbed. In fact, when the post mortem was done the pathologist stated that the killer had made some attempt to cut out her heart.'

Hunter and Grace exchanged looks.

Deakins ran his fingers down the typewritten script. 'Uniform were first on scene. A dog man did a follow through the woods and some farmer's fields, which led towards the village of Great Houghton, in your area. He lost the track there unfortunately.'

Deakins set down the papers.

'And that's where I came in. I was part of the team which did enquiries in your area. We joined up with a few of your detectives and did house to house. We circulated the e-fit and got an anonymous tip-off, which pointed us in the direction of Gabriel Wild. I knew as soon as I started interviewing him that something wasn't right. He was so nervous and cagey. We found a bonfire in the back garden, some clothing and what looked like a pair of trainers had been burned, but it was four days after the murder and everything was ashes. His mother covered for him. She said he was with her in the house at the time of the murder. Gabriel hardly said anything in the interview and we couldn't knock what his mother said. She stood firm even though we threatened her with perverting the course of justice.'

The DS's mouth set tight.

'Gabriel remained, and still remains, our strongest suspect for Kelly Johnson's murder.'

'Just one question,' said Hunter, 'did you find a playing card with Kelly's body?'

The enquiry stopped Deakins in his tracks.

'Do you know, that rings a bell.'

He flicked through the mounds of paper and dragged out several stapled sheets. Sliding a finger slowly down the notes he stopped halfway down the second sheet and looked up at Hunter and Grace.

'Yes, it's here, on the exhibits list from the scene — a playing card found in Kelly's left hand. It was photographed in situ; the two of hearts.'

'Kelly Johnson was his second victim,' said Hunter.

DAY THIRTY-FOUR

The back door of the Wilds' semi-detached house — original wood and glass from the early fifties when the house was built — lay in pieces. It initially resisted the Task Force firearms team battering ram, but on the third run the oak door had exploded from its frame in spectacular fashion. Splinters of wood and shards of glass had flown everywhere.

'Clear,' one of the Kevlar-armoured firearms officers shouted as he swept the last remaining room on the ground floor and moved on towards the stairwell.

Hunter and his team shared an air of nervous excitement as they stood outside, waiting and listening for their signal to enter. An earlier clear blue sky had given way to a slight drizzle and despite it still being the last dregs of summer the air seemed dense with cold moisture.

Set out in front of them was a meticulously tidy garden. Neatly trimmed hedges and tall bushes surrounded a newly mown lawn.

Hunter strained his ears, following the sounds of the searching firearms team who were currently moving rapidly through the upper rooms. Even though he was anticipating it, when the call for them to enter came it made him jump.

Hunter went in first. Despite the daylight, the lights were on in every downstairs room. A television was on somewhere in the lounge to his left and Hunter could see the flicker of blurred images against the dark patterned wallpaper. He bounded up the threadbare carpeted stairs, quickly followed by Grace, Tony and Mike. On the landing, he was surprised to be met by Paul Goodright, garbed head to toe in standard protective Task Force clothing, a Heckler and Koch rifle strapped across his chest. He'd forgotten Paul was part of the firearms team. It was the first time he had seen him in uniform. He looked quite a commanding presence.

'Fancy meeting you here,' Hunter said.

Paul's features were grim. 'The target's not here, Hunter, and you're not going to like what we've just found.' He pointed to the front of the house.

Hunter pushed the bedroom door fully open and the four MIT detectives trooped in. The room was gloomy, with a single shaft of light piercing the dimness. One of the windows was open and the velvet curtains were lifting in the breeze.

He picked out the sheet-covered mound on the bed. Using thumb and index figure he carefully lifted the top edge of the white linen cover to reveal the figure of an ageing woman curled up in the foetal position. A gut-wrenching smell emanated from the body and he held his breath as he bent over the corpse.

Lividity was rampant throughout her torso, a clear sign she had been dead for some days. Looking into her wide, staring eyes he knew that the blood-shot effect meant that the blood vessels had blown, usually the result of strangulation — a feature in all the murders they had been investigating. A grotesquely swollen tongue had forced its way between her lips, filling the entrance to her mouth.

'Looks like he's got to her as well. I wonder if she found out about him and was going to drop him?' Tony Bullars broke the silence.

'The bastard. His own bloody mother. The evil bastard.' Grace seemed to stumble over her words. 'I need some fresh air.'

She hurried down the stairs and made her way to the back door, stepping out into the fine rain. She leant back against the house wall and took in deep gulps of air.

Hunter joined her. 'You okay, Grace? This is not like you.'

'Things have just caught up with me, Hunter. It's been a long couple of months with very little break and now this.'

She pushed herself back off the wall.

'I want to personally nick this twisted bastard,' she said loudly. 'Want to look him in the eye, take a leaf out of Barry's book — hope he puts up a fight so I can give the bastard some of what he deserves.'

Her bottom lip quivered as she fought back the rage. She took a deep breath.

'But we've dealt with his type all the time, haven't we, Hunter? When they come up against someone who's a match, they totally bottle it. They're wimps and cowards. And I bet this pervert's just the same.'

'You finished venting your spleen now? Because we've got work to do.'

'Yeah, I feel better after that,' Grace said, giving him a wan smile as she turned to go back into the house.

He wanted to wring that fucking woman detective's neck — just like his mother's. Saying things like that about him.

I'm not a wimp and a coward and I'm certainly not a pervert. I'll show her.

He slunk back into the bushes, away from the officers' gaze.

He had only just managed to hide. The arrival of the police had taken him by surprise. He had been in the shed looking for some sacking to take his mother's body away and bury, now it was starting to smell, when he heard the cars screeching up to the front of the house.

That sound could only mean one thing and confirmed in his mind that he had been right to do what he had done. Before he had ended his mother's miserable life, she must have telephoned the police and tipped them off about him. What had she said to him? 'Enough is enough.' Those were her words.

I knew she had, that's why she had to die.

By rights he should have punished her a long time ago.

How could she betray me after all this time? I'd only let her live this long because she had helped me. How many times had she washed his bloodstained clothing without question? *It wasn't just my secret. It was our little secret. It was the only thing we actually shared since that day she caused my dad to leave.*

When he saw the armed police smash down the door and then watched them all scuttle inside to search, he had decided to make himself scarce, and was about to emerge from the bushes at the bottom of the garden when that black lady detective and her colleague had come out, and she had started to slag him off. He listened to every word she had said, wanting to ring her fucking scrawny neck. She was just like all the others. The moment the detectives had gone into his house he'd managed to sneak away and he had intended to disappear but now he decided he had one more job to do before he left.

She has to be taught a lesson. She can't say those things about me without being punished.

DAY THIRTY-SIX

Grace cupped a mug of hot coffee in both hands and stared at the small TV screen in her kitchen. The sound was on low but she could still pick out Detective Superintendent Michael Robshaw's words. The local news broadcast was replaying footage from last night's press conference held at the front of the Wilds' home.

'There has been a significant development with the discovery of the body of an elderly woman, and a post mortem examination will be carried out to determine cause of death,' he was announcing to the world's press in his best police speak. 'We urgently need to trace and speak with her son, Gabriel, in relation to this incident.'

His face was solemn, though Grace knew that inside he was elated because they finally had a name for their serial killer. Gabriel Wild was on the run.

Next came an aerial shot of the Wilds' rear garden, where a white forensic tent had been erected beside the wooden shed. They had already dug up the remains of Gabriel's dog, but more disturbing was the fact that ground penetrating radar had indicated at least one much larger form buried beneath the flowerbeds. They were expecting to find the body of yet another teenage girl.

Grace flicked off the television, crossed the kitchen, snatched up the wall phone, scrolled down the contacts list and hit the speed dial button. She trapped it between her head and shoulder, listening to the ringing tone as she put the finishing touches to the polish on her nails.

'Come on, come on — answer,' she muttered under her breath. She blew on her sticky nails. She had a lot to do after yesterday's discovery.

'Hello,' said a deep voice.

'Hi Dad, it's me.' She moved the phone from between her head and shoulder, pressing it against her ear.

'Oh, hello, Princess.'

Grace screwed up her eyes. She loved to hear her father's Jamaican accent, and knew it was just his term of affection towards her, but she still cringed when he used that word.

'Dad, I wish you wouldn't still call me Princess, I'm thirty-seven years old.'

'You will always be my princess, no matter how old you are.'

With the surname Kelly, she'd often wondered why her father and mother decided to call her Grace. As a young child she hadn't realised the significance of the name, but when she reached comprehensive school, she had been brunt of much taunting and mocking, her first experience of prejudice because of her colour.

She shook away her thoughts.

'Dad, I need a favour. I've got to work late again. Something really important has cropped up.'

'I know, it's been on this morning's news,' he said.

'Can you pick up the girls from school and give them their tea? I've got them booked into a holiday school sports scheme for this week. I wouldn't ask you under normal circumstances but David's still trying to sort out his new job so he's been working late as well.'

'Anytime, Princess. You know you don't need to ask. Me and your mother love having them.'

'Thanks, Dad, you're a star.' She didn't give him the chance to respond further. She just didn't have time, especially as she had to drop off the girls before she drove in.

The Wilds' home had become another murder crime scene. Mrs Wild's body had been removed on the instructions of the Coroner's Office and now lay with all the other bodies, in cold storage at the mortuary.

Hunter, Tony Bullars and Mike Sampson, together with forensics, had gone over every inch of the house, rifling through cupboards and drawers to search out evidence. On the second sweep of the loft, Hunter shouted as he began prising at a corner of what looked like a section of wall, but was in fact painted plywood. It was a false wall covering the chimney breast and he tugged it away from its frame.

'Bloody hell, just look at this lot.'

He reached inside and pulled out a glass storage jar. It had a label near its base and he turned it around and held it up to the single bulb which provided the loft's only illumination. The jar was filled with a discoloured liquid and something slopped around inside.

'Frigging hell!' He recoiled, almost dropping the jar. He caught it with his other hand and brought it closer to get a better look. Claire Fisher's name was written on the label in bold black ink. In the dim light he studied the contents, then thrust the jar at Mike Sampson.

'Christ, Mike, is that what I think it is? The sick bastard. The press are going to have a field day when they get hold of this.'

Mike scrutinised the contents and nodded. 'It's a heart. The bastard cut out and stored her heart. And look — there's a couple of more jars behind there as well.'

Hunter handed the jar to Mike and leaned back into the space. He could make out three more jars lined up on a narrow shelf. Above, on another shelf, he spotted several box files and he took one down and flicked it open. It contained an array of newspapers and photos, which he began to study. He recognised some of the faces in the photographs and yellowing newspaper cuttings. Claire Fisher, Rebecca Morris and Carol Siddons were among them. Sellotaped to Carol's photo was the ace of hearts playing card: foxed and discoloured, it showed clear signs of ageing.

She was his first victim, Hunter said to himself. Hers was the first body they had found with its heart cut out. And he bet there would be a jar on the shelf with her name on it.

There were images of other teenage girls who looked familiar and he guessed they would match some of the missing from home files back in the office. They were filed in date order and he speed-read the newspaper story lines of young girls who had disappeared over the past fifteen years. He picked out the ones they had already found murdered. But there were other girls whose bodies hadn't been found and Hunter knew they were in gravesites not too far away, waiting to be uncovered.

Inside clear plastic pockets he found graphic and gruesome photographs. Gabriel had taken shots of the girls before and after he had killed them. Some of the faces bore looks of horror, and some were pleading. For a moment he thought about the parents of these girls. Once this got to court, they were going to see the looks of their children's last moments and he shuddered. It didn't bear thinking about. *Sick fuck!* As he took out more files, Hunter found a large-scale local map of the Dearne Valley and surrounding area. At the old Manvers Colliery site were four areas ringed in red ink. As he scanned the map he spotted, circled, the old farm complex near to the village of Harlington, and at the top left-hand section another circle covered a wooded area close to the village of South Elmsall.

Hunter knew he was looking at where Gabriel had buried his victims and there was further digging to do, especially around the Manvers complex.

Outside Wild's home the media circus had gathered. The team could hear the Sky News helicopter hovering above. A description and photograph of Gabriel Wild had already been circulated and it had been plastered across every news channel the previous evening. Numerous sightings were currently being followed up and they had put out an all ports warning to prevent Gabriel from leaving the country.

The search to capture Barnwell's serial killer was in full swing.

It was easier to get back to his car than he had anticipated. He slipped on the spectacles and his father's duffle jacket, which were still in the boot and then scooped a handful of hair wax from its tin and rubbed it into his hair. He sat in the car for a good ten minutes, cursing. Things had come to a head quicker than he had ever anticipated. He would be punished for sure. They'd found the body of his mother before he'd had time to bury her, and sooner or later the detectives would tear apart the house and find all his little secrets.

A tingling sensation coursed through his body as images of all his victims washed around in his brain. He closed his eyes, trying to hold the vision of each one as he recalled what he had done to them.

Their names slowly filtered through. Carol Siddons had been the first. He smiled. He could see the surprise on her face like it was only yesterday. Then there was Kelly Johnson. She had been a right tart. He'd soon sorted her, though. He'd never forget the two girls from the children's home near Doncaster; Amy Clarke and her friend Katie Nichols. He'd met them on Nether Hall Road, a notorious place for prostitutes. He'd been cruising the area when he spotted them.

'Fifty quid for both of us,' Amy had said. 'You're getting underage you know.'

Those two bitches had chosen themselves.

Though it had proved difficult killing them. The girls had been edgy the entire journey to the Manvers complex and when he pulled onto the track behind the coking plant they had tried to escape. Thank God his car had only been two-door; they couldn't get out of the back.

They had put up a hell of a fight though. He had scratches and bite marks everywhere and the car was a real mess when he had finished. It had taken days of cleaning before he could use it again. He'd buried those two together in the same grave. And then there was Claire Fisher — posh little rich kid. If only her parents had known what she was really like. He didn't need to rape her. She had given in to him so easy, but he'd killed her anyway — gullible bitch.

Three years ago there had been Zoe Green. She was so pretty. He spotted her while he was mooching around Clifton Park, in Rotherham. She was walking her dog and had let it off its leash. Luring the mutt into the bushes had been easy and when she had come looking, he'd pounced. He could still see the shocked look on her face. She had frozen and he'd killed her in less than a minute.

Smuggling her body into the boot of his car had been the hard part. He'd waited until dusk and then moved her before anyone had come searching. He'd driven home and secreted her behind his garden shed, covering her with bin bags and garden rubbish and the next day buried her between the hydrangea bushes and the back fence without his mother noticing.

Finally, there had been Rebecca Morris. She was his bad omen. Killing her had proved his downfall, but now wasn't the time for recriminations. He still had things to do.

He started the engine, took a good look up and down the street, then when he had satisfied himself that no police officers were in sight, he set off to the quiet country lanes he knew so well.

Earlier that day it had not been too hard following Grace's people carrier. *She obviously has other things on her mind.*

He smiled to himself as he wove in and out of the traffic, two, and no more than three cars behind. He had picked her up late in the evening leaving the police station and followed her home. He was elated when Grace had emerged at 8 a.m. with her two children. He hadn't thought about the detective having kids — and they were girls.

He liked the look of the eldest in her school uniform. He was surprised to see her dressed like that because the kids were on school holiday. Then he recognised which school she was at — a private school. He guessed they must have different holidays and he took a shortcut, anticipating where Grace would be driving. He was right, and was comfortably parked a good hundred yards from the entrance to the school when Grace arrived. He used the zoom lens on his camera to watch the girls get out, then snapped off a shot.

He was sure Grace would be working late again because of the hunt for him and he guessed her daughters would be making their own way home.

For the remainder of the day he put things in place and rehearsed his lines, and ten minutes before the school day was due to end, he parked his car into a marked bay opposite the school gates and sat back to wait.

It wasn't long before he spotted the eldest girl coming towards him, chatting with a bunch of mates.

He slipped out of the driver's seat and strode purposefully towards her.

'Miss Marshall?' He showed the fake warrant card he had made earlier on his laptop. She looked taken aback. 'Miss Marshall, I'm Detective Wild. I work with your mum. She's had an accident and I've been sent to take you to the hospital.'

The girl paled.

'I need to speak with someone.' She reached for the mobile in her blazer pocket.

'We need to hurry, Miss, your mum needs to go to theatre. You can phone who you need to tell on the way there.'

She dropped it back into her pocket and followed him, hurrying to keep up as he jogged to his car.

Back in the MIT office, Grace and Barry had been given the task of logging all the evidence gathered and brought from the house. They were in the process of separating the vast array of forensic bags when Grace's ringing mobile phone disturbed them. The ring tone was a baby laughing and she loved it. It reminded her of her own two giggling girls when they were babies, and how she would end up in fits of laughter with them. This time, though, she tried to ignore it, she had important work to do, but it rang again and she snatched the phone out of her handbag and flicked up the screen. It was Robyn. It must be important; she knew not to ring her at work.

'Hello, Robyn? Mum's busy, tell me what you want quickly,' she said.

'I gather I am speaking with Detective Grace Marshall,' said the man's voice.

'Who is this? Is that the school? Is there something wrong with Robyn?' Grace asked anxiously.

'Not yet, but there soon will be.' The voice was cold and menacing.

Grace froze, her mind racing.

'You know who this is, Grace, don't you?' he said. 'It's Gabriel Wild. You've been bad-mouthing me, Grace, and you need to be punished.'

'Is Robyn there? I haven't been saying anything about you,' Grace stammered.

'You're lying, Grace. I heard you. I was hiding in the bushes. You said I was a coward and a wimp and a pervert. Those were your words, Grace, and for that I'm going to hurt you where it hurts the most.'

There was a long pause. Grace's face turned ashen. She saw Barry was trying to get her attention, he knew something was wrong.

'Do want to speak to Robyn?'

Grace could hear her daughter sobbing in the background. The sobbing got nearer.

'Robyn. Robyn!' she screamed down the phone.

The sobbing drifted away and Gabriel Wild was back on the line. 'Do you know what I did to all the other girls?'

'If you hurt her. If you harm one hair on her head, I'll fucking kill you!' Grace shouted, an edge of hysteria in her voice. Tears of anger and desperation welled up in the corner of her eyes.

The line went dead.

DAY THIRTY-SEVEN

Detective Superintendent Robshaw was running the operation from the command suite at the police station. He had called in a hostage negotiator, briefed the Task Force firearms unit and turned out as many police vehicles as he could muster and ordered them to park up at strategic points throughout the district. Finally, he had called in phone technicians from headquarters to fix tracking and recording equipment to Grace's phone. As soon as her mobile rung again they would be able to get a fix on the user.

In less than four hours he had managed to get everything in place. He was praying nothing had happened to Grace's daughter and that Gabriel Wild had a big enough ego to make contact.

He didn't have to wait long. Grace's mobile started to ring.

Suddenly the ring tone was not so funny.

She watched the technicians operate their equipment and when they gave her the okay signal she flipped up the screen.

It was Robyn's phone. 'Hello, Robyn?' she said nervously.

'Hello, Grace, it's me.'

She recognised Gabriel's voice.

'Let me speak to Robyn,' she said.

'You're in no position to make demands, Grace. And I'm guessing there's someone else listening to this so I'll be hanging up before you can get a trace. I just want you to say goodbye to your daughter.'

Grace could hear Robyn's cries coming nearer to the receiver. Soon she was sobbing in her ear.

'Help me, Mum,' she snivelled. Then her weeping drifted away.

'The next time you see your daughter, Grace, will be in the mortuary with all the other bitches.'

Gabriel hung up.

Grace dropped her mobile.

For several seconds there was silence in the room. It was broken by one of the technicians.

'Traced it,' he shouted and stabbed an index finger on a blown-up copy of a map of the district. 'They're here, behind one of the units on the Manvers Industrial site.'

The early evening sky was rapidly filling with grey clouds. With it came a fine rain which sprayed across the windscreen of the parked MIT car, diminishing the view of the main Dearne parkway. Hunter and Tony Bullars were in the unmarked car. They had tucked the Vauxhall Astra into a lay-by and were monitoring their radio sets. Watching and waiting.

When the shout went up with a location for Gabriel Wild, the two detectives bolted upright and stirred into action.

Seconds later, a car came screaming towards them.

It was Wild's Toyota, and it rocked the MIT car as it shot past.

Hunter revved up the engine and slammed into first gear.

Tony Bullars snatched up the radio handset to call it in.

The wheels spun, churning up loose gravel, and Hunter pressed harder on the accelerator, spurring the car in the direction of the speeding Toyota. Whipping through the gears, Hunter soon had the unmarked police vehicle registering seventy mph and was making ground in their pursuit. From the radio chatter, he knew other police cars were coming to their aid. Whisky nine-nine — the police helicopter — had lifted off from its base at Sheffield to join in the hunt.

As an advanced driver, trained in pursuit from his drug squad days, Hunter handled the car faultlessly, jerking around the many roundabouts, before pointing the bonnet towards the middle of the road as he straightened out to continue the chase. He blared the car horn then readjusted his fingers to flick on the beam of his headlights.

As Wild's car swerved up ahead and the brake lights illuminated, Hunter knew his driving had had an effect.

Beyond the Toyota, Hunter spotted whirling blue lights in the distance, heading towards them. The response on the radio told him that it was the marked firearms vehicle and he began to ease off. The Task Force vehicle had a far more powerful engine and was better placed to take over the chase.

Gabriel Wild almost lost control when he spotted the CID car's flashing headlights in his rearview mirror. For a second his car snaked and he stamped on the brake and whipped down the gears. Hitting the accelerator, he could hear the Toyota's engine scream as he began to widen the gap again. His concentration on the car behind meant he didn't spot the oncoming marked police car until it was too late.

The police Volvo lined up towards the Toyota and then swung sideways across the road. The action had the desired effect. The Toyota's tyres protested with a concerted squeal, jarring, as Gabriel braked hard. He could do little to stop the car crabbing sideways as he lost control of the steering. In a panic he hit the accelerator. The engine screamed, drowning out the exploding front tyre. The car bounced up the kerb, onto the grass verge, smashed through wooden fencing at the side of the road and, picking up speed on the muddy surface, it careered wildly down a small incline. The Toyota slid for ten yards before flipping over and rolling twice onto its roof, finally coming to a halt when it hit a metal gatepost.

Gabriel's head had taken out the side window and only his seatbelt had saved him from being thrown out. As he kicked open the buckled driver's door, he caught a glimpse of himself in the rearview mirror. His face was barely recognisable. His forehead had a wicked gash and blood poured from numerous cuts. His right cheek was swollen, causing his eye to close. His lip had split. He reached up, fingers probing his blood-marked face.

'The bastards. The fucking bastards!' he screamed.

Robyn was slumped in the passenger seat. He could see she was stunned but uninjured. He snapped off her seat belt and dragged her by her hair across the front seats, pulling her through the driver's door, snatching his Bowie knife from the doorwell as he stumbled out onto the grass.

The CID officers following had already alighted, as had the two uniformed officers who had cut off his path, and they were armed; their short rifles were pointing in his direction.

Panic set in.

Gabriel pulled Robyn closer to him, pressing his head tightly against hers. His focus was on the two armed officers. He could see their mouths moving but he couldn't hear what they were saying. The detonation of the airbags had temporarily deafened him.

He pushed the blade to her neck, digging the point into her soft flesh and drawing blood.

'I'll fucking kill her!' he screamed. 'I'm telling you she's fucking dead.'

If Gabriel Wild could have looked in a mirror at that moment, he'd have known how wrong he was.

But he couldn't see the red laser dot from the tritium illuminated sight dancing on his forehead.

The 9mm lightweight round left the Heckler and Koch MP 5 muzzle at 400 metres per second. The illegal dum-dum bullet punched into Gabriel Wild's head just above the eyes, smashed through his skull and fragmented into the frontal lobe of his brain.

He had no time to realise why none of his limbs would move like he wanted them to. The force flung him backwards and before he hit the ground, he was dead.

A little blood splattered Robyn Marshall's cheek and for a second she stood there, frozen. Then she let out a shriek and the shriek became a scream.

The officer secured the cocking handle of his gun, cleared the round in his chamber and pulled away the fifteen-round magazine holder. He turned and handed his weapon to his supervisor.

'Sorry, Sarge, I felt I was left with no option. You heard me shout to him three times to drop the knife but he took no notice. I thought he was going to kill her,' he said.

As he strolled back to the armed response vehicle, Paul Goodright thought back to the night the CID car was stolen. He saw his sister lying in intensive care, the doctors telling her that her boyfriend had been killed and she would be crippled for life by the joyrider who had run them off the road.

He had sworn there and then to her that he would track him down and, after all these years his efforts had paid off.

Paul dropped his chin, trying to suppress a smile.

He had finally delivered Gabriel Wild's punishment for all the misery he had caused.

Now he could lay his own demons to rest.

'What were Gabriel Wild's last words to the firearms officer just before he shot him…?'

In between drinks, sniggers and laughter erupted from the group of detectives at yet another one of Mike Sampson's serial killer jokes.

Hunter smiled and shook his head.

The MIT team had taken over half of the lounge. It was a good job the pub had only the handful of regulars that the team all knew. Anyone else might take offence.

An hour earlier he and the rest of the team had been elated to see Grace hugging her fourteen-year-old daughter tightly in the back yard of the police station.

He'd tried to put a reassuring arm around his partner, telling her it was all over but one look at her face told him her head was elsewhere. All she kept repeating was that she needed to get Robyn home.

Grace had left with her daughter in the back of a traffic car, in a daze.

The detective superintendent had wrapped things up quickly with one of the fastest de-briefs Hunter had ever known, ending the short conference with a promise of a more thorough scrum-down early the next morning and finishing the preamble by standing everyone a drink to celebrate the end of the investigation.

Hunter pushed his way to the bar, half-listening to the end of Mike's joke. It was these moments that bonded a team.

On his way he spotted Paul Goodright tucked into a corner, hunched over a beer, rubbing a hand over his shaven head. He was alone.

Hunter decided to spend some time with him once he'd got himself a drink. He hadn't seen Paul since the shooting.

He ordered a pint and then walked across to his old colleague.

'How're we feeling?' Hunter asked, sliding onto a seat opposite.

Paul's head shot up. He'd been lost in thought.

'Not too bad — had better days.'

Paul made a brave attempt to crack a smile, but it was half-hearted.

'Glad it's over?'

'You bet.' Paul pushed himself back against his seat, his squat, muscular frame stretching his black T-shirt.

Hunter could remember when Paul had been a very slim twenty-something detective with a full head of hair. That's when the memories tumbled into his head. He would never have guessed the decisions he and Paul made on that fateful night in October 1993 would have brought about such a tragic chain of events involving so many people. As the episodes had unfolded during the past few weeks, he had questioned himself many times. Should he have done anything different? He was unable to answer and that was one of many things he would dwell on over the next few weeks.

'Thanks to you the result is good though, eh?'

Paul's mouth tightened and he rested his strong bare forearms across the table and gripped the bottom of his glass. His beer had lost its head. Hunter wondered how long he'd been nursing it.

'You say that but it doesn't really take away the feelings I have over what happened all those years ago. That psycho tore my life apart.' He looked up with sad hazel eyes. 'I thought that when I shot him it would have made me feel better but it's already short lived. I still feel so responsible for what happened. If I hadn't have gone off shagging that night this wouldn't have happened.'

'Paul, you've got to stop beating yourself up. You weren't to know what was going to happen that night. People happened to be in the wrong place at the wrong time. You have to put it down to fate. The guy was a killer — born and bred — full stop. There was nothing — and I repeat, nothing — you could have done about it.'

Hunter pointed at Paul's flat beer.

'Let me get you a fresh one, you've earned it, believe me. There will be a lot of people out there grateful for what you've done. Just think about the parents of the girls he murdered, for one. Secondly, we won't have the expense of a trial and the worry that some smart barrister will exploit a loophole or a jury will do an OJ Simpson and allow him to walk free.'

Hunter drained his own beer and wiped the corner of his mouth.

'I'd be honoured if you'd allow me to buy you a drink.'

Paul smiled weakly. 'Another beer would be great, thanks.'

Hunter pushed himself up from his seat and edged through the throng once more towards the bar. He ordered another two pints of Timothy Taylor and returned to his old colleague. He placed the beer in front of Paul and then raised his glass.

'Cheers.'

Paul picked up the pint. 'Cheers.'

Hunter took a swig. 'I'm gonna get some fresh air in the garden. You're more than welcome to join me but I'm going to have this and then disappear. I'm knackered. It's been a long day.'

'No, you get yourself off. I'm having this and then I'm going as well. Anyway, I wouldn't make good company at the moment. We'll catch up some other time, eh?'

'You bet,' Hunter acknowledged with a quick nod and then turned away.

Easing himself past a couple blocking his path, Hunter pushed open the French doors that led out into the garden. The sunlight momentarily blinded him and he closed his eyes for a second. Blinking them open, he saw the earlier evening drizzle had given way to the beginnings of a spectacular sunset. The temperature had risen, although the air was still fresh from the rain.

He leant against one of the wooden benches and took in all the smells of the surroundings. That burst of rain had invigorated the landscape. He took another swallow of his second pint, casting a glance over the hedgerow at the bottom of the beer garden to the countryside beyond.

For the first time, he realised the pub's location gave him a clear view of the scene where this mayhem had first started five weeks ago. In the distance, he could just make out the collection of old tumbledown farm buildings where Rebecca Morris's body had been discovered. That find had started this whole roller coaster of events, uncovering the actions of a demented killer who had devastated the lives of seven innocent teenage girls and their families, and culminating in the abduction of Grace's daughter — one of their own. It had made him realise just how vulnerable they could all be.

Yet somehow Hunter no longer had the appetite or indeed the energy to rejoice. It felt as if every last drop of adrenaline had been squeezed out of him. He was drained. The long days and sleepless nights had finally caught up with him. He'd only drunk one full pint, and a little of his second but it had gone to his head.

He was so deep in thought that he started when the hand was placed on his shoulder. He jerked around to be greeted by Barry Newstead's beaming face.

'Penny for them, Hunter.'

'Crikey, Barry, you made me jump. I was somewhere else just then.'

'Thinking about Grace and Robyn?'

'Yes, them and Paul Goodright, and the families of the other victims.'

'Careful, Hunter, you'll have someone thinking you've gone soft.'

They both grinned.

'Anyway, what are you doing out here?' said Hunter. 'Why aren't you celebrating with the others? That's not like you. People will be talking that Barry Newstead is going on the wagon.'

Barry dug Hunter in the ribs. 'I'm on a promise.'

Hunter's eyes widened. 'My, my; we are a dark horse. Tell me more.'

'Sue Siddons.' Barry paused.

Hunter gave him a pleased look.

Barry continued, 'The enquiry got us back together, made us both realise what we had lost. Not just Carol, but years of friendship. She's going to straighten herself out now that she's got closure. She's started going to AA meetings.'

Hunter patted Barry's upper arm and gave him a reassuring look. 'Hope it all goes well for you, Barry. I really do, you deserve it. You've been a good ally to me on this investigation...'

Barry pulled him up short. 'Getting soft again, Hunter.' He winked and downed the remainder of his beer. Wiping the dregs from around his mouth with the back of one of his huge hands, he said, 'Fancy another?'

Hunter shook his head. He glanced at his watch. Beth would be just getting the boys' supper ready before their bedtime. He emptied his glass and set it down onto one of the wooden benches.

'No thanks, Barry, that's me done. I'm not even going to say goodbye to the team — I'm knackered. I just want to get home, put my feet up and watch the ten o'clock news for once.'

As he made for the side gate, he knew what he was going to do. It was an eternity since he'd last had some R & R, even though they'd done a family holiday at half-term in Minorca. He was going to suggest to Beth they book a cottage on the North-East coast for them all — at one of his favourite spots. He might even be able to smuggle along his paints.

A NOTE TO THE READER

My journey into writing crime fiction began in my early teens, inspired and encouraged by an uncle, who was a lover of books, had a wonderful imagination and who taught me the basics of crafting a novel. In the autumn and winter months we would spend many an evening together in front of a roaring coal fire working on plots, developing characters and opening chapters.

Becoming a police officer in 1976 was the stepping stone for crafting my crime stories. The on-the-job experiences provided me with the ideal material to weave into my writing and it was around this time that I discovered the work of Ed McBain. I devoured many of his 87th Precinct novels and knew that this was how I wanted to formulate my own novels.

I got that opportunity upon my retirement in 2006 after 32 years in the police. During that time, I had dipped in and out of writing groups, writing short stories and numerous first chapters, based on my experiences, promising myself that one day I would complete a novel. Now there was no excuse, and I had so much rich material to draw upon — I mean, how many crime writers have experienced first-hand the true gruesome horror of death.

Added to that, I also had my many experiences as a detective. I began my plain clothes work in Vice Squad during the Yorkshire Ripper era. I progressed to CID, and was involved in many notable murder investigations and then as a Detective Sergeant I entered Drugs Squad working undercover. My last job was as an Inspector, in charge of a busy CID, whose work was centred around sex offenders, child protection, domestic violence and racial incidents — a rich vein to draw upon.

The inspiration behind part of the plot for *Heart of the Demon* came courtesy of a brutal spree killing committed by psychopath, Anthony Arkwright, who lived in a neighbouring town. In the early hours of Sunday the 8th of August, 1988, he broke into his disabled neighbour's house and stabbed him 70 times. Taken into custody, Arkwright was placed in a room where a pack of cards had been left on the table. He picked them up, took out the four of hearts, and told detectives, 'This is the mastercard. It means you have four bodies and a madman on the loose.' Hours later police found the butchered bodies of his grandfather and his grandfather's housekeeper.

For the villain in my story I drew upon knowledge of another local psychopath, Peter Pickering — The Beast of Wombwell — who was first convicted of attacking two schoolgirls in 1966 and jailed for six years.

In 1972, five months after his release, he abducted 14-year-old schoolgirl Shirley Ann Brody in his home town of Wombwell, near Barnsley, drove her to secluded woodland, where he raped her and stabbed her while wearing yellow washing-up gloves — a detail that gave rise to his other tabloid nickname, the "maniac in the marigolds".

Following that murder he was locked up in a psychiatric hospital, but it was always believed he had committed more attacks and murders and he was interviewed by detectives on numerous occasions over several decades. The focus of those interviews were the murders of 14-year-old, Anne Dunwell, from Rotherham, in 1964, and 14-year-old, Elsie Fox, from Bradford, in 1965.

He refused to cooperate.

However, following another investigation, detectives found evidence linking him to the rape of a Sheffield woman, committed just weeks before he abducted and murdered Shirley Ann Brody, and in 2017, at the age of 80, he was convicted of that rape.

The year later Pickering died, taking his secrets to the grave.

My protagonist, Hunter Kerr, first appeared in 1995 as a rookie cop in my first police procedural 'Loitering with Intent.' That novella still sits on my shelf but elements of it have been redrafted, forming the basis of my prequel to this series, *Hunter*.

It would be fair to say that there is a fine membrane between myself and my character Detective Sergeant Hunter Kerr. My stories to date are interwoven with my own experiences as a cop or linked to incidences involving former colleagues and I've taken liberties with them. Hunter's thoughts, feelings and emotions are mine as is much of his background. Where we differ is, I didn't lose my first love to a serial killer.

BOOK TWO: COLD DEATH

PROLOGUE

November 1971
Glasgow's East End, Scotland

Iain Campbell wound down the window and switched off the headlights of the black Mercedes, swung the car into Fielden Street and straddled the middle of the road for several yards until his eyes adapted to the dimness. Then, following the pointing finger of his front seat passenger, he switched off its throaty engine and coasted quietly towards the nearside kerb where he slowed to a halt.

For a few seconds, the three occupants of the Mercedes sat motionless, watching and listening. Outside there was deathly silence.

As he stared out through the windscreen from the passenger seat, Billy Wallace's slate grey eyes darted from side to side, scanning the high tenement buildings each side of the street. Billy knew the area well. He'd lived here as a child, until his family went up in the world.

But the area had deteriorated over the past few years. Only recently, it had made headlines as one of the toughest, poorest places in Britain. Most of the people he'd grown up with here had moved out, leaving behind unfortunates who had fallen into the hands of the drug dealers and money lenders.

This was his turf.

He flung open the passenger door and used it as a springboard to launch himself upright onto the pavement, rocking for a second on the balls of his feet. Arching his back, pulling at the lapels of his signature black Crombie, he uncoiled his six-foot, four-inch, muscular frame and looked around. The old overhead street lights still hadn't been replaced, leaving most of the street cast in eerie shadow.

Some people had a fear of the dark, but Billy loved it — it was the perfect cover for what he had to do.

Raking fingers through his chestnut, collar-length hair, Billy surveyed the street again, searching for activity, narrowing his eyes to search within the shadows.

A light wind disturbed the dead leaves cluttering the gutter. Other than that, there was no other sound or movement along the road.

Good. He had a score to settle and he needed the element of surprise on his side.

He beckoned the back-seat passenger to join him. Rab Geddes was his most trusted henchman, chosen for his fearsome reputation, especially his penchant for violence.

Billy stuck his head back into the warmth of the car's interior. 'Just keep the engine running, Iain, we shouldn't be long,' he said quietly.

On Billy's nod, Rab nudged his door closed.

Somewhere nearby a dog started barking, its sudden bawl fracturing the stillness. Billy waited for the barking to stop, had a quick look around and, seeing only an empty street, set off at a jog across the footpath, dodging into the nearest passage that led to the rear of the tenement.

At the stairwell, Billy was greeted with the strong whiff of bleach and disinfectant, which was doing its best to disguise the stench of stale urine and animal faeces that stained the bare cement floor. He screwed up his nose as he mounted the concrete steps two at a time, Rab matching his pace, and, despite the rubber soles of their shoes, every footfall echoed in the enclosed stairwell.

At the first floor, they slackened their pace and slunk back against the wall. Their dark overcoats helped them melt like phantoms into the shadows. They slipped onto the walkway. For a few seconds Billy checked his bearings, then he nudged Rab and they moved on. At number 34, Billy paused, holding up a hand for them to stop. Satisfied that he had the correct address, he put an ear against the panelling and listened. He could hear a television playing inside and took another look along the walkway to check for witnesses. Not a movement. Then, stepping back two paces and flexing his muscles, he launched himself against the door. The flimsy lock was no match for Billy's fourteen stone and the door flew inwards, smashing against the interior wall.

The pair sprinted towards the well-lit room at the end of the corridor and were only a few feet from the doorway when a slim dark shape appeared as a silhouette in the opening.

The start of a scream was instantly silenced when Billy smacked the unknown individual square in the face. There was a sickening crunch of bone and gristle and the slender form flew backwards to the floor.

In the light from the lounge Billy recognised who he had thumped; for several seconds Morag McCredie lay motionless. Then she slowly opened her eyes, her face tightening as she strained to focus. A film of tears blurred her vision and she moaned as she squeezed her eyelids to force away the teardrops.

As she finally focused, Billy took pleasure in seeing the colour drain from her face, guessing from her reaction that she recognised him. He edged forward, leaning over her, pushing his face within inches of hers.

'Where's Davie, Morag?' Billy growled.

'He's —' She broke off, her voice trembling as she suppressed a sob.

'Nobody fucking rips me or my family off, Morag. Davie knows what's coming to him.' Billy pressed within an inch of her, giving her his hardest stare. 'Now — where — is — he?'

She pulled her head away. 'He's not here,' she spat out, cupping a hand over a nose that had already swollen to twice its size, then staring at the bright globules of blood dripping through her fingers. 'You've broken my fucking nose,' she groaned in her broad Glaswegian dialect.

'That's not all I'm going to break if you don't tell me where fucking Davie is,' Billy snapped back. He reached down and grabbed a handful of bottle-blonde hair and yanked hard, hoisting her upwards.

Morag swung up an arm to protect herself and a handful of hair ripped from her scalp. She yelped and bit her lip. Tears welled up again.

Billy fixed her with a hate-filled stare. 'I'm going to ask you one more time, Morag. Where's Davie?'

Quivering, she tried to move away but Billy grabbed hold, snaring his hands around her chin and jaw, seizing her in a vice-like grip. He dug his fingers into her skin until he was squeezing bone.

Morag gave a piercing scream and Billy raised a hand to silence her. At that moment the instinct to survive kicked in — she snatched up the kitchen knife from the nearby coffee table and with one swift movement lashed out. It slashed Billy's cheek, opening up his flesh.

He let go of her, stumbling backwards, slapping both hands over the gash. Blood was pouring from the wound, seeping through the gaps in his gloved hands and onto the front of his coat.

Rab Geddes had been too late to stop the damage to Billy's face, but he reacted to prevent a second attempt, smashing his fist into the side of Morag's head. She reeled back, flipping over the arm of an armchair.

Billy stared at the blood staining his gloves. His face contorted, taking on a demonic look. The pupils of his eyes became so dilated they were almost black.

'You fucking bitch,' he snarled, kicking aside the armchair. He towered above Morag, who was scrabbling around in a puddle of her own blood, a badly swelling face disguising once pretty features. She was groggy, trying to get up.

Billy reached into his Crombie, pulling the handgun from the waistband of his trousers. It became an extension of his arm as he aimed.

Morag tried to swallow. Her eyes pleaded and she swung up an arm to protect herself.

The bullet passed through her hand and into her right eye. She was dead before her head smashed against the tiled fireplace.

The reek from the cordite caught the back of Billy's throat and he swallowed hard and jerked back his head. Then he spotted movement to his left, a small shapeless form at the periphery of his vision. He spun around.

Rab followed suit.

In the doorway stood a dark-haired little girl, dressed in striped pink pyjamas, aged no more than four. She was rubbing the sleep from her eyes and under one arm she clutched a teddy bear. She stared at them through sleepy eyes. Then her gaze fell upon Morag lying prostrate, a puddle of blood spreading around her.

'Mummy,' she whimpered.

Billy raised the gun again and fired. The shot drilled a neat hole in the front of the child's head and smashed out of the back. Blood, brain and bone splattered the wallpaper behind her. She hit the ground at the same time as her teddy bear.

A halo of crimson began to form around the girl's head and Rab glared at his boss, stunned.

'Jesus Christ, Billy, she was just a kid.'

Billy stared back. 'She was a fucking witness,' he said brusquely. Then Billy looked down at the bloodstains on his overcoat. He tugged at the front of his Crombie, focusing on the wide lapels. 'Look what the bitch's done to my fucking coat.'

Billy raised the Smith and Wesson again, spun around and fired the remaining four rounds into Morag. Her body never moved; the first shot had taken her life. Billy continued clicking the trigger well after the gun had emptied and Rab had to grab hold of his arm. He fixed Billy's wild stare.

'We need to get out of here, Billy, before someone calls the cops.'

Slotting the handgun back into his waistband, Billy surveyed the carnage around him. Bending down, he grabbed the hem of Morag's dress and wiped the blood from his leather gloves.

'We need to set fire to the place Rab…' He paused for breath, getting back his composure. 'Get rid of any incriminating evidence. Know what I mean?'

Rab nodded and began scanning the room for suitable material to ignite.

Iain Campbell fidgeted in his seat. He had the driver's window down and was listening and looking nervously around — he had been doing so ever since Billy and Rab had disappeared. He looked at his watch and wondered how much longer they were going to be. They had already been gone twenty minutes.

This wasn't the job he'd been asked to do. 'Look after my son's back!' was what Billy's father had instructed and paid him for, but all he had done over the past three hours was chauffeur around the two thugs while they picked up drug debts. He had already seen them give one guy a good kicking, and from their conversation he knew they were chasing up another man who owed Billy the best part of two hundred pounds.

They could stuff the job after tonight.

He scoured the streets again. He felt cold and yet he was sweating. Fight or flight! It was a long time since he'd felt like this. He was sick to his stomach.

He was about to wind up the window when he heard a loud crack that sounded like gunfire.

No, it couldn't be!

He strained his ears. There was another! His heart leapt against his chest and he felt his stomach churn.

Four more shots followed in quick succession. He stiffened and gripped the steering wheel.

Less than a minute later, both nearside doors were yanked open, making Iain jump.

Billy threw himself into the front seat, his face covered in blood. Then Iain spotted the gun in Billy's hand.

'Billy, your face.' Iain could see Billy had lost a lot of blood. His shirt collar and the front of his coat were drenched and more was still oozing from a deep gash that snaked from the bridge of his nose and across his right cheek.

'Never mind that. Just get us the fuck out of here.' Billy threw the gun into the footwell. 'Come on, hurry the fuck up.'

Iain Campbell sharply engaged first gear and gunned the accelerator, spraying up loose road chippings beneath the spinning wheels, hurtling into the darkness as a second-floor window in the tenement exploded.

DAY ONE

24th August 2008
North Yorkshire

Tentatively, Hunter Kerr stepped to the cliff edge of the Cowbar and looked over. Only yards below, seagulls screeched and swooped, their fleeting shapes silhouetted white against the backdrop of Staithes, cloaked in early morning shadow. Opposite, above the harbour, the sun was beginning its ascent over the drab rock face of the Nab; an orange glow blurred the top of the hill giving the surroundings an almost mystical appearance.

Hunter raised his camera, clicked off a couple of frames and took a step back to where his painting easel had been set up some twenty minutes beforehand. He squeezed his blue eyes to slits and studied the vista, separating shape and tone in the landscape. Then, setting aside his camera, he picked up a brush and hurriedly mixed together some of the colours on the palette. From his previous painting ventures, he knew he had another thirty minutes to capture the first light bouncing across the haphazard rooftops of the white-washed cottages and punching its way through the narrow alleyways to the Beck, before the majestic effect disappeared and the blueness of the day took over.

As Hunter settled into his painting, switching his gaze between the tranquil scene of old fishermen's cottages perched above the Beck and the canvas board holding the start of his painting, he could feel the stress and tension of the past few weeks easing from his body.

Scrubbing in large blocks of colour, feeling the breeze brushing his unshaven face, he realised how glad he was that Beth had persuaded him to take this weekend off and spend time with her, their two sons and his mum and dad, in the cottage she had rented. When they had left home the day before yesterday, he had packed his painting gear because he rarely got the opportunity to paint these days, what with juggling his career as a murder detective and the needs of his family.

When he had seen the weather forecast last night, he realised this morning would be an ideal opportunity to complete a small oil sketch, and he had sneaked out of the cottage before daybreak without disturbing anyone. As he now built up his painting, he thought of them all still tucked up in their beds, and smiled.

Aspects of his last case had broken into his thoughts, too. Before leaving work on Friday he had given his team a list of instructions now that the investigation had finished, though he knew deep down they didn't need them; the squad was more than capable of closing down the enquiry they had been working on so intensely over the past five weeks.

He had handed his partner, DC Grace Marshall, supervisory responsibility and he could visualise her now, mothering the team in her own inimitable way, organising the clearing of the incident room, stacking the house-to-house documentation, categorising witness statement papers, sealing the hundreds of exhibits, and storing all the gory photographs into box files ready for the Coroner's Court inquest in a few months time.

This last case had been his most intense and testing to date — not just since his appointment as Detective Sergeant into Barnwell Major Investigation Team, but throughout his fourteen years as a detective.

When he had left to take this break, CSI had just removed the forensic tent from the back of the serial killer's home. One of his victims had been discovered in the house and the remains of another had been found buried in his garden. The week previous to that, the bodies of two more teenage girls had been unearthed from shallow graves at an old colliery site.

They had managed to identify all of the victims and matched them to missing persons reports, thanks to documents and photographs the killer had secreted behind a false wall in his loft.

The killing spree of the now infamous 'Dearne Valley Demon' — as the press had dubbed him — had shocked them all and would have lasting repercussions. So many revelations had come to light during the enquiry, some involving colleagues, some unwittingly involving him, and they had caused him much personal angst and soul-searching over the past few weeks.

The phrase 'tangled web' came to mind and a chill shot down Hunter's spine as he fought once again to push away any thoughts of the case.

Dismissing his thoughts, Hunter returned his gaze to the view across the Beck. The morning light had become less intense over the landscape. In another ten minutes, the artistic quality of the atmosphere would be gone.

A few more brush strokes and I'll head back for breakfast.

Ten minutes later, he set down his brushes, smoothed his hands into the base of his spine and teased the tension from his back, stretching himself up to his full six-foot-one. Before calling it a day, he took another couple of photographs that would enable him to finish the painting when he got back home, and was just lowering his camera when he spotted his dad on the opposite side of the harbour, leaning against railings that overlooked the beach.

Dad's up early as well.

He clicked off another frame and as the shutter snapped, he caught a fleeting movement to one side of the nearby Cod and Lobster pub. He was sure he'd seen someone dart into the shadows. His policeman's sixth-sense piqued, he zoomed in as far as the camera would allow, targeting the side entrance of the pub where he had last seen the figure.

He was right. There was someone, slinking against the wall, looking in the direction of his dad. Something wasn't right. He snapped another shot but the zoom was at its maximum and the image was blurred. All he could make out was a squat, stocky, white guy with a shaven head. His features were fuzzy.

Quickly lowering his camera, Hunter looked back at his dad, Jock, who was still leaning on the metal railings, one foot resting on the bottom bar, staring out to sea. From the relaxed posture, Hunter could tell his dad was unaware of the man ten yards away. Hunter dug his mobile from his pocket and flipped up the screen.

Damn. He'd forgotten he couldn't get a signal here.

He moved closer to the edge of the Cowbar, ready to shout, hoping his dad would hear. Then he saw his dad spin around — the shaven-headed man had emerged from the shadows and was striding towards him. The stranger halted just feet away and jabbed a finger inches from Jock Kerr's face. Although Hunter couldn't hear, their body language was telling him this was not friendly banter. He raised his camera again and shot off a succession of quick frames, not checking if the images were good or not. That was when he saw Jock slapping away the man's hand, slamming a punch into the stranger's chest, dumping him onto his backside. Towering above, Jock speared his own finger only a foot from the man's face. There was a frank exchange of words and then as quickly as it had started it was all over. Jock turned from the stranger and marched away.

The shaven-headed man picked himself up, dusted down his knees and took out his mobile. Seconds later, he pushed it away again in disgust.

'He can't get a signal either,' Hunter muttered to himself.

As the man turned, Hunter raised his camera again and rattled off several more frames before the stranger strode out of view.

At the edge of the cliff, Hunter scoured the cobbled High Street, straining his eyes into the narrow alleyways of the thrown-together houses but he couldn't see either his dad or the stranger. With a sense of urgency, he collapsed his easel and packed away his things.

Half-jogging, half-marching, and breathing heavily, Hunter trooped up the steep incline out of the old village and up towards the newer part of Staithes and their rented cottage.

He'd been keeping watch for the shaven-headed man but the only people he had come across were fishermen preparing their boats. As he neared the top of the hill, he saw his dad a hundred yards ahead, ambling along, hands thrust deep in pockets, as if nothing had happened.

Hunter took a deep breath and shouted after him. Jock stopped and waited. By the time Hunter had caught up he was gulping for air and beads of sweat were trickling from his hairline and down the sides of his face.

'I thought you were supposed to be fit, son,' Jock said in his strong Glaswegian accent, pointing to the glistening sweat on his son's brow.

Hunter set down the easel and wiped his forehead with the back of his hand, flicking the residue onto the footpath. 'I am. It's that bloody hill, it's a killer.' He took in several deep breaths. 'I've been trying to catch you up to see what that was all about.'

'What was what all about?' said Jock, matter-of-factly.

'You know what I'm on about. Don't give me the all-innocent. That argument you've just had with that guy.'

'That wasn't an argument, just a case of mistaken identity. He thought I was someone else.'

'You don't dump someone on their arse because of a case of mistaken identity.'

Jock flushed. 'Leave it, son, it's nothing to do with you.'

'What do you mean it's nothing to do with me? My dad smacking someone is nothing to do with me? I don't think so.'

Jock held up a hand for silence. 'No, you don't think so at all. That was my business down there. I said leave it — and I mean it.' He spun on his heels and marched away.

It had been a mild day but the evening was giving way to a sheet of fine drizzle. It peppered the windscreen of Hunter's Audi, obscuring the view of the main road through Sleights village. Hunter flicked on the wipers to clear the screen. As he began the steep incline up towards Blue Bank, he saw his dad's car in front was almost at the top.

Hunter dropped down a gear, squeezed the accelerator and sped towards the summit.

Since they had set off from the cottage, Hunter had been at odds with himself. Beth had sensed it, asking what was wrong. He'd shrugged it off, telling her he was back to thinking about work. But he couldn't get the incident involving his dad and the shaven-headed man out of his mind. What made it worse was that his dad had lied and then dismissed him when he had tried to probe deeper. He'd tried to catch his dad's attention during the day but he had deliberately avoided eye contact.

Something wasn't right, but Hunter didn't know what — and it was frustrating the hell out of him. He'd thought he knew his dad, but a couple of things had altered his view recently. Throughout his childhood, teenage years and into manhood, he had never seen his dad lose his temper, and then three weeks ago that had changed. Hunter was getting a good hiding from three family members of someone he had just put into prison when his dad had come to his aid. Such was the viciousness of his dad's onslaught that Hunter had to drag him off before he caused a really serious injury to one of the guys. The man had ended up in hospital with a fractured jaw and a couple of busted ribs.

Today's incident had brought that flashing back and it was unsettling Hunter. He clutched the steering wheel tighter, willing his Audi faster up the hill. As they crested the brow of Blue Bank, he eased off the accelerator and began cruising along the moorland road that passed through *Heartbeat* country. Ten yards in front, it looked as though his parents were chatting. He wondered if his mum, like Beth, sensed something wasn't right.

Hunter didn't see the silver BMW until it shot past. It was so close that it rocked his car, almost catching the wing mirror, and for a split-second he lost control, veering towards the grass verge. He braked sharply, corrected the steering and swung back into lane.

'The bloody idiot!' Hunter shouted, then halted his tirade, remembering that Jonathan and Daniel, his young sons, were in the back.

Up ahead, the speeding BMW was getting dangerously close to his parents' car and he dropped into third gear, squeezing the accelerator, so that he could make up ground and take note of the car's registration number.

Just when it looked as though the BMW was about to hit the rear of his parents' car, it swung out into the opposite carriageway and began overtaking. Hunter heaved a sigh of relief. Then, without warning, the BMW swung hard left, smashing against the driver's side. His parents' car snaked and blue smoke emerged from beneath the wheels as the vehicle began to crab. Chippings flew up from the surface as the car lurched sideways and began to bounce out of control. It hit the damp moorland grasses at the road edge, throwing up huge tufts, then bucked into a ditch, bounced back out, flipped over onto its roof, before returning back on its chassis, rebounding into the heather and finally coming to a standstill when it thumped into a peat bog.

Hunter stamped on the brake, bringing his Audi to a screeching halt as he flung open his door. It felt as if everything had gone into slow motion.

He was conscious of Beth fishing around in her handbag trying to find her mobile, while on the back seat he caught a quick glimpse of the boys, straining against their seatbelts, both pale-faced and frightened. Fifty yards ahead, he saw the BMW's brake lights flash on as it skewed to a halt.

About to sprint to his parents' rescue, he stopped mid-pace as the BMW driver's door flew open.

Hunter heaved another sigh of relief. He had initially thought this was going to be a hit-and-run. Now the car had stopped he guessed it was just bad driving and the driver was coming to help.

That was until he recognised the man who emerged. It was the shaven-headed guy he had seen arguing with his dad earlier.

The man took a long hard stare at Hunter, and with outstretched hand he reached across the roof of the car and pointed towards his parents' upturned car. He fashioned two fingers and a cocked thumb into a makeshift pistol, and jolting his hand, mimicked a firing action. He never took his eyes off Hunter, fixing him with a malicious grin before mouthing the word 'pow!'

Then the shaven-headed man jumped back into his car and the BMW squealed away, throwing up a film of spray in its wake.

Hunter clocked the registration before it disappeared over the brow.

He shouted to Beth to dial 999 and then bounded across the moor to where a plume of steam was masking the predicament of his parents.

I just know this is going to be cold, Katie Williamson thought to herself as she stepped into the murky waters of Barnwell Lake, disturbing the stillness of its surface with her fins. Once she was fully submerged beneath the water, it would be even colder; from a previous dive here, she knew in a few minutes the pain inside her head would be as intense and sharp as if she had eaten ice cream.

'I'll be only a couple of feet behind you. Remember the signals?' her dive instructor, Craig Palmer, said.

Katie formed an 'O' shape with her thumb and forefinger, feeling the resistance in her neoprene gloves as she forced them together.

'Good. And if you need to come up quickly?'

She stuck a thumb in the air and jabbed it skywards several times.

'Okay. Final checks.'

Katie watched her dive-buddy's eyes roaming over her body — not eyeing her up, just double-checking all her diving equipment was in place.

'This is your last dive and then we can sign your logbook up for your first qualification. Looking forward to it?'

'In these freezing waters? You're joking!'

A smile creased her instructor's face. 'You are such a wimp. Twenty minutes and the ordeal will all be over and this time next year you'll be able to take a novice out yourself. Now check your air pressure and make sure your hoses are not tangled.'

Katie slotted the mouthpiece of her breathing regulator into her mouth, adjusting it so that it fitted snugly between teeth and lips. She purged the demand valve and a blast of concentrated air shot into her mouth, plumping out her cheeks. She swallowed, tasting the freshness and purity of the compressed air and formed another 'O' with her fingers.

'Okay, mask on and let's make our way to the centre of the lake.'

Katie fitted her facemask, waited a few seconds for the glass to clear and began walking penguin-fashion over the loose stones and moss, edging slowly into the waters.

As she reached chest height, she felt her buoyancy jacket taking up her weight, keeping her afloat, enabling her to flip her fins and push towards the middle of the lake. She could hear Craig splashing closely behind. After five minutes of gentle kicking, Katie felt a tap on her shoulder.

'Okay, this is it. Let the air out of your jacket and let's drop to the bottom. We're going to swing left and circle the lake, okay?'

She formed another 'O', and then slowly released the air out of her buoyancy jacket, feeling herself sink below the surface. It wouldn't be long before she hit the bottom, the depth was only five metres.

Katie felt the slippery fronds of the reeds brush against her as she gradually dropped. Four metres down, the water was so murky that her visibility was just a couple of feet and she had to sweep her hands before her, feeling her way through the gloomy depths. Turning left as instructed, she was surprised that the water wasn't as cold as she had expected.

This is not going to be too bad after all, she said to herself, kicking hard and dragging one hand along the silt bottom.

Katie felt a sudden tap on her calf and guessed Craig wanted her to take in another turn. She pulled her wrist close to her mask and checked her watch. They had been diving for just over ten minutes.

Halfway there already, time has flown.

With a series of quick kicks, she propelled herself left again and adjusted her movement with a graceful flip.

Then her knee hit something solid, taking her by surprise and she stumbled across the object. She spun around, seeking out her dive-buddy. He was only a couple of yards behind and she began waving frantically for him. Seeing him stop kicking and using his hands to slow she jabbed her thumb downwards.

Katie dropped to her knees, sitting almost astride the entity and began rubbing her hand over it. She could make out what appeared to be a rolled-up carpet, enmeshed in the weeds. Curious about the bundle she felt for an edge to unfurl and, finding a corner, she tugged hard. Something appeared from one end. For a split-second her mind wouldn't take in what was peeking out. Then it hit her. The bloated green-grey distorted blob had a face — a human face. Katie was looking at a dead body. Gasping, she almost released her mouth-piece. In that instant the water rushed into her mouth, hitting the back of her throat and causing her to gag. There was no time to signal to her dive-buddy. Blind panic took over and Katie kicked frantically for the surface.

With increasing pace, Detectives Grace Marshall and Mike Sampson quick-marched along the path that led from the car park to the entrance of Barnwell Country Park.

In the two-hundred yards from where they had left their car, the blazing heat had got to them. Mike was gasping for breath, having difficulty keeping up with Grace, and she was hot and sweaty and her shirt and jacket were starting to stick. Grace slackened her pace to let Mike catch up, unbuttoned her jacket and gathered her mane of tight black curls into a tidy bunch and fastened it with an elastic band.

Picking up her pace once more, she threaded between two lines of tall laurel bushes that marked the route towards the lake. For a moment her thoughts drifted. Being here brought back happy memories of strolling around the lakeside path watching the world go by with her two daughters and husband. They were times she still treasured in her bank of memories, especially now that the girls were teenagers and no longer wanted to do such things.

Coming across a young-looking PC, who had been given the job of preventing the uninvited from getting to the crime scene, Grace and Mike flashed their IDs, announced their names and waited as he scribbled down their arrival on his log.

They ducked below the blue and white police tape, passed another line of laurel bushes and entered the inner cordon.

Grace paused by the second line of police tape and surveyed the scene. Three CSI Officers were already in situ, dressed in their white forensic suits. Two were in the process of cordoning off a small wooden jetty which led out into the lake, while another was taking photographs. Grace recognised the cameraman as Duncan Wroe, the Force's experienced Scene Manager.

At the lake's edge, a uniform sergeant was briefing her team before they began a search of the area.

On the water, a couple of yards from the edge of the quay, two wet-suited police frogmen steadied their motorised dinghy. A third was in the water, placing his breathing regulator into his mouth. Grace assumed that beneath the dinghy was where the body had been discovered and the Underwater Search Unit was now going to haul it up.

By picnic benches, next to the country park reception centre, Grace spotted two other divers. The female was seated on one of the benches, doubled-up, her head in her hands. A male with a tanned complexion and short crew-cut hair stood over her, resting a hand on her shoulder. She guessed these were the two who had found the corpse. She took out her warrant card again and popped it into her breast pocket with the police crest on display. Hunter had handed her the mantle of Acting Sergeant while he was away and she was going to show she could handle it.

'What do you want me to do, Grace?'

Mike's question broke into her thoughts. 'I'm guessing those two are the ones who've found the body,' she said, pointing in the divers' direction. 'You go speak to them and I'll go and have a word with uniform and also see what SOCO have got for us.'

Mike set off, tugging the sleeves of his oversized jacket away from his pudgy fingers. Mike had to buy jackets several sizes larger so that they would fasten over his beer-belly, which meant the sleeves were always too long.

'Oh, and Mike,' Grace shouted after him. 'Be professional. Don't start playing pocket billiards while you're interviewing her.'

'I shall ensure my afflictions are kept under control at all times, Acting Sergeant Marshall.'

Grace smiled to herself. Despite Mike being the joker in the pack, when he was given a task, he always approached it as the consummate professional.

By the time Grace reached Duncan Wroe, the SOCO manager was aiming his camera at the Police Frogmen. There was still no sign of the body being brought to the surface.

'What have you got for me, Duncan?'

The SOCO manager turned, lowering his camera. 'Oh, hi Grace, I saw you arrive but I was busy.'

With his sharp features, unruly hair and unshaven face, Duncan looked nothing like the sharp-minded and experienced forensic specialist that he was. Fortunately for Grace, any prejudices she had about his appearance had been blown away early in her career. He had attended her first rape case as a detective, a teenage girl attacked while out walking her dog. A good quarter of a mile from the scene, Duncan had found trainer marks and several discarded cigarette butts in some bushes and, acting on a hunch, he had recovered them. Within a week they had DNA of the perpetrator, and while carrying out a search of the young man's home, Duncan had found his trainers secreted amid the rubbish in a wheelie bin. It transpired the man had carried out two other similar crimes and at court he was given a life sentence. Since then, Grace had worked with Duncan on many cases and knew his technical craft and knowledge of forensics were second to none. He was one of the very few civilian scenes of crimes officers in the country to be promoted to the position of manager — most supervisors were police officers of rank.

Grace nodded towards the lake. She watched air bubbles bursting on the surface. 'No sign of the body being brought up yet?'

'I'm told it's in a bit of a mess. I think they're trying to secure it tightly so it doesn't lose any of its limbs when they bring it up.'

'What do we know then, Duncan?'

'Well, we don't know anything about the body yet. I've been told it's bound inside a carpet or rug of some kind so I don't think we'll know anything straight away. When we do get it to the surface, I'll give it a once-over, but we don't know how long it's been in the water, so we'll need to get it to the mortuary as soon as possible because once its exposed to the air there will be a rapid acceleration to the decomposition.'

'Have you got anything in the forensics line yet?'

He shook his head. 'Too early, Grace. What I can say is that I'm pretty confident the body was thrown off the edge of the jetty there.' He pointed to the wooden platform leading from the banking out into the lake. 'You see where the Search Unit's dinghy is? Well, that's roughly above where the body is. That's about six feet from the edge of the jetty and that's why I say thrown. Because of how far away it is from the jetty I would say at least two people were involved in dumping it.'

'Two?'

'Yep, two — at least. If one person had carried that body they would only have been able to drop it or roll it off. It's virtually impossible for one person to sling a dead body any distance. With two people, they would have been able to get enough swing to heave it that far into the water.'

'Couldn't they have used a boat?'

'And only gone out a few feet?' He dismissed her suggestion with a curt shake of the head. 'No, it was thrown, trust me.' He tapped his nose and a smile crept across his wizened features. 'Simple when you've dealt with as many bodies as I have,' he added. 'Because the body's wrapped up I'm running on the assumption that the person was more than likely killed elsewhere and bought here and dumped. Nevertheless, we're taping off the jetty and checking it for bloodstains, hairs and fibres. It's a hands and knees job, but we'll be searching for footwear marks as well. I'm also setting up a search grid and looking for tyre tracks. The underwater search unit will be bringing the body up to another landing stage and then I'll secure the body to be transported to the morgue. I understand Miss Marple is already making her way there and will be performing the post mortem later this afternoon.'

He was referring to the forensic pathologist Professor Lizzie McCormack, who had acquired her nickname not only because of her ability to catch killers through her forensic skills but also because of her uncanny likeness to the actress Geraldine McEwan.

Grace thanked Duncan with a smile and headed to where Mike Sampson was still talking to the two divers who had found the corpse. As she was running through everything again inside her head, marrying what the homicide investigation manual recommended together with her experience of attending murder scenes, her mobile rang. She delved into her jacket pocket and pulled it out. The screen displayed the name of her work partner — Hunter. He was somewhere up in the Whitby area in a rented cottage with his family.

I bet someone back in the office has rung him and told him about this and now he's phoning to check up that I can cope.

Even though she knew he would be enquiring in that nice, caring and unobtrusive way of his, he was still checking on her. She needed to do this without someone holding her hand — to prove to herself more than anything that she was capable.

'Well, Sergeant Kerr, I am coping very well, thank you,' Grace muttered beneath her breath. 'And I don't need you checking up on me.'

As she waited for the call to go through to voicemail, she heard a shout from the lake and turned to see the police frogman's head break the surface. His hand was raised. It looked as though they were about to bring the body up.

Her phone stopped mid-ring. She would listen to the message later. She placed it back into her pocket, telling herself she'd ring him this evening — once she had got everything up and running.

Screeching to a halt in the rear car park of the Medico Legal Centre, Grace checked her watch for the umpteenth time. She cursed; she was running late and regretted not having followed the body carrier from the Country Park as she should have done. Instead she'd sat in her car, on her mobile, updating her Detective Inspector, Gerald Scaife, who was setting up the incident room back in the MIT department.

She had given him as much information as she could, but because the post mortem was yet to be done she couldn't answer the majority of his questions. It only reinforced the fact that she should have followed the body.

To cap it all and cause further delay, the DI had then passed her across to DC Isobel Stevens, the HOLMES (Home Office Large Major Enquiry System) supervisor, who had begun logging the information onto the National network, and she had found herself listening to another round of questions which she was unable to answer. Fortunately, because she was the same rank as Isobel, she was able to politely fend her off, promising to get back to her the minute the post mortem had concluded.

Grace entered the Medico Legal Centre through the rear doors and hurried along the corridor to the post mortem suite, pulling off her elastic hair fastener and shaking out her thick mane of curls. In the locker room, she slipped quickly into a protective body suit, and in her haste, as she slotted the shoe coverings over her ballet pumps, she stumbled forward, shouldering the wall. She cursed again under her breath, rubbing the top of her arm as she barged through the double set of doors which gave access to the autopsy room, causing the occupants to snap their heads in her direction.

'Quite a dramatic entrance — Miss?' Professor Lizzie McCormack said, glancing over the rims of her spectacles.

The way the pathologist had paused and then added 'Miss' made Grace feel like a schoolgirl. She smiled apologetically. 'DC Marshall,' she responded, feeling herself blush. 'Grace,' she finished and scanned the faces of Detective Superintendent Michael Robshaw and Scenes of Crime Manager Duncan Wroe, who not surprisingly, had beaten her there. Disconcertingly, the Superintendent was frowning.

'Ah yes, of course — Grace. You have to forgive me, I'm terrible with names these days. We met several weeks ago at the old farm near Harlington, a fourteen-year-old girl mutilated by our infamous serial killer, if my memory serves me right.'

Grace nodded. 'Terrible business that. You finally got him, though.' Grace felt her chest tighten as a flashback of the images of the murders burst inside her head. Although twelve days had gone by since that fateful evening, the memory was still as sharp as if it had happened yesterday. That last investigation had caused her mental pain and left her physically exhausted. She had only just got back to work after taking a week off sick to get her head right. The mental pictures from that night were going to live inside her for quite some time to come; the Force's counsellor had told her so.

She took in a deep breath, held it, and let it out slowly — just like she'd been advised at the onset of a panic attack.

'Anyway, that's all in the past now. Back to the present, eh!' Lizzie McCormack's voice snapped Grace out of her reverie. 'Well, Grace, you're not a moment too soon — we are just about to start.'

The petite grey-haired woman peeled on her latex gloves and pulled a metal trolley closer. Upon it, laid out in pristine condition, glinting beneath the bright artificial lighting was every surgical tool and evidence collection container imaginable.

The body, still wrapped up in its bundle, was laid out on one of the steel mortuary tables. Despite being covered by a substantial amount of silt and broken reeds, Grace could now see the body was shrouded inside a rug of Asian design.

Professor McCormack reached up and switched on a microphone above her. In her soft Scottish accent, she began her PM preamble, beginning with the time and date. Instructing her technician to cut away the bindings, she took a step back and slid the green scrub mask up over her mouth and nose.

He began to snip at the cord securing the rug. The binding was white plastic-coated washing line.

'Careful as you unwrap it,' said Duncan Wroe to the technician, moving in closer with his camera. 'In the past I've known the murder weapon to be included when the killer has wrapped up the body.' He looked from Detective Superintendent Robshaw to Grace. 'By dumping the body in the lake, the murderer was obviously hoping it would never be found and therefore they might just have thrown in the weapon.'

The second the technician carefully peeled the sides of the rug away from the cadaver, the stench hit Grace and she quickly pulled on her facemask. The air conditioning that was supposed to deal with the smell of rotting and decaying flesh did not dissipate it completely.

The body was grotesque; bluish-purple and swollen beyond recognition, though there was no mistaking it was female. Long, black, matted hair covered most of her face and neck, and she was naked.

The technician moved aside and Professor McCormack took over, exploring the cadaver inch by inch, pausing from time to time to scrutinise certain marks before moving on. She cleared her throat and continued with her commentary.

'The covering has been removed to reveal the body of a woman of Asian appearance in a state of advanced decomposition. This is manifested by skin slippage, discolouration, bloating and the presence of a foul odour.' With thumb and forefinger, she began sliding the long strands of black hair away from the deceased's face. 'Well, well,' she said. 'I think I've more than likely found this young lady's cause of death.'

Angling a slender forefinger over the corpse's neck, she stepped back to allow the SOCO manager to take more photographs. Grace and the detective superintendent took a step forward, leaning in to see what the pathologist had discovered. The gash stretched almost ear to ear across her throat.

Photographs taken, Professor McCormack continued with her examination. 'On the left-hand side of the neck, approximately two and a half centimetres below the jawline, is an incision which is approximately fifteen centimetres in length. The large vessels either side of the neck have been severed. The larynx has been severed below the vocal cord through to the intervertebral cartilages. The arteries and other vessels contained in the sheath have all been cut through. The cut is very clean, very precise.' She raised her eyes and caught Grace's gaze. 'Her death would have been immediate.'

Professor McCormack returned to the corpse, picking up limbs, examining the hands and fingers. Then she began to turn the body. As she rolled the cadaver onto one hip, she gave off a surprised, 'Mmm,' and beckoned to the SOCO Manager. 'Mr Wroe, I take my hat off to you.' She supported the bloated body as he shot off a series of frames. After he had finished, she pulled out an object which had been hidden beneath.

Duncan was doing his best to suppress a triumphant grin.

'In all my years as a pathologist I have never seen anything like this,' she said, holding up something which closely resembled a knife.

Grace stared at the object and exchanged glances with her colleagues. None of them had seen anything quite like it.

Professor McCormack dropped it into an exhibit bag and handed it to Grace, who eyed it again through the plastic, turning it over repeatedly.

'A real vicious looking thing,' said Detective Superintendent Robshaw from over Grace's shoulder.

The weapon was twenty centimetres long and had a curved blade. Half of it consisted of a black metal handle or grip with two small metal hoops at either end.

'These loops look like where your fingers should go — you know, like a knuckle-duster,' Grace said. She searched for agreement from her boss but he merely shrugged. She scrutinised it one further time before handing it over to the SOCO manager as the pathologist began her internal examination of the body. Picking up a scalpel, Professor McCormack began the Y-shaped incision at the front of the torso, cutting from the breastbone down to the pubis.

A rancid gas erupted from the body and Grace gagged. She pressed her head down into her chest and tried to breathe in the perfume she had sprayed herself with in the car before entering the centre but that didn't help much.

An hour later, after careful removal and examination of the corpse's internal organs, Professor McCormack rounded off her head-to-toe examination, reported on her findings and wrapped things up. She reached up, switched off the microphone, snapped off her latex gloves and turned to face everyone.

'The girl has taken a severe beating prior to her death. I've found at least thirty blunt trauma wounds to her head, upper torso, buttocks and legs, caused by clenched fist and boot. Three of her ribs are broken — she would have been in a great deal of pain before she died.' She shook her head in disgust. 'Duncan should be able to get at least one good sample of a shoe print from the girl's left thigh. She also has defence wounds to her hands and arms. Several of her nails have been broken and I have managed to swab them for perpetrator DNA. There is also bruising to the inside of her thighs and genitalia. In other words, she was raped prior to death.

'I have examined the girl's trachea and lungs and there is no airway froth or sediment indicative of drowning. And there is no fluid in the paranasal sinuses or stomach. Therefore, she was already dead before she went into the water. In conclusion, death was the result of the severe haemorrhaging of the carotid artery in the neck caused by a sharp-edged instrument. Forensics will no doubt match the wound to that weapon we've found.' She dropped her latex gloves into a biohazard bin. 'The incision across the throat is left to right and the penetration angle of the cut suggests that the killer was above or on top of her to carry out this action. That leaves me to believe your killer is left-handed.'

'What about identification of the girl?' enquired Grace.

'Other than what I have already said, height, weight, of Asian appearance etc., that's all I am able to give. The bloating and decomposition has put paid to physical identification. She has also lost a number of teeth from the blows she received but dental records might be still of use, and of course I have taken a blood sample for DNA purposes, but that only helps if she or her family are on the database.'

'I will sort out the dental impressions and fingerprints,' interjected Duncan Wroe. 'I've had a look at the ridges and they are in a bit of a mess. There is a lot of skin slippage because of the length of time the body has been submerged. What I can do, however, is cut around the top section of each finger and peel off the flesh and then put them over my gloved fingers and roll an impression. I've done that once before and it worked.'

Grace felt her skin go goosey.

'I can show you how to do it and then let you have a go if you want,' he added with a mischievous grin

'Duncan, that is gross.'

'Needs must, Grace, needs must!'

It was well after 9 p.m. before Grace eventually got home, and she was mentally and physically drained.

She had spent the past two hours apprising DC Isobel Stevens so the HOLMES system could be updated ready for the following day's briefing. She had also begun the timeline sequence on the incident boards, finishing the task by Blu Tacking photo images of the crime scene, including a sequence of mortuary shots — rug-wrapped body, unwrapped body and the unusual looking weapon used to kill the unknown woman. She'd then sat down with DI Scaife to fill in the gaps in his journal ready for the 8 a.m. briefing. It was only when she had finished all that that it hit home to her what the responsibility of acting Detective Sergeant meant. She'd never given any thought before to how much additional work Hunter put in after they had headed off home or down to the pub. She made a mental note — from now on she would always ask him at the end of a busy day if he needed any help.

She unlocked her front door and called out. There was no reply. She headed for the kitchen, where she found a note on the table, picked it up, headed back into the hallway and climbed the stairs slowly, reading as she went. It was a mixture of scribbles made by David, her husband, and Robyn and Jade, her daughters. They had gone out for food and then onto the cinema to see the *Twilight* movie. The note ended with 'love u lots', and kisses, three times in different handwriting. She mouthed the words silently and smiled to herself.

Grace stripped off her things on the landing and dumped her clothes in a pile without going into the bedroom. The stench of rotting flesh still clung to them and she decided to wash them straight away and not put them in the dirty clothes basket for fear of contaminating the rest of the washing.

She turned on the shower, cranking the temperature gauge up a couple of notches before climbing in, then lingered longer than usual under the powerful jet of hot water and scrubbed herself until her skin tingled.

Ten minutes later, feeling cleansed, she towelled herself off in front of the bathroom mirror. As she dabbed the moisture away from her tawny coloured skin she lingered over her reflected image. She turned sideways and clenched her stomach muscles and liked what she saw. Although she maintained her fitness through regular swimming sessions, Grace owed her lithe well-toned figure and height to her Yorkshire-born mum, while her hair, skin colour and burnt umber eyes were the product of her Jamaican father's genes.

Half an hour later, dressed in a T-shirt and joggers and clutching a glass of chilled Chardonnay, Grace flopped onto the sofa. She tucked her legs beneath her and began to run through the day's events. Graphic images kaleidoscoped around and she reflected on the post mortem, especially how indifferently Professor Lizzie McCormack had treated the corpse. She had seemed so brutal, slicing open the young Asian woman, almost defiling her — but then Grace recalled how gently she had washed and combed the hair and washed out the nasal passages for evidence. She recalled what the forensic pathologist had said as she had gone about her work: 'The body gives up so much of where it has been before it has had its life ended. Pollen or fibre samples can be matched to the place where it met its death,' and Grace had resolved to store those words for the future.

She jumped out of her reverie, remembering the early phone call which she had left to voicemail. She had forgotten to return Hunter's call. She scooped up her mobile from the coffee table. She couldn't wait to tell him how she had coped being in charge of her first murder.

Jock Kerr stirred and gave a low moan as he shuffled uneasily in the bed. The groaning snapped Hunter out of his doze and he drew himself up in the bedside chair in time to see his dad's face twisting in pain. He'd been in and out of a restless sleep since his admittance to the hospital ward that afternoon, despite being heavily dosed with a strong painkiller and sedative.

'Okay, Dad?' Hunter asked. 'Do you need me to call a nurse?'

Jock eased opened his eyes. 'I'd rather have a dram, son.' He started to laugh, then winced. 'Jeez, son, I feel like I've gone ten rounds with Muhammad Ali.' He licked his dry lips. 'What's the doc's verdict? What's the damage?' Jock's voice was brittle and more laboured than normal.

Hunter leaned forward, resting an elbow on the edge of the bed, and cupping his chin. He was in need of a shave. 'Bruised ribs, a few cuts and bruises and a couple of stitches above your right eye. You'll live.'

'How's your ma?'

'She's on Ward Two.' Hunter saw his dad's anguish and concern. 'Don't worry, she's only there for observation. She's had a nasty bang to her head — she actually *looks* like she's done ten rounds with Muhammad Ali.' He cracked a wry smile. 'Beth and the boys are with her, keeping her company.'

'I'm glad she's okay, son. I wouldn't know what I'd do if anything happened to your ma.' An attempt to clear his throat sent Jock into a paroxysm of coughing. His chest shook fitfully and he groaned.

Hunter felt helpless as tears welled up in his dad's eyes.

'Bloody hell, that hurt,' Jock moaned, clutching his chest. 'What happened, son?'

Hunter recounted the incident, the silver BMW ramming the car and how they somersaulted across the moorland. 'You're lucky to be alive.'

'Some accident, eh?'

'That was no accident, Dad. The BMW deliberately rammed you.' Hunter sat upright. 'And I recognised the driver. It was the guy you were arguing with this morning.'

Jock tensed. 'I've already told you what that was about. Leave it,' he snapped.

'Look, you and Mum were nearly killed today. You need to tell me what's happening.'

'And I said just leave it. I'll sort this once I get out of here.'

'Dad, you're in no state to sort anything out. Leave me to deal with it. That's what I get paid to do. That's my job. You need to tell me what that was all about this morning. It's too much of a coincidence that what happened with the car was only a couple of hours after you've dumped a guy on his backside. What are you hiding, Dad?'

'Nothing,' Jock snapped again. 'Just leave it, I said.' He suddenly paled and dropped back against his pillow, his face glistening with sweat.

Hunter got up. 'Do you need me to get a nurse?'

'I could do with a couple of painkillers. I hurt all over.' Jock closed his eyes.

Hunter thought his dad looked tired and drawn, almost frail. He made for the nurse's station and was asking a staff nurse for extra painkillers when he felt his mobile vibrate in his pocket. He quickly fished it out and viewed the screen — Grace. He'd been trying on and off for most of the afternoon to get hold of her. He answered the phone, indicating to the nurse that he needed to take the call and jogged away from the nurse station and along the corridor.

'Hi Grace,' he answered, exiting the ward and stopping in the corridor. 'I've been ringing you most of the day and all I've been getting is your voicemail.' He didn't wait for her to reply. 'Listen, I need a favour.'

Hunter rattled off what had happened that morning — how he had seen his dad arguing with the shaven-headed man, following up with details of the incident involving his parents' car — barely pausing for breath. 'I've only managed to get a part index, and I've given that to North Yorks police but I could do with someone following it up.' He paused for breath. 'Grace, do you remember a few weeks ago when we dealt with Steve Paynton?'

He was trying to visualise her reaction. It was Grace who had found the photographs behind a bath panel during the search of Paynton's home; undraped images of pre-pubescent children. He had seen how it had disgusted her.

'Do you recall I had a run in with his two brothers and a cousin shortly after we got him remanded? I think they might have something to do with this. I think the Payntons could be trying to get back at me and Dad, and they may have sent a heavy to deal with us, but my dad won't tell me anything. Could you do me a favour and find out where the Payntons were today and see if they have access to a silver BMW? It'll have some nearside damage to it.'

'Hunter, I can't.'

Hunter stopped and listened as Grace explained about the body at Barnwell Lake. In the glass panel of the door he was facing, he caught his ghost-like image. He looked disappointed and he was glad she couldn't see him. As she finished, he composed himself.

'A real baptism of fire, eh? Good for you. Okay, Grace, don't worry. I can see you're going to have your hands full and it sounds as though you've got it all well under control. Listen, I'm going to be up here for another couple of days until they release my parents. You crack on and I'll ring you daily so you can update me.'

Hunter ended the call brightly but deep down he was agitated. He needed someone to do some discreet and maybe underhand digging for him. Someone he knew he could trust — and Grace had been his best hope. Then someone else sprang to mind; someone who he knew always got a result. Hunter scrolled down his contacts, selected the name he wanted and made the call.

DAY TWO

Warm sunlight streaming in through the windows and the scent of fresh furniture polish greeted Grace as she breezed into the MIT office. She must have missed Angie the cleaner by minutes, she thought to herself. A pity, because she loved having girlie chats with Angie, who knew all the building's gossip, especially the real juicy stuff — like who was having an affair with whom.

She shrugged off her jacket and draped it over the back of her seat before sitting down, then pulled a bunch of papers from the top of her tray, sifted them out over her desk and fired up her computer.

Grace had got into work early. In Hunter's absence she was responsible for pulling together the inquest file for 'The Dearne Valley Demon' case, and she wanted to make inroads into it before things got manic.

As she waited for the program to load, her mind wandered — mulling once more over the events of August 12th — and she felt her chest tighten. The blood pounded inside her head, causing a rushing sensation in her ears and she took several deep breaths in an attempt to regain control. She felt sick to her stomach. She hated the sensation these attacks brought and wondered if they would ever go away.

This isn't fair. I want my life back.

After a couple of deep breaths, she felt the tight band across her chest slacken. Regaining control, she returned to the job in hand, opening up the inquest document folder. She'd already drafted a large part of the summary prior to being called away to the lake yesterday and she speed-read back over it. Closing her eyes, she thought about the final points she needed to add. Moments later, her next steps decided upon, she snapped open her eyelids, scanned the screen, scrolled to the point where she needed to pick up and began typing.

Footfalls along the corridor outside the office broke into Grace's deep concentration. She glanced at her watch; the past hour had flown. The first detectives were beginning to filter into the office and as the doors opened a new aroma assaulted her nostrils — the greasy smell of bacon sandwiches from the canteen. Her stomach rumbled and she realised how hungry she was. She had given breakfast a miss.

Mike Sampson and Tony Bullars, her team members, were among the first in. She acknowledged them with a smile and a nod. Mike headed for the office kettle. He stopped mid-stride, caught Grace's attention and mimed the act of bringing a cup into his mouth, silently mouthing the words, 'Want one?'. She nodded gratefully and began bundling up her papers. Less than a minute later, Mike was clonking down a mug of freshly brewed coffee in front of her as she was saving her report. She glanced up at his cheery, well-rounded face. 'Right, let's get ready for briefing,' she said, closing down the computer.

Detective Superintendent Michael Robshaw took up position next to the incident board, giving it the once-over and flicking through his notes. He had been appointed the Senior Investigating Officer for the Barnwell Lake murder.

He peered over the top of his spectacles, taking a deep breath that swelled his muscular chest, straining his crisp white shirt. 'Good morning, ladies and gents. In the words of the old adage it never rains but it pours — we have just cleared up one set of nasty murders and now we have another particularly grisly one turn up.' He paused, then added, 'This is playing havoc with my budget.'

A ripple of laughter filled the room.

He tapped the mortuary photograph of the bloated grotesque face. 'Okay, on a serious note, our job is to find out who murdered this young woman. As you can see from the decomposition she is unrecognisable. She was found stripped naked and with no identification marks. We have her DNA and her fingerprints but we do not know who she is or anything about her life.' He moved to the next photo. It was a full body shot of the victim prior to the autopsy. 'But what we do know is that three to four weeks ago she was badly beaten, raped, had her throat cut, was bundled inside a rug and then dumped in the bottom of Barnwell Lake, where she lay until yesterday afternoon when two divers on a training session found her.

'Our main priority is to find out who this young lady was. We also have quite a wide time frame between the murder and the body being found and as yet we don't know where she was killed, only where she was dumped.

We are up against it, but we have all been here before and I know you lot will fill in the gaps.'

He tapped the incident board again, glancing behind him before focusing on the faces of the detectives.

'What we do have is the rug she was found wrapped up in and the weapon that was used to slit her throat. These appear to be foreign and these are our leads at the moment. If no one has any questions, you can now all report to DI Scaife who will give you your tasks so you can get out there and clear this up.'

There were no questions. The briefing broke up and the MIT detectives picked up their assignments for the day.

Grace was still acting DS. The DI told her Hunter had been in touch and wouldn't be back for at least another three days. She collared Mike and Tony.

'Right you two, we've got the job of checking missing persons because of our experience with the last set of murders, and also finding out about the murder weapon, especially to see if there are any local outlets who sell anything like it.' She snatched her jacket off the back of her chair, picked up the car keys and slung them towards Tony. 'Bully, you're driving,' she said and led the way out of the office.

Hunter paced the hospital corridors, frustrated and tired. He had slept very little the previous night. They had managed to book a family room in a motel not too far from the hospital but he had spent a restless night going over the events in his head. The more he mulled over the incident, the more frustrated he became.

Now he had another long day before him at the hospital, unable to make any inroads into finding out the identity of the shaven-headed man responsible for doing this to his parents.

Beth and the boys were flitting between Ward Two, where his mum was 'comfortable and stable', and the ward where his dad was resting. He was having trouble being in the same room as his dad, who refused to say anything. Hunter had tried to be patient but he knew his dad was holding back on some secret and was refusing to give it up. It had got to the stage where his dad lay with eyes shut, refusing to respond to his questions.

Hunter had tried several times to call the number he had rung last night but it was switched off and on divert. His head was swimming.

Even though he hated drinking out of plastic cups, Hunter strolled down to the drinks machine on the floor below and dropped some change into the slot. They were out of tea. He kicked the bottom panel and growled. Then his mobile rang. He viewed the screen. 'Withheld' flashed up.

'Hello?' Hunter answered.

'Hunter, it's me.'

He recognised the voice. It was the Major Investigations Team's civilian investigator, Barry Newstead. Barry was one of the few workmates whom Hunter also counted as a good friend. They'd met twenty years ago, shortly after Hunter's first serious girlfriend — Polly Hayes — had been found murdered.

Barry had been one of the investigating detectives on the case and early on in the enquiry he had interviewed Hunter as a suspect. Barry's questions had been so probing that Hunter had been glad he'd had a solid alibi. Polly's killer had never been found and it was Barry who had broken the news to him that the enquiry was being wound down because all leads had been investigated. That was twelve months after her murder — Hunter had been almost eighteen years old. And it was when he decided to join the police.

He bumped into Barry four years later, as a nineteen-year-old uniform cop. Barry had been at the peak of his career and had taken Hunter under his wing, showing him all the tricks of the trade. That learning had gained Hunter an early entry into CID and they had formed a formidable team until Hunter was promoted to Detective Sergeant eight years ago and transferred to District CID. Since then Barry had retired, but following the 'Demon' case, Hunter had persuaded him to come back as a Civilian Investigator.

Barry was the only person, other than Grace, that Hunter trusted enough to help investigate his dad's secretive behaviour.

'Have you got anything for me?' Hunter asked.

'Sorry mucker, afraid not. I've made quite a few phone calls but there's not a whisper down here. I also went round to all of the Payntons' houses, and the lock-ups they have access to, but there's no sign of a silver BM. And everyone I spoke with yesterday had never seen any of the family driving one, or in one. I've checked with Intelligence and nothing with that part registration features on our system. It's a blank at the moment but I've put a few feelers out, so if I turn up anything, I'll bell you. Okay?'

Despondently, Hunter thanked him and rang off, though he knew he shouldn't feel down. If villains from his back yard had carried this out, then his source would get to hear. He would have to rely on that for the moment — until he could get back to base and shake some trees himself.

DAY FOUR

Keeping to the shadows of the dilapidated buildings on Sauchiehall Lane in Glasgow, Fraser Cullen slowly made his way to the entrance of the derelict car park, constantly checking behind him. There he stopped, leant against the crumbling brickwork and lit up another cigarette. He'd only just finished the last one — but he was nervous.

He pulled up the collar of his jacket. Was it his imagination or had the temperature dropped in the past half hour? It must be the damp, he told himself.

Every time he heard a car's engine, he stuck his head out from behind the wall and scoured the partly cobbled street. Fraser glanced at his stolen Rolex; he'd give them another ten minutes, then he was off.

He almost missed the silver BMW. It coasted past, hardly making a sound. He took a final drag on his cigarette, dropped the burning remnant and scrunched it underfoot before he stepped out into the lane.

The car pulled up sharply, then reversed and halted alongside Fraser, its nearside tyres squealing as they scraped the kerb. Fraser bent down, blowing the smoke from his mouth as the passenger window slid down.

The front passenger wafted a hand in front of his face. 'Fucking hell, do you have to do that?' he said.

The deep gravelly tones had not changed, even after all this time, thought Fraser, though the man's appearance had. The hair was ravaged by grey and he couldn't miss the scar that ran from the bridge of his nose down towards his jaw. The occupant of the front seat had been a hard bastard thirty odd years ago, now he looked even harder.

'What have you got for me, then, Fraser?'

Fraser bent forward, resting a hand on the car door and meeting the stern gaze of the front passenger. 'I found him, Billy. It wasn't easy, mind,' he said in his harsh Glaswegian dialect. 'You'll find him drinking regularly in Lauders on Sauchiehall Street. He's there most days. Goes in about four in the afternoon and usually leaves about half-seven. He comes down this way to get to the subway. I've followed him three times now without him knowing. And there's nae CCTV,' he said, his eyes roaming around the high buildings lining the narrow lane.

Billy smiled, reached inside his coat pocket and brought out a handful of notes. He peeled off five 20s. 'There's a ton, Fraser. Now piss off and keep your mouth shut.'

Before Fraser could reply, the dark-tinted window powered shut and the rear wheels burned rubber as the BMW lurched towards the main road.

Alistair McPherson stood at the front of Lauders bar, tapping the cigarette on its packet before popping it into his mouth. He lit it in cupped hands, an old habit from his army days. His first drag was a long one, which triggered a spluttering cough. It lasted several seconds before he banged his chest and brought it under control.

Jesus, these things are going to kill me one day.

He stood for a good minute, taking in the sights and sounds of Sauchiehall Street. How it had changed over the years! It had gone upmarket since his time working here. It was now a busy thoroughfare full of high-class shops, and many of the gracious houses had been converted into offices.

He stepped onto the pavement and began his steady meander home. He'd pick up a fish supper on the way back, he told himself. He turned into Sauchiehall Lane, heading for the subway on Bath Street. As he rounded the corner, he heard a car slowing behind him and guessed it would be someone wanting directions — lots of tourists got confused by the Glaswegian traffic system.

He stepped to one side, waiting as it drew level and, removing the cigarette from his mouth, he held it in his cupped hand. The window coasted down and Alistair turned to talk to the driver but could only see his chest and shoulders. He bent to get a better view and was met by a piercing stare from the scar-faced passenger leaning across the shaven-headed driver. There was something about that face that registered.

'Remember me, Mr McPherson?' said the passenger. The voice was deep and menacing and a wave of panic shot through Alistair.

The DOA — 'dead on arrival' — call was logged at 7.50 p.m., discovered by a young waiter who had slipped out through the rear emergency doors of the restaurant into the derelict car park for a smoke-break. He'd got the shock of his life when he tripped over the crumpled mess. At first, he'd thought it was a pile of rags — people were always dumping their rubbish here — but then he'd spotted the thick congealed blood beneath his feet. The sight of the mush, which had once been a head, had almost made him throw up.

He had dialled 999 on his mobile, requesting an ambulance — because the body was close to the fire-escape he had assumed the dead guy had accidentally fallen from the top. Then he'd fled back inside the restaurant and dragged out his boss to bear witness to what he had found.

The ambulance crew who turned up could see the horrific injuries were not the result of an accident and they requested immediate police attendance.

The first officers were on scene in a matter of minutes; Pitt Street police station was only three-hundred yards away. The uniform sergeant studied the dead man but the victim's face had taken such a severe hammering that he was barely recognisable.

'Looks like somebody's tap-danced on his heed,' he said to his colleague, slipping on a pair of latex gloves.

He began to search through the dead man's pockets for some ID, found the man's wallet in an inside jacket pocket and began rummaging through the cards. In the back section, he found a laminated National Association of Retired Police Officers membership card which grabbed his attention. He stared at the name and then at the photograph. He glanced at his junior colleague in disbelief.

'Bloody hell, I know this guy,' said the sergeant. 'He was in CID at Shettlestone nick.'

By 8.15 p.m., the full length of Sauchiehall Lane had been cordoned off. A murder enquiry was underway.

DAY SIX

Grace took a final look over her notes to gather her thoughts and then turned her attention to the colleagues seated around the room. She had centre stage this morning because Detective Superintendent Robshaw had been called into headquarters to liaise with the press office. He had a meeting booked with the local press and TV news teams to give an overview of the murder investigation and to make an appeal for witnesses.

Grace's stomach turned. Pangs of nervousness drifted from her gut up into her throat. This was her first up-in-front briefing and she was outside her comfort zone. She sought out Mike and Tony, who were giving her the thumbs up. It made her realise how much support her two team-mates had given her during her spell as acting Sergeant. She gave them a grateful smile.

The three of them had not stopped over the past two days in their attempts to identify the murder weapon. She'd split the jobs between them. They had searched the internet, made dozens of phone calls, and finally had teamed up to trawl the many and varied Asian artefact and martial arts shops in South and West Yorkshire.

Their efforts had paid off. Late the previous morning they had found their answer in Bradford, in a small warehouse that sold Asian ceremonial weapons — items more for show than for use. Along with a brief history of the weapon, she had watched in amazement as one of the young male storekeepers had given a demonstration in its application.

Grace had requested a list of people who had purchased such a weapon, but they only dealt in cash and kept no till receipts. Even Mike's veiled threats of letting the tax man know of their accounting methods hadn't taken them any further forward, other than to provide the store's distribution outlet over in Pakistan. Grace and her team settled on a free replica of the murder knife, and left.

Grace perched herself on the corner of her desk ready to feed her information into the morning's briefing. She cleared her throat, picked up the replica murder weapon and began. 'A bagh nakh.'

She held up the knife with its curved angled blade and brass knuckles fixed into the hilt. Behind her, pinned to the incident board, was the SOCO photo of the weapon found with the girl's body. The weapon from Bradford was identical to the killing instrument on the photograph.

'An Indian hand-to-hand weapon designed to fit over the knuckles or be concealed against the palm. This is a variant of a traditional weapon that consisted of four or five curved blades and is designed to slash through skin and muscle, mimicking wounds inflicted by a wild animal. The bagh nakh features in many of the video games the kids play these days. It was originally developed primarily for self-defence, but in this case, as we know, it was used to attack and slit the throat of our victim.'

She explained how they had got hold of the replica.

'Unfortunately, even though this is a strange knife to our eyes, among the Asian population it is not. There are a number of outlets for this weapon both in this country and abroad and at this moment we are unable to find out who purchased it. Detective Superintendent Robshaw will be showing this as part of his appeal so we're hoping it will jog someone's memory.'

Grace put the knife down on the desk and went on to explain that they still had no positive identification of the body. She had gone back into the National Missing Persons database but such was the putrefied state of their victim that it was hampering the search parameters, and despite the DNA database having some six million indexes and the National Fingerprint Database having eight million individuals they still had no trace.

'We can only hope that the Super's TV broadcast will give us a lead,' she finished, and dropped down off the edge of the desk and returned to her seat so that DS Gamble from the other Syndicate could finish off the morning's briefing.

Mark Gamble took Grace's place in front of the incident board, picking up where she had left off, running through yesterday's day long footslog around the traditional Asian carpet stores in Bradford.

Two of his team had eventually tracked down rugs of a similar make and design in a warehouse on an industrial unit on the outskirts of the city. Shipping receipts held by the owner identified they were part of a large consignment from the Punjab province of Pakistan. They had pressed the owner to narrow down the location but he had been unable to help — many of the rugs were crafted in small factories and family homes to a specific design, picked up weekly and delivered to a warehouse by the docks. Dozens of villages would be involved in one single design; it was impossible to pinpoint where the rug had been made.

DS Gamble cleared his throat. 'We also had the task of gathering any CCTV evidence at the country park. There is some, and it does have night vision software, but unfortunately it only covers the Lakeside Café, reception area and storeroom and is a good hundred metres from the jetty where we believe the body was thrown from. Having said that, there is some coverage to the outside of the building for security and so anyone passing close by would be picked up by the system. They store discs for a month before they are reused so we have got our civilian investigators currently going through days and weeks of footage. If whoever killed this girl carried the body past the main building before dumping it off the jetty, they will have been picked up by the cameras.' Mark paused again, massaging and stretching the back of his neck. 'It's a long shot but fingers crossed.'

The briefing broke up with the DI handing out fresh enquiries for the day. Grace scanned the half-dozen sheets generated by the HOLMES team. She had been given the task of tracing and interviewing the Countryside Rangers at the park. She handed them over to Mike and Tony to complete; she still had the Coroner's Inquest file from the last case to finish.

Hunter drove the two hours back from Scarborough District Hospital hardly uttering a word. His head was thumping. His dad, beside him, had sat throughout the journey with his head back and eyes shut. Only Beth and his mum had struck up any conversation, and that had been idle chit-chat between themselves. Even the boys were unusually quiet. It was a very strained journey and one he was glad to bring to a close as he pulled up outside his parents' home.

He followed his dad in through the front door, carrying their overnight bag which he set down in the hallway. He checked Beth and the boys were helping his mum, then strode after his dad who had made for the kitchen.

His dad had filled the kettle and was reaching into the cupboard for crockery. 'Tea, son?' he asked rhetorically, setting out four cups. He grimaced, gritting his teeth and biting down, doing his best to disguise the pain.

Hunter edged forward. 'Let me do that, Dad.'

'Nae, I'm fine, son, it's only a twinge.' Jock spooned in sugar for himself and Hunter.

'Look, Dad, I don't want us to fall out over this,' Hunter said quietly. He could hear Beth fussing over his mother in the next room.

'And neither do I, son.'

'I know something's not right, maybe it's the policeman in me, I don't know. You haven't wanted to talk about it, but just think about what happened up on those moors. If I hadn't been following, you could have been there for hours. You and Mum could have been killed. I don't know what you're covering up but it seems to me to be too dangerous not to share it.'

Jock turned and touched Hunter's arm, looking at him squarely. A film of tears flooded his intense blue eyes; eyes so like Hunter's. 'Give me some space, son. I won't promise you anything but I need some time to think it through.'

Grace ducked beneath the police crime scene tape and stepped towards the edge of the lake next to the jetty, focusing on the spot where six days earlier she had watched the Underwater Search Unit haul up their so-far-unnamed body.

She listened to the sounds around her; the lapping of the water and the regular thunk of the moored rowing boats against the damp wooden pilings of the quay. Behind her she could hear instructions being shouted to the line of officers who were on hands and knees carrying out a fingertip search in one of the areas marked out by the forensics team. Most of Barnwell Country Park was still off limits, cordoned off as the search for evidence continued. She scanned the park, a place she had visited so many times and which she normally associated with peace and tranquillity.

She had come for some fresh air after finishing the Coroner's Inquest file half an hour ago. It had taken longer than she had anticipated. All that was needed now was for Hunter to read it through before it was submitted. She wondered when he would be back.

DAY SEVEN

Hunter sat at his desk at Barnwell police station, running fingers through hair still damp from his shower twenty minutes earlier. After a restless night he had awoken just after 6 a.m. and decided to run into work to clear the past week's cobwebs from his head.

He booted up his computer, preparing to tackle an abundance of emails waiting for him and leaned back in his chair. As he waited for the system to go through its firewall security checks, he gazed at his desk calendar, then picked up his pen and crossed off several past dates. He'd been away from the office for eight days.

Tomorrow would be the first of September — the date pricked his conscience. It was on that date twenty years ago that he received news which tore his world apart. Polly had been walking her dog in woodland close to her home when she was attacked. The dog returned home without her, sparking off a search. Police found her body three hours later. She was the reason why he had joined the Force seventeen years ago.

Polly's killer had never been caught and he always hoped that one day he would get justice — not just for himself, but for her parents too. They were still around, and he called on them from time to time — though those times were becoming less frequent with the passing of years. He made a mental note to visit in the next couple of days, especially with it being the anniversary of her death.

He broke out of his reverie, looked away from the calendar, lifted the handset of his phone and dialled the Force's voicemail system. Upon hearing the mechanical voice, he switched to speaker phone and punched in a six-digit password to retrieve his personal messages.

'Hi, its Zita,' the first communication greeted him. 'It's three-thirty on Friday afternoon. Just wanting a quick chat about the country park murder. I think I might have something for you. I'm in the office tomorrow from eight. Can you give me a call? You've got my number.'

Hunter gave a wry smile — a quick chat was definitely not what she meant. Zita wanted the heads up on the investigation but he wasn't in a position to help her. He had met her six months ago at an awards ceremony at Barnwell Museum and Art Gallery, where he had won the Open Art Exhibition. She'd introduced herself as the reporter for the *Barnwell Chronicle* and wanted to do a piece on him. Once she had discovered he was a DS with MIT she had rung him almost weekly. Deep down, he didn't mind. He never gave anything away which would compromise an enquiry, though he had called her first after the 'Demon' case.

Hunter made a note to get back to her once he was up to speed and then hit the next message button, got up and made for the office kettle. He was in need of a strong, sweet, cup of tea. He switched on the kettle and listened to the next recorded call as he dropped a teabag into his mug. It was an ex-colleague who was now the safety officer at his beloved football club, Sheffield United. He had a couple of tickets in the directors' box for next Saturday's home game and asked Hunter to give him a call. That was too good an offer to miss. Hunter checked the time on his watch — he would make that his priority call straight after the morning briefing.

He took his hot drink back to his desk and returned to his emails. Most of them were in-force spam — good news, because he had come into work early to clear up as much of the accumulation of paperwork as he could before the start of the day's play. Grace's Coroner's inquest file was at the top of his pile. He picked it off and opened it.

Twenty-five minutes of reading, chewing on his pen top, saw him making headway and as he finished the last paragraph of Grace's report, he became aware of the clamour of voices further along the corridor. He checked his watch and cursed. The team were already beginning to filter in for briefing and he'd not made a dent in his 'to do' tray. He was in for a long day.

Hunter picked up the bundle of papers, jostled them together into a semblance of neatness and added a post-it note reminding Grace to have all the exhibits ready for the inquest proceedings, including photographs and video evidence.

He signed it off with 'good job' and 'thanks' before dropping it onto her desk, and finished by fixing the well-chewed plastic pen top back onto his biro. He glanced at the damaged pen and shook his head. Terrible habit, but better than biting his nails like he used to.

Scraping back his chair, he pressed the stiffness out of his back and made for the office kettle again; he'd let the last cuppa go cold before he had finished it. As he listened to the water boil, he updated himself with the timeline sequence on the incident board and studied the mortuary shots for the first time. They were horrific; such appalling violence had been meted out by someone before they had snuffed out her life. And she still had no name, despite the detective superintendent's TV appeal. He had caught it twice last night, first at the end of the early evening news and then after the ten o'clock news.

Hunter double-checked the log to ensure nothing significant had happened overnight. The HOLMES team would have been covering a late shift yesterday evening to take any calls prompted by the news plea.

Grace entered the office at bang-on 7.30 a.m. and followed a similar ritual to his, slipping off her jacket and making a beeline for the kettle.

A few minutes later, hugging a steaming cup of coffee, she sunk gently into her chair. He saw her react as she spotted the post-it on the front of the inquest file. After a few seconds, she looked up with a smile and responded with a thumbs-up and 'thank you' before placing the file into her tray.

The morning's briefing was a low-key affair. The HOLMES team were still checking through all last night's calls but there appeared to be nothing new to add to what had already been uncovered. DI Scaife issued some fresh priorities but Hunter's team still had a couple of the park's rangers to interview. Hunter asked Grace if she, Mike and Tony could finish off the actions without him. He made the excuse that he wanted to clear his tray, but in reality, he had more personally pressing things to sort out.

'Fine, Hunter, no problem. We should be able to clear them all by late this afternoon, but do you fancy working a bit over tonight?' said Grace.

'Not really,' he hesitated. 'Why, is there something urgent to follow up?'

'Not urgent as such. One of the park rangers we tracked down yesterday said something which could lead somewhere.'

'What's that then?' Hunter asked, leaning across his desk, resting his elbows and interweaving his fingers.

'Apparently, after the park closes, the back of the car park is occasionally used by courting couples in cars. The rangers have been told by their boss that whoever covers a late shift should try to discourage it, because there had been a few complaints from dog walkers. One girl in particular turns up quite regularly in different cars and with different guys. They know her as Tanya and it seems she has spun them some yarn about being a Russian dancer who has fled her brutal husband and is trying to make ends meet.' Grace rolled her eyes and clucked her tongue against the roof of her mouth dismissively. 'It's obvious she's a street worker who's using the car park as a regular spot. I just thought that if she is a regular visitor, she'll know the comings and goings of other regulars and there's the off chance she will have seen something suspicious but is afraid to come forward because of what she's doing there. I thought we could stakeout the lake for a couple of evenings, and see if she turns up.'

Hunter unlocked his fingers and pushed himself back into his seat. 'I'd love to say yes, Grace, but I've got something else planned tonight.'

'Oh, okay, sorting out your parents — I understand.'

'In a way — just something I need to follow up, that's all.'

Grace's gave him an inquisitive look. 'That all sounds rather mysterious, Hunter.'

'That's because it is,' he said, rising from his seat. 'It's top secret and if I tell you I might have to kill you.' He smiled, tapped his nose and headed towards the door.

Hunter tracked MIT's civilian investigator, Barry Newstead, to the CCTV room, where he found him going through footage from the country park's security system. Barry was sitting at one of the viewing consoles concentrating on speeded-up images floating across the screen. Pausing the footage, Barry acknowledged Hunter with a quick nod and then returned to the TV monitor.

Hunter fondly ruffled a hand through Barry's rumple of dark dyed hair. 'How's it going, big man? Found anything?'

The thickset investigator grunted, shaking his head away from Hunter's rifling fingers.

Hunter pulled up a chair next to his old friend and colleague.

'Not a damn thing so far,' said Barry, not taking his eyes off the screen. 'I've been here looking at this lot for the best part of a day and a half and I'm getting square eyes. The most exciting moment was watching a female mallard and her seven chicks waddle across the front of reception. This is almost as boring as going through all the missing-from-home files from the last job.'

Despite Barry bemoaning the task, Hunter knew it would be done thoroughly. He edged his seat closer. 'Glad I've caught up with you. Sorry to have put you on the spot with those enquiries, but I was stuck up in North Yorks and there was only Grace and you I could trust with something so sensitive, and Grace had just taken on this job.'

'No problem, that's what buddies are for.'

'Anything new cropped up?'

Barry pressed pause again and faced Hunter. He smoothed a thumb and forefinger across his dark, bushy moustache. 'I followed up a few calls late yesterday but there's nothing on the grapevine at all about what happened. I've only given my snouts half a story, they've no idea it's your parents, just told them it's a hit-and-run near the east coast. That way if someone does come back with something I'll know if they're telling me the truth.'

Hunter patted Barry's shoulder. 'Cheers for this — I owe you one.'

'No problem, Hunter. You getting me this job has more than paid a debt. I was bored stiff at home. It's great to be back in the thick of it, especially after being thrown on the scrapheap.'

Six years ago, Barry had been forced into retirement. A newly promoted Chief Inspector, wanting to make his mark, had targeted him because of his unorthodox methods. It had happened while Hunter was at District, and word had got back to him that the new man had threatened to discipline Barry for bringing the force into disrepute, before finally side-lining him to a desk job which he knew he would hate.

Hunter had caught up with Barry at his retirement do and ended up laughing with the rest of those attending when Barry had ended his retirement speech with 'I'm going to call it a day before I smack that bastard.' Word had got back to the Chief Inspector but it was too late for him to do anything about it.

Since then there had been regular phone calls and the occasional beer together, getting fewer over the years. Then six weeks ago his ex-buddy had come back into his life again. Barry had rung him out of the blue with vital information on the serial killer case which they had just put to bed, and Hunter had managed to persuade the boss to take him on as a civilian investigator at a time when their backs were against the wall and the team needed more experienced staff.

'Fancy doing some night-fishing?' Hunter asked. He caught Barry's smile. They had used the term so many times over the years, their coded phrase whenever one of them had decided to engage in underhand activities and needed backup.

'I've nothing much else on. What do you have in mind?' Barry said, interest piqued.

The Masons Arms on Barnwell High Street was a drab Victorian pub that had not changed much in decades. It had a reputation and decent local folk and anyone with an ounce of sense gave it a wide berth. Such was the clientele who frequented it that a simple brawl always turned into a wild-west saloon fight.

It was the first time Hunter had been there for a drink — under normal circumstances he would have avoided the place — but tonight he was on a mission.

Hunter and Barry entered the lounge, or at least that's what it said on the door. They stepped into an interior that belonged somewhere in the past — dingy, low-lit, and with the smell of stale tobacco hanging heavily in the air. Because of the smoking ban, Hunter guessed it was emanating from the pores and clothing of the dozen or so customers who hugged the bar. But then he took a closer look, recognising some of the faces, and wasn't so sure. Some of the people in here didn't give tuppence for society's rules and regulations.

The room fell silent as the regulars clocked them, but as Hunter and Barry strode past, they returned to their drinks and continued their conversations in low voices. Although they appeared to be minding their own business Hunter knew eyes would be covertly watching them until they left.

He scanned the room and spotted his quarry, sporting a Mohican style haircut, tucked into a corner, nursing what looked like a half-finished pint of lager.

He and Barry had snuck over and pulled up chairs before David Paynton realised they were there.

'Mind if we join you?' Hunter said, squatting down on his seat, slotting his legs under the small round table that separated him from his foe. Barry took up a position at the side, leaving David Paynton boxed in.

Paynton's eyes burned with hatred. 'What the fuck do you two want?'

'Now that's not a very nice greeting for two old friends of yours, David, is it?' Hunter surveyed Paynton's disfigured nose with satisfaction. It gave him the look of a boxer who had lost more fights than he had won. It was Hunter's handiwork and had been well deserved. A month ago, David, his brother Terry and his cousin Lee had ambushed Hunter coming out of his dad's gym. Thankfully, Barry and Jock had come to his aid and between them they had hospitalised all three of the Paynton clan. It was at the forefront of Hunter's thoughts as he said, 'How's your Steven? Heard from him?'

David looked menacing. 'You fucking know how he is. You and that bitch are the ones who got him banged up. He's on the nonce's wing for his own protection, thanks to you.'

'Now, now David, don't get yourself worked up,' said Barry. 'Steve has only himself to thank for that. He was the one who raped those women and abused those children. He admitted it, remember?'

'So you say, so you say.' Paynton pushed his wiry six-foot frame back into the faux-leather seat. 'Anyway, what do you two fuckers want?'

'A little chat, that's all,' said Hunter.

'A little chat, my arse.' Paynton took a sip from his pint, never taking his eyes off them. As he set it down, he said, 'Just piss off and leave me alone.'

'Look, David, we can do this the easy way or the hard way.' Barry snapped one of his shovel-like hands across Paynton's knee, then squeezed, digging his fingers into the joint. The man twitched. 'The easy way is we ask you some questions to which you give some honest answers. The hard way is I walk over to that bar, buy a fresh pint of lager, set it down in front of you, drop you a tenner on the table and we walk out of here. I'm sure those at the bar will not be too impressed, especially if they think you're a grass.' Barry released his grip. 'Now, which is it to be?'

Paynton pushed Barry's hand away. 'What do you want?' he growled.

'That's better,' said Hunter. He leaned in towards Paynton. 'First question — what car do you own?'

Puzzled, Paynton raised his eyebrows and seemed to think about the question for a good ten seconds, then said, 'Astra, blue, O five plate, you know that. It's on your computer.'

'Second question; which one of you or your mates owns a silver BMW?'

The puzzled look deepened. Paynton shook his head. 'None of us.'

'Sure about that?'

Paynton swelled his chest and stroked at uneven tufts of bristle peppering his jawline. 'Sure, I'm sure. We've never owned a BMW — German crap.'

'Who do you know that owns a silver BMW?' Hunter persisted.

'No one. BMs are for flashy-gits and pimps.' Paynton looked back and forth between Hunter and Barry. 'Look, where is this going? All these questions about a silver BMW. Was it used in a robbery or something?'

'A hit and run,' Hunter said, watching for a reaction. There was none.

'Look, I'll say this once more and only once more. None of us have ever owned a BMW. It's not our style. British every time. We're patriots. And as far as being involved in a hit and run, I have absolutely no idea what you are on about. When was this? Was it in Barnwell?'

'On the North Yorkshire moors six days ago,' Hunter told him. 'Ring any bells?'

'I can't even remember the last time I was anywhere near the moors.' Paynton stroked his chin, then blurted out, 'Six days ago! Ha! It can't have been me! I was with our Terry. We had to go to the Job Centre for an interview — they were going to stop our benefits. A bloody waste of time that was as well.' His face creased into a smile. 'Check it if you want.'

'Don't worry, we will,' said Hunter, scraping back his chair. He tried to hide his disappointment.

Paynton looked more confident. 'Now, wind your neck in and get off my case.'

Barry leaned to within an inch of Paynton's face. 'Watch your mouth. We can still do the dirty on you.'

Paynton stared back defiantly, picked up his pint and took a long swallow.

Hunter and Barry kicked back their chairs and left the way they had come.

Outside, Hunter paused on the footpath and studied the quiet High Street. It was just turning dusk, an orange glow low on the horizon poked between a band of grey cloud.

'Think he's telling the truth?' he asked.

'It wouldn't be hard to check out, would it?' Barry replied. 'I hate to say this, Hunter — because he's a Paynton — but I think he is.'

DAY EIGHT

The sky had been filled with dark leaden clouds all day but the rain had held off and all that was left of the northerly weather front was a gentle breeze. At Barnwell Country Park, Grace and Hunter stood at the lake edge, listening to the water lapping against the shale. The surface undulated as a cool evening wind whipped across the murky lake.

Hunter looked skywards to watch tufts of pink cloud scoot across a blue-green sky. The sun was beginning to drop low. He glanced at his watch. 9.10 p.m. The summer was drawing to a close. Another month and autumn would be here.

It had been a day of mixed fortunes so far. Hunter had listened to the briefing earlier that day with a degree of enthusiasm. It was a mixture of bad and good news. Although the team had been working flat out for over a week, the enquiry was stalling. None of the detectives were bringing anything new. They were still no nearer to identifying the victim; there had been no luck with dental records, fingerprints or DNA, and they hadn't been able to match the rug the victim had been found in to a crime scene.

But the Detective Superintendent ended the session on a high as he told them about a phone call from Professor Lizzie McCormack. The pathologist's niece was a forensic medical artist whose skills lay in facial reconstruction and she had agreed to rebuild the victim's face so a fresh appeal could be made on TV. Work to build up the victim's facial features was to begin in the next few days and should be finished in a week.

After the briefing, Hunter had got to grips with his overdue paperwork. Then he'd caught up with Grace and fixed up the stake-out at the country park to see if Tanya would turn up. An hour earlier, they had left their unmarked car near the reception centre and begun their reconnaissance of the car park where the street worker had been frequently spotted.

Dressed in fleeces, they looked like any other couple on an evening stroll around the lakeside. And thanks to a ranger's advice they were in a hidden spot with a clear view of where Tanya parked up with her clients. It was now a waiting game.

From the corner of his eye, Hunter studied Grace, watching the gentle breeze lift the curls from her face, revealing dark summer freckles. He'd often commented on how they made her look like a cute little schoolgirl and she'd responded by slapping his arm.

He grinned — she always blushed at his comments but sometimes used her naive schoolgirl look to good advantage. On several occasions, he had watched on in amusement as villain after villain, as well as the odd Alpha male colleague, had been thrown off guard by Grace's innocent childlike-look and demeanour. It was like watching a python hypnotise its prey.

She turned and he averted his gaze; he didn't want her to know he'd been watching her. After a couple of seconds, he said, 'By the way, Grace, I've been waiting for the right moment to say that you've made a cracking job of leading your first murder case. You've made it so easy for me to pick up. I've been conscious about taking it back from you, especially as you've put in so much hard work. And you've managed to fit in the inquest file as well, that's no mean feat.'

'To be honest, Hunter, I'm glad you came back when you did. Don't get me wrong — I loved it and the team have been stars but I was feeling the pressure. In fact, I've not being able to switch off when I've got home and just now, I need to.' She looked out over the lake. 'Anyway, did you get done what needed to be done last night? You don't have to tell me if you don't want.'

'No, I don't mind. I just didn't want to say anything yesterday. Not that I don't trust you but I needed to check things out.' He outlined the previous night's events with David Paynton, constantly switching his gaze between Grace and the car park — he didn't want to miss their target.

'So, you're no nearer to finding out who ran your mum and dad off the road?'

'No, and it's doing my head in. I know my dad's hiding something but he's refusing to talk about it. I thought it might have been that bother we had with the Payntons after you and I locked up Steve. But after last night I think I need to be looking elsewhere.'

'What about the photos you got of the shaven-headed guy? Have they thrown up anything?'

Hunter shook his head. 'Unfortunately, they're not that good. I've tried messing about with them on the computer but the light wasn't that brilliant and he was too far away to identify.' He gazed down to the water's edge as a line of ripples broke across its surface. 'Anyway, enough about my family's problems, how are you coping?'

'Oh, so, so. It's Dave I feel sorry for. It can't be easy being married to a copper, especially as this cop's burdened him with so much just lately. I've promised to make it up to him. I'm going to take him away for a long weekend. Paris or something — once this job's wrapped up.'

'We're worse than teenage kids, aren't we?'

Their attention was diverted by the sound of crunching gravel across the lake. After a few seconds, a dark blue Rover saloon appeared in a gap in the laurel bushes and headed towards the rear of the parking area. It was in view for a moment and then disappeared behind another line of bushes. Hunter and Grace waited for it to reappear but when it didn't, they swung into action, bursting into a jog. An earlier test run had shown they could be at the location in just under three minutes — more than enough time to catch the mysterious Tanya if she was with a punter.

Two-hundred yards from the car park, they slowed to a fast walk. They could make out a front grille and headlights of a car through a gap in the bushes. Crouching low, Hunter and Grace moved off the path and onto a stretch of grass which would bring them up behind the vehicle. It gave them a chance to get their breath back.

The blue Rover was rocking from side to side on its suspension as they approached. Hunter and Grace smiled at one another as they moved to either side from the rear.

Hunter banged on the roof and yanked open the driver's door. 'Police,' he shouted.

Simultaneously, Grace had the front passenger door open.

Inside were two very surprised faces, a man in his early forties, and a much younger woman, both in the early stages of undressing — the man had his trousers around his knees and she was dropping her leggings. They grabbed at their clothing in a state of panic.

'Okay,' Hunter said loudly, 'put it away, sir, and get out of the car.'

'And you rearrange yourself, young lady, and do the same,' said Grace.

The two detectives turned their heads away but kept a firm grip of the door handles as the pair got themselves sorted.

Minutes later, the driver was standing before Hunter, trying to fasten the belt of his trousers, finding it difficult because of his shaking hands. He looked a nervous wreck, avoiding any eye contact and was most apologetic. As Hunter checked out his details, the man kept repeating that he was sorry and asking if his wife would find out about this.

Hunter glanced at Grace. She was enjoying watching the guy squirm.

The driver checked out; no convictions for anything. Hunter berated him for his actions and told him this was a warning and to sling his hook. He couldn't get away fast enough, slamming the car into reverse and throwing the girl's red high-heeled shoes and matching handbag out from the passenger seat, while Grace held onto her as the car moved backwards.

In less than a minute, the blue Rover was heading towards the park exit, a cloud of dust spinning up from its rear wheels.

Hunter and Grace got their first good look of Tanya. She was skinny, with pale skin and couldn't have been more than nineteen.

She bent to slip her shoes on and then hoisted up her leggings over a black thong that left nothing to the imagination. 'Bastard,' she mumbled with not a hint of embarrassment.

'Now, young lady,' began Grace, 'you and I are going to have a long chat.'

'I didn't do anything wrong. You can't prove it.'

'Oh, believe me, we can.' Grace grabbed the girl's handbag, unclipped the fastener and turned it upside down. Lipstick, a compact case, half a dozen twenty-pound notes and at least ten condoms spilt out onto the grass. 'That should be enough evidence for a police caution — unless you've been cautioned before and then it's a court appearance.'

'Bitch,' Tanya snarled and snatched her handbag. She dropped to her knees and began picking up the scattered contents, mumbling under her breath.

Grace bent down and aligned her face with Tanya's. 'I need to ask you some questions. If I get the right answers, then you and I will part the best of friends. If I don't, it's back to the station, and you make no more money tonight. Have I made myself clear?'

Grace's opening gambit reminded Hunter of his and Barry's interview technique with David Paynton the previous night. He turned away to hide a smile.

The girl stuffed the spilled contents back into her handbag, checked the ground to make sure she hadn't left anything and hoisted herself up.

Hunter looked her up and down, studying her face. Her dark eyes were sunken. Foundation and blusher had been heavily applied to cover blemishes and soften her prominent cheekbones. He realised she wasn't slim and petite because of her build, but because of her habit. He had seen the tell-tale signs many times during the three years he had served in the Drug Squad. This girl was a druggie, heroin by the looks of her.

'First what's your name?' asked Grace.

'Tanya. I'm Russian.'

Hunter tried to place the accent. It had a foreign twang to it but somehow it didn't sound Russian.

'Not what people call you. What's your real name?'

'Tanya.'

'Didn't I make myself clear?' said Grace, pushing her face nearer. 'This is not a good start. It looks like you and I are going back to the station to do a few checks. We'll take your fingerprints and photograph and bring in immigration if you persist with this.'

With a pissed-off look on her face, Tanya switched her gaze between Grace and Hunter for the best part of ten seconds, then slamming her hands onto her hips she responded, 'Okay, it's not Tanya.'

The foreign accent had gone, replaced by a broad South Yorkshire dialect. It sounded to Hunter as if she was from the Barnsley area.

'It's Kerri — Kerri-Ann Bairstow,' she continued, looking down at the ground. 'I found I could make more money with a foreign name and fancy background.'

'Right. Now we've got that sorted, let's stop mucking about because I've got some really important questions to ask, and I don't want any more of your bullshit.' Grace placed a hand under Kerri-Ann's chin. 'Look at me now. I want to see your face when I ask you these questions.'

Kerri-Ann lifted her head and Grace drew back her hand. The girl looked sorrowful and lost.

'I believe you use this place quite a lot. Bring your punters here on a regular basis?'

Kerri-Ann nodded. She began fiddling with her fingers, picking skin at the side of her cuticles.

'How many times a week, would you say?'

'A couple of times in mid-week, but quite a lot at the weekend, that's when there's not so many people about the place.'

'And how long have you been using this park for your sessions?'

'Six — seven months.'

'And do you always get the guys to park up where we found you?'

Kerri-Ann nodded again. 'It's out of the way if people are walking round the lake.'

'Have you heard about the body recovered from here just over a week ago?'

Kerri-Ann gulped and coloured up, turning away.

Grace grabbed Kerri-Ann's chin again and looked at her squarely. 'You have, haven't you?'

Kerri-Ann shook herself free. 'Course I frigging have. You can't miss it. It's all over the news.'

'Look, Kerri-Ann, this is very important. A young woman's body was dumped in that lake just over a month ago, and where you park up with your punters is in clear view of the jetty over there.' Grace pointed towards the mooring dock. 'I need to know if you saw anyone on there during any of your visits here. Especially if you saw anyone carrying anything.'

Kerri-Ann looked away again. That told Hunter she was hiding something.

'This is very serious, Kerri-Ann,' he said. 'A young woman has been murdered and her body dumped over there. If you've seen anything we need to know.'

'I don't want to get involved. I'm only talking to you now because I want you off my bleeding back. What if whoever did it comes looking for me?'

'You don't need to think about that. There is no way we are going to give out a witness's name. Anyway, what are you worrying about? You've been using a false name for ages — just change it again and do your trade somewhere else,' said Grace.

'I don't know. I feel scared about this.'

'Kerri-Ann, listen to me, so far you're our only lead. You really might be able to help us catch this girl's killer.'

'I didn't see that much.'

From that comment, Hunter knew Grace had managed it. This could be the breakthrough. A tingle of excitement ran through him. He wanted to jump in but this was Grace's call.

Grace touched Kerri-Ann's arm and looked into her sunken eyes. 'That's the hard part over. Now just tell us, slowly, what you saw.'

'Look, if I tell you will you stop hassling me and let me earn some money? I've got a two-year-old at home and I didn't see the dad for dust once I told him I was pregnant. I can't manage on the benefits they give me.' Her eyes darted between Grace and Hunter.

There was silence for a good thirty seconds and Grace was about to prompt her again when Kerri-Ann blurted out, 'All right, if it'll keep you off my back and you promise I won't go to court.' She began to pick at her fingers again. 'It was either a Friday or Saturday evening. I know that much because those two nights are my busiest time and I was with my fourth punter. Probably be about half past ten.'

'Can you remember how long ago?'

'You're joking. As you said could have been four to five weeks ago. I don't keep a diary.'

'Okay, Kerri-Ann, that's a start. You said it was about half ten at night?'

'Yeah, that's roughly the time because the guy I was with said he needed to get back into town for eleven. Anyway, we'd finished business and I needed a piss so I got out of the car to go behind the bushes. I was just about to get back in the car 'cos he'd promised me a lift, when I heard voices near that jetty thing you've pointed out and it made me jump. I sneaked a look through a gap and saw these two guys struggling with a bundle half way along it. I thought they were just dumping rubbish.

'Anyway, I went back to the car and the guy starts having a go at me. He'd had second thoughts about giving me a lift and we ended up having a row. Finally, he agreed to drop me off in a pub car park near town. I jumped in his car before he had chance to change his mind and we'd just set off when this white van came from nowhere. Almost cut us up. It had no lights on and really freaked us both out.

'At first, I thought it was cops, especially 'cos the guy said he didn't want to get caught by them. He stopped for a good couple of minutes. He was really freaked out by it. In fact, he wanted to leave me there and then and piss off back home. I told him there was no way I was leaving the car.

Anyway, after about five minutes he decided to leave, but he drove really slowly and I could tell he was nervous all the way to where he dropped me off.'

Hunter said, 'Kerri-Ann, you've just said the guy you were with said he didn't want to be caught by them — as if he knew who they were. Am I right in thinking that?'

'That's what I thought when he said it.'

Hunter exchanged a look with Grace. This interview had just thrown up something he hadn't expected.

'Kerri-Ann, this punter you were with — do you know him?'

'No, it was a first time and I haven't seen him since.'

'Can you remember what he looked like?'

'Vaguely. He was in his early twenties and quite good looking — most of them are fat or ugly.'

Hunter and Grace both grinned.

Hunter asked, 'Anything else you remember about him?'

'He was about your height and build, and he had brown curly hair, which was about shoulder length if I remember rightly. Oh, and he was wearing a suit, like a businessman or something.'

'Where did he pick you up?'

'Down by the industrial estate where I normally hang out.'

'Can you remember the car he was driving?'

'Now cars I'm good at — have to be — you know, in case something happens? I text it into my phone.' Kerri-Ann unclasped her handbag and fished out her mobile, flicked it open and began tapping the keys. Thirty seconds later she looked back at them before glancing back at the screen. 'A silver Volkswagen Golf. I've entered the first few letters and numbers.' She turned the screen to let Grace see the registration.

'YP02,' Grace read out loud.

'I'm sorry, that's all I had time to put in.'

'Don't apologise, Kerri-Ann, that's brilliant. Did you manage to get his name?'

Kerri-Ann started to laugh. 'You are kidding, aren't you?'

Grace blushed. 'Sorry, stupid question. Anything else you can remember about him — distinguishing marks, scars, etc.?'

Kerri-Ann shook her head.

'Did your punter drop you back off?'

'Yeah, eventually. In the end, I got him to drop me off near the bus station. He wouldn't drop me near the pub. As I say, he was a nervous wreck.'

'Can you remember roughly what that time would be?'

'Elevenish, or something like that.'

'Okay, that's good. Now I just want to take you back a bit. We'll not keep you much longer. Did you manage to get a make or number of the white van?'

'No. As I say it just came out of nowhere. It scared us to death. It wasn't a big van like a Transit or anything, just a small one. I didn't get a number, it happened so fast.'

'Did you notice anything special about the van? Anything written on the sides?'

Kerri-Ann seemed to think about it a few seconds, then shook her head. 'Sorry, it was dark and as I say it hadn't got its lights on.'

'What about the two guys you saw with the bundle on the jetty?'

Kerri-Ann shook her head again. 'Sorry, it was so dark. They were just shapes. I never got close enough to even see what they were wearing. As I say, at the time I just thought they were dumping rubbish.' She paused and studied Grace and Hunter's faces. 'I'm not lying, I really didn't see their faces or anything — they were too far away and it was dark.'

'Okay, Kerri-Ann, I believe you,' Grace replied. 'Well done. Now let's get back to our car and get a statement from you.'

As they set off towards the car park Hunter knew that this was the kick-start the investigation needed.

Rab Geddes flung open the car door and flopped into the driver's seat. 'Still no sign of anyone — could be he's on his hols.' He examined his shoes in the footwell. 'Jeez, just look at the state of these. The fields are full of mud. Your turn next time.' He wiped his loafers on the car mat and checked them again.

'Will you shut the fuck up moaning,' said Billy Wallace, leaning forward. With the back of his gloved hand he rubbed the condensation from his side of the windscreen. Though bushes prevented them seeing their destination, he continued staring out along the uneven track. From an earlier reconnoitre, Billy knew the secluded bungalow they had been searching for lay less than a hundred metres away.

This was the third parking spot they had chosen that afternoon, spending the time in between going for a drive around, so that they didn't attract attention from the locals.

Billy powered down the window. Outside, a strong wind whistled through the trees nearby, making an unpleasant sound as resisting branches squeaked and creaked. In the past hour the weather had turned; the wind had picked up fiercely and was whipping across the fields. He thumbed the window back up. Splodges of rain were beginning to scar the windscreen, distorting his view ahead. He wasn't complaining, though. It meant people wouldn't be straying far from their homes. The last thing he needed was witnesses.

They had driven the hour or so to Killin early that morning. At first, he wasn't sure he had heard the name right when he'd eventually beaten it out of Alistair McPherson four days ago, and he'd had to search for the place in the road atlas. But when he had found the small village and confirmed the name it made him smile.

What an appropriate name. Especially for what he had in mind for his next quarry.

He and Rab had entered the picturesque village mid-morning, by the stone bridge which spanned the Falls of Dochart. As they crossed, Billy got a sense of déjà vu and for a few seconds it had puzzled him. Then he realised why as he stared across at the foaming water pounding between the huge grey rocks and boulders below. He had seen this location so many times. It featured in the 1950s film, *The 39 Steps* — one of his all-time favourites. How ironic that the film was about a fugitive on the run and he should be here, though in his case he wasn't an innocent man. It had prompted another twisted smile.

They had checked out the place, driving up and down the main street. Rab had made a few enquiries about the man they were looking for, explaining he was an ex-colleague, they were on a fishing trip and wanted to catch up with him. It had not taken long to find out he was a regular in the bar of the Clachaig Hotel located beside the falls. A quick visit there and the pair had left armed with the man's address. That was seven hours ago.

Now they lay in wait, watching for the occupant to return to the white-washed bungalow in the middle of nowhere.

Billy climbed out of the car, stretched and then relieved himself by the bushes that were keeping them hidden. He fastened his zip and glanced at his watch. 'We'll give it another hour,' he called back over his shoulder, 'and then call it a day if he doesn't return.' He stood, peering over the top of the brambles, feeling the breeze brush his face, looking towards the property. He was still there as dusk settled and seemed unmoved by the sudden biting north easterly and slanting rain.

Then his heart jolted. A light appeared through the bushes — the bungalow's windows were lit up. In the warm, yellowing glow he saw a human shadow passing across the right-hand window. He stood transfixed for several moments, watching for more activity, but there was none. He stretched his gloves tighter over his hands, so tight he could see the outline of his knuckles against the black soft leather. He turned sharply. 'Come on, Rab, get your arse in gear. He's back.'

They crossed the field, hugging the bushes, Billy leading, his Crombie flapping in the wind. Rab had to put in a jog every couple of paces to keep up. Twenty metres from the rear of the bungalow Billy halted and pushed against the hedgerow. He stared about him, listening. There was only the sound of the wind and the rain lashing against the tops of the trees.

'Right, remember what we rehearsed?' Billy whispered.

'Sure.'

'Okay, let's do the business.'

Rab brushed droplets of rain from the front of his jacket and tiptoed towards the door. Billy never took his eyes off him. Rab knocked and a few seconds later the door opened. The man who answered had put on some weight since Billy had last seen him and the hair was thinner and greyer, but this was definitely the guy they were after.

Billy caught up as the man was asking for Rab's ID. He jammed a foot in the gap before he had time to close the door. 'Mr McNab — long time no see.' He grinned menacingly.

Ross McNab's face was a picture.

Billy slammed a clenched fist into his pudgy belly. It dropped him to the floor and as Billy was about to deliver a kick, he caught movement through the open door which led into the lounge to his right. A woman, who he guessed was Mrs McNab, stood open-mouthed only a few yards away.

There was terror in her eyes. He strode into the room and had a hand clenched around her jaw before she had time to scream.

'Rab, get the fat bastard up and get him in here!'

Mrs McNab jerked her head and pushed out with her hands, trying to get free of Billy's grip. He responded by digging his fingers deeper into her mandible and then smacked her across the ear. He felt her jaw pop and she wailed as she fell from his grasp, to the floor.

Rab forced Ross McNab's arm up his back, hoisting him forward, hustling him into the lounge.

'Put him there, Rab,' Billy said, pointing to an oval dining table with a seating arrangement of six chairs.

Rab manhandled McNab towards the table, kicked out the nearest chair and slammed him into the seat.

McNab was fighting for breath, his face covered in sweat.

Billy checked on Mrs McNab — she was out of it. In two strides, he was beside McNab, delivering a vicious blow to the man's head. McNab jolted sideways, almost taking the chair he was seated on with him. Rab pulled him back upright.

'Right, you fucking bastard, do you remember me?' Billy hissed.

The man groaned and brought his hand up to his reddened cheek. 'Course I do, how can I forget you? Billy Wallace — the bastard who murdered Morag McCredie and her wee bairn.' He paused. 'For nothing.'

Billy had a flashback. They were becoming far more frequent of late. His mind transported him back to that night, re-living the horror when that junkie slag had ruined his looks. And, as if it was happening there and then, he felt a sharp sting across his nose and cheek and reached up and stroked the outline of the ugly, irregular, leathery scar, snaking across half of his face.

'And you're one of the fuckers who helped put me away,' he growled.

'And you're going away again for this, you bastard. If I was ten years younger…'

Before he had time to finish the sentence Billy smashed his fist into McNab's face, breaking his nose.

'Grab his hand,' ordered Billy.

Rab Geddes snatched hold of McNab's wrist and forced his hand flat, palm downwards, onto the table. He tried to resist but Rab was too strong.

Billy pulled out a knife from his Crombie. 'Now, you bastard, me and Rab here have spent thirty-six years in prison because of you and that Campbell who grassed us up. It's payback time.' He sprang the switch-blade and held it over McNab's hand.

Ross tried to pull away again but Rab's grip held him firm.

'I want to know where Iain Campbell is. I know you know where he is.'

McNab's face turned white and a stain-patch of sweat began spreading across the front of his shirt. 'I don't know what you're on about. Stop this now, Billy. This is your final chance or you'll be back to Barlinnie and you'll nae see the light of day again.'

Billy started to laugh. Then a look of malevolence crept over his face. 'You are in no position to threaten me, Mr McNab. One more chance. Where does that bastard Campbell live?'

'Don't be so fucking stupid.'

Billy slammed the blade down onto Ross McNab's little finger, using his other hand as a lever. The knife sliced through the digit easily, cutting through into the dark wood of the table in the process. The finger shot across the surface and a gush of blood sprayed out across the polished veneer.

A guttural scream exploded from McNab.

Billy started jumping up and down, patting his hands together like an excited child. 'Oh, I bet that hurt,' he said laughingly. 'Did — it — hurt?'

McNab was drenched in sweat now. It was running in rivulets down the sides of his waxen face, and his chest was heaving, breathing as fast as if he had been jogging.

Billy heard loud moaning noises behind him and realised Mrs McNab was coming to. He slipped the knife back into his pocket, took the few steps to where she was laid out and grabbed a handful of her hair, hoisting up her head. Her eyelids snapped open from the pain. A gurgling sound broke from her and she tried to shout, but her jaw was hanging at an awkward angle and all that came out was an incoherent mumble.

Reaching into another pocket of his coat, Billy took out a washing-up bottle. He popped the plastic top and squeezed the contents over her head, then dropped the empty bottle and let go of her hair. She dropped back onto the carpet into a crumpled heap, then forced open her eyes and blinked as the liquid trickled over her eyelids and onto her cheeks. Her face took on a look of unimaginable horror.

The vapours had invaded her nasal passages.

The smell of petrol filled the room.

Billy took out a disposable lighter from his trouser pocket and held it above her.

'Now, this is your last chance, McNab. Tell me where that bastard Iain Campbell is.'

Billy and Rab returned to familiar territory in Glasgow and dumped the car in the labyrinth of roads around one of the notorious sink estates of Easterhouse.

The pair wiped much of the interior clean with petrol-soaked rags and Rab dropped the keys onto the driver's seat before closing the door and striding away with Billy.

Billy had thought it all through. He had spent enough time in prison to make his plans and consider all eventualities. This was all going to plan and he liked the feeling of being in control. He took another look back at the silver BMW. Sooner or later, one of the gangs around here would realise it wasn't a police trap and nick it. Hopefully the crew would get involved in a chase with the cops and get arrested.

If by chance anyone had clocked the car near the scene back in Killin, that would throw them off his scent for quite some time: enough time for him to do what he needed to do.

I've come too far now to get caught.

Billy checked he still had the package in his coat pocket, nudged Rab and pointed to a gap between the high-rise buildings. They increased their pace, slipping between the tenements, melting into the dark.

The salt in his sweat stung Jock Kerr's eyes and he closed them. He took a step back from the punch-bag and wiped away the perspiration from his brow. Opening his eyes, shaking away the residue from the back of his training glove, he resumed his session, bobbing and weaving around the sand-filled bag hanging from one of the gym's roof beams.

He dashed off a series of quick-fire blows to the bag. It hardly moved; it was momentum he was aiming for rather than impact. Catching his reflection in one of the mirrors that ran along the length of a wall, he smiled to himself. If he saw one of his boxing trainees performing like this, he would have bawled them out.

Stop tickling it, he would have barked. *Give it a good thumping.*

Thankfully, Jock was alone and wouldn't be embarrassed by his performance. His chest still hurt — the heavy breathing was causing a strain. It was his first time back in his gym since the accident and he'd decided to go in after everyone had finished, to give things a try out.

The session had not gone too badly. Another week, he told himself, and he should be back to tip-top condition. He gave the bag a final punch, wincing as sharpness gripped his rib cage, forcing him to clasp the sides of his stomach.

He caught another glimpse of his image in the mirror. In spite of his injury, he still looked in pretty good shape for his fifty-six years, though, he had to admit, his face looked tired and drawn. He put the hangdog look down to the lack of sleep over the past week and things being strained at home. Fiona, his wife, was pressing him to talk to someone, and on a couple of occasions he had reacted towards her like he had with Hunter. Unlike Hunter, however, there was a reason behind her pushing him — she knew what lay behind the attack.

Two nights ago, they had sat down and discussed at length how his past had finally caught up with them, and they gone over, time and time again, the 'what ifs', were they to tell Hunter. He felt guilty that Fiona had got dragged into this and cursed himself for being so naïve as to believe he could bury everything that had gone before. The crux of all their deliberations was not if, but when, they should tell Hunter. Fiona felt it was time, he wasn't so sure. Having made his decision an hour ago, Jock had pulled on his training top and jogged down to his gym.

The past half hour on the bag had reinforced his thinking. It was time to make that call.

Jock pulled off his training gloves, slung a towel around his neck, and began to steady his breathing, gazing around his gym. For a split second, a wave of satisfaction washed over him. He could remember the sight that had greeted him the first time he walked into this place thirty-five years ago. Then, it had been a derelict drill hall once used by army cadets. It had swallowed up all of their savings and taken lots of physical work to lick it into shape before he could open it up as a gym. But it had been worth it. Now it was one of the best boxing academies in the Yorkshire region.

Jock had gained a reputation as a boxing coach; he had a good stable of future young champions-in-the-making, and as an added bonus it was a profitable business. As he dabbed the last remnants of sweat from his face, he hoped against hope that what he had achieved over the years wasn't going to come crashing down around him because of one night from his past.

Jock wandered into his office and dropped into his Grandfather's old captain's chair behind his desk, leaned back on its springs and surveyed the cluttered room. For a few seconds as he pondered putting off the inevitable, his gaze skimmed the walls, checking out the boxing promotion posters hung all around. Every one of his achievements was recorded on them, all of the fights he had won in his heyday as a professional.

He shivered, mulled over in his head what he needed to say and then yanked open the desk's top drawer. After ferreting around in the loose paperwork, he found the card that had been buried at the back for years. He took up the handset and punched in the number and listened to the ringing tone. It took what seemed an eternity before anyone answered. He had almost given up hope and was ready for hanging up, then a voice came on he didn't recognise — a woman's voice. It sounded younger than he expected. The voice just said a simple 'Hello,' to which Jock repeated the same greeting.

'Who is this?' said the woman.

'Jock — Jock Kerr, who is this?'

'Detective Chief Inspector Dawn Leggate,' she answered. The voice was slow and distinctive with an air of confidence. 'Who is it you are after?'

'Sorry, I must have the wrong number. It was Ross McNab I was after.'

'Oh, you have the right number, all right.'

DCI Dawn Leggate closed her driver's door and pulled on her windbreaker. As she zipped it up, she stood for a few seconds taking in the surroundings, preparing for what lay ahead. She'd deliberately parked twenty metres away from the scene, where the lane turned into the driveway and gave her a clear view of the setting.

Ahead, parked on the gravel hard-standing were two marked police vehicles, a fire engine and an ambulance, crowded together, blocking the entrance to the McNabs' bungalow. Spinning blue and white strobe-lights picked out the shapes of surrounding trees and hedges and skirted across the fields, lighting up the waving fronds of wild grasses before washing over the white walls of the secluded dwelling.

For a split-second there was darkness as the blue lights spun away and then everything lit up once more as they continued their sweeping sequence. The image felt staged, like the opening sequence to a TV drama, yet Dawn knew this was for real. Thirty-five minutes ago Communications had rung her work mobile while she was in the middle of her evening meal and she'd had to leave it and break the speed limit to get here. Thank goodness the roads had been relatively clear.

She'd driven like a mad woman — a mixture of frustration and resolve — but it was her turn as the on-call SIO and as she'd tore up the A84, she'd told herself this was what her job was about. Though having just finished yet another long day at the office, and with her personal life in chaos, she didn't need this pressure right now.

Another gust of wind rose over the hedges, whipping Dawn's ginger hair across her face. Coaxing the shoulder length strands into a loose ponytail, she tucked it into her jacket collar and walked up to the McNabs' home, slipping on a pair of latex gloves as she avoided the puddles in the divots along the track.

Passing between the emergency vehicles, the only light she could pick out inside the smoke-ridden place appeared to be coming from torches, dancing back and forth through the soot-stained windows. She guessed the fire had taken out the electrics. A couple of the windows were open and wisps of white smoke drifted through the gaps before being whisked away by the north easterly and up into the leaden night sky.

She let herself into the darkened hallway. No one was on the door, the crime scene had not been sealed off yet. She mentally ticked it off as one of her priorities.

The air was heavy with soot and smoke and it clogged the back of her throat, making her gag. She clasped a hand over her mouth and loosely pinched her nose.

'Hello — anyone there?' she called, despite the activity in the bungalow.

A bright beam appeared from the doorway to her right and flashed across her eyes, temporarily blinding her.

'Sorry, ma'am, didn't hear you arrive,' she heard a man's voice say. The light had blanked her vision for a few seconds, she couldn't see a thing.

'The bodies are this way.'

She blinked frantically, desperate to see. Gradually, through a haze of orange flashes, a silhouette appeared. She picked out the shape; a uniform cop barred the door. She recognised his face from back at the station but couldn't remember his name.

'They're in a bit of a mess,' he said, stepping back.

She took out her own powerful Maglite and switched it on. An intense beam of light pierced the drifting fire smoke, hitting the opposite wall of the hallway. She swept it through the open doorway into the room, along the floor, up onto the walls, picking out bits of furniture.

She deduced this was the lounge area of the bungalow. The smell in here was different, soot and smoke, but in the pungent mix was something sweeter. It reminded her of a barbecue. Then her beam fell onto a body and she realised why.

Mrs McNab — from the remnants of a charred dress which was still smouldering. Her upper body was chargrilled black, except where the skin had split from the intense heat and gashes of raw pink flesh gaped through. Eyes stared back at her and white teeth glistened because the soft tissue of the eyelids and lips had shrivelled away. It was a surreal sight.

'The fire officer says she's been set alight with an ignitable solvent of some type — probably petrol,' said the uniform cop who had followed her into the room. 'When I got here, they were just dousing her out. She was the seat of the main fire.'

Dawn shuddered. She felt her skin prickle.

'It's even worse back here ma'am.'

She followed the light from the officer's torch as it settled on a human form seated and slumped over a dining table.

Striding around the charred remains of Mrs McNab, she stepped warily towards the table arrangement. Moving to the left and right of the humped figure, she said, 'And this must be Mr McNab?' His head was face-down on the table, a halo of thick cloying blood surrounding it. A chunk of flesh was missing from his frontal lobe; it looked as though attempts had been made to scalp him. His skin and clothing were in the main charred and blackened, though parts of his bare forearms displayed heat blisters.

'It looks as though he's been tortured,' said the officer. The beam from his torch flooded the grimy mahogany surface and settled on an outstretched hand. 'Three of his fingers have been chopped off,' he continued, 'and look at this, here.' He flicked the torch light over to a packet of fish fingers resting in the centre of the table. 'There's a note underneath them. I've already read it but not touched.'

Dawn crossed the officer's ray with her own Maglite beam, fixing onto an A4 sheet of paper. Despite the film of soot, she could make out the black capital letters scrawled across it, which read — THESE ARE TO REPLACE THE MISSING ONES.

She tried to make eye contact with the uniform cop but he was in semi-darkness. Her gaze flickered between the disfigured hand of Mr McNab and the fish finger box.

'What sick bastard would do this?' she said, then shook herself back from her thoughts, quickly turning to crime scene investigation mode. She went through a check-list in her head.

Earlier, while speeding towards the scene she had been told over the radio that SPSA were on their way; getting the Scottish Police Services Authority forensics team here was one job she could tick off.

'I want you to start the visitor log please.' She threw the cop her car keys. 'There's a clipboard and paperwork in my boot. And seal the area off with tape before you come back to the house. Oh, and before you go, point me in the direction of the senior fire officer.'

Her instructions were interrupted by the ringing of a telephone. It was coming from somewhere back in the entrance hall. She paused in mid-flow, waiting for voicemail or an answer machine to kick-in but that didn't happen and the phone continued to ring.

She stepped around Mrs McNab's body and strode into the hallway where she found the ringing phone on a small table close to the front door. Lifting the handset, she could feel a slimy, greasy film covering it as a result of the fire and she raised it towards her ear; close enough to hear, yet not mark her face.

'Hello,' she answered. There was no response but she could make out someone breathing heavily at the other end. 'Hello, can I help you?' No response. 'Who is this?'

'Jock — Jock Kerr.' She thought she heard the man say. She made a mental note of the name for later, tried to determine the region of the Scottish accent but somehow it had lost its twang. 'Who is it you are after?'

She listened carefully to the answer, making another careful record in her head.

When he had finished, she answered, 'Oh, you have the correct number all right. This is Detective Chief Inspector Dawn Leggate. Can you give me your details and telephone number? I'm investigating Mr McNab's murder.'

The caller hung up. She was left listening to a long, purring noise. She checked her watch and noted the time; she would make a request for caller ID when she got back to the incident room.

Returning the handset, she stepped to the front door and took in a couple of deep breaths of fresh air. At the entranceway she took a long look around to see if any neighbours overlooked the bungalow. There were none. This was going to be a difficult case.

While she was thinking about the phone call, a flitting movement up to her right surprised her. A couple of black shapes flashed in front of a pale moonlit sky — bats taking to the night.

Dawn stood and watched, fascinated by their swift movement, zipping and swooping and zooming so close to the trees and at the last moment diving and swinging away. Living in the city she didn't usually see such a stage-show. It made her night.

For several minutes she stood there, mesmerised. Then she shook herself out of her reverie and fished her mobile out of her pocket. It was time to bring in the Procurator Fiscal and call out the troops.

DAY TEN

Hunter stepped through the French doors from his kitchen and onto the patio, nursing a steaming mug of tea. He took a long and measured look over the garden. Most of the flowers were beginning to fade and needed deadheading, he thought. With the exception of the potted plants, most of them were looking tired. What with the events at work over the past few months he had hardly had time for any gardening. In fact, it seemed like he'd missed summer altogether this year. He'd never experienced a year like this before.

He settled down onto one of the four chairs arranged around the mosaic tiled patio table and put down his drink. He loved the view from here. This was where he and Beth sat on warm summer evenings, sharing a bottle of wine, grateful for a little peace and quiet after they had tucked Jonathan and Daniel up in bed.

Hunter felt relaxed. Last night, he had finally put an end to all those restless nights. It had been his best sleep in ages. It also helped that he didn't have to go in early to work. He had arranged to have a coffee and chat with Zita, the reporter with the *Barnwell Chronicle*, and then he was off to the Forensics Lab to see how Professor McCormack's niece was shaping up with the facial reconstruction.

He'd spoken on the phone with the forensic medical artist yesterday and she'd invited him up to see the work in progress. He was looking forward to the trip. From an artistic point of view, he couldn't wait to see the result of the application and flair employed by another artist, and as a cop, he was eager to see the likeness that could possibly lead to the identification of their victim.

It had been arranged for him and Grace to visit the lab, but last night those plans had changed; Detective Superintendent Robshaw had requested that Grace join him at Barnwell Country Park that morning, where he was making a televised plea for witnesses. When Grace had told Hunter about appearing in front of camera, he had seen how nervous she was and had reassured her, saying she would be fine — it was all good experience for a future promotion board. But as they parted, he could tell his words hadn't allayed her fears.

Before leaving work, he'd asked Mike and Tony to make a start on the vehicle owner checks; the information from Kerri-Ann Bairstow had given the enquiry fresh impetus. Not only had she provided them with a partial index number of a Volkswagen Golf, but from further questioning, they had gleaned the white van was a Renault Kangoo, and Kerri-Ann felt confident it was a 53 plate — registered in 2003.

It was a real boost and the investigative machinery had cranked up as a result. The HOLMES team had submitted the Golf's partial registration number to the DVLA for a search. At the same time they had extracted the names of all the local owners of Renault vans and tracking them down was the fresh focus of the MIT teams.

Barry Newstead had been given new CCTV work — to scrutinise town centre footage, especially around the bus station, and also identify and flag up any white vans seen around the country park, including searching through stills obtained from speed site cameras.

The enquiry was slowly, but surely, gathering pace.

Hunter was meeting Zita in a coffee shop tucked away inside a ladies' high-end fashion shop on the High Street. When Zita had invited him, he'd had to double-check the address. He'd passed the shop many times over the years — in fact, it was one of Grace's frequent shopping haunts — but never realised it had a cafe. He was even more surprised as he ambled past the racks of ladies' clothes to the back of the shop and found a bright and airy bistro-style cafe, furnished in a contemporary style. The original artwork adorning the walls brought him to a standstill for a moment as he browsed.

Zita was waiting for him at a table in a corner of the room. She was wearing a white cotton shirt tucked into a pair of jeans and her shoulder-length flaxen hair was tied back, accentuating her high cheekbones.

Hunter pulled back a chair, slipped off his jacket, hung it over the back and seated himself opposite.

'I've ordered a pot of tea for us. It is tea you drink, isn't it?' Zita flashed him a welcoming smile. 'I told them I was waiting for someone and to serve it when you come in. Is that okay? You said on the phone you could only spare an hour.'

'Yeah, thanks, Zita, that's fine.' As Hunter made himself comfortable, he told her about his visit to the forensic lab and his reason for going.

'Oh, wow, that's cool. You will let me have an early look at the results, won't you?'

'I'll be getting some photos done of it so I'll get one of those across to you as soon as they land on my desk.'

'I appreciate that. Anyway, how are things with you?'

Hunter was just about to reply when a shadow fell across the table. A young girl dressed in black was sidling towards them, carrying a tray of cups and the pot of tea Zita had ordered. He waited as she set it down, acknowledging her with a smile before she returned to the kitchen. He picked up a cup and locked on to Zita's hazel eyes. A hint of peacock blue mascara lined them, highlighting their colour.

'When you say, how are things with you? I'm guessing you don't really mean in my personal life. You really want to know how the investigation is going, don't you?'

Zita held up her hands in mock surrender. 'There's no flies on you, Hunter Kerr. I guess that's why you're a detective.' She flashed another bright smile. 'Are there any new leads?'

'We have one lead, Zita, but it's in the very early stages. In fact, the team are following it up this morning. If it comes to anything, you know I'll give you a call.'

Zita turned her attention to the teapot, lifted the lid, glanced inside and then picked up a spoon and began stirring the contents.

'Will it lead to the killer?'

'I honestly don't know. We only came across the information two days ago and as I say the team are out there following it up.'

'Is there nothing you can give me for our next edition?'

Hunter pursed his lips. 'We still have no idea who the victim is. We don't even know where or when she was killed. All we know is that whoever killed her wrapped her up in a rug and dumped her in the lake. We're obviously going through the routine stuff to try to identify her, but locally there's no report of anyone missing who matches her description, so we don't even know if she's a local or not.'

'Nothing to identify her then?'

Hunter shook his head. 'Nothing. I'm hoping the facial reconstruction will do that. And as I've said, once I get some photos done you are first on my list to get a copy.'

Zita replaced the lid on the teapot and poured some tea into Hunter's cup. 'Well, I might be able to help you out in return.' She filled her own cup.

'You mean identify her?'

'Maybe. When I got the info regarding the murder, especially that the victim was Asian, I made a few phone calls to some of my contacts. One of those contacts is a woman who runs an Asian women's refuge across in Sheffield. I've done a few stories in the past about domestic violence and this lady provided me a couple of horror stories which affected Asian women. Anyway, she told me that recently a couple of young girls had approached the refuge for support and one in particular had made arrangements to stay there but failed to turn up and had not contacted her since. She told me she had tried the girl's mobile several times but it was always switched off.'

Zita took a sip of her tea and Hunter fixed her gaze.

'It may be nothing, Hunter, but it's obviously concerned the woman who runs the refuge enough for her to mention it to me.'

'And it's certainly enough for me to raise an enquiry and check it out. Can you give me her details?'

'I need to hold on that, Hunter. I haven't told the woman I was going to have this conversation and I don't want to betray her trust. I'll need to get back to her and fix up something for you. I'm sure she'll be all right because she does deal a lot with the police, but just to make sure, if you know what I mean.'

'No problem, Zita. It's good of you to tell me. And anyway, if it comes up trumps you can splash across the headlines how the *Chronicle* helped with the murder enquiry.'

Zita gave him another smile.

It took Hunter slightly over an hour to drive to the Forensic Lab at Wetherby. As he slowed for the gate, he pondered upon how long it was since his last visit. *It must be at least 10 years*, he thought, as he approached the main gate. He had been a young detective, given the task of safely delivering evidence — now civilian drivers delivered the exhibits.

He flashed his warrant card to the uniformed gate guard and answered a few security questions before being pointed towards the visitors' car park. Strolling towards the laboratory, he could see that with the exception of the increased protection since his last visit, very little of the physical structure had changed. The building was a 1960s design — flat-fronted concrete and glass — though up-to-date colourful signage did its best to break up the grey drabness.

The reception area was remarkably light and airy and he checked in with the receptionist, telling her that he was expected.

Hunter had only just taken a seat when Frankie Oliver — he saw her name badge — breezed into reception. She thrust out a hand and greeted him with a beaming smile, displaying a set of perfect white teeth — so white in fact that Hunter wondered if they had been cosmetically bleached.

Frankie was slim and petite just like her aunt, Professor Lizzie McCormack. Hunter guessed she was in her late twenties and he could see that she had been blessed with a faultless complexion and pretty features. A hint of mascara framed soft blue/grey eyes. What made her stand out though was her hair — short and chopped and dyed jet black with hints of burnt copper.

As she led him to her lab, Hunter explained the dual purpose of his visit — his fascination to learn the process, but more importantly, to see the artistic representation.

'A detective with a soft side, eh?' Frankie commented as she swiped her security card. 'That's unusual, and refreshing. At least for once I'll know my work will be appreciated.' She opened the door and held it for him to pass through. He caught a whiff of her perfume, a hint of flowers, subtle, expensive.

As she led the way to her work-station, Hunter saw half a dozen other white-coated technicians beavering away in the lab. From her station, Frankie pointed at a tall white plinth a few metres away. On it was a grey half-executed bust, with all the appearance of a head but without fully formed features. Plastic teeth and prosthetic glassy eyes were set but not covered, giving it a surreal effect.

'I'm afraid I haven't finished it yet, but I can take you through what I've done so far,' Frankie said, slapping a hand over the lumpy cranium.

Hunter was studying the craftsmanship that had gone into the project. 'Give me the full works. I'll let you know if you're boring me.'

She laughed, displaying those perfect white teeth again. 'Don't beat about the bush, will you! Okay, pin back your lugholes and if there's anything you don't understand, stop me. I must warn you that once I'm in full-flow I take some holding back.' She moved closer to her sculpture. 'Firstly, I did a cast of the girl's skull. My aunt helped me with that. In the past, I have worked with clean skulls from skeletons dug up, but in your case the body was intact, despite its state. Anyway, I digress.'

She pinched some of the clay away from the head and worked it into a lump. 'We use an oil-based clay.' She thumbed it back onto the bust. 'Sticks easily to the cast and can be manipulated for longer. First, plastic pegs are inserted at specific anatomical sites around the skull to indicate the level of tissue required. Those enable me to begin the muscular build up with the clay — like I have done here.'

She stroked an index finger around contour lines of the face. 'Big muscles which form the sides of the face onto the jaw, around the eyes,' she continued, stroking the clay form to make her point. 'Once the muscle structure is in place, I can think about the thin fatty layer which lies on the surface — the connective tissue as it is called. A lot of formation was already there on your body, even though it was bloated and disfigured. For instance, creases and folds from the underlying muscle structure, especially the mouth and shape of the nose, were in place. The nose is generally one of the most difficult facial features to reconstruct because the underlying bone is limited. However, because the girl's face is almost intact this model should be exact.'

As she was talking Hunter through her handiwork, Frankie was smoothing dainty, slim fingers around the clay head. She picked up a cloth from a tabletop and wiped some oily deposit from her hands. 'Another couple of days and I'll have the face finished. Then it'll undergo a paint job. I can match the skin tone exactly from the body colour. Finally, I'll add a similar style and colour hairpiece and you should have a vision of your victim. It won't be an exact portrait but the main features will all be there to enable you to have as near a match as possible for identification purposes.'

Hunter thanked her. This is what he had been waiting for. Having a name for the victim always gave an enquiry an extra dimension — family, friends, associates and a background — which provided a wealth of additional information to point them in the direction of the suspect or suspects. He couldn't wait to see Frankie's completed work.

DAY TWELVE

'Okay, what have we got?' DCI Dawn Leggate asked, pushing open the door to the CID office, fighting with her waterproof jacket as she wrestled to free an arm from its sleeve. Every member of her team was hard at work at their desks. They looked up as she entered.

'I wouldn't take your coat off yet, boss,' said Detective Sergeant John Reed, rising from his seat. He snatched his coat from the back of his chair and picked up a file from a mountain of paperwork strewn across his desk. 'We've got a meeting with Glasgow A Division CID,' he continued. 'I said we'd join them —' he glanced at his wristwatch — 'ten minutes ago.' He skipped past her and held the door while pointing down the corridor, urging her to hurry up.

Dawn fought to slot her arm back into her waterproof as she dodged past the DS.

He handed over the folder he was holding. 'That's the file for the job. I'll fill you in on the way.'

In the rear yard of the station John Reed started the engine of the CID car and waited for the screen to de-mist. Dawn shot him a sideways glance as he combed his fingers through his dark, wavy, collar length hair.

'You're going to love this job, Dawn,' he said as he drove out of the yard, leaning across and tapping the paperwork spread open on her lap. 'Traffic spotted a silver BMW in the early hours of this morning cruising around one of the Easterhouse estates. The car's registration number pinged up on their ANPR.'

John was referring to the Traffic car's on-board computerised Automatic Number Plate Recognition system linked to the National Vehicle Centre.

'There were three recorded hits for various parts of the registered number. Firstly, a hit-and-run in North Yorkshire, secondly, it was clocked driving away from the scene of a murder on Sauchiehall Street, and finally, as you know from our enquiry in Killin, a silver BMW was spotted by a local walking her dog, who was suspicious about its activities around the village. Anyway, traffic had a hell of a blues-and-twos chase last night, but they finally caught it when it crashed into a lamp post.' He tapped the paperwork again. 'It was two-up. Unfortunately, the little bastards didn't get hurt — not even a scratch, would you believe?' John gave a wry smile before returning his gaze to the road in front. 'And look at the intel sheet of the two they arrested.'

Dawn licked a forefinger and turned several pages until she found the section she was looking for. She started to read the typed sheet following the route of her shaking finger because of the erratic motion of the car. John was trying to make up for lost time, but she wished he would just slow down a fraction; she was being bounced around uncomfortably in her seat.

'Driver was Sandie Aitkinson and front seat passenger was Bruce McColl. Both are well known and have form for burglary and car crime and a bit of anti-social behaviour, but none for violence. It turns out the car is on cloned plates. We visited the address of the registered keeper according to the number plates on it and they still have their own silver BMW on the drive. Anyway, after Traffic checked out the chassis and engine number, they discovered that it belongs to someone living at an address in Bellshill. We asked uniform to do a visit there for us early this morning and they've found the house broken into and the guy who lived there battered to death.'

Dawn gave a low whistle.

'Told you you'd love it.'

'Are the two prisoners saying anything?'

'No one's interviewed them yet. We're letting them stew in their cells.'

'Do we know any of the victims of the other two jobs — any links to our case at Killin?'

'The names are somewhere in the file, I can't remember them off-hand. North Yorkshire faxed us a copy of the statements from the man and woman who were rammed off the road. They're from Yorkshire.'

Dawn began to search the folder.

'The murder on Sauchiehall Street happened just over a week ago. And get this, it's another retired cop — worked out of Shettlestone nick many years ago.'

'Just like Ross McNab?'

'Exactly.'

Dawn pursed her lips and gave a low whistle. 'Did they work together?'

'Don't know much about the Sauchiehall Street murder at all, other than he was found dumped near a subway and had been given a real good hiding. His face apparently was barely recognisable — IDed from his NARPO card. That's why I've fixed up our meet with CID from Stuart Street nick. They are dealing with the job and they're now at the scene of this latest killing in Bellshill. It's a DI McBride we're liaising with there.'

Dawn knew that name and was trying to put a face to it. She continued picking through the file and found faxed copies of the witness statements of the hit and run in North Yorkshire. One of the witnesses was a DS in South Yorkshire — Hunter Kerr.

A Yorkshire man with a Scottish surname.

Then the alarm bells started ringing in her head. Kerr — she had heard that name recently.

Now, where was it? Then the light switched on. It was the guy on the phone at the McNabs' bungalow. He was a Kerr — Jock Kerr. She recalled him telling her that before he hung up.

She flicked through the faxed statements. And there it was, the driver injured when his car was rammed off the road by the silver BMW. He was also called Jock Kerr. 'This is just too much of a coincidence,' she muttered.

Through the windscreen she saw the sign for Bellshill and closed the file.

They entered the old part of the town, driving past row upon row of high-rise old pink sandstone tenements, now refurbished. Within five minutes they were turning into a newer estate. The road was cordoned off and they had to leave the car at the junction because of abandoned police vehicles blocking their way. After locking up, they headed for the blue and white tape strewn across the street.

The first people they came across were press photographers, but they pushed their way through to the PC guarding the scene. Dawn and John flashed their warrant badges and she asked for DI McBride. They were pointed towards a tall, slim man, with thinning wavy hair, who had his back to them watching the forensic team erect a blue tarpaulin around the front door of a pair of modern semis.

Dawn called his name as she got closer. The detective spun around. She recognised him; they had been on the same hostage negotiator's course.

He flashed a smile and held out a hand for her to shake.

She took it and introduced her DS.

'You know the reason why we're here, don't you, Alex?' She recollected his first name.

'Aye, your DS told me over the phone. You've trapped up two who were caught in this victim's car. It was on false plates, I'm told.'

'Aye,' replied Dawn. 'And we've linked the car to a murder we're dealing with in Killin five days ago. A retired cop and his wife tortured and then set on fire. A local saw the BMW driving around the village several times on the day of the murders, thought it was suspicious so she noted down its number.'

'So I heard. And the same car could be linked to a murder just off Sauchiehall Street. We've got CCTV evidence of a silver BMW driving away, close to the scene around the time. We're currently enhancing the images to see if we can identify the driver. My team are dealing with that. I suppose you've heard that the victim was also a retired cop?'

'Aye.'

'Well, this latest killing is going to grab you as well. I've just been told he's a retired DS who also used to work out of Shettlestone CID. He retired back in 1994. Whoever killed him has left him in a right old mess. I've not been inside yet. Forensics are setting up things so we can walk around the scene.'

Three retired detectives murdered, and all from the same station.

DAY THIRTEEN

In the busy lounge of the George and Dragon, Hunter nursed the last of his beer and stared into space. His mind was elsewhere — revisiting the images he had seen several times that morning.

The bound book of colour photographs had been waiting on his desk for him and he had viewed them the minute he had got in. He was impressed with Frankie Oliver's work, especially the life-like features she had managed to form on the reconstructed skull of their victim.

The photos had been revealed to the team during the Detective Superintendent's morning's briefing and were going out on the local news broadcast later that evening.

The announcement had caught Hunter by surprise and he had shot out straight after the briefing to get a set over to Zita at the *Chronicle*. The last thing he wanted was for her to see them on the TV when she hadn't got her own copies as he had promised.

Hunter wondered if Grace would be on tonight's local news. He remembered their conversation three days previously, how nervous she had been about being with the boss for the press conference. He hadn't spoken with her since. He'd been so wrapped up in things that he had forgotten to ask her how it had gone.

'Penny for them, Hunter.' Grace sidled up next to him.

'Crikey, you made me jump! I was just thinking about you and your fifteen minutes of fame.' He pointed to a wall-mounted TV playing without sound. The national news was on. 'Are we going to see your bright, cherubic features this evening?'

She dug his arm. 'Hey! Less of the cherubic. That means fat, doesn't it?' She took a drink of her wine. 'After spending all morning tramping round the country park the other day, I didn't even get a look-in with any of the TV crews. All they wanted was Mister Robshaw. It was a waste of bloody time. And I'd got myself all done up for it as well.'

Hunter smiled. He knew what Grace was like for her make-up and fashion, even on a normal working day. She would have spent hours the night before sorting out a suitable wardrobe for her TV debut, and here she was telling him she didn't get a look-in.

'That's because to the press you're a lowly detective, while he's an interesting, high ranking Detective Superintendent who's running a murder enquiry.'

'Are you saying I'm uninteresting?' Grace dug Hunter again. 'It's us who does the leg work and solves the crime.'

'Ha, but that's not what the public think.' Hunter drained his beer and thrust out the empty glass. 'Fancy another?'

Grace swilled the remnants of the Chardonnay around the bottom of her glass before swallowing the last mouthful. 'Just get me a Coke. I'll have that then make tracks home, I daren't be late this evening. I promised the girls I'd take them out for a bite to eat. And I need to catch up with Dave. Things have not been easy over the past couple of weeks.'

'Know that feeling. The job just gets a hold of you, doesn't it? I sometimes wonder why Beth puts up with me.'

'Must be those rugged good looks!'

'Flattery will get you everywhere,' Hunter said, taking her empty wine glass. 'One more won't do you any harm.'

'Oh, go on then, you've twisted my arm. Then I definitely must go.'

Hunter yawed his way to the bar. The MIT team had taken over half of the lounge. They had left work early to have a couple of swift drinks and to watch their SIO's appeal on the local news broadcast before they all headed home.

Hunter squeezed between a small group of regulars congregated at the bar and caught the eye of one of the staff. He ordered a pint of Timothy Taylor and a glass of Chardonnay. As he ferreted around in his pocket for money, a loud cheer and several wolf-whistles went up behind him. He spun round to see a sea of detectives' faces all fixed on the television.

Someone shouted to turn it up and Hunter began to decipher the sound. The shot was zooming in on their Senior Investigating Officer, Detective Superintendent Michael Robshaw, and the announcer said they were speaking from the lakeside at Barnwell Country Park. The newscaster was dubbing the storyline 'The Lady in the Lake'.

Michael Robshaw was commenting on the status of the enquiry, and as he began to make his plea for witnesses the scene panned out and was replaced by the stills of the reconstructed face of their victim. Blown up and backlit, the result looked spectacular.

Someone just has to recognise this woman, Hunter thought.

DAY FOURTEEN

Hunter didn't hear Grace approaching, his thoughts were elsewhere and he jumped as she slapped a fresh sheet of paper on top of the small pile of vehicle enquiry forms he was scrutinising. The paperwork had been left on his desk from the previous day's tasks and he was checking if all the outstanding enquiries had been completed before he handed them over.

'Come on. Get your lazy butt in gear, we've got a prime witness to interview.' Grace stabbed at the pink form she had deposited across his papers. As Hunter started to read, she snatched it up. 'Isobel from the HOLMES team has just handed this to me. She said it's the breakthrough we've been after.'

Hunter tried to grab back the paper Grace was waving but she spun quickly away, snatching her jacket from the back of her seat. She fixed him a look. 'What are you waiting for?'

Hunter picked up his coat and wrestled the car keys out from a pocket before following Grace out of the office.

'Are you going to tell me what we've got then?' Hunter asked as he swung the CID car out through the gates of the station's rear yard. 'All you've said so far is drive to the hospital.'

Grace pulled down the passenger visor and checked her make-up. She smoothed a hand across her nose and cheek before turning to Hunter. 'We're off to see a junior doctor, name of —' she took a quick glance at the paperwork — 'Chris Chambers. He works on Medical Ward Three at the General. Isobel says he rang in last night after the news and he's certain he knows who our victim is.'

Taking the back roads through the woods, Hunter was able to push the car faster than the speed limit because there was no traffic, so he made the hospital in just over quarter of an hour. He parked the car in one of the mortuary visiting bays, took the POLICE VISITING card from out of the glove box, slid it on top of the dash and then he and Grace took a rear entrance to the lifts. They knew the hospital layout like the backs of their hands.

'Ward Three you say?' said Hunter, pressing the lift button.

Grace double-checked the document and nodded.

They rode the lift in silence. It squealed and juddered up the two floors before opening up to a directional sign for the ward they wanted. They followed colour-coded tramlines along the corridor, taking a sharp left when the yellow line peeled off from the red.

Medical Ward Three lay behind a set of closed doors, behind which Hunter could hear a commotion and he wondered what was happening. After dispensing a large dollop of antiseptic handwash, he opened the doors with his shoulder as he cleansed his hands. He entered a world of chaos, bustle and raised voices and it stopped him in his tracks. Everything seemed to be happening behind a screen around one of the beds.

He exchanged looks with Grace and shrugged, before branching away to the nurse's station. That was busy too.

After a few seconds, Hunter caught the attention of an auburn haired, plump woman, dressed in dark blue. Her name badge identified her as the ward sister. He flashed his warrant card. 'I bet the last people you want to see right now is us?' he said, nodding towards the commotion.

The sister sighed. 'They brought in a twenty-two-year-old girl in the middle of the night, suffered a stroke just after she'd had a baby. Looks like we've just lost her.'

Hunter gave a sympathetic look as he returned his ID to his wallet. 'We contacted the hospital this morning. We were told a Dr Chambers would be on duty.'

'That's right. He's behind the screen.'

Hunter and Grace took another look down the ward.

'We need to speak with him, I'm afraid,' said Grace, returning her attention to the ward sister. 'We can disappear for half an hour for a coffee and then come back.'

'Is it urgent?'

'Could be. He contacted us last night.'

'Okay, just give him twenty minutes. It looks as though we can't do anything else for her anyway. They've been working on her for over ten minutes now, he'll be calling time soon and should be out in a bit.' Her response to the young girl's death seemed matter-of-fact, devoid of any feeling. Hunter guessed her job was very much like his — in times of crisis you remove the emotion in order to cope.

They had just taken a seat in the sister's vacant office when Dr Chambers tracked them down. Dressed in a light blue, open necked shirt tucked into a pair of jeans, he looked very young. In fact, if it hadn't been for his nametag and the stethoscope draped around his neck Hunter would never have guessed he was a doctor. He remembered Grace mentioning he was a junior but this guy didn't even look like he'd started shaving yet.

The doctor shook their hands and dropped into a seat, beckoning them to two seats next to a filing cabinet.

'We'll try not to take up too much of your time, we can see how busy you are,' opened Grace.

'A bit like your job, eh? No rest for the wicked.' The doctor ruffled his fingers through his light brown hair, leaned back in his seat and crossed his legs. 'Is this about my phone call last night?'

'You left a message that you think you know who the victim is?' Grace passed across one of the colour photographs of the facial reconstruction.

The doctor accepted it and took a long, lingering look, then nodded. 'The guy on TV said this is the girl found at the bottom of Barnwell lake, right?' He sounded nervous.

'Yes, a couple of weeks ago. She was murdered and dumped there.'

'Shocking. Truly shocking.' He shook his head.

'Do you recognise her?'

'Well, it certainly resembles a girl I used to go out with. Samia. But I can't believe it, she's such a lovely girl — or was, if it's her.'

'Samia?'

'Yes, Samia Hassan. She lives, or rather she used to live, with her parents in Hoyland before we went out together.'

'Are you certain? That photo is just a facial reconstruction. She was in a bit of a mess because of how long she'd been in the water,' said Hunter.

'It definitely looks like Samia. Has anyone else phoned in — her family, or maybe her friends?'

'You're the first.' Hunter paused, gathering his thoughts. 'You said you used to go out with her?'

'We were at Sheffield Uni together. I was doing my last year when she came. A group of us hooked up with her and her mates on rag week. That's how we met.'

'When was this?'

'Year before I started my doctor's training — 2006.'

'Do you know how old she was then?'

The doctor thought for a moment. 'I'm 23 now so I would have been 21 back then,' he appeared to be talking to himself. 'She would have been 18 or 19.' He paused and then said. 'We went out for a short time. Well, until we had all that bother.'

Hunter glanced at Grace.

'Bother?' said Hunter.

'Yeah from her cousins. As I say, we met on rag week. We got chatting. She was doing her first-year medicine and she wanted to know what to expect. We just hit it off, you know. After that she'd come round to my place from time to time to borrow some notes and chat through stuff. After a couple of months, I asked her to go out for a meal and she agreed. I was in student accommodation and she was in halls of residence and she started staying at mine on a regular basis. Sometimes even at weekends when she should have gone home. That's when the trouble started.'

'What trouble?'

'Let me just give you some background. Samia's parents are Pakistani but she was English. She told me they owned a shop in Hoyland and lived in the flat upstairs. She had her heart set on being a doctor but they continually badgered her to go to Pakistan for an arranged marriage to her cousin. Apparently, the only way they allowed her to come to university was because she promised she would go to Pakistan to meet the cousin during the summer break. She was dreading it because she had never been to Pakistan in her life and didn't want to marry any cousin. She'd seen a photograph of him and he was a lot older than her — in his thirties, I think she said — and she didn't know him or fancy him. I heard her a few times on her mobile having a row with her father about wanting the freedom to choose who she wanted to marry.'

'What about the trouble?'

'That was about a year ago. I had just finished uni and started my medical training. I got a newer flat and she moved in with me. She didn't tell her parents because she knew it would cause problems, though she had told them she was seeing me. They had another blazing row. They were threatening to disown her and said she was bringing shame on the family and should marry the cousin in Pakistan. I know it upset her a great deal. She tried to speak with her mother a few times but her mother would hang up.

'Then one night we had just come out of this bar and this car pulls up. Two Asian guys get out and just set about me, gave me a right hiding. They tried to drag Samia into the car, but there were quite a few people about that we knew, thank God, and they intervened and phoned the police. The two guys took off before the cops arrived. Samia told me they were relatives, she'd seen them before at her house. She didn't like them. She said one of them had been in trouble with the police. I was going to make a complaint but she persuaded me not and said she'd sort it. She guessed it was because her parents had found out about us sharing a flat.'

'So, you never made a complaint?'

'I wanted to. My face was in a right mess. I couldn't work for a couple of days and I got a rollicking from my consultant for turning up to work all bruised. Said I didn't set the right image for a doctor.'

'Was that the end of it?'

'Christ, no. There was a couple more. One night we came home and the flat was trashed, and I mean trashed. Everything was in pieces and they had cut up all of Samia's clothes.'

'Did you report that?'

'I did that time. I had to, for the insurance. We told the police about Samia's relatives, but there were no witnesses, and they didn't find any evidence to connect them, so that was that. The final straw came when I was on lates one day. I finished my shift just before midnight and I was walking across the hospital car park when the same two guys grabbed me. They'd wrecked my car. One of them got me by the throat and told me in no uncertain terms I had to finish with Samia or I'd end up at the bottom of a lake. Those were his exact words.'

DCI Dawn Leggate's alarm woke her at 6.30 a.m. and despite having only had five and a half hours sleep, it had been undisturbed and she felt remarkably refreshed. As she brushed her teeth, she could already feel a buzz as she thought about her day. She always felt like this when a big investigation was running.

She made herself coffee, put bread from the freezer into the toaster and dialled Alex McBride's mobile.

From his voice she could tell she'd woken him and she apologised when he said it had been 2 a.m. before he'd finally got to bed. She offered to ring him later, but he responded by telling her he needed to be up to brief his team.

'I've got an early briefing as well, and I just wondered if you had any update from things your end?'

He brought her up to date on the Bellshill murder and told her he was sending over two detectives from his team to join her briefing.

Entering the office, Dawn saw several new boards had been set up. The Glasgow city centre and Bellshill murders had a board each, abutted onto the Killin enquiry. Already, the important components of the investigation were on there. Looking them over, she rubbed her hands. The compilation, which included the three victims' names, addresses, witnesses, timelines and photographs, now took over the entire frontage of the room.

She checked the three timelines — the handwriting was wonderfully neat, a rarity among police officers. Also attached were copies of the gruesome Scenes of Crime shots, plus crime scene locations and maps of each of the surrounding areas. Her eyes moved from log to log. Everything was here. Thorough updates on those charts kept them all in touch with the case. The information they contained invariably pointed them in the direction of the perpetrator. Dawn made a mental note to find out who'd made the effort and congratulate them.

She double-checked the contents and recollected the notes she had made during her phone call with DI McBride, the morning's briefing was going to be intense.

She opened her journal, picked up a dry-erase pen and added a couple more notes to the boards, doing her best to replicate the script. Stepping back for one final look, she saw that the link to each case was the stolen silver BMW, presently with forensics.

Ten minutes later, standing in front of the incident boards, Dawn waited for her team to finally settle down. She could tell they were fired up. It had been a long time since they had been involved in a major joint investigation and the fact that each of the victims had been one of their own would make them even more determined to catch the culprit.

She banged a hand on the nearest board. 'Guys, we've got a busy day ahead of us, lots of work to do, so give me your eyes and ears for the next half hour.' Then, pointing to the furthermost panel, she continued, 'Firstly, our own Killin enquiry. Ross McNab, aged sixty-four, and his wife, sixty-three, were murdered on the afternoon of the thirty-first of August, at their isolated bungalow. As you know they were both beaten and Ross was tortured prior to his death. Everything about that scene indicates that more than one person was involved in their deaths.

'A sharp instrument, most probably a knife, was used to remove three fingers from Ross's right hand and those have not been found. It looks as though the killers took them from the scene and then left behind a box of fish fingers with a handwritten note which stated —' she paused and glanced at a photograph of the message recovered next to Ross McNab's body — '"These are to replace the missing ones." Before the killers left, they set fire to Mrs McNab using an accelerant. The PM indicates that she was still alive when they lit her.'

Dawn paused for maximum effect. She scanned the detectives' faces again. 'A woman walking her dog in nearby fields spotted smoke coming from the bungalow and called the fire brigade. The same woman also spotted a silver BMW driving along a track close to the scene. She had seen this car earlier driving around the village and thankfully had noted its number because she thought it was acting suspiciously. The resulting fire has damaged forensics but we might be lucky with the note and box of fish fingers. As you all know Ross was a retired detective. He retired thirteen years ago in 1995.'

Dawn took a side-step. 'Okay, moving on.' She stabbed a finger below one of the scenes of crime photos depicting a battered face, barely recognisable as a man's. 'Alistair McPherson, sixty-one years, another retired cop, was found beaten to death near a subway close to Sauchiehall Street, at 7.50 p.m., on the 27th of August. We have him on CCTV coming out of Lauders bar on that street ten minutes prior to his body being discovered. A very small time-frame.

'CCTV also picked up several sightings of our silver BMW driving in and around Sauchiehall Street before and after the attack. The images have been enhanced but both the driver and passenger had their visors down and so there are no clear images of their faces. What we can distinguish, however, is that it is not the two young men we have trapped in the cells.'

Dawn moved back from the second board. 'Finally —' she slapped her hand over several photographs taken from different angles, of an elderly man slumped in a carver type chair — 'Donald Wilson, a retired DS, 69 years old. His body was discovered two days ago in the lounge of his home at Bellshill. His hands had been nail-gunned to the arms of his chair and there was an iron burn mark in the centre of his chest. His throat had also been cut. The pathologist has indicated he was killed approximately two weeks ago. The body had early stages of decomposition. The silver BMW on false plates, which we have recovered, belonged to him.'

Dawn studied the faces of her team — they were focused. 'There are two links to all these three killings, firstly the BMW owned by Donald Wilson, which was stolen from outside his house and which has been sighted around the locations of the other two murders. The two young men, Sandie Aitkinson and Bruce McColl, who were caught driving it, have form but it's petty stuff and one of them has a cast-iron alibi for the Killin murder. They are sticking to their story, that they found it parked up with the keys on the front passenger seat and we can't knock that. By the end of play this afternoon the Procurator Fiscal has indicated we should bail them.'

Dawn was in full flow now. 'There is another incident involving the BMW but I don't know if that is linked yet or not. On the 24th of August, three days before the murder of Alistair McPherson, it was involved in a hit and run in North Yorkshire. The driver and his wife were injured in that accident and we have discovered from statements that they have Scottish surnames.'

Dawn hadn't told the team about her telephone conversation with the man who had called himself Jock Kerr. That was one enquiry she and her sergeant were going to follow up personally. 'Coincidence or not, we will be looking into that as one of the actions. The other link, as you all now realise, is that they are all retired detectives who at one time worked out of Shettlestone CID. The key tasks which are being pushed out from this briefing are related to that. I want to know the relationship, working or otherwise, that these three had and what jobs they worked on together. There are checks to be done with Personnel and the Retired Police Officers' Association. I want everyone traced who knew these three. I am convinced our answer lies in their past associations. I want the evil bastards who did this trapped up as soon as possible.'

DAY FIFTEEN

Hunter left the station locker room after a shower and change of clothing. He rolled his neck and flexed his trapezius. He felt tight but sharp after an intense training session and three-mile run into work.

He'd risen a good hour earlier than normal, promising Beth before he left that he'd get a flyer and take the boys to their football coaching session that evening. Then he headed to his dad's boxing gym where he'd let himself in and trained alone. He'd spent twenty minutes working the punch-bag, twenty minutes pushing weights, and ten minutes doing sit-ups before locking up and running into work.

As he passed the Detective Superintendent's open door, he saw his boss at his desk.

'Morning, boss,' Hunter greeted him as he passed.

He had only gone a few yards when Michael Robshaw called out, 'Hunter, have you got five minutes?'

'Sure.' He stepped into the tidy office and stood by the desk. The Detective Superintendent was writing a memo on the front of a CPS file. Behind him, warm light cascaded through a huge window, backlighting the SIO. His reflection bounced off the surface of his polished desk. Hunter glanced around the room. It was plush and organised — just what he'd like to aspire to, he thought.

Robshaw signed off his paperwork with a flourish, clicked the top onto his fountain pen and laid it square across his jotter. He slipped off his spectacles and lined them straight, alongside his pen. Raising his head, he regarded Hunter seriously. 'I've had a complaint about you.'

Hunter looked puzzled. 'A complaint about me! What am I supposed to have done now?'

'David Paynton ring any bells?'

Hunter took a long, hard look at his boss. The last thing he wanted was to give him any bullshit. He'd known the Superintendent far too long, and trusted and respected him too much to pass off an answer which would be an insult to his intelligence. When Hunter was a fledgling detective constable, Michael Robshaw had been his DI. Robshaw had achieved his current status because of his ability to juggle the management of many successful teams as well as handle the politics which came with his rank. Hunter also knew him personally — they had trained together at his dad's gym and they had run together many times during lunch-breaks.

He settled for, 'What's he said I've done?'

The Detective Superintendent interlinked his fingers. 'Apparently, you and one other, and I'm guessing from the description that the one other was Barry, waylaid him in the pub a few nights ago and gave him the third degree about your father's hit and run. Says you were trying to fit him up with it.'

'Just a minute, boss, I never...'

Unlocking his fingers, Robshaw held up a hand. 'I'm not going to quiz you on what you did or didn't say to David Paynton. I'm here to tell you to lay off him. He's flagged as part of an ongoing drug squad operation. He's giving them a couple of major players knocking out cocaine, so they want him around. Besides, I can tell you he definitely wasn't involved. I got a call from North Yorks police late yesterday afternoon. It would appear the silver BMW involved in your parents' road accident has been found in Scotland on false plates and two young thieves are locked up for aggravated vehicle taking. I suggest you give them a call.'

Robshaw handed over a post-it with a telephone number. 'That's the officer in North Yorkshire who's dealing with the incident.' He leaned back in his chair. 'Hunter, you're a great cop, don't put your career in jeopardy for that little shit, and besides you've still got an unsolved murder here to focus on.'

The morning briefing focused on Hunter and Grace's meeting with junior doctor, Chris Chambers.

Perched on the corner of his desk, nursing his second cup of tea, Hunter repeated, almost word for word, what Dr Chambers had said. In addition, the doctor had given them the names of some of Samia's close friends from university who would need chasing up. And the doctor had also made time to do a composite e-fit of the two Asian men who had beaten and threatened him.

Printed copies of the computer-generated images, together with a note stapled to them — stating that the doctor had confirmed they were good likenesses — had been waiting on his desk that morning. Hunter handed them around as he briefed, but he could tell that no one recognised the pair.

Overnight, the HOLMES team had done background checks on the address of Samia's parents. There were three incidents logged — all 999 calls requesting police attendance for detained shoplifters. A voter's check listed Samia Hassan at that address, along with her father, Mohammed, and mother, Jilani. There was no record of her being reported missing.

'We don't know what we are walking into today,' Hunter concluded. 'The doc is convinced our body from the lake is his ex, Samia Hassan, but no one else has called us about her being missing, including her parents, so we don't know what kind of reception we're going to get when we visit. Grace and I will do a softly-softly approach and check out if she is still living there, or if not, if they have heard from her recently. We'll meet back after lunch for a scrum-down once we've done the visit.'

Hassan's convenience store was nestled between a hairdresser's and a small post office on one of the arterial roads leading into the small town of Hoyland. It had only taken Hunter and Grace ten minutes to drive there.

As they entered the brightly-lit store, the first thing that hit Hunter was the pleasant aroma of spicy food.

To their immediate left, a long counter spanned the frontage. An Asian man, who appeared to be in his early fifties, was working behind it. Hunter looked him over. The man was slightly smaller than he was and overweight, a well-rounded stomach strained the bottom buttons of his blue and white striped shirt and sagged over his trousers. Thick black hair skirted the sides of his head, but he was bald on top. His most striking feature was his hooked nose.

Hunter thought of the image of Samia — if this was her father, then she didn't get her looks from him. He surveyed the shop. Most of the brightness came from overhead fluorescent lighting. It was set out like a miniature version of a supermarket, with well-packed shelves of fresh produce, tinned and packet foods. The back shelves were stacked floor to ceiling with wines, beers and spirits, and close to the door newspapers and magazines took up the remainder of the space. There was a large flat-screen TV suspended behind the counter, its screen split into six sections, each showing a different part of the store. The CCTV images were of good clarity for a change, Hunter thought. He made a mental note; they might need that to back-check footage.

'Mr Hassan — Mohammed Hassan?' Grace said.

The man greeted them with a cheery smile, suspicion in his eyes.

'Don't worry, we're not selling anything.' Grace showed her warrant card.

He looked surprised and nodded.

'Mr Hassan, we're just making some enquiries regarding an investigation we have running. We're trying to track down people who we think might be of help and a witness has given us your daughter's name, Samia. Is she around?'

Good start, Grace, thought Hunter, focusing on the man's face. Watching and listening was just as important as talking when it came to interviews, and having a partner who was on the same wavelength was a big advantage.

The man looked down for a second or two, enough for Hunter to realise Grace had hit a nerve.

'Samia? Er no, she's not here.' He stumbled over his words.

'Do you happen to know where she is?'

Hunter became conscious of someone moving at the back of the store. Into view appeared a slim, petite Asian woman, dressed in a peacock blue sari. She ambled towards them and despite being older she bore a remarkable likeness to the photograph of the facial reconstruction. There was no doubt this was Samia's mother. She was talking rapidly in her mother tongue as she approached.

Mr Hassan responded in the same language. The conversation lasted for a good thirty seconds.

Hunter could only pick out the words 'police' and 'Samia'.

Grace said, 'Mr Hassan, could you speak in English please?'

He turned to Grace. 'Sorry about that. My wife doesn't speak any English. I told her you were making enquiries about Samia. She wants to know what type of enquiries you are making?'

'There is no easy way to say this, Mr Hassan, but we are concerned as to her whereabouts.'

Mr Hassan's eyes shifted again and he shared a glance with his wife. Her eyes were wide and searching. There was a slight delay in his response. 'Why are you concerned?'

'Well, we're trying to track her down but we don't know where she is.'

Mrs Hassan started chattering unintelligibly again. Her husband replied, his hands animated.

'Mr Hassan, if you wouldn't mind?' checked Grace.

'Sorry,' he apologised, 'my wife is asking what is going on — why are the police here?'

'Do you know where your daughter is?'

'Of course I do, she is in Pakistan.'

'In Pakistan,' said Hunter. 'Are you sure about that, Mr Hassan?'

'Of course I am. Why are you asking me these questions about my daughter?'

'As my colleague has already said, we have concerns about her whereabouts.'

'Who has said these things? Who is causing us this trouble?'

'No one is causing you any trouble, Mr Hassan. All we are here for is to check on your daughter's whereabouts,' continued Hunter.

'She is in Pakistan.'

'Where in Pakistan?' said Grace.

'She is staying with my family.'

'Where?'

'Look, what is this all about. All you keep telling me is that you have concerns about her. What concerns?'

'That she might have come to some harm.'

'My daughter has not come to any harm. She is with my family.'

Hunter looked from the man to his wife. Something was not right between them but he did not want to damage the enquiry at this early stage. 'Mr Hassan, we're not here to cause you and your wife any anguish, it's just that a close friend of hers has not seen her for a while and has not been able to get hold of her and therefore reported it to us because they thought it was unusual,' he lied. 'Now, if you can just give us a little more information as to where she is, so that we can contact her, it would be a great help.'

After a short delay, Mr Hassan answered. 'You won't be able to get hold of her, it's a small village in the mountains. My family do not have a phone. It is not like it is here in England. They are quite poor. They have to walk miles to the nearest town.'

'What about your daughter, did she not take her mobile?'

After a hesitation, he replied, 'It will not work in the mountains.'

'When did she go to Pakistan?' interrupted Grace. 'And where did she go from?'

'I can't remember the exact date. It was about two months ago. She flew to Lahore from London. I can't remember if it was Gatwick or Heathrow.'

Grace scribbled some notes in her notebook. With a warm fake smile, she said, 'Thank you for that. That's a big help.'

'Mr Hassan, just one final thing before we leave you in peace,' Hunter said. 'It's just a procedural thing, but in all cases where someone reports something like this to us, we have to check physically for ourselves that they haven't come to any harm in their own home. You do understand, don't you? We would be heavily criticised by our bosses if we didn't do that check.'

There was an uneasy silence for the best part of twenty seconds. Mr Hassan glanced down, seemed to be checking his hands, then shot a glance at his wife before turning his attention to Hunter. 'I don't suppose we have any choice.'

'It's not a matter of choice, it would just help us with our enquiries. We'd be able to report back to our bosses that we're okay with everything.' Hunter dished out his own fake smile.

Mr Hassan spoke to his wife in their language, to which she responded with a loud huff and made an exaggerated gesture of throwing part of her sari back over her shoulder before turning and making for the back of the shop.

'My wife is not happy with this interference. We are very private people. We have not done anything wrong.'

'We're not accusing you of anything, it's just a formality we have to go through,' Hunter replied. 'If you can just show us Samia's room, then we'll leave you.'

Mr Hassan locked up the shop, turned the sign to 'closed' and pointed them through to the rear.

The entranceway at the back led them into a small, dimly lit stairway. It was cooler back here. Beyond, Hunter could see a large breeze-blocked room full of boxed goods, obviously the store room.

Bare wooden stairs led up to a door marked private and beyond it they found themselves in a lavishly carpeted hallway. There were five doors off the hall. A couple were open and Hunter could make out the lounge and what appeared to be a kitchen area. He guessed the other three rooms were the bathroom and two bedrooms.

'This is Samia's old room,' said Mr Hassan, pushing open one of the closed doors.

Hunter and Grace followed him inside. The room looked more like a guest room than someone's bedroom. It was devoid of any personal effects. There had been pictures or photographs hung up at one time, judging by the marks on the wall. The bed had a duvet draped over it, but the duvet cover and bottom sheet had been removed and were neatly folded and lay across the pillows. It looked like it had not been slept in for some time. Against one wall was a bare chest of drawers and next to the window on the back wall was a wardrobe.

Hunter slipped past Mr Hassan and moved towards it. 'Do you mind?' he asked, but didn't wait for an answer.

He looked inside. The wardrobe was empty, except for a few wire coat hangers dangling from a metal rail. Next, he checked the chest of drawers, tugging open the bottom drawer first. Moving up, Hunter slid out the next three drawers, asking background questions of Mr Hassan as he went along — how long had he and his wife owned the business? How long had they been resident in this country? Which region of Pakistan did they come from? What was the name of the village where the family lived and the place and date of Samia's birth? He tried to make the questions sound unimportant, making a mental note of the answers to keep the man at ease.

Pushing all four empty drawers back into place, Hunter straightened and did another scan of the room, gaining a mental picture for his next visit, which he knew would not be too long away. This room is soulless, he thought. Things were definitely not right, but they couldn't move too fast under the circumstances. He had to be patient — make the enquiries first and cover all angles.

'Did your daughter take all her belongings with her? Did she not leave anything behind?'

'My daughter has gone to join my family back in Pakistan. If you want to know, she has gone to marry my cousin out there and make a new life for herself.'

While Hunter had been checking out the bedroom with Mr Hassan, Grace had slipped away. He found her in the lounge with Mrs Hassan. She was trying to talk to Samia's mother but the woman was having none of it, repeating 'No speak English.'

This would be a good time to withdraw and plan the next steps.

'Well, Mr Hassan, thank you for your time. You have been most helpful. You have put our minds at ease I'm sure this can be sorted out now.'

'I hope it can, officer, I hope it can,' the shopkeeper responded.

Hunter and Grace sat in the CID car. He had started the engine but not yet set off, just sat running his hands around the steering wheel, staring out through the windscreen, not focused on anything in particular.

'Are you thinking what I'm thinking?' he asked.

'You bet I am. It is Samia we've found in the lake, isn't it?'

Hunter nodded in agreement. 'Having just done that search and watching Mr Hassan and his wife while you were talking, I'm convinced that they're either responsible for or involved in her death. We've got some digging to do to match our hunch.'

The Major Investigation Team regrouped at 2 p.m., the meeting called by DS Michael Robshaw who had sat with the HOLMES team as updates came in. Information had come in thick and fast and for the first time since the investigation had started, he could see a clear picture emerging as to where the enquiry was heading.

The timeline sequence on the incident board had been brought up to date, with the addition of new photographs. Only ten minutes earlier, DC Isobel Stevens, the HOLMES manager, had added information ready for the meeting.

Michael Robshaw took a look at the board and slipped off his glasses. 'Okay, guys. Firstly, well done everyone, you've made some significant inroads this morning. As a result of your feedback from the tasks you were given, we now believe we know who our victim is.' He folded his spectacles and popped then into his shirt pocket. 'Hunter, you and Grace have been to see Samia Hassan's parents. Would you tell the team what you have learned?'

Hunter scooted out his chair beneath his desk and faced the squad. 'As you know, Samia's parents, Mohammed and Jilani Hassan, are the owners of a convenience store in Hoyland. They have lived there for the past 15 years and have been resident in this country for 24 years.' He glanced at his scribbled notes. 'Samia was born here 21 years ago, on the 25th of July, 1984.'

As accurately as he could, Hunter recounted the morning's visit to the Hassans, only occasionally reading from his notes.

'I managed to tease out of him that the place where he says Samia has gone. It is a very small village set in the foot of the mountains, twenty miles from a town called Sul Banda. It's in the North East of Punjab, at least a day's journey from Lahore. He says the cousin she has married is also called Mohammed. He was edgy but I think that was because of us. I'm pretty sure he hasn't seen yesterday's news bulletins. If he had, he would have been far more guarded. However, from now on, there is no doubt he will be, especially when he sees this week's local newspaper.'

'You did a cursory search as well?' asked Robshaw.

'Yeah, without making it too obvious.' Hunter recounted what he had done. 'There is nothing left in that flat to indicate Samia ever lived there. All her personal effects have gone and there are no photos of her anywhere. Grace managed to check out the lounge as I was looking over Samia's room and there were no pictures of her there either. It's like she never existed.'

Robshaw thanked him, taking back the briefing. He turned to Detective Sergeant Mark Gamble, supervisor of Syndicate Two. 'Mark, will you input your team's info?'

Gamble made his way to the incident board. Three new photos had been added, shots of Samia Hassan with a group of girls of similar age. They were smiling, happy images and from the background lighting and red-eye effect it looked as if they had been taken either in a pub or nightclub. The pictures of Samia bore a striking likeness to the facial reconstruction done by Frankie Oliver.

This just has to be our lady from the lake, Hunter thought.

'My team were given the job of tracking down the girls named by Dr Chambers during her time at Sheffield University. We have so far caught up with four of her closest friends. They all describe her as a very bubbly, intelligent girl. Two of the girls shared rooms with her for several months, prior to her moving in with the doc. She discussed much of her relationship with all of them at some point and there is no doubt she had formed quite a good relationship with Dr Chambers.

'Her friends said everything changed when Samia told her parents about that relationship. Mr and Mrs Hassan completely disapproved, and one of the girls recalled that one Friday afternoon, both her mother and father turned up at the flat they were sharing and had a stand-up row with Samia and tried to get her to come home, which she refused to do. She saw Mr Hassan smack Samia across the face. After that visit Samia was in floods of tears. She said her parents were threatening to disown her because she had brought shame on the family.'

Gamble leaned against the panel. 'All of them mentioned the attack on Dr Chambers by two Asian men. It happened one Friday night, just as they had all come out of a wine bar near the university. The girls confirm it was unprovoked. The guys appeared from nowhere in their car, jumped out and attacked him. One of the men tried to drag Samia into their car. They describe it as an old battered white Corsa.

'Anyway, the girls bravely went to Samia's aid and managed to attract a crowd, so the guys backed off and drove away. The police were called but Samia persuaded the doc not to make an official report and said she would sort it out. She later told the girls the two men were her cousins. They confirm the damage to the doctor's flat as well, and they have confirmed that the e-fits which the doc has done are very good likenesses of the two men.'

Gamble tapped the three new photos on the board. 'These pictures are from Samia's Facebook page. They were posted after she had finished uni. She kept in touch with all four girls and occasionally phoned them. They all say she was down, that her parents were continually pestering her to marry a cousin who lived back in Pakistan and that she didn't want to. The last contact anyone had with her was on the 29th of July. They have tried phoning her but it goes straight through to voicemail. We have the number to see if the "techies" can put a trace on it. We've also posted messages on her Facebook page but that's not been updated since the 29th either.'

Robshaw puffed out his chest, took out his spectacles, wiped them with a handkerchief and put them on. 'Thanks everyone, the case has moved on with some real momentum today and I think we all know where it is going.

I have no doubt that we are dealing with an honour killing here. I'm sure you have drawn the same conclusion. Because of the sensitivity and the repercussions it could have, I want a sealed lid on this. No one discusses anything outside this room. Everything we get from here on we follow up with the utmost discretion, just on the off-chance that we might have got this completely wrong. I want no backlash.'

Robshaw turned to the incident board and the list of actions he had written. Looking back to the room, he said, 'Okay everyone, these are the tasks and there are quite a few. The majority are phone calls and will involve diplomacy and patience from you guys. For some of these enquiries you will have to go through the British Embassy in Pakistan and Interpol, okay?'

He checked the first bullet point he had written. 'First on the list, we will need to check if she was ever on any flight out of this country into Lahore. We will also have to check with Border Control here and in Pakistan, and we need to check the Passport Agency to see if Samia was ever issued with a passport. And now we have Samia's details I want another check done of local dentists here and in Sheffield, to see if we can come up with an identical match to our body. I also want triangulation done of her phone — see if we can pinpoint where her last call was made from. Finally —' he tapped the two e-fit images on the incident panel — 'I want a check of the intelligence system and I want these faxed to surrounding forces. We need to find out who these two are. My guess is these are the guys our witness Kerri-Ann Bairstow saw dumping the body off the jetty.' He put his hands on his hips, taking in a deep breath. 'When we have got all those answers — and only when — we go and pay an official visit to the Hassans.'

Hunter pulled his sons' sports bags from the boot of his car as Jonathan and Daniel bolted from the back seat and into the house. As he slammed down the tailgate, he saw they had left the car doors wide open and was about to call them back when Beth shouted from inside the house, 'Dirty boots off now,' and 'Jonathan, where have I told you to put them?'

He smiled and shut the doors himself. *Typical lads.*

Hunter had managed to leave work shortly after four and he was glad. It meant he could take the boys to their football coaching session. He enjoyed it, especially the final twenty minutes when the session ended with a 'dads against lads' kick-about. It reminded him of the days when he'd played regularly for a Sunday pub team in his 20s. The last time he had been able to play with any regularity was two years ago — weekly five-a-side games while he was in the Drug Squad.

He walked indoors to find Beth at the bottom of the stairs bawling up to emptiness, 'Put your smelly clothes in the wash basket the pair of you and then get in the shower. I'll be up in ten minutes to dry you off. And no putting on SpongeBob SquarePants until you've done that!'

Hunter closed the front door with his heel. As it slammed shut Beth spun round and glared. He held up his son's sports bags. 'What?' he said, trying to suppress a smirk. 'I've got my hands full.'

'You're as bad as they are. How am I supposed to get them to treat the house with respect if you won't take any notice?'

He put on his best scolded-boy look and leaned in to plant a kiss on her cheek.

She held him off with her hand, breaking into a smile. 'You stink as well. You can have a shower before you come anywhere near me. Here, give me the bags. I'll sort them out, and for your sins you sort out the boys.'

She relieved him of the sports bags and he gave her bottom an affectionate tap before sprinting up the stairs.

'You're not too big to feel the back of my hand yourself, Hunter Kerr!' Beth shouted as he arrived at the first of the boy's bedrooms, bundling up Jonathan's discarded football kit and confining it to the wash basket.

Fifteen minutes later, clean and refreshed and dressed in jogging bottoms and T-shirt, Hunter skipped into the large dining-kitchen, a rear extension of their three-bedroom semi.

Beth was taking a hot dish from the oven. He slid behind her, wrapped his hands around her waist and nuzzled the nape of her neck.

'Smells good.'

'Home-made lasagne.'

'Hmm, yummy. Fancy a kir?'

'Oh, I'd love one Hunter. I've had a pig of a day. A man had a heart attack in the waiting room this morning. We managed to get his heart beating again, thank goodness, but by the time the ambulance came we were an hour behind with patients. And you can imagine that some of them were in a state themselves after witnessing it. I've been in catch-up mode all day.'

'And I think my day's been tough!'

Hunter took a bottle of wine from the fridge and two glasses from the cupboard, then placed a small amount of Frais des Bois liqueur into the glasses and added chilled Muscadet. He took a sip and savoured the crisp, cold fruitiness of the French aperitif.

He handed a glass to Beth before sliding into a chair at the farmhouse table that took centre-stage in their kitchen. Hunter ran his palm over the oak surface and remembered when they had bought the table. They'd spotted it in an antique shop when they'd spent a week in the Yorkshire Dales a few years ago. It was old and battered and only three of the chairs matched but they'd fallen in love with it and bought it on the spur of the moment. It was an ideal gift to one another and suited the shabby-chic appearance of the rest of the kitchen perfectly.

'I've left the boys in Jonathan's room. I said they could play on their Xbox until tea was ready,' he said. 'I called in at Mum and Dad's with the boys on the way back.'

'Oh yes, what did they have to say?'

'Mum was in on her own. I asked her where Dad was and she said he'd had to go back up to Scotland for a funeral.'

'Oh, that's sad. Anyone we know?'

'She mentioned a name, Archie something, but it didn't ring any bells.'

Beth stopped what she was doing and turned around. 'This is going somewhere, isn't it, Hunter? Come on, spit it out. I can read you like a book.'

'It was just the way she said it. She said it was an old friend of his — she couldn't remember his full name. I asked a few questions but I could tell she just wanted me to shut up.'

'Well, you've given your dad a hard time just recently.'

'And rightly so, after what went off. I saw him arguing with someone and he denied it. What am I supposed to do when he won't say anything? I know he's hiding something but I don't know what. Now this sudden disappearance up to Scotland — he's not been back there for years and years. In fact, come to think about it I can't ever remember him going back up there.'

'You're too suspicious, Hunter, do you know that? It could be a genuine funeral for all you know. Think about it, all your dad's pals from his past will be getting on in years now.'

'I can't help but feel that if I hadn't called in to see them it wouldn't have been mentioned.'

'I know what you're saying, Hunter, but there's nothing you can do about it, is there? He'll tell you when he's good and ready. Just give him some space.'

'There's something not right,' he muttered. 'I'm going to get to the bottom of this if it's the last thing I do.'

'Cop!' Billy almost upended his fish supper onto his lap as he fought frantically to pull his baseball cap down over his eyes.

'Where?' said Rab, sliding lower into the driver's seat.

'There!' growled Billy, pointing over the dashboard. He pulled the peak of his cap lower and, satisfied that he had hidden enough of his face, lifted his head and peered through the windscreen, watching the dark-haired man in the short grey overcoat leaning against the driver's door of a dark blue Vauxhall twenty yards up the road. The man was scanning the street and he shot a fleeting glance in their direction.

Rab went for the key in the ignition but Billy snapped a gloved hand around his wrist.

'No, just wait! I don't think he's spotted us.'

'How do you know he's a cop?'

'I saw him a couple of weeks ago at the bail hostel, talking to the supervisor.' He leaned forward to get a clearer view. 'I wonder what he's doing in this neck of the woods? Let's just wait a moment and see what he's up to. If he clocks us then we piss off.'

Billy leaned back in his seat and returned to his supper. He loaded a couple of chips into his mouth, his eyes not straying from the plain-clothes cop. Five minutes later a slim, dishevelled man, appeared from a side street opposite where the cop was waiting. He stood, looking around.

'Well, just look who it is.' Billy's eyelids screwed into hardened slits as the man strolled across the road and struck up a conversation with the detective. 'I wonder if we're on their agenda by any chance?'

The shabbily dressed man accepted a cigarette from the detective. Billy reached beneath his seat, grabbed hold of the wheel brace and began to slide it out. 'Once they've finished their cosy chat, you and I are going to have a wee word with our pal. I don't like it when people go behind my back.'

DAY SEVENTEEN

'What's the address again?' Hunter asked, pulling the car into the kerb. He had been driving around back streets, searching for their destination, for the past five minutes.

Grace handed across the note she'd written back in the office. They were following up yesterday afternoon's telephone call from Zita. She had got back to Hunter with the address of the Asian Women's Refuge and had fixed up a meeting with the owner.

They'd found the street easily enough — off the Wicker in Sheffield — but all the buildings looked the same, three-storey Victorian red-brick houses with dusty windows and soot encrusted frontages. At first glance, it looked like most of them were empty or used as storage for the small shops or last remnants of businesses which still operated in this run-down area, but given the absence of a number, and because the secret address would have no signage to advertise itself, finding it was proving extremely difficult.

'Give the woman a ring, will you, Grace? Tell her where we're parked and ask her to come out and make herself known, otherwise we'll be here all day.'

Grace reached into her handbag, took out her mobile and tapped in the telephone number from the note. Within seconds it was answered. Less than thirty seconds later, Grace ended the call and slipped the phone back into her bag.

'She'll be down in a minute. She's been watching us drive up and down from her office somewhere up above us, but because we're in an unmarked car she didn't come down.'

Hunter turned off the engine and, as he was parked on double-yellow lines, placed the 'police visiting' card on the dashboard.

A sharp rap on the front nearside door startled them. Hunter turned to see a middle-aged Asian woman crouched down looking in. She was smiling but half of her face was covered by a white cotton veil.

They got out of the car and introduced themselves to Nahida Perveen. She greeted them with an energetic shake of the hand.

She was dressed in a long, white cotton dress, embroidered with a gold neckline. Hunter could see she was tall and slender, though he still couldn't make out her features because of the veil.

'Sorry I didn't come down and make myself known. We have to be very careful here as you can guess. I forgot to ask Zita what you looked like and some of the husbands and fathers of the women who are staying here will do anything to find this place.' Her voice was perfect BBC English — not a hint of an accent.

The building she showed them into had an old but solid door badly in need of paint. The entranceway was gloomy, but Hunter could pick out detailed Victorian tiles covering the lower half of the hallway and the floor that told him this had once been a fine residence.

They followed Nahida up a stone stairway to the first floor where the lighting was better.

'We have ten ladies with us at present but I don't think any will make an appearance. They've gone through such a lot and have come here for safety until we can help them turn their lives around. They knew you were coming but you still won't see any of them. Some of them don't trust the police, unfortunately.' She led them to the top of the stairs, only occasionally looking back as she spoke.

Unlocking another solid-looking door, Nahida guided them along a corridor and through a door at the back of the building. It led to a sitting room, big and brightly lit, with a high ornate plaster ceiling, again in need of a fresh lick of paint. It was furnished with four sofas and three armchairs, draped with throws, though none of the fabrics matched. They were arranged around two low wooden coffee tables. The carpet was thin, stained and threadbare. The place had been furnished on a tight budget.

Nahida sat on one of the chairs and pointed to one of the sofas. Crossing one leg over the other and leaning back, the veil fell away and that was when Hunter saw her badly scarred face. A clump of pink leathery flesh marred the left side of her head.

'You're probably wondering how I got this scar?' she said.

Hunter concentrated on her warm brown eyes. He felt embarrassed. He had taken too long looking at her face and could feel his cheeks flush.

'Don't be embarrassed.' Nahida smiled. 'I've lived with this for almost twenty years. That's what made me set up this place.' She pulled back her cotton veil a fraction, enough for Hunter to see the full extent of her injuries. The scar wound its way from the side of her left eye, over her ear and down towards her jaw. A portion of her hair was missing. In its place was a lumpy piece of scarred flesh.

'My boyfriend did this with drain cleaning fluid — a powerful acid.' She re-covered her face. 'It ended my career. I was a TV news journalist working in London — an in-front-of-camera reporter.' She gave them an awkward smile. 'I'll not bog you down with the details because I know you're here on other matters, but it's why I set up this place. The man who did this was chosen for me to marry. He came from my parents' village in Pakistan, was from a family who had been very good friends with them. My father and his father had been business partners before my parents came to live here.

'I'm British born and although I've been brought up with my parents' values, I quickly discovered that his values and culture were far stricter. I knew it wasn't going to work within weeks of meeting him. Firstly, he wanted me to pack in my job. He started to accuse me of flirting with my colleagues. After nine months, I told him I had taken enough and wouldn't be going through with the marriage.

'I left him one night when he was at work and went to stay with a friend. He started pestering me with phone calls, threatening me, so I changed my number. Then he'd turn up at work and security had to intervene. Anyway, one night we were celebrating a colleague's birthday in a bar and he turned up. He started accusing me of having an affair and then threw the cleaning fluid in my face. Fortunately, some quick thinking by my friends prevented me from serious injury — they poured drink all over me and used water from behind the bar, but it still left me with this.' She smoothed a finger over the scar. 'The police arrested him but he was given bail and fled back to Pakistan to his family. He's still on the run out there.' She shrugged. 'I continued my career as a journalist but it was all desk work. My editors didn't say as much but I realised my career in front of the camera was over and so I persuaded the company to make me redundant and I used the money to come up here where no one knew me, and to set up this place so that I could help protect other Asian women from what happened to me.'

'And have you been able to help many?' asked Grace.

'Hundreds over the years. Word of mouth and contacts through solicitors have made this a very popular place for women to turn their lives around.'

'And from what you've told Zita, I gather that you believe the women we've found in the lake contacted you for help, had made arrangements to come here but never turned up. And that you haven't been able to get hold of her since?' Hunter said.

'That's right. I've tried her mobile several times since our meeting and it went to voicemail. In fact, I rang it as late as yesterday and now it appears to be dead. Not only that, but I saw the reconstructed face on the news the other night and it looks remarkably like the girl who came to me for help. She told me her name was Samia.'

Hunter and Grace glanced at one another. Grace opened her folder and slid out an A4 colour copy of the facial reconstruction. She also took out pictures from Samia's Facebook page and slipped them across the coffee table.

'Is this the girl you met?' asked Grace.

Nahida lined up the photographs and picked up one which showed Samia holding a drink to camera. She scrutinised it for a few seconds before setting it back on the table. She tapped the photograph. 'This is definitely the Samia I met and spoke with.'

'When did she come here?'

'Oh, she never came here at all. She originally left a message on our answer machine and left her mobile number. It would have been a good six months or so ago now. I arranged to meet up with her at a coffee place at Meadowhall. It's a place I always use. It's public and it's busy. I also need to suss out the people I'm meeting with before they find out where we are. You wouldn't believe the tricks the husbands and parents pull to track down the girls who flee here. I have had people posing as police officers, social workers, solicitors — you name it, I've had to deal with it.' Nahida leaned forward, hands clasped. 'I suppose my job is a little bit like yours. When I meet up with the people who request my help, I have to sort out who is genuine and who is not.'

Hunter knew where she was coming from. He nodded.

'Can you remember what she said to you?' said Grace.

'Not word for word but I can give you the gist of our conversation.' She settled back. 'She wanted to get away from her parents but needed somewhere to hide while she sorted out somewhere permanent. She said her parents were putting pressure on her to go to Pakistan to marry a cousin out there and that she didn't want to. I told her I could help her out with that.

'Samia said she had been constantly watched since she finished university, her parents wanted to know virtually her every move. She felt she was being followed and mentioned two cousins. At our first meeting, she also gave me details of other problems she had encountered because of a relationship with a young doctor.

'At the end of that meeting I gave her a number of options, which included talking to the police as well as meeting me again. She felt she couldn't go to the police because she didn't want to get any of her family into trouble and felt it would just make things worse. She really just wanted to get away.'

'Did you meet again?'

'We did, but that didn't go to plan. She contacted me a couple of times beforehand and told me she couldn't get away without anyone knowing. Then right out of the blue, about six weeks ago, Samia rang me. She was on a train coming to Meadowhall and asked if I could meet her again at the coffee place just by Marks and Spencer. She was in a bit of a state when I finally got there. She was agitated, looking around. She made me nervous even though I've been involved in so many of these cases. I was really glad that there were a lot of people around.

'She'd managed to sneak out of the flat while her father was at the warehouse and she'd brought some things for me to store for her until she could get everything together and leave. She was in one hell of a state and I suggested she should come with me there and then. I said I could arrange with the police to pick up her other bits she needed later, but she didn't want anyone else to be involved. Especially not the police. I didn't want to leave her to do all that but she said everything would be okay, she was confident she could finish getting together the last of her things. She said she'd contact me and arrange to be picked up in a couple of days.'

'Can you remember when that was exactly?'

'It will be in my diary.'

Nahida got up and left the room. A few minutes later, she returned carrying a red knapsack and a large diary. She set the knapsack down on the coffee table, covering the photographs of Samia, then sat back in the chair, flicking open the book. Her roving finger drifted over several pages, checking each one before moving onto the next. After a couple of minutes she stabbed at a page. 'It was Monday the 28th of July,' she announced, looking across at Hunter and Grace. 'She was already at the coffee shop waiting for me.'

Hunter caught Grace's eye. Her friends had last reported speaking with Samia the day after — the 29th of July. Since that day on no one had heard from her.

Nahida closed her diary. 'From what I remember it was about half ten in the morning. As I said, she was really agitated. She was convinced someone was following her. I said I could call security or the police if she wanted and I would bring her here, but she said it was only a feeling she had, that she hadn't seen anyone. Also, she wanted to pick up some final things before she left home permanently.' She leaned forward and tapped the red knapsack. 'This is what she asked me to keep safe for when she got here.'

Hunter pulled the bag towards him. 'Have you had a look inside?' he asked, unzipping the top.

Nahida shook her head.

The section he had opened contained items of clothing and he lifted out each piece in turn, laying them down across the coffee table. He counted out two pairs of jeans, four T-shirts, a hooded sweat top, several items of underwear and a pair of trainers.

He ran his hand around the inside lining, empty. He then switched his attention to the side pockets, where he found make-up and a few items of jewellery — a mix of expensive gold items, a bracelet, two necklaces and a pair of gold loop earrings, together with inexpensive costume jewellery, which consisted of various bead bracelets.

Finally, he zipped open the front and couldn't hide his surprise. With forefinger and thumb he removed the item and carefully placed it on the laid-out garments. It was a British passport. He opened up the back section for Grace and Nahida to see.

The personal details and photograph left them in no doubt that it belonged to Samia Hassan.

DAY EIGHTEEN

Jock Kerr poured himself a generous shot of Lagavulin.

Just a wee dram after a hard day in the gym.

He reclined in his captain's chair and propped his feet on the desk. Swilling the golden liquid around the crystal tumbler he cradled it against his upper chest, allowing the peaty aroma to tease his nostrils. In dream-like state, his gaze roamed around the room, surveying the many framed photos and promotional posters adorning the walls; memories of his past boxing career. Then the dream switched to nightmare as the vision of how it all finished tumbled into his thoughts.

Just when he'd been on the cusp of greatness, with a Commonwealth medal to his name, his prospects were ended prematurely with a single punch, thrown after the bell, which sliced open an irreparable deep wound above his right eye. At the tender age of 20 his career was over. That one punch had ended everything and landed him where he was now — in one hell of a mess.

Deep down, he knew some of it had been his own fault — if only he had known at the time what he was getting into.

Foresight is a wonderful thing.

Back then, he had been a young, naïve man with a living to make and his fists were the only tools of his trade. He'd even used that phrase to the two detectives who interviewed him three days ago in his native Scotland.

Detective Chief Inspector Dawn Leggate and Detective Sergeant John Reed had picked up Jock from Motherwell railway station and driven him to a quiet hotel where they'd questioned him in the empty bar. They said they'd chosen it because they did not want anyone to know he was back in Scotland. At first, they hadn't asked him about the three detectives who had been murdered, but whether he thought he had been followed on his journey. And they had driven a long, circuitous route to the hotel. Jock had watched the Detective Sergeant constantly checking his mirrors, satisfying himself that they did not have a tail.

That was when he had told them about the shaven-headed man in Staithes and the subsequent hit and run on the moors.

The DCI said it confirmed their worst fears.

They had talked for well over two hours, piecing everything together between them. Jock had been able to add much of the background to their investigation, and although initially he sensed the two detectives were suspicious of what he told them — he recognised the signs from his son — once they had double-checked his story with information on their briefing notes, they had ended the interview by thanking him for his help, which had significantly moved on their enquiry.

Before they dropped him back at the railway station, they had advised him about his personal safety and the DCI had given him her direct mobile number.

Time and time again during the past two days Jock had run through everything they had talked about — checking that he hadn't left anything out. He knew deep down he hadn't — it had been locked away in his memory for so long. He shivered, staring back at the framed photographs. He'd done his best to bury the past but it had caught up with him.

What a bloody mess.

Jock swilled the single malt around the glass and drained it in one gulp. For a second, he considered pouring another but he checked himself. He had to keep a clear head. It was time for home.

He wiped the tumbler with a paper tissue and placed it back on his desk. Then he returned his whisky to the bottom drawer before turning off the lights and locking his office

He made his way through his gym, returning a couple of misplaced dumbbell weights to their respective spots on the rack, before taking a last look back — like he always did — and turning off the last of the lights.

Outside, the temperature had dropped. Jock shivered and zipped up his training top. The car park was empty save for his rented Toyota; the insurance company was still assessing the damage to his car.

He was about to step away when he noticed a padded envelope at his feet. Puzzled, he surveyed the car park again — this time with a critical eye. It was quiet.

He bent to pick up the small brown package. There was nothing written on it. He turned it over to see that someone had scribbled 'JOCKS GYM' in thick black lettering. The handwriting was poor.

He felt the envelope — there was something lumpy inside — then pulled open the seal and peered in.

Jock recoiled in horror and dropped the package, causing the contents to roll out. He gasped as his stomach leapt to his throat. Three severed fingers lay in front of him.

DAY TWENTY

Hunter leaned back in his seat, stretched his arms and folded them behind his head, interlacing his fingers. Physically he felt drained, yet mentally he was energised. Since he and Grace had met with Nahida Perveen, the investigation had clicked up a gear.

Samia's passport had been the catalyst. Fingerprints found on it matched those from the body.

He mulled over what they had uncovered in the past few days. The team had tracked down a dental practice near to the university in Sheffield where Samia had been a patient. Records held there matched the x-rays from her post mortem. They now had official confirmation — the body recovered from Barnwell Lake was Samia Hassan.

Phone calls to UK Border and Immigration Control and the British Embassy in Lahore confirmed no air ticket had been purchased in Samia Hassan's name. There was no record of her passing through Immigration Control in the UK, or of her arriving at Allama Iqbal International Airport in Lahore.

Locally, they had tracked down and interviewed several more of Samia's friends and acquaintances, found through her Facebook page. The interviews had reinforced many facts they already knew; the attack on Dr Chambers, the burglary and damage to the flat, and Samia's fear of a forced marriage, and they had also determined that no one had spoken with her since the 29th of July. Presently, they were tracking down the police officers who had turned out to those incidents, in the hope that one of them might have recorded the names of Samia's cousins. It was a long shot.

Civilian Investigator Barry Newstead had been assigned to Meadowhall to liaise with the police and security team there and view CCTV footage. Nahida had provided times, dates and the exact place where she had met Samia and Barry had been given the job of locating the footage to check if anything could be of help.

There had been a meeting with Duncan Wroe from Scenes of Crime and his counterpart from the Forensic Science team, and Task Force had been booked for that Sunday to execute a warrant at the Hassans' shop and residence.

Things were coming to a head, thought Hunter, as he viewed the work in progress on the incident board. Long lists of actions and names had now been added to the timeline. In big red capitals 'MOHAMMED HASSAN, JILANI HASSAN and SAMIA'S COUSINS?' had been ringed as main suspects.

Everything was taking shape.

'Who's the redhead with the gaffer?' asked Tony Bullars, entering the office.

His appearance brought Hunter back to the present. He unlocked his fingers and came out of his stretch. 'Redhead?'

'Yeah, good looking, late thirties. I've just come past the office and they seem to be thick as thieves. The door was open and she sounded Scottish.' Tony stopped and gave a wry smile, then said, 'It's murder!' in the style of TV detective *Taggart*. He laughed and dropped a bundle of papers in front of Hunter. 'That's the operational order and the warrant for this weekend's raid at the Hassans. The magistrate asked a few questions but nothing I couldn't handle. I just flashed my bestest smile at her and she signed it up.'

Hunter smirked. Tony had been a ladies' man for as long as he'd known him. He was tall and slim, with blue grey eyes, chiselled features, gelled and styled light brown hair and was always immaculately dressed. He was 28, still single and a charmer. In fact, Hunter couldn't recall seeing him with the same girl more than twice, and they were always stunners. He glanced at the warrant and then back at Tony. 'Bully, don't give me half a story. What do you mean good looking redhead, Scottish accent, in with the gaffer?'

Tony shrugged. 'I smell cop — and senior cop at that.' He tapped his nose and turned away. 'Get you a cuppa?' he shouted, making for the office kettle.

Hunter's head was suddenly elsewhere. Hadn't the gaffer told him the offenders arrested in the car that ran his parents off the road were from one of the sink estates outside Glasgow? Since then, he'd managed to track down the officer in the case from North Yorkshire, only to be told he'd handed over the paperwork to a female DCI up in Stirling. After several phone calls he had finally found out who the Detective Chief Inspector was and he had left four messages for her, none of which had been returned. There had to be a reason why she hadn't phoned him back.

Well, there's only one way to find out.

He picked up the signed magistrate's warrant for the Hassans. It was a good excuse to get a foot in the door.

The Detective Superintendent's door was ajar. Hunter slowed his pace and strained his ears, hoping to pick up some of the conversation. A woman's voice drifted out. Definitely Scottish, though he couldn't make out what she was saying. He paused at the door for a second and then knocked.

'Come in.'

Hunter stepped inside Michael Robshaw's office. The redhead was in one of the comfy armchairs, looking relaxed. She glanced up and flashed a smile. He remembered what Tony Bullars had said. She certainly was attractive and looked to be in her late 30s, wearing a well-tailored dark blue trouser suit over a white cotton blouse. A visitor's badge was clipped to her jacket pocket but he couldn't make out the name. A folder lay open across her lap. He tried to get a glimpse but she snapped it shut as if she knew what he was doing.

He flashed a false smile, greeted her with a nod and turned to his boss. 'Got the Op order and warrant for the Hassans this Sunday, boss.' He held out the documents.

'Okay, Hunter.' Robshaw took the paperwork from him and dropped it onto his jotter. 'I gather no problems with it?'

Hunter shook his head.

'Smashing. Everything in place as well?'

Hunter nodded.

'Right, thanks for that. Tell everyone briefing's at 7.30 on Sunday.'

It felt like Hunter was being dismissed. He turned to the redhead. 'I couldn't help but notice your Scottish accent. My dad's from Glasgow.' That was a good opener.

'Oh yes? I'm from Stirling.'

'This is DCI Leggate,' interjected Robshaw.

'Not DCI Dawn Leggate?'

'Yes,' she said, sounding surprised.

'I've been trying to track you down for the past few days. I was told by North Yorkshire Police that you'd taken over the enquiry into my parents' hit and run. Apparently, you've arrested two for it.'

'Oh yes — yes, of course. You're Hunter Kerr?'

She sounded hesitant.

'Have they been charged?'

'Has your father not said anything to you?'

'No, I wasn't sure if he knew or not. It's been like getting blood from a stone just lately.'

'Well, things have been discussed with him. He knows where we are in our enquiry.'

'Can you tell me then?'

'Well — er.' She seemed flustered. 'You should know better than that. Confidentiality, DS Kerr.'

'But this is different. I'm a cop.'

'So, you should be even more aware then. I'm afraid I can't tell you anything. It's an ongoing investigation. I suggest you speak with your father.'

'Sorry to interrupt, Hunter, but I have a few things to discuss with DCI Leggate,' Robshaw interposed. 'If you could excuse us.'

Hunter knew that his probing had been brought to an end.

'And if you could close the door behind you, Hunter? Thank you,' added Robshaw.

Hunter sank into his armchair and rested his eyes. He felt drained, had a thumping head and the TV was interfering with his thoughts; everything was spinning around so fast that he couldn't make sense of any of it. From the muddle of his mind, the sound of Beth coming down the stairs dragged him back to the present. He snapped open his eyes as she entered the lounge.

'You look tired,' she said, dropping down on the sofa with a big sigh. 'Boys were lively tonight.'

'Sorry, Beth, I should have taken them up and given you a break.' He tried to focus on the TV programme but it was washing over him.

Beth pushed herself up. 'What's the matter, Hunter? You've been at odds with yourself since you got home. Something at work?'

He shook his head. 'It's my dad again.' He told her about the brief meeting with DCI Leggate. 'I called in at Mum's on the way home but they weren't in. I've rung their mobiles and Dad's gym but there was no answer.'

'Look, Hunter, do you think you might be reading into this more than you should?'

He pursed his lips. 'I thought that myself, but it was the way both the superintendent and the DCI reacted when I tried to probe about Mum and Dad's incident. She gave me all the confidentiality crap. You know cops don't do that with other cops.'

'She might just be a stickler for procedure, Hunter. She's from another force. She doesn't know you from Adam.'

'No. There was something in the way she answered me. She was bullshitting.'

'Well, you can't do anything about it, can you? You're going to have to wait until your dad tells you himself.'

Hunter closed his eyes again.

I'm going to get to the bottom of this if it kills me.

DAY TWENTY-TWO

By 7.30 a.m. the incident room was overcrowded with Murder Squad detectives, Task Force Search Team members, Scenes of Crime officers and Forensic specialists, squeezing into any space they could find. It was standing room only.

A large-scale street map and a blown-up aerial photo of Hassan's store, together with a hand-drawn layout of the property — both the store and flat — dominated one of the white boards at the front of the room.

Hunter led the briefing; he was orchestrating the raid. He handed around photocopies of the operational plan setting out the purpose of that morning's sortie and then quickly got into his preamble. He summarised the investigation to date and then outlined everyone's tasks.

Although the team had the Hassans as TIEs (Trace, Interview, Eliminate), they had not been able to identify the attack site where Samia had been killed. That was the crux of the day's task and the purpose of the warrant and he deliberated over his final words. He wanted no stone left unturned.

Shortly after 8 a.m., as the Police and Forensic teams were heading out of the station's yard, daylight had just broken through a heavy grey sky. The day ahead looked promising.

Hunter and Grace were leading the convoy and in less than 15 minutes they were hitting the outskirts of Hoyland. Hunter eased off a fraction but took the turning into the road at the side of the convenience store quicker than normal and had to brake sharply to avoid hitting a parked car. He mumbled an apology to Grace as the car rocked to a halt.

He was wired. A highly-charged tingling sensation surged through him. He was always like this on raids: a memory from the Drug Squad days flashed through his thoughts and just as quickly disappeared as he studied Hassans' convenience store.

In less than twenty seconds they had the premises surrounded. Hunter glanced at his watch: 8.20 on a Sunday morning and the shop was already open.

He and Grace entered first, Hunter holding out the warrant, while Task Force, Scenes of Crime and Forensics disembarked, sealing off the area and sorting out their equipment.

Mohammed Hassan was serving a customer with a morning paper. His jaw dropped as they entered but within seconds he had composed himself and his face hardened.

'What is the meaning of this?'

'We have a warrant to search these premises, Mr Hassan.' Hunter thrust the rolled-up document in his face. Simultaneously, he threw the customer an 'I want you to disappear now' look and followed up by using his head to indicate the door. The customer took the hint and left quickly.

'What for? I have done nothing wrong.'

'When we came the other day making enquiries about your daughter, do you remember me asking you a series of questions as to her whereabouts? You told me she had flown to Pakistan.'

Hunter paused and studied Hassan's face. Tiny beads of sweat had appeared on his forehead.

'We now know she was never there, because as you will have realised by now from the local news broadcasts we have recently found her body. She has been murdered and I suspect your involvement in her killing.'

'No, no, you have got this all wrong. I haven't done anything to Samia.'

'Mr Hassan, I am arresting you on suspicion of your daughter's murder,' finished Hunter.

Ten minutes later, in handcuffs and protesting loudly, Mr and Mrs Hassan were helped into separate police cars as officers sealed off the front of the store with crime scene tape. The premises were secure and ready to be searched.

Hunter took out a forensic oversuit from the boot of his car and slipped it on. He watched everyone else kit themselves out as he picked up his clipboard from the back seat. He made a beeline for Duncan Wroe, the Scenes of Crime manager, and the Task Force Sergeant, wanting to double-check their tasks. Grace was corralling her team together. She had responsibility for the search of the rear store-room.

For the next three hours, Hunter repeatedly moved from one doorway to another, watching the Forensics Team photographing, swabbing walls and furniture, lifting carpets, selectively dropping various items into evidence bags, while Task Force overturned chairs, sofas and beds and rummaged through and behind units and cupboards. The work was slow and methodical but the exhibits were soon stacking up on the landing, ready to be removed for tests.

As Hunter was about to call time for lunchbreak, the first positive call went up.

'Got something, Sarge.' It came from one of the Task Force officers in the kitchen.

Hunter strode excitedly to the doorway and waited; he didn't want to contaminate the search grid. A slightly built, dark haired female greeted him with a broad grin. Her white forensic suit hung loosely in baggy folds.

'Is this what you're looking for on your list?' She offered him an A4 folded document. He slotted the clipboard under his arm and took it, casting his eyes over the DVLA V12 form. As he peeled over the front sheet, he couldn't help but smile. It was a registration document for a white Renault Kangoo van — on a 53 plate.

Hunter loosened his tie and undid his top button. He glanced at Tony Bullars. 'Right, let's see if we can wrap this up,' he said, opening the interview room door.

The two detectives strolled into an already warm and stuffy room and eased themselves down on seats opposite Mohammed Hassan and his solicitor. Mr Hassan was looking uncomfortable, a damp patch stained the front of his shirt.

Another hour of questioning and I'll have you soaking wet with sweat.

Hunter pushed his legs under the table and for effect dropped his paperwork and exhibits onto the table with a resounding slap. He slowly and deliberately unfastened his cuffs and rolled back his shirt-sleeves to reveal sinewy muscled forearms.

Tony Bullars flicked on the tape recorder.

'Mr Hassan, you understand why you have been arrested, don't you?' said Hunter. 'We have explained to you that your daughter's body has been recovered from Barnwell Lake and that she has been murdered.'

Hassan nodded.

His bearded, overweight solicitor began making notes.

'Mr Hassan. I would appreciate a verbal answer. The tape cannot pick up nods.'

'Yes, yes,' he stammered, licking his lips. 'But you have got it wrong. I haven't done anything bad to Samia. I haven't killed her.'

'We'll get around to that in a minute.' Hunter steepled his fingers and looked over them. He tried to lock onto Mohammed's eyes but they were darting around, avoiding eye contact.

A classic sign of guilt. 'When I was at your place a week ago you told me Samia had flown to Pakistan to get married to a cousin of yours. Do you remember telling me that?'

'I can recall saying something like that but I think you misunderstood what I meant.'

'Why would I misunderstand you?'

'Because I might not have explained myself.'

'Would you like to explain yourself now?'

'What I should have said is that I guessed Samia had flown to Pakistan to marry my cousin. You see she packed up all her things a couple of months ago and told me she was going to Pakistan to marry my cousin.'

Hunter gave a wry smile. He pulled his fingers apart and pushed himself back. 'Well, that is very interesting, Mr Hassan — because we have statements from several people which clearly state that she did not want to go to Pakistan to marry any cousin. In fact, those witnesses have said you were forcing her to go there.'

'They are lying.'

'Why should six different people all say the same thing? That you were trying to force her to go to Pakistan, to force her into a marriage with someone she didn't know?'

'She probably told them one thing but really meant another. Samia was happy to marry my cousin.'

'If she was happy to marry your cousin, why should she pack some of her things together with a view to taking refuge from you?'

'That is a lie.'

'No, it is not, Mr Hassan. We have a statement to that effect and we also have the things she packed ready to leave. We also have a statement from someone who states you went to Sheffield while she was staying with friends and argued with her about going to Pakistan to be married, and when she told you she didn't want to go you slapped her across the face.'

'They are lying. We rowed because I found out she was living with someone. She was bringing dishonour upon herself.'

'Because she had a white boyfriend?'

Mohammed's face coloured up. 'No, no, you are trying to put words in my mouth. She was bringing dishonour upon herself because she was sleeping with him before she was married.'

Hunter wanted to probe further about the two men who had assaulted Chris Chambers and tried to drag Samia into their car, but the team had not yet been able to identify them. He didn't want to alert Mr Hassan to the fact that they were aware of this incident, for fear his two relatives would go to ground, or even disappear out of the country — if they hadn't already done so. Anyway, he still had something else he wanted to hit him with. 'I put it to you, Mr Hassan, because Samia had made her mind up not to enter into a forced marriage and to get away from you that you decided to do something about it?'

'No, no, that is not right.'

'That you were angry with your daughter. That by her refusal to agree to marry your cousin, you thought she was bringing dishonour to yourself and so you murdered her.'

'No. You are making me out to be a bad man.'

The solicitor stopped scribbling and gave a loud throaty cough. 'I think my client has fully answered all your questions relating to this terrible act against his daughter. If you press him any further, you will be in danger of intimidating him.'

'Oh, I wouldn't want to do that.' Hunter leaned forward, rested his elbows on the table and interlaced his fingers. He fixed Hassan with a glare. The man stiffened. 'Okay then, Mr Hassan, seeing as everyone is lying against you and your solicitor is unhappy with my line of questioning about you being involved in the brutal murder of your daughter…'

'Detective Sergeant Kerr, that is out of order,' interrupted the solicitor.

Hunter shrugged and gave the solicitor an innocent look. 'I apologise if you find my questioning offensive, but my job is to discover the truth and all your client has given me are answers which are evasive. I don't want to get into a cat fight here on such an important issue so I'll move on — okay?' He paused. 'Mr Hassan, this morning when we searched your flat...'

'You had no right to do that,' Hassan interrupted.

Hunter raised his clenched fists a fraction then dropped them back down with a thump.

Both Hassan and the solicitor jumped.

'Sorry about that,' Hunter said, unlocking his fingers. 'Now, where was I before I was so rudely interrupted? Oh yes, this morning when we searched your flat — with a warrant,' he added in an exaggerated tone, 'we found this at the back of one your kitchen drawers.' He slid out a clear plastic exhibit bag which contained the registration document for the white Renault Kangoo van. 'I am showing Mr Hassan exhibit RA One.' He slid the document into the centre of the table. 'This VR Twelve relates to a white Renault Kangoo van registered in 2003. Is this yours, Mr Hassan?'

Hassan blushed. A droplet of sweat ran down the side of his face.

'It was mine. I used the van for collecting stock from the warehouse.'

'Where is it now? It's not at your premises or parked nearby.'

Hassan looked up to the ceiling.

'Mr Hassan, can you give me an answer?'

'It, it,' he stammered, 'it has been stolen.'

'And when was it stolen?'

'I — I can't remember exactly,' he paused. 'I think it was taken a couple of months ago.'

'Did you report the theft to the police?'

'No.'

'And why didn't you report the theft of your vehicle, Mr Hassan?'

'Because I didn't think it was worth it.'

'You didn't think it was worth it?' Hunter returned dryly.

'Well, it wasn't worth that much.'

'Detective Sergeant Kerr,' interjected the solicitor again. He rested his pen on his notepad and stroked the line of his beard to its point. 'Is there some significance to this line of questioning, or are you on some fishing expedition?'

'No, I am not on some fishing expedition. There is something I am working towards.'

'And what would that be?'

'Mr Hassan — your client — has so far indicated that everyone is lying against him and also there is a big coincidence here that I am struggling with.'

'A coincidence?'

'Yes, a coincidence that your client owns a white 2003 plate Renault Kangoo van and a similar one was seen in suspicious circumstances at Barnwell Country Park, shortly after we think Samia's body was dumped in the lake.'

'You say *shortly* after you think Samia's body was dumped.' Hunter wished he had chosen his words more carefully. 'I gather by that comment you do not know for certain that was what exactly happened. These might be coincidences, Sergeant Kerr, I'll grant you that, but as you well know coincidences do not make a case. Now, unless you have any pertinent questions for my client, I suggest we finish things here. That is unless you have something more concrete?'

The solicitor had the upper hand and Hunter realised it was futile to carry on unless he wanted to reveal the information about the two men seen dumping Samia's body, men the team strongly felt were related to Hassan.

Hunter pushed himself back in his chair and pasted on a false smile. 'Mr Hassan, I am going to bring this interview to a close. We have a number of further enquiries to make, especially to track down your Renault van which has been so conveniently stolen. But I'm sure that when we will find it there will be some further questions for you.'

Hunter picked up his papers and the exhibit bag and scraped back his chair. He maintained his false smile as he nodded to Tony to turn off the recording machine and then he cast Mohammed Hassan a threatening look. 'In the words of the Canadian Mounted Police — we always get our man.' Before the solicitor had the chance to challenge, he turned and strode purposefully out of the interview room.

As he closed the door behind him, Hunter gripped the handle, squeezing the very life out of it. In the corridor, he turned to Tony. 'Fuck, fuck, bastarding fuck,' he muttered through gritted teeth.

Tony smirked. 'I gather by that outburst, Hunter, that one is a tad fractious and frustrated. You could always resort to torturing him for a confession.'

His colleague's words lightened Hunter's mood and he smiled. 'Now, now, Bully, you know that's not my style.' He winked and let go of the door handle. 'That smug solicitor may have won that battle but he hasn't won the fucking war.'

As Hunter walked into the incident room, half a dozen members of the murder squad, including Grace and Mike, turned expectantly in his direction. He raised his hands in surrender. 'Sorry guys — I failed. No cough, no job. It's back to the grindstone, I'm afraid.'

The detectives returned to their tasks as Hunter beckoned to Grace. Flopping down opposite her, he asked, 'You have any joy with Mrs Hassan?'

She shook her head.

Hunter's shoulders dropped and he sighed. 'What a bummer.' He picked at his nails as he recounted the interview to Grace. 'And I'm afraid SOCO can't help us either,' he added, 'I rang Duncan Wroe ten minutes ago and he says the Hassans' place is definitely not the attack site.'

'Me and Mike haven't made any progress either,' said Grace, picking up where Hunter had left off. 'We couldn't get any momentum going with Mrs Hassan. Every time we asked a probing question, she'd say she couldn't understand what we were saying. Going through an interpreter as well as a solicitor was bloody awful. I even tried the mother-daughter approach to empathise with her. You know, tell her what I'd do if it was my daughter and I thought my husband was responsible? But she just sat there, stony-faced. The woman is a real heartless bitch. I'll tell you what, though, I'll be ready for her next time.'

She tried to put on a brave face but Hunter saw through her veneer. He nodded. 'The one solid thing from this is it reinforces my belief that these two are guilty of some involvement in their daughter's death. Neither of them has shown any sorrow or remorse.' He leant forward. 'Unfortunately, a jury won't convict them for that. I hate to say this but we're going to have to release them on bail.' He pushed himself up from his desk. 'Come on, no time for dwelling on our misfortunes. We owe this to Samia if nothing else. We've still got to find the white van. If that was used to dump Samia's body — and my guess from Mohammed's reaction is that it was — then it should have some forensics.' Hunter headed towards the door. 'And we'll also seize their mobiles before they leave. With a bit of luck, they might give us the names of the faces from the e-fits.'

DAY TWENTY-FIVE

Marcus Hill had been a police officer for fifteen years and had developed a nose for sniffing out when something wasn't right. And as he watched the grey Ford Mondeo in the distance, circling ever so slowly around the recently cropped field, he had the feeling something was wrong.

Firstly, because the farmer who owned this field had a red Nissan Navarro and he'd only ever seen the farmer's tractor going around in that field. And secondly, there had been quite a few complaints over the years about fly-tipping in this area. Thirdly, the lane above the field was where a couple of burned out stolen cars had been found in recent months.

Marcus had spotted the Ford Mondeo two minutes earlier. He was heading back to the station for his meal, having spent the past twenty minutes driving around the countryside section of his beat, where the roads were less congested and the scenery was better. It had been an unusually quiet afternoon and he was savouring the tranquil moments. These instances were few and far between, especially on the afternoon shift.

The car attracted his attention when it emerged from a copse of trees which he knew was the site of a ruined eighth-century chapel. He had an interest in local history, and he knew the place had protected status.

Marcus pulled his police car off the road, mounting the grass verge and settling next to a gap in the hedge where he hoped for a better view. The Mondeo had come to a stop, but such was the angle of its parking that he was unable to get a view of the number plate. He watched as the passenger door opened. A man dressed in a long, dark coat disembarked.

Leaning across the passenger seat, Marcus strained his eyes to get a clearer description but he was too far away. The dark clothed man made his way to the rear of the Mondeo, where he popped open the tailgate.

Marcus had seen enough. His suspicions aroused, he radioed in, telling the communications room operator what he could see and asking for backup. Then he pulled back onto the road and set off towards a track which led to where the Mondeo was.

The public bridle path he turned onto was rutted and undulated and lined by heavy hawthorn bushes, and it took him much longer than he had anticipated to find an opening into the field.

Marcus spotted the gap at the last moment. He pulled the steering wheel hard left, bounced up and over a tufted incline and dropped down onto the recently harvested field. The heavy landing knocked the wind out of him and he slammed on the brakes. The police car skidded to a halt. As he fought for breath, he scoured the fields to gather his bearings. The Mondeo was twenty yards away, though both front doors were open and the car was devoid of passengers. He had lost the element of surprise.

Marcus flung open his door and sprinted towards the car, giving an update over his personal radio while scouring the field to see if anyone was making a run for it.

There was no sign of life. He guessed they had dashed into the copse where the old chapel stood. Once his colleagues arrived Marcus knew that there would be nowhere for them to hide. They'd soon flush them out.

He stopped at the Mondeo, craning his neck inside just in case one of them was laying low in the seats. The car was empty. Then he walked to the rear where the tailgate was still up.

Now let's see what you were up to, shall we?

Curled up in the foetal position lay a man, and Marcus had seen enough corpses in his time to realise this man was dead.

The rustle of leaves from the coppice made Marcus jump. A stocky built man emerged through the bushes, a black woollen ski mask hiding his face. Marcus reached for his baton, simultaneously depressing the emergency button of his radio — a signal which overrode all other communications on that channel and let colleagues know that he was in danger.

Marcus never heard the footsteps behind him and never felt the blow to his head, though his ears registered the sharp crack as his skull fractured.

The last thing he saw before his vision pitched into darkness was the galaxy of stars that exploded inside his head.

DAY TWENTY-SIX

It took Hunter ages to find a parking spot. He had never seen the police station car park so full. And inside, the station was no better. The rear foyer and corridor were crammed with uniformed officers milling around. He didn't see any familiar faces.

As he reached the first-floor stairwell, he recognised one of the duty group sergeants, who was carrying a clipboard and seemed deep in thought.

'What's going on?'

The sergeant looked up. 'Oh, morning, Hunter. You mean the Task Force officers? Haven't you heard?'

'Heard what?'

'Marcus Hill was attacked last night. He's in a bad way.'

'Marcus!' Hunter knew him. A few years ago, he had joined Hunter's team as a CID aide, but had then passed his sergeant's exams and decided to go back into uniform where he would have the regularity of 'acting-up'. Hunter had chatted to him a couple of weeks ago when they'd bumped into each other in the canteen. Marcus had smiled as he shared the news that he'd just passed the last round of sergeant's boards and was waiting for a suitable vacancy.

'What happened?'

The sergeant elaborated. 'Fractured skull. And he suffered a bleed to the brain. They operated on him late last night and he's heavily sedated. We won't know anything else about his condition until later this morning.'

'Have you got who did it?'

The sergeant shook his head. 'He called in a grey Mondeo acting suspiciously in one of the fields opposite the Crown Inn at Barnburgh and called for backup. Then he went status-zero, but it took the first car a good ten minutes to get to him. By that time the Mondeo, and whoever had attacked him, had left. We've got everyone available out looking. Task Force are going out to do a thorough search of the area.'

Hunter patted the sergeant's shoulder. 'Okay, let me know how you go on, and keep me updated about Marcus.' He turned and climbed the stairs to the MIT room, his thoughts drifting.

As he shouldered through the doors, Hunter sensed the atmosphere in the office. It was a complete contrast to downstairs. This place was buzzing and it brought him back from his gloom.

He slipped off his jacket and left it on the back of his chair. Grace glanced at him as she put a mug of coffee down on her desk.

'Morning, Grace. Have you heard about Marcus?'

'Yeah, terrible, isn't it?'

Hunter nodded. He pointed to his colleagues who were at their desks, cradling their own hot drinks and chatting excitedly in small groups.

'Something going on that I should know about?'

'That's appeared this morning.'

Grace thumbed towards the incident boards at the front of the room. Beside them, stacked on a trolley, was a large flat screen TV on stand-by and a DVD player.

'I called in to speak to Isobel first thing and she said we were in for a treat this morning. There's been a breakthrough but she wouldn't tell me what.'

Before Hunter and Grace could discuss things further, they were interrupted by Michael Robshaw and Barry Newstead making a noisy entrance. Barry swaggered to the television, his face beaming as he switched on the monitor, while the SIO took up centre stage.

'Okay everyone, settle down. I'm guessing you've all heard a whisper that progress has been made in this case, especially after the disappointment of the interviews with the Hassans.' Robshaw turned to Hunter and Grace. 'And that's no reflection on you two by the way. We had nothing to go on.' He grinned. 'That was until yesterday afternoon.' He rubbed his hands together. 'When Barry discovered what you are all about to see. All yours, Barry.'

Barry smoothed a hand over his loosened tie. He took a deep breath and made a vain attempt to pull in his beer belly. 'As you know, I was given the task of visiting the security team at Meadowhall to see what, if any, CCTV footage they had of Samia Hassan and whether there was anything of significance which could take the investigation further. Well, thanks to the dates, times and precise location provided by Nahida Perveen, I was able to isolate the cameras which might have images of Samia. This is what I have found. The footage is disjointed because I have taken clips from hours of original CCTV film and cobbled them together.'

He stepped back from the TV and pressed the remote. A section of the huge shopping mall interior flickered onto the forty-eight-inch screen.

'Okay, this is where we first pick up Samia.' Barry pointed with the remote and homed in on a young, dark haired Asian woman strolling through the ground floor of Marks and Spencer's store and out through the entrance to the mall.

The murder squad was glued to the pictures playing out over the TV. Samia weaved her way between a throng of people seated in an open plan coffee lounge and took up a place at an empty table.

'At the bottom right, you'll see the time and date of the footage; the 14th of March — a good six months ago. I'll fast forward it a bit.' Barry zipped through to a point where another woman joined Samia and then pressed play. 'That's Nahida Perveen. I'll not go any further but I can tell you they have coffee and are obviously in conversation for about 25 minutes. Then Samia leaves and makes her way back into Marks and Sparks before heading off for the train.' Barry clicked the remote again. 'Okay, this is the second piece of footage. We jump forward to the 28th of July.'

Again, images played out of Samia walking through the ground floor of Marks and Spencer's to the coffee lounge. Samia sat at a table and Nahida joined her. Barry speeded up the footage, showing Samia handing over a red knapsack and then froze the picture. He turned to Hunter. 'I think this is the same knapsack where you found Samia's clothing and passport, is it not?'

Hunter nodded.

'Okay, there's not much conversation on this occasion.' Barry increased the speed of the footage for a few seconds then hit the play button. 'They're only together for ten minutes and as you can see they split up and leave.' Barry stopped the footage, looked away from the screen and scanned the room. He had the attention of every detective. 'Now, this next bit is very interesting,' he continued, clicking the remote back into play.

All eyes watched Samia travel the escalator to the first floor of Marks and Spencer's, stride through the aisles and leave through the exit doors. At one stage it looked as though she was heading for the ramp to the train station, but then changed direction towards the car park. She was continuously glancing behind her.

'At this stage, like you, I was wondering why she was looking around as much as she was, so I pulled up footage from other cameras and I found this.' Barry clicked the remote again, changing the image. The shots were back inside Marks and Spencer.

The picture zoomed in and a grainy image of an Asian male, mid to late 20s, dressed in white T-shirt and jeans, came into focus. He was dodging from one rack of clothing to another, acting suspiciously.

'As I pan the shot out, you can now see that this guy is following Samia and I'm guessing because of her reaction she has sussed this. Okay I'll play it out a bit more.'

The picture juddered for a split-second and then the drama was back on. Samia was picking up her pace, slipping between parked cars. In the background, visible but out of focus, the Asian man took something out of his pocket and put it to his ear.

'He's on his mobile.'

Samia took a final look in the direction of the Asian man before dashing into one of the stairwells which gave access to the ground floor car park.

'And finally this,' said Barry.

The image changed again to a low-lit underground car park. The view was wider and longer, taking in a considerable amount of the parking area, but the action being played out was unmistakable. Samia sprinted out of the stairwell like a chased rabbit, looking back over her shoulder. From out of nowhere, a blur at first to the right of the screen, another Asian man, taller and much stockier than the first, steamed into her like a rugby player, bowling her over onto the concrete floor. He was on top of her in a split-second, straddling her, one hand covering her mouth to prevent her crying out, the other pummelling her chest.

Seconds later, the man who had been initially following Samia emerged from the stairwell at pace, slipped on a wet patch at the bottom of the stairs, caught himself, re-balanced, and joined in the attack.

It was over in thirty seconds. Samia slumped under the onslaught. The stocky man pushed himself off her and sprinted away out of camera view, while the first Asian man stood over her looking around, but there was no one else in sight.

Less than a minute later a white van entered the picture and pulled directly in front of Samia's prostrate body, blocking the camera's view.

Barry glanced around the room. All eyes were fixed on the screen, the detectives unable to pull themselves away from the scenes unfolding before them. He turned back to the screen in time to see the two Asian men bundling Samia's limp figure towards the rear of the van. They slung her into the back like a rag doll. The doors slammed shut, both men jumped into the front and then the vehicle tore away.

'All that took less than three minutes,' Barry told them. 'The last footage I have is this.' It was a short snippet of the white van heading towards the exit of the ground floor car park, at the point before it entered the major road system around the Meadowhall Centre. Barry freeze-framed a close-up image and there were the faces of the two Asian men who had attacked and abducted Samia.

The eyes of the murder squad darted between the e-fit images on the incident board and the TV screen. There was no doubting they were an exact likeness. Just as important was the index number on the front number plate of the van — it was the same registration as the VR 12 vehicle document which had been recovered from the Hassans' home.

DAY TWENTY-EIGHT

Hunter's eyes were glued to the TV in the incident room. It was the third time he had watched the attack and abduction of Samia.

He shook his head as the violent images replayed — this time inside his brain. He cringed at the sheer brutality meted out to the young woman. Samia was so slight. She'd not resisted or put up a fight and yet those two men had beaten her mercilessly and tossed her into the back of the van like a sack of rubbish. He reflected on what the post mortem had revealed — the catalogue of injuries inflicted upon her and the violation she had suffered prior to her death.

What he'd like to do to those two bastards.

As he shook himself out of his reverie, he found himself trying to squeeze the life out of the plastic TV remote. He glanced around, red faced, hoping no one had noticed as he set it back down on the trolley.

Hunter strode back to his desk, dropped down onto his chair and began to immerse himself in the paperwork which had accumulated over the past couple of days. The majority of it was written off actions or reports as a result of his team's footwork and foraging. As he pored over their content, he summarised what they had learned to date.

The MIT teams had not eased up since Barry had discovered the CCTV footage; the investigation was now a manhunt. Blown-up footage of the two Asian men had been given to the Intelligence Unit, who had circulated it throughout South Yorkshire as well as to neighbouring police forces. On the back burner was a visit to the *Crimewatch* studios but they wanted to exhaust their own enquiries first. The pictures were so good that everyone was confident it wouldn't be long before they were caught.

Simultaneously, checks were being carried out at scrap dealers and car dismantlers for the white Renault van. It hadn't been found dumped or burnt out yet, and experience told them that if it wasn't still secreted away somewhere, these were the usual means of disposal.

Now they had the fixed time and date parameters for the attack and kidnapping, the technicians at force headquarters had been able to make a quick examination of the SIM card memory and mapping hardware inside

Mohammed Hassan's seized mobile. The wizards had made a crucial breakthrough. From the downloaded data, they had discovered activity on his phone within minutes of his daughter's abduction and traced a name and phone number.

The name Ari was registered in his contact details and the same number had been dialled persistently over several days following Samia's kidnapping, with the last call recorded at 10:33 p.m. on Friday, the first of August. Since then there had been no activity to the number and the technicians were reporting the line was now dead — the phone switched off or more than likely dumped, especially since the raid at the Hassans'.

Kerri-Ann Bairstow had seen a white van driving away from the country park on either a Friday or Saturday. Hunter was sure that was when they had dumped Samia's body into the lake, which meant she had been held captive for almost five days.

The hairs at the back of his neck prickled; the post mortem had shown she had been raped and butchered. He couldn't imagine what she must have gone through during that time.

Hunter continued picking over the reports. The mobile number Mohammed had contacted was a pay-as-you-go phone bought in Sheffield with cash and the details of the purchaser were false. Nevertheless, from discussions during briefings the murder squad were confident Ari was the man's real name.

Together with the photographs from the CCTV footage, Hunter knew this was as good as they were going to get.

'Hunter, didn't you hear what I said?'

Grace broke his concentration. He looked up from his paperwork and caught her glaring. She was holding up the handset, pointing at the receiver.

'Sorry, Grace, I was elsewhere.'

'Yeah, I could see,' she said. 'I just said they've found the white van.' Her voice was up several octaves. 'It's Communications on the phone. Uniform have found it at a car dismantler's in Rotherham. A low-loader's on its way to pick it up and SOCO are heading out there.'

Later that afternoon, Hunter drove into the force's forensic examination facility and swung into an empty parking space. Excitedly, he jumped out, not bothering to lock the car, and quickly made for the drying room. Grace hurried after him.

Duncan Wroe, in a blue forensic suit, was just climbing out of the rear of the white Renault.

It looked in remarkably good condition considering it had been languishing in a car dismantler's for several weeks, though it was missing its rear number plate.

Hunter shouted to Duncan, who turned and acknowledged them with a wave, a small fluorescent light in one hand and a bottle of blood reagent spray in the other. He sauntered over.

'Hi, Hunter, Grace. Wondered how long it would be before you got here.' He set the spray down on a table.

'We wanted to give you enough time to work your magic on it, Duncan,' Hunter said.

Duncan smiled and mussed his fingers through his already tousled hair. 'Too early for miracles just yet, I'm afraid, though I have made a start on it.' He picked up the Luminol spray. 'Come on, slip on some overshoes and I'll show you what I've got so far.'

He left Hunter and Grace to fit on latex shoe coverings, still talking as he walked away. Hunter hobbled after him, struggling to fit on one shoe protector while trying to concentrate on what the SOCO manager was saying.

'I've only done a preliminary examination, you understand. The van's been out in the open for months and will need at least a couple of days in the drying room before we can bottom it. However, I have made a start.' Duncan stopped by the open rear doors as Hunter and Grace caught up.

'Is it the right van?' said Hunter, pointing at the absence of the rear number plate.

'Absolutely. The engine and chassis number are a match. This is definitely the van belonging to Mr Hassan.'

'And what have you got so far?' asked Grace.

'Well, I have found traces of blood — just small amounts. I've given it the once-over with the Luminol and it shows up under the fluorescence. Whose it is at the moment I won't be able to say, but my guess is Samia's. Her throat was cut as I recall and despite the fact she was bundled up in the carpet, I think some will have seeped out. I'll swab it and send it to the lab.'

'Anything else?'

'The impossible I can do, miracles take a little longer, Hunter. Once it's thoroughly dried out I'll be checking for fibres and DNA. I've got the samples from the carpet she was wrapped up in, so I'll be able to examine them and see if there is a match. I'll certainly be able to confirm if this was the vehicle she was carried in.'

Hunter returned a thank you smile. 'All very technical for me, Duncan, but I have faith in you.'

'In layman's terms it's a bit like the fluorescent lights in a nightclub picking out white clothing.'

Hunter and Grace nodded, understanding.

'I'll also be checking for soil samples in the wheel arches and on the wheels and see if I can marry them to the samples I've taken from the car park at the country park. Lastly, we'll swab the cabin's interior and see if there is a DNA composite for the driver and passenger. With a bit of luck, in a day or two I should have all the answers.'

Hunter found Barry Newstead reaching across his desk as he entered the office. Grace was only a few strides behind.

'Caught you!' Hunter said. 'Snooping through the boss's things while he's away?'

'It would take a real detective to ever catch me doing that,' Barry said, looking over his shoulder. 'I thought you'd disappeared for the day. I'm just leaving you a note before I knock off.' He finished scribbling on an A5 pad, then tore off the top sheet and handed it to Hunter. 'A couple of things I wanted to leave for you before tomorrow morning's briefing.'

'What's that, Barry?'

'Firstly, we might have identified Samia's cousins — the two men from the Meadowhall CCTV footage. I've been chasing up the Intelligence Units throughout the Force and Sheffield think they have a positive ID on the pair. It looks as though they're known to Drug Squad, so I'm just waiting on final confirmation of that. It looks promising.'

'Great stuff. And the second thing?'

'Remember we set up a trace search of the part index number of the Volkswagen Golf that Kerri-Ann Bairstow gave us, belonging to one of her punters?'

Hunter pursed his lips. 'Yes?'

'Well, you're going to love this. Guess who it comes back to? You've already interviewed him.'

Hunter shook his head. 'Surprise me.'

'Mr Christopher Chambers. An address in Sheffield.'

Hunter's eyes widened and Grace looked surprised too.

'Told you you'd love it.'

Hunter snatched up the phone, punched in a number and waited for a response. His feet were tapping ten-to-the-dozen. After a brief conversation, he slammed the handset back onto its cradle and turned to Grace. 'Have you got anything pressing this evening?'

'Nothing that can't wait. I'll just make a quick call to Dave to sort out the girls and then I'm with you.'

Hunter patted Barry on the shoulder. 'Cheers for this. Now I've got some arse to kick.'

Hunter listened as soft footfalls padded towards him. He looked away from the car park for a few seconds to check his watch. He and Grace had been waiting in the entranceway to the hospital generator room for less than half an hour.

While they were waiting, the last light of dusk had faded. The car park security lighting had activated, giving everything a blue-white tinge.

Hunter saw the shadowy outline of the man a few yards away. He recognised him from their previous visit to the infirmary.

'Good evening, Dr Chambers,' Hunter greeted him, stepping out of the shadows. Grace slipped in beside him.

The doctor started, slapping a hand over his heart.

'Christ, you made me jump!' Chris Chambers gasped.

'Good.'

The doctor looked perplexed.

Hunter took a few determined steps forward, stopping inches from his face. 'Give me one good reason why I shouldn't haul you down to the station right now for perverting the course of justice!'

Even in the low light from the glow of the security lighting Hunter could see Chris Chambers had coloured up.

'I — I,' he spluttered.

'Why, after contacting us and giving us all that information about Samia's cousins assaulting you and threatening you, didn't you tell us that on the evening of Friday the first of August you recognised them leaving the country park in their white van?'

The doctor's head drooped.

'You could have saved us a lot of time — do you not realise that? Instead, you gave us a storyline half pointing us in their direction. Is it because you were with a prostitute that night?'

Chambers nodded. 'I'm close to finishing my time as a junior doctor. If the hospital finds out about this I'll not get a post. Believe me, I didn't want to obstruct your investigation. I thought if I gave you enough to lead you to Samia's cousins and help catch them, this wouldn't come out.'

'Well, it's backfired, hasn't it? We've wasted time tracking down the owner of a VW Golf for weeks as a potential witness and all this time it was you. I'd be very careful how I'd answer this next question. Did you see the two men dump Samia's body in the lake?'

The doctor shook his head vigorously. 'Christ, no! I didn't spot them until they'd cut us up in the car park. When I saw who was in the van I thought they were after me again, because of my past fling with Samia. I thought they'd followed me there and I was going to get another hiding. When they drove away, I couldn't fathom it out. Then when I saw it all on the news, I put two-and-two together and realised what I had seen.' He paused and dropped his gaze again. 'I'm sorry. If it hadn't been for the prostitute I would have told you all this.'

'You might be able to save some face here. Can you definitely say you recognise the two people in the white van as Samia's cousins who previously beat you up?'

Chambers nodded. 'Yes, it was definitely them.'

DAY THIRTY

'These are our targets,' announced Michael Robshaw, holding aloft a pair of A4 size colour photographs. They were head and shoulders mug shots of two Asian men holding custody reference boards — at some stage they had obviously been arrested and charged.

'Ari and Pervez Arshad. 29 and 27 years old, from the Attercliffe area. These were taken just over five months ago when they were charged with witness intimidation after an assault on a young man at a taxi rank. Three witnesses stated Ari and Pervez pushed in on a queue and when a 22-year-old man challenged them they set about him. They punched him to the ground and witnesses say Ari jumped on his head with both feet several times. That young man is now permanently brain damaged and the three witnesses who initially came forward have refused to give evidence in court after being visited by the pair.'

Robshaw turned and pressed the images onto the incident board, directly beneath the two earlier e-fits, joining the enlarged CCTV image of the two Asian men driving away from Meadowhall in the white Renault van.

Everyone could see the likeness.

Robshaw turned back to the room. 'These two are well known to the Sheffield police and also to Drug Squad. They have been strongly suspected of knocking out cocaine and heroin to clubbers for some time but subsequent raids have only found enough gear for possession charges. Ari has been arrested twice for assault and aggravated burglary when he went to collect drug debts owed to him, though once again victims and witnesses refused to give evidence in court.' Robshaw scanned the room. 'However, their luck has finally run out. We now have clear identification placing these two at Barnwell Lake on the night Samia's body was dumped. It's by Christopher Chambers, who was previously assaulted by the pair. And he is willing to testify in court.

'So not only do we have CCTV footage of these two abducting Samia, we can now place them on the night her body was dumped in the lake. What we don't have is their address. They no longer live at the flat where they were arrested five months ago. That has been let to another couple who were living there on the date of Samia's abduction. Detectives from Sheffield have paid this couple a visit and given the place the once over. There is no suggestion these two people have any links to our targets or to the Hassans and therefore our priority now is to identify where they are currently living and bring them in. Tasks today relate to their known associates with a view to tracking them down.'

Mike Sampson raised his arm. 'What about bringing Mohammed Hassan back in, now we've found Ari's number on his mobile?'

'Not yet. I don't want him to know how much we've got until we have Ari and his brother Pervez in custody.' Robshaw tapped the incident board. 'All our efforts now are focused on these two. Good hunting, everyone.'

Prompted by an early finish from work — they still hadn't discovered the Arshads' address — Hunter made a last-minute decision to detour on his way home and call into his dad's gym for a quick training session to unwind.

As he took his bag out of the boot, he casually looked around the car park. There were a good dozen cars — more than usual at this time of day. *Must be a few in.* He might be able to get in a bit of sparring for a change.

As he set down his bag to close the boot, out of the corner of one eye he spotted movement in one of the parked cars. A grey Mondeo, its engine revving, was parked at the end of the row. It looked out of place here; not the type of car he normally saw in the car park — most of the trainees who used his dad's gym were young men who drove old bangers, the best of them done up with body kits which shouted boy racer.

After everything that had happened recently, Hunter went on alert — something didn't feel right. And weren't they looking for a grey Mondeo in relation to the attack on PC Marcus Hill?

He slowly closed the boot and slipped down the side of his car to get a better look at the Mondeo, especially the driver and passenger. It looked as if the two men were concentrating on the entrance to the gym.

Crouching, he shifted for a better angle. The passenger was the nearest. He was a middle-aged man with long straggly, greying hair and a neatly trimmed beard. Hunter was too far away to get a look at his face. The driver, also middle-aged, had crew-cut sandy hair. His head was back against the headrest and although Hunter couldn't see his features, there was something familiar about him.

As Hunter took another step forward the passenger sat bolt upright. He'd been eyeballed.

The Mondeo roared into life, its front wheels whipping up gravel as it jolted forward, fish-tailing for a split second before straightening and shooting out of the exit onto the side-street.

He had just enough time to log the registration number in his head before it disappeared.

As the squeal of tyres faded into the distance, his hackles rose. It was the look the passenger had thrown him — a cold-blooded granite stare. It was an animal-like expression he had seen only a few times in his career — usually when someone wanted to kill him.

Those two meant business and he had disturbed them.

DAY THIRTY-ONE

Billy Wallace looked up for a break in the clouds as more drizzle floated from a murky sky. Around him, puddles were forming. He gave an involuntary shudder as droplets of rain ran down his neck and onto his back.

It had been raining on and off for most of the day — but that wasn't a bad thing, he'd told himself as he sloshed through the wet that afternoon. It had enabled him and Rab to do what they had needed to do and not draw suspicion as they had scoured the streets for their target's address.

He wiped drips of rain from his hair and stepped into the smoking shelter at the rear of The Station public house, his slate grey eyes never leaving the station ticket office and waiting room fifty yards away. He was listening for the next train, the connection train from Edinburgh.

He stroked the recently grown beard that covered his craggy features and hid most of the hideous scar which made him stand out, mulling over his decision. They'd needed some extra muscle to finish the job, and the only way he could arrange that was by calling in favours with old contacts. It had meant a flying visit to his hometown two days ago. He felt uncomfortable; he always liked to know who he was working with, needed that level of control and trust, but this time he had no choice. It had cost him a few grand, but it would be worth it.

'Get that down your neck.'

Rab Geddes made him jump. He was edgy.

He took the pint of lager from his partner in crime and stepped to one side so he could come into the dry.

Neither of them smoked. They were using the shelter in the hope of not attracting attention — two strangers with Scottish accents would stand out.

'Not arrived yet?' asked Rab, sweeping a hand over his newly grown hair.

It was a long time since Billy had seen Rab with hair. It was still sandy in colour but it was now thin and wispy and he realised why Rab had taken to shaving his head over the past ten years.

Nevertheless, it was necessary. They needed a change in appearance for a few more days.

'Nope. It's a couple of minutes late,' Billy replied, looking at his watch again. He glanced back to the station. The rain clouds were easing and the light was failing, another half an hour and darkness would cover them.

His thoughts drifted to their recce earlier in the day. After they had finally found the house, Billy had done a circuit of the surrounding streets. Instinct told him cops would be close by, on protection duty, and he'd been right. He'd spotted the unmarked police car on the second sweep and had to smile as he checked out the Peugeot. Even after all these years in prison, though the make and models had changed, the police radio in the centre console was still a dead giveaway.

He mentally noted its number and position; it would have to be taken care of so they could make their getaway after the job. The car was empty and he guessed the detectives would be in a house somewhere nearby keeping observation, though he didn't stay around to check. He and Rab had driven back to the railway station, finalising their plans, making sure that when they parked the Mondeo it was well away from view. Since they had been clocked by that nosy bastard at Jock's gym they had kept a low profile. *It's only for a few more hours.*

In the distance he heard the rumble of the train and it brought him back to the present.

'Come on, Rab, they're here,' he said, nudging his partner and swallowed the remains of his lager. He swiped the residue from his mouth with the back of a gloved hand, then wiped a handkerchief around the edge of the glass several times. *No room for error,* he told himself, holding it up to the light before leaving it on a bench.

As he stepped into the car park, he pulled up the collar of his coat.

'Got the masks?' He turned back to Rab who jogging to catch up.

Rab waved two black woollen ski masks.

The corners of Billy's mouth creased into a malevolent smile.

The late evening news was starting as Jock Kerr set his steaming mug of tea on the coffee table and flopped onto the sofa. He was about to shout through to Fiona, who was in the kitchen opening a fresh packet of shortbread, when the telephone rang. The handset lay on the coffee table and its display was glowing. He snorted and glanced at the clock on the mantelpiece, even though he knew the time. He snatched up the receiver.

'Hello?'

'Do you know who this is?' said the harsh voice. 'I always said I'd catch up with you and I have. Your day of reckoning is almost here.'

The line went dead.

Jock stiffened as continuous purring berated his ears. An image from the past flooded his mind. He recognised the voice and now his head was in turmoil. As he pushed himself up from his seat the lounge window exploded. Shards of glass flew everywhere and the closed blinds were torn from their fastenings, as a weighted lump appeared through the opening.

Jock froze. His eyes registered what lay before him but his brain was grappling with the vision; confusion, disbelief and fear were all manifesting at the same time. The head and bare shoulders of a man's lifeless body lay flopped over the windowsill, entangled in the wreckage of the blinds. He felt cold as he stared at the long, unkempt hair hanging from the bloodied head and became conscious of an awful gut-wrenching smell.

His wife's piercing screams jolted him into action — the instinct to survive taking over. Jock jumped up and made a dash for the hallway. Flinging open the front door, he ran out onto the path. It took a few seconds for his vision to adjust, but then he saw clearly — slumped half-inside, half outside the front window was a naked man. The paleness of the flesh told Jock he was dead.

Out of the corner of his eye, he caught movement at the top of his drive and turned. A tall silhouetted figure stood looking at him. Behind the shadow, against the kerb, a hatchback had its engine revving loudly. In the half-light he could make out at least a couple more people in the front and rear, all staring at him. The figure at the top of his drive was slowly pulling off a ski mask. Jock caught sight of a beard, and as the woollen mask was completely removed straggly, wavy hair dropped, framing the man's face.

A shiver ran down Jock's spine. Despite the greying beard and hair, he still recognised his nemesis. Billy Wallace's eyes were wide and staring, glistening with hate.

In the distance Jock could hear the faint wail of a siren; the police were on their way and a wave of relief washed over him.

There was a stand-off as Jock scrutinised Billy, who stood, motionless.

For a moment Billy remained, staring back at him. Then he lifted a hand and dragged a finger across his exposed throat — a slow slicing movement.

He gave a menacing smile before turning and climbing into the front passenger seat of the car. His door was still open as the wheels squealed on the wet tarmac. It shot away from the kerb, tearing towards a side street.

Hunter sank into his armchair with a tumbler of single malt whisky. He swilled the amber liquid around, listening to the chink of ice against the cut glass, then savoured his first sip, enjoying the pleasant afterburn tickling the back of his throat, drifting down his gullet and into his stomach.

It had been another long day.

He took another small sip, this time holding it in his mouth. Momentarily, he closed his eyes as the oak-aged flavour caressed his taste buds. He swallowed.

Moments like this were rare these days.

He'd got home an hour ago, in time for Beth to make her girls' night appointment. He hadn't even taken off his jacket before she was kissing his cheek and telling him his salmon was in the microwave and there was salad in the fridge.

'I'm only around the corner at Julie's,' she shouted over her shoulder. 'You know where I am. See you about eleven.' She disappeared out of the door.

He'd only just managed to get Jonathan and Daniel settled down. As he'd ruffled their hair affectionately and kissed their foreheads before tucking the boys in, it had jolted his conscience. He wished he had more time for this.

Hunter picked up the remote from the coffee table and powered on the TV; he would try and lose himself for a couple of hours before Beth got home.

He took another glug of whisky and listened to the sounds of the house. The central heating pipes creaked upstairs beneath the floorboards. He sank into his armchair, feeling himself relax. He swilled the contents around again; the tumbler was almost empty.

One more, and that's it.

He enjoyed a drink at home but never more than a couple to unwind. Many of his colleagues used it as a crutch to ease away the tensions of the day, only to find themselves relying on it too much. For some cops, drinking was second nature and he'd seen the disastrous consequences. He was determined not to go down that route.

Twenty minutes later, as he set down his second empty glass, he felt his eyelids drooping. He was close to exhaustion.

Time to call it a day.

He couldn't stay awake much longer. Not even for Beth. Never mind, he knew she'd understand.

As he eased himself up, the phone rang.

It was his parents' names on the screen, and he slipped the receiver out of its stand and answered.

Before he had time to speak, his mum's voice screamed down the line. Her panicked cries rattled him to the core. He tried to interrupt, make sense of her high-pitched ramblings. Finally, unable to get a word in, he shouted, 'I'm on my way!' and ended the call.

He speed-dialled Beth's mobile — she was only two minutes away — and bolted upstairs to sling on jeans and a sweat top. By the time he came downstairs again, Beth was falling through the front door, her face flushed.

'Sorry about this,' he said, snatching up the car keys from the hallway table. 'Something's happened at Mum's. I'll ring you as soon as I find out what!'

Hunter raced at break-neck speed towards his parents' home. The tiredness of ten minutes earlier had gone and it was like he'd never touched a drink. He was alert and trying to make sense of the hysterical screams he'd heard on the phone.

Within twelve minutes of leaving home he was screeching into his parents' road — to be greeted by mayhem.

The street was awash with police officers, and emergency vehicles of all descriptions lined the road, their whirling strobes lighting the area like a disco. Blue and white crime scene tape was everywhere — sealing off the approach to his mum and dad's semi and keeping neighbours back.

His stomach turned. This was the scene of a major incident.

Hunter slewed his car into the kerb and leapt out, leaving the driver's door open as he sprinted towards the house. A young uniformed officer was about to head him off but moved aside when Hunter flashed his warrant card.

He slackened his pace as he neared the driveway — he had never seen so much activity. Uniformed cops, plain clothed detectives and Scenes of Crime officers were swarming around the front of the house. It seemed surreal. This was his old home, he had moved here when he was twelve years old and had spent his teenage years growing up in its warm and loving environment. And this was close to where he'd met Polly, who had lived three streets away and with whom he'd fallen madly in love as his first girlfriend. It was here where he had heard about her murder. Finally, it was where he had made his most life-changing decision — telling his parents he didn't want to go to university to study fine art, instead, he wanted to be a cop and catch his girlfriend's killer.

A lot of water had flowed under the bridge since then.

He tried to focus as he walked up the drive. Much of the activity was by the lounge window which had a gaping hole in it. Two forensic officers were draping a plastic sheet over something half-inside the window and as he got nearer Hunter realised it was the naked shape of a gaunt, lanky man. This is why his mum was in in such a state.

On the front lawn, the skeletal frame of a forensic tent was in the process of being erected by SOCO. He recognised Duncan Wroe.

Then he spotted his boss emerging from the front door. In the hallway, behind him, stood the red-headed Scottish DCI. He tried to recollect her name but his brain was mush.

'Hunter!' shouted Detective Superintendent Robshaw.

Hunter's pace had dropped to a fast walk. 'What the hell is going on? Who on earth's this?' he pointed at the body. 'Where are my mum and dad? Are they hurt?' He machine-gunned questions one after another.

Robshaw held up a hand as Dawn joined him.

Hunter pointed at her. 'Why's DCI Leggate here?' He'd remembered her name. 'What's she got to do with this?'

'Whoa! Just a minute Hunter, calm down. Both your parents are okay. Shook up, but neither of them are hurt. They're on their way to the Victim Interview Suite at Maltby police station. The FME is en route to check them over.'

'Who's that?' Hunter asked again, pointing at the naked corpse which had finally been covered up.

'Steady down, Hunter, and we'll tell you.'

Robshaw glanced sideways at the Scottish DCI.

She shrugged and took a deep breath, pushing her hands into her rainproof jacket. 'That's the body of a junkie.'

'A junkie?'

Dawn nodded. 'He was abducted two weeks ago near to where he lived in Glasgow.'

Hunter was dumbfounded. Everything was spinning round in his head.

'What's having the body of a druggie from Glasgow thrown through the front window of my mum and dad's home got to do with them?'

'It's all linked to an investigation I'm involved in,' Dawn said.

He looked from Dawn to Robshaw and pointed his finger at her like a weapon. 'I knew you were down here for something. What's this shit you're hiding from me?'

'That's enough, Hunter,' said Robshaw. 'Don't say something you'll regret later.' He took a step forward. 'DCI Leggate is here under my sanction, and she and her team have been trying to protect your father. As I have already told you, your mum and dad are safe and should be at Maltby police station by now. I want you to go there with DCI Leggate and when you get there, she and your dad will fill you in with everything you need to know.'

Given the time of night, the main roads were quiet, enabling Hunter to step on the accelerator as he headed towards Maltby Police Station.

Beside him sat Dawn Leggate.

'The junkie's name is Fraser Cullen. He was a snout for one of my DSs.'

Hunter watched her out of the corner of his eye. She never took her eyes away from the windscreen.

'It's a long story, but basically, me and my team have been investigating the murders of three retired detectives and just over two weeks ago Fraser contacted my DS with information about one of the murders. Fraser gave us the names of two men who had beaten to death a retired detective in Glasgow. Ten minutes after the meeting between Fraser and my DS, we got an anonymous phone call to the effect that someone had seen Fraser being bundled into a grey Ford Mondeo. We've been searching for him, the car, and the two men he named since that call.'

There was the grey Mondeo again. The same colour and make of car that was involved in the attack on one of Hunter's uniformed colleagues, and which he had disturbed in the car park of his dad's gym yesterday.

What the fuck is going on? 'I don't get it. What's the relevance of Fraser's — whatever his name is — dead body being thrown through my parents' front window? Are you saying my dad's involved in drugs?'

'Cullen. Fraser Cullen. And no, it's nothing to do with drugs. As I've said, it's a long story, and soon you'll be told everything. Let's just see if your mum and dad are all right first. That's the main priority. Then if your dad's in a fit state to talk he can tell you everything. I promised him he could be the one to tell you when the time came.'

Hunter's head was in a whirl and he was doing his best to focus on his driving. He gripped the steering wheel so tightly that a tingling sensation shot through his fingers and into his forearms. His brain was desperately trying to make sense of the muddle and as he glanced down at his hands, he felt nothing but frustration and vexation.

He spotted the road sign for Maltby police station — the journey had flown. He flicked down the indicator and turned off the main road.

Pulling into a visitor's bay, he killed the engine and took a deep breath.

Dawn Leggate grabbed Hunter's forearm.

He stared at her.

'I'm not trying to hide anything from you, DS Kerr, believe me. I made a promise to your father and I'm simply keeping it. In another ten minutes you'll know everything. Some of what you are going to hear is not going to sit comfortably so I'm warning you to be prepared.'

Hunter led the way into the station; he had been here before. They both flashed their warrant cards to the receptionist and she buzzed them through and directed them to where they needed to be.

The Victim Reception Suite was where rape victims and abused children normally came to be supported, examined and questioned. Hunter had used similar rooms at other stations when he was in CID.

Hunter pushed through the door into an overbearingly warm room furnished like someone's front lounge. His mum launched herself from the sofa and flung her arms around his neck.

Hunter felt her body convulse as she mumbled his name. It took him aback; he had never witnessed an outburst like this from his mum — she was such a strong character.

It deflated his anger and frustration, bringing him to his senses. He looked over to his dad who was slowly rising from one of the seats, his face a picture of shock.

Hunter gently eased his mum away. Her eyes were bloodshot.

DCI Leggate guided her back to the sofa and sat next to her.

Hunter dropped into a chair facing them.

Dawn flashed an awkward smile at Jock. 'I've not told your son anything yet, Jock, but now it's time for him to know. We agreed that if things ever came to this it would be the right thing to do, didn't we?'

Jock nodded forlornly.

Dawn turned her attention to Hunter. 'Before your father tells you his bit, I'll explain where I fit into all this. Just over three months ago two prisoners serving life for the murder of a 24-year-old woman and her four-year-old daughter were released from Barlinnie prison after spending 36 years behind bars. Those two prisoners are Billy Wallace and Rab Geddes. I didn't know either of them — way before my time — but I know them now. Billy had the nickname Braveheart in his younger days. He had a fearsome reputation and used to boast that William Wallace was his ancestor. I'm not sure that's true, and knowing what I now know about Billy Wallace I think it's an insult to a great Scottish hero.

'Billy comes from bad stock. His father, Gordon, did time for a couple of warehouse robberies and was involved in the black market during the 1950s in Glasgow. Throughout the 60s, Gordon built up a bit of a criminal empire and formed one of the leading gangster families in the suburbs, offering protection to pubs and clubs and at one stage he was peddling guns around to criminals.'

She leaned forward, clasping her hands. 'Gordon introduced his son into the fold when he was about 18. Billy was a real tough-nut who could handle himself and he quickly made a reputation for himself because of the extreme violence he used. Rab Geddes was a lifelong school friend and between them they began to run the Wallace family business. Billy started to push drugs — something unheard of in the gangs back then — and began to amass quite a fortune.

'Then things took a turn for the worse for Billy and his family. The police began to crack down. A few rogue cops who had been taking backhanders to turn the other cheek, or in some cases lose evidence, were investigated and dismissed and many gang members had their collars felt. Rival gangs started to turn against one another.

'The Procurator Fiscal and the CID from Shettlestone nick began looking at the Wallace gang round about 1970 and Gordon decided to call it a day, happy to live off the wealth he had amassed from his earlier criminal activities. His son Billy didn't, and one night back in 1971, when he went to collect a drug debt, things boiled over. He couldn't find the dealer who had ripped him off and so in a fit of temper he shot the guy's girlfriend and her four-year-old daughter before setting fire to the flat.

'Within days, snouts from opposing gangs had dropped Billy and Rab for it and detectives got a breakthrough with a witness who had been there on the night of the murders and who provided crucial evidence. The upshot was that they were both arrested and as a result of the evidence they were convicted and sent to prison for 36 years.

'You will have gathered by now that Billy is a bit of a psycho, and even in prison he continued his violence. He was responsible for at least one prisoner's murder and he was also involved in the stabbing of two others.' Dawn sat back and crossed one leg over the other. 'He vowed revenge against the team of detectives who'd arrested him and the main witness who had helped to convict him. And that's where I've come in. Several weeks ago, Billy and Rab disappeared off the radar when they did a bunk from a bail hostel. Shortly after, four people — three men and a woman — were brutally murdered. The man and woman were from my neck of the woods — Stirling, the other two men lived near Glasgow. The men are all retired detectives — the same detectives who were responsible for getting the convictions and putting Wallace and Geddes behind bars. My team from Stirling are involved in a joint investigation with Glasgow CID and we have enough evidence to link Billy and Rab to the murders.' She uncrossed her legs and hunched forward. 'Your dad recognised Billy Wallace this evening. The grey Mondeo he came in got away before we got there but we have circulated it. There are a lot of officers on the ground looking for them as I speak — but you'll have guessed that.'

The mention of the grey Mondeo flashed an alert inside Hunter's head. Now he remembered where he'd seen the driver before. The newly grown, thinning, sandy hair had tricked him. It was the shaven-headed man he'd seen arguing with his dad at Staithes. It was all fitting into place.

Dawn continued. 'Me and my team are down here for two reasons — one, to track down Wallace and Geddes, and two, and just as important, to protect the main witness from that trial back in 1972 — your father.' She looked across at Jock. 'I'll let you take over.'

Jock took a deep breath and glanced at his wife. Then, as he had done so many times recently, he avoided eye contact, instead staring down at his clasped hands.

'This is very difficult for me, son,' he began. 'I've not tried to hide this from you — I just didn't know how to tell you what you're about to hear, especially with the important job you have. I suppose naively I hoped it would never come to this. What do they say about the best laid plans?' Tears welled up in Jock's eyes. 'You know I've told you all about my younger days as a boxer and how my career ended and how me and your ma came down to Yorkshire where you were born and I set up the gym?'

Hunter nodded. He felt his stomach knot as his dad wiped the corner of an eye with the back of a hand.

'All that is true but I have never told you why, have I, son?' He looked at Hunter for the first time, took his wallet from his trousers, fished into it, extracted a folded piece of paper and held it out.

Hunter took the yellowed, Sellotaped news cutting, which he unfolded. The headline read: GLASGOW GANGSTERS SENTENCED FOR BRUTAL SLAYING OF MOTHER AND DAUGHTER. Below that was a smaller sub-heading: SUPERGRASS TURNS QUEEN'S EVIDENCE. Hunter started to read.

'That's what I've been trying to avoid all these years, you finding out the full facts. My name's not Jock Kerr — or rather my birth name wasn't that.'

Hunter felt like he'd been punched in the guts. His stomach turned. From the look on the faces of his mum and the DCI, he knew he had heard right. His head started to throb.

'I'm sorry, son, I know this has come as a bit of a shock but now you know. I've been living under an assumed name for years. I was forced to change it after the trial. I took on your grandfather's name from your mother's side, and the Procurator Fiscal and the detectives on the case helped me to relocate to Yorkshire.'

'So, you're the supergrass in the article?'

'No — no, nothing like that. That was just what the papers wrote. Let me tell you the full story before you judge me.'

'I think you'd better.'

'After I had to give up my boxing, I didn't know what to do, and Billy's dad — Gordon Wallace — came to me one night when I was in the club having a beer. He said he'd heard good things about me and maybe he could put some work my way. I was good with my fists so he offered me some door work looking after a couple of clubs. I knew Gordon as being dodgy but I genuinely didn't know the level of crime he was involved in. Then one day he turns up at the flat I had with your ma and says he wants me to keep an eye on his son, Billy. Some people were after Billy and he asked me to drive him around and watch his back. Said he'd pay me a hundred pounds a week. Well, I jumped at the chance, didn't I — where else could I earn that type of money? All he said to me was I wasn't to ask too many questions, just watch his son's back.

'Well, the first time I picked Billy up he introduced me to his pal Rab and asked me to drive them to this tenement because he had some business to sort out. I had no idea what he was up to until he and Rab came running back to the car and told me to get them out of there. There was blood everywhere. Billy said the woman in the flat had slashed him with a knife. Him and Rab were arguing over shooting a kid and Billy was flashing this shooter about. I was really scared, Hunter. I drove them to some wasteland and watched them bury the gun and then they told me to drop them off.

'I was physically sick when I got home. The next day, I saw on the news that they'd killed a woman and her four-year-old bairn. I told your ma what had happened and she told me to go to the police. I didn't at first but I called anonymously and gave them Billy's and Rab's names. I don't know how, but a couple of days later two detectives came to the flat and asked me about the murders. I told them everything and they told me to find somewhere else to live until the trial. I knew I wouldn't be safe, especially when I found out about the gangster connections and it came out about my links to Gordon Wallace, and so I agreed a deal with the police. I said I would give evidence if they gave me a fresh start — and they did. I stopped being Iain Campbell.' For a second Jock closed his eyes. 'Little did I realise what repercussions there would be. Do you realise now why I wanted to hold this back?'

'And that guy I saw you arguing with in Staithes?'

'Rab Geddes. It was sheer bad luck he recognised me, especially after all these years. Apparently, he was visiting an old girlfriend.'

For a few seconds, Hunter felt like a great weight was pushing down on him. He was trying to make sense of what he had been told. What kind of person was his dad, and just as important, who was he?

'This may seem a strange question, Dad. Is my name really Hunter Kerr?'

Jock looked shocked. 'Of course it is. Only I changed my name. It was done by deed poll. Your mum was already a Kerr so she reverted back to her maiden name. You were christened Hunter and your birth certificate says that.'

Hunter dropped his head into his hands and rubbed his face. He could feel a migraine coming on for the first time in ages. In another hour or so the pressure would be so great that he'd see flashing stars and be physically sick.

DAY THIRTY-THREE

Hunter adjusted the rear-view mirror, stared at his reflection and noted the dark rings under his eyes. He stroked his jaw-line — he was in need of a shave.

Overall, you look like shit, Hunter Kerr.

'You look crap,' said Grace.

It was like she'd heard the voice in his head. He glanced across at her in the passenger seat.

'I feel it. I've hardly slept the past couple of days.'

'Your dad?'

Hunter nodded. 'He and my mum are staying with us.'

'They'll catch this Billy Wallace and his mate soon and then you can all put it behind you. It sounds to me as though they've got them bang to rights and they'll be going back inside and die in prison.' Grace examined her fingernails. The pearlescent polish glinted in the sunlight.

'We won't be able to put it behind us, though, will we? It's always going to be there, isn't it?'

She fixed him with a glare. 'Oh, for goodness' sake, Hunter, stop feeling sorry for yourself. How will it affect you in the future? It's your dad this has happened to.'

'Grace, he's not the man I thought I knew. All these years he's lied to me.'

'Listen to me, Hunter. This is me talking to you, not only as a colleague but as a friend as well. Your father has not lied to you and never has done. Yes, he's held back the truth but that is not lying. And the way I see it he did it with all best intentions, especially with the job you've got. How could he have told his son — a cop — that he was involved with gangsters in his past? Think about it for a second — would you tell your sons?'

He held her stare. He had no response. He hadn't looked at it that way.

'And from what you've told me it seems to me he had little choice. He was only 20 at the time with all kinds of problems to deal with, especially how to make a living for him and your mother after his promising boxing career had ended. I'm sorry but I don't agree with you on this one. I feel for your dad. It must have been a living nightmare for him the last couple of months. Can't you imagine what must have been going on inside his head? He was trying to protect your mum and you from this. You need to take a long, hard look at yourself, Hunter. You've only got one set of parents. You know how much they've been there for you and how much you've got in common with your dad. He's your friend as well as your father. If you carry on like this, you'll be in danger of destroying your relationship. Anyway, what's Beth say about all this?'

Hunter hesitated. He'd had a similar hushed conversation with his wife. Finally, he said, 'Practically the same as you.' He felt a lump in his throat.

'Well, there you are then. Listen to her. I don't know what you men would do without us women. For god's sake, take him out for a beer and clear the air.'

Suddenly, their radios broke into the conversation.

He, Grace, and the majority of the MIT team had been on plot since 7 a.m., in unmarked cars at locations dotted around Parkhill Flats in Sheffield, lying in wait for Ari and Pervez Arshad.

Grace yanked across her seatbelt and Hunter started the car, straining to hear the report coming over the radio net.

The information he was listening to spirited his thoughts away from the problems of his dad and took him back to the previous afternoon, when Superintendent Robshaw had bounded into the office with the news that they had found out where Samia's killers were hiding. A Drug Squad informant had revealed the location — a flat which the team was now staking out. The pair had false passports and were making plans to leave the country in the next few days.

'They should be coming into view in the next minute or so,' Grace said, ear close to her radio.

Hunter was listening too. DS Mark Gamble and DC Paula Clarke were on foot and had Ari and Pervez in their sights. They gave the targets' descriptions and location.

Hunter parked on an elevated section of road overlooking the concrete monoliths, which he had read somewhere were now an icon of 60s architecture. Many of the blocks were in the throes of refurbishment and their frontages had been given a vibrant colour scheme of red, blue and yellow in an attempt to hide their drab greyness.

Within seconds, Hunter had the targets in sight.

The two Asians appeared to be in no hurry. They were sauntering across a grassy slope 150 metres below. The pair were dressed identically in dark hoodies and baggy jeans and the glint of gold in the bright mid-morning sunshine revealed that both wore a number of lengthy chains around their necks, dangling to mid chest. They were huddled together and appeared deep in conversation.

Hunter leaned forward as the pair made a surprise sharp movement. They stopped in mid-step and turned to look behind.

Something had spooked them, thought Hunter.

A split second later the brothers were off and running, with DS Mark Gamble scrambling after them. His voice was screaming over the airwaves, letting everyone know that the foot surveillance had been compromised.

Hunter kept watch on the fleeing figures, checking where they were heading before he made a move. Gripping the handbrake, he squeezed the accelerator and felt the engine surge. He was ready for the chase.

The pair dropped from view, disappearing into a line of trees at the edge of the estate. They were making for the road.

Mark Gamble was doing his best to keep the commentary going, his voice trailing off now and again as he tried to make ground. Within seconds his excited tone was alerting the team.

'They're getting into a new-shaped silver Astra!'

Hunter craned his neck, scouring the road system beyond the line of trees. He heard the Vauxhall before he saw it as tyre rubber screeched on the tarmac. Then it sped into his sightline, heading away from the estate and towards the suburbs of Halfway. Hunter locked the steering wheel sharply and pulled away from the kerb. Whipping through the gears quickly he soon made the junction and he guessed he would be a fraction in front of the speeding Astra. He could hear over the radio that two other cars were in hot pursuit but trailing.

Hunter slung his car at an angle to stop the Vauxhall turning into the road. He tightened his hold on the steering wheel and braced himself.

Ten seconds later the Astra gunned into view, rocking out of a right-hand bend and veering towards them.

Hunter gritted his teeth and in one swift movement spun the steering wheel sharply, hitting the accelerator and the brake almost simultaneously.

His car jumped forward into the carriageway, giving the impression he was going to deliberately ram them.

The action had the desired effect. There was a long screech as the Astra tyres crabbed across the road. It slewed sideways, the nearside wheels smashing into the opposite kerb.

Hunter could see Ari, the driver, fighting with the wheel, trying to straighten up as the car bounced back into the road. His actions were in vain. It bucked and scythed violently, whipping into a screaming 180-degree turn before smashing its back end against a street lamp.

Hunter threw open his door, released his seatbelt and leapt out of the car.

Ari was as quick, kicking open his door so that it smacked Hunter's legs and spun him sideways, giving Ari the few seconds break he needed. He was out of the blocks like a sprinter on a running track.

Hunter winced at the pain to his right thigh but then adrenaline kicked in and he set off in pursuit.

Ari had gained ten yards. Hunter could make out the word SEMTEX in large white letters across the back of his black designer hooded top and thought how much he'd like to demolish him once he got hold of him.

Within moments his chest was pumping in rhythm with his arms and legs. His lungs clawed for air as he put in an extra burst. In less than fifty yards Hunter was in grabbing distance and he lashed out with a swift kick. It connected, crashing one leg into the other, sending Ari sprawling into a heap. Hunter was on top of him and wrestling an arm up his back before he had any time to react.

He screamed as Hunter yanked his shoulder joint against the socket.

'You're breaking my fucking arm!'

'Think yourself lucky it's not your fucking neck,' Hunter snarled. 'You're nicked!'

As he turned to drag his prisoner back, he saw the chaos behind him. Uniform and CID cars were everywhere and Grace was trying to snap handcuffs on the wrists of a dishevelled Pervez. He was being restrained by Tony Bullars, who had been the lead car in the chase.

As Hunter neared, jamming Ari's arm up his back, forcing him to walk on his tip-toes, he could see Pervez was doubled up, struggling with Tony Bullars, trying to rub his face and moaning loudly.

'What's the matter with him?' he asked, releasing his prisoner to Mike Sampson who was waiting with cuffs.

Pervez raised his head. Tears were streaming down his face and he was having difficulty opening his eyes.

'That fucking bitch has CSed me,' he moaned.

'Stop rubbing your eyes, you'll only make it worse,' Grace said with a smirk, slipping the CS gas canister back into her jacket pocket. She turned to Hunter. 'I thought he was going to attack me so I gassed him.'

'Fucking liar, I said I was coming quietly.'

Hunter kept a straight face. 'I don't know, Grace, what have I said to you about police brutality and that temper of yours?' He opened the back door of his car and shoved Ari onto the rear seat. 'I wouldn't dream of doing anything like that. I don't know, I can't take you anywhere.'

He turned to see her rolling her eyes and shaking her head in mock despair and he shot her a wink.

'Well done, everyone,' he said, slamming the rear door shut. 'Let's wrap this up and get these two back for questioning.'

Hunter picked up a Pakistani passport, flicked through the inside pages and added a few more notes to his pre-interview record. He set it back down on the pile of evidence laid out across his and Grace's desks.

Upon their return to Barnwell with their prisoners, the team had emptied the contents of Ari and Pervez's Vauxhall Astra. In the boot they found clothing in three holdalls, together with two single airline tickets to Allama Iqbal International Airport and two Pakistan National passports bearing Ari and Pervez's photographs, but under other names.

The Drug Squad informant had been spot-on about the brothers making ready to flee the country, thought Hunter as he looked across to where Grace was still logging the evidence.

The incident room was empty. Mark Gamble and Paula Clarke had shot out to Hassan's convenience store. They were going to arrest Mohammed and Jilani, now the Arshads were in custody, while Andy France and Alex Mills were in Sheffield, trying to find an address for the brothers. They had refused to divulge where they lived when they were booked into custody and nothing in their possessions had offered a clue. However, they had recovered the brothers' mobile phones, which were now with the technical experts in the hope that they could locate the last spot where a signal was emitted. It was a long shot.

'Ready?' Hunter asked. He and Grace were to interview Ari, while Tony Bullars and Mike Sampson had the job of questioning his brother Pervez. They were already in one of the other interview rooms.

Grace nodded.

Hunter pushed back his chair and gathered his notes. He took a final lingering look at the incident board, confirming and double-checking in his head that he had it all lodged, ready for when he needed to dig in to his memory banks. He nodded. He was prepared.

'Okay, Grace, let's put this job to bed.'

Ari Arshad looked cocky despite the painful pink graze to his right cheek, caused when Hunter tripped him prior to arrest. He had bleated to the Custody Officer about assault when he was booked in. He leant back on the rear legs of his chair; arms folded defensively.

The duty solicitor was next to him, making notes in his legal pad. As the two detectives walked into the room, Hunter saw the solicitor check his watch and make a note of the time.

Hunter slapped his paperwork on the table, making the solicitor jump and scowl at him over his spectacles. Hunter cracked a false apologetic smile. 'Sorry about that.' He took a seat opposite, nodding to Grace and she started the tape-recording machine.

Hunter went through the customary preamble to an interview, flicking open his folder even though he knew he wouldn't need to refer to it.

'For the tape, can I confirm you are Ari Arshad?'

The prisoner exchanged a look with his solicitor, who shrugged his shoulders and nodded.

Ari rocked slightly on the back legs of his chair. 'That's right, I am the one and only Ari Arshad,' he said.

'And not Habib-ur-Begum, as it says in the Pakistan National Passport we found in your car?'

'No comment.'

'Why were you in possession of a false passport and a one-way airline ticket to Pakistan?'

'No comment.'

'Okay, if that's the tack you wish to take, Ari, I'll ask you a less incriminating question. Just for the record, what relation are you to Mohammed Hassan?'

Ari glanced at his solicitor again, who gestured with raised eyebrows that it was okay to answer.

'Mohammed is my uncle.'

'And so Samia Hassan, his daughter, is your cousin?' Hunter removed a photo of Samia from beneath his papers. It was a blown up shot from the Meadowhall CCTV footage. 'For the tape, I am showing the defendant a colour photograph of Samia Hassan. Is this the Samia we are talking about?'

Ari nodded. 'Yes.'

'When was the last time you saw Samia?'

Ari bunched his shoulders. 'Can't remember.'

'Rough guess. Couple of weeks, couple of months?'

'Couple of months, I guess.'

'Where was that?'

'At my uncle's place.'

'What address is that?' Hunter was hoping for a slip up. They still did not know the attack site.

'His shop in Hoyland.'

'You have already been told the reason for your arrest this morning, haven't you?'

'Yes, but that's shit. I haven't murdered Samia. You've got the wrong man, Mr Smart Detective.'

Hunter rolled with the sarcastic retort. 'I'm guessing you've seen the TV news and the newspaper headlines about Samia's murder?'

'Yeah.'

'When did you first become aware of her disappearance?'

'Can't remember.'

'Who told you about it?'

'My uncle, I think.'

'Can you remember when that was?'

'Nope.'

Hunter needed to move things forward. He replaced the photograph in his folder and took out another. It was of the white Renault van recovered from the Rotherham car dismantlers. 'Ari, slight change of questioning now. Do you recognise this van?'

Hunter clocked Ari's reaction. He dropped his chair back on to its four legs but didn't respond.

'I'll ask the question again. Do you recognise this white Renault van?'

Ari coughed. 'I think so.'

'You think so?'

'My uncle owned a similar van.'

'This is the van owned by your uncle, Mohammed Hassan — I can confirm that from its index number. Have you ever driven this van?' From Duncan Wroe's SOCO report, Hunter knew Ari's fingerprints and DNA were all over the van and that he had been seen in the Country Park by Dr Christopher Chambers.

There were a couple of seconds silence then Ari replied softly, 'Yeah, I used to do deliveries for him.'

'When was the last time you drove or were in this van?'

There was a delayed response again. 'Can't remember.'

'Let me help you remember. Have you ever been to Meadowhall in the van?'

Now there was a clear reaction. Ari locked his arms tighter and his face hardened.

Hunter waited for twenty seconds but there was no reply. 'I'll ask again. Have you ever driven to or been in this vehicle at Meadowhall shopping centre?'

Ari turned to his solicitor as if seeking help with an answer. His solicitor picked up on the look. 'DS Kerr, is this line of questioning going anywhere?'

Hunter opened up a CD case, took out a DVD and slid it across to Grace, who slotted it into a small TV/DVD player set in the corner of the room. The screen flashed from dark grey to blue.

Hunter turned to the solicitor. 'There is some significance to this line of questioning which your client obviously finds uncomfortable answering. Could it be he has something to hide?'

'DS Kerr, that is out of order.'

Hunter fixed Ari with a determined stare. 'Mr Arshad, my question relating to your use of your uncle's white van at Meadowhall has in my view hit a raw nerve. I am therefore going to show you some CCTV footage which may help jog your memory.'

He nodded to Grace, who hit the play button on the TV. Over the next five minutes the horrific attack on Samia by Ari and Pervez in the underground car park at Meadowhall played out across the screen. The entire time Hunter studied his prisoner's face. He put on a front as he watched the damning evidence but from the continued movement in the young man's Adam's apple, Hunter knew he had him rattled.

Grace stopped the footage.

'Do you want me to play that again or are you happy for me to ask you questions in relation to what you've just seen on the TV?'

Complete silence.

'You have just watched an attack upon Samia Hassan in the underground car park at Meadowhall shopping centre which was carried out by two men on the 28th of July this year. Do you recognise the two men you have seen carry out that attack?'

Ari's eyes widened. He glared back in defiance.

'Mr Arshad, I would appreciate an answer. From what you have just been shown, do you agree that the one of the people who beat Samia Hassan until she was unconscious was yourself?'

Ari unfolded his arms and slammed them onto the table. 'No comment. No fucking comment.'

The solicitor reached across and tapped Ari Arshad's arm. 'DS Kerr, I would like ten minutes with my client,' he announced.

The ten minutes went beyond twenty minutes. Hunter leaned against the wall outside the interview room, his eyes on the gap at the bottom of the door. He knew that inside the room there was some serious client solicitor storyline being hammered out. A smile played on his lips; they had Ari on the rack.

Just as he was checking his watch again the door opened and the solicitor stuck his head around it. 'My client is ready to answer your questions.'

Hunter and Grace started with fresh tapes. Grace switched on the recording machine and Hunter reminded Ari of his rights. 'Okay, before we had a break you were shown CCTV footage of an attack upon Samia Hassan by two men. Was one of those men you?'

'Yeah, but I didn't kill Samia.'

'And who was the other person who carried out the attack with you?'

'You know who it is. It's Pervez, my brother.'

'Why did you attack Samia?'

'We were forced to do it.'

'Forced?'

'Yeah, you don't know what my uncle Mohammed is like. He's a violent man, we're scared of him. He told us to do it.'

This didn't ring true, especially given the criminal records of the pair, but Hunter encouraged Ari to continue.

'Mohammed used to ring me lots, telling me Samia was dishonouring the family. He told me she was sleeping with a man outside of marriage and wanted us to warn her and get her to come home. Then a few months ago he came to see me and Pervez and said we had to do something about Samia. She was refusing to marry a cousin of ours after agreeing to the marriage and he wanted us to make her go to Pakistan. I told him we couldn't do that but he threatened me and Pervez. He is a very violent man. That day at Meadowhall, me and Pervez were making deliveries for our uncle and he phoned me up shouting and swearing. He said Samia was at Meadowhall threatening to run away and he told us to go and get her and bring her back. I know on that footage it looks worse than it was.'

'Looks worse than it was,' interrupted Hunter. 'You beat her unconscious and threw her in the back of the van like a rag doll.'

Ari shrugged. 'We didn't mean to beat her like we did, we just got carried away.'

'So, what happened after you left the car park?'

'Mohammed met us on an industrial site near Rotherham and took her out of the van and drove her away. We didn't kill her. The last time I saw her was when we helped put her in the back of Mohammed's car.'

Hunter hadn't expected this response. He had damning evidence to refute what had just been said. His spirits lifted.

'You say you took Samia out of the van and put her in her father's car?'

'Yeah.'

'Was she conscious or unconscious?'

'Conscious. She was struggling.'

'Then why did you get need to get rid of the van. To dispose of it at the car dismantlers like you did?'

Ari lowered his head for a few seconds before looking up again. 'Because Mohammed told us to. If he tells you something, you obey.'

'Did you do this straight away?'

'No, we hid the van in a garage for a few days then took it there.'

'Did anyone else use it?'

'No, we hid it.'

'Ari, I've let you go on a bit but that's because I wanted to give you enough rope to hang yourself. What you have just told us is complete bullshit. And how do I know that? Well, firstly, how do you account for fibres being found in the rear of the van? Fibres which match the rug in which Samia's body was found? Before you try and dig your way out of that one, I also want to introduce some other evidence as well. Do you remember a few years ago when Samia was at university and she had a relationship with a young man who was training to be a doctor?'

Ari looked up to the ceiling.

'A young man who you and your brother assaulted because of their relationship?'

Ari's eyes lowered. 'No complaint was ever made about that.'

'No, it wasn't, but we know you and your brother paid him a visit another time when he was working at Barnwell Infirmary and you warned him off and also damaged his car. And the bad news for you is that he just happened to be driving his car at Barnwell Lake on Friday, the first of August, the night you and your brother dumped Samia's body in the lake, and he recognised you driving your uncle's white van.'

From Ari's expression, Hunter knew he had him. The man closed his eyes for a few seconds then snapped them open. 'I've told you what happened, now I'm saying fuck all else.'

Hunter tried a few more probing questions which Ari batted off with 'no comment'. He'd lost the impetus of the interview and decided to sum things up, draw it to a close, and return Ari to his cell.

Hunter and Grace waited in the custody suite. Tony Bullars and Mike Sampson had not fared any better with Pervez, who had also made no comment to the majority of the questions. Once he was shown the CCTV footage of the attack on Samia, he refused to talk to the detectives except to demand to be locked up back in his cell.

They still had to interview Mohammed and his wife Jilani. At least Ari's evidence had implicated Samia's father and would provide a wedge, though Hunter doubted the truth of that, especially as they knew Samia had been violently raped prior to being murdered. That just didn't feel like something a father would do. They had made inroads that afternoon but were still no nearer to getting a clear-cut confession.

As they returned to the incident room for debriefing, Hunter knew the priority was to find the attack site. It would provide them with so many answers and much needed evidence to swing the enquiry.

DAY THIRTY-FOUR

Hunter pulled another bacon sandwich from the pile that Angie, the cleaner, and Grace had made. He'd heard them chatting and laughing in the small kitchen next to the incident room and wondered what they had found so amusing. He guessed they were gossiping about someone in the station.

Most of the team were in, hugging mugs of tea or coffee, munching on the surprise breakfast and chatting as they waited for the morning briefing.

This enquiry had just turned the corner, despite the lack of confessions to Samia's murder. The implication from Ari that his uncle Mohammed was responsible for his daughter's final days and hours was the starter for the day, and with a bit of luck it might just be the lever for obtaining the proper story.

Grace walked in with another plateful of sandwiches. 'That's it, all the bacon's gone now,' she said, plonking the plate down between hers and Hunter's desks.

'What muck have you two raked up on someone then? You were going at it hammer and tongs back there.'

Grace flopped into her seat and leaned across. 'You will never guess what I've just found out from Angie,' she said in a hushed voice.

'Go on, enlighten me.'

'The boss is only having a thing with that DCI from Scotland.'

'You are joking?'

'Nah, nah. One of her friends is waitressing at the Stables restaurant. The pair have been in there most evenings.'

Hunter shook his head in amazement and grinned. 'Well, the crafty bugger.'

Grace smiled, settling back in her chair.

Hunter took another bite of his sandwich. The mention of DCI Dawn Leggate caused him to drift away for a few moments. His parents were still staying with them. He'd wanted so much to sit down and sort things out with his dad but he hadn't had the chance because of the investigation. He had talked about it to Beth, who said his dad was moping round the house like a caged animal and wasn't eating properly. Hunter's mum had taken

Beth to one side and told her his dad was desperate for some time with Hunter to explain everything.

The sooner we put this enquiry to bed, the sooner I can get things sorted with him.

'You lot owe me a gallon of beer,' announced Barry Newstead, as he strode into the room, breaking Hunter's daydream. 'You are going to really thank me for this.' He waved a CD aloft and headed for the TV, switched it on, inserted the disc into the player and grabbed the remote. 'I spent most of yesterday afternoon with the neighbourhood team for the Parkhill Flats. Did you know most of it is covered by CCTV?'

The screen fluttered into life.

'There are 20-odd cameras fitted around the outside of the place, plus they have lift cameras at each floor inside the flats. I searched various time frames between the 28th of July, when we know Samia was abducted from Meadowhall, right through to the first of August when we believe her body was dumped in the lake and I found this little lot.'

Barry grinned widely. He loved to take centre-stage. He fired the remote at the DVD player like he was shooting a gun. A grainy image fluttered onto the screen.

'This was captured at 9.36 p.m. on the first of August. This camera is looking down on a grassed area in front of one of the buildings.'

Suddenly, in the right-hand corner of the screen, two men in dark hooded tops stumbled into view, struggling with a rolled-up bundle. Barry zoomed in on the hazy images.

One of the men had his back to the camera and was bent over, dragging what appeared to be a large rolled up rug along the ground.

Although their hoods were up, hiding the men's faces, Hunter could clearly make out the white lettering on the back of one of the designer hooded tops. The word SEMTEX was visible. He felt a surge of excitement.

The team watched in silence. The play continued with the two men disappearing off camera with their bundle.

'I also found this footage,' said Barry.

Another image flashed onto the screen. The pan of the camera was a lot wider and covered a larger portion of the complex. Into view came a section of road below a grassy knoll. Along the bottom of the screen was a line of parked cars.

'This is one of the slip roads just below the flats.'

From the top of the screen, the camera picked up two fuzzy images, silhouettes at first, but their movement was evident and they were obviously the same two characters, from their clothing. And they were struggling with the rolled-up carpet. The one at the back slipped and his end of the carpet slumped to the ground.

The person humped it back up towards his midriff and then the pair continued waddling down the slope with their bundle until they reached the road.

Barry zoomed in on the footage again. It was grainy but the images could be made out, though not well enough for facial recognition.

The pair pulled the rug towards a white van parked in a row of vehicles. The one wearing the SEMTEX designer top opened its rear doors and the pair loaded in the bundle. Both jumped into the front of the van and it pulled away and drove out of camera view.

Barry freeze-framed the shot. In the top left-hand corner was the time and date sequence 9.52 p.m., 01:08:08.

It all fitted. The time to travel from Sheffield to Barnwell Lake was approximately 40 minutes. It meant that their witness, the sex worker, Kerri-Ann Bairstow had been spot-on with the timings of her sightings of the two men and the white van at the Country Park.

'And for my encore,' Barry added with a flourish. He restarted the DVD player. 'This was captured in the entranceway of one of the internal lifts.'

The image which flickered onto the screen showed a floor area with a section of lift doors at the top quarter of the screen. From the angle of the shot, this was captured by a camera at ceiling height.

Suddenly the person in the SEMTEX designer hoody came into view. He was bent double, dragging the rolled-up carpet. Quickly following, lumping the other end of the rug, came another hooded figure. The clarity of these images was excellent and sections of pattern on the carpet were a perfect match to those of the rug in which Samia's body had been found. Hunter had no doubt he was watching the first stages of her being taken away from the place where she had just been raped and butchered.

The pair stopped by the lift doors, dropping both ends of the carpet and the one in the designer hoody straightened, easing out his back with his hands. As he pressed for the lift, he flicked back his hood and stretched his neck. There was no mistaking that face — it was Ari Arshad.

Hunter wanted to punch the air.

'That lift is on the fifth floor. Now all you've got to do is some old-fashioned door-knocking and you should have your attack site.'

Hunter studied Barry. A pneumatic drill couldn't remove that contented smirk on his face. He was so pleased for him and so glad he had brought him onto the team.

'Ever thought about being a detective, Barry?' said Hunter, straight-faced, leaping out of his seat.

Barry scrutinised him for a second then said, 'Detective Sergeant Kerr, if I didn't know you better, I would say you're jealous because an old hand has beaten you to the end-game.'

They grinned at each other.

'One up to you, Barry,' said Hunter, wetting a finger and striking it in the air. 'Well done, you old fart.'

As he switched off the TV, Barry said, 'I'll take that as a compliment, shall I? By the way I will accept payment with several pints of John Smith's amber nectar.'

'Let me have a go at Jilani,' Grace said to Hunter.

At briefing, Superintendent Robshaw had decided that now they had the CCTV evidence damning Ari there was no rush to re-interview him — the team should focus on Samia's parents because no one had spoken with them since their arrest the previous afternoon.

He had allocated that task to Hunter and Grace, sending the remainder of the team across to Sheffield to find Ari and Pervez's place, now Barry had narrowed down the flat location and floor level.

Hunter looked up from his notes.

'Let me try the empathy approach — mother and daughter thing again. It might work this time. I can guess she's been subservient to Mohammed for years and even afraid of him, but I can't believe deep down that she is involved in all this. My gut instinct is she's keeping silent because she's more afraid of her husband than she is of us.'

Hunter stroked his chin. 'Okay, let's go for it.' He clicked the top back on his pen and slid the folder of evidence across the desk. 'She's all yours.'

Jilani looked haggard. Her dark hair was unkempt, her red and gold sari was crumpled and black streaks stained her cheeks from crying.

Grace could see the woman had suffered a sleepless night and guessed she was feeling jaded and vulnerable. It all stacked in her favour.

An interpreter and her solicitor were present.

Hunter started the tape recording machine.

'Jilani, I want to make things easy for you. Yesterday we interviewed your nephews Ari and Pervez and one of them has admitted to being involved in the abduction of your daughter Samia.' Grace concentrated on Jilani's face, looking for reactions as the interpreter repeated her opening lines in Urdu.

'He has also implicated your husband Mohammed in this, saying your husband forced them to carry out the abduction under threat of violence.' Grace deliberately held back Dr Chambers's evidence.

There was a flicker in the woman's eyes and she gave a quick shake of her head.

'Mrs Hassan, I don't want to prolong this agony for you, because what happened to your daughter was horrendous. But we have a duty to investigate this thoroughly and if we find you are involved in her murder then you will suffer the consequences. Do you understand what I am saying?'

Jilani nodded before the interpreter finished and Grace realised the woman had a better understanding of English than she had initially made out. That was good. It would be easier for her to look for the signs in her facial expressions and body language.

'I'm going to show you some film footage now that was captured by CCTV cameras about two months ago at Meadowhall. I must warn you, it is disturbing, but I want you to concentrate on it.'

Hunter got up, switched on the small TV, and started the DVD rolling with the same footage they had shown to Ari Arshad the previous day.

As it played Grace kept her eyes on Jilani. Five minutes had gone by when the woman dropped her head onto her chest and started to weep. As the tape came to an end, Grace said, 'I'm sorry you had to sit through that, Mrs Hassan, but I needed to show you just how your daughter started her suffering. I also have to tell you that we now believe she was held for five days before she was killed and during that time she was violently raped.'

The woman's anguish increased to a sob.

'I can tell you that we now have enough evidence to take this to court and prosecute for murder. Ari has implicated your husband in your daughter's murder and your prolonged silence in all this is not going to help you. If you continue to refuse to talk then we will suspect you are involved and you will also go to court.'

Jilani looked up at Grace. Black kohl eyeliner ran down her cheeks.

'Mrs Hassan, I am a mother of two daughters and if I thought my husband had been involved in their deaths I would move heaven and earth to see him punished. As a mother yourself, I do not believe for one second you would want anything different. Am I right?'

With glazed eyes, Jilani nodded. Then she began to speak in Urdu. After about twenty seconds, she stopped. 'I never realised they had done that to my Samia,' she delivered in broken but understandable English.

Grace took hold of Jilani's hands, giving her a sympathetic look. 'Mrs Hassan, do you want to tell us what you know?'

Jilani hung her head and dropped her gaze. 'I never wanted Samia harmed. I went along with my husband and told her I would disown her after what she had done with that young doctor. She knew our values and she went against them but I never wished any harm against her. It was Mohammed — he wouldn't let it go. He arranged for her to marry a cousin of his back in Pakistan. He said it would be the best thing for her but she flung it back in his face. Then he discovered she was planning to run away and he got very angry.'

'What did he do?'

'I knew he was arranging things with Ari but I didn't know what he intended. I know Ari and Pervez are not good people — that they have been in trouble, but I do not know what for. I pleaded with Mohammed to let things be, just disown her, but he wanted to punish her for bringing dishonour to him.' She broke into a fresh sobbing fit.

Grace let Jilani's hands go, fished a tissue from her jacket and handed it over.

Jilani dried her eyes. The kohl smudged further.

'Please go on, Mrs Hassan.'

'I never knew it was going to go this far. Mohammed told me Ari and Pervez were going to force her to go to Pakistan and everything would be sorted. When you came to the shop and I heard you say you were investigating her murder I was shocked. It was only then that I realised what Mohammed had done to Samia. Believe me, I did not know this. What you have shown me on the TV, the thing that has happened to Samia — it is evil.'

'Are you willing to give a statement?'

Jilani wiped her eyes again. Then she nodded.

For evidential purposes the first statement was written in English followed by a second in Urdu, by the interpreter. The evidence against Ari and Pervez Arshad and also Mohammed Hassan was damning and Hunter couldn't wait for that evening's briefing. He was eager to get back into the incident room to find out if the flat had been found.

Hunter followed Grace out into the custody suite corridor and closed the interview room door. He could hear Jilani Hassan sobbing. He turned to Grace with sparkling eyes and gave her a 'you did it' look, then planted a kiss on her forehead. 'You little beaut,' he said, before strolling back to the incident room.

Hunter and Grace rode the clanking lift to the fifth floor; they were looking for flat 508.

An hour earlier they had returned to an empty incident room and learned from Isabel Stevens that the whole team were over in Sheffield — the Arshads' flat had been found and they were doing house-to-house enquiries. They decided they wanted to be in on the action. Scooping up a set of car keys, Hunter told Grace that Pervez and Mohammed could sweat in the cells a little longer.

They lodged the statements made by Jilani Hassan with Isobel and quickly drove to the Parkhill Flats complex.

The instant the metal doors screeched open, Hunter was greeted by a strong smell of pine disinfectant and he could hear activity somewhere out along the corridor.

As he stepped out of the lift, he recognised the location from the CCTV footage Barry had shown them. He looked to the ceiling, at the small black dome housing the CCTV camera, and wondered how the pair could have been so stupid. He pointed it out to Grace and then made his way to number 508.

Blue and white police crime scene tape was draped across the dim corridor and a uniformed officer barred their way. Hunter ducked under the tape, flashing his warrant card.

The door to flat 508 was ajar and he rapped loudly before gently pushing it open. The hallway was in shadow, but they could see light from the gap of a door at the end and hear activity behind it. He and Grace walked towards the light and Hunter pushed open the second door. It was the lounge and Duncan Wroe was on his haunches, carrying out a careful examination of the carpet. Two other SOCO Officers were in the room, spraying and swabbing a wall. A bare bulb in the centre of the ceiling gave the only illumination. Close draped curtains covered one wall and were thick enough to keep out most of the daylight.

The room was sparsely furnished with a flimsy two-seater sofa and a single armchair of cheap quality, and yet fastened at chest height on a wall above the fireplace was a huge flat screen TV.

'They've obviously got their priorities right,' Hunter said wryly, pointing at the TV.

Duncan looked over his shoulder. 'I wondered how long it would be before you two arrived,' he said and returned to his task.

'You know us, Duncan, can't keep our noses out. Anyway, I thought you'd have finished with the scene by now. Are you holding out for overtime?'

'Very funny, Hunter. Very funny.'

'On a serious note, Duncan, is this the place where Samia was killed?'

'Oh, this is it all right.' Duncan slowly eased himself up. His knees cracked. 'I'm getting too old for this, roll on my pension.' He sauntered to the far wall where the two SOCOs were working. 'Attempts have been made to clean down the walls but we're already picking up blood spatter patterns low down, close to the skirting. By the looks of this lot I would say this is from a cut — a slashing effect. Didn't she have her throat cut if I remember rightly?'

Grace nodded.

'And there is also a pooling effect soaked into the carpet down to the floorboards.' Duncan lifted an edge of cheap nylon carpet to reveal a dark stain ingrained in the light wood flooring beneath. 'She'd obviously lost a substantial amount of blood.' He returned to the centre of the room. 'Finally, I have this for you. Switch off the light behind you.'

Hunter reached behind him and pitched the room into semi darkness. Just a little daylight poked between the gaps in the heavy drapes.

'Remember when I showed you how fibres could be lit up by a light source when I examined the white Renault?'

Hunter and Grace nodded.

'As you know, fragments of fibres are transferred when they come into contact with another surface. I mentioned different fibres can give off different wavelengths which can be picked up by fluorescent lights. I already told you that we had the wavelengths of the fibres from the Asian rug because of its unique make-up.'

Hunter acknowledged again with a nod.

'Well, this is what I've found.'

Duncan switched on a low voltage, hand-held fluorescent light and began scanning the carpet. As if by magic a line of bright blue fibres became distinguishable from the remainder of the room carpet. As he swept the area, an oblong outline began to appear over the surface. 'What would you say if I told you the perimeter of this is the exact same size as the rug Samia's body was found in? In other words, the rug once fitted in this exact spot.'

'You're a genius, Duncan.'

'Science actually, Hunter, but I will accept that accolade.' Duncan turned off the lamp, plunging them back into semi-darkness.

Hunter switched the room light back on.

'Another four or five hours and I'll have this room telling me what exactly went on — but at least for now I've given you something which will help to hold them in custody.'

Hunter and Grace thanked him and made their way back to the car.

It was just after four p.m. when they got back to Barnwell. Other members of MIT were still out on enquiries and expected back within the hour. They had gathered enough statements and material evidence to place Ari and Pervez in flat 508.

Armed with this information, Hunter and Grace headed to the custody suite to re-interview Pervez.

He was waiting with his solicitor in the sticky, warm interview room. He didn't have his brother's cockiness, but fixed them with a penetrating glare.

As Hunter and Grace sat down, Pervez folded his arms defensively and gave a smug grin.

Hunter loved a challenge.

Grace switched on the tape recorder and turned around to switch on the TV/DVD player.

'Mr Arshad, during your last interview you chose to make no comment and that is your prerogative. However, it is only fair to tell you that, since that last interview, things have moved on considerably. We have interviewed your brother Ari and I have to tell you that he has implicated you in the abduction of Samia. We have a statement from a witness placing you at the scene where Samia's body was dumped and I must also tell you that Jilani Hassan, Samia's mother and your aunt, has also made a statement implicating you and Ari.'

Suddenly his eyes were restless. He searched out his solicitor who had his head down making legal notes, then looked back across the table. 'You're bullshitting.'

'Mr Arshad, would I be telling you this in the presence of your solicitor, and on tape, if it wasn't true?'

Pervez rolled his eyes to the ceiling, unfolded his arms and wiped the palms of his hands down the thighs of his trousers.

'I know you have been shown CCTV evidence of you following Samia in Meadowhall and your involvement in her attack down in the car park and you chose not to respond when that evidence was presented. Now I want to show you some more footage we have recently acquired.'

Grace switched on the DVD player and started to play the latest footage compiled by Barry.

Hunter kept his eyes glued on Pervez, watching the sweat trickle down his face as he viewed. Hearing Grace switch off the machine he leant across the table, locking together his fingers. 'We have now found the flat shared by you and Ari. As we speak, forensics are going through the place with a fine-toothed comb. We already know this was where you held Samia where she was killed, and you've seen from that CCTV footage that we now have you on camera taking her body to dump in the lake. You have every right not to say anything, but I hope your brother will be as loyal when he sees this.'

Hunter watched Pervez's face change. He was rigid with fear.

'Ari raped and killed Samia,' Pervez said. 'I thought we were only going to kidnap Samia and force her to go to Pakistan. That's what Ari told me. He said Uncle Mohammed wanted to teach his daughter a lesson because she had brought shame on the family and we were to take her to our place and hold her there.'

'Is that what happened after you put her in the back of the van at Meadowhall?'

Pervez nodded feverishly. 'Yes, yes. We took her back to our flat and Ari tied her up in the bedroom. He phoned Uncle Mohammed and told him we had her and asked what he wanted to do with her.'

'What did your uncle say?'

'I don't know. Ari was always the one who talked to Uncle Mohammed, though he came to the flat the next day and started hitting Samia, swearing at her and saying she had brought dishonour to him and she didn't deserve to live.'

'Is that when she was killed?'

'No, no, he busted her mouth and nose and I cleaned her up with a towel from the bathroom. She was still alive. She begged me to let her go and then Ari came into the bedroom and dragged me away. Uncle Mohammed left and I could hear him and Ari talking in the hallway.'

'What were they saying?'

'I don't know — I couldn't hear. They were whispering together.'

'What happened next?'

Pervez's eyes moistened. He dabbed at them with the back of his hand. 'Nothing that night, but the next day Ari told me to go out and get some food for us. I went to the local Spar and when I came back Samia was dead. Ari had killed her.' Tears welled up in the corner of his eyes. 'That's the truth. I swear on the Prophet Mohammed.'

'When you say she was dead. Describe what you saw.'

'There was blood everywhere. Up the walls and a huge puddle around her head. She was lying on the carpet in the lounge near the armchair. When I left her, she was tied up in the bedroom. When I got back, he was pacing up and down and he had that knife-thing in his hand. He'd cut her throat with it.'

'Was she still tied up?'

'Her hands were behind her back but he'd untied her feet.' Pervez gulped and looked down at the table. 'She wasn't wearing her jeans or her knickers. I knew what he'd done.'

'When you say she was dead, did you check at all to see if she was still alive?'

'I looked at her but you could tell. There was a big pool of blood. Her eyes were wide open. She wasn't breathing.'

'What did you do?'

'I panicked. I couldn't believe he'd done that. We argued and I asked him why. He said Uncle Mohammed wanted him to do it. I didn't know whether to believe him or not.'

'What happened then?'

'Ari said we had to get rid of the body. He wrapped Samia in the carpet, wiped the knife-thing and put it in with her and then he asked me to help bind her up. After that he rang Uncle Mohammed.'

'Did Ari tell your uncle what he had done?'

'He told him she was dead. But I don't know what my uncle was saying. I couldn't hear that part of the conversation.'

'Is that when you brought Samia across to Barnwell and dumped her in the lake?'

'No, we kept her body in the flat a couple of days. We put the rug in the bath so no more blood seeped out. Ari said Uncle Mohammed was going to ring him and tell him where to take the body. Then that Friday evening Ari took a call from Uncle Mohammed and said he had found a place to hide Samia where no one would find her. That's when we drove to the lake and dumped her.' His voice started to quiver. 'That is the truth. I didn't kill Samia. It was Ari. My Uncle Mohammed told him to do it.'

It was after 6 p.m. when Hunter and Grace finally returned to the incident room, having completed another interview with Mohammed Hassan. He had been more stubborn than his nephews, had refused to accept their testimonies and the evidence presented and continually bleated that everyone was lying about him — including his wife. However, as they had walked him back to his cell, they had witnessed the first cracks. As Hunter slammed the reinforced door, he'd taken a final glance through the hatch. Mohammed had looked up from the bench with glazed eyes, before dropping his head to his chest.

With a satisfied smile, Hunter had slid the metal hatch shut with a resounding clang.

Feeling energised, despite the long day, he bounced into the MIT office. It was full, the Office Manager, Detective Inspector Gerald Scaife, and the SIO, Detective Superintendent Michael Robshaw, were among the team waiting.

Hunter could sense them searching his face. He guessed Grace would be experiencing the same good feeling. He surveyed the room before grinning widely.

'Result. Pervez has coughed. And he's given us enough to send down his brother and Mohammed.'

The cheer was deafening.

Jock Kerr slowly scanned the four walls of his son's and daughter-in-law's lounge. Though he had the place to himself he felt anxious and agitated. It was like being in prison.

This is doing my head in. I've had enough.

He picked up the car keys from the coffee table and left the house, jumped into the hire car provided by his insurance company and fired up the engine. Before pulling off the drive he phoned DS John Reed on his mobile.

'I'm coming down to the gym. I'm sorry but I can't take any more of this. I can't keep hiding away.' He listened to the detective's response, before replying. 'Look, there are four of you nearby. If Billy and Rab turn up then you'll nick them, won't you?' He hung up before the sergeant could object.

Jock kept watch in his rearview mirror more than usual but spotted nothing untoward and was feeling quite relaxed by the time he reached his gym.

The entrance doors were locked and he checked his watch. The boxing coach who had been looking after things in his absence must have gone home early. Jock unlocked the doors and let himself in.

The place was fairly tidy with only a few weights out of place. He took a long, lingering look around. The pristine whitewashed walls gave the gymnasium a clean and bright if not clinical appearance. A full-size boxing ring took up half of the floor space, with one side for weight training and another for bag work. This place was his pride and joy. It had taken him a long time to build it up. Most of his life was in this place.

I'm buggered if I'm going to lose all this because of those two evil shites!

Hunter swilled the remaining dregs of his pint around the bottom of the glass as if it was the finest whiskey and swallowed. He said, 'That never touched the sides.' Nudging Barry next to him, he added, 'Fancy another? I owe you one.'

Barry drained the remainder of his pint in one mouthful and wiped the froth from his dark, bushy moustache with the back of his hand before answering, 'I'll not refuse a free pint.'

Hunter weaved his way through the squad to the bar. They had congregated into small groups, as was usual at these celebratory gatherings. A couple of his colleagues gave him a congratulatory tap on the shoulder as he squeezed by.

Plonking the empty glasses down on the bar, Hunter took a look around at the faces of his workmates. He recalled the first words instilled into him on that first day in CID, after Barry Newstead had taken him out and got him rolling drunk. 'The spirit and bonding of a team is created in the pub,' Barry had said. 'Putting a frustrating, complicated and exhausting enquiry to bed with a celebratory drink is what gels everyone together.' How true that had proved over the years.

As he waited to be served, Hunter mused over the hurried briefing given by Superintendent Robshaw less than a half hour ago. The SIO had made energetic scribbled notes on the incident board, creating cohesive actions for tomorrow.

He and Grace had been given the job of charging Ari, Pervez and Mohammed with murder and the task of putting together the remand file for court, while the remainder of the MIT were to tie up all the loose ends, logging evidence and collecting statements to make everything stick.

The hard work wasn't yet over; their aim was to stack the evidence so much in the prosecution's favour that a guilty plea was inevitable.

Hunter was just trying to grab the attention of one of the bar staff when he felt his mobile vibrate in his trouser pocket. He dragged it out and took a look at the incoming caller. The word 'gym' flashed onto the screen. It had to be his dad. He took the call.

For a second all he could hear was heavy breathing then his dad's voice came on the line. He sounded frantic.

'Hunter, get down here quick,' he heard his dad say. 'It's Billy and Rab — they've just turned up.'

Then the phone call ended.

DS John Reed and his partner DC Craig McDonald stared out of the large plate glass window into the car park below. They had been in the first-floor office of the empty warehouse since 7 a.m. that day. It was their fourth stint in the observation post and they were weary.

John Reed was thankful for the sunshine beaming in through the large window. There was no heating in the building and it was all they had for warmth. He'd be glad when they had Billy Wallace and Rab Geddes so he could get back home. He hadn't seen his family for the best part of a week and the motel room he was sharing with his colleague was not exactly luxurious. To make matters worse, his working relationship with Dawn Leggate was compromised because of her dalliances with the local Detective Superintendent. Reed had dropped in on her last night and he had been there. She looked embarrassed as she explained they were just discussing the joint operation. All in all, he wasn't pleased with how things were progressing.

The hiss of the radio crackling into life broke his thoughts. Jock had just left his son's house and was alone.

John Reed huffed in frustration. He had only just got off the phone with Jock, trying to persuade him not to come to the gym. He made an entry in the log and set the video camera rolling.

Ten minutes later, Jock's car cruised into the car park below and the camera captured him making his way into his gym.

The screeching of tyres two minutes later startled John Reed. He saw the green Range Rover sway to one side as it swept into the car park, slewing into a skid before rocking to a halt. The passenger door flew open and he was mesmerised for a second as a stocky built man wearing a ski mask leapt out. Reed was on his radio in a second, shouting for backup. Grabbing the sleeve of his partner, he bolted towards the stairwell leading down to the car park.

Billy Wallace watched the Range Rover tear into the car park and slide to a standstill. Opposite the entrance, he pressed himself against the trunk of one of the trees lining the road, the shade from the canopy of leaves masking his features. Rab was close by. As one of the masked men leapt from the passenger side his slate grey eyes became watchful. He was ready and waiting.

It soon paid off. He saw the two detectives tumble out through the doors of a derelict warehouse and onto the car park.

He gave the signal and the masked man jumped back into the car. Before he had time to close the door, the back wheels were chewing up gravel as it sped away.

Billy smiled to himself. It was all going to plan.

The two officers weren't far behind. Sprinting across the car park DC McDonald aimed the key fob at a dark blue Vauxhall Vectra, triggering the locks as John Reed shouted an update into his radio and leapt into the front passenger seat.

Less than thirty seconds later, the unmarked car's engine was being gunned as it tore off in hot pursuit.

Jock saw Billy Wallace stroll into the gym. He was still wearing that signature Crombie of his.

After all these years and he still dresses like he's the 'big I am'.

Billy looked menacing as he stepped further into the room. His pupils were so dilated that his eyes appeared almost black. It was a look Jock had seen in those eyes before — the look of cold death.

Suddenly everything seemed to fast-forward. Billy made a quick jabbing movement with right arm and Jock saw the glint of a long blade emerge from the end of his sleeve. A tremor raced through him. Then he realised he was still clutching one of the free weights and it gave him a strange reassurance. He tightened his grip around the barbell.

'Don't be stupid, Billy. If you do anything to me you're going to go away for a very long time. You'll probably die in prison,' Jock said, doing his best to sound calm. 'You can walk away from this right now and no one will be any the wiser.'

'I've done 36 fucking years already because of you. It will be worth it,' Billy growled, edging closer.

Jock was mesmerised by Billy's cold-blooded stare as he stepped closer.

Jock took up a defensive stance, lodging the barbell against his hip and balling his other hand into a solid fist. Two combatants locked in a fight to the death.

Billy catapulted forward, whipping his right arm across.

The knife slashed across Jock's forearm before he had time to react and he staggered back, clattering against the metal racks. The blood spread through the sleeve of his sweat top, though surprisingly he felt no pain. It bought back memories of his boxing days — he'd not recognised pain back then, either.

Billy pulled back the knife again, preparing for another attack. Every sinew in Jock's body tightened, stretched as tight as a bow as he felt an immense power surge through him. He dropped back on one leg and exploded forward, swinging the barbell up in an arc. It smacked Billy's jaw and his eyes went blank. Jock had seen that look many times during his boxing bouts. He followed up with a left hook, smacking the side of Billy's head. The knife clattered to the floor and Billy's legs buckled. Just before he sank, Jock caught him with the swinging barbell again, a dull thwack to the back of his head.

Jock dropped on top of him, took a handful of hair and yanked back Billy's head. He slipped an arm to the front of his neck, slotted his windpipe into the crook and began to squeeze.

Hunter grabbed Barry Newstead within seconds of the line going dead. 'My dad's in trouble,' he called, bolting for the side door of the pub.

A rush surged through Hunter as he jumped into his car and fired it up. Slamming into first and stamping the accelerator, he revved his Audi's 1.9 litre engine and tore out of the pub car park towards the gym.

Beside him, Barry was making an emergency call on his mobile.

Less than ten minutes later they sped into the gym car park, skidding to a halt.

Hunter flew from the car, leaving the engine running and propelled himself through the doors into the gym, with Barry only seconds behind.

Rab Geddes was waiting in the corridor, legs astride, smacking a baseball bat into his palm.

Hunter stopped a few yards from him. 'Where's Billy Wallace?' he yelled.

'You're too late!' Rab said with a sneer.

For a few seconds there was a stand-off. Hunter eyed the baseball bat bouncing in Rab's hands. Then anger took over. He flew at him, aiming for his face, mauling with clawing hands, gouging at his eyes like a rugby player in a ruck. The force spiralled Rab sideways smashing him into the wall. Hunter heard the breath explode from his lungs and felt the warm breath on his cheek, and in a white heat of berserk fury he pulled, punched and pummelled.

Barry jumped into the fray, forcing in his bulk. Within seconds Rab was pinned against the wall, the baseball bat clattering to the floor as he tried to protect himself.

Hunter fell away, gasping for breath and drenched in sweat. He doubled-up, retching, as Barry slammed in a couple more punches to the ribs before Rab collapsed into a heap.

'My dad,' Hunter gasped.

'You go and help him,' Barry said. 'This guy's going nowhere.'

Hunter turned on his heels, hitting the swing doors into the main training area with his shoulder. He readjusted his balance and scanned the room. His dad was by the weight rack, draped across a prostrate figure who he immediately realised was Billy. At first Hunter wondered what was happening, then the reality hit home. His dad was strangling Billy. He sprinted across, snapping his arms around his dad in an effort to drag him off but he had Billy locked tight.

'Dad! Dad!' he screamed. 'He's had enough, let him go. You're going to kill him.' He hooked his fingers into a gap and prised at Jock's wrists. 'Dad, I said let him go — NOW!'

Hunter saw the shout had registered. He prised at his dad's hands again and this time they yielded. Billy's head smacked the wooden floor.

Hunter pulled his dad to his feet, pushed him away and went to Billy's aid. He checked his airway, manoeuvred him into the recovery position and checked him again. He stared at Billy's chest and prayed.

Suddenly a spluttering cough burst from Billy's mouth.

'Thank god for that!' Hunter turned to face his dad, who was ashen-faced. 'Christ, Dad — you could have killed him.'

Jock stared at the blood pouring from the wound on his forearm, clamped a hand around it and started to shake.

From the entrance to the gym, Hunter watched Billy and Rab being loaded into the back of an ambulance. They had a catalogue of bumps and bruises between them, and Billy had a deep wound to the back of his head, but neither was seriously hurt. A couple of minutes later they were off to hospital with an armed police escort

DCI Dawn Leggate appeared with two members of her team. The man in the ski mask and the other hired help had been detained and were en route to the custody suite. The pair were known back in Scotland as petty crooks but since they hadn't done anything, except act as decoys, they had nothing to hold them, she added — although she'd make sure they had a night in the cells while checks were made to see if they were wanted elsewhere.

That was ten minutes ago. Now Hunter, Jock, Barry and Dawn were seated around Jock's desk. Jock had refused to go in the ambulance but one of the paramedics had put a bandage on the laceration and told him it required suturing and must be treated before the day was out.

Jock had promised he would. Now he sat in his chair, nursing his arm.

In a couple of weeks' time Hunter knew his dad would be showing off the scar, just like the one above his right eye, saying, 'Scars are the medals of heroes'. Hunter wished he had a pound for every time he'd heard his dad say it. Hunter shook his head and smiled to himself. At least there was no lasting damage.

Dawn needed to question them about what had happened. Hunter asked for a little time with his dad and for it to be carried out after he'd visited the hospital. He needed to check what his dad was going to say and prime him to use the words 'trying to restrain' in his defence.

Dawn agreed. Hunter could tell by her face that she knew what had really happened and he revised his earlier opinions of her. He gave an appreciative smile.

Suddenly Jock announced, 'I could do with a stiff drink.' He opened the bottom drawer of his desk and pulled out a bottle of single malt. Then he shuffled together four mugs and poured a generous amount into each.

'They say it's good for shock,' he added, handing Hunter, Barry and Dawn a mug each. 'Sláinte! Doon the hatch,' he toasted, chinking each mug.

Hunter glanced at his dad. The colour had returned to his face.

You and I need to sit down and talk.

DAY THIRTY-FIVE

Hunter flopped back on the small sofa in his conservatory. He had inserted a Michael Bublé CD into his Bose system and closed his eyes, allowing 'Summer Wind' to sweep into his mind. His head was thumping. The Detective Superintendent had given the team a lie in, allowing them all to work an afternoon shift that day. There was still a fair bit of mopping up to do to close the investigation — Ari, Pervez and Mohammed were to be charged with Samia's murder, and a remand file had to be put together for court.

Disturbing images from the previous day flashed into Hunter's already aching head. Sometimes he wished he could turn off his brain. He shook his head and replaced them with more pleasant ones.

Beth and his mum had joined them at the gym, thankfully after the melee had ended, and as his dad had poured them all another 'wee dram' Beth had given him a quick check-up and saved him from going to the hospital by applying several Steri-strips to close the wound to his forearm, before re-bandaging and giving him a clean bill of health.

Then he, Barry and his dad had returned to the pub to rejoin the celebrations at the end of the Samia Hassan enquiry.

Everyone was keen to hear what had happened but Hunter gave a potted version of events and promised to fill them in the next day. He needed a few more beers to bring him back down from the adrenaline rush and wanted to be beside his dad, to let him see he was there for him. Barry had lightened the mood in their small group but the conversation between Hunter and his dad had been stilted and shallow. Despite this, Hunter had a feeling the ice had been broken between them.

They had fallen through the doors at 1.30 a.m. that morning and now Hunter was suffering.

'Morning, son.'

His dad's voice brought him back. He rolled his eyes.

'Feeling delicate?'

'An understatement. Rough as a bear's arse springs to mind.'

Jock chuckled. 'Here, get that down you. I've just mashed.'

Hunter took the cup of strong tea, just how his dad drank it. 'Thanks.'

Jock sat down beside him and put his cup on the coffee table. 'Son, I need to apologise.'

'Don't, Dad.'

'No, I do, don't stop me. I know I should have told you about this but I thought I was doing the right thing. I now realise I was wrong keeping you in the dark.'

'Dad —' Hunter tried to interrupt.

'Let me finish, son. I'm not proud of what I got myself into and with foresight I would have gone nowhere near that crew, but at the time I was a 20-year-old man with a career in tatters. I thought I was making a fast buck and didn't know what I was getting myself into. Nevertheless, I think I made the right decision to protect your ma and I haven't made a bad job of bringing you up. You've turned out a son I'm very proud of and I hope when things settle down you'll feel the same way about me. Just remember this, Hunter — even though I changed my name, you are of the Kerr clan. Your mum's a Kerr and you have every right to wear that tartan.'

Jock picked up his cup and took a drink.

Their eyes met again.

Jock said, 'You know, one thing has come good of all this. For years I've had to stay away from my family for fear of putting them in danger. Going back up there to meet the DCI when I did made me realise just how much I've missed them. I've been in touch and already fixed up a meeting. What about you, Beth and the boys coming up with your ma and me and I'll introduce you to your family?'

EPILOGUE

21st November 2008

Hunter took a couple of steps back from his easel, angling his head, slowly scanning sections of his latest oil painting — a seascape of Robin Hood's Bay. Every few seconds he halted his gaze to focus on a particular part of the scene, checking that he had resolved it before letting his artistic eye move on. Five minutes later, pleased with how he had managed to capture the stormy mood in the piece, he set his brushes down on his palette and wiped his hands with a rag.

Time for a cuppa.

Before making for the kitchen, he took another lingering look. It was a process he always went through before he put the canvas to one side. He would get it out again in a week's time and repeat his actions. From speaking with other artists, he knew he was not alone in going through this critique.

As he focused on the blustery, rain-leaden clouds, brushstrokes laid down in tones of purple, ultramarine blue and pink, it reminded him of a word he had heard his dad use — *dreich*. That summed the spirit of the painting perfectly, he thought.

Bringing that word to mind conjured up feelings from the recent turmoil within his life. For a few seconds, images rode a carousel inside his head.

He shook himself and they cleared. It would be a while before they left him permanently — if ever. The main thing was that he and his dad had reconciled their differences. And he had discovered new members of his family. He had travelled up to Scotland with his dad to support him during his visit to Glasgow High Court for the plea and directions hearing for Billy Wallace and Rab Geddes, charged with five counts of murder and the attempted murder of his dad.

That court visit had been shorter than expected. The pair had refused to come out of their prison cells for the hearing and refused to enter a plea and in their absence the judge had set a trial date for the second week in January the following year.

Hunter mentally diaried the date so that he could take time off to support his dad when he returned to give evidence.

He had seen DCI Dawn Leggate at the court and taken her to one side to check on the prosecution's case. This time she was far more amenable, telling him that the evidence against the pair was overwhelming. She was expecting them to enter a guilty plea at the last moment and added that the Procurator Fiscal was requesting an indeterminate life sentence for both men. The likelihood was they would die in prison.

After that, they had gone on to Bellshill — his dad's old home town — and he had been introduced to his dad's cousins. It had been a weekend of celebrations, resulting in very thick heads for both of them. Since then he had witnessed a change in his dad's demeanour and they had spent some very enjoyable sessions together, especially down at the gym.

The ringing telephone in the lounge broke his reverie. He heard Beth answer it.

'Hunter, it's for you,' she shouted, walking towards him, holding out the handset. 'It's work.'

He held up his hands to her, indicating they were smeared with oil paint.

She switched it to speaker phone.

'Hello,' he said.

'DS Kerr?'

He recognised the voice of one of the duty group inspectors. 'Speaking.'

'Sorry to disturb you at home. I know it's your long weekend off, but I've been asked to call you in. Some of my officers are at the scene of a derelict pub. A couple of builders there have found the remains of a body in the cellar.'

A NOTE TO THE READER

It would be fair to say that none of my books make for comfortable reading and are certainly not for the faint-hearted. They are based on my own, or my colleagues experiences and that is the case with *Cold Death*. This story came courtesy of two cases, one of which I was in charge of and the other I worked on the periphery of.

Samia Hassan's story was sparked by a call from a British born Asian lady of Bangladesh parents who'd had her flat trashed, and was being harassed by cousins of her father, simply because she was in a relationship with a young man she had met at college, that hadn't been chosen by her father. Myself and a colleague visited her parent's home to be confronted by an angry man who wanted nothing more to do with his daughter and whom had obliterated any existence of her from his home. It was a very sad situation for the young lady and my first experience of prejudice through culture. Unlike Samia in the story, this young lady did not come to any harm and progressed well through college to begin a career in nursing.

The character Billy Wallace came about following my attendance at the scene of a brutal attack on a woman by a man she was in a relationship with. The scene I visited was one of the bloodiest I have ever been to. The woman had been hacked at with a boning knife and machete. She'd been stabbed 37 times, had her throat cut and several fingers severed. She only survived thanks to the quick actions of a neighbour who was a nurse, and she was eventually able to give evidence against him in court and see him jailed for a minimum of 22 years. When we looked into the background of the man it was discovered he was someone who targeted women at various church groups by pretending to be a religious Christian man who had fallen on hard times. He was nothing of the sort. He was evil. Once he befriended them, he subjected them to sado-masochistic sex and brutal violence. He came to South Yorkshire following his release from prison after an 8-year sentence for a brutal attack upon a man who tried to protect one of his victims. The man was left with severe brain damage. Within weeks of being here he targeted his next victim, a vulnerable woman who went to a church support group having already suffered domestic violence. Whilst on remand for his latest attack, knowing he had severed three fingers from his victim's hand, he sent a packet of fish fingers to her with a note 'These are to replace the ones you're missing.'

The scenario where Billy launches the dead body through Hunter's parent's window was also based on a true event. It happened where I worked in Barnsley, during a turf war over drugs. One gang broke into the mortuary at Barnsley hospital, took a body from the cold storage and as a threat of what was to come launched it through the window of their rival drug leader who lived at home with his mother. Can you just imagine the fear she must have faced that evening?

BOOK THREE: SECRETS OF THE DEAD

PROLOGUE

14th November 2008
Barnwell, North Yorkshire

A sudden wave of panic washed over him and his chest tightened.

Slowing his pace and pausing for a moment, he checked his bearings. It was a long time since he had been in these woods and the memory of that last visit bore no resemblance whatsoever to the area he was currently scanning. In fact, nothing was familiar.

He cursed beneath his breath. He had especially chosen this morning because of the foul weather but hadn't anticipated it working against him. The veil of early morning fog was thicker than he had expected — he could only just make out his boots, never mind the landmarks he was seeking.

Ten minutes earlier he'd left his car parked in the layby, at the edge of the coppice, in almost the same spot as he had done all those years ago, and now he was attempting to retrace the route he had taken that night. But it was proving more difficult than he'd expected. So much of the terrain had changed. The wood was much denser, and, of course, it had been nightfall back then.

If truth be known he wouldn't be here now, had it not been for that letter he had received a week ago. Inside the Sheffield-postmarked envelope had been a single sheet of paper with five words typed upon it — *'It's time for the truth'* — and those words were a shadow of peril hanging over him.

Since then, he had slept fitfully. When he had dropped off, he had been haunted by images of that night. They had replayed over and over, and no matter how hard he tried to dismiss them, they lurked in the deepest recesses of his mind and leapt out whenever he had closed his eyes. Two days ago, it had led him to kill again.

He'd thought that would put paid to his problems, but he had discovered that there was another loose end to eliminate. Since then, he had dwelt on little else. Finally, last night, he had convinced himself what he needed to do. *Silence the bastard!* Only then would he be able to bury the past.

Before that, though, he had one more important thing to check out.

When he had heard the weather forecast this morning, he had immediately realised that today would be his best opportunity; only the most ardent of dog walkers would be braving the woods in these conditions and even then, they wouldn't be stepping away from the track like he was about to do.

Taking another quick look around, convinced he must be close to the spot, he stepped off the main path and cut deeper into the undergrowth.

Tramping through the dying ferns, he spotted his first landmark and let out a sigh of relief. He was surprised he had not seen it sooner — the laurel bush before him had grown so much; it was almost as big as a tree.

He picked up his pace. The bracken beneath his boots was soft and springy — the moisture-laden atmosphere had flattened the mass, making his trek easier, though he found himself catching his breath and beads of sweat had begun to form on his brow. It was a sign of how much out of condition he was. Always so fit as a young man, the toll of his over-indulgent lifestyle over the years had finally caught up with him.

Stopping in mid-stride, he scoped the way ahead. Silvery tentacles of fog weaved before him, caressing the woodland floor, wrapping themselves around tree trunks, making the search for his second marker harder. He strained to listen. Nothing: everything was so still. Not even birdsong this morning.

He walked on through the damp undergrowth, yawing from his course every dozen or so steps. The manoeuvre had the desired effect, for within five minutes he spotted the oak tree he had been looking for. It was bigger and more majestic than his last memory, but then that had been 25 years ago. He increased his pace, striding into a small clearing and ran a hand over the bark. Then, turning to his right, he re-fixed his bearings and focused on the spot where he had buried her all those years ago.

A thicket of holly overhung the site. Nothing had been disturbed.

My secret is still safe.

He smiled to himself. In that moment he felt an overwhelming sense of reassurance and let out a satisfied sigh. Reaching into his coat pocket, he slid out his cigarettes. Shuffling the pack, he removed one with his lips and, cupping his lighter, lit it. Taking a deep breath, while raising his head towards the mist laden sky, he held the smoke longer than normal until he could feel the kick from the nicotine fuzz his brain. Now he was relaxed.

Removing the cigarette, he bowed his head and said a silent prayer for himself.

Confident that his business was done, he took a final drag on his cigarette, nipped the remains and flicked the stub away. Then, taking a last look around, he turned on his heels and began the stroll back to his car.

DAY ONE

24th November, 2008.

Detective Sergeant Hunter Kerr booted up his computer whilst eyeing the statements, notes, and evidence littering his workspace. He didn't like it when his desk was untidy; it messed with his head.

The paperwork related to the death of a young woman whose body had had been found in the cellar of a derelict pub three days earlier, and in spite of all the enquiries he'd made so far, Hunter was still without a name for her.

Pressing back in his seat, pushing a hand through his dark brown hair, he brought the case file up on screen and drifted his gaze to the ceiling, thinking about what evidence he had, and wondered for a moment if he had missed anything. Swiftly coming to the conclusion he hadn't, he returned his eyes to the screen and scrolled through the 'Circumstances of Death' page, speed-reading its content.

A small team of builders carrying out renovation work had discovered the woman lying face down on the cellar floor, immediately realising from the bloated face and pungent smell that she was dead and not just sleeping rough. Although Hunter was still awaiting results from toxicology samples taken during the post-mortem, all the indications were that she had died of a heroin overdose. There had been at least a dozen empty syringes surrounding her body. Added to that, the numerous discarded foil wrappings and a couple of spoons which showed signs of being heated over a naked flame had clearly set the scene that the cellar was being used by addicts as a shooting den and she had accidentally ended her life there.

For a brief second, Hunter recalled the first images he had of her, lying amid the detritus of a damp old pub cellar, in the early stages of decomposition and with bits of her missing — vermin had begun to nibble at her purple-coloured bloated flesh. Under normal circumstances this would have been a job for uniform but Hunter had been called in because the pathologist had picked up on an injury to her right cheek; there was some bruising and the cheekbone was cracked.

The cause of that injury was inconclusive, though Hunter had pointed out that she had been found lying face-down on hard concrete ground. If the toxicology report came back that it was a heroin overdose which had caused her premature death, then he could clear its 'suspicious death' status and leave it in the hands of the coroner.

Before that, though, Hunter was determined he would do his level best to put a real name to Jane Doe so that he could give her family, wherever they were, disclosure. *They deserved that*, he told himself, as he returned to the front page of his report. Initially, everyone who had attended the scene and viewed the corpse, himself included, had thought that the body was that of a young teenage girl, but then the autopsy had revealed that the girl was in fact a petite woman aged late teens to early twenties.

With regards to proof of identity, all he had so far was that she had grey-blue eyes, shoulder length light brown hair, a good set of teeth and the initials 'J. J.', together with a pink butterfly, tattooed just below the hairline at the back of her neck. There was nothing on her body, or in the cellar, that revealed who she was.

The Scenes of Crime Officer had done his best to fingerprint her at the mortuary but it had been the ends of her fingers that rats had nibbled first, making it near impossible to get a good enough set of whorls from any of her digits that they could work with to get a fingerprint ident. There was the DNA the pathologist had collected, but Hunter knew that if the woman wasn't in the system then that was of no use.

So, except for the tattoos, the only other things he had as clues to establish her identity were the three items he'd found in her jeans. First of those was a torn photograph. He'd found that, together with a Christmas card, in the same rear pocket. The ripped photo featured the head and shoulders of a man who looked to be in his early 30s, who was clean shaven, with thinning dark hair. Hunter thought the face seemed familiar, and he'd shown it round the office to see if any of his colleagues recognised him, but that had drawn a blank.

The Christmas card, folded and heavily creased, appeared to be an old one. Inside, it had been simply signed 'Mr X'. Hunter wondered if Mr X was the guy in the photo.

The third item, a worn brass key, he'd found in one of her front pockets. It didn't fit the door to the cellar she'd been found in, and there was nothing else that assisted with an address where she had lived.

Hunter had done a lot of leg-work these past two days, even reacquainting himself with ex-colleagues from his drug squad days, but the woman's description didn't fit any of the druggies they knew. Hunter had already decided that if by lunchtime he was no further forward with identifying her, he was going to speak to his contact at the *Barnwell Chronicle* and ask her to run a piece in the paper as a last-ditch attempt to identify the body.

A thwacking sound and the sudden appearance of a newspaper landing on top of his paperwork made Hunter jump. He looked up to see his partner DC Grace Marshall with a big grin on her face. He had been so absorbed in the drafting of his narrative that he neither heard nor saw her breeze into the office.

Barry Newstead, Civilian Investigator for the Major Investigation Team, followed in her wake, looking rumpled as ever. He had his jacket slung over his shoulder, allowing Hunter the view of a white shirt straining over his ample belly. The tail of one side had escaped from the waistband of his trousers and it was open at the collar, from where the two ends of a striped tie dangled at an odd angle from its untidy knot.

As Hunter switched his gaze from Grace, tall and slim, in her designer grey linen suit, to Barry, clothed the way he was, Hunter couldn't help but smile to himself. They were so far apart when it came to dress and style, and yet complemented each other with their ebullient character and respective work ethic.

'You're a bit of a dark horse, Detective Sergeant Kerr!' Barry arrowed a finger towards the newspaper Grace had just dumped over Hunter's paperwork, shooting Hunter a wink as he sucked in his stomach, squeezed himself around his desk and slunk into his chair.

Hunter picked up the weekly *Barnwell Chronicle* that was open to one of the inside pages. There, in full colour, he was pictured proudly holding before him one of his recent paintings. Below it was the headline 'A Brush with the Law'. He could feel himself colouring up. A month ago, his contact at the paper had interviewed him about his recent success within the art world. Two of his seascape oil paintings had been selected for The

Mall Gallery's 'Royal Society of Marine Artists' exhibition. It had been the most defining moment of his artistic career to date and had brought him an invite to showcase his work with a leading London gallery.

Barry said, 'Detective Sergeant Hunter Kerr uses the long arm of the law for more than just collaring criminals.'

Hunter caught Barry's smug grin but chose to ignore the jibe. Instead, he silently read the opening paragraph of the article.

'Fancy a cuppa?' Grace asked, as she made for the kettle, which sat on top of one of the filing cabinets. She flicked it on. Looking back over her shoulder, she said, 'Take no notice of him, Hunter, he's jealous. I'm very proud of you. At least someone has a bit of class in this office.'

Hunter lifted up his gaze and caught Grace pulling her braided hair back from her face. The summer freckles peppering her cheeks, so prominent a few weeks ago, were just starting to fade.

Hunter shook the tabloid straight and quickly scanned the couple of paragraphs which made up the remainder of the article. His initial embarrassment had subsided; now he beamed inside. He folded the paper and set it aside. He would read it and digest it again tonight when he got home and showed it to Beth.

Grace settled a mug of tea in front of Hunter. 'Oh, and there's a full-page spread on page five about the "Lady in the Lake" murder. They've covered the case really well.'

'I bet you're really pleased with that result, aren't you?' said Hunter, catching the glint in Grace's eyes as she plonked herself down in her chair at her desk opposite. He was referring to the recent guilty verdict returned on the two men who had raped and murdered a 23-year-old female; her battered body had been discovered at the bottom of Barnwell Lake three months ago and Grace had been lead investigator.

When the job had been called in, Grace had been 'acting' DS while Hunter had been away on a long weekend break with his family. He recalled how admirably she had coped during his absence, both with the investigation and with being in charge of the team. There had been many times since that case when Hunter had lain awake at night, rerunning the difficulties of the enquiry in his head, wondering how on earth she had coped with everything, especially seeing as only two weeks before that case, Grace's eldest daughter, Robyn, had been abducted and almost killed by a serial killer they had been hunting in a previous investigation. He knew she was still seeing the force counsellor, and still suffering the occasional panic attack, and yet outwardly, she continued to display remarkable resilience.

'Chuffed to bits,' Grace replied. 'The judge gave me a commendation as well.'

'And rightly so — you deserve it. I hope the gaffer's said something to you?'

'He has actually. Told me a couple of days ago that he'd put me forward for a Chief Superintendent's commendation.'

'I can see we're gonna have to get the joiners in to make some wider doors for that big head of yours.'

'Huh! Hark who's talking. At least I don't have to suck up to journalists to get an article done about myself.' Grace licked the tip of a forefinger and struck an invisible mark in the air.

Hunter laughed and picked up the tabloid again, flipping back to page five, where he found a full-page spread about the 'Lady in the Lake' investigation and court case, together with a series of colour photographs. In the office one of the phones rang and he heard Grace answer. Within a few seconds her voice became excited — the way it did when something was breaking.

Hunter lifted his eyes from the newspaper and saw Grace making notes on a pad, the handset clamped between ear and shoulder. A couple of minutes later she set the receiver back.

'That was the duty inspector. Uniform are at a suspicious death. A woman made a 999 call ten minutes ago. She's turned up at her father's and found him dead and thinks his house has been broken into. Mike and Bully have just been sent to the scene.' Grace was referring to the other two members of Hunter's team, Mike Sampson and Tony Bullars.

Hunter set down the newspaper. 'Got any other details?'

'The address they're going to is listed to a Jeffery Howson. The Inspector believes he's a retired cop.'

Barry launched himself out of his chair, banging his knees on the edge of his desk in the process. He made a pained face. Rubbing the tops of his knees vigorously, he said loudly, 'Bloody hell, did you just say Jeffery Howson?' Grace nodded. 'Mind if I go to this with you? If this is the Jeffery Howson I think it is, then there's something I need to tell you.'

They dashed to the address, using a series of side streets as shortcuts to avoid rush-hour traffic on the main thoroughfares. From the back of the CID car, Barry gave Hunter and Grace a potted version of a phone call he had received two days ago from the retired detective.

'It was a couple of nights ago, around 11 p.m., I think,' Barry told them. 'Howson rang out of the blue and said he needed to meet with me. He wanted to talk to me about the Lucy Blake-Hall murder case back in 1983. He said he knew the wrong man was convicted and he knew who really killed her. He claimed he had evidence. I went to meet with him yesterday, but he never turned up.'

'Are you sure he said that?' said Hunter, driving one-handed, his other hand flexed around the gear stick, constantly changing up and down as he sped through one small estate after another, weaving between tightly parked cars.

'Positive. I know I was dead to the world when the phone went but I can remember most of what he told me.'

'And you were supposed to meet him yesterday?' asked Grace.

'Yes, at the George and Dragon in Wentworth. He said to meet him there at 12 o'clock. I went with Sue and we waited until half two, but he never showed up.'

'What happened in the Lucy Blake-Hall case?' Grace asked. 'Were you involved in it, Barry?'

'No,' Barry replied. 'They arrested the guy who'd done it pretty quickly and so we weren't called upon to help. Lucy was in her early 20s, married with a kid — a daughter, I believe — and was having an affair with a local guy. She was last seen arguing with him outside a pub in town and then no one saw her after that. Husband reported her missing, and within days they had tracked down her lover, arrested him and charged him with her murder. He pleaded not guilty, alleging that he had been fitted up by the police, but the jury found him guilty. He got life, but they never found Lucy's body.'

The cul-de-sac of Woodlands View, which held less than a dozen 1930s style semi-detached houses, had already been cordoned off by the time Hunter, Grace and Barry arrived. Blue and white 'Police Crime Scene' tape had been fastened between two gate posts to stretch across the entrance to the quiet street. It was a big area that had been isolated, but Hunter knew that someone had done their job right; it was better to start off with a large cordon, which could be reduced, rather than a small one which might need expanding and which could also get contaminated in the interim.

Up ahead, wearing a high-vis jacket, a female police officer was standing guard by another barrier of plastic ribbon stretched across the road. An inner cordon had also been established.

Pulling into the kerb and switching off the engine, Hunter took a longer look at the surroundings. He had not been on this street for years. It was a route he had frequently taken back in his uniform days when he had needed some peace and solitude, recalling that a footpath cut between the house to his right led to a 50-acre patch of much-used woodland, which was also the site of an ancient Roman ridge. It was a shortcut to a private golf club and a popular place for dog-walkers.

If this is a murder, he thought to himself, as he climbed out of the car, *we are certainly going to have our work cut out, given the number of people passing regularly through this location.*

Hunter gazed along the line of parked-up cars already here. One of the department's unmarked Ford Focuses, two beat vehicles, and a SOCO van had already beaten them here to number 12. To his left, he saw that uniform had already started knocking on doors.

Hunter went to the boot, took out three packs of forensic suits, handed one each to Grace and Barry, and began to get changed.

Less than five minutes later the three of them were heading towards the crime scene, Hunter already wondering what would be facing them, switching his thoughts into investigative mode.

By the gateway of number 12, another uniform officer wrote their names down on his log and allowed them down the drive. They took the path to the side door, which was wedged open. Hunter immediately noted the damage to the glass panel in the upper section. The corner closest to the key-lock had been smashed, and fragments of glass lay scattered over a portion of the tiled kitchen floor inside.

A yellow coloured Scenes of Crime marker — number one — had been placed in the middle of the broken glass and a series of strategically placed forensic foot plates snaked their way into the depths of the house, from where Hunter could hear muffled voices. He recalled the earlier phone call

Grace had taken back in the office, especially the part about the daughter believing that the house had been broken into, and as he took another look at smashed glass in the upper panel of the door, he conjured up an image of a hand reaching through and turning the key to let themselves in.

Before stepping inside, Hunter pulled on his latex gloves and mask. Grace and Barry followed. The side door opened into the kitchen, a small area with fitted floor and wall units in dark oak, many of which had lost their polished lustre. Decades-old green and white tiles decorated the walls.

Hunter stepped over the reinforced foot-plates in the direction of the voices. The lounge was where all the activity was taking place. The moment he stepped into the room, his sense of smell was immediately assaulted by the fetid and musty mix of stale urine and tobacco, and he screwed up his nose. The room was untidy and drab. Artexed walls, which he guessed were originally cream in colour, had become stained a dirty brown, and the mahogany furniture, dating from the 1980s, looked tired. Heavy drapes partially drawn across the window blocked out most of the natural light, only adding to the gloom of the room. The fireplace had been fashioned from a patchwork of Yorkshire stone, which spanned across from one alcove into another to make up a low unit, on which perched a large flatscreen TV. It was the only modern item Hunter had so far spotted.

This is a place that has seen better days, Hunter thought to himself.

DC Mike Sampson acknowledged their arrival with a nod. He had his hands locked into his sides, his squat rotund shape stretching the fabric of his forensic over-suit. He was standing over the pathologist, Professor Lizzie McCormack, who was crouching to examine the head and neck of a lifeless man slumped in an armchair close to the fireplace.

Hunter ran his eyes over the body and noticed a dark stain covering the crotch of the man's trousers. He realised why he'd been greeted by the strong stench of urine. Next to the body was an overturned low table and an upturned ashtray, the contents of which had scattered everywhere across the patterned carpet, which explained the tobacco smell. Also, on the floor, close by the side of the armchair was the handset of a cordless phone. Its holder was several metres away, the phone lead ripped from the wall socket. Strategically placed forensic pyramids earmarked that a struggle had taken place.

The dead man had an emaciated look; his facial features were waxen and stretched tight over his skull. Every outline of his bone structure was evident beneath the yellowing flesh. Wide open eyes were set deep inside dark ringed sockets. The shirt and jumper he wore hung in folds on his thin, frail body.

Hunter's initial thought was that the body looked to have been dead for some considerable time and yet he knew that Barry had last spoken with this guy only two days previously. He also recalled Grace saying the deceased was a retired detective. If that was the case, then this looked like someone who had been out of the game for a long, long time.

'Lung cancer,' said Mike Sampson.

Hunter shot his colleague a glance.

Mike returned a rueful look. 'I saw the way you were looking at him. I thought exactly the same when I first saw him. And you can obviously see what the cause was,' he said, pointing at the cigarette butts spilt across the floor. 'When me and Bully arrived, his daughter was still here. Bully's taken her home, by the way. She only lives in the next street. He's getting a statement from her.'

Hunter nodded. 'Has she touched anything?'

'No, everything's as she found it. She came with her daughter, and the moment she found him like this, she whisked her daughter away and rang us on her mobile. She was waiting for us on the drive, and as you can imagine she was in a bit of a state, so Bully's taken them both home. She believes someone's been through his stuff.' Mike pointed to several books spilled across the floor next to a bookshelf. Then he indicated a writing bureau. The writing flap was down and various papers and envelopes were strewn across it — some had fallen onto the floor. 'She said she last saw him on Saturday afternoon and the place was tidy then.'

'Does she know if anything's been taken?'

Mike shrugged. 'To be honest, Hunter, I didn't ask that question, but given what she told us, it's my guess she hasn't checked. We'll have to bring her back here once we've got things sorted and the body's out of the way.'

'And she's confirmed that this is her father, Jeffery Howson, and that he's a retired detective?' Hunter looked the body over once more. He didn't recognise the man. Howson must have already left the job by the time he joined CID. He switched his gaze to Barry, throwing him a questioning look.

Barry responded with, 'Hair's a lot thinner, and he's lost a lot of weight, but this is the Jeffery Howson I knew.'

'Daughter says he retired as a DC over ten years ago. She can't remember exactly when that was,' continued Mike Sampson. 'He was diagnosed with lung cancer four months ago. Terminal. Given six months.'

'That's not the cause of this man's death, though,' said the pathologist, pushing herself up and stretching out her back. Slim and petite, with grey hair and spectacles, Lizzie McCormack bore an uncanny resemblance to the actress Geraldine McEwan and as a result had gained the nickname Miss Marple. 'This man's eyes are very badly bloodshot and there is some evidence of trauma around the mouth and nose. I'll be able to tell you a lot more once I've done the post-mortem, but my initial findings are that he has died as a result of asphyxiation. It looks very much like he has been suffocated by someone, or something was used to smother his nose and mouth.'

Professor McCormack paused, looking around. Her gaze settled upon a brown cushion on the floor, a foot or so to the side of the chair. It lay beside the upended low table. She stabbed a finger towards it. 'I'd have forensics check that out. That just may be the weapon.' She turned back to face them. 'Oh, I've also found what appears to be extensive bruising to the wrists. Looks as though he's put up a bit of a struggle while being restrained. With a bit of luck, there might be contact DNA from the perpetrator. Will you ensure his hands are bagged up?'

Hunter nodded. 'So, you're indicating that he was held tight by the wrists while being suffocated or smothered?'

'Eloquently summed up, DS Kerr.'

'Which means at least two people carried this out?'

'Nail on the head again. My, my, we'll make a detective of you yet.'

'I'll take that as a compliment.'

'You and I go back too far for it be anything else, DS Kerr.' Professor McCormack delivered Hunter a cheery smile and, looking at her watch, said, 'I've taken an initial core body temperature reading and that indicates to me that he has been dead at least 24 hours. Once again, I can be a lot more accurate once I do the PM. And if you manage to get things sorted and can get the body down to the morgue inside the next four hours, I can start that late this afternoon.'

She pulled off her latex gloves, slipped them into her oversuit and returned a sideways glance as she made for the kitchen. 'Nasty way to die, you know, suffocation. Like drowning. Panic, lots of panic. That's what the victim endures. Terrible way to go.' She shook her head as she disappeared through the door.

The disposable shoe covers Hunter was wearing rustled and echoed along the corridor as he headed towards the post-mortem suite of the Medico Legal Centre. As he pushed through the slap-doors into the walk-in freezer area the familiar smell of formaldehyde greeted him.

A mortuary technician was just offloading a male body from a gurney into the minus-20-degree fridge. Hunter spotted the large sewn-up Y-section incision extending from the chest down to the pubic bone of the naked cadaver, a clear sign it had undergone a recent post-mortem. One half of the face was gone — no jaw, no cheek and no eye socket, just a dark mush.

'What happened to him?'

'Suicide. Blew half his head off with a shotgun,' the technician answered, sliding the corpse into the fridge.

'What a mess. Must have been desperate,' Hunter commented, taking another look at the grisly self-inflicted injury.

'Farmer about to be evicted from his farm, I understand. Told his wife he was just going to clean out one of the barns. Must have been a hell of a shock for her, finding him like that.'

The tray made a metallic clang as it hit the back of the freezer.

Hunter pressed through a second set of doors leading into the main cutting room. The smell that greeted him here was even stronger and he soon saw that it was coming from the stale blood of that last post-mortem, which hadn't yet drained off the gurney.

The appointed SIO, Detective Superintendent Michael Robshaw, was already there, along with Scenes of Crime Supervisor Duncan Wroe. Before leaving 12 Woodlands View, Hunter had contacted the police communications room asking for the pair to be updated and requesting that they meet him at the Medico Legal Centre. He had left Grace in charge of the scene, to liaise with forensics, gather the exhibits and especially gather information from the door-to-door enquiries to determine if there were any witnesses.

Professor McCormack was also present. In her green scrubs, she was just snapping on latex gloves in preparation for her examination. Jeffery Howson had already been stripped and lay on a metal cutting table.

She acknowledged Hunter's arrival with a nod, and then in her soft Scottish brogue began her preamble as she scrutinised the corpse. Name, age, height and weight were dictated in clear voice captured by the built-in recording system.

Hunter was not surprised when the pathologist announced that the body of the retired detective weighed just 7st 8lbs. He could see almost every bone poking beneath the man's yellow waxen flesh; the cancer had eaten away at him.

The pathologist began her examination at the head, hooking an arm beneath the neck and raising it from its table prop. With her free hand she pinched back the nose, pulled at the lips and ran a finger around inside the mouth. She swabbed inside the nostrils and the mouth and dropped the swabs into clear plastic exhibit phials.

'It's just as I surmised from my initial examination of this body at the scene. Clear signs of trauma around the mouth and nose and I've swabbed some trace evidence of fibres from those areas. He's bitten down on his tongue as well — most probably as he's struggled.'

She moved onto the arms, down to the hands, removing the plastic forensic bags encasing them, and individually checked each finger, taking several swabs beneath the nails.

'Can you photograph these, please?' she said, as she raised the corpse's stick-thin wrists.

Duncan Wroe had been hovering behind Professor McCormack, taking the swabs from her, scribbling on the labels of each of the samples and laying them out on a trolley beside him. He picked up his digital camera with its macro lens and began shooting off a series of frames as the professor rotated each forearm.

'There are clear signs of haemorrhaging into the soft tissue of both the right and left lower forearms, especially around the wrists.' She pointed out a series of deep purple patterns, clearly evident because of the paleness of the flesh.

'Looks as though he put up a hell of a struggle,' Hunter said.

'I thought that myself at first, but these contusions are particularly evident because this man was taking Warfarin. I saw in his notes that he had a heart condition, which was controlled by the drug. The least little knock can look as though he's been in a bar-room brawl. These marks, exaggerated though they may be, look like finger-grip marks. He has definitely had his wrists pinned down hard, probably against the arms of the chair he was sitting in.'

She picked up another two swabs and washed them over the bruised areas.

'There might be trace evidence of DNA if the offender wasn't wearing gloves,' she announced, sealing the swabs and handing them over to Duncan Wroe.

For the next two hours, Hunter watched the pathologist methodically going about her job. Firstly, with a precision steel scalpel, making the standard Y-shaped incision into the cadaver's chest, down through the stomach and finishing in the pubic bone region. This enabled her to crack apart the ribcage, providing access to the internal organs. She removed and inspected the heart and lungs carefully, weighed them, sliced into them and examined them again before dropping them into a bucket for a final analysis later. Throughout this, she continued with her dictation.

Partway into the dissection, the removal and the cutting opening of the stomach provided a surprise. Initially the vile stench caught them unawares and caused each of them to take a hurried step back.

It was some moments before Professor McCormack looked into the contents, but then she cried out, 'My, my, what have we got here?' Between thumb and forefinger, she brought out an inch-long object. It looked to be metal but was covered in sticky yellow globules of slime. She wiped it into the palm of her gloved hand and then held the object up to the light. It was a small brass key.

'This was something he didn't want anyone to find.' She passed it to Duncan. 'Now, if I was a detective, I would be thinking that key had something significant to do with his death,' she added.

She completed the autopsy at the head, slicing into the lower part of the neck and removing the trachea, before finally removing and examining the brain.

Hunter had watched this so many times over the years, and while he had seen many of his colleagues turn away in revulsion, he found himself drawn to the performance with a sense of morbid fascination.

After two and a half hours, the pathologist set down her scalpel and snapped off one of her surgical gloves.

'To sum up, gentlemen, the post-mortem has uncovered petechial haemorrhaging to the eyes and there is determined damage to the external airways around the mouth and nose. Fibres removed from the nasal passages and from the victim's mouth leave me to conclude that asphyxiation is the cause of death, as a result of him being smothered with a cloth-covered article. And the injuries to the wrists suggest that you are looking for at least two killers. He was definitely held down while being smothered.'

Professor McCormack turned, peeled off her other latex glove and dropped the pair into a biohazard bin as she retreated to her office.

Hunter looked at Superintendent Robshaw. He guessed that right now their thoughts were similar. Some cruel bastard had pressed a cushion over Jeffery Howson's face until he'd stopped breathing. *But why? And, what's the significance of that key he swallowed?*

That evening, Hunter met back up with the rest of the team at their favourite local Indian restaurant to celebrate their recent successful solving of the 'Lady in the Lake' murder case. The Major Investigation Team had been going for a curry on a regular basis since its inception two years ago, and tonight they had invited their respective wives, husbands or partners to share in the celebrations. Hunter knew it wouldn't be long into the meal before Beth would be kicking his ankles beneath the table as talk inevitably drifted towards police work.

Barry Newstead leaned into Hunter's ear and said in a hushed voice, 'A few years ago celebrating a result was a lot different from this. Do you remember? It was a pie and a pint and a lock-in at the pub and you paid for it with a thick head the next day.'

Hunter did remember. Surprisingly, the memories of those nights were as fresh as if they had happened only yesterday. The venue had nearly always been the George and Dragon, owned by a retired cop, where there would be a lock-in, and a couple of the lads would get their guitars out from the boots of their cars and everyone would join in with slurred renditions of songs until the small hours and then stagger home with croaking voices. And just like Barry had said, the following day Hunter would feel as if his head and guts were going to explode.

'Yeah, good nights, eh?' Hunter responded. 'But things move on.'

'Not always for the best if you ask me. I don't know, this bloody job's gone soft.' Barry took a long slurp of his beer, demolishing half the pint.

Hunter glanced across at Beth who had already found a seat in the foyer and was chatting away to Barry's girlfriend, Susan Siddons. The four of them were the first to arrive at the Indian restaurant.

'I don't know, Barry, I quite like these nights out. You get to know more about the people you work with.' Hunter took a sip of his chilled beer. 'Do you know why I think you don't like these evenings?' Hunter deliberately turned his head away, hiding a smile.

'Go on, surprise me,' Barry replied gruffly.

'Because you're afraid of letting your mask slip, or that someone might reveal your secrets. We might find out that the ruff-tuff brusque detective is really a pussy-cat with a liking for crochet and basket-weaving.'

Barry dug Hunter's arm with his elbow. 'Daft pillock!' He took another swill of his beer, then said softly, 'Anyway, what's wrong with crochet?'

They both cracked a laugh.

Grace and her husband David were the next to arrive. David joined Hunter and Barry at the bar, while Grace sidled off to greet Beth and Susan.

Mike Sampson arrived just after them. He made straight for the bar. Hunter knew that his first beer would hardly hit the sides before Mike was ready for the second. And he was right. Mike had devoured the pint before the second had been dispensed from the pump.

Mike clonked the empty glass down onto the bar and wiped the corners of his mouth. 'Christ, I needed that,' he said, taking the second drink from the barman while digging into a pocket for cash.

Hunter returned the nod and raised his glass. 'Down the hatch.'

Mike took another sip of his beer. 'I'm taking it easy tonight.' He patted his rotund belly. 'You know I'm not a lover of alcohol.'

Hunter chuckled as he eyed Mike. He wasn't the biggest of coppers, and for as long as Hunter had known him, he had been overweight. But what he lacked in stature he made up for with his sanguine character. He was a good thief-taker, a very good interviewer and he had a dry wit. When you were at a low ebb or there was a dark moment in an enquiry, you could always rely on Mike to lighten the moment, but he was also the consummate professional who did more than his fair share of the workload. Hunter had known Mike frequently come in on his day off to do an hour or two on his paperwork, and then spend an hour distracting others with his gossiping and joke telling.

Mike was also a complex character and very guarded when it came to his personal life. Hunter knew that he loved fishing and shooting, with a wide circle of mainly male friends, and he was very knowledgeable when it came to pub quizzes, but that was where it ended. He had never known Mike to be in a personal relationship. Mike had always lived at home with his mother until her unexpected death from a stroke three years ago and since then had lived alone.

Hunter had been to the house a few times to pick him up or drop him off when they were going out for a drink and a curry and had been surprised when he had seen the interior. Not that it was untidy or dirty, in fact the opposite was true — the house was pristine. But the furnishings, the carpets, even the décor, were stuck in a time warp in an era which belonged to Mike's mum. Nothing had been upgraded or changed.

Yet, despite his seemingly lonely home life, Hunter had never seen Mike down in the dumps. He was always the life and soul of both the office and the party and Hunter guessed that by the end of this evening, he would have everyone's attention with another of his funny stories.

Barry nudged Hunter when Tony Bullars came through the doors with a very attractive raven-haired woman on his arm. Flaxen-hair with sparkling blue-grey eyes and chiselled features — 'very handsome,' as Beth had ribbed him on more than a few occasions — Hunter knew that Bully had an eye for the ladies and never settled with any girl for very long. He had seen him with this girl on the last two departmental gatherings.

'Things must be getting serious. Next thing he'll be telling us he's decided to settle down,' he said to Barry through one side of his mouth.

Hunter ordered another round of drinks and slipped away from the bar to take Beth a glass of white wine. Suddenly, the lounge went quiet. He caught the look on his wife's face, eyes wide and eyebrows raised, her gaze was fixed somewhere over his shoulder. Turning sharply, he spotted Detective

Superintendent Michael Robshaw making for the bar. Just as quickly, stepping out from behind him, he saw a flame-haired woman. She offered a meek smile.

'Well, that's certainly killed the conversation,' Robshaw said good-humouredly, his keen eyes searching out the faces of his team. 'I think you've all met DCI Dawn Leggate?'

She strode the short distance to Hunter, hand outstretched. The gesture took him aback. He felt his insides flutter. Seeing her heavily freckled face brought uncomfortable memories flooding back.

Hunter had last seen Dawn Leggate eight weeks ago in the rear yard of the headquarters' custody suite. She and her team had been preparing to return to Scotland, where she was based, with two murderous villains that he and Barry had helped to lock-up. She had shaken his hand then and he had thought it would be the last time he would have to see her.

He reluctantly reached out and took hold of her hand.

'Hello, Hunter, nice to meet you again. How are you?'

'I'm fine, thanks.'

She held his hand for a few seconds. 'Good. No hard feelings then?' It was a rhetorical question. She slipped her hand away and turned back to her escort. 'I'd love a glass of red wine, thanks.'

Robshaw ordered drinks for everyone, then one of the waiters showed them to their table. They had all pre-ordered their meals during drinks and as they selected their places at the long table, the first course of mixed pickle and chutney with poppadums was already waiting.

Fighting spoon against spoon to battle for the lime-chillies with Barry helped Hunter to relax slightly, though he couldn't help but shoot repeated glances to the end of the table where Dawn Leggate was seated next to his boss.

There had been office gossip about Michael Robshaw and the Scottish DCI being an item, and there had been several sightings of the pair at a local restaurant over the past few weeks. This was now confirmation.

It couldn't be easy carrying on a relationship with six hours' driving time between them, Hunter thought as he watched the pair chatting. He just hoped it wouldn't be permanent. He felt uncomfortable in her presence; she knew too much about him and his family.

As they all finished the first course, two waiters glided in and cleared away the crockery. A sudden repetitive tinkling of metal against glass grabbed everyone's attention. Robshaw was tapping the side of his beer glass with his fork. It brought the team to order.

'I just want to say a few words.' Robshaw set down his fork but still held his pint glass. 'This is not a night for speeches, but there are three celebrations tonight. First and foremost, to the team, for another successful outcome. Your hard work during the past eight weeks has paid off. We got a good result last week — guilty verdicts with a 25-year minimum life sentence. It was well deserved after all the hard work you all put in and I'd like you to raise your glasses.'

There was a resounding response around the table. 'To us!'

'And now, secondly. This has not been an easy decision. I have thoroughly enjoyed my time with you lot. This is probably the best team I have ever worked with in my career, but I have decided that with three years to go before I can officially retire, I'm going to take a back seat. Though you all know I dislike the politics of the job, sometimes in your career you have to run with the devil. Next month I am moving on to headquarters. I am being promoted to Force Crime Manager.'

'And not a moment too soon,' Barry shouted from his seat. 'We'd thought we'd never get rid of you, gaffer,' he added with a mocking grin.

There was a ripple of laughter around the table.

'Thank you, Barry. I'll take that as a compliment. Now, for the last celebration. I invited Dawn tonight for a specific reason. Not just so you could all gossip about us, and yes we are an item, but I wanted you all to share and celebrate her success.' Robshaw glanced to his side and Dawn met his gaze. 'Dawn has made a life-changing decision in the past few weeks. From today she is a member of South Yorkshire Police and more importantly she is here on promotion to Detective Superintendent.' He thrust forward his half full glass of beer. 'Dawn will be shadowing me on this case for the next month and then she will be taking over. Please raise your glasses to your new SIO.'

Hunter's head snapped up. Those words struck him like a tsunami. He didn't join in the celebration — it wasn't a deliberate snub, but his thoughts were elsewhere. When he turned his attention back to the table, the second course had been put in front of him. He picked at the spicy pieces of chicken in crispy pancake casing.

Suddenly he wasn't hungry anymore.

DAY TWO

The next morning, in the female toilets of Barnwell Police station, Dawn Leggate checked her appearance in the mirror. She ran a finger around her lips, softening the edge of the gloss which she had applied just two minutes earlier.

Not too much make up, she told herself.

She straightened her dark blue jacket, flicked at the collar of her white blouse and stepped back a few paces to take in her overall image. Outwardly she looked calm, but inside her head and heart were racing like a clubber on speed.

It was the first day of her promotion, and she had a new team to manage.

Meeting the MIT squad last night had filled her with trepidation, particularly after what had gone on two months previously with DS Kerr. She couldn't afford for things to be edgy between her and one of her team supervisors, not with an investigation in full flow. She needed Hunter back on side.

First opportunity, she would have a clear the air session with Hunter, especially given that on her very first day she was in at the deep end of a major enquiry and working with a team she knew very little about.

This had been a giant leap for her and the past couple of months had been a whirlwind. At the heart of it had been Michael Robshaw, who had filled a void in her life. After an evening meal with him, she had done something which she had not done since university — she had jumped into bed with a first date. Her marriage had just ended and Robshaw offered her the kind of love she had craved for years.

The sudden chasm in Dawn's life had been partly her own fault. Since her teenage years, she had always thrown herself into everything she had done — love life, as well as job. Recently, she had chosen the job; she had been promoted as DCI into a very busy divisional CID. But she had thought she had done a pretty good job juggling both, until four months ago. Getting home late from work that Friday evening, she found the note on the kitchen side from Jack, her husband of eight years, telling her that it was all over and that he had left her. He hadn't even had the guts to face it out.

Over the following weekend, she discovered that he had moved in with a female colleague from his work — a liaison which had been going on for 18 months.

She, one of Scotland's top detectives, hadn't even suspected.

Going for that promotion board a month ago had been the hardest decision she had ever made. She already had a distinguished career and worked with some pretty damn good colleagues who were also friends. But at this stage in her life, a fresh start was required.

Hunter made his way up to the office. The rest of the squad were in and there was a buzz about the room. It was always like this the first day of an investigation — everyone was eager to get a quick result.

Hunter eased himself into his chair, looking to the front of the room. The incident board had been set up but there was very little written on it. The personal details of Jeffery Howson ran along the top of the white board and below that the timeline sequence had begun. A head and shoulders shot of him was Blu Tacked above his name.

Hunter checked the time-date sequences. The first was the sighting by Howson's daughter, who had visited him three days prior to his death and seen nothing out of place. The second time-frame covered the phone call with Barry Newstead that same evening, and the third denoted the finding of Jeffery dead by his daughter with his lounge ransacked.

'Okay, guys, listen up.' Detective Superintendent Robshaw brushed past Hunter's desk and made his way to the front. The incident room fell silent. Robshaw banged a hand on the incident board. 'Give me your eyes and ears for the next half an hour. We've got a lot to get through.'

Out of the corner of his eye, Hunter caught Dawn Leggate settling herself down on the edge of Mark Gamble's desk. He was met by her smile and forced one back — it felt awkward. He looked away and concentrated on his SIO.

Robshaw opened up the briefing. 'Victim is 63-year-old Jeffery Howson, a retired detective. He was last seen by his daughter when she visited him on Saturday afternoon. She brought him some shopping, put it away, did a bit of tidying up, made him a snack and left about 4.15 p.m. She was with him just under an hour. Our victim had heart problems and had recently been diagnosed with terminal lung cancer. Because of that, he had trouble getting around, but when she left him, she says he was settled in his chair, watching football on television. Apparently, he spent a lot of time in that chair, even taking to sleeping in it recently because he couldn't get comfortable in his bed. We also know that later that day, just before 10.50 at night, he made a phone call to Barry Newstead here, with a request to meet. Barry, will you give us the heads-up on your conversation with him?'

Barry ran a hand through his dark rumple of unruly hair and pushed himself back in his seat. In his gruff voice, he outlined the conversation he had had with the murder victim three days earlier. Upon finishing, he also repeated the details of the Lucy Blake-Hall murder case.

'Thanks for that,' said Robshaw. 'We know from phone records that the call to Barry was made from Howson's landline and at this stage we have no reason to believe that the caller was not our victim. What we do know is that Jeffery never made that meeting. In fact, we know from the PM that he probably met his death shortly after the phone call with Barry. We haven't got anything of significance yet, though house-to-house has thrown up something interesting from his next-door neighbour.

'Mr. Farmer, who has been Jeffery's neighbour for the past 15 years, has told officers that just before 11 on Saturday evening his dog started barking and he noticed the outside security light had come on. He went out to do a quick check, but he didn't see or hear anything, and just assumed it was a cat or a fox, and went back inside, locked up for the night and went to bed. He was specifically asked if he heard the sound of breaking glass, as we know that the offenders got in via the side door, but he says he heard nothing like that, and he definitely didn't hear any signs of a struggle or arguing coming from Jeffery Howson's place. So, until anything more definite comes in regarding time frames, I am holding on to the fact that Howson was attacked just before 11 p.m. when his neighbour was disturbed by the dog barking.'

Robshaw drifted his gaze between detectives. 'What we don't have at the moment is a motive for Howson's murder. We know about his phone call with Barry, the crux of which was his concern over the murder of Lucy Blake-Hall back in 1983. And we know about the mysterious key found in his stomach contents, which he obviously swallowed for a reason. But we don't know yet what that reason is, or what that key opens up.

'I guess when we discover that, all will become clear. Until then, there is another element we need to focus on. There are signs of a search, certainly in the lounge area, so we also have to ask ourselves if this is a burglary gone wrong.'

Robshaw faced the room again. 'Guys, Howson was one of our own. We owe it to him and his family to get a quick result. Forensics are at a very early stage. They will be returning this morning to do a thorough examination of the house. House-to-house has only been done with his immediate neighbours. Besides Mr. Farmer's information, we have learned that Jeffery was a relatively quiet and private man who had very few visitors. So far, no one has reported anything else out of the ordinary.

'We're casting the net a little bit wider this morning. Task Force will be continuing with the door-knocking and will also be doing a fingertip search of the garden. That will be extended. Beyond his garden fence there is a footpath leading into the woods.

'Okay, actions. First, we re-interview the daughter, get a thorough background. Everything she knows about her father. I also want to know what that key fits. See if the daughter knows. He swallowed it for a reason, and as I have already mentioned, my guess is that reason got him killed. But we don't reveal that to her or to anyone outside this room how we found it.

'Second, he made great stay about the murder of Lucy Blake-Hall back in 1983. Barry has already given an insight into that and I want a copy of that file and to know everything about it. Contact the cold case review team.

'Third, we trace Jeffery Howson's colleagues. I know he's been retired a good few years now, but a number of his ex-colleagues should be around. I want to know who he worked with at divisional CID. Who did he regularly partner with? I also want someone to speak with the Intelligence unit. Has there been a spate of burglaries recently? Who is active in that area?

'And finally, for today, we make a request for his telephone records. We know about his phone call to Barry, but I want to know if he made any other calls after that, and anyone else he spoke with in the week leading up to his murder. Given his state of health, the phone was his lifeline to the outside world and we need to know if the list throws up anyone of interest.'

Robshaw tucked his hands into his trouser pockets. 'That's it for now, everyone. We meet back here at eight p.m. for another briefing.' He took a deep breath and steadily scanned the room. 'Team, it would be nice to put this one to bed quickly. I want the bastards who did this nailed, and pronto.'

Hunter and Grace had been tasked with collecting the case file relating to the disappearance and murder of Lucy Blake-Hall, and after putting in a call to the cold case review team, they headed over to newly built Maltby police station where they were based.

They had only been waiting in the foyer of the station for a little over five minutes when Detective Sergeant Jamie Parker, the officer in charge of the team, appeared in reception. The DS was tall and slim and looked business-like in a charcoal grey suit. His short dark hair was giving way to grey and a neatly trimmed half-beard and moustache lined a cheery smile. He introduced himself, shaking their hand, and showed them through into a carpeted, brightly lit corridor lined with doors, many of which were open with lots of activity going on behind them.

'We've got a murder running — just started this morning,' Parker said. 'They've drafted in detectives from other stations. It's a bit manic today.'

'Always is at the start of a job,' added Hunter, thinking about his own team's new case.

Parker nodded. 'We're up on the first floor,' he said, pointing them along the corridor to a set of double doors.

A metal stairwell took them up to the next floor. The cold case review team was housed in the first office along the corridor. It was a long oblong room, made cramped by metal filing cabinets, filling almost the length of the back wall, and six desks, which took up most of the floor space. Three detectives were at their desks. They cast Hunter and Grace a quick glance before returning to their work.

Parker took up his own seat at his desk and offered up two empty seats either side of him. 'It's a good job the other two DCs are out on enquiries, otherwise it would have been standing room only,' he said, leaning forward and pushing back the desk jotter to make room to rest his arms. 'We drew the short straw when we moved in here. We were the last team in. I think they gave us the janitor's storeroom by mistake,' he said. 'Can we get you a cuppa?'

'I'd love one,' Hunter said.

'Coffee, if that's okay,' added Grace.

One of the detectives stepped over to the filing cabinets, shuffled together a load of cups and left the room carrying a laden tea tray.

'How long have you been here?' asked Hunter.

'It'll be two years in January. We were set up not long after the Major Investigation Units started.'

The DS's comments jogged Hunter's memory. His own unit had been one of many set up by the Force in 2006 to investigate major crimes as a result of a government review. One of the remits had been to pick up old rape and murder cases which still lie undetected in station vaults and would benefit from modern policing and scientific techniques, particularly using the advancement of DNA.

Originally, his team had cherry-picked a few cold cases, but then along had come current major crime and those investigations had taken a back seat. He guessed this was why the cold case review team had been formed.

'How many cases are you working on at the moment?' Hunter asked.

'We usually pick up two or three each at a time and juggle them around between us. Some of them are really fascinating and it's especially gratifying when we can go back to a complainant or a parent after all those years and tell them we have enough evidence to take their attacker to court.'

'How many cases are there still outstanding?'

'Too many to mention. This Force has records stretching back to 1974 when it was formed and there are also records from when it was the West Riding. The oldest file I have seen is an undetected murder from 1962.'

Hunter pursed his lips in a silent whistle.

'The case you're after is the murder of Lucy Blake-Hall from 1983, is that right?'

'Yeah. Well before my time. I didn't join the job until 1991.'

'Well, it's all there.' Parker pointed to an array of cardboard file boxes stacked next to a metal cabinet.

Hunter guessed there must be at least a dozen stacked boxes. He hadn't expected that amount.

'You're in luck. We've had a quick scan through and it looks as though everything is there.' Parker pushed himself up from his seat and moved to the pile. Giving a cursory glance at its label, he prised open the lid of one box and lifted out a thick file with both hands. 'This is the summary, main witness evidence, and suspect interview file which was presented at the trial.

In the other boxes are the house-to-house forms, original witness statements, scene of crime photographs and the Home Office forensic forms for the science labs. Oh, and in your case quite a few of the boxes contain the original index cards for the job.'

'You got this quick. We only rang about this case a couple of hours ago.'

'There was a message left on my voicemail this morning from a Detective Superintendent Dawn Leggate. I got in at 7.30, so I was able to arrange a driver to pick up the box files first thing.' Parker handed Hunter the file.

Hunter weighed it in his hands, turned it and fanned apart some of the pages. The file had the patina of ageing but was easily readable. He glanced at the strapline, reading it off inside his head, *Regina v Daniel Weaver*.

'You're very lucky,' Parker told him. 'Many of the really old case files have been destroyed. Forces have had to be ruthless because of the lack of space, and I know from experience that huge swathes of paperwork have been binned. I've had a cursory look inside the boxes of this case. There's an inventory at the top of each one. And although all the paperwork appears to be there, I'm afraid there're no exhibits. I don't know yet if those have been destroyed or not.'

Hunter shot a quick glance at Grace.

'No need to look downhearted,' Parker said. 'I do have some good news. Since I've been doing this job, we've discovered that the forensic science labs, unlike the police, have kept files and samples from every job ever submitted to them. So, somewhere in their system will be samples taken during the Lucy Blake-Hall investigation. Once you sort through the paperwork, I can set things in motion to check with forensics, if you'd like?'

Hunter thanked Parker and returned the file to its box. He cast his eyes along the stack of other boxes. *There's a lot of paperwork to go through here*, he thought, setting the lid back on and heaving it up.

'We'll give you a hand to load it,' offered Parker. He picked up a box from the pile and hoisted it mid-chest. 'Listen, we have loads of experience of dealing with cold cases, especially tracking down witnesses. We have found it can be tricky tracking down female witnesses. Many women get married, change their surname and also move away, but we have tried and trusted ways of finding them. Once you've gone through the boxes and sorted everything out, if you get stuck with anything just give us a bell.'

Hunter thanked him.

'Just a bit of advice as well,' Parker continued. 'When the time comes for you to speak with the detectives who previously worked on the case, I know from experience that some of them get very nervous when you start going back over things, because methods that were used during their time were not always the right ones. Just remember that was then, this is now. Your focus shouldn't be about how the case was detected.'

Hunter got an image of Barry Newstead. He knew exactly what Parker was talking about. He'd been introduced to many unorthodox methods in his pursuit of villains during his early CID days; all of them instigated by Barry. He couldn't help but crack a grin as he turned towards the door.

Detectives Tony Bullars and Carol Ragen knocked on the front door of Jeffery Howson's daughter's four-bedroom detached house and waited for it to be answered.

Katherine Edwards answered with her mobile pressed to her ear. Pointing to it, mouthing the words, 'My mum,' she ushered in Tony and Carol, and bid them to follow her through to the kitchen. As she walked into the kitchen, she said on the phone, 'Yeah, the police are just here now. I'll give you a ring later when I find out what's what, okay? Yeah, love you too, bye.' She ended the call and placed the mobile on the central work island.

They were in a bright and airy L-shaped kitchen diner with contemporary black and white high gloss units lining soft cream walls. Most of the light came from a large set of French doors, which gave a view out to Katherine's well-tended garden. The expensive, well designed look of the kitchen reminded Tony that she had told him the previous day that she used to work as a sports injury therapist for a professional football club but now worked privately from home and that it was very lucrative.

'Sorry about that. That was my mum. I've only just managed to get hold of her to break the news. She didn't get back from Gran Canaria until the early hours of this morning.' Katherine picked up the electric kettle and filled it from the tap. 'Can I get you a drink? Tea? Coffee?'

Both agreed on tea.

'Sorry to burden you at a time like this, Katherine,' opened Tony with a sympathetic look. 'But as you can probably appreciate, we need to move on this quite quickly in order to find your father's killer. I know I bombarded you with quite a number of questions yesterday, but I need to go back over things with you. We have gaps that need filling, both in terms of his past history, as well as recent events in his life. We're hoping you will be able to fill those in?'

'I couldn't sleep last night. I can't believe what's happened. Dad being murdered. All those murders he's investigated in the past and now he's been killed.'

Katherine filled the kettle, switched it on, and plucked out three cups from a cupboard, arranging them around the kettle. Turning back to face the detectives, she swept a hand through one side of her dark hair, tucking it behind her ear and fixed them with her grey-blue eyes. 'This has come as such a shock. Thing is, I thought I'd done most of my grieving for him several months ago when I found out he'd got terminal cancer. I've been to hospital so many times with him these past few months when he's gone for his chemo that I'd thought I'd become hardened to the fact that he was going to die.' Her voice trailed off on a brittle note. Dabbing a forefinger into the corner of one eye, she turned quickly back to face the boiling kettle. 'But this... I mean, Dad murdered. It's just so hard to imagine.'

'Katherine, I want to introduce you to DC Carol Ragen.' Tony swapped his gaze from Katherine to his colleague. 'After today, Carol will be spending quite a lot of time with you and your mother throughout the duration of this enquiry. She will be here to support you both and give you everything you need. If there is anything you don't understand, just ask her. She will keep you up to date with the enquiry. Is that okay?'

Katherine nodded, switching her gaze to Carol.

Carol met her eyes. 'As Tony says, if you want to know what is going on or anything you don't understand, I'm here for you. The only thing I ask is that what I tell you is kept to yourself.'

Tony continued, 'It's a bit of a cliché, Katherine, but do you know if your father had any enemies? Or if he'd had an argument with anyone recently?'

Katherine shrugged her shoulders. 'He'd been a detective for 30-something years, I guess he made loads of enemies over that time. If you mean, did I know of anyone who hated him that much to do this to him, then the answer is no. However, I do know something was troubling him of late.'

Tony's eyebrows raised. 'What do you mean, troubling him?'

'Well, because I've been spending quite a lot of time with him recently, we've caught up on a lot of things from the past, and Dad talked a lot about some of the cases he'd been involved in. To be honest, I switched off most of the time because he started to ramble, I'm guessing to do with the morphine, but some of the things he said stuck with me, because I thought they were a bit strange.'

'Strange?' prompted Tony.

'Yes. A couple of times he said, "I've done some bad things in my time. I've done stuff when I was detective that I shouldn't have done." He'd say other stuff like, "I've not always been a good husband or a good dad," as well, but he'd keep going back over the fact that he'd done something bad when he had been a detective.'

'Did he mention what that was?' Tony asked.

'Not exactly. You have to understand, he was so high on the morphine that some of the time he didn't make sense. He'd start with one thing and then start rambling on about something completely different, so I only half-listened to what he was saying. I do recall him saying that "he was going to put things right."' Katherine paused for a second, then shook her head. 'Sorry, I don't think he expanded on that.' She pulled a face. 'I feel awful now that I didn't listen properly or push him to tell me more.'

'When you say he said he was going to put things right, did he say how he was going to do that?'

Katherine shrugged her shoulders again. 'Sorry. I feel terrible. I wish I'd have listened better to what he was saying.'

'Don't worry about it. It's one of those things. You weren't to know this was going to happen. Would there be anyone else he might have talked to about this? Any other visitors? Close friends?'

'I'm not quite sure. I know he kept in contact with a couple of his ex-colleagues. I've turned up a couple of times with bits of shopping for him and he's been on the phone. I picked up on him reminiscing about jobs he'd been involved in and just guessed it was people he'd worked with. I know he was particularly close to someone from the old days. Someone called Alan. I know that at least once a month they'd go off for the day, usually out to Derbyshire, and they'd stop off at a pub for a couple of beers and lunch. He'd talk about working with him but I've never met him. Other than that, he seemed to keep himself very much to himself. I've only really got to know him since I moved back here five years ago.'

Katherine looked up, swallowed hard and returned her gaze. 'He's been on his own since he and Mum got divorced back in 1984. I don't think there was anyone else romantic in his life since then, but to be honest that's not something I would discuss with him. It's taken quite a lot of time just getting to know him again. It's not been easy for him, or me. I went with Mum when she left him.

'Mum wouldn't talk about why they'd split up and so I just shut myself off from it all. I was 17 at the time. I swapped schools for a year, got my A levels, and then I went off to uni. While I was there, Mum met Derek, my stepfather, and she moved in with him and they married. I went back to Derek's for a short while to be with Mum but it just didn't feel right. Not that I didn't get on with Derek or anything, but being away for three years, you know, I'd moved on.

'Then, I got a job as a sports injury physio at Skegness hospital for a short time, before getting that job at Lincoln City, and that's when I met Sean who was one of the coaches there. It was a bit of a whirlwind romance. We were married within 18 months. Amy, our daughter, came along a few years later and that was it. I had my own family to focus on and Dad didn't feature. He didn't come to the wedding and hadn't seen his granddaughter until five years ago. It's taken a lot to get to know each other again. I only came back here because Sean and I separated and I decided to return to my roots.'

Katherine stirred her tea and took a long sip of the hot drink. 'We've never really picked up on the lost years. I had my new house and was starting my business so I was always busy. I did catch up with him, and I used to nip round a couple of times every week, and he would have Amy quite a lot when I had my evening clients. We did touch on old times but whenever I'd raise anything about them splitting up, he'd just say he'd rather leave that alone. After a while, I just stopped asking him questions.'

Katherine switched her gaze between the two detectives. 'Don't we all lead such complicated lives? If only we could go back, eh? The sad thing is, I was always going to ask why he never came to my wedding and why he never acknowledged the birth of Amy but it never seemed to be the right moment. Even when I knew he was going to die with cancer.'

'Sorry to push you, Katherine,' Tony said. 'Just to take you back a little to where your dad mentioned about putting things right. You said that you had overheard some of his phone calls with his old colleagues, reminiscing about jobs. You mentioned this colleague, Alan. Do you recall anything of the conversations about him?'

Katherine shook her head. 'Nothing springs to mind at the moment. I'll think it over, and if anything comes to mind, I'll contact you. There's so much to take in, you understand? It would be worth your time speaking with my mum. Like Dad, she's never really discussed why they split up. I have broached it a few times but all she used to say is what's done is done. I'll give Mum her due, she never slagged him off when I was around.'

'We'll be doing that as part of our enquiries,' Tony assured her. 'And don't worry about not remembering. Something might come to you later. Think about it in your own time. Now, just to take you back to Saturday. What time did you last see him?'

'It would roughly have been 4.15 p.m. I'd done a bit of shopping for him. I was chatting to him as I put it away. He was watching football on Sky.'

'Can you recall anything of what was said?'

'Not exactly. I'm afraid I was going off on one. I told him off about the full ashtray again. Cigarettes are what caused his lung cancer. But I do remember the conversation we had on Saturday night when he rung me late on. I remember it because of the strange thing he said.'

Tony raised his eyebrows. 'Tell me about that.'

'When the phone rang, I'd only just poured myself a glass of wine and put my feet up. I let Amy stay up a little later on Saturdays, so it was just after 10.30. I'd not long tucked her up, and got out of the bath myself, so I was going to ignore it, until I saw it was Dad and I thought he might have taken a turn for the worse. But he hadn't. In fact, I was surprised how chirpy he sounded.

'He apologised for ringing me so late, and then asked if I would do him a favour on Sunday and run him out to the George and Dragon pub in Wentworth where he was going to catch up with someone. Unfortunately, I couldn't. I had a couple of clients and I apologised and asked him if he could wait until two, when I was free. He said he'd promised to meet him at lunchtime, and no worries, he'd get a taxi. I said if it was anything important, I could cancel one of my clients, but he said, "No, it was only one of my old colleagues I wanted to catch up with. I'll sort it."' Her face took on a look of concern. 'I feel guilty about it now, especially because of what's happened.'

Tony guessed that when they checked the records, the timing of the phone call to Katherine would follow the one with Barry Newstead. He said, 'You said your dad said something strange?'

'Oh, yes. Sorry — about going around the houses. Just before he hung up, he said, "If anything happens to me, Katherine, I want you to look in the safe." That's what he said. Those were his exact words. When he hung up, I remember thinking, what a weird thing to say.'

'Look in the safe?' Tony repeated.

'Yeah, the safe in the back room. He has it hidden beneath a panel in the back bedroom's fitted wardrobes. It's covered by his shoes. He showed me where it was not long after he was diagnosed. He told me that everything was in there that I would need to settle his affairs, and that he would leave me instructions inside it which he wanted me to follow. He said the house deeds, insurance policies and important papers were all in there.'

Tony's eyes lit up. He reached into his suit jacket pocket and retrieved the exhibit bag that contained the brass key removed from Jeffery Howson's stomach. He held it up to Katherine. 'Do you recognise this key, by any chance?'

'Yes. That looks like my dad's safe key.'

Tony stepped outside and rang Detective Constable Mike Sampson, who was working with forensics at Jeffery Howson's address.

Mike answered and Tony filled him in on what Katherine had said.

'Has anyone found a safe?' Tony asked. 'Katherine says it's secreted inside one of the wardrobes in the back room.'

'Hold on, I'll check,' Mike replied.

Tony heard the sounds of Mike climbing the stairs and then Mike asking someone, 'Have you been through the wardrobes yet?'

A woman's voice said no, and then Mike said, 'Mind if I take a quick look inside?'

There was a few minutes silence, before Mike said, 'Bingo! Tony, there's a green metal safe tucked away here. It isn't large, roughly 30 centimetres square. There's a handle and a keyhole, but it's locked.'

Tony Bullars turned up at Howson's property ten minutes later, bounding up the stairs to join Mike. He had left DC Ragen with Katherine.

Mike pointed out the safe and Tony removed the small brass key from the exhibit bag. On bended knees, he leaned inside the wardrobe and tried it.

'Fits,' he called back over his shoulder, turning the key.

The door, though surprisingly heavy for its size, opened smoothly. In the gloom, Tony could make out a number of packages and envelopes. He took each one out individually, using only finger and thumb, and passed them back to Mike who laid them out on the sheeting.

Running a hand around the inside of the safe, satisfying himself it was empty, Tony pushed himself up and turned to his colleague. In better light he was able to see the contents from the safe more clearly. There were two small Jiffy bags and three A4 envelopes. Each was marked in neat copperplate handwriting. He scanned the packages, picking out the words 'last will and testament' and 'life insurance' on two of the envelopes.

'That's the one we want,' said Mike, picking up a brown envelope.

Tony read the words written across the front and felt at the package. It felt like it contained a small wad of paper. He turned the envelope over. It had been stuck down and additionally sealed with sticking tape. He turned it back and re-read the sentence neatly written in black ink: 'For the attention of Barry Newstead'.

Hunter stretched up in his chair, hooked his hands behind his head and gazed around the incident room. It was the first time in over an hour that he had looked up from his desk. He and Grace had got back from the cold case unit at midday, and over a sandwich he had immediately delved into the Lucy Blake-Hall file.

Now, he became conscious of the noise levels and activity going on in the room, realising that he had immersed himself so much in the story of the 1984 trial of Daniel Weaver, who had been charged with the killing of Lucy, that he'd been oblivious to the work going on around him. He spotted his counterpart, DS Mark Gamble, leaning back in his chair, one leg propped upon the corner of his desk, the phone handset clamped between his right shoulder and ear, doing more listening than talking.

Grace was at the front of the room leaning over a long table, moving around postcard-sized buff-coloured cards like a croupier at a Blackjack table. In front of her were row upon row of similar cards and she appeared to be switching or adding to the piles she had created. He realised she was sorting out the old recording index from one of the case boxes.

'Having fun?' he called over.

Grace looked up. 'Having fun? This is a nightmare. It's like sorting out a 1000-piece jigsaw with some of the bits missing. I can't make head nor tail of most of the cross-referencing or the information written on some of these cards. I'm hoping that when I start going through some of the paperwork it will all fall into place.'

Hunter unhooked his hands and pointed to the prosecution file he had just finished. 'This is an interesting story. The summary is a lot more long-winded than some of today's files but it makes for good reading. In fact, having read it, I'm puzzled now why Jeffery Howson said the things he did to Barry, because on paper the job seems cut and dried. The evidence against Lucy Blake-Hall's killer is so strong.'

Grace stretched out her spine. 'Give me a quick run-down then. It might help me make some sense of this lot.'

'Okay, briefly, Lucy was 22 years old when she disappeared back in August 1983. At the time, she was married with a young daughter.' Hunter paused and glanced down at some notes he had made. 'Jessica,' he added and continued with his narration. 'It appears she'd been having an affair with a guy called Daniel Weaver for approximately six months and he'd made arrangements to rent a place near Cambridge, where they were going to live together. On the night of her disappearance —' Hunter checked his notes again — 'Friday the 26th — the start of the Bank Holiday weekend — witnesses saw her and Daniel together in a pub and an hour later they were seen arguing in the marketplace. That's the last anyone saw of her. Husband reported her missing the Saturday morning, and when Daniel was paid a visit, a day later, on the Sunday, he had scratches to his face, so he was arrested.

'Jeffery Howson and Detective Sergeant Alan Darbyshire were the arresting officers and they had several interviews with him. Initially, he denied the affair and denied meeting her on the Friday. On the second interview he changed his story. He admitted the affair and admitted seeing her that Friday. He also admitted that the marks to his face were caused by Lucy. He said they had rowed because she had changed her mind about running away together. His place was searched and they found Lucy's handbag hidden among some sacks in his garden shed. In a third interview, Weaver confessed to killing her. That's it, in a nutshell.'

Grace threw Hunter a puzzled look. 'But didn't Barry say that Lucy's body's never been found?'

'It hasn't.'

'Well, if Weaver admitted to killing her, why didn't he tell the interviewing officers where he had buried her?'

Hunter hunched his shoulders. 'Well, he did in a fashion. In his last interview he coughed to strangling her during a row back at his place, and then, when he realised she was dead, he drove her body up to Langsett Moor in his works van and buried her somewhere up there. He said he couldn't remember where because he'd been drinking and it was dark.'

'But I thought he pleaded not guilty?'

'Oh, he did. At his trial, Weaver alleged that he'd been fitted up. I'm hoping to find the details of his defence among the paperwork in one of the boxes I've yet to go through. This file just has the main witness statements and his interview notes.'

The unexpected ringing of his desk phone made Hunter jump. He reached across and snatched it up.

'DS Kerr, Major Investigation Team.' After listening for a minute, Hunter launched himself out of his chair, and exclaimed, 'Get your coat on, Grace. That was Bully on the phone. The key found in Jeffery Howson's stomach was for a safe which they've found hidden in a set of wardrobes. He says he's found something of great interest.'

Jockeying his way through heavy traffic, Hunter managed the journey to Woodlands View in less than 20 minutes. He tucked the CID car behind one of the SOCO vans parked at the head of the cul-de-sac.

A TV camera crew team were now at the scene. They had set up by the first taped cordon slung across the road, the backdrop of their focus being number 12. A reporter appeared to be in the middle of a shoot.

Hunter nudged Grace. 'Make sure your lippy is on, girl, you'll be on *Look North* tonight.' He flashed a wink as he pushed his driver's door to and popped the locks.

Approaching the top of the drive of number 12, Hunter saw that a large blue canvas had been erected against the side door, protecting as well as hiding the entrance. He flashed his warrant card to the uniform logging officer and trooped off down the drive with Grace, squeezing past Jeffery Howson's 10-year-old Volkswagen Polo, as he made for the side door.

They found Tony and Mike in the dining room at the back of the house, hunkered over an oval mahogany table. The well-polished surface was littered with a raft of paperwork sealed inside exhibit bags. Most of the documents appeared to be handwritten police interview forms.

Hunter noted that this room, although slightly musty, had none of the stale tobacco or urine smells which had disgusted him during his visit the day before. And it was a lot brighter. Patio doors, overlooking the overgrown rear garden, took up half of one wall, letting bright afternoon sunshine flood in.

'I thought you might want to see this little lot before forensics take them away,' said Tony, looking up. He pushed a couple of the bagged pages towards Hunter. 'They've all been photographed and Duncan's promised me he will have the images emailed to me for tomorrow morning's briefing, but I wanted you to read this interview record and cast your eye over these documents we found.' Tony tapped the A4 envelope with a handwritten inscription across the front. 'They were inside this envelope addressed to Barry. It's pretty interesting stuff. If it's the real deal, then it certainly opens up our investigation!'

Hunter stared at the array of documents across the table. There must have been at least 20 pieces. Six of the clear plastic forensic bags contained newspaper cuttings, yellowed and pitted with age. Hunter saw that someone had taken the time to cut out, organise and neatly paste a series of different tabloid articles onto separate sheets of paper. He took in a couple of the headlines 'DISAPPEARED WITHOUT TRACE'; 'THE LAST PERSON TO SEE LUCY'; 'LUCY BLAKE-HALL — MAN CHARGED WITH MURDER'.

Several black and white photographs were dotted throughout the articles. Hunter recognised a shot of the Coach and Horses pub in Barnwell town centre, which he knew from reading the Daniel Weaver prosecution file earlier was one of the last places where witnesses saw him and Lucy together.

Another was a head and shoulders shot of a smiling young woman, blonde hair piled up and fashioned into a bunch at the crown. Dark mascara ringed glistening eyes and a thin slender nose complemented a face with high cheekbones. The caption gave Lucy's name, with the addition of 'Where is she?'

Very pretty woman, Hunter thought to himself. It was his first sighting of Lucy; previously she had just been a name on paper. He would like to have read them further, but at the corner of his eye he could see Tony anxiously beating a tattoo over one particular piece of evidence.

Hunter pulled the plastic bag from beneath Tony's forefinger, spinning it around to its correct way up. He saw that the exhibit pouch contained the first sheet of a formal record of interview form identical to the ones he had seen in the murder file that morning.

Reading his way down, he picked out that it was the contemporaneous account of an interview with Daniel Weaver, conducted by Detective Sergeant Alan Darbyshire and Detective Constable Jeffery Howson on Monday 29th August 1983. Questioning started at 2.20 p.m. and was concluded at 3.25 p.m. that same day.

Hunter began reading the script, penned in black biro and still very clear and legible after all this time. In fact, unlike the clipped out foxed newspaper articles, it looked as though it hadn't seen the light of day since it had been written.

As he inched his way down the text, he felt more and more confused. Why had such an important document been locked away in Howson's safe? It should have formed part of the prosecution file against Daniel Weaver.

For the next 20 minutes, Hunter meticulously read every handwritten sentence of the chronicled interview. As he put aside each separate sheet, Tony fed him another, until all the 12 pages had been digested.

Taking in the last sentence of the final page, Hunter set it aside with the others. He let off a low whistle and then said, 'I think I now know why Jeffery Howson was killed.'

DAY THREE

A gloomy start to the day meant that the overhead fluorescent lighting in MIT had to be on for the morning briefing. The bright lights bathed the room in a warm glow, masking the cold outside.

Hunter watched as Dawn Leggate took her place beside the incident board at the front of the room.

'Good morning, everyone,' she said. 'Mr Robshaw has had to start at Headquarters today to sort out the budget for the investigation, so he's asked me to take the briefing. We have quite a lot to go through this morning, especially the find yesterday, so we'll run this from the top.' She tapped the incident board with her pen. 'We all know that 63-year-old retired detective, Jeffery Howson, was found murdered at his home on Monday and the likelihood is that he was killed late Saturday night. We also know that before his death he made a phone call to Barry here, stating he wanted to meet and tell him about the murder of Lucy Blake-Hall in 1983. That the wrong person had been convicted of it and that he knew who had done it. Have I got that right, Barry?'

Barry nodded.

'I can also see from the write-up on the board that we now have the background to the Lucy Blake-Hall murder. Hunter, you and Grace had that enquiry. Can you expand on the information on the board?'

Hunter picked up his loose notes from his desk and made his way to the front.

'Yes, boss,' he replied. 'We picked up the case files from the cold case unit yesterday. We haven't had time to go through everything, as you will appreciate, but I have read the prosecution file and the report on the appeal, and Grace is currently trying to organise the old card index system for inputting into HOLMES. She has also spoken with the Forensics lab at Wetherby. It would appear they still have the exhibit slides from the original investigation and they have their own set of comprehensive notes, which is a real plus.'

Hunter outlined the Lucy Blake-Hall case. He gave a brief resumé of her family circumstances — married with a five-year-old daughter, back in

1983, and then focused in detail on the last sightings of her on Friday 26th August, when witnesses saw her with her lover, Daniel Weaver, in the Coach and Horses pub, and then later that same evening arguing in the marketplace in Barnwell.

'Jeffery Howson and DS Alan Darbyshire, whom, I've been informed by Barry, retired as a DCI in 1992, arrested Daniel the day after Lucy had been reported missing, following a visit to his home when they saw scratches on his face, which he refused to account for. Weaver was known to the police. He had previous for a chemist break-in and also possession of a controlled drug with intent to supply. He did 18 months in a young offenders' institution in 1977.'

Hunter outlined the interrogation of Daniel Weaver at the police station, in which, after initial denials, he admitted to his affair with Lucy and confessed that it was she who had scratched him during an argument on the evening of her disappearance. He revealed how Jeffery Howson and Alan Darbyshire had also discovered Lucy's handbag hidden under sacking in Weaver's garden shed, and that after making another initial denial Weaver had gone on to give a full admission as to how he had strangled Lucy and then buried her body up on Langsett Moor.

'A team of police officers spent a fortnight up on the moors searching for signs of her burial site, but at that stage Weaver had been appointed a solicitor and refused to cooperate with the investigation further, so her body was never found. The trial of Daniel Weaver took place in April, 1984. He did go in the box and give evidence.

'I've also got the next bits from the newspaper articles covering the trial. Weaver admitted to the affair and to the argument with Lucy in which she had scratched his face. He said they were caused while trying to reason with her and she had pulled away from him. He admitted making a number of statements during his interviews, but he flatly denied making the one where he admitted to strangling her and burying her body up on Langsett Moor. He accused the police of planting the handbag. After a three-week trial, he was found guilty of Lucy's murder and given life. His defence submitted an appeal but it was turned down on the grounds that the trial was conducted fairly, and that without fresh evidence the conviction was deemed to be safe.'

Hunter glanced up from his jottings. 'On my first reading of the file, I thought everything was cut and dried. That was until we found the set of contemporaneous notes in Jeffery Howson's safe. Last night, I re-examined the case file. There were three sets of interviews, all written on the same forms we found in Howson's safe. The first two, in which Weaver admitted the affair with Lucy and how he came about the scratches, following his argument with her, were signed by Weaver. The third set of notes, which contained his confession he did not sign. On those, where his signature should have been, the words "refused to sign" have been penned.'

'Sorry to steal your thunder, Hunter,' said Dawn, 'but can I come in here?' She tapped her biro against the sides of the incident board, where reduced photocopies of the contemporaneous notes recovered from Jeffery Howson's safe were fixed in the top right-hand corner. 'This find could change everything about the trial and conviction of Daniel Weaver. The originals of these are currently on their way to Forensics for chemical dating analysis and for fingerprint identification. What we have here, team, is a set of recorded interview notes conducted with Weaver during the time he was in police custody on 29th August, 1983.

'As we have heard, the interviewers were Jeffery Howson and Alan Darbyshire, and going by the handwriting, which matches that on the envelope they were found in, it looks as though they were completed by our murder victim Jeffery Howson. For those in this room who were not around before tape-recorded interviewing was introduced, all interviews were handwritten. The notes take the form of a question and answer session between the police officers and the defendant, known as contemporaneous notes, and had to be read and witnessed by the defendant upon their completion.

'The notes found in the envelope in Howson's safe bear the signatures of Daniel Weaver and bears no resemblance to any of the notes on the original prosecution file. In fact, recorded on them is a clear denial of Lucy's disappearance and there is certainly no admission to her murder. In fact, quite the opposite. Daniel Weaver states that he last saw Lucy when he argued with her in the marketplace at about 9.30 p.m. on the Friday evening. He says she told him she was going home, that her husband had found out about their relationship and was holding onto their daughter Jessica, threatening Lucy that she would never see her again if she left. She told Daniel that she couldn't leave her daughter behind, so was calling it off. In the notes, Daniel states he did his best to make her change her mind, and at one stage grabbed hold of her and that's how he got his face scratched when she pulled away.

'He goes on to say that he went straight home to his flat, drank a few whiskies and watched some TV, and then went to bed where he remained until the next day when he went to his parents' house about 11 a.m., where his mother made him some breakfast. When he was asked about the handbag being found hidden under sacking in his shed, he said, "Someone must have planted it".

'This could overturn the conviction against Daniel Weaver for Lucy's murder. If those notes are the real thing and had been submitted as part of the original prosecution file, then I am not convinced he would ever have gone to trial. In fact, they would have opened up the entire investigation into Lucy's disappearance. It would have been nice if Jeffery Howson had left a note to explain all this, but I'm guessing that he didn't leave one because he was fully intending to explain everything to Barry when they met. And, as we all know, he was murdered before he could make that meeting. So now, in the absence of any other information, we are left to speculate why they were never submitted. Their discovery certainly supports the comment he made to Barry in his telephone call on Saturday night that the wrong person was convicted.'

Dawn glanced at the incident board. 'There are only three people who can provide the answers to the validity of those notes. One is Jeffery Howson, who is now dead. The second is retired DCI Alan Darbyshire. And the third person is Daniel Weaver, who is currently serving life for Lucy's murder. Hunter has already told us that on the original file, he found that the contemporaneous notes outlining Weaver's admission were not signed. The ones we have recovered from Jeffery Howson's safe are timed and dated, exactly the same as Weaver's admission interview notes. Only one of those sets can be the original notes and I know which ones I am inclined to go with.'

Dawn studied the faces of the detectives. 'I don't want to even mention the unmentionable here, that two police officers perjured themselves to convict an innocent man of murder, but if the notes from Howson's safe are the originals of Daniel Weaver's final interview, then that is what we are looking at. And if that is the case, we have to ask ourselves why did Howson hold onto them? Why not destroy them? They clearly incriminate him and Alan Darbyshire. Were they some kind of insurance policy?

'Again, I am speculating. There are a lot of unanswered questions at the moment. But one thing is for sure — someone found out about the existence of those notes and wanted desperately to get their hands on them, even if it meant killing Jeffery Howson. And I guess that is also the reason why Howson swallowed his safe key to protect the evidence. Without doubt, the finding of this piece of evidence has opened up Pandora's box, and for now we need to keep a lid on it. The last thing we want is an out of control media frenzy interfering with our enquiry. If anyone gets a whiff that the press is onto this, they report back to me immediately, okay?'

Dawn returned her gaze to her tasking notes on the board. 'Right, new set of actions. Tony, I want you to talk to Howson's ex-wife. I want to know everything about his life. Who his friends and associates were during his CID days. I especially want you to see what you can learn about him during 1983, when he was involved in the Lucy Blake-Hall case. We know from Katherine, his daughter, that he was separated and divorced a year later, so something had gone wrong in his marriage during this time. I want to know what that was.

'Hunter and Grace, I want you two to find out where retired DCI Alan Darbyshire is living and go and talk to him about his CID days, particularly his partnership with Howson. I do not want him to know he is under scrutiny at this stage and I especially don't want him to know about the discovery of the interview notes. See if you can sneak in the Lucy Blake-Hall case without throwing up suspicions.

'We also have additional tasks, which DI Scaife will allocate after this briefing. The house-to-house forms have thrown up a number of enquiries, none earth-shattering, but they need to be bottomed, and he has also drawn up a list of fresh actions from the Lucy Blake-Hall case. At this stage we have potential links, and although it doubles our workload, they need to be established.

'I want all the main witnesses from the original investigation tracking down, and I want them interviewing as if it was a fresh enquiry. And find out which prison Daniel Weaver is serving time in. That's it for now. Thank you all for giving me your fullest attention. There is a lot of work to do but I know you will come up trumps.'

'Push up girl, let me get in,' Barry said, scooting his chair next to Grace and moving her chair aside so he could tuck his legs under her desk. He glanced between her and Hunter before leaning over Grace's desk. 'Listen, I did a little bit of digging last night,' he said, lowering his voice. 'I contacted a few of my old colleagues to get the low-down on Jeffery and Alan Darbyshire after you told me about those interview notes. I'll just tell you what I found out before you go and see Alan.'

Hunter's brow creased.

'Don't worry, I didn't tell them anything about the investigation, especially about the Lucy Blake-Hall link. I made out I was just after background stuff about Jeffery and his work and was chasing up anyone he knew or worked with. It wasn't easy getting stuff out of them. You know what the job was like back then. Nothing was ever straightforward and detectives took chances. Some are starting to distance themselves from Jeffery and they're not so forthcoming about what he got up to. And I'm afraid I can't be of much help. Although I knew the pair to say hello to, they were at Division, so the only time we ever got together was during major incidents, and even then, we worked with our own partners. To be honest, I avoided Alan Darbyshire as much as I could. He was a bit too flash for my liking. He used to turn up and act as if he was the bees-knees. And he used to shout his mouth off. He'd always act like he'd done a job better than anyone else and used to criticise everyone. I guess that's why he got promoted.'

Hunter cut in, 'Do I detect pangs of jealousy, Mr. Newstead?'

'Jealousy, my arse! I could match him any day, but I didn't go about shouting off to all and sundry like he did. Anyway, that's what I remember about him, and I'm afraid I can't help you with the years we're focusing on here because I worked on a job with Serious Crime Squad for 18 months. So I've tracked down who was in the office with him and Jeffery at that time to see what they could recall. I never mentioned Alan by name, but a couple of my old colleagues said he and Jeffery were thick as thieves. A couple of the lads have said to me that from what they remember Alan and Jeffery sailed pretty close to the wind at times.'

'Didn't every detective during the 80s?' said Hunter. 'You've already acknowledged that detectives took chances. I remember some of the things I learned from you, and your stories.'

'Not like that, Hunter. This was outside of the job. It appears the pair of them were regular visitors to a strip joint. It was also believed to be a knocking-shop. Back then, places of that ilk were well dodgy, and it was an absolute no-no to frequent them unless you were doing an op on them. Talk in the office was that these two were regular visitors, and it was even hinted at that they were taking favours from the girls, and in exchange tipped off the owner every time it was due to be raided. Also, one of my ex-colleagues mentioned that the pair were renowned for holidaying in Spain. Two, to three times a year, they'd go with their wives. Benidorm, I've been told. In the same villa every time. Belonged to some businessman.

'No one's said anything about them being bent or anything, and to be honest they were renowned for working loads of overtime, so they could easily afford holidays abroad. Their arrest rate was very good, especially on the important jobs, and because they kept the detection figures high, they were the gaffer's blue-eyed boys.' Barry pushed himself back in his chair. 'What would you do without a real detective being around, eh?' he grinned. 'Well, that should give you two a little bit of a heads up when you start pumping Darbyshire for background stuff.'

Alan Darbyshire lived in a semi-detached refurbished police house nestled amid half a dozen others in a small cul-de-sac. He had been easy to find from the pension payroll list.

Hunter and Grace decided to do a cold-call on him; they wanted to see his reaction when they turned up unannounced flashing their warrant cards. Recalling what Barry had told him earlier, Hunter knew that guilty cops felt the pressure just as much as guilty villains when they were being interviewed by one of their own.

As they pulled up outside the retired DCI's home, Hunter glanced across at Grace, wondering if she could tell he was uneasy — even though Alan Darbyshire was retired, it was the done thing to observe and respect rank, and Alan was unofficially two ranks above him.

Hunter checked his watch as he alighted from the car. Just after 10.30 a.m. He made a mental note of the time as he opened the front garden gate.

Double-glazed windows and a side extension had been added to the property in an attempt to differentiate it from the other police houses around it. Hunter knew that many other cops who had bought their police houses during the Thatcher era had done the same.

The man who answered the door was the same height as Hunter but easily twice his build. He was vastly overweight, with a double chin that blended into a flabby neck. His hair was thinning and Brylcreemed back in a style which Hunter thought lent itself more to the early 1960s than today's fashion, and he had a neatly trimmed pencil-thin moustache.

Hunter held up his warrant card in front of Darbyshire's face and introduced Grace and himself. 'We're here about the murder of Jeffery Howson. I guess you saw it on the local news last night?' He watched for a reaction. There was none.

Casually, Darbyshire answered, 'I got a phone call on Monday afternoon about it, actually. You know what the police grapevine is like, even if you are retired. I guessed you'd be coming sooner or later to talk to his old colleagues.' Then he checked with, 'It is a social visit?'

Quick off the mark, Hunter replied, "Course — why shouldn't it be?'

'You'd best come in then. Oh, and if you wouldn't mind taking your shoes off before you come in the lounge.'

The room they entered was tastefully decorated, though a little too chintzy for Hunter's tastes.

Alan Darbyshire lowered his bulk into the armchair using his arms for support and indicated for Hunter and Grace to take the sofa. 'Make yourselves comfortable,' he said, then added, 'Now, what can I do for you?'

'We're trying to build up a picture of Jeffery. We know you were a colleague of his for a good few years.'

'We started out as DCs together,' Darbyshire said. 'And then I was his DS when I got promoted. I was lucky — they kept me in the department and we carried on working together on the same team until I was promoted again. We were close, me and him, socially as well as professionally. We kept in touch even after retirement.'

Grace had already taken out her notebook from her handbag and had begun making notes.

'How did he die, if you don't mind me asking?' Darbyshire asked.

'You'll need to keep this to yourself, because it's not been released yet, but he was suffocated,' Hunter told him.

Darbyshire inhaled sharply. 'Good God. Poor Jeff.'

Hunter watched Darbyshire's face. He looked genuinely shocked.

'When did you last see Jeffery?' Hunter asked.

Darbyshire took another deep breath and composed himself. 'It'd be about two weeks ago now. I called in to see how he was. As I've already said, we still kept in touch, though visits had dropped off over the years. You may have already gathered that Jeff was very much a recluse. I don't think he really got over his wife leaving him. She took his daughter as well, which made it even worse. And when she married again, well, that really hit him hard. It's awful to say, especially with what's happened to him, but I thought at one stage he was going to top himself, so I spent a lot of time with him. That's why I asked you how he died.'

'It definitely wasn't suicide.'

Darbyshire nodded an acknowledgement. 'So, what else do you want to know?'

Hunter responded, 'As much as you can tell us. You know the type of thing we're after. We've only spoken to his daughter so far.'

Darbyshire nodded slowly for a couple of seconds before answering. 'He thought the world of Katherine. Her being taken away was the hardest part for him, though they're back in touch with one another now, which I'm guessing you will already know. He rang me and told me when she'd moved back and said she'd found a house just around the corner from him. That made a world of difference to him, I can tell you.'

'Why did he and his wife split up?'

Darbyshire shrugged. 'You know how it is. Being a copper's not easy. The unsociable hours and everything that comes with it. Being married to a detective is even harder for some wives. The long hours.'

'When did things start to go downhill for him?' Hunter already knew from Katherine's statement that his wife left him in 1984, the year following the Lucy Blake-Hall case, and he wanted to check how much Darbyshire was prepared to reveal.

'Jenny, that's his wife, was always a bit of a funny bugger. In our early days me and my missus and Jeff and Jenny went out such a lot together, but to be honest I always got the impression she did it just for Jeff's sake. She could be a bit stuck-up. I know she used to give him some right earache when we went out on drinking sessions. I don't think she was happy with him being a detective. What I'm getting at is that things between them were always strained and they just deteriorated. I personally thought good riddance when she went, but Jeff was devastated. He did everything to try to get her back but she wasn't having any of it. In fact, to spite him she went off with someone else. If you ask me, I think she had a fancy man all along. I used to tell him he was better off without her.'

'Okay, thanks for that,' Hunter replied. 'Now, when did you last see Jeffery or speak with him?'

Darbyshire rubbed his flabby chin and looked up to the ceiling, then replied, 'To be honest, once we both retired, things drifted away between us. I took on a part-time job doing some security work, while Jeff became a bit of a recluse. I think the only time he went out was to nip down to the bookies. He used to like his horse-racing. Then a good couple of months ago Jeff phoned me up after getting his bad news about the lung cancer, so I called round to see him. Not surprisingly, he was pretty down. I offered to take him for a beer but he didn't feel up to it. I nipped over at least once a week during the past few months. I watched the cancer eat him away. It wasn't a nice thing to see.'

'When was the last time you saw him?'

'The Monday of the week leading up to his murder. He was killed over the weekend, right?'

Hunter nodded. 'Late Saturday night, we believe.'

'I was at home with Pauline, my wife.'

The defensive response surprised Hunter and for a moment he caught an awkward look on Darbyshire's face. But Darbyshire quickly retrieved his composure.

'That's the ex-detective in me, answering like that. Everyone you interview is a suspect, right?'

Hunter masked his thoughts by returning a forced smile. He recalled what Barry had told him about the nights that Darbyshire and Howson had spent together in the strip club, and the holidays with their wives, courtesy of an unknown businessman, and wondered if he should raise it as a series of questions, but just as quickly he remembered what Dawn Leggate had said at that morning's briefing. Keeping on track with what he had rehearsed inside his head, he asked, 'What was he like as a detective?'

'Brilliant. Good thief-taker, good interviewer. Worked hard and played hard. Everything a good detective should be.'

'Sorry to have to ask you this, Alan, but you were his DS and his friend — did he get up to anything dodgy?'

'I don't mean to be funny, but where is this going?'

Hunter hadn't managed to throw him off guard. 'I'm not trying to draw you into anything. I'm trying to establish if you were aware of anything untoward in Jeff's past. We haven't got a clue at the moment as to why he was killed.'

'Depends on what you're hinting at. We did things differently back then. We didn't have all that fancy forensic help that you lot have got today. We had to do things the hard way. We took more chances to get our results. Let's just leave it with the fact that Jeff was a good detective.'

Hunter sensed an edge to Darbyshire's voice. 'I'm not trying to accuse him of anything, or you for that matter. I know that policing was different during your era from working with Barry Newstead when I first went in CID. I'm working with him now. He's a civilian investigator with us and I have to listen to his ranting on about how the job's not what it used to be on almost a daily basis.'

Darbyshire's face creased into a smile. 'I remember Barry as a fresh-faced detective. He was a good thief-taker himself, from what I remember. Not as good as me mind, but if you were taught by Barry then you can't be all that bad.'

Hunter continued, 'Going back to that last question. Did Howson have any enemies, or do you know of anyone he'd come up against in the job who could have held a grudge against him?'

Darbyshire dipped his eyes down to the carpet. That diversion of his gaze was enough for Hunter. He knew he had hit on something. But now wasn't the time to push. He'd store it for later and see first what Darbyshire was prepared to tell them.

'I've been thinking about that since I found out about Jeff. You could say all the collars we felt became our enemies. It's like I said, we did things differently when he and I were in CID. There were no custody suites like there are now. Just a couple of cold cells and if the villains didn't play ball they got banged up for the night without a blanket. They were so cold that the next morning they'd sell their grandmother for a cup of warm tea. And I know a couple of the lads in the office would give their prisoners a bit of a slap to make them confess. That's just how it was.'

'Was that Jeffery's style?'

'Not giving anyone a slap. I never saw Jeff hit a prisoner. He could talk the hind leg off a donkey. His villains would cough just to shut him up.' Darbyshire gave off a short laugh.

'What about any cases he worked on?'

'We worked on so many over the years and you always got the odd villain whingeing or threatening to make a complaint about you because they weren't happy with their treatment.' Darbyshire's eyes danced between Hunter and Grace. 'You know how it is.'

'Any high-profile ones that spring to mind?' *There*. Hunter had given him the opening. It was his ideal opportunity to introduce the Lucy Blake-Hall investigation.

'Well, there was one I recall. The Terry Braithwaite arrest brought lots of publicity. The papers referred to him as The Beast of Barnwell. It was before your time, probably before you were born. There were a number of indecent assaults and rapes on women in the late 60s and early 70s. Always in late autumn and winter and during a full moon — that's how he got his nickname. For five years he ran amok, and then late one night in the woods he was disturbed by one of the night fishermen at Barnwell Lakes. The man heard screaming from inside a van parked in one of the car parking areas.

'The man went to investigate and disturbed Terry Braithwaite in the middle of carrying out a rape on a young girl. The man ended up in a scuffle with Terry, banging his hands on the roof of the van, but Terry managed to get away. The next day the body of 17-year-old Glynis Young was found in bushes at the edge of the wood.

'Terry Braithwaite had been one of our suspects for a couple of the assaults because he matched the descriptions of the e-fits the victims had given us, and he owned a van like the one described. The next day Jeff and I locked him up. He'd cleaned the inside of his van but he'd forgotten to do the outside as thoroughly as the inside and SOCO found the man's handprint still on the roof.

'It was one of Jeff's first big jobs; he'd been in CID about a year. The upshot was that Braithwaite got life in 1973 with a minimum 30-year sentence. He sent word out from his cell that he was going to get us back for that. He said we had stitched him up even with the evidence from the witness. He had two appeals turned down. He did over 30 in the end and was released two years ago. The *Chronicle* got wind of his release and didn't know if he'd come back to Barnwell to live. I read that the Probation Service stated Braithwaite was in a bail hostel in another county.

'Terry Braithwaite would be a good start for your enquiries. He was a nasty piece of work and never forgave us. Jeffery and I visited him in prison on quite a few occasions over the years because we were always convinced he had done more rapes than he was convicted of, either in neighbouring forces, or because some of the women he'd attacked hadn't come forward, but he refused to talk to us. He'll be in his 60s himself now, but he looked after himself inside.'

Hunter spent the next half an hour teasing out aspects of Jeffery Howson's career, and although Darbyshire freely talked about Jeffery's working style and about their drinking sessions together, he avoided mentioning the visits to the strip club, and gave away no revelations which would take the enquiry forward. Bearing in mind what Dawn Leggate had said, Hunter decided to bring the interview to an end.

'Well, thanks for that, Alan,' Hunter said, pushing himself up from the sofa. 'You've been a great help.'

Grace shut her notebook and returned it to her handbag.

They shook hands and made for the door.

'Oh, there was just one thing, Alan,' Hunter said, a clever lie suddenly forming in his brain. 'We've found some of Jeffery's old pocket notebooks.'

'Pocket books?' Darbyshire frowned. 'They should have all been handed in when he retired. They destroy them after seven years.'

'That's what we thought. Well, it seems he hung on to a couple. We've got to go through them thoroughly but they seem to feature a case you haven't mentioned. What was it now, Grace?'

'Oh, the Lucy Blake-Hall murder back in 1983.' Grace had quickly latched on to her partner's wavelength.

Hunter could have sworn Darbyshire gulped. Despite the pudgy neck, there was a clear movement.

'Lucy Blake-Hall.' Darbyshire seemed to stumble over the words. 'Sorry, you caught me unawares. I had to think hard for a bit then. It was so long ago now. Jeff and I interviewed the man who killed Lucy. He confessed to her murder. Yes, I remember now. He was found guilty at Crown and got life. I've forgotten most of the details. Senior moment and all that. It's strange he should have kept those. Did he leave anything else relating to that case?'

'Don't believe so.' Hunter raised another fake smile and followed Grace out onto the path. 'Well, thank you for your time, Alan. If anything else crops up, we know where to find you.'

DAY FOUR

Hunter dropped his right shoulder and exploded forward with a deft uppercut. He followed up with a left jab, and a swift right, before dancing away into the centre of the ring and setting up his guard again.

Sweat dribbled into the corner of his eyes. He experienced a momentary sharp stinging sensation before blinking and wiping the salt water away with his training mitts. He switched his footwork and took up a leading position in readiness for another onslaught.

'Come on, son, last 30 seconds,' barked his dad, Jock. 'Then you're done.'

Flexing his shoulders, Hunter sprang forward again. Two hard and fast punches, right and left, smacked the leather training pads Jock held. He dodged away and took in a great gulp of air. He had only been sparring with his dad for ten minutes, but he was drained.

It had been two months since Hunter had last trained this hard with Jock. He had visited his dad's boxing gym during that time, but he'd only had time to lift weights and work the training bag.

There was also another reason they had not trained together. Hunter still felt a certain awkwardness in Jock's company. He had tried to put the events of the past two months behind him, but in the background they had niggled away. His father had deceived him, covering up his past that had got people killed. And although Jock had finally told Hunter the truth, it seemed as if he was now just wiping it under the carpet as if nothing had happened.

'Your dad will talk about it when he's good and ready,' Beth had said to Hunter on more than one occasion during the past few weeks, but it was jarring away at him again. *The moment this case is over, I'm sitting down with him and sorting this out, once and for all.*

Barry Newstead grabbed Hunter the moment he set foot in the department.

'I've been trying to get hold of you on your mobile most of the morning,' he said excitedly.

Hunter pulled his phone from his pocket and examined it. 'Sorry, Barry, I've had it on silent. I've been down at my dad's gym.'

'You'll never guess what I've discovered.' Barry thrust a sheet of paper at Hunter.

Hunter saw that it had a list of numbers, in time, day and date order. Barry stabbed a finger over one number highlighted with yellow fluorescent ink.

'That's the top copy of Jeffery Howson's itemised phone bill for his landline. Guess who he rung on the afternoon of his death.'

Hunter scrutinised the telephone number. It didn't mean anything.

'Alan Darbyshire. He rang Alan Darbyshire just before five p.m. on the day he was murdered. It's one of the last numbers he called that day. The next one was mine and the last one was his daughter Katherine.'

Hunter fixed Barry's glistening brown eyes. 'Good God, Barry, this is a real turn up for the books. It completely contradicts what he told me and Grace yesterday. He told us that he had last spoken with Jeffery on the Monday prior to his death. Does the gaffer know about this?'

'Yeah, I fed it into this morning's briefing. She's chasing up forensics to prioritise examination of some of the exhibits to see if we can find something good enough to bring Alan in.'

Hunter stamped his feet on the damp grass and blew into his hands. The cold was beginning to get to him. A biting north-westerly wind had picked up since he had emerged from the warm church and was disturbing the fallen autumn leaves around the headstones in Barnwell cemetery. The dry rustling noise disturbed an uncanny silence. He flicked up the collar of his overcoat and buried his hands in his pockets as he examined the faces of the mourners huddled at the graveside.

Ten minutes earlier, he had followed up the rear of the slow procession as Jeffery Howson's casket had been carried from the church to his final resting place in the cemetery. The coffin now rested upon two wooden posts above an open grave. Four of the coffin bearers, two either side of the grave, grabbed hold of the end of a rope, and took the weight of the casket as the supporting props were slid away. The bearers began to lower the coffin.

Hunter watched the casket being slowly lowered, then looked at the burial group, scanning their faces. It wasn't a large assembly, mainly made up of elderly men whom Hunter guessed were ex-colleagues of Howson. Three women were among the burial party. Katherine and her daughter, Amy, were two of them. Katherine was sobbing uncontrollably. The third, a slender, dark-haired woman, who looked to be in her mid-60s, had a comforting arm around her. Hunter guessed it was Katherine's mother, Jeffery's ex-wife.

Hunter hated funerals. He had been tasked with attending Jeffery Howson's service, and he knew nearby there would be a member of the Intelligence unit covertly filming everything. It was standard procedure; it was not unknown for the killer to turn up at the funeral of his victim.

That thought made him lock onto Alan Darbyshire, who was huddled amid the congregation. The man looked up, as if he had known he was being watched. He quickly turned away and dropped his head down again.

If that wasn't the actions of a guilty man, thought Hunter.

Hunter's concentration was disturbed by the machine-gun rattle of a solitary magpie somewhere to his left. He turned his head and 50 metres away, by the boundary hedge, he caught a sudden and unexpected movement. A broad, squat figure, dressed in a black padded jacket and wearing a dark woollen hat that covered most of his head and his ears, disguising his features, was standing close to a gap in the hedge.

Hunter eyeballed him for several seconds. The unknown guest was staring in the direction of the funeral party. Hunter took a few steps back, pulling out his radio from inside his coat. He switched it into life. It had been pre-loaded onto the same frequency as that of his colleague from the Intelligence unit. Although he couldn't see him, he knew he would be somewhere nearby.

Turning away from the gathering, Hunter pressed the handset close to his mouth and in a low tone requested the plain clothed officer's attention. The radio crackled but there was no response. He tried again, in a firmer tone this time, and began striding toward the stranger.

Hunter knew he was in the open but he had little option. Instinct was telling him that something wasn't right. He'd only made a half a dozen steps before the stranger saw Hunter and began edging away.

Hunter picked up his pace and hissed into his radio as the stranger made the gap. In a flash, the man had disappeared.

DAY FIVE

'Hunter Kerr, I'm surprised at you,' scolded Grace, over the rim of her coffee cup. 'It's not like you to be a nine-o'clock-critic.'

'I'm just so frigging miffed. We could have caught that guy at the funeral. Instead he did a runner and we've no idea who he is.'

Grace leaned forward. 'It was a mistake. Anyone could have made it. The Intel guy had simply switched off his radio for the church service and forgot to switch it back on. End of. He wasn't to know that that guy was going to turn up in that part of the graveyard. His job was to film the congregation of Jeffery Howson's funeral and he did that.'

Hunter held up his hands. 'Yep, fair comment, Grace. It just would have been nice to find out what that man was doing there.'

"Course it would, but we didn't, and so we have to live with it.' Grace rested her elbows and took a sip of her drink. 'Anyway, he did manage to get some good footage of Alan Darbyshire. Did you see the look on his face as you were chasing after the guy?'

Hunter nodded.

'Picture, wasn't it?' Grace continued. 'You could tell from his reaction that he knew who that man was.'

'There's no doubt Alan Darbyshire is somehow up to his neck in this. I'd love to bring the lying toad in, but the gaffer wants us to hold off for the time being, see if we get something concrete that will link him physically with Jeffery Howson's death.'

'It'll happen. We know he told us one lie about the last time he spoke with Jeffery because of the telephone records, and don't forget his signature on those notes we found in Howson's safe. If they are the originals, then we've at least got him for perjury in the Weaver trial. That will be enough to arrest him and quiz him about Jeffery's murder.'

Hunter nodded again. 'I can see where the gaffer's coming from. Because Darbyshire's ex-job, especially an ex-DCI, she wants us to get enough evidence, so that when we do finally give him a tug, we can make it stick, but it's so frustrating.'

'It'll come good in the end.' Grace pushed herself up, taking a last sip of her coffee. 'Anyway, we've enough work to handle just now. You weren't here for this morning's briefing, but the Super's back and he wants us to speak with Daniel Weaver before the press get wind that we've reopened the Lucy Blake-Hall case, especially as Weaver's already had one appeal turned down. I've already set things in motion. Weaver is currently in Wakefield Prison, and I've also managed to track down his barrister from the trial back in 1984. I've left a message with his secretary for him to get back to me.'

'Good job, Grace. Once you sort out a time and date with him to meet, I'll contact the prison and fix up a visit. This'll not be an easy one, you know. If those notes from Howson's safe prove to be original, he's going to be more than a little pissed off. He's served 24 years for a murder he might not have done.'

'And we're going to come in for some flak from the media,' Grace added. 'They just love a miscarriage of justice story like this.'

'That's why it would be nice to have Alan Darbyshire in a cell before we go and speak with Daniel Weaver.'

'Trouble is we need the evidence, and we haven't got enough.'

'Talking about evidence — how've you gone on with the old card index?' Hunter asked.

'It's been a nightmare. I've managed to get it in some semblance of order, but only thanks to Isobel from the HOLMES team. She's worked on the old card system on quite a few murders in the past, so she helped me piece it all together. It's currently laid out over two desks in their office, and the team are slowly inputting it into the computers. She's estimated that it's going to take at least a fortnight before we're up to speed enough to be able to run the Lucy Blake-Hall enquiry from HOLMES. And once it's loaded up there's still going to be a lot of leg-work. We're going to need some help from the cold case team.'

'How do you mean?'

'Well, Isobel's already identified that quite a few of the witnesses are dead. Added to that, some of the addresses no longer exist because the old terraced streets have been knocked down. And, to complicate matters further, some of the female witnesses have changed their names. Got married and moved. This is not going to be an easy investigation.'

'It certainly isn't, Grace. It's a tangled web and we've only just started to unwind it. Who knows what else it's going to bring up? What started out as a murder of a retired detective has turned into something I don't think any of us has dealt with before, and we've dealt with some pretty nasty cases just lately.'

'You mean the possibility of a couple of bent detectives fitting-up an innocent man for murder?'

Hunter nodded. 'There's that. But we've also now got the original crime Daniel Weaver was jailed for. Lucy Blake-Hall's murder. Was that covered up by Jeffery Howson and Alan Darbyshire for a reason? Did they actually have a hand in her murder and needed a scapegoat?'

Grace's mouth dropped open. 'Bloody hell, Hunter, I never thought of that.'

Tony Bullars rang the front doorbell of Katherine Edwards' home and, together with Carol Ragen, waited for a response. From deep inside, they heard a shout to 'Come in' and so let themselves into the hallway.

As the two detectives entered the kitchen, instead of finding Katherine, they found Jeffery Howson's ex-wife, Jennifer West — they recognised her from the video footage from his burial — standing by the open French doors. She was taking a long draw on her cigarette. She acknowledged them with a raised hand, and then flicked the smouldering remains out onto the paved patio.

Tony and Carol watched her shiver as she took a last look out across the rain-sodden garden before stepping back into the warmth and closing the doors.

'Gosh, it's brass-monkey weather out there today,' she said. 'You won't tell Katherine you caught me smoking, will you? I'll not hear the last of it if you do. I've told her I've quit since Jeffery was diagnosed with lung cancer. It's easier to tell a white lie than to argue with her. I've been smoking since I was 14 and it's hard to break a 50-year habit.'

'Cross my heart,' Tony replied, drawing a sign over his chest.

Jennifer smiled, fixing him with twinkling grey eyes. 'Katherine's already filled me in. You want to know about Jeffery?' she said.

'If you don't mind. We've obviously got some recent stuff from Katherine, and we've talked to some of his ex-colleagues, but as his parents are now dead, you're the person who probably knew him the best during his younger years.'

'Only until 1984. That's when I left him.'

'Yes, we know, and that's the period I want to focus on, if you don't mind?'

Jennifer looked puzzled.

Tony continued. 'You appreciate that I can't go into things in any detail, because the investigation is still in its infancy, and we haven't arrested anyone yet for Jeffery's murder, but a few things have cropped up since we started this enquiry which makes us want to look into his past, and the 1980s are a period of his life we are interested in.'

'Oh, I see. I realise you have your reasons why you can't say too much but it's during that time that he and I had our differences.'

'Yes, we've gathered that. That's why I want to ask you a few questions.'

'Yeah, okay, but you'll have to appreciate this is not going to be easy. I don't want to paint Jeffery in a bad light, especially for Katherine. I've never really told her anything about why me and her dad split up. She's only really just got to know him.'

'Don't worry, Jennifer, we'll treat what you tell us with confidence. We're only interested in anything which may point us in the direction of his killer. Having said that, it's also important that we have the right picture painted of him. Especially his background.'

Jennifer wrung her hands. 'This is going to be awkward. I've never sat down and discussed with anyone what went on in Jeff's and my life before I left him. Don't get me wrong, when I first left, I told snippets of it to a couple of close friends, and I have mentioned the odd thing here and there to Derek — he's the man I'm married to now — but I didn't even tell my solicitor some of the stuff Jeff had done, because I knew it would lose him his job.'

Tony caught a pained expression drift across her face. He said, 'All I can say, Jennifer, is that we'll do our best with what you tell us. But it is important that we get to know everything about Jeffery. It might give us our best clue as to who killed him.'

She nodded. 'This is so weird. So many times in the past, I've listened to Jeffery's stories of some of the enquiries he has been involved in and how he has interviewed witnesses. Never did I think I would be one of those witnesses myself.'

Tony exchanged a quick glance with Carol. She had her journal open, ready to take notes. He said, 'Tell me a bit about yourself and Jeffery. When you married and a bit about your early life together. Just for background. Speak freely. I'll interrupt if I want something different, okay?'

Jennifer nodded again, switching eye-contact between Tony and Carol. 'I first met Jeffery in 1964, not long after he'd joined the job. He was 19 and I was 20. I worked at Woolworth's and I'd caught a young lad shoplifting. Jeffery came to arrest him and he asked me out while he was taking a statement from me. It was so spontaneous and he was so handsome. A man in uniform and all that.' Her solemn look suddenly transformed into a smile. 'He took me to the cinema to see *Goldfinger*. I know it's corny and all that but I saw a resemblance in Jeffery to Sean Connery. And that was it, I was smitten.

'We went out together for just over a year and I got caught with Katherine. It was a real blow for both of us. We had talked so much about what we wanted to do before we settled down but that put paid to both our dreams. Don't take that the wrong way. Once we got our head around things, we were both overjoyed, and Katherine's made my world perfect, but it was just at the time, you understand?'

Never having had a child, Tony didn't understand. Nevertheless, he nodded.

'We had to get married before she was born,' Jennifer continued, 'because the job frowned upon it. But they gave us a police house to live in. A three-bedroom semi. It was better than what both our parents had. Those early years were good times. We were short of money, but we had such happy times as a family. And then he went in CID.' She glanced at Tony. 'Sorry. I didn't mean that to sound like it did, because we still had some good times even in his early CID days. The extra money he brought in from his overtime was more than welcome. It helped us get together the deposit for the house at Woodlands View. But it also meant he was spending a lot of time at work. Sometimes I didn't see him from one day to the next, especially if he was on a murder. And especially when he got in with that Alan Darbyshire.'

Tony straightened up at the mention of that name. 'What about Alan Darbyshire?'

'Oh, don't read too much into that comment — he was just a bad influence. Jeffery was never one for drinking, but when he got in with Alan, they seemed to be never away from the pub. It was putting a strain on our marriage and I told him so. And I told him that he had a daughter to think about.'

'Can you remember roughly when this was?'

Jennifer glanced away momentarily, a look of concentration on her face. For a couple of seconds, she started worrying her bottom lip, then said softly, 'He went in CID in the summer of 1972, and he was probably three or four years in when he started with the regular late drinking sessions with Alan. He didn't come in rolling drunk, it was just that it'd be the early hours of the morning before he got home. He always used to say he'd been working late. It caused quite a few rows, I can tell you.'

'Did you get to know Alan Darbyshire well?'

'Oh yes. I saw a lot of Alan. We used to go out as a couple — me and Jeffery and him and his wife Pauline. She was nice, and he was quite a character.'

'It's been mentioned that you used to go on holiday together?'

'Yes, that was in the early 80s. Alan knew someone who had a place in Benidorm, and so it only cost us for the flights and our spending money. We'd go there a couple of times a year. It worked out cheaper than a holiday in England.'

'What kind of place are we talking about in Benidorm?'

'It was a two-bedroom villa with its own pool — lovely place.'

'Do you know who it belonged to?'

'This is where it gets a bit awkward.' Pursing her lips, Jennifer added, 'To be honest, at first, I didn't think anything about it. As cops, and you'll know what I mean when I say this, you get to know a lot of people, from all walks of life, and Jeffery used to tell me it was a case of "you scratch my back and I'll scratch yours". He told me that he and Alan had done a businessman a favour and in return he was letting them use his holiday home when he didn't need it.' She fixed on Tony's expression. 'And before you ask, no, I don't know what that favour was. But I don't believe it was anything underhand. Jeffery wasn't like that. He loved his job. I have to say though, I was never too sure about Alan. I always used to say to Jeffery that I thought he was a flash git. He got promoted and he had a bit more money and used to throw it around a bit.'

'What do you mean by throw it around?'

'Well, things were a bit tight for us, even with the overtime. I didn't work and we had Katherine. Alan and Pauline didn't have children, and she worked, so it always seemed as if he had a lot of money and he liked to show off.'

'Did you ever get the impression Alan would do anything dodgy?'

'Not to my knowledge, no. But Alan always acted like he was Jack the Lad and after a while it grated on me. I felt as if Jeffery was a bit of a lap-dog around him, both at work and when we were out, and I didn't like it. I told Jeffery my thoughts and we'd end up rowing over it. It wore me down in the end and I deliberately forced some space between us when it came to going out as couples. I used to make excuses about not feeling well, or say we couldn't get a baby-sitter, and then I told Jeffery I couldn't face going on holiday with them.

'I guess that's when I realised our marriage was in a mess. I did try to make a go of it but I could tell Jeffery wasn't happy and that's when he and Alan started going out boozing regular. We started to drift apart. And I started to re-evaluate my life. The final straw was when he came home with the new car. A brand-new BMW. I went spare because money was tight enough as it was, but he told me that the businessman Alan and he had done a favour for brought them over from Germany, because he fiddled the VAT, and he'd got the car on a nought per cent interest deal. It was at that stage I felt something wasn't quite right. I know the police are sticklers when it comes to accepting gifts, or even credit, and I wanted him to give it back. I told him he could lose his job if anyone found out. All he kept saying was that it was all above board and he was paying for it but without the added interest and that Alan had got a similar deal as well.'

'Is that what caused your marriage to break up?'

'Not exactly. It was well on its way by then. I started to get suspicious about Jeffery's late-night jaunts. I've already mentioned about his drinking sessions. Well, on a couple of occasions when he came home, I could swear I smelt women's perfume on him, and I fronted him up about it, but he just told me it was because of this nightclub he and Alan went to. I got a friend of mine to follow him one night and I discovered he was visiting a private club in Wakefield, which I found out was a strip club.

'That was it. I dolled myself up one night and turned up at the club. I found Jeffery and Alan entertaining a couple of women at the bar. Dressed like whores, they were, and for me that was the last straw. I came straight back home, packed two suitcases, got my dad to pick me up, and I left with Katherine and stayed at my parents' caravan in Skegness until I could fix myself up with a place for us both. Then I filed for divorce. I never came back. Jeffery came to the van and pleaded on bended knees, but by then I'd really had enough. I knew I'd be better out of it. Jeffery had changed so much as a person.'

'When was this, Jennifer?'

'1983. And I got divorced the following year on the grounds of his unreasonable behaviour.'

'That year's important to our enquiry. You've mentioned earlier that Jeffery used to tell you about some of the jobs he was involved in. Can you recall him ever mentioning the name Lucy Blake-Hall?'

Jennifer nodded. 'I certainly do. It was splashed all over the local papers as well. He and Alan played a big part in that job. Jeffery told me that they had arrested the man who had murdered her.' She straightened sharply. 'In fact, that was the night I caught him and Alan with those women. He tried to tell me, once I'd caught him out, that he was celebrating because they had charged Lucy's killer with her murder. You see, the strip club belonged to Lucy's husband.'

DAY SIX

Hunter had the house to himself and it was peaceful. The only sound came from the crackling logs burning in the grate; he had lit the fire the moment he had got up, having seen the state of the weather when he opened the bedroom curtains that morning.

Taking a spell out from his paperwork, he stared into the dancing flames. They reminded him of his and Beth's very first viewing of this house. Passing by after a shopping trip, they had spotted the owner's home-made sign fastened to the post at the top of the drive and he had stopped the car and reversed to get a better look. They had decided to knock on the owner's door. By sheer chance they were the first viewing since the sign had gone up, and the minute they had entered the brightly lit hallway they knew this was a house with potential. Once they had been greeted by the roaring fire, Hunter had looked into Beth's eyes and knew this was the place for them. That was ten years ago, and since then it had become a family home with the births of Jonathan and Daniel.

Hunter returned his gaze to the documents spread out over his coffee table. The previous evening, he had brought home the Daniel Weaver prosecution file together with the bundle of photographs taken by SOCO. At work he had already read through all of its 500 pages twice but he wanted to fully ingrain the important elements of it to memory before he and Grace visited Daniel Weaver in Wakefield Prison later that day.

He flipped through the bound file, searching for the first statement he wanted. He had four hours to plough his way through the file before Beth joined him for lunch; it was her half day today, and she had dropped the boys off at school on her way to the surgery, leaving him to get on with his task.

Jeffery Howson's witness statement was the first Hunter had earmarked, and he pinched together the dozen or so typed sheets and settled back in the sofa to slowly read through it again. This was one piece of evidence he couldn't afford to rush through — this, and the testimony of Alan Darbyshire, were the crucial accounts which had condemned Daniel all those years ago. The previous afternoon, the forensic results had come back on the interview notes found in Jeffery Howson's safe — the tests on the paper and the ink had confirmed that they dated back to 1983.

Daniel Weaver's conviction was now unsafe and Hunter knew that Detective Superintendents Robshaw and Leggate had a meeting scheduled that morning with CPS to discuss the latest developments. The likelihood was that Daniel Weaver's case would be presented before the High Court inside the next seven days and he would be released on bail pending a re-trial. Hunter knew that this afternoon's interview was not going to be easy. Weaver's solicitor had already started asking pointed questions.

Next to Hunter were several pieces of paper, which all had a series of boxed grids drawn on them — his own personal index system to record and summarise the evidence from each witness statement. In the grids on the left-hand side of the sheets were the names of all 32 witnesses contained in the file and in the right-hand grids were spaces for making any relevant notes from their testimony.

Some of the witnesses had very little to say, but others had played a crucial role in Daniel Weaver's prosecution. The evidence was in two parts — independent witnesses, who had seen Daniel and Lucy together on the night of her disappearance, and police witnesses, including forensics. Hunter knew some of the detectives — though only briefly — who had been involved in the investigation. They were all retired now and he wondered what their reaction would be when he broke the news that the case was being re-opened. Given the new nature of the investigation, he wondered if they would be willing to talk. He knew this was going to be a very uncomfortable case to examine, for everyone involved.

As he read through Jeffery Howson's statement, he paused and made notes on important points. When he got to the part detailing the first visit to Daniel Weaver's flat, two days after Lucy Blake-Hall's disappearance, he turned to the pile of black and white crime scene photographs, picked up the booklet containing the interior shots of Weaver's flat, and slowly thumbed through the images. The ones he was especially interested in were those of the garden shed where Lucy's handbag had been discovered.

There were two close-up shots of a small, fake leather bag, which Jeffery Howson's statement told him was cream coloured, poking out between a pile of hemp sacks beneath a bench. The discovery had been crucial to the prosecution's case and was now one of the pieces of evidence being put under the spotlight.

Hunter sighed as he finished reading Jeffery Howson's statement. The evidence appeared so precise, yet most of Howson's testimony was in doubt because of the paperwork found in his bedroom safe. *If only he had left a note*, Hunter thought.

Hunter drove into HMP Wakefield car park, slotting the car, nose first, into a visitors' parking space and killing the engine.

'What do you think our reception's going to be like?' Grace asked.

'I think Daniel Weaver's going to be pretty pissed off,' said Hunter, gazing over the front of the fortified Victorian prison. 'And I guess he's every right to be. I've read the prosecution file three times now and I know it back to front. At the time of his trial, you can see why the jury returned a guilty verdict. Several witnesses saw him and Lucy arguing that night and no one saw her again after that. And because he lived alone, there's no one who could alibi him after he left the marketplace. The only defence he could present was that Lucy was alive when he last saw her, that he had no idea where she went after that, and that the police planted the handbag in the shed and then fabricated his confession. We now know the last part of that could be true.'

'I spoke with Prison Intelligence yesterday to get a bit of background on Weaver,' Grace said. 'It appears he's kept himself very much to himself. They have him down as a regular complainer and he's refused to engage in any prisoner therapy. That's why he hasn't been considered for parole or early release. So, how do you want to play this?'

Hunter pulled a bulging folder from the back seat. 'I've made notes and I'd like to lead him back through that night, but it all depends on what his brief has advised him to say.'

Tucking the folder beneath his arm, Hunter locked the car and strode towards the entrance gates. Grace followed him.

At reception, Hunter produced his warrant card and appointment letter, after which he and Grace passed through metal sliding doors into the search area, where they emptied their pockets into trays and stepped through the airport-style electronic security portal. Then they were taken to the main hall, where the families of the prisoners had all congregated to meet their loved ones and where children were chasing around yelling at one another.

Taking in the mayhem, Hunter was glad when the officer escorting them told them they had their own interview room. As the door closed behind them, most of the noise muted. In the centre of the room was a table, the surface of which had been well-graffitied, together with four chairs, all secured to the floor. Hunter and Grace each took a seat.

They had been waiting for less than ten minutes when the door opened and Daniel Weaver appeared. He was dressed in a sweatshirt and jeans. Behind him was a well-groomed man in a suit, who Hunter guessed was his solicitor. A prison officer stood behind the pair.

Daniel had his hands in his pockets and, as he took a seat opposite, he lifted them out and folded his arms in a defiant pose.

Hunter remembered the shots he had seen of Daniel from the SOCO photos. He still had his curly hair, though it was showing distinct signs of thinning and much of it was greying. He was roughly the same size as himself, with well-developed shoulders and arms, but he was carrying a paunch.

Hunter asked him if he wanted a drink. Daniel Weaver shook his head.

'Daniel, do you know why we are here?' Hunter began.

'Yeah, my brief's told me. You're here to apologise for fitting me up and to negotiate the amount of compensation I'm due.'

The reply threw Hunter for a second. He fixed his gaze and forced a smile. 'That's not my job, Daniel. That's something for your solicitor and the Home Secretary. I'm here to tell you that we're re-opening your case and I want to ask you some questions.'

Daniel leant forward and rested his folded arms upon the table. 'You've got a fucking nerve. The last time I was asked questions by your lot, I got 30 years.'

'That wasn't me, Daniel.'

'No, but you're all the same.'

'Believe me, we're not all the same,' said Grace.

Daniel Weaver pushed himself back in his chair, tightened his mouth and shrugged. 'Whatever.'

'Daniel, I have read your prosecution file,' Hunter continued, 'and I want to go back over the events of what happened between you and Lucy on the night she was last seen.'

'No offence like, but if you think you're gonna get any help from me, you've got another think coming. You lot got it so wrong back then and fitted me up. Now you're trying to make amends. I've done 25 fucking years for something I didn't do and you come here with your false smiles and expect me to help you? You can take your questions and shove them up your fucking arse.'

'I realise there's a lot of things going through your mind right now, Daniel,' Hunter said. 'And you've every right to feel bitter towards the police, but I can assure you this time things will be different and I hope you will be willing to co-operate.'

'Co-operate! You have got to be fucking joking. Look what happened the last time I co-operated.'

'Okay, Daniel, let me try a different approach. Are you aware of the reason why we have re-opened the investigation into Lucy's disappearance?' There was no reaction. 'Okay, I'll tell you. A detective involved in that case has been murdered and has left behind some evidence which raises questions about one of the interviews with you when you were arrested.'

'Is it Darbyshire or Howson?'

'Jeffery Howson, and I can't go into any details about that at this moment, but what I can tell you is that we have a new piece of evidence that casts doubt over one of your initial interviews.'

'Well, you'll understand when I say I'm not fucking sad to hear he's been topped, after what he's done to me. Darbyshire will get his payback as well, once I'm out of here.'

The solicitor, who had been making notes with a straight face, quickly looked up. He reached across and grasped Weaver's wrist, then turned to Hunter. 'As you can appreciate, Detective, my client is a little frustrated. This news has been a complete shock.'

Daniel shook off the solicitor's grip. 'Frustrated! That is an understatement! I'm fucking furious. You have the audacity to come here after 25 years and ask me to help you out with your enquiries into a murder which you lot stitched me up for. That's a fucking joke.' He pushed himself up. 'At least you can't fit me up for Howson's murder, I've got a pretty good alibi this time, but I want you to pass on a message to Darbyshire when you see him. You tell him, he'd better keep looking over his shoulder.'

'Is that a threat?' Hunter asked.

Daniel made for the door. Grabbing the handle, he turned around. 'You bet it is,' he shouted, then stormed out of the room.

The solicitor quickly scooped up his papers and made to follow his client. 'Mr Weaver doesn't mean anything by that. I'll have a word with him once he calms down.' He almost sprinted out of the room.

Hunter could hear him shouting after his client, his voice drifting away into the distance. Hunter pulled together his paperwork, tapped the edges level and slipped them into his folder. Snapping shut the cover, he said, 'Well, Grace, that didn't turn out the way I had planned.'

She gave him a weak grin. 'Yes, I wouldn't say it was one of your best interviews, would you?'

Barry Newstead still had a flush on from his evening bath and had just got to the bottom of the stairs, tucking his T-shirt into his jogging bottoms, when the doorbell went. Through the frosted glass of the front door he got a view of the top half of a silhouetted figure and wondered who it could be at this time of night. He opened it. Standing in the porch was a man, the same size and shape as himself, with close-cut, salt-and-pepper, greying hair. His hands were thrust deep into a long, camel-hair coat.

'Is Sue Siddons in?' the man enquired, his voice nasal and high-pitched.

'You are?' Barry replied, sucking in his belly and sticking out his chest.

'Guy Armstrong,' said the man, holding out his hand to shake. 'I used to work with Sue on the *Barnwell Chronicle* many years ago.'

Barry didn't take the hand. He thrust them into his pockets. 'She has mentioned you.'

'You must be Barry. She's told me about you as well.' Barry's face set tight. 'Sue's mentioned that you're working on the murder of a retired detective who was involved with the Lucy Blake-Hall case back in 1983. I worked on that case and I have a source who believes they know who killed her all those years ago; I only want a quick chat — a bit of background about this detective's murder. I won't mention Sue's name.'

'Mr Armstrong, you and Sue may have been colleagues all those years back, but she is no longer a reporter, and I would prefer it if you left her alone. She has nothing to say to you about either the Lucy Blake-Hall case or about the death of one of my former colleagues.'

'Are those her words, or yours?'

Barry could feel the frustration welling up inside him. 'This conversation has finished. I want you to leave. Do I make myself clear?'

'Look, Barry. If you've spoken with Sue, you know I worked on the original story when Lucy went missing. I know there are links between the murder of the detective and Lucy, because my source has told me, and I've also made a phone call to Daniel Weaver's solicitor and he's told me that detectives interviewed him earlier today. The story is going to come out soon; you know how it is. I'm just wanting to be ahead of the game — put the police's side of the story first.'

'Then you're talking to the wrong person. If you want a quote, contact the press office.'

'Is this a miscarriage of justice?'

'I said, conversation over.'

Guy Armstrong shook his head. 'I can help you with your investigation. I spoke with the witnesses back then. I dealt with Lucy's family and I also know Daniel Weaver's family. I scratch your back and you scratch mine.'

Barry started to close the front door. 'Goodbye, Mr Armstrong.'

The reporter placed his foot over the threshold.

Barry glanced down at the reporter's black scuffed shoes and then fixed him with one of his meanest looks. 'You take that foot away now or I'll break it. Then I'll put my own foot up the crack of your arse and boot you all the way back up the drive. Do I make myself clear?'

Armstrong withdrew his foot, looking sheepish. 'Is that a quote?'

'No, but this one is. Fuck off!' Barry slammed the front door shut and kept his huge hand tight on the handle, watching as the blood drained from his knuckles. He waited until he saw the silhouette of Guy Armstrong fade away. *Fuck me, they've made the links already.* After this, he knew that other reporters would be in on the chase. He made for the phone. He needed to let the gaffer know.

DAY SEVEN

Hunter got into work just before 7 a.m., brewed himself a cuppa, booted up his computer and immediately attacked his pending work. Opening his emails, he found three relating to the suspicious death of the girl found in the cellar of the derelict pub ten days earlier. He still had a number of gaps waiting to be filled, and with the recent murder case he hadn't had time to conduct any further enquiries into identifying the victim, and he desperately wanted to tie-up the loose ends and put it to bed.

His first email was from the coroner's officer. The opening paragraph read: 'The girl has been identified as 23-year-old Jodie Marie Jenkinson, who goes by her nickname "JJ".' They had managed to identify her by her fingerprints, despite the damage caused by the rats. She had a previous conviction for drunkenness and assault, and she had been on probation for shoplifting. The coroner's officer had listed her probation officer and his telephone number.

Hunter scribbled down the details onto his blotting pad. He'd put in a call and fix up to see him tomorrow morning after briefing. He skimmed through the remainder of the email and saw that the cause of death was drug related. The syringe found beside Jodie contained heroin of a purer concentration than that normally found on the streets. Hunter had known this happen on many occasions; users get so used to injecting cut-down stuff that when they get decent gear their bodies can't take it. He guessed that is what had happened to Jodie. That information took his enquiry a giant leap forward and he rattled off a thank you back to the coroner's officer, adding that he owed him a drink.

Hunter's luck continued with the second email. It was from an old colleague, now attached to one of the community beat teams, whose patrol area took in the derelict pub. The email explained that the pub was one of the places he regularly checked because residents had complained that it had become a haunt for drunken teenagers. He hadn't found any teenagers, but he had come across a homeless man, nicknamed 'Chicken George', who was using the place to doss down. The officer had last spoken with him just over a month ago and was now trying to track him down to ask if he had seen the girl or anyone else in the premises. Hunter responded with another thank you and requested an update once he had caught up with him.

The last email was from Duncan Wroe, the Scenes of Crime manager, which stated that he had forwarded on an album of photographs relating to Jodie's death. Hunter looked at his pending tray and lifted off a couple of reports from the top. Tucked between the paperwork, he found a blue A5 bound photograph album. He opened it to reveal the first colour print — a front view of the derelict pub. Its sign was missing, as was the lettering above the front windows and door, though he knew it used to be called the Barnwell Inn. Once white plaster was heavily stained, and large clumps had fallen away from the walls to reveal crumbling red brickwork beneath.

It looks a mess, thought Hunter, though he knew from the builders that it was about to get a new lease of life as a pub-cum-diner. The next picture showed the view from the entrance door — a narrow strip of corridor toward the beer cellar. He could make out the absence of the bottom door panel of the cellar door and knew from the statement from one of the builders that it had been caused when it had been booted through to get access.

The next view took in most of the cellar itself. Jodie was slumped face down on the concrete floor, arms by her side, legs tucked beneath her in a child-like sprawl. Hunter concentrated on this photo. It was a stark reminder of what he had encountered when he had been called out that day. A combination of stagnant beer, damp surroundings, and stale faeces, mixed with the decay of someone long dead had greeted him, and as he stared at this photograph the images and smells returned, making him shudder.

Hunter put it aside and looked at the remaining shots. These were close-ups of the girl. The images were vivid. It wasn't just the decomposition, but the damage caused by the vermin attacks. As well as her fingers, the tip of Jodie's nose was missing and part of her right ear had also been chewed. Two of the remaining photographs were close-ups of her heavily blanched arms, which bore multiple healed criss-crossed scars, the tell-tale signs of self-harm. The next couple focused on the drugs paraphernalia surrounding her — the used syringes, strips of burnt foil, and two spoons which showed signs of being heated.

Hunter closed the album and thumbed his way back through the pages again. Something about those images was bothering him, but he couldn't think what. He tried to conjure up visions from previous drug-related deaths he had investigated during his time on the Drug Squad, but that wasn't helping. He went over the shots a second and third time — a little slower — but he still couldn't put his finger on it.

It might just be me, he told himself. He might be reading something which wasn't there. For now, he decided to fill in the gaps with this recent information, hopefully speak to her probation officer tomorrow and then revisit the photographs once he had done that.

Clomping footsteps outside in the corridor snatched him back to the present. He checked his watch as the office doors opened.

Barry Newstead barrelled in like someone entering a Wild West saloon. 'Now then, me old mucker, touch of insomnia, have we?' he said gruffly, slipping off his coat.

'Got in early to try and sort out some paperwork. No rest for the wicked.'

'Talking about the wicked, I had a visitor last night I want to tell you about. But first, the most important job of the day, I'll stick the kettle on.'

Hunter watched Barry sling his coat across his desk and head for the kettle. The tail of his shirt was hanging out of his waistband again. Hunter smiled. Sartorial elegance was certainly not one of Barry's strong points.

Barry made two drinks, dunking teabags into mugs of hot water, adding milk and sugar to both before sidling back to Hunter's desk. He dropped down into Grace's empty chair opposite and slid across a mug.

Hunter looked at the weak contents, decided it was the best he was going to get and picked up the steaming brew, muttering his thanks.

'What about this visitor of yours then?'

Barry pretended to spit. 'Time to circle the wagons! The press have got wind. They're linking Jeffery Howson's murder already to Lucy Blake-Hall.'

'Who's that then? Local or national?'

'He was local, worked with Sue on the *Chronicle*, but he's freelance now. I threatened to put my boot up his arse.'

'Good to see the old Barry Newstead is still alive and kicking.'

Barry took a sip on his tea. 'Well, they get on your bloody nerves, don't they? And the cheeky bastard had managed to get to Sue before she could speak to me.'

'Has she said anything?'

'She's told him a little. He obviously knows about Howson's murder, and because he worked on the Lucy Blake-Hall case, he's made the link, but he doesn't know about the notes we found.' Hunter watched Barry's eyebrows knit together. 'He caught her on the hop unfortunately.'

'One of those things, Barry. It's not Sue's fault. I guessed it wouldn't be long before someone would sniff out our investigation.'

'Yeah, I guess so. Anyway, just in case you come across the leech, his name's Guy Armstrong. Sue tells me that he made his name from the case and got a staff job with the *Mail* as a result. He became one of their northern crime reporters, but Sue tells me that didn't last long. She's certain that a few years ago he was involved in an accident in which a cop got killed and she's almost sure he went to prison because of it. I'm going to follow that up and see what's behind it.'

'Okay, thanks for the heads up. Keep me posted once you find out something, will you? And let me know if he contacts you again.'

'Somehow, I don't think he will. My size tens are a fearsome weapon.' Barry winked, picked up his mug, pushed himself out of Grace's chair and sauntered to his own desk.

Morning briefing was short. Robshaw took it with Dawn Leggate looking on.

It was Hunter's first opportunity to feed in the results of his follow-up enquiries from his interview with Alan Darbyshire.

'As you know,' he began, 'when I asked Darbyshire about anyone who might have a grudge against Jeffery, especially from high profile cases that he and Jeffery had been involved in, instead of him mentioning Lucy's case he referred to the Beast of Barnwell investigation from the 70s. He told me that he thought the offender, Terry Braithwaite, had been released to a bail hostel two years ago. I've made a couple of phone calls and found that Terry Braithwaite was relocated to Bridlington. He's 72 years old now and living in an old folks bungalow. He suffered a stroke when he was inside and still hasn't fully recovered. I'm going to put in a call to his probation officer to see if we can rule him out or not.'

Hunter then reported on his and Grace's visit to Daniel Weaver.

Robshaw sympathised and responded with an update from his meeting with the Head of the Crown prosecution service. An appeal had already been lodged with the Home Secretary by Weaver's barrister and listed for next Friday. Robshaw added that, given the new evidence, the Appeal Court Judges would not hesitate to grant bail and Daniel Weaver would likely be out by next weekend.

Robshaw then asked Barry to give an update as to which of the original witnesses from the Lucy Blake-Hall case were still around. Barry had been working with the HOLMES team who had been transferring information from the old card index system from the 1983 investigation onto the computers. He was the ideal choice for this work. Not only did he have experience with the previous recording method but was also familiar with the current protocol for capturing information.

Barry replied, 'The girls on HOLMES have been working round the clock, and they're not far away now from listing all the witnesses and summarising what's in their statements. I've been checking the electoral register against the names and doing some chasing up with phone calls to see who's still around these parts. What I've learned is that Weaver's mum died of a heart attack six years ago. And the landlady of the Coach and Horses, where Weaver and Lucy had their last drinks together, has also died.

'The three witnesses who saw the pair arguing in the marketplace — a man and two women — lived on a street which was knocked down 15 years ago. I've got the council going back through their records to see if they were rehoused locally. We're having difficulty tracing the two women because they were just young girls at the time, 18 and 20, so the likelihood is they've got married and changed their surnames. We're also having trouble finding Lucy's best friend, Amanda Smith. Once again, we're guessing she's got married.'

Hunter remembered his earlier conversation with DS Jamie Parker. It looked as though they would have to bring in someone from the cold case unit to help with the tracing.

'On the plus side,' Barry continued, 'we've tracked down Lucy's husband, and her parents are still around, living at the same address in Bakewell, Derbyshire. And, we think we know where Lucy's daughter, Jessica, is. She's now married and has a daughter of her own. With regards to the detectives who worked on the case, we know where they all are from the Force's pensions records. That's it, boss.'

'Okay, good work, Barry,' said Robshaw. 'Right, actions everyone. We've got our work cut out on two fronts. Firstly, the murder of Jeffery Howson, and secondly, the reopening of the Lucy Blake-Hall murder. The links between the two enquiries are the interview notes found in Howson's safe.

'With regards to the murder of Jeffery Howson, our major suspect to date is Alan Darbyshire. As we know from the pathologist's examination of Howson's body, two people were involved in his killing. Plus, the finding of the notes in Howson's safe now indicate he perjured himself in the Lucy Blake-Hall murder trial. We know from Howson's phone call to Barry that it seemed he was about to spill the beans on the whole affair, so it gives Darbyshire the motive for wanting Howson dead.'

Robshaw tapped the top of the incident board. There was now a photograph of Alan Darbyshire stuck alongside those of Jeffery Howson. It was an enlarged shot of him in a collar and tie, from Force archives, taken when he was in his early to mid-forties.

Robshaw continued, 'Because of who he is, I want to make sure we have as much solid information as we can possibly get before we bring him in for interview. Therefore, I want as many of the witnesses as possible from the Lucy Blake-Hall enquiry tracing and re-interviewing. If we are still struggling to track down people by the middle of the week, I'm going to make an appeal through the media. Sooner or later the press are going to learn of our enquiries and I'd rather have them with us than against us. Especially now that we know Daniel Weaver is going to be released.'

Hunter exchanged a quick look with Barry, wondering whether he was going to mention Guy Armstrong, but Barry kept quiet.

Hunter and Grace had the job of speaking to Lucy's husband, Peter. They had been told he was living in a renovated farmhouse in the picturesque village of Hooton Roberts. Hunter knew the area well; he had painted there in the past. It was a relatively small village, separated by the busy main A630 Rotherham to Doncaster road.

As Hunter swung the car in through a wide opening onto a gravel chipped driveway, he saw that Peter Blake-Hall's home included a linked barn. It looked a lavish and impressive conversion with sand-blasted stone walls. The barn entranceway was set with huge panelled glazing and roof window-lights.

'This must have set him back a bob or two,' Hunter said to Grace, as he slowed the car to a halt. 'I want to play this just the same way as we did with Alan Darbyshire. No pushing. Try and let him do most of the talking and see what he gives.'

Grace nodded.

'I'm not going to mention the re-opening of his wife's case unless he asks about it,' Hunter continued. 'I'm going to come at him from the angle of being someone Howson was closely linked to in the past and see where that leads to. I'm only going to let on that we've spoken to Howson's ex if he's not forthcoming. I want to see what he is prepared to offer without encouragement.'

Hunter turned off the engine and opened his door. Immediately, he heard raised voices. It sounded like two men, and the conversation was heated. One of them was swearing and loudly.

Hunter threw a quizzical look at Grace. 'Someone's venting their spleen. We'll take a shufty, shall we?'

Locking the car, Hunter trotted past the entrance and edged around the side of the building where the two voices had now reduced to one. Behind him, Grace's low-heeled shoes scrunched over the loose gravel chippings. There would be no element of surprise.

He turned the corner in time to witness a man in a camel-hair coat being pushed from a doorway, his arms wind-milling, as he fought to keep his balance, and in doing so a small hand-held tape recorder flew up in the air and landed behind him. Hunter recalled what Barry had told him about being door-stepped by a reporter the previous evening. The description Barry had given fitted this man to a tee.

In the doorframe a tall, beefy man was spearing a finger in the direction of the journalist. He reminded Hunter of the actor Ray Winstone.

He shouted, 'Now for the last time, fuck-off.'

Hunter stepped into view. 'Having a spot of trouble?'

Both men turned his way.

'And who the fuck are you?' said the beefy one.

Hunter dug into his jacket and pulled out his warrant card. 'CID,' he announced, flashing his badge.

'Well, you're just in time to witness me kick this reporter off my premises for trespassing.' The thickset man moved from the doorway and onto the drive.

Grace quickly stepped in front of the reporter to protect him. He was scrabbling in the wet gravel, attempting to recover his tape recorder.

'There's no need for that now we're here. I'm sure this gentleman was just leaving.' Hunter turned to the reporter. 'Weren't you, sir?'

The man huffed, made a quick visual check of his tape-recorder, wiped it on his coat sleeve and turned on his heels without saying a word.

Hunter turned back to the Ray Winstone lookalike, who he gathered was Peter Blake-Hall. 'Local reporter?'

'I'm guessing so. Fucking leech.' Peter turned to Grace. 'Pardon my French, miss.' Then he turned back at Hunter. 'He says you're re-opening the case into my wife's murder. Is that right?'

Best laid plans... Hunter reflected. Quickly gathering his thoughts, he replied, 'Well, Mr Blake-Hall, we're investigating the murder of a detective who worked on the case. That's what we're here for. Can we come in and have a word?'

'Yeah, sure.' Peter stepped to one side and invited them into the house.

From a short hallway, Hunter and Grace stepped into a large, airy, open-plan house. The lounge and dining room were one, and at the far end, through a set of open glazed doors was a bespoke fitted kitchen of cream painted units and light oak work surfaces.

Hunter found himself staring around the cavernous room. 'This is a beautiful home, Mr Blake-Hall. The nightclub business is obviously doing well.'

Hunter eyed the man carefully. Peter Hall-Blake looked to be in his mid- to late-50s. He still had most of his light brown hair, but it was beginning to grey and the front had thinned to a widow's peak. At some stage he had used weights regularly but now the muscle-tone was giving way to fat, though, viewing the bulk of his upper arms straining the sleeves of his casual striped shirt, Hunter thought that he still looked as though he could handle himself. It had been a good thing that Grace had got between him and the reporter, or they would likely now be interviewing him under caution for assault, rather than chatting with him as a possible witness in their murder enquiry.

'I see you've done your homework on me.' Peter sank down onto a large three-seater sofa, offering them a matching one opposite. 'I'd prefer it if you wouldn't refer to my place as a nightclub. It's licensed as a private lap-dancing club. I offer something totally different to one of those vulgar places. Maybe in the old days my place was viewed as being somewhat lascivious, but thankfully the world has moved on. And yes, in answer to your question, it has allowed me a good lifestyle over the years.' He draped a leg over his knee. 'You'll have to pay us a visit. And I don't mean in the official sense. Come socially one night, on me. Bring a couple of colleagues.' Peter turned to Grace. 'My offer extends to you, but it might not be to your tastes, dear.'

Hunter could sense Grace shuffling beside him. He knew the remark would have wound her up. Before she had chance to bite, he replied, 'Thanks for the offer, but that might not be a wise idea under the circumstances.'

'My, things have changed. I guess this is what I've heard your retired colleagues moan about. Political correctness and all that. The detectives I knew in the past would have jumped at my offer.'

'Well, I wouldn't say it's political correctness, but yes, things have changed.' Hunter flipped open his folder. 'Let me just tell you why we are here.'

'I've been expecting you. I believe you want to ask me about Jeffery Howson.'

Hunter was caught off guard again. He asked, 'Did that reporter tell you that?'

'No, Alan Darbyshire rang me and told me what's happened. Terrible shock.'

'Oh? When was that?'

'A couple of days ago.' Peter paused. 'Yeah, it was either Thursday or Friday when he rang me.' He shook his head and smiled. 'There's nothing sinister about Alan ringing me up and telling me about Jeffery. We go back a long way. But then you know that, otherwise why would you be coming to see me about Jeffery Howson? Let me just say on record that I'm indebted to those two guys. If it hadn't been for them, my wife's killer would never have been caught. Since then, we've kept in touch. In fact, when Alan retired from the Force, I gave him a job.'

This was news to Hunter. 'He didn't tell us that when we spoke with him the other day.'

Peter shrugged his shoulders. 'It's no big secret. I took him on to manage the staff in my club. He was with me until about 18 months ago.'

'Did Jeffery work for you as well then?' asked Grace.

'Jeffery? Good God, no. Jeffery kept himself to himself when he retired, although I'm guessing Alan would have told you that. No, Jeffery changed after he got divorced. To be honest, I'm partially to blame for that. I don't know if you know, but Alan and Jeffery used to come to my club regularly, more so after they arrested Danny Weaver. I treated them to a few beers and the entertainment. I know officially it was frowned upon, but it was my way of saying thank you.

'One night, Jeffery's wife turned up at the club and caught him chatting with a couple of the girls. There was a right to-do between them. She accused him of carrying on with one of them, slapped him across the face and stormed out. That was the end of their marriage. It was Alan who told me that she had left him.

'Jeffery did come in a couple of times after they split-up but it wasn't for long. To be honest, I had to politely ask him to stop coming — he was so bloody miserable around the punters. I kept in touch with Alan, though, and as I say he worked for me once he retired.'

'When did you last see or speak with Jeffery?' asked Hunter.

'Crikey, that's a question.' Peter gazed up into the roof space. A few seconds later, he said, 'It wasn't that long after Danny Weaver's trial. That's when I had to have a quiet word with him. As I said, he became a right miserable sod. He just seemed to prop the bar up and drown his sorrows. My regulars were starting to complain about him. He took the request well, though. There was no animosity between us about it.' Peter unhooked his legs and hunched forward. 'Can I ask you something?'

'Sure.'

'That reporter I threw off my doorstep said you were re-opening my wife's case. Is that right? And do you think Jeffery's murder has something to do with that?'

Inwardly, Hunter was cursing. He vowed to track down that journalist and give him a piece of his mind. He said, 'You have to appreciate, Peter, there are some things we can't discuss. As a result of Jeffery's murder we are looking into the possibilities of why he was killed. That includes looking at some of the previous cases he was involved in. Your wife's case is one of those. Does that answer your question?'

'I guess so.' Peter leaned back against the cushions. 'Does that mean you're looking at Danny Weaver? I thought he was still inside?'

Hunter didn't want to mention the previous day's interview, or the likelihood that Daniel would be shortly released. Before he had time to magic up a response, Grace rescued him.

'Did you know Daniel Weaver prior to his arrest?' Grace asked. 'I have noticed that on a couple of occasions you have referred to him more personally as Danny rather than Daniel.'

Peter switched his gaze. 'I did know him before his arrest for Lucy's murder. Danny worked for me. I used to import cars from Germany — Mercedes and BMWs. It was very lucrative. Before the 90s you could get away with bringing in cars, and so long as you registered the car to an individual, and not a business, you'd get away with not paying any VAT. It was a loophole in customs. I'd have a circle of people, including Danny, who'd bring the cars in and register them in their names. I'd keep them garaged for six months and then move them on. I made a nice tidy profit.' His mouth suddenly tightened. 'I looked after Danny and that's how he repaid me.'

'When did you find out about him having an affair with Lucy?'

'I didn't. Not until after he'd been arrested. It was a complete surprise. I found out they'd been carrying on under my nose for over six months.'

'So the news was broken to you by Alan Darbyshire and Jeffery Howson?'

'I think it was Alan who told me.'

Hunter interjected, 'I'd like to just clarify one or two things from your original statement after Lucy disappeared, if that's okay?'

Peter spun his gaze back to Hunter. 'You're asking something there. That was such a long time ago.'

'Don't worry about that. I'll prompt you as we go along.' Hunter had read the prosecution file so many times now that he had all the information from the key witnesses locked in his head. He said, 'You said in your statement that the last time you saw Lucy was on Friday, tea-time, 26th of August. Can you remember that?'

'Yes, that's something I'll never forget. It was August Bank Holiday, and I went in early to the club because Bank Holidays were our busiest times.'

'And you stated that when you got back in the early hours Lucy wasn't in the house?'

Peter nodded.

'Yet, you didn't report her missing straight away. In your statement you reported her missing late the next morning. Is that correct?'

'No, that's wrong. I actually reported her missing in the early hours of Saturday. When I got back from the club, about one a.m., Lucy wasn't at home and that was unusual, so I phoned her parents, but they said they'd not heard from her. I told them I'd ring the police, which I did. The guy at the station said that as she was an adult, they wouldn't make any enquiries until she had been missing for 24 hours and that I should ring back then if she hadn't returned home. I then rang around a couple of her friends, but they hadn't heard from her either. And the next morning, when she still hadn't shown up, I contacted Alan Darbyshire. I told him it was unusual for Lucy to disappear like that, and he took it seriously. He and Jeffery came round to see me straight away.'

'They took your report and instigated a search for her?'

'Yeah. Alan rang his boss and the next thing I knew, the whole place was swarming with cops. Later on that day, Alan rang me and told me that Lucy had been seen arguing with a man in the marketplace the evening before and gave me a description of him. I told him I thought it fitted Danny.'

'And the next day, the Sunday, they arrested Daniel?' Hunter asked.

'Yeah, that's right. Alan told me that Danny had scratch marks to his face. They had also found Lucy's handbag hidden in his shed.'

'Did you see the handbag they found?'

'Yeah. Alan and Jeffery brought it round. It was definitely Lucy's. Her purse was still inside. Later on that night, Alan and Jeffery turned up at the club and told me that Danny had confessed.'

'Did they say anything else about Daniel's confession?'

Peter's eyebrows knitted together. 'I'm intrigued now. Why are you asking about Danny's confession?'

'It's just an angle in a number of enquiries we're following up.'

Peter shrugged. 'Fair enough. I suppose you'll tell me at some point.' He pursed his lips. 'Well, as I say, they came to the club to tell me that Danny had given them a statement and he would be charged with her murder. I was so delighted at the time, I just wanted to treat them to a drink.' He paused again and cleared his throat. 'I may have used the wrong word there. I think the word I should have used was relieved. Relieved that I knew what had happened to Lucy, and yet also sad, of course.'

'Of course.'

'Anyway, we had a couple of drinks together and they told me that Danny had told them that he had strangled Lucy during an argument at his flat and then put her in the back of his van and taken her to Langsett Moors and buried her there. And she's still up there somewhere. They searched but they never found her body.'

'Just to clarify, you said they told you Danny had confessed. Was it both Alan and Jeffery, or was it one of them?'

Peter screwed up his face in deep concentration. 'It was Alan who told me.'

'I know it's a long time ago now, Peter, but can you remember what Jeffery Howson was like that night when they came to your club and gave you the news?'

'Not really. You have to appreciate it all came as a surprise. All kinds of things were going around inside my head.' Peter paused again. 'Although now I come to think about it, Jeffery was a little subdued about it all. Usually, if they'd had a good result from a job and came into my club, the pair were buzzing. That night Jeffery was a lot quieter than normal. Why? Is that significant?'

It was Hunter's turn to shrug. 'We don't know yet. As I say, our enquiries are really in the early stages.'

'Do you have any clues as to who killed Jeffery then?' Peter asked.

Hunter gave him a smile. 'I'm afraid I can't tell you that. Let's just say, we have a number of leads we're following up.' He pushed himself up from the sofa. 'Well, Mr Blake-Hall, you've been most helpful. We'll leave you in peace now, but we may be back with some other questions before the investigation is over.'

Rising, Peter Blake-Hall proffered an outstretched hand. 'Well, you know where to find me.'

Everyone was back at their desks before 6 p.m. and Michael Robshaw took briefing early. Except for Hunter's and Grace's feedback from the meeting with Peter Blake-Hall, there was very little in the way of information and things were wound-up early. En masse, the team decamped to the George and Dragon for a drink.

Hunter didn't immediately go into the pub. He sat in his car and phoned Beth, telling her would be home within the hour. He had just disconnected the call when his passenger door opened and Barry Newstead climbed in. He kept the door open, leaving one leg dangling outside. He leaned in towards Hunter.

'I'm glad I've caught you. I wanted to have a quick word with you about your visit to Peter Blake-Hall this afternoon.'

'Oh yeah? Actually, I've got something to tell you, because guess who was at the house when we got there?'

A frown creased Barry's forehead.

'None other than that journalist friend of yours.'

'Guy Armstrong?'

'We didn't get his name, but from your description it certainly fitted him. Blake-Hall was giving him the same reception as you did. Grace had to step in to protect him. It looked as though he was about to get more than just a boot up his arse.'

'You should have let it happen.'

'Now, now Barry. This is the modern police service.' Hunter smirked. 'Anyway, what's so important it can't wait till we get in the pub?'

'I got a phone call today from an old CID buddy about Alan Darbyshire. Peter Blake-Hall was a snout for Alan for years. You know how I said about Alan showing off about all the arrests he made?'

Hunter nodded.

'Well, it seems that most of those were down to Peter. It seems as though Alan and Jeffery had a right old thing going on with Blake-Hall. It's my guess, he was giving them info to keep the pair sweet, and in return they'd tip him off if any raids or other stuff was coming his way.'

'Have you told anyone about this?'

'Not yet. I only got the phone call an hour ago. This old mate of mine doesn't want to get involved if he can help it. He used to work on the same team as Alan and Jeffery and had a lot of time for them. He said that he respects Alan and that he was a very good gaffer to work for.'

'Yeah, but it looks now as though he's not only bent but he may have murdered Jeffery as well.'

'I know. Just keep it under your hat for now. I'll make some more calls, and see what I can come up with from other sources.'

'Look Barry, you know how important this is. I'll give you a couple of days to do your digging and if you don't get anywhere then I'm afraid this friend of yours is going to have to stand up and be counted.'

Barry gave Hunter's wrist a gentle squeeze. 'Give me until Thursday.'

Just after 8 p.m. Hunter left the pub feeling hungry and tired but relaxed. He'd only travelled half a mile when he spotted a dark coloured saloon car tucked next to the stone wall of the small village brewery to his right. There was someone in the driver's seat. Under normal circumstances it wouldn't have attracted his attention because cars frequently park there during the day, but at night, when the brewery was closed, the place was usually deserted. He eased off the accelerator and started using his rear-view mirrors.

Less than 100 yards on, in his driver's-side mirror, he saw the car's headlights suddenly blaze and watched it pull onto the road. Thinking he was being followed, Hunter floored the accelerator. The Audi's 1.9 diesel turbo kicked in, and within seconds he had reached 70 m.p.h., the car's low-profile tyres humming off the wet tarmac as it thundered along the stretch of unlit road.

The winding roads ahead were in total darkness but Hunter knew this area of the countryside like the back of his hand, and although he could still make out the headlights of the car behind, he saw that they were slowly diminishing as he left it behind. Taking a sharp left, he tore up a switch-back climb of road, and then, 200 yards along, he hit the brakes, wrenched the steering hard left and swept into a side lane. As his car rocked to a standstill, he turned off its lights.

15 seconds later, the saloon flew past. He had enough time to get a fleeting look at the driver and he was sure that it was the reporter Guy Armstrong.

Hunter banged into first gear and booted the accelerator. He whipped his car back onto the glistening road. In less than 30 seconds he had caught up with the speeding reporter. He turned on his headlights and hit high-beam.

Hunter saw the saloon's brake lights flash on and the rear end wobble. Then it began to angle sideways and slide. He hit his brakes as Armstrong's car scythed sideways for several seconds before bouncing against the grassed verge, bucking to a halt.

Hunter flung open his door and dashed towards the driver's side of the still-rocking saloon. He yanked open the door and composed himself. 'Mr Armstrong, if I'm not mistaken. And I thought I was the one with the certificate in surveillance.'

'You bloody idiot,' Guy Armstrong spluttered. 'You could have got me killed.'

'That'll teach you for trying to sneak up on me. Now, why are you following me?'

The reporter took a deep breath and sank back in his seat. 'I wasn't sneaking up on you. I just wanted a quick word with you about Peter Blake-Hall.'

'Well, I don't want to have a word with *you*. Especially to do with Peter Blake-Hall. This is a murder investigation and you know that.'

'This will be off the record. Just you and me.'

'Off the record. How many times have I heard a journalist say that?'

'But this is. Believe me. I think I can help you. I have a source who —'

Hunter held up his hand. He choked back the words he wanted to use and instead forced a tolerant smile. 'Thank you very much, Mr Armstrong, for your kind offer, but I don't need your help.'

'I really can help you.'

'Mr Armstrong. This conversation is over. Goodnight.' With a mighty fling, Hunter slammed the door shut.

DAY EIGHT

At morning briefing, Hunter gave details of his encounter with Guy Armstrong, cautioning the team to watch out for him.

Michael Robshaw followed up Hunter's warning by telling everyone that he had been forced into a press conference that afternoon because of Friday's High Court Appeal requesting the release of Daniel Weaver. 'There's a lot of interest in this case now. I'm already having to fend-off calls from the media,' he explained. 'We really are going to be on our guard from now on,' he concluded.

On a lighter note, Barry Newstead ended briefing by relaying his success at tracking down Lucy's best friend, Amanda Smith. 'She got married in 1985, the year after Lucy's murder trial and moved away. Her husband was a serving soldier in the Military Police and he was posted to Germany. They came back to this country in 1988 when he left the army and the pair are now living in Cumbria. In fact, both she and her husband have joined the police up there. She's now called Rawlinson — Amanda Rawlinson and she's a uniform sergeant stationed at Kendal. I spent ten minutes chatting with her on the phone late yesterday afternoon and I've told her someone will be going up to interview her within the next few days.'

Following morning briefing, Hunter put in a phone call to the local probation service. He caught up with Jodie Marie Jenkinson's probation officer, a man called Ray Austin, as he was about to leave the office for his first court appearance of the day. He could tell from the man's reaction that the news of her death had come as a surprise. He told Hunter he would be back in the office for 11 o'clock and could spare him an hour then.

Hunter settled down to catch up with his own paperwork and at 10.40 a.m., he picked up the folder containing Jodie Marie Jenkinson's sudden death report and headed off out for his meeting with Ray Austin.

Barnwell Probation Service was housed in a large double-fronted Victorian building in a cul-de-sac of similar style dwellings. It had once been an area where the well-to-do businesspeople of the locale lived, but over the years, as people's lifestyles and status had changed, the place had altered.

Some of the houses had been sold on to developers, who had divided them into flats, and the two buildings either side of the probation service had been sold to a firm of accountants and a dental practice.

Hunter entered the reception area, gave the woman behind the reinforced glass screen his name, and told her of his appointment with Ray Austin.

Hunter had only been waiting for a couple of minutes when a door next to the reception counter opened and a man appeared in the doorway. For a second, Hunter was thrown off-guard, because the man bore a striking resemblance to the torn photograph recovered from Jodie Marie Jenkinson's jeans pocket. He quickly recovered his composure, hoping the man hadn't spotted his startled look.

The man said, 'DS Kerr?'

Hunter nodded.

'We spoke earlier. I'm Ray Austin. Would you like to come through?' He stepped to one side.

He led Hunter up a stairway to the first-floor landing. There, a security door prevented them going any further. Ray Austin punched a four-digit code into a key-pad and the door clicked open. He directed Hunter down a dimly lit corridor and then showed him into an office. On the door plaque Hunter saw that Ray Austin's title was Senior Probation Officer.

Ray slipped past Hunter and dropped down into a high-back chair behind a cluttered desk. He offered Hunter a seat, then parted some of the paperwork and rested his forearms. 'Can I get you a drink?'

Hunter shook his head. 'No thanks. To be honest, I'm in the middle of a murder enquiry at the moment and I've a tight schedule today. I'm fitting our meeting in between enquiries.'

Ray threw him a puzzled look. 'You've confused me, Sergeant Kerr. You said on the phone you were investigating Jodie's sudden death and now you've just said you're involved in a murder enquiry. Has Jodie been murdered?'

Hunter shook his head. 'Sorry. I explained myself badly there. Yes, I am investigating Jodie's sudden death, and I am also involved in a murder enquiry, but the two are not related.'

Ray gave an understanding nod. 'So, how can I help?'

'Well, I'm led to believe you were her probation officer.'

'Yes, for my sins. Jodie came to me after her last court appearance six months ago.' Ray leaned further forward. 'When I say for my sins, I don't mean that in a derogative way. Jodie had her faults, but like a lot of our clients, once you got past the veneer there's a different person under the surface. You might find that difficult to believe, I guess, from your dealings. But they come to us having received their punishment and the majority just get their heads down.

'Jodie wasn't like that though. I realised long ago that her probation gave her structure and purpose in her life and she embraced it. She always did everything we asked and was always on time for her appointments, unlike many of our other clients. Hearing of her death this morning has come as a real shock, I can tell you.' He paused. 'To be honest, I was about to write her up for breaching her sentence. She missed her last two appointments. That was unusual, as I've just explained, and so I cut her a bit of slack because of how good she had been in the past. But when I rung her mobile and she didn't return my calls, I thought she'd done a runner.' He shook his head. 'I know why now. When did Jodie die?'

The comment about him trying to contact Jodie on her mobile jolted Hunter's brain. *Where was her mobile?* It hadn't been in her possession or at the scene where she had been found. He stored that thought away and then asked, 'Can I ask when those appointments were?'

Ray switched his gaze to his computer. For a few seconds he browsed his monitor. 'The first one she missed was on Tuesday 18th November. She was booked in for 3.30. The second one was last Tuesday, the 25th, at two o'clock. We had another scheduled for tomorrow afternoon. I had just reduced them to weekly appointments because she was doing so well.'

'Jodie's body was found on the 21st, but we believe she had been dead for the best part of a week.'

'Gosh, that's terrible.'

'So, if her appointments with you were weekly, the last time you saw her was Tuesday 11th?'

Ray looked back to his monitor. 'Yes, the 11th. Three o'clock. For the past couple of months, they were always mid-afternoon because it fitted in with her job.'

'She was working?'

'Yes, she'd got herself some work in a bar, though I don't know where that was.'

'Do you know where she was living?'

'Yeah. I actually fixed her up with a place before she went for sentence. She said she had nowhere to go and as we have a list of landlords who are prepared to take our clients, I made a few phone calls and got her a place. I thought that if I could get her a more permanent residence then there was a fair chance of her getting probation, and so I fixed her up with a flat in one of the houses at the top of this road. I also sorted out her benefits, so she had enough money and didn't need to go out shoplifting again. You might find this strange, but I had a bit of a soft spot for Jodie.'

'What do you mean by a bit of a soft spot?'

'In the strictest professional sense, of course. I've known Jodie a long time, almost nine years. She did her first probation sentence when she was 16. Don't get me wrong, Jodie could be a pain in the backside at times, but she also had a heart of gold once you got to know her.'

'And how well did you know her?'

'Probably better than any of others in the office. She caused some of the girls here a bit of grief at times. Jodie had a temper on her. Especially when she'd had a drink. And so I used to get her every time you lot had charged her. Everyone else wanted to avoid her, but I got on well with her.'

'Why do you think that was?'

'I don't know. I suppose I didn't give up on her like others had done. She had a pretty shitty life you know.'

'Were you fond of her?'

Ray's brow creased into a frown and his mouth tightened. 'Fond of her. I don't get what you mean?'

'Mr Austin, I won't beat about the bush. When we found Jodie's body she had a photograph of you in her pocket.'

'A photo of me?'

Hunter flipped open the cover of Jodie's file, withdrew the plastic evidence bag containing the torn photograph, and turned it so that it was facing Ray. 'That is you?'

'Wow. Now I know where that photograph went. It went missing from my desk at the start of the year. I wondered where it had gone to.' He reached out to a wooden photo frame next to his desktop computer and turned it around to face Hunter. 'This is another copy of the same photo. I replaced it.'

Hunter studied the framed photograph. He saw that the image contained not only Ray's head and shoulders but he had his arm around the shoulders of a woman in her 30s. There was no doubt that the torn section of photograph they had recovered from Jodie's pocket was one half of this one he was looking at.

'That's my wife, Sarah, with me. We've been married almost ten years.' Ray returned the framed photograph to his desktop, nudging it into roughly the same position it had been before. A smile creased his face. 'Now I realise why you were asking me the type of questions you were. You thought something was going on between Jodie and me?'

Still guarded, Hunter said, 'Was there?'

Ray's face straightened. 'You're being serious, aren't you? Look, when I say I was fond of Jodie, it was nothing like you think. It was strictly probation officer and client. But like I said, I did have a soft spot for her. You didn't know Jodie like I did. She had a bad life and it wasn't getting any better.'

'Tell me about it.'

'As I said, I first came across Jodie when she was 16. She'd got drunk and badly assaulted a younger girl at the care home she was in. I'm afraid Jodie was yet another failure in our care system. She had suffered a life of neglect and abuse by parents who drank heavily and went into care when she was 12 as a result. She was fostered out a few times but caused havoc with every family she was placed with and so in the end no one would have her. She started drinking heavily when she was 14, and by the time she was 15 had been cautioned three times.

'The assault was her first court conviction and I was given her file. After that, I got her paperwork every time she went to court. As I've said, I just seemed to be able to get on with her. Even when she wasn't on our books, she'd pop in to see me and have a chat. She did say to me once that I was the only person who listened to her and understood what she was going through. I don't know if that's true or not, but she obviously felt she could confide in me. Can I ask you now how she met her death? Was it to do with drink?'

'No. Drugs actually.'

'Drugs?'

'Heroin.'

Ray looked startled. 'Heroin?'

'Yeah. An overdose. She was found in the cellar of a derelict pub. The place had been used as a shooting den. You sound surprised?'

'That's because I am. As far as I was aware, Jodie never touched drugs. Maybe the odd spliff now and then, but not the hard stuff. A couple of the care staff from the home where she lived told me that Jodie used to come back there from time to time and if she found any of the kids using gear, she'd end up preaching to them about the dangers of the stuff. She had some success as well. Helped get a few of the kids clean. She was actually a role model for some of them.' Ray paused, then he said, 'Are you sure it was heroin?'

'Absolutely. A really pure concentrate as well. Not the normal street smack.'

'I really find that difficult to believe. If you'd said she'd died as a result of choking on her own vomit from drink, then yes, I'd believe that, but not drugs.'

Hunter pushed himself back into his seat. Ray Austin's response was setting alarm bells ringing. He thought back to the crime scene photographs, especially those relating to Jodie's post-mortem. And then it hit him. The scarring on Jodie's arms from her years of self-harm had distracted his investigative eye. Everything was suddenly a whirl. He shook his head in an attempt to dismiss the chaos emerging in his thoughts.

Ray eased himself back. 'You look a little concerned, DS Kerr?'

'That's because I am. I think I've been walking down a blind alley over this. What you've just said has completely changed my thoughts about Jodie's death. I thought she'd overdosed. Now I'm going to have to go back and check things.' He glanced at Jodie's file. 'There're just a couple more things to sort out before I leave you in peace.'

'Oh yes?'

'First thing, what's her address?'

Ray wrote down Jodie's address and passed the note to Hunter. 'Her flat's on the top floor. It's a one-bedroom place. She shared a bathroom with two other flatmates on the same floor. There're ten flats in that place, mainly DHSS clients.'

Hunter glanced at the address on the note. 'Thanks. We found a key on Jodie, so I'm hoping it's for this place. I'm going to nip up there next. We also found a Christmas card in her possession. It's signed Mr X. You wouldn't know anything about that, would you?'

Ray's face creased into a smile. 'Goodness me, has she still got that? I sent her that donkey's years ago. It was sent as a bit of a joke, but I know she appreciated it. I've already mentioned that she used to pop in the office from time to time for a chat, even when she wasn't on probation?'

Hunter acknowledged with a brief nod.

'Well, one Christmas when she was 18 or 19, she called in for a chat and she saw all the cards on my desk and mentioned that she'd never ever been sent a Christmas card. I found that comment so sad, and so I sent her one and signed it as Mr X as a bit of a joke. She knew I'd sent it, because she turned up at my office waving it around and thanked me. I thought she was going to cry.' Ray pursed his lips. 'That's quite sad, don't you think? The only person to ever send her a Christmas card was her probation officer.'

Hunter flipped Jodie's file shut. 'It obviously brought comfort to her, because she'd held on to it after all these years.'

Ray's eyes suddenly glistened. Swallowing quickly, he said, 'Do you know, the mention of Christmas has just triggered something Jodie said to me the last time we met.'

'Oh? What's that then?'

'Well, I don't know if it's relevant to your enquiries or not, but after she'd told me this, I asked her what she was doing for Christmas and she said, "With a bit of luck going on holiday." It wasn't the reply I expected, so asked her if she'd won the lottery, as a joke, and she said: "Just as good as. I know a secret that's going to make me a lot of money".'

Hunter repeated, 'A secret?'

'Yes. I'm afraid she wouldn't tell me what the secret was. She just said I'd read about it in the papers.'

'You're sure she said that?'

'It wasn't word for word, but it was certainly something close to that. I looked her straight in the eyes after she'd said it and I could tell by her face that she was serious. I told her to be careful, that she couldn't afford to get into any more trouble. She just laughed at me and told me not to worry, that she could look after herself.' Ray exchanged looks with Hunter. 'Are you thinking what I'm thinking? That secret could have just got her killed?'

Hunters brain went into overdrive. Closing Jodie's death report was certainly not going to happen today. There were too many unanswered questions. He replied, 'That is just what I need to find out.'

Hunter glanced at the address scribbled on the note stuck to the dashboard, slowing his car and turning it in towards the kerb. He got out of his car and walked up to the doorway. Twisting the dirty brass doorknob of the original Victorian panelled door, he opened it slowly. The hallway was gloomy and dingy. Many of the original black and white floor tiles were chipped and scuffed. A couple were missing and concrete patches replaced them. Torn, woodchip wallpaper covered the walls.

Trying not to make too much noise, he climbed the staircase up to the second floor where Ray Austin had told him he would find Jodie's bedsit. At the head of the second stairway, the landing split left and right with a door at either end. Jodie's room was to his right.

He approached Jodie's room. Three steps along the landing, he faltered. He could hear sounds from inside. He saw the Jodie's door was open a fraction and clocked that the jamb around the lock was splintered.

Senses heightened, he clenched his fists and edged forward. Inches from the door, he paused and listened. The earlier noise had stopped, and the only sound now seemed to be from a television set in one of the flats below.

Using the toe of his shoe, he inched the door open. It creaked on its hinges. As the gap widened, he tried to get a better view inside, but the curtains were drawn and all he could see was the silhouette of various pieces of furniture. He was about to step in when a dark shape shot into view, rocketing towards him, taking him by surprise. Instinctively, he threw up his hands into boxing stance, but it was an instant too late. He never saw the blow. It caught him full in the mouth, knocking him sideways, sending him crashing against the wall. Before he had time to react, a blow to his midriff sent the air exploding from his lungs. His legs buckled and he only just managed to throw out his hands in time to stop himself from smacking against the deck.

Hunter felt the figure brushing past but couldn't do a thing about it; he was still scrambling around, trying to recover. He could just make out the sound of someone fleeing heavily down the stairs.

Hunter yanked himself up. He was just in time to see a squat, stocky man, in a dark padded jacket with a woollen hat pulled low over his ears disappearing through the front door. His assailant looked to be of the same build and shape as the man he had chased three days earlier at Jeffery Howson's funeral.

Hunter's head was in turmoil. There was no reason why this should be the same person. There was no link between Jeffery Howson and Jodie. He took a deep breath, closed his eyes, committing the description to memory and then let out a heavy sigh. If it was the same man, then that was the second time he had let him slip. There wouldn't be a third, he told himself as he thumped the handrail in frustration.

Taking another deep breath, he felt his strength returning and delved into his jacket for his mobile. He needed to call this in. Back-up would be too late to capture the fugitive but he needed to preserve the scene and get forensic support here quickly. He was confident now that Jodie's death was no accident, that he may have just missed her killer, and that this was as fresh a crime-scene as he could possibly have.

The marked Response Car got to Hunter inside five minutes. He quickly briefed the driver and his partner as to what had happened and left them to get on with coordinating a search, while he began to fathom out how best to secure the premises.

Next to arrive were Grace and Mike Sampson. They had been about to set off to interview Lucy's parents, when they'd picked up his distress call and had immediately diverted.

'Which way did he run?' asked Grace.

Hunter shrugged. 'Don't know. Best guess is he made a left into the side streets. There're quite a few alleyways he could've shot down and from there he could have made the town centre or out towards the hospital. I don't even know if he had a car or not. I didn't hear one, but to be honest it took me a good couple of minutes to get my breath back and get down the stairs. He packed a hell of a punch.' Hunter dabbed at his mouth and saw that the side of his hand was smeared with fresh blood. 'I'll punch his fucking lights out when I get hold of him.'

Grace shook her head and threw him one of her looks.

He reacted with, 'What?'

She pointed to his mouth and said, 'Don't worry, it's not made any difference to your looks. You're still just as ugly.' Then she smiled. 'Come on then, Sergeant Kerr, start dishing out the orders, tell us what you want us to do.'

'We need to check out who lives in these flats. I'm going to secure the area between the first floor and second floor. SOCO are on their way.'

Within ten minutes Hunter had donned a white forensic over-suit from the boot of his car and sealed off the staircase between the first and second floors. Below, he heard the entrance door open, followed by the clipped sound of heels on the tiled hall floor. Hunter peered over the banister and caught sight of Dawn Leggate coming up the staircase.

She called out, 'Hello. DS Kerr?'

'Up here, ma'am.'

Dawn craned her neck to meet Hunter's gaze. 'Please don't call me ma'am, Hunter, I bloody hate that word. Makes me sound like the Queen. Just call me boss or guv.' She paused on the last step before the landing. She was wearing a brown checked duffel coat, which she started to unbutton as she climbed. 'I'm afraid you're going to have to put up with me, DS Kerr. Mr Robshaw's going to run the Howson enquiry and I'm running this one. I hope you're okay with that?'

Hunter nodded. He felt a sharp tinge from the cut at the side of his mouth.

'Good, 'cos I wasn't giving you an option.' Dawn flashed him a mischievous smile as she reached the landing. She started to pull on a pair of latex gloves. 'Right, Hunter, tell me what you've got. I've heard over the radio that they're still searching for the guy who slugged you, though it looks as though he's gone to ground.'

Hunter felt his face flush. He was still smarting. Not just from letting someone thump him without any form of retaliation, but also knowing that he let his quarry get away. He gave Dawn the background to the case, explaining how he had initially thought that Jodie's death was the result of a drugs overdose. He relayed the earlier conversation with Ray Austin.

'And so, you're thinking that this guy who you've disturbed had something to do with her death?' Dawn asked, when he had finished.

Hunter nodded. 'Too much of a coincidence, don't you think?'

'And you got the impression that this guy was the same person you chased at Jeffery Howson's funeral?'

'I couldn't swear on it 100 per cent. But he was certainly dressed the same. Though, it doesn't make sense why the same guy at Jeffery Howson's funeral should turn up here.'

'Just hold onto those thoughts for now. We've got a lot of enquiries ahead, and you say that uniform are still out there searching for him, as well as the CCTV crew, so we might be able to rule him either in or out later on, okay?'

Hunter agreed with a nod. He flipped open Jodie's file. 'This is what I've got in terms of evidence.' He showed Dawn the Scenes of Crime photographs. 'These are shots of the pub and the cellar where Jodie's body was found and also of her PM.' Hunter pointed at a couple of the post-mortem photos, which focused on her arms. 'I'd looked at these a couple of times, and there was something I wasn't happy with but I couldn't put my finger on it. Since learning this morning about her stance on drug abuse, I gave them the once-over again, and I realised what had been concerning me. There are no track-marks on her arms, or anywhere else on her body for that matter.'

He flicked back a page to the sequence of images SOCO had taken of the premises. 'There was something else bugging me as well.' He pointed to a close-up shot of the door to the cellar with its broken panel. 'The foreman told me that they had to kick this in to get access. This door was fitted with a mortise lock. The only key we found on Jodie was for this flat, and that's a Yale make. No other key was found on site. Also, the cellar was too clean to be a shooting den. Just look at the photograph which shows her slumped along the floor.' He thumbed to the next shot in the album. 'All that's around her is a couple of syringes, a couple of spoons and a few silver wraps. That's it. There was no cigarette lighter or matches, either on her possession, or in the cellar. This was staged for our benefit.'

Hunter closed the evidence album. 'The absence of any lighting material means that someone else was in the cellar to heat up the heroin on the spoon before it was injected. And, whoever it was, locked her in there and left. With that in mind, I've phoned the foreman at the site and told them to stop what they're doing so we can do a thorough forensics job and extend the search area. Thankfully, he tells me that they've not touched the cellar since Jodie's body was found.'

'What about witnesses here?' Dawn asked.

Hunter told her what Grace and Mike were doing.

'Well, you seem to have got everything covered.' Dawn checked her watch. 'It's just gone one o'clock. My guess is it will take SOCO a good hour to get set up and it's going to take a while for Grace and Mike to get round the residents, so I'm going to leave everything in your capable hands while I sort us out an incident suite. I'll need to get onto the coroner as well and fix up a second PM.' She glanced down at Jodie's file. 'Can I take this back with me, so I'm up-to-date with everything and can get the incident board set-up?'

Hunter nodded and Dawn set off back down the stairs.

Hunter was leaning over the balcony with his eyes glued to the front door. He had been like this for the best part of an hour and was beginning to feel cold. He could see that there was a single radiator below him in the hallway, but he couldn't tell if it was working or not. It certainly wasn't throwing out enough heat to reach him up on the second floor. He cursed, wondering why it was taking SOCO so long to get here.

Then the front door opened with a jerk and Duncan Wroe appeared. He called out, 'Hello. Where is everyone?'

'Up here, Duncan,' Hunter responded, checking his watch, noting the time for his log: it was 1:55pm.

By the time Duncan had reached Hunter he was out of breath. He dropped his aluminium case onto the landing and pushed his free hand through his unruly mop of straw-coloured hair. Duncan straightened his back. 'What have you got for me then?'

Hunter repeated what he had told Dawn Leggate. 'This is Jodie's bed-sit, Duncan. The only person I'm aware of who's visited the place since her death is that guy who socked me one and no one's stepped a foot inside the place since that happened.'

'Good.' Duncan climbed into his white suit and picked up his case. 'I noticed you've kept a sterile area down to the first landing. That's good as well. Did you notice if the guy was wearing gloves or not?'

Hunter shook his head. 'It all happened so fast. He was wearing a woollen hat and padded jacket. That's all I had time to clock.'

'No problem. We'll soon see once we start sprinkling the magic dust around.' Duncan made towards Jodie's door, stopping to scrutinise the splintered lock. 'That wouldn't have offered much resistance,' he said, glancing over his shoulder. 'Who's the exhibits officer?'

'Everything's down to you and me at the moment, Duncan. We're a bit thin on the ground, what with the retired detective murder case that's running, plus we've just re-opened a cold case murder from 1983 that looks as if it's linked.'

'Yeah, I heard that.' Duncan pushed the door open wider with the edge of his case and switched on the light.

Hunter looked over Duncan's shoulder. It was his first opportunity to get a proper view inside Jodie's room and it didn't take him long to cast his eyes around — the space where Jodie had lived was no bigger than ten-feet square.

The place looked like a hurricane had ripped through it. The mattress from the single bed had been flipped over onto the floor, its duvet and pillow shredded. A set of double cupboards above a small sink and draining board were open and, judging by the debris over the floor, its contents had been emptied. A single wardrobe had its doors wide open and various items of clothing littered the floor. A portable TV had been upended, and a large number of photographs, DVDs and CDs covered the threadbare carpet.

Duncan glanced back. 'I think you're onto something here, Hunter. I would say this is no ordinary burglary. Someone was looking for something in particular.'

'Well, I hope he didn't find it.'

'We shall see, we shall see.' Duncan turned and handed Hunter his clipboard. 'I'm going to make a call back to the office. I'm going to need a hand here.'

It was 6.10 p.m. before Hunter, Grace and Mike got back to the office.

Hunter had left Scenes of Crime still examining the scene and managed to get the duty inspector to provide a uniformed officer to stand guard over the scene.

So far, door-to-door enquiries by Grace and Mike had not revealed anything startling about Jodie. A couple of the tenants had spoken with her, but only by way of acknowledgement and not to chat. However, a young man in the flat below had been helpful. He told them that he had seen a skinny girl, with dyed blonde hair, roughly the same age as Jodie, going up to her bedsit on several occasions and he had heard them partying together quite a few times.

After one such party, about a month ago, he'd got so pissed off with the pair making noise that he'd banged on Jodie's door. The skinny blonde one had answered and when he'd complained she'd just laughed in his face and told him to fuck off. He'd collared Jodie the next day on the stairs and she'd apologised. He told Grace that he had seen this girl twice in the past week going up to Jodie's room. Realising the significance, because Jodie had been dead for well over a week, Grace had pushed him to expand on the girl's description, but he hadn't been able to and so she had fixed up for him to do a digital e-fit in a hope that it would help identify the girl.

Beside themselves, the only person in the office was DI Gerald Scaife. He was sat at a spare desk, head buried in paperwork.

Hunter said, 'Only you in, boss?'

Gerald looked up. 'There are a few of the HOLMES team next door. The rest have gone. The DS sacked it early. He's had to go over to Sheffield to the BBC studios to do a piece for *Look North* tonight. Everyone is in for eight a.m. briefing tomorrow. Oh, there's a couple of messages on your desk. That reporter, Guy Armstrong, has been trying to get hold of you. He's left his mobile number and home number and asked if you'd call him the minute you got in. I think he's also left a message on your voicemail. Sounds desperate.'

Hunter saw several scrap pieces of paper on his desk blotter. There were four notes in all, two of them with phone numbers. He bundled them together and dropped them into his pending tray. 'He's a determined man, if nothing else. He'll have to wait until tomorrow now. I've got a glass of whisky with my name on it waiting for me back home.'

DAY NINE

When Hunter entered the office, it was bustling with activity. Two members of the cold case unit had joined the team. Despite the new arrivals, he knew they were still going to be stretched, especially now there was *his* investigation to add to the mix.

Hunter settled into his seat. Grace was already at her desk nursing a steaming mug of coffee.

'Much happening?' he asked her. 'I see a couple of lads from the cold case unit have joined us.'

'Yeah, apparently they came in late yesterday to help the HOLMES crew man the phones following Robshaw's appeal on *Look North*.'

'I saw that on the late evening news. Did anything positive came out of it?'

'I had ten minutes with Isobel this morning and she tells me that they only took a dozen or so calls. She said a few of those were helpful. One of them was from a witness at Daniel Weaver's trial. She was a friend of one of the witnesses who saw Weaver and Lucy arguing in the marketplace before she went missing. She gave Isobel her details and details of her friend, who she says is now married and lives near Yarmouth. Isobel's expecting to get a call from the woman this morning.

'And one call has given us a lead in the Jeffery Howson case. A couple coming back from the pub on the Saturday night saw a car parked up close to the bottom of the path which leads up to the back of Jeffery's garden. I've had a quick chat with one of the new lads as well. He told me that their brief is to help with tracing the remaining witnesses from the Lucy Blake-Hall case.' Grace set down her cup. 'By the way, have you heard the other news?'

'News? You mean TV/radio news, or police gossip news?'

'Guy Armstrong's dead!'

'Guy Armstrong, as in nosy, pain in the arse reporter, Guy Armstrong?'

Grace nodded. 'Killed in a road accident last night.'

'You are kidding me?'

'No. Isobel told me that she bumped into the duty inspector last night just before she went off. He was just turning out to the accident. I don't know all of the details but it looks as though he missed a bend on his way home from the pub last night and crashed into a tree. His car went up in flames.'

'Jesus, poor guy. I know I said he was a pain in the arse, but I wouldn't wish that on anyone.' Then Hunter remembered yesterday evening's conversation with Gerald. He rifled through his pending tray, pulling out the four scribbled notes he had tidied away. He spread them out on his blotter and read each one. None contained any specific details, other than to state that Armstrong wanted to speak with him. Two contained a mobile and landline telephone number.

He felt guilty about not calling. Hunter punched in his voicemail number and code. He had six messages on his list — five of them were old ones he had saved. Guy Armstrong's was the only fresh one. The message lasted 20 seconds.

When it had finished, he shot his gaze across the desk, attracting Grace's attention. 'Listen to this message Armstrong left me,' he said excitedly.

He punched the play key again, engaging the speakerphone.

'Detective Sergeant Kerr, this is Guy Armstrong. It's important that I speak with you. I've just learned that Jodie Jenkinson is dead and that you are investigating it. The reason why I am ringing you is because Jodie was the source I mentioned to you the other night. It was she who tipped me off about the Lucy Blake-Hall case. A couple of weeks ago, she overheard a conversation between two people which leaves me to believe that Daniel Weaver really is innocent of her murder. I sent an anonymous note to the person who I believed killed Lucy to lure him out, but I fear it may well have got Jodie and that retired detective killed. I'm going to call into the George and Dragon tonight to hopefully catch you. As soon as you get this message, please call me.'

Hunter struck the store key on his desk phone and slowly set down the handset. 'Talk about a voice from the grave.'

It was almost 10.30 before morning briefing started.

Following Hunter's phone call, Dawn Leggate hot-footed it back from District Headquarters, and with his help, set up an incident board displaying all the information associated with the death of Jodie Marie Jenkinson.

A sea of eyes followed Detective Superintendents Michael Robshaw and Dawn Leggate as they made their way to the front of the incident room.

There were now three separate incident boards side-by-side. The two SIOs stopped beside the one displaying information relating to Jodie's death.

Robshaw opened the briefing. 'First things first. Last night's TV appeal. I'm guessing you all saw it. We've got a couple of good calls. A couple who live three streets away from Jeffery were on their way back from the pub just before half-past-ten on the Saturday evening, when we believe he was killed, when they noticed a dark coloured four-by-four parked very close to the entranceway of the path which runs past the bottom of Jeffery Howson's garden. I want that call following up as a priority this morning. See if we can identify that vehicle, and more importantly, if they saw anyone with it.' He paused and looked around the team. 'We don't happen to know what vehicle Alan Darbyshire drives, do we?'

'I can make a discreet phone call regarding that,' piped up Barry Newstead.

Robshaw spun his attention to Barry. 'Okay I'll leave that one with you.' Then he returned to the room. He slapped a hand, palm-flat, against Jodie's incident board. 'Okay, Jodie Marie Jenkinson. Until yesterday, it was believed that her death was an accidental overdose. The information Hunter gained yesterday afternoon, the discovery of the burglary at her bedsit, and the message left by reporter Guy Armstrong, who incidentally was found dead in his crashed car last night, has changed all that. It's my firm belief, given everything we have learned in the past 24 hours, that she has been murdered.

'We also have tenuous links to Jeffery's murder, as the man Hunter disturbed burgling Jodie's bedsit fits the same description as the man he chased at Jeffery's funeral. This may be just a coincidence, but until anyone brings me anything different, I am linking Jodie's death to our current investigation. And it may not end there. Guy Armstrong's accident is also just too much of a coincidence. So, with that in mind I'm also organising tasks this morning relating to Armstrong.' Robshaw's face took on a look of earnest. 'In the past year we have had our fair measure of harrowing and complicated cases, but never have I known one with as many twists and turns as this. It would be fair to say we have a lot of work ahead.'

After briefing, Hunter caught up with his journal, putting in the details of his conversation with Ray Austin and also logging the incident at Jodie's bedsit. He revisited the scene in his head, trying to magic up a better image of the man he had encountered, but no matter how hard he concentrated, he was stuck with the mental picture of a faceless man in dark clothing.

He realised there were still a number of gaps about Jodie's personal life and he put in a call to the probation service. Ray Austin had not yet gone off to court and the receptionist put Hunter through.

The second he answered, Hunter said, 'Ray, DS Kerr here. Did you manage to find out the name of the bar where Jodie worked?'

Ray replied, 'I'm afraid I've not had much luck, Sergeant. I've wracked my brains since you left yesterday but I can't remember what she told me. I've asked the receptionists to check with a couple of clients who knew her. Other than that, I can't help, I'm afraid. If I do get anything, I've got your number.'

'When you say clients, do you mean friends of hers?'

'Not as such. Jodie didn't have many close friends. She knew a lot of people, but I wouldn't class any of them as friends. We have one associate on file, who I remember she was close with, but I checked her status out this morning and she's currently in Newhall Prison serving 18 months for shoplifting.' He gave Hunter the woman's details.

Hunter relayed what the tenant living below Jodie had told them about the blonde woman who had been seen in Jodie's bedsit.

Ray answered, 'Sorry again, Sergeant Kerr, that description doesn't ring any bells. I've made some notes and I'll ask my colleagues here and go back through Jodie's paperwork again and see if I can come up with the name of anyone that might fit.'

Hunter thanked him and hung up. Looking across the desks, he saw Grace's eyes glued to her computer screen.

'You good to go?' he asked.

She lifted her gaze. 'Just clearing my emails.'

'I want to go out to where Armstrong had his crash last night. You okay with that?'

Hunter steered Grace out of the office and jockeyed her down the stairs, and then tossed her the keys to one of the team's unmarked cars. 'You drive, Grace.'

'Aye, aye, Captain,' she said, pointing the key fob at the blue Vauxhall Astra, popping the door locks.

He caught her playful smile as he jumped into the passenger side. As she climbed in beside him, he said, 'Sorry, Grace. I've got a million and one things on my mind this morning.'

'So have I, and not all of it's police work,' she responded, slotting the key into the ignition. 'I was reminded by the girls this morning there's no cereal left and David has asked me if there's any chance of us sitting down as a family and having an evening meal together any time in the near future.' She started the car.

Hunter tried to catch her gaze. 'Point made.'

'I forgive you, Sergeant.' She engaged gear. 'Anyway, don't you want to know how I've got on this morning?'

Hunter gave her an inquisitive look.

'I was given the job of tracking down who Guy Armstrong worked for.' Grace swung the car out of the station yard onto the main thoroughfare. 'Well, he wasn't freelance at all. For the last five years he's been employed at *The Star* in Sheffield. I've spoken with one of the newsroom editors and he tells me that he was one of their investigative reporters. And a good one at that, by all accounts. He told me that Armstrong was onto a hot lead with regards to the Lucy Blake-Hall murder and was planning to file copy this morning for this lunchtime's deadline. You can imagine he was in a bit of shock when I told him what had happened. He asked me if the accident was being investigated as suspicious. I tried to give him the usual bullshit about it being a fatal and as such would be investigated thoroughly, but don't be surprised if a few reporters start following us around.'

Hunter blew out a soft whistle. 'So, Guy Armstrong really was on to something.'

Grace picked up the road which led to Wentworth. The crash site was on a sharp bend half-a-mile outside the village.

Ten minutes later, as they were nearing the crash site, they spotted a liveried Range Rover, roof lights flashing, blocking their way. A small posse of journalists were huddled next to it.

Hunter nudged Grace and nodded. 'You were spot on about reporters,' he said.

Pulling alongside the Traffic car, Grace showed her warrant card to the driver and then zipped through a gap that led to the scene. The small country lane was littered with all manner of marked and unmarked cars.

Over the hedgerow to their right, where the field dipped down from the road and met a line of trees ten metres away, a large white forensic tent had been erected. Hunter spotted Dawn Leggate and Duncan Wroe disappearing inside it.

He slipped off his overcoat and quickly donned a protective suit. Grace followed, and the pair picked their way through a break in the hedgerow and down the embankment to join their colleagues.

Duncan was stood in the entranceway of the tent. His head was down and he was writing on his clipboard.

Hunter approached him. As usual Duncan's hair was unkempt, but this morning at least a good day's growth sprouted from his jawline and his eyes were red rimmed.

Hunter said, 'You look bleary-eyed, Duncan.'

'You would be as well if you'd only had four hours' sleep. Do you know what time I finished your job last night?'

Hunter shrugged.

'Ten o'clock, that's what time! And then I'd just got back to the office when they called me out to this. It was four a.m. before I crawled into bed, and then your gaffer dragged me back out an hour ago and told me they wanted me to go over this scene again.'

Hunter said, 'Just think of the overtime.'

'Pah! They don't pay me enough for this.'

Hunter blew into his hands. He was beginning to feel the cold. 'Anyway, Duncan, to digress a second, did you find anything at Jodie's place?'

'Lifted a few different sets of prints, you'll be pleased to learn. I'll try and get them off later today, though I don't think they belong to your burglar. I've recovered some fibres and it looks like he was wearing gloves.'

'Dare I ask you about The Barnwell Inn, where Jodie's body was found?'

'The answer is no. It's on my to-do list. With 101 other jobs. It might even have to go out to another team, depending on how long and how much I have to do here.' With that Duncan made an exaggerated stab with his pen onto his clipboard and stepped inside the tent.

Grace nudged Hunter and mouthed, 'Tetchy.'

Hunter held back a smirk as they moved into the tent.

The first thing Hunter noticed as he entered was the nauseating mixture of rubber, petrol and cooked pork and he swallowed hard. His eyes took in the scene. Guy Armstrong's Citroen C5 was a heap of charred metal. Wire framework was all that remained of the seats and Guy's body was still in the driver's seat, slumped forward over the melted remnants of the steering wheel, his chargrilled head welded into the framework. Guy Armstrong was no longer recognisable.

The concertinaed front end of the saloon was wedged into the trunk of a tree. The bark had also succumbed to the flames, and the ground around the base of the car was blackened and oily.

'It must have been one hell of a fire,' Hunter commented.

Looking up, Dawn Leggate said, 'A fireball is how the first fire officer on scene described it. The petrol tank exploded just as Fire Service got here. Guy Armstrong had no chance. Traffic didn't get here until the fire was almost out.'

'Any witnesses?' Hunter asked.

'Not to the accident. A couple driving back from the bistro in the village called 999. They said it was well ablaze when they came across it and there was no one else around. They hung on for the Fire Service and Traffic. Their call was logged at 11.09. Fire Service got here at 11.21. Traffic about ten minutes after that. They got Armstrong's details from the chassis number on the car. One of the Traffic Officers has already been to his address, but no one answered. One of the next-door-neighbours says he's lived on his own for as long as she's known him. We'll check on his personal status when we speak with his employers at *The Star* again.'

'Do we know if he'd been drinking? The message he left me on my voicemail said he was going to wait for me at the George and Dragon last night.'

'I got one of the Traffic lads to nip up there. The landlord confirms he was in there until late on. He remembers him because it was a quiet night, but he says he wasn't drunk when he left. He had a couple of pints and finished off with a couple of Cokes. Left just before 11, which, given the distance between here and the pub, ties in nicely with the timing of when his car was found by that couple.'

'And was it an accident?'

Duncan answered, 'Oh, the car was certainly involved in an accident. It has a dent to its rear offside and I've found remnants of its back-light cluster up there on the carriageway.' He pointed a finger up towards the road and then slowly traced it back. 'You can see the wheel ruts where it's crashed through the hedge, before colliding with this tree. As to the fire, however, that was definitely not caused by the accident. The petrol cap had been removed and I've found burnt remnants of cloth which had been pushed down inside the inlet pipe to the tank.' He recovered his clipboard. 'In terms of evidence, I'm afraid that so far we have very little. The entire surface of the car has been burned. We have the petrol cap, but all I've found on that is a couple of partial prints, which could be Guy Armstrong's, and some fibres, which indicate that someone has handled it with gloves on. There're quite a number of footprints around here, so I've photographed them and I'm going to take a number of casts. We might get lucky, but don't hold your breath — this place was swamped with Fire Service and Uniform last night. When I got here, everyone and their grandmother was trampling around the scene. Your best bet is if you can track down the vehicle that rear-ended Armstrong's car. At least we should be able to match paint samples.'

Dawn shook her head, announcing, 'Okay, no time for hanging around, we've got a murderer, or murderers, to catch.' She turned to Hunter and Grace. 'I want you two to go straight across to Guy Armstrong's place and see what you can find. If you can't find a key lying around, and he hasn't left one with neighbours, force entry. Get someone else to help you search.'

'What about Jodie's PM this afternoon?'

'It's not going ahead today, Hunter. The coroner rang Mr Robshaw this morning. He only got the message first thing, and we can't get hold of another pathologist to carry it out until tomorrow. To be honest it will give us a bit of breathing space, especially as headquarters have told us there are no more resources. There was a double fatal shooting yesterday evening in Sheffield, so we've got to make do with what we've got.'

'What about Task Force?'

'I've managed to snaffle one search team. The bulk of the team have been drafted into Sheffield for the shooting. It's believed to be gang related. I'm meeting with them here —' she paused and took a quick glance of her watch — 'in the next half hour or so. They're gonna do a search here first, and then I've earmarked them to go over to the Barnwell Inn to carry out an extensive search of the building and grounds.'

As they trudged back to the car, Grace mumbled, 'That's me in the bad books again when I get home tonight.' She turned to Hunter. 'Correction, *if* I get home tonight!'

Mike Sampson and Tony Bullars were already outside Guy Armstrong's 1970s semi by the time Hunter and Grace showed up.

'You've taken your time,' Mike said, as they got out of the car. 'We've checked the house and it's all locked up. And we've had a good look around to see if there's a spare key hidden away, but if he has, we can't find it.'

'We got tied up at the crash scene with the new gaffer,' Grace replied.

'What do you make of her?' asked Tony.

'I'm having difficulty understanding what she's saying,' said Mike. 'I'm having to watch back-to-back episodes of *Taggart* so that I can get to grips with her accent.' He paused then said, 'There's been a murderrrrrr,' exaggerating the rolling of his 'r's.

They all burst out laughing.

'You'd better not let her hear you say that,' said Grace. 'Anyway, I think she's lovely. It's just what you men need — a strong woman to put you in your places.'

The four of them split into two pairs and set about door knocking in the hope that one of Guy Armstrong's immediate neighbours might hold a spare key to his house. No one did. They did another check to see if he had hidden one away but didn't turn anything up.

Disappointed, Hunter said, 'No other option but to kick the door in.' He nodded to Tony. 'The back door looks the best bet, Bully.'

Using the heel of his foot, it took Tony half-a-dozen attempts before the lock finally gave way. With a resounding crack, the door crashed against the kitchen wall with the hasp shooting across the laminate floor.

'Right everyone,' said Hunter, stepping into the kitchen and slipping on a pair of latex gloves, 'we take a room each. I'll take the lounge.'

Unpleasant smells greeted him as he stepped further into the house. As he passed through the kitchen into the hallway, his nose picked up the stench of old cooking fat. The untidy work surfaces were spilling over with various plates and cups, stained by remnants of food, and a frying pan, which contained globules of furred fat floating on top of an oily surface.

Slowly opening the door into the lounge, the sight which met him was not pleasant. The pattern of the carpet was barely visible, every inch covered by a sea of paper. Some of it was torn handwritten sheets from notebooks, but the majority was from newspapers. The furniture in the room was piled high with books and more newspapers.

Hunter sighed. *This lot's going to take an eternity to sift through.*

As he scooped up a handful of papers from the floor, a cry came from upstairs. It was Mike Sampson.

'Get up here, you lot, and just have a butchers at this!'

Hunter took the stairs two at a time and met Mike on the landing. Grace and Tony were not far behind.

Mike was pointing into one of the rear bedrooms, the door of which was wide open.

Hunter poked his head inside. What he saw took him completely by surprise. The room had been kitted out as an office. It contained a desk and chair and a bookcase crammed with books. The desk overflowed with pile upon pile of handwritten notes. However, it was the stuff on the walls that grabbed his attention. Pasted, Sellotaped, stuck, and pinned to every conceivable inch of space on the walls was an array of photographs, newspaper cuttings, hand-drawn diagrams, and copious Post-it notes containing scribbled information. Some of them were new, but the majority had the patina signs of ageing.

Hunter turned to his colleagues. 'You know what this is, don't you? This is everything relating to the Lucy Blake-Hall case. This is Guy Armstrong's very own incident room.'

DAY TEN

The incident room was crammed to capacity for the morning briefing. More members of the cold case unit had been drafted in and Task Force were represented by an inspector and a sergeant. The two SIO's, Michael Robshaw and Dawn Leggate, stood side-by-side at the front of the room. Another incident board had joined those of Jeffery Howson's, Lucy Blake-Hall's and Jodie Marie Jenkinson's. This one was full of information and photographs from the fatal crash involving Guy Armstrong.

It had been 7 p.m., the previous evening, before Hunter, Grace, Mike and Tony had left Armstrong's house. They had uncovered newspaper cuttings and original black-and-white photographs chronicling every event from Lucy being reported missing up to the trial with guilty verdict of Weaver in 1984. They had spent almost seven hours going through Armstrong's collection but had only scratched the surface before calling it a day. They planned to continue sorting and cataloguing that morning.

Hunter highlighted all this when he addressed the room, following Robshaw's request for an update from him.

'It looks like Armstrong's laptop and Dictaphone are missing,' Hunter said. 'They were not found in his car and they are not at his home. It's his editor who's brought that to our attention. The editor assures me that he took them everywhere with him.'

'So that's one of the priorities,' said Robshaw. 'Find that laptop and Dictaphone and we should find out who our killer is. We already know that he had a lead on a story which was going to prove Daniel Weaver's innocence. Someone has gone to great pains to silence three people who all had stories to tell about the murder of Lucy. Everything seems to centre on that case and so that's where we are going to start. We strip everything back to that original investigation.

'I know some of the witnesses have died but we still have quite a number around. And now that we've managed to track them down, I want them all visiting. I also want everything we can get on Guy Armstrong. Not just recently, but what he was up to back in 1983, when he originally covered the Lucy Blake-Hall investigation. We are up against the clock on this.

Daniel Weaver's appeal court hearing is this Friday and I have no doubts he will be freed. In a few days' time, we are going to be under the spotlight. Every aspect of this current enquiry, as well as the original case into Lucy's murder, will be scrutinised. I don't need to emphasise the pressure this places on us all.'

Hunter, Grace and Mike pulled up at Guy Armstrong's house shortly before 10 a.m. and trooped down his drive, each holding an armful of exhibit bags.

Hunter opened up the back door with the new key the locksmith had supplied to him the previous evening. He was anticipating a long day. Ahead lay the task of cataloguing and collating the things they had discovered in the study, the lounge and the dining room. It didn't help that they were a team member down; Tony Bullars had been tasked with speaking with Lucy's parents and had set off with Carol Ragen to their home in Derbyshire.

The stale and musty smell greeted them once more, though, as Hunter opened the door into the kitchen, he thought that it wasn't as bad as yesterday. As he made for the stairs, he decided to leave it ajar and let some fresh air blow through.

Much of the paperwork from the floor and desk in the study had been stacked into piles the previous day, and today's mission was to sift through and record and bag the items relevant to the Lucy Blake-Hall investigation. As Hunter entered the small room and looked around, he knew that this was going to be a laborious task.

'Okay, let's get this organised,' he said. 'Mike, you record and log, and Grace and I will gather and bag.'

The team missed lunch, deciding to work through because they were making significant inroads, though they had munched through a sealed packet of biscuits they had found in Armstrong's kitchen cupboards and Grace had busied herself scouring out three mugs so that they could have a warm drink.

Hunter had almost cleared two of the room walls when a cry from Grace broke his concentration.

'Bloody hell, just look at what I've found!'

After confirming their visit with Lucy's parents, Tony Bullars and Carol Ragen took the route across the Strines to Bakewell. Richard and Margaret Hall's home was a pretty cottage built of Derbyshire stone and slate with rolling hillsides as a backdrop.

Richard Hall had the front door open before they had stepped through the garden gate. He greeted them with a warm smile and then stepped to one side to let them enter.

'Nice place,' said Tony, lowering his head to pass beneath the low-lintel front door and into the sitting room.

Two small sofas arranged in a broken L-shape just about filled the small room and Margaret Hall was sat in one. Slightly hunched forward, she had her hands clasped loosely together, resting in her lap. She had a bob of soft greying hair, which framed a well-rounded, cheery face.

Richard offered Tony and Carol the other sofa and then lowered himself into the space beside his wife.

'You said on the phone that you're re-investigating Lucy's murder?' Richard said, leaning into the arm of the sofa.

'Yes, that's right,' Tony answered.

'Does that mean Danny Weaver is innocent after all?' Margaret asked.

'I don't want to use those words, Mrs Hall. All I can say is that we have discovered something that casts doubt on what was presented at Weaver's original trial.'

Richard glanced sideways at his wife. Then he returned his gaze to Tony. 'Have you found Lucy?'

'No, but we're carrying out another search. You will be the first to know if we find Lucy. I promise you that.'

Carol met Margaret's eyes. 'Do you know something about Weaver that you didn't tell the police during the original enquiry?'

'Oh no. It's just that I was really surprised when those detectives told me that Danny had confessed to killing her. You see, I told those two detectives at the time that Lucy seemed to be so happy, especially those few days before she disappeared.'

Tony had been separating their witness statements for them to read. At this comment, he looked up from his folder. 'Did you see and talk with her regularly then, before she went missing?'

'Oh yes. I saw Lucy and Jessica, that's our granddaughter, at least three times a week. She'd come up to the house or we'd go into Barnwell shopping.'

'What, she'd come all this way?'

'No, no. We haven't always lived here. We used to live in Wortley. That's where Lucy was brought up. We lived on Constable Row, just behind the church. We came here a couple of years after the trial. We couldn't bear staying in the same village anymore. We came here with Jessica.'

'Tell them the truth, Margaret,' Richard butted in. 'We couldn't abide to be anywhere near that supercilious husband of hers.' He switched his look between Tony and Carol. 'We found stuff out about him that never came out in the trial. It was no wonder she was unhappy.'

Tony said, 'Now you've lost me. Margaret, you said Lucy was happy just before she disappeared and Richard, you've just said she was unhappy.'

'Lucy never told us anything,' Richard replied. 'We've found out stuff about Peter from Amanda, Lucy's best friend from school. We never realised the half of it.' He shot a quick sideways glance at his wife again. 'It was heart-breaking for us. Have you spoken to Amanda? She's a sergeant up in Cumbria. Married with a daughter herself now. She's kept in touch with us over the years. In fact, we rang her last night when we knew you were coming.'

'I wished we'd have known you were still in touch with her,' Tony said. 'It could have saved us a lot of time. You wouldn't believe the effort we've put in to track everyone down from the original enquiry. Someone has spoken to her on the phone and we've made arrangements to see her in the next day or so.'

'Well, she'll be able to tell you a lot more about Lucy and what went off,' Richard said. 'We've found out little bits from her over the years that have shocked us, I can tell you, but we don't think she's told us everything, because she didn't want to upset us any further.'

'If you could just tell us what you know that's relevant about Lucy's disappearance, it would help us immensely,' Tony said.

'Where do you want me to begin?' Richard asked.

Tony opened his notebook. 'Shall we start where she met Peter, and I'll nudge you from time to time if I need you to elaborate on anything.'

Clearing his throat, Richard said, 'Lucy met Peter just before her 17th birthday. He was older than her, early 20s, but to be honest that didn't bother us, especially when we first met him. He was well turned out, polite and acted a lot more mature than some of the other boys Lucy was friends with. We'd never met him before — he lived at Thurgoland with his gran, but he used to come to The Wortley Arms drinking. That's where he met Lucy. She was underage to drink but it's such a small village that the landlord used to let her and a few mates go in there and just have soft drinks. When she first introduced him to us, Peter was working as a mechanic and as a side-line, he bought and sold his own cars. He was a good worker and always seemed to have plenty of money. Lucy was certainly happy with him back then. Then we heard one or two whispers about him.'

Tony glanced up. 'Whispers?'

'The landlord at the Wortley Arms and a couple of regulars in there said to keep an eye on Peter. They told that his dad was a rum 'un. That he was in prison because he'd killed someone. We decided not to say anything to our Lucy. We just hoped the relationship would run its course and they'd finish, but it didn't. Lucy got caught with Jessica and then Peter asked if he could marry her. What could we say? We mentioned to Lucy what we'd heard about Peter's dad and she said he'd told that his dad had broken into a shop in Sheffield and had got caught by the owner and that he'd killed him in a fight.' Richard paused. 'He's dead himself now. Stabbed in prison, I think. Peter and Lucy went to his funeral.'

Tony made a few quick notes. 'Tell me about Peter and Lucy's marriage.'

'It was a rushed job. A registry office wedding, three months before Jessica was born. I have to say that back then Peter was good to her. He got together enough money for a deposit for an old cottage in the next village at Tankersley. For the first year of their marriage he worked really hard. He began making quite a bit of money importing cars from Germany. BMWs and Mercedes, if I recall. Then in the second year of their marriage he bought a big old nightclub near Wakefield, spent thousands doing it up, and changed it into a private members' club.

'That's when we noticed the cracks beginning to appear in the marriage. Peter seemed to be out all hours. Then we found out the club Peter owned was in fact a strip club. We were mortified. We tried hard not to interfere, but felt we needed to talk with Lucy about it. When we did, we could see that she wasn't happy about it herself, but she stuck up for him. She just kept saying that Peter was working very hard because he wanted to make lots of money for them. Sure enough, he did that, and he bought an old farmhouse, just outside the village, which he had done up for Lucy and Jessica, but we could see things weren't right.

'Then, a few months before Lucy disappeared, we noticed a difference in her. For about a year, her regular visits had dropped off. Then, around June time in 1983, she started turning up two or three times a week again, just like she used to, and she was her old self again. So bubbly. Of course, what we didn't know at the time was that she was having an affair with Danny Weaver, and that was the reason for her happiness.'

'And that's why I was so surprised when those two detectives came to our house that Sunday evening and told us he had confessed to killing Lucy,' added Margaret. 'She was so happy in the months and weeks leading up to her disappearance. It was such a shock when we learned how long things had been going on between her and Danny. Although Amanda did cushion us from some of it.'

'Did Amanda know about it all then?'

'Oh yes. Lucy and Amanda were like that.' Margaret formed her index and middle finger into an X. 'Lucy told Amanda everything. Amanda told us that Peter had started knocking Lucy about. Though she never said that in the witness box. Apparently it wasn't relevant!'

Tony held her look. 'What do you mean, not relevant?'

'I don't know. Those two detectives who were in charge of the case told Amanda to just talk about Lucy's affair with Danny. Supposedly, that was all the judge wanted to hear. I've spoken with her many times since then and she says now that she wished she'd mentioned that Peter had beaten Lucy.

'Since the trial, we don't have anything to do with Peter. It isn't just because of what went off with Lucy, but what he has done to our Jessica. We looked after Jessica once Danny was charged. Peter just said it would be for the best while he got his head around everything. Then after the trial he asked us if we would adopt Jessica, because she reminded him too much of Lucy and he wanted to just forget it all and start a new life.' Margaret shook her head. 'How can a father do that to his daughter? She's had some terrible nightmares. In the end we had to take her to a psychologist. She doesn't have anything to with her father now. Good riddance, that's what I say.'

Tony offered a sympathetic look. 'Just one more question. Peter's name, Blake-Hall? Is the Hall part of his name a coincidence?'

'No, that was Peter's idea before they got married. He was called Blake. He thought changing it to a double-barrelled one would be good for his business.'

Michael Robshaw had called evening briefing early. By 7 p.m., everyone had returned to the incident room. Robshaw opened by announcing, 'I'm going to bring in Detective Superintendent Leggate first. She went to Jodie Jenkinson's second post-mortem this afternoon.'

Dawn was standing alongside Robshaw. She said, 'The second PM has uncovered something which was not picked up the first time around. Under different lighting conditions, the pathologist has discovered bruising beneath the skin of both wrists, consistent with Jodie being restrained. Her skin has been swabbed for DNA. Secondly, I can confirm she was not a drug user. There are only two needle puncture sites over her entire body, and those are on her left arm. One of those missed the vein, the other didn't. Again, we've taken DNA swabs. So, it looks as though someone restrained her, either by taking hold of her wrists, or by using something, and then injected her with a lethal dose of purer than normal street heroin.'

'So that's where we are with Jodie,' Robshaw said, taking back briefing. 'Hunter, I want to bring you in now. Tell everyone what you and Grace found at Armstrong's place today.'

Hunter picked up an aged yellowing newspaper and held it aloft for everyone to get a good look. The large headline made for a powerful statement. The word 'BUTCHERED' was only slightly smaller than the newspaper masthead. 'This edition of the *Sheffield Telegraph* is dated the fifth of October, 1974 and outlines the story of the murders of Frank and Cynthia Pendlebury. They ran their own small family jewellery business in Attercliffe. Early morning of the fifth, they were found dead by an officer. He found the shop's front door open. Frank's body was found just behind the counter, and his wife Cynthia was found at the top of the stairs just inside the entrance to their flat. Both had been stabbed several times. At the bottom of this article there is a quote from a DCI Burrows, who was leading the enquiry, to the effect that the case was being treated as murder, and that it was believed that Frank and Cynthia had disturbed robbers at their premises.'

Hunter tapped several more newspapers that lay across his desk. 'These papers here all contain follow-up articles relating to the murders. To summarise them, the safe in the Pendlebury's shop had been blown open and a large quantity of jewellery had been stolen. They mention the search for the robbers and have the usual stuff the papers put out about any manhunt. But this one —' he said, putting down the broadsheet he was holding and then picking up another from the top — 'contains the story of the arrest of three men for the murders.'

Hunter showed everyone the front page. It bore the headline 'MURDER SUSPECTS DETAINED.' 'This edition is dated a week later, and describes the raids on two homes, the discovery of items of jewellery and the arrest of three men. The names of the suspect are not revealed, as per protocol. However, down the side of the article, written in pen, are three names.' Hunter tapped the edge of the newssheet. 'From other samples of handwriting, we believe this is Guy Armstrong's writing. He has entered the names of George Blake, Peter Blake and Ronald Bishop.' He tapped the pile of papers again. 'Later editions outline that a George Blake, 39 years old, from Sheffield, was charged with the murders of Frank and Cynthia Pendlebury, and on the 20th January 1975, he pleaded guilty at Sheffield Crown Court and was given a life sentence.'

Robshaw held up a hand. 'I'll just stop you there for now, Hunter, because I want to bring in Tony. Tony, you went to see Lucy's parents over in Bakewell this afternoon. Tell the team what you learned from them.'

Tony repeated what Richard and Margaret Hall had said. 'They told us that Peter Blake-Hall changed his name by deed poll after his marriage to Lucy. He was born Peter Blake.'

Robshaw said, 'Today's enquiries have turned up some very interesting information. It doesn't solve who murdered Jeffery Howson, Jodie Jenkinson, Guy Armstrong and Lucy Blake-Hall, but I think it takes us down another avenue regarding the suspects. It also provides the answers as to why Guy Armstrong had so much of a fixation with the Lucy Blake-Hall enquiry, and why he'd given so much of his time carrying out his own investigation into Daniel Weaver's trial. He knew from the outset that something wasn't right. Now all we've got to do is determine who actually killed these four. And although we still mustn't lose sight of uncovering Alan Darbyshire's role in all this, today's enquiries have thrown up another possible lead — Lucy's husband.'

Robshaw rattled off a long list of tasks, writing them up on the dry-wipe boards and checking back with everyone.

One of the key tasks was to see if DCI Burrows, who had been in charge of the Pendlebury murders, was still around to discuss the case. Barry Newstead volunteered for that job. He told the room that 'Ted' Burrows had been his DCI when he had been attached to Headquarters Serious Crime Squad in the early 1980s, and that although he knew he had retired in the 90s, he believed he was still living somewhere in Sheffield.

DAY ELEVEN

Hunter got into the office shortly after 7a.m. and was surprised to find the place bustling with detectives. It had been a while since he'd seen it this full; generally, he was first in, with a good quarter of an hour at least to himself.

He booted up his computer and checked through his emails. Among them was an update regarding 'Chicken George' — the homeless man who occasionally dossed down in the old Barnwell Inn. There had been a sighting of him around Barnsley town centre and officers had been instructed to watch out for him.

Hunter felt a tap on his shoulder. He looked up as Grace slid past him, dumping her handbag and coat onto her desk.

'Cutting it a bit fine,' Hunter said, looking at his watch. 'Domestic issues?'

'Nightmare of a morning,' she responded, slumping into her seat. 'I'd forgotten it was the school Christmas party and disco today. Both girls were on my case. I ended up losing my rag with them. And then to cap it all David wanted me to iron him a shirt for work. I tell you, I'm up to here this morning. The sooner this enquiry is put to bed, the better. If it goes on much longer, I can see me heading for the divorce courts.'

Hunter smiled. 'Deep breaths, Grace. Deep breaths. You get yourself sorted and I'll get you a coffee. The only job we've got today is to finish off at Guy Armstrong's house. We've lost Mike and Tony because they've got other jobs, but you and I should break the back of it by mid-afternoon and then you can take a flyer. I'll finish off here and stay for de-brief.'

'Are you sure about that? I would really appreciate it.'

'Sure I'm sure. That's what kind-hearted sergeants are here for.' He winked.

Hunter and Grace entered Guy Armstrong's house shortly after 10 a.m. They had one remaining room to search — the lounge.

Hunter had given the room a fleeting look during their first visit and now getting a second view of it he let out an exasperated sigh. Stack upon stack of papers filled every nook and cranny. There was barely an inch of floor space showing.

Hunter and Grace exchanged looks.

'This is going to take ages,' said Hunter.

Grace smiled. 'It's a good job you've got someone as organised as me on your team.'

As Hunter began sorting through the various piles, he soon realised that hardly anything was relevant to their investigations, but after an hour and a half, he spotted a pile of A4 colour photographs. He called out, 'Bloody hell! Just look what I've found, Grace.' The three photographs were a sequence of shots taken only seconds apart. They depicted three men standing close together on the top of some steps, at the front of what appeared to be a club entrance. They appeared to be stills of an argument between two of the men. The clarity was exceptional and there was no mistaking who the two arguing were — Alan Darbyshire and Peter Blake-Hall. It looked like Blake-Hall was stabbing a finger into Alan Darbyshire's chest. But it was the third man, who was looking-on, who especially caught his eye. Hunter couldn't be certain, but he was a similar height and build to the man who had assaulted him. *Now this is interesting*, he told himself, scooping up the photographs.

At the front of the incident room, Robshaw bounced on the balls of his feet. In an elated voice, he said, 'Not one, but two breakthroughs today. Firstly, Road Policing Unit took a call from a man who lives in Wentworth. He's told them that about 11 o'clock on Monday night, he'd just let his dog out and was standing on his doorstep when a dark coloured four-by-four went speeding past, travelling towards Harley. Although he wasn't able to clock its reg, he's said it was a Mitsubishi Shogun Sport with blacked-out windows. That could link with the car spotted at the bottom of Jeffery Howson's garden on the evening we believe he was murdered. For the second piece of good news, I'm going to hand over to Hunter.'

Hunter held up two of the photographs he had recovered from Guy Armstrong's place. He said, 'I found these in Armstrong's lounge.' He separated the photos, placing one in each hand and continued, 'I think you can all make out that these feature Alan Darbyshire, and the person who is poking him in the chest is Peter Blake-Hall. The third person, who has his back towards us, is the same size and shape as the man I disturbed at

Jodie's. On the back of the photos, the names of Alan Darbyshire and Peter Blake-Hall have been penned, plus one other, Ronald Fisher.'

'I can see what you're all thinking,' said Robshaw. 'But there's just one more person I want to bring in before I outline what the next lines of enquiry are.' He turned to Barry Newstead. 'Barry, you've spoken with retired DCI Burrows today.'

Barry responded, 'Yeah boss, I caught up with Ted Burrows earlier today at his home in Ecclesfield. He's 74 now, but his mind is still sharp as a knife and he can certainly remember the Pendlebury case. Ted says it really was a vicious attack. The couple had over 50 stab wounds between them and in old man Pendlebury's case, his head had almost been severed.

'The robbers had got away with quite a bit of gear. As well as some of the jewellery from the displays, the safe had been expertly blown and emptied. The Pendleburys, however, had kept good records. The couple had described all their stock in a ledger upstairs, which meant that the investigation team were able to compile a list of what had been stolen and get it circulated quite quickly. Within a couple of days, they were given a name of someone who was trying to sell on some of the stuff — Ronnie Fisher.

'Ronnie was known to Sheffield police, but only as a car thief. He'd been pulled a few times and got 12 months for nicking a couple of cars when he was 15. Ted says that once they started doing some digging about him, they learned that a few months before the Pendlebury job, there was a rumour circulating that he'd stabbed a man during a pub fight. The man he'd supposedly stabbed was himself a well-known villain, with a bit of a hard-man reputation. He was more than happy to grass on Ronnie Fisher. He not only confirmed that Ronnie had stabbed him in the shoulder and in the leg, after an argument over a girl, but he also told the team that it was all round the grapevine that Ronnie had been involved in the Pendlebury robbery and was desperate to get rid of the gear.

'He not only dropped Ronnie's name but also George Blake and his son Peter. In George's case, everything fitted together. They had lots of intelligence about him. He'd done time in his early 20s for house and shop burglary and had apparently learned how to blow safes during his first prison spell. In the early 70s, there'd been a spate of safe-jobs at working men's clubs up and down the country and George's name had been put forward on quite a few occasions, but the evidence hadn't been there to convict. There was also a rumour that he was doing jobs down in London for some of the gangs there.

'The team raided George's house in High Green and Ronnie Fisher's mum's house at Ecclesfield. Peter Blake lived with his dad back then. He was an apprentice mechanic working for a local garage. Although they didn't find any of the stolen jewellery at their homes, they had info about a lock-up garage which Ronnie used and they searched that as well. It was there they found most of the gear. All three were arrested and the upshot was that George confessed.

'Ted Burrows tells me it took the team completely by surprise as to how quickly George rolled over and admitted everything. There were a lot of inconsistencies in George's story, but no matter how hard they pushed him, he stuck to his confession. Even when they charged him, they believed he was only admitting it to protect his son and Ronnie.

'They pulled Peter and Ronnie in on several occasions, but they couldn't get a cough out of the pair — both alibied one another and George indicated he was happy to plead guilty to the Pendlebury murders. In 1975, he got life. Ted Burrows told me they were convinced that it had been Ronnie who'd murdered the Pendleburys. They did a couple of prison visits to George, but he stuck to his story and then, in September 1998, he was found dead in his cell. Someone had cut his throat. They never found who'd done it.

'That's it regarding those murders, but I'll tell you what else I've found. In 1986, there were several entries in our intelligence system linking Peter and Ronnie to drugs. It's low-grade intelligence from a couple of users, and it's not supported by hard information, but they all state the same thing — that they were bringing in amphetamines from Holland and banging it out in Wigan and Leeds at night venues.

'Now, we've already been told that Peter was importing cars from Germany during the 1980s. The suggestion was that he was bringing in the drugs hidden inside those cars. As I say, none of the intelligence is corroborated by any of the agencies and there's nothing on the system indicating if it was acted upon or not.'

'Until now, we haven't listed Peter Blake-Hall or Ronnie Fisher as suspects,' interjected Robshaw. 'From now on, all that changes. Thanks

Barry, you've done some good digging there.' Robshaw rubbed his hands together. 'Okay everyone, time to draw up fresh lines of enquiry.'

DAY TWELVE

Hunter intercepted Grace the moment she entered the office. 'Don't take your coat off,' he said, grabbing her by the elbow. 'Full day for us today, partner. Loads to do.'

'What, not even time for a cuppa?'

'Nope.' He led her back through the doors and down the stairwell to the car park.

'Not even time to put on my lippy?'

He glanced back at her, rolling his eyes. 'By the way, how did your evening go? Back in the good books again?'

'Oh yeah, great thanks. The family thing didn't work out exactly as I'd planned — the girls went around to their mates — but it did give me and Dave some time to catch up. We even cooked together. That's the first time we've done that for what seems ages. And I got to wrap up some of the girls' Christmas presents.'

'Crikey Grace, I hadn't even thought of Christmas.'

'Anyway,' said Grace, pulling open the passenger door, 'how did briefing go last night?'

Hunter started the engine. He told her what Barry had revealed, watching her face light up. 'Good stuff, eh? It's certainly opened up the enquiry now. Everyone's buzzing this morning.' He dropped his folder onto Grace's lap and tapped it. 'I've managed to snaffle us a nice trip out for the day. We've been given the job of speaking to Amanda Rawlinson, Lucy's old school friend. I spoke with her first thing and she's day off today, so the timing's perfect.'

Hunter drove out of the yard, heading in the direction of the motorway. 'But before that, we've got a deviation to make into Sheffield. They've tracked down "Chicken George" to a homeless shelter. George apparently booked in late yesterday afternoon. I've managed to get two PCSOs down there and they're babysitting him so he doesn't do a runner. Also, we've confirmed that George had been staying at the old inn where Jodie was found. Task Force found a couple of carrier bags containing some of his stuff in the loft during their search yesterday. There was an old mattress up there and some other bits of furniture as well. It looks as though he was using the place regularly. The sergeant says that it looks as though George made a quick exit. I've got my fingers crossed it's because he saw something which scared him off.'

'That'd be good if he has. Why's he called Chicken George?'

Hunter smiled. 'I asked my old mate that. He walks the beat where George used to live. He tells me George used to own this big sprawling house with quite a bit of land, which he ran as a smallholding, breeding chickens, but the council took out a possession order against him, because it was slap bang in the middle of where they needed to run a new bypass. He held the council off with a shotgun and we had to get involved. He was headline news for the best part of a week. Some of the locals held a demonstration around his property in support. The upshot was that eventually they managed to talk him around and he gave himself up. He was compensated and the council re-housed him but he wasn't allowed to breed his chickens anymore and ended up becoming a bit of a drinker and a recluse. In the early 90s, he started dossing around the town centre, worse for wear in drink and caused quite a few problems for shopkeepers and stallholders in the market. In the end he got locked up a couple of times and did a short spell in prison.

'Aw, that's really sad.'

'*C'est la vie*, Grace, *c'est la vie*,' Hunter responded, turning onto the M1.

The charity-run homeless building was on the edge of the city, close to Hallam University. Hunter managed to find a parking place in one of the side streets.

They were greeted by a thin, wiry man with wavy ginger hair. Hunter showed him his warrant card and the man said, 'You're here for George.'

'Yeah, someone called us last night,' Hunter replied. 'I sent a couple of PCSOs just to make sure he hung around.'

The man swung open a door. 'I've put them in a room down there,' he said, pointing down the corridor. 'They're having a cuppa with him. Can I ask what you want to see him about? Has he done something wrong? Not that I'm nosy, but we have responsibility for him while he's here. '

'I can understand that,' said Hunter, slipping his warrant card back into his pocket. 'As far as we know he's not done anything wrong, but we think he might have witnessed an incident at a place he was dossing down in.'

'I'll show you where they are,' answered the man, setting off down the dim corridor. 'He's not too good, is George. He's been sleeping rough under the railway arches, and the drink's got hold of him now. He's in a sorrier state than when I last saw him here.' The man paused by a door at the far end of the corridor. 'They're all in here,' he said, opening the door and standing to one side to allow Hunter and Grace through.

As Hunter stepped into the room, two things greeted him. The first was the smell — a dirty, unclean, and unpleasant stench of decay and stale body odour, and the second was the heat, which emphasised the pong. He crinkled his nose.

Hunched forward in a well-worn wing-back chair, was the saddest looking human Hunter had set his eyes on in a long time.

George glanced up. His face was sallow and waxen and Hunter couldn't help but notice his tinted yellow eyes. His collar-length unruly hair was a mix of greys and he had a thin, wispy beard. His clothes had seen better days and the trousers were heavily stained, especially around the crotch area. It looked as though he had wet himself, thought Hunter. On his feet was a pair of new-looking fawn slippers and Hunter guessed the centre had provided him with those.

Hunter nodded to the two male PCSOs who were standing by a wide-open window, their faces close to the gap, breathing in fresh air. It was their cue to go, and they seemed only too happy to leave Hunter and Grace to it.

Hunter took a deep breath, pulled another wing-back chair from the side and placed it in front of George. Grace made her way to the open window.

'George, do you know who I am?'

'A detective, I'm guessing. Those two young coppers said CID wanted a word with me.'

'In a way that's right, but we're not exactly CID. We're from the Major Investigation Team at Barnwell. We're making enquiries into a murder.'

'Oh aye, and what's that to do with me? I ain't killed no one.'

'I'm sure you didn't, George, but I think you know why I'm here, don't you?'

Hunter was watching him carefully. George's yellow eyes darted towards him and then just as quickly turned away. That exchange was enough. Hunter said, 'George, you've been sleeping rough at the old Barnwell Inn recently, haven't you?'

George made a grunting noise.

'You've been sleeping in the loft. I know that because we found some of your stuff up there.'

George shrugged. 'No harm in that.'

'No, of course not, but I'm interested in why you left so quickly.' Hunter searched his face again. 'Shall I tell you what I think, George? I think you left so sharpish, because you saw something which scared you.'

The yellow eyes met Hunter's.

'I'm right, aren't I, George? Come on, tell us.'

'Din't see nothing.'

'I've been in this job a long time and I know when someone is not telling me the truth.'

George lowered his head so that Hunter could no longer see his face.

'Come on, George, you saw a girl get hurt there, didn't you?'

'Din't see nothing.'

'Well, maybe you didn't see, but you heard something.'

George glanced up. He had squeezed his yellow sunken eyes to slits.

'Please, George, we really need your help.' Hunter waited for a few seconds. 'What if I tell you that we know what went off, and we have a fair idea who killed her but we just need confirmation. Come on, George, you can do that, can't you? What if I show you some pictures of the people who we think killed the girl?'

Hunter reached into his folder and pulled out one of the photographs of Alan Darbyshire, Peter Blake-Hall and Ronald Fisher that he had found at Guy Armstrong's. He thrust it in front of George's face, making him jump.

'George, please help me. This is really important. A young girl lost her life in that pub and this is a photograph we have of the three people who we think killed her.'

George seemed to study the photograph.

Hunter said, 'What if I say what you tell us stays in this room? No one will know what you've told us. This is just between us three.'

George lifted his head and eyed Hunter suspiciously.

'Promise, George. Just help me out and we'll leave you in peace.'

George shook his head, answering, 'Just two.'

Hunter tapped the photo. 'Two people in this photo? Is that what you mean?'

George nodded. 'Yeah, just two, not three.'

'Can you point out which two for me, George?'

A grubby hand with dirt beneath the fingernails hovered over the photograph for a couple of seconds. Then he stabbed an index finger at two of the images.

'Those two. They carried the young lass in. I heard them pull up in their big car and then I heard her screaming. I looked out of the window. They were dragging her. Then they disappeared inside with her. I heard screaming some more and then everything went quiet. I hid upstairs. I was shit-scared. Then they left without her. I didn't see what they had done to her, but I guessed it must have been something bad, 'cos they took off so quickly.'

'When you say they had a big car, George, what do you mean by that?'

'One of them big four-by-four things. A big black 'un with blacked-out windows.'

Hunter tapped the photograph. 'And you're quite sure it was these two you saw dragging the girl into the pub?'

George nodded.

Hunter and Grace left the centre. Hunter stood on the damp pavement for a second looking up into the murky grey sky. He started smiling.

Grace said, 'I don't know why you're looking so smug. We can't use any of that, you know?'

''Course I realise that, Grace, but what other way were we going to get out of him what we did? You can see the life he leads. How is he going to make a good witness? Do you think he'd stick around if we told him we wanted him to be a witness at Jodie's murder trial? Didn't you notice his eyes? They were yellow. That's a sign his liver's packing up. Even if we were to get him as a witness, he'd probably never live long enough for the trial. He's probably looking at another few months at best.' Hunter shook his head, tapping his folder tucked beneath his arm. 'No, that was the best way of doing it. Now we know who killed her. We've just got to get the evidence, that's all.'

He set off back to where he had parked the car.

Within minutes of entering Derwentwater, Hunter found the address they were looking for. Lethargic after the long drive, Hunter pulled himself out of the car and indulged in a wide stretch. A cold snap of wind whipped past his cheeks and ears, bringing about an instant freshness. He leaned back into the car, retrieving his folder from the back seat and turned toward the house.

A pebbled-concrete path led to a porch-covered front door. Hunter pressed the bell.

Amanda Rawlinson greeted them with a warm smile. 'I bet you two could do with a warm cuppa.' She beckoned them inside and said, 'It's DS Kerr and DC Marshall, isn't it? Come on in, we'll go into the kitchen, its warmer in there — the range is on.'

Hunter and Grace followed Amanda into a kitchen that was dominated by a large Aga set into a feature fireplace. A solid oak table with four chairs sat in the middle of the room.

Amanda pulled out one of the chairs. 'Please, take a seat,' she offered. 'I'll just put the kettle on.' She filled a kettle and set it on the Aga. 'I'm so glad to hear you've re-opened Lucy's case.' She dropped some teabags into a teapot. 'It's just been on the one o'clock news by the way,' she continued, bringing three cups together, pouring a drop of milk in each. 'There wasn't much about it on, just the fact that Daniel Weaver had been granted leave to appeal and was being allowed out on bail. I guess there'll be a longer piece about it on tonight's news.'

It didn't take long for the water to boil and Amanda soon brought three steaming cups to the table. She pointed to the sugar bowl in the middle. 'Help yourselves,' she said.

Hunter slipped off his coat and hung it on the back of the chair. Then, from his folder, he retrieved a copy of Amanda's witness statement from 25 years earlier.

'Is that my statement?' she asked, sitting down opposite Hunter and Grace. She pulled one of the mugs towards her.

Hunter nodded. 'I'm not going to show it you just yet, Amanda, because as you'll appreciate, we're speaking with every witness as though it was the first time. I know it was a long time ago now, but I'm sure there'll be a lot you still remember without me needing to show you your statement.'

'That suits me fine, because if I remember rightly the two detectives who took my statement never put in everything I told them anyway.' Amanda looked from Hunter to Grace. 'There were quite a few times when I'd tell them something, and the sergeant, I don't recall his name now, just kept saying that wasn't relevant because they'd got somebody locked up for it and he'd confessed. Of course, knowing what I know now, with the job and everything, I realise it should have gone in, and that I should have said a lot more than I did do in the witness box. But I was so naïve back then — I was only 22. And I've thought about this a lot just lately, especially when I heard you were re-opening the case. I can't make my mind up whether those two detectives were just being lazy or there was more to it. I mean, I was really surprised when they first told me that it was Danny Weaver who'd murdered Lucy.'

'Why do you say that?' asked Grace.

'Well, for the last few months before Lucy disappeared, all she ever talked to me about was Danny. And he didn't sound like someone who wanted to harm her. Now, if it had been Peter, well that would be different.'

'Peter, her husband?' said Grace. Amanda nodded and took a sip of her tea. 'He used to bash her about, didn't he?'

Amanda's hazel eyes searched out Grace's. 'God, he was a right bully. She showed me some of the bruises he used to leave her with. He used to punch her at the top of her arm or in the back, near her kidneys, where it didn't show. He was a right bastard. When she told me about Danny, I told her to go for it. She seemed so happy.'

'When did you first meet Lucy?' Grace asked.

'We met at Barnwell Comp. We hit it off in the first year — sat next to each other. We went through five years of school together. In fact, we went everywhere together.'

'And you were around when she met Peter?'

'Yeah. A gang of us would go up to the Wortley Arms on a Thursday and Friday to meet up once we'd finished school. Peter used to be in there with a couple of his mates and after a few weeks he got around to chatting Lucy up. He was different back then. Or at least, he seemed it. There were the rumours of course, about his dad being in prison for killing someone, but that was his dad, not Peter. He always had lots of money, and he was quite generous with it, 'cos we were always skint. He was a mechanic at a local garage and he told us he made some extra money by buying cars and doing them up.'

'When was this?'

'1978 it was. Next thing, Lucy told me she was late, you know, thought she was pregnant — she was of course. Then they got married at Barnsley Register Office. I was her chief bridesmaid. Peter had bought a place in the village. It was a lovely cottage. Then Jessica was born.'

'And everything was okay between her and Peter at that point?'

'Oh yes, really good for a couple of years. I was working for the local council back then, but I'd see her at least three times a week and we'd catch up. Peter worked long hours and made lots of money and he bought a bigger house — an old farmhouse. It needed some work on it but Peter paid for it and Lucy oversaw the building work. It was a beautiful home by the time they finished. He also bought an old working man's club out near Wakefield — the one he still has — though I didn't know at the time he was turning it into a strip club. When Lucy told me about it and she learned what it was, she wasn't happy. That was when things started to go wrong with the marriage. It was probably about six months after him opening the club when she first told me he'd hit her.'

'How did she tell you?'

'I can't remember exactly how she told me, but she said that she'd suspected he was seeing someone and thought it was one of the girls. She said that they'd rowed one night and he'd hit her. I didn't see the marks but she told me he'd blacked her eye and she'd had to stay indoors for almost a week. I wanted her to go to the police, but she wouldn't. She said she daren't. She told me that even if he was locked up, she still wouldn't be safe 'cos he would set Ronnie on to her.'

'Ronnie?'

'Ronnie Fisher. He was Peter's best mate. They went everywhere together. I never liked Ronnie. Have you not come across him?'

'He's just featured in our enquiry,' said Hunter.

'Now, if they'd have told me Ronnie had killed Lucy, and not Danny, then I could have believed that.'

'Why do you say that?' Hunter asked.

'Just intuition I guess, but there was just something about him. The way he acted. The way he looked.' Amanda shuddered.

Grace continued, 'But you never saw Ronnie being violent?'

'No, I didn't. But I heard that he'd stabbed someone once. Over a girl, I think. I was always wary of him. We all were.'

'Okay, moving on. When did you first learn about Danny Weaver?'

'Again, I can't remember an exact date or anything. It was roughly six months before she disappeared, so I suppose it would be around March time of 1983. I suddenly saw a change in Lucy's mood — really upbeat, the way she used to be. I did know of Daniel; I'd met him before because he'd been doing some of the work on Peter and Lucy's house and I think he did a bit of driving work for Peter. Peter used to bring cars in from Germany, some tax fiddle, and Danny was one of the drivers.

'There was no doubt Lucy was happier in herself and Danny was a real good looker. And he had a nice personality. If I'm honest, I was a bit jealous at the time. Now I look back and feel a bit sad about things. I mean, I used to think she was so lucky. She had the big house, loads of money, but I now know I was the lucky one. I was the one never covered in bruises.'

Grace gave her an understanding look. 'Did Lucy tell you any details of her relationship with Danny?'

'Not as such. I did know that when she met up with Danny she left Jessica with her mum and dad on the pretence of doing some shopping. And I have to confess that a couple of times I looked after Jessica for her.'

'Did she ever mention if she thought Peter knew about the relationship?'

Amanda shook her head. 'Nope, though she did once tell me that Danny had asked her to run away with him. Start afresh.'

'When was that? Can you remember?'

'No, sorry. Though it was pretty close to the time she disappeared.'

Hunter looked up from his notes. 'Amanda, a couple of times now you've used the word disappeared instead of murdered or killed. Is there something you know about Lucy going missing?'

She returned a thoughtful look. 'No. I guess I've said it subconsciously, that's all. I'm not hiding anything, if that's what you mean. It's only because they've never found her body, have they? The last time she was seen was in the marketplace that Friday night. And yes, I know people saw her arguing with Danny. But that was it. No one saw him attacking her or manhandling her.'

'Do you think she's dead?' Hunter asked.

'Deep down, I do. Especially after all this time. We were such close friends that if she were still alive, I'm convinced she would have contacted me before now. And she absolutely doted on Jessica. Jessica was her world. No, I'm sure she's dead.'

'And who would you put money on killing her?'

'I don't want to point the finger, and I don't know what evidence you've got, but knowing what I know now, I think I'd be looking at Peter and Ronnie.' She switched her gaze between Hunter and Grace again. 'And that's what I told those two detectives all those years back, especially after she told me that she was going to tell Peter about the pregnancy.'

'The pregnancy?'

Amanda frowned. 'Yes. Isn't that recorded anywhere? Lucy was pregnant with Danny's baby. That's why she went into town to meet him that Bank Holiday Friday. She was going to tell him.'

DAY THIRTEEN

Staring across the MIT office, Hunter stifled a yawn. He had struggled to drop off last night and had awoken well before dawn this morning, his brain replaying everything he had learned yesterday. He was eagerly awaiting the 8 a.m. briefing as he and Grace hadn't been able to get back in time for the previous evening's debrief.

He caught sight of Grace coming into the office and he watched her make a path to the kettle. He acknowledged her with a raised hand as he clicked open his email list. He had one waiting for him from Duncan Wroe, with the bold title of 'Prints identified'. Hurriedly, he opened it and scanned the short text. His face lit up as Grace delivered his tea. 'They've identified some of the prints found at Jodie's flat.'

She raised her eyebrows.

'Kerri-Ann Bairstow. Remember her?'

Grace nodded. They had come across Kerri-Ann Bairstow a few months ago, in August. She was a sex-worker, feisty and loud-mouthed, who had reluctantly become a witness for them in the 'Lady in the Lake' case.

'What's the betting that Kerri-Ann is the girl the downstairs neighbour saw in Jodie's room?' Hunter said. 'The one who gave him a bit of a slagging.'

'It would certainly fit her character.'

Hunter nodded in agreement. 'I'll feed that in this morning, as well as what we learned yesterday, and then you and I will see if we can track her down and have a little chat. Fancy her cropping up in two murders in such a short space of time. She's certainly going to be pleased when she sees us two again — not!' A smile creased his face. 'I'm betting she can tell us something.'

Morning briefing took over an hour. Both Detective Superintendents were present and Michael Robshaw led the session.

Tony Bullars and Mike Sampson were first to speak. They had completed the search of Jodie Marie Jenkinson's bedsit but hadn't found any significant evidence. Her mobile was still missing, and she hadn't been the type of girl who kept a diary, so they were struggling to build up a recent picture of her life.

That was when Hunter broke the news about the identification of the prints found in Jodie's room. As expected, he and Grace were handed the job of tracking down Kerri-Ann Bairstow. Then he told everyone what he and Grace had learned the previous day. First, he reported on the interview with Amanda Rawlinson. He saw the looks around the room when he revealed Lucy's pregnancy. 'She was meeting Danny Weaver that night to tell him.'

'So that could be the reason behind the flare-up in the marketplace,' interjected Robshaw. 'But why didn't Danny Weaver explain that when he was interviewed?'

'He might have, boss, and Alan Darbyshire and Jeffery Howson chose to suppress it,' said Hunter. 'We now know that Danny wanted Lucy to run away with him and the pregnancy would certainly complicate matters. It could well have been the trigger behind the argument that night. I guess the only other person who'll be able to answer that question is Danny Weaver himself, and he certainly wasn't forthcoming in prison.

'There is also the added element of her husband, Peter. We don't really know if he knew of all this and that's the reason why she and Danny were arguing. There is nothing in the file which tells us who was looking after Lucy's daughter that night. Someone had to be. What if that person was Peter, and he was telling Lucy to end it, or something to that effect? We know from Amanda that he used violence towards her.

'When we spoke with Peter the other day, he said he didn't know about Lucy and Danny's affair, but we only have his word for that. Amanda certainly paints Peter Blake-Hall in a bad light. And she was also extremely critical of Alan Darbyshire and Jeffery Howson. They steered what she should put in her witness statement and then primed her about what to say in court. Weaver never stood a chance.'

Hunter gazed across the room; his mouth set tight. 'I got something else as well yesterday.' He related his meeting with George. When he got to the part about the photograph identification, he felt his neck reddening. He swallowed hard when he saw the look on Robshaw's face. 'I know I didn't go about it right, gaffer, but it was the only way I was going to get anything out of him. And he has given us something really positive to work with. He pointed out Peter Blake-Hall and Ronnie Fisher as being the two he saw carrying Jodie into the Barnwell Inn. He said she was kicking and screaming. Under the circumstances, I don't think I could have got a better result.'

Robshaw's look softened. 'Okay, Hunter. I guess I would have preferred if the identification had been carried out according to procedure but needs must in the circumstances. And it does give us something concrete to work with, but are you confident he told you everything? You're happy that he definitely didn't see what they did to her?'

'He said not, boss. And I believe him.'

'And he told you they had a black four-by-four?'

'Yeah, with blacked-out windows. No prompting.'

'Okay, that's good.' Robshaw's eyes swept the room. 'This is our first real break-through. The link to the recent murders is the black four-by-four and so one of the main priorities is to find that car. The witness at Wentworth seems to think it could be a Mitsubishi Shogun. I want to know if Peter or Ronnie own one, and if they do, where it's garaged.' Robshaw then asked Barry Newstead for an update.

Barry said, 'I mentioned before that there was intelligence about Peter and Ronnie bringing in amphetamines from Holland and it was believed they were using imported cars from Germany to carry the stuff. They had been flagged up by number-three-crime-squad as targets. I managed to track down the DI who was in charge of the team doing surveillance on Peter and Ronnie. He's called Tom Stone.

'Tom said they started following Peter and Ronnie around in March of 1986. All they had was evidence from a couple of users that Ronnie was the one who was knocking out the gear. And they had nothing on Peter, other than a whisper that it was his money being put up. The fact that he was using the imported car business to bring in the gear came from a significant source six months into the surveillance. That intelligence highlighted where the collection point was in Holland and some of the distribution outlets in Sheffield and Leeds.

'Tom says that the job was running really smoothly, and that they were putting together the evidence, slowly but surely, but then nine months into it things started happening which made the team suspicious that Ronnie and Peter were on to them, especially Ronnie. It was nothing concrete, but occasionally during the surveillance, he'd suddenly deviate, double-back, or put his foot down and lose them in a side street. Then they had regular sightings of two detectives at Peter's club.' Barry paused and looked around the office. 'Yes, you've guessed it, Alan Darbyshire and Jeffery Howson. There was nothing to say they were tipping off Peter or Ronnie, but their visits to Peter's club were too frequent for the Crime Squad's liking and so they decided to introduce an undercover officer.

'And that's where it went belly-up. To digress a little, when I became aware that Guy Armstrong was sniffing around at the beginning of this enquiry, Sue, my partner, told me that she used to work with him when he was a reporter with the *Chronicle*, and when he moved to the *Daily Mail*, he was involved in a road accident in which a cop was killed. Well, this is where it gets very interesting. The cop who got killed in that accident was none other than the undercover detective placed in the club.

'Tom Stone told me he has no idea how Guy Armstrong got involved in all this. He only became aware of the reporter's involvement after the fatal crash. The officer had established himself with Ronnie and had gained enough trust to set up a sting-deal. He had ordered a couple of kilos of amphet and was arranging a delivery. On the night of the crash, the detective went to Peter's club to hand over money as a deposit for the gear, and Tom and his team were waiting at Rawmarsh police station for a call to tell them the deal had been set up.

'Just before midnight, Tom received a call from traffic that the detective had been involved in a car accident and that he had been killed. He had been a passenger in Guy Armstrong's car. Armstrong was taken to hospital seriously injured. He was two and a half times over the drink-drive limit and Tom was told that his car had left the road on a bend near Millhouse Dam and had hit a wall. When they interviewed Guy in hospital, a couple of days later, he insisted they had been run off the road.'

Barry paused and stared around the room. He had a captivated audience. 'Sounds familiar, doesn't it? Especially with recent events. The bottom line, however, was that they could find no evidence to substantiate Armstrong's story and so he was charged with causing death by careless driving. He offered the same story at court but he was found guilty and given an 18-month prison sentence suspended for two years.

'Because of Guy's job, and because of the sensitive nature of the op, they decided not to speak to him. And so they never knew what connection Guy had with the undercover detective, or if he ever knew he was working undercover. The guess was that he was just following his nose for the story and the UC man was a source for him to tap into.' Barry glanced down at his notes. 'Anyway, there was an internal enquiry, and it was decided to hush the whole thing up and to shelve the ongoing operation against Peter Blake-Hall and Ronnie Fisher. But there is one interesting snippet arising out of this. I mentioned earlier that Crime Squad got significant information which changed the course of their investigation. Well, that source was none other than Daniel Weaver. He apparently wrote to them from his prison cell.'

Hunter and Grace got Kerri-Ann Bairstow's address and drove straight there after briefing. She wasn't at her flat and a neighbour told them she hadn't seen her for at least a fortnight. A further probe of the intelligence system gave them more addresses, and they spent most of the morning driving around Barnwell, banging on doors, trying to locate her.

Finally, after two and half hours, they got lucky. At one address, they were told that Kerri-Ann had left the previous evening and that she was in a bit of a mess — drinking heavily and not eating properly. The woman revealed that Kerri-Ann had told her that someone was wanting to kill her. She gave the detectives another address to try.

The bungalow at Oak Drive was registered to a pensioner. The front curtains were closed, but as Hunter approached the door, he could hear signs of life inside.

Grace slipped around the back as Hunter banged on the front door.

He saw the curtains of the window twitch and then he heard raised voices coming from the rear, before his partner shouted, 'She's round here, Hunter.'

He found Grace grappling with Kerri-Ann Bairstow, trying to pin her against the wall. The girl was doing her best to squirm out of her leather jacket in an attempt to get free.

Hunter grabbed hold of her arm and made sure she was going nowhere. Kerri-Ann's bleary blue eyes burned with a mixture of fear and hate.

'Get off me, you bitch!' she screamed at Grace. Her breath reeked of stale booze.

Hunter tightened his grip. 'Kerri-Ann, calm down.'

After a couple more failed attempts to break free, she stopped struggling. 'I ain't done nothing. What're you fuckin' 'arassing me for?'

'We're not harassing you, Kerri-Ann. All we want is a chat,' said Grace. 'Now, I'm going to let go of you. If you kick-off again, or try to do a runner, then you will be arrested.'

Grace and Hunter both released their grip.

Kerri-Ann shook herself back into her leather jacket. 'I'm going to make a complaint. You can't do this when I ain't done nothink.'

'Fine, Kerri-Ann,' said Grace, 'Come on. We'll take you to the police station and introduce you to a nice inspector, if that's what you want.'

Kerri-Ann scanned the two detectives' faces. 'Pair of fucking smart-arses.' She zipped up her jacket. 'Anyway, what do you two want again?'

'How do you know it's you we want to speak to? It might be Mr Thompson, who lives here,' said Grace.

'You ain't here for Len, 'cos he ain't done nothing. I'm not stupid. I know you're looking for me.'

Hunter blocked off Kerri-Ann's escape route and then let Grace continue with the questioning. On their last meeting, it had been Grace who had broken down Kerri-Ann's defences and persuaded her to be a witness in a murder trial.

'Well then, you'll know what it's about, won't you?' Grace said,

Kerri-Ann said, 'No,' and attempted to look innocent.

'Yes, you do, Kerri-Ann, because for the past two weeks you've not been at your flat. In fact, we know you've been dossing around with whoever will put you up. If that's not the actions of someone who's scared, or got something to hide, then I don't know what is.'

Kerri-Ann's face flushed.

Grace pointed at her. 'You see, that tells me that you do know something. We've found your prints all over a friend of your's bedsit. A friend who's been murdered.'

Kerri-Ann stared at the floor.

'I think you and I need to have a little chat.' Grace took hold of Kerri-Ann's arm.

Kerri-Ann shook it away. 'I'm coming. No need for the rough stuff.'

Grace and Hunter exchanged glances. They followed Kerri-Ann to their car. She got into the back without any prompting.

Grace and Hunter jumped into the front seats.

Grace continued, 'Look, Kerri-Ann, please don't make this hard for us. We know you've been a regular visitor to Jodie because you had a bit of a spat with one of the tenants. And we also know that you know something about Jodie's murder.'

'I don't,' Kerri-Ann said sharply.

Grace leaned her head over the back of her seat. 'This is not a game. For the past two weeks you've been avoiding someone, and we know from talking to the people where you've been staying that you've been scared witless. In fact, you told one of them that someone was out to kill you.'

'Big mouth,' Kerri-Ann said.

'Maybe, but that's because they care about you. I know you don't see eye-to-eye with us, but you know from last time that we looked after you when you were our witness and we can do the same again. Your friend Jodie has been murdered. And the people who did it tried to make it look as though she'd overdosed. Jodie didn't deserve to die, and we know she died because she knew something and was hiding it. You don't need me to tell you that those same people will find you and you could suffer the same fate unless you let us help you.'

'I don't need no help.'

'Yes, you do, Kerri-Ann, because these people will stop at nothing until we put them away. And the only way we can put them away is with evidence.' Grace paused to let her words sink in. Then she said, 'We need to know what Jodie told you — what secret she was keeping.'

'You don't know what these people are like.'

'Oh, I think we do, Kerri-Ann. And if you help us, I promise they won't harm you.'

Kerri-Ann nervously picked at her fingers. She studied her hands for several seconds and then she looked up at Grace. 'Can you promise me?'

'Yes.'

'It involves a cop you know ... well, an ex-cop. At least that's what Jodie told me.'

'Go on.'

Kerri-Ann lowered her chin and muttered, 'She overheard something where she worked.' Tears had collected in the corners of her eyes. 'Jodie didn't do anything wrong. She was the bestest mate you could wish for. She got me off heroin, you know.'

'That's what friends are for, Kerri-Ann. There to look after you. Now it's your turn to return the favour.'

'But I'm shit-scared about these guys. They don't mess about, you know. And what's to say 'cos it's one of your own, you won't protect him?'

'Do you think if we wanted to protect him, we'd be going to all this trouble to find you and offer to look after you?'

Kerri-Ann shrugged.

'Think about it, Kerri-Ann. We want to put the people who killed Jodie away. I can assure you of that.'

Kerri-Ann first looked at Grace, then at Hunter.

He nodded his head in assurance.

Kerri-Ann said, 'I only know what Jodie has told me. I didn't hear or see anything myself. Now I wish she hadn't told me. If she'd have just kept her mouth shut, she might not be dead.'

'When you say if she'd have kept her mouth shut, do you mean her telling that journalist?'

Kerri-Ann's mouth dropped open in astonishment. 'You know about that?'

Grace nodded. 'I told you, we know a lot. We know she told her secret to a journalist, but we don't know what that secret was.'

'She just wanted to make some money to start a new life. I told her to be careful.'

'It's too late now, isn't it? But you can help us get those responsible. We really need to know what Jodie told you.'

Kerri-Ann fiddled with her hands again, this time rolling a ring around her finger. She chewed her bottom lip, then responded, 'I want screens at court. I don't want these guys to see me.'

'We can arrange that.'

Kerri-Ann studied their faces for a few moments, then said, 'She heard an argument at the club where she was working.'

'The club?'

'Yeah, Jodie had a job working behind the bar of a strip-club near Wakefield.'

'Owned by Peter Blake-Hall?'

'I don't know who owned it, but she did mention a guy called Peter and another one called Ronnie. She didn't tell me the name of the ex-cop involved. She just told me she knew it was an ex-cop 'cos she'd heard them arguing with him.'

'Do you recall when this argument took place?'

Kerri-Ann shook her head. 'No, she told me about three weeks ago.'

'And what did Jodie say about what she heard?'

Kerri-Ann seemed to study the question, and then she answered, 'I can't remember what she told me word for word, 'cos she told me one night when we'd had a drink.'

'But you do remember what she told you?'

'Yes. She said she didn't know they were in the club. She'd gone in with the bar manager to help stock up. She was in the cellar and came up 'cos she heard arguing. She thought it was the manager at first. That someone had come in while they were shut and was trying to get a drink. When she got to the door, she realised it was the owner, that Peter guy, and his mate Ronnie.

'She'd told me about Ronnie before. He tried to tap her up once and she told him to back off. She didn't like him at all. She told me he was a scary freak. Anyway, once she saw who it was, she decided to stay where she was until they'd done arguing. She said that there was this other guy there — an older guy — and he was shouting something about his mate wanting to go to the cops or something. And Ronnie was telling this older guy that he needed to keep him in order and tell him what's good for him. That if he grasses, then he, as an ex-cop, had a lot more to lose. That's when Jodie picked up on the older guy being one of your lot.'

'Did she manage to get this man's name — this ex-cop?'

'She never told me that. The only names she mentioned were Peter and Ronnie.'

'What else did she hear?'

'The ex-cop apparently said something about the other man having some evidence which could send them all down for a long time. Ronnie just went off on one after he said that. Jodie told me she got really scared 'cos he pulled a knife out and started shouting that he'd sort him. And Peter said if there really was some evidence, then they needed to make sure it disappeared.'

'Do you know what evidence this was all related to? Did she tell you that?'

'Jodie said that she'd found out later what the argument was all about, because she mentioned it to this reporter she knew, and he'd given her 100 quid and was going to give her more if she could find out more. She told me it was to do with murder of a woman from a long time ago.'

'Did the reporter tell Jodie the name of the woman?'

'Jodie didn't tell me any name, but the reporter told her it was Peter's wife. That's when I told her she needed to be really careful.' Kerri-Ann looked solemn. 'And I was right, wasn't I? This got her killed. You can see now why I'm scared, can't you?'

DAY FOURTEEN

Shortly after 7.30 a.m. a convoy of three MIT cars, a Task Force transit and a Scenes of Crime van, turned off the main thoroughfare and coasted into St. Margaret's Avenue. 20 seconds later the five vehicles fell neatly into line, pulling up nose-to-tail in the cul-de-sac.

Hunter and Grace were first to step out onto the street, followed by Tony Bullars and Mike Sampson. They closed their car doors with as little noise as possible and tiptoed across the road to Alan Darbyshire's semi-detached home.

As Hunter neared the gate, he glanced back over his shoulder and signalled to the search team to hang back. Then, followed by Grace, he trotted down the drive to the front door. Tony and Mike slipped around the side and secured the rear.

Hunter checked his watch, noted the time in his head and banged sharply on the front door. Then he took a step back and glanced up at the bedroom window. He saw the light come on and ducked back out of sight.

Less than a minute later the hallway light came on and he heard heavy footfalls coming down the stairs. As the key turned in the lock, he heard Alan Darbyshire's voice call out, 'Who is it?'

'Police,' Hunter shouted back.

For a few seconds there was no movement, then Hunter heard a security chain being released and the door opened.

A blast of warm air greeted Hunter, as did a bleary-eyed Alan Darbyshire, wearing his dressing gown. He was fastening the belt around his oversized stomach.

Alan said, 'What do you two want at this godforsaken hour?' but Hunter could tell from the look of resignation that he knew why they were there. When any cop called at this time of the morning it was only for two reasons — to be the bearer of bad news, or to arrest. Alan Darbyshire's face paled as he stared over Hunter's shoulder and spotted the line of cars parked opposite. 'What the fuck is this?'

Hunter wanted to say so many things but he composed himself. Stepping into the hallway, he said, matter-of-factly, 'Alan Darbyshire, I am arresting you for perverting the course of justice.'

Grace followed Hunter into the carpeted hallway, speaking softly over her radio, telling everyone they were in. She left the front door open.

Still drained of colour, Alan said loudly, 'You'd better have something bloody good on me, because you're not going to hear the last of this. You'll be on fucking traffic-duty by the time I'm done. I still know people, you know.'

'Is that a threat, Alan?' Hunter narrowed his eyes. 'I don't think you are in any position to make threats. And, in answer to your question, we certainly have the evidence. Believe me. I think you'd better get dressed, because we've got a nice warm cell waiting for you.'

Darbyshire's eyes widened. 'You need to be very careful about what you say to me, young man. Do you understand?'

Hunter was about to respond when he felt a tap on his shoulder. He turned to see Dawn Leggate.

She said, 'Mr Darbyshire, I am Detective Superintendent Leggate. I am in charge of this operation. I am here to make sure this job runs professionally.' She paused and then said, 'After all, there can be no room for error, can there? We don't want anyone accusing us of a miscarriage of justice, do we?'

Hunter could have sworn there was a twinkle in her eye. He returned his gaze to Alan Darbyshire, whose face was drained of colour. Hunter said, 'I want you to get dressed now, Alan, and then we're taking you down to the station for questioning. You'll already know this, but you'll be able to contact a solicitor once we get there.'

'Meanwhile, I'll be overseeing a search of your home,' added Dawn. 'Is there anyone else in the house we need to be aware of?'

'My wife, Pauline, but she's not very well. She's laid up with flu. She's sleeping in the back bedroom.'

'Well, we'll inconvenience her as little as possible, and we'll try our best not to damage anything. Now, if you'd get dressed, please, my officers will escort you back to the station. I will see you later and update you.' Dawn beamed a broad smile at him. 'After all, we want to make sure you have no grounds for complaint.'

Hunter thought he heard Darbyshire swear beneath his breath as he trudged his way upstairs to dress.

Alan Darbyshire was escorted to the custody suite by Tony Bullars and Mike Sampson. Hunter wanted as little contact as possible with the retired DCI before interviewing him. He knew that what lay ahead would challenge everything he had learned over the years and so, when he returned to the office, he drafted an outline plan of how he intended to approach things. 20 minutes later, his pre-interview notes completed, he read through them, double-checking that he matched times and dates against the evidence they had. Finally, he selected the exhibits he required, checked they were all labelled correctly, and that they corresponded with his notes and bundled everything together.

'Ready?' he asked, looking across his desk. Grace was resting her head in her hands.

'This is a first,' she said getting up. 'You making notes prior to an interview. After all these years, you're finally going to conduct an interview according to the rules.'

He smiled. 'You know what they say about wit?'

'Anyway,' said Grace, 'while you were preparing your stuff, I nipped next door to the HOLMES team and had a chat with Isobel. Things are really stepping up a gear.'

'Oh yeah?'

'She tells me that they've done loads of checks on Peter Blake-Hall and Ronnie Fisher. Associates, vehicle ownership and premises, the lot. They've got an address for Ronnie and guess what?'

Hunter raised an eyebrow.

'Swansea have confirmed a black Mitsubishi Shogun listed to that address. Ronnie is right in the doo-dah now. The boss has asked Tony and Mike to do some discreet enquiries to confirm if he's still living there and see if they can spot the vehicle. The gaffer's apparently trying to get hold of Headquarters' Surveillance Team to target him and Peter, now that we've pulled in Alan Darbyshire.'

'Well, we'd better make sure we can sign, seal and deliver everything at our end then.' Hunter picked up his pen and made for the door.

In the interview room, Alan Darbyshire was seated at a table with duty solicitor Miles Harper. As solicitors went, Hunter knew that Miles was one of the more amenable ones, who, providing the rules were adhered to, would allow the interview to flow without interruption.

From chest height, Hunter dropped his bundle onto the table, letting the papers and exhibits spill out like a pack of cards. He wanted Darbyshire to see exactly how much evidence they had against him, without letting him know all of the content.

Hunter was determined to take a psychological advantage. He lowered himself opposite his adversary and fixed him with a confident stare. Darbyshire immediately dropped his gaze. Hunter unfastened his shirt collar and slackened the knot in his tie. Then, slowly, he unfastened his shirt cuffs and rolled them back over his forearms. He clasped his hands in front of him, resting on the table.

Grace reached across and switched on the tape recorder. A buzzing noise filled the room. When it stopped, Hunter said, 'This interview is being tape recorded.' He went into the starting preamble, strengthening the tone of his voice as he reminded Darbyshire that he was under caution. 'You understand why you have been arrested this morning?' he asked across the table.

Darbyshire was beginning to sweat. 'Yes, and all I want to ask is when this is supposed to have occurred?'

'1983, following the arrest of Daniel Weaver. Ring any bells?'

'Yes, I remember it.'

Hunter straightened his paperwork back together and picked out his pre-interview notes. He scanned them and then looked up. 'Mr Darbyshire, in 1983 you were a detective sergeant in Divisional CID, is that right?'

'Yes.'

'And in August of that year, the 27th to be precise, you received a phone call from Peter Blake-Hall to the effect that his wife was missing. Is that correct?'

'It is.'

'Can you lead me through what you did regarding that missing person enquiry?'

Darbyshire answered, 'Peter rang me early that Saturday morning and told me that his wife, Lucy, hadn't come home, and that he was worried because he had rung her parents and round her friends and no one had seen or heard from her. I went to his house with Jeff Howson, made the decision that this was not a usual missing from home and, after taking some details, went back to the nick and began making enquiries.'

'And what did you do after that?'

'You know what happened after that, because I'm guessing that since we last spoke you will have read the file, otherwise why would you be asking these questions?'

'Yes, I have read your file, but please, Alan, will you go through what you did regarding your enquiries?'

Darbyshire shook his head, huffing loudly. 'Well, as you know, we found out that Lucy had been seen arguing with a man the night before in the marketplace. It was Bank Holiday Friday and there were quite a few folks about who had witnessed it. Anyway, we found out that the person she had been seen arguing with was a Daniel Weaver. That was the last anyone had seen of her and so, early Sunday morning, me and Jeff went around to his flat and had a chat with him, hoping that Lucy was there. He allowed us to search it and she wasn't, of course. He admitted he'd been having an affair with her and that he'd asked her to come and live with him, but she'd told him it was over and they'd ended up rowing about it.

'We noticed scratches to his face and when we asked him how they'd come about, he said that Lucy had done them when he'd grabbed hold of her and she'd pulled away. When we asked him what had happened after the argument, he told us she had left to go home. We weren't happy with that story and so we arrested him and carried out a more thorough search of his flat.'

'And did you find anything?'

'Not in his flat, we didn't. Later, Scenes of Crime found her prints there, but we knew from what he'd told us that she had spent some time there, so they were valueless. But we did find her handbag in a shed in the garden at the back of the flats, which was his. It was hidden in some sacking. He couldn't account for it being there.'

'And it was definitely Lucy's handbag?'

'Definitely. Peter identified it.'

'So you then interviewed him back at the station?'

'Yes.'

'And what form did that interview take?'

'I interviewed him and Jeff wrote down everything.'

'You made contemporaneous notes?'

'Yes, that was how interviews were conducted in those days. We didn't have tape-recording like now.'

'These notes?' Hunter removed three exhibit bags from his pile. Each bag contained a set of interview notes from the original prosecution file. He lined them up in front of Darbyshire. 'I am showing the prisoner exhibit numbers HK one, HK two and HK three.'

Darbyshire looked carefully at the three exhibit bags before replying. 'Yes, these are the original notes of those interviews with Daniel Weaver.'

'And they are all signed and dated by yourself and Jeffery Howson?'

Darbyshire nodded. 'Yes, as I've already said, that is what we did in those days. Once the notes were completed, Daniel would be invited to read them and, if he agreed with their content, he signed them and then we signed them.'

'I want you to look carefully at the notes. Numbers HK one and HK two were signed by Daniel, but on HK three, instead of Daniel's signature there are the words "refused to sign" at the bottom of each page.' Hunter saw Darbyshire's face starting to flush. He added, 'Why is that, Alan? Especially given the fact that in those notes he has admitted to killing Lucy and burying her on Langsett Moor.'

Darbyshire gulped. 'I can't remember the reason why he didn't want to sign them. He just didn't. You have to appreciate this is a long time ago now, but what's in them is almost word for word what he said.'

'Okay, fair enough, I will come back to that later, but for now we'll move on.' Hunter put the three exhibit bags to one side. 'So, based on his admission and the evidence of the handbag found in the shed, Daniel Weaver was charged with Lucy's murder and remanded to prison?'

'Don't forget there were witnesses who saw him and Lucy arguing in the marketplace on the night she disappeared.'

Hunter nodded. 'And in May the following year, he went for trial and you stood in the witness box and gave evidence regarding everything you have just said.'

'Yes, you know all that. It's in the file.'

'Okay, thanks Alan. I want to move it on a bit now. You know we are investigating the murder of your old colleague, Jeffery Howson, because we told you that when we came to see you.'

'Yes, terrible thing that. Have you found out who killed him?'

'We have some leads.' Hunter paused, watching for a reaction as he let the words sink in. Darbyshire's look remained steadfast. 'While we have been investigating his murder, we have come across some disturbing evidence which impacts on the Daniel Weaver trial.' Hunter pulled out the plastic bag containing the notes from Jeffery Howson's safe. 'In his house we found these. I want you to look at them carefully and see if you recognise them?'

Hunter turned the clear exhibit bag over and pushed it across the table. He watched as a trickle of sweat fell from Darbyshire's hairline, down the side of his face, collecting at his jawline.

Darbyshire spent the best part of a minute scrutinising the evidence inside the exhibit bag before looking up. He shrugged.

Hunter asked again, 'Do you recognise them?'

'Should I?'

'Is that your signature at the top and bottom of the notes?'

Darbyshire glanced at the exhibit again for a few seconds, then looked at Hunter. 'Looks like mine.'

'Well, those notes are timed and dated exactly the same as the ones I have previously shown you, exhibit HK three, but they are signed by Daniel Weaver, and what is interesting, Alan, is that in those notes, just like as in exhibits HK one and HK two, he denies his involvement in the murder of Lucy Blake-Hall.' Hunter paused a moment. 'What if I also tell you that those have been analysed by forensic scientists and they can be dated back to 1983. You'll know what I mean when I say they've been analysed, won't you, Alan? The grading of papers and the watermarks have been compared, as well as the chemical compositions of the inks.'

'Yes,' Darbyshire said.

'Testing found indentations of lettering transferred through from exhibit number HK two. You know what that means, don't you, Alan?'

'Enlighten me.'

'These notes from Jeffery Howson's house must have at some stage been beneath the contemporaneous notes, exhibit HK two, for the handwriting impressions to have indented through. I therefore put it to you that these notes are the original ones Daniel made during your interview with him, and that notes HK three are a fabrication you and Jeffery Howson put together after interview to convict Daniel Weaver.'

Darbyshire stared hard at Hunter. The corners of his mouth set tight and then he answered, 'No comment.'

'You went into the witness box at Crown Court and told lies, didn't you?'

'No comment.'

Hunter sat back in his seat and grinned. After several seconds of silence, he leant forward. 'I want to now ask you questions about the murder of Jeffery Howson.'

'What?'

'When we spoke with you at your home, one of the questions we asked you was when did you last speak with Jeffery. If I remember rightly, your response was about two weeks before he died. We know from phone records that Jeffery rang your home on the evening of 22nd November, the day he was murdered.'

Darbyshire bit down on his lower lip. For a few seconds he didn't answer. Then, he said, 'I think you need to check your notes there. If I remember rightly you asked me when I had last seen Jeff, not when I last spoke with him.' He threw a smug grin back at Hunter.

Hunter glanced at Grace for support. She shrugged. He quickly gathered his thoughts. 'Okay Alan, my mistake. Regarding that call he made to you — what did he say?'

'Nothing much, just passing the time of day. I think he just wanted to talk to someone.'

'It wasn't to tell you then that he was going to go to the police and tell us about the miscarriage of justice he and you had been involved in regarding Daniel Weaver?'

Darbyshire coloured up. 'No, definitely not.'

'DS Kerr, that is out of order.' It was the first time the solicitor had intervened.

Although Hunter knew he had struck a nerve, he also knew he needed to back off. He held up his hands in surrender, then said, 'Changing tack, Alan, how well do you know Peter Blake-Hall?'

It was another few seconds before Darbyshire answered. 'You'll probably be aware if you've done your homework that Jeff and I used to pay him a visit at his club in the early 80s. We used to drink there occasionally.'

'And you used to work for him?'

'Yep, no secret. I needed a job once I retired and he had the ideal position of a club manager going vacant. I used to make sure everything ran smoothly at the club regarding his licence and the hiring of staff.'

'And when did you last see him?' Hunter paused, then added, 'Or speak with him?' He put on a fake smile. 'I don't want my questions getting misinterpreted.'

Darbyshire glared before answering, 'It'd be a good year or so. I don't have anything to do with Peter anymore. I don't need to.' His words had an edge of anger.

'Or Ronnie Fisher?'

Darbyshire's face reddened further. 'Look, where is this going?'

'What if I tell you we have a witness who overheard a conversation between you Peter Blake-Hall and Ronnie Fisher, discussing the murder of Lucy, as recently as early November this year, when you made mention of evidence which could get you all sent down?'

'I'd say she was wrong.'

Hunter instantly zeroed-in his look upon Darbyshire. 'I never said the witness was a she.'

Darbyshire's eyes widened.

Hunter released a sly smile. 'We have put a lot of work into this investigation and it would be fair to say that we are building up a case which is not putting you in a very good light. We have a lot of unanswered questions, especially regarding Lucy's disappearance all those years ago, and now the murder of your ex-colleague Jeffery Howson. This is your chance to redeem yourself.'

'And now I, DS Kerr, have decided I wish to say nothing further.'

'You're certain about that?'

'Yes.'

'Well, I'll give you one last opportunity.' Hunter shuffled out several more exhibits from his folder and laid them out in front of Darbyshire. 'You have just said that the last time you saw Peter Blake-Hall was about a year ago. How do you account for these photographs taken just over three weeks ago, on the tenth of November? It looks to me as though you, Peter and Ronnie were having a heated exchange of words. What was that about, Alan?'

Darbyshire's chair almost fell over as he jumped up, his face filled with fear. He smashed a fist down hard on the table. 'You think you're fucking smart, don't you? You've no idea who you're dealing with here.'

Two phones rang at the same time at opposite ends of the office, breaking Dawn Leggate's concentration. One of the phones stopped ringing and she waited for the other one to switch across to voicemail. After 30 seconds of continuous ringing she realised that wasn't going to happen, and giving out a long sigh, she scooted back her chair and strode across.

'DS Leggate,' she said, snatching up the phone.

The downstairs receptionist was on the other end. She explained that a woman had come in asking for someone from MIT — that she had information about the Lucy Blake-Hall case.

Dawn was about to tell her to take down details, and that someone would go out and see her later, when she changed her mind. 'Tell the woman I'll be down in a couple of minutes,' she said, hanging up. She swept out of the office.

Dawn opened the door into the foyer to see a slim, dark haired woman looking out through the plate-glass windows.

The woman turned and met Dawn's gaze.

Dawn said, 'Mrs?' and waited for a response.

'Aldridge. Lisa Aldridge.' She took a step forward and removed a newspaper from beneath her arm. 'I've come about this,' she said, holding up the paper.

It was the latest edition of the *Barnwell Chronicle*, with 'INNOCENT' emblazoned in large print across its front page. Dawn had already read the article and knew that it featured Daniel Weaver's release pending his appeal and the re-opening of the Lucy Blake-Hall case.

'Would you like to come through?' she said, keeping the door open. She led the way down the corridor and showed Lisa into a small ante-room, used mainly for taking complaints or statements. As such, it had very little in the way of comfort — just a table and four chairs.

Dawn pulled out one of the chairs and gestured for the woman to sit opposite. As Lisa sat down, she slid across the newspaper.

Dawn thought she appeared to be agitated and gave her a reassuring smile. 'I'm Detective Superintendent Dawn Leggate,' she said.

Lisa stabbed at the paper. 'I've come because I think I saw what happened to Lucy that night.' There was a nervous inflection in her voice.

Dawn felt the hairs on the back of her neck prickle. She said, 'Oh yes?'

'I saw what happened to her after that argument in the marketplace.'

Dawn flipped open her notepad, thumbed to a blank sheet and wrote down the woman's name quickly. 'Did you not make a statement to the detectives investigating her disappearance back in 1983?'

There was an awkward silence before Lisa answered, 'No. I'm sorry. My mother told me you had arrested someone for Lucy's murder, and so I never did. It's only seeing this in the paper that's made me realise I should have done.'

'What do you mean?'

'I'm not explaining myself very well, am I?' Lisa held Dawn's gaze for a second. 'I was in the marketplace that Friday and saw what went off. I'd been out with some mates in town. We were celebrating me getting a job in Canada. Halfway through the night, my friends decided they wanted to go on to Rotherham, to a nightclub, but I didn't, so I told them I was catching the bus home. I went to the bus stop near the market. I'd forgotten it was Bank Holiday and there was a limited service, so I had to hang around there for a bit, and that's when I saw Lucy arguing with him.' Lisa stabbed at the newspaper again, directly over the photograph of Daniel Weaver. 'It was a right old shouting match between the pair of them and I got a bit nervous about it because it was going off just across the street from me, and so I hid by the side of the shelter. I could still see and hear it though.'

'And what was going on?'

'I can still see it as if it was yesterday. He had hold of Lucy by the arms, shaking her and shouting something about how it didn't matter — he still wanted her and he'd sorted out a place for them to go. Well, words to that effect anyway. And she said that she couldn't go because of Jessica. Then she said something like, "You don't know him. You don't know what he's capable of." She was trying to pull away from him and he pulled her back. That's when she pushed him away again. I think she caught his face, 'cos I saw him put a hand to his cheek and then look at it. Then she screamed at him to go away and he stormed off.'

'So Daniel Weaver walked away from Lucy?'

Lisa nodded. 'He went off up the hill and she stood there, watching him go. She started crying and I stayed where I was hiding, 'cos I was a bit embarrassed. I didn't want her to see that I'd been watching them argue in case she turned on me — you know what I mean?'

Dawn nodded. 'And then what happened? Did Lucy walk away as well?'

'No. She was watching him go, crying, and at first I thought she was going to run after him, but then this car comes screaming up and stops. It pulled up right in front of her. That's when she got scared.'

'Scared?'

'You ought to have seen her face, she looked scared to death! Especially when the bloke got out of the car.'

Dawn couldn't stop herself looking surprised. She quickly prompted, 'Then what happened?'

'Well, he grabbed hold of her by the arms, virtually picking her up off her feet. She tried to wrestle him off but he was too strong. He shouted at her. Told her to get in the effing car. Yes, that's what he said, "Get in the effing car, Lucy," but he swore properly. He was really mad with her.'

'Did you know who this man was?'

Lisa shook her head. 'No, but you could tell by Lucy's reaction that she knew him.'

'And then what happened?'

'Well, he flung open the passenger door and pushed Lucy in and then he took off. Wheels were spinning and everything.'

'Did you get a good look at him? I know it's a long time ago now, but can you describe what he looked like?'

'I can remember at the time thinking that he was a pretty big guy. By that, I mean tall and muscular like. He'd be a bit older than Lucy, late 20s, maybe early 30s, and he had dark brown hair. I think he had a centre parting. It was collar length.' Lisa shrugged her shoulders. 'I mean, he'll have changed since then, so I don't know if I'd recognise him now, but if you showed me a photo of him back then, I'd maybe be able to recognise him.'

'What about the car he was driving?'

'Big red thing. A posh car. I think it was a Mercedes. It was one of those cars with a big silver badge on its grille. A three-pointed star inside a ring. That's a Mercedes badge, isn't it?'

'This is a wild shot, Lisa, but did you get the number?'

'No, but it wasn't a British number plate. It was foreign.' Lisa held up a hand. 'And, sorry, but no, I don't know which country. I only remember thinking it was foreign.'

'Don't apologise, Lisa, that's good. Just another couple of questions. Was he alone in the car, or was there anyone else with him?'

'He was alone.'

'After all this time, why have you decided to tell us this? Why didn't you tell us this back in 1983?'

Lisa coloured up again. 'Well, because of my mum.'

'What do you mean?'

'As I've already said, I'd got this job in Canada and I was going down to Heathrow on the Saturday to fly off there. I told my mum when I got home what I'd seen and asked her if she thought I should go to the police. She said that it might not be anything and that if I went to the police I'd miss my flight and maybe lose my job, so she said she'd keep an eye on the news, and if it was anything important she'd let me know and I could report it if it was serious. A couple of days later, when I'd settled in and phoned her, she told me that the argument and fight I'd seen was to do with a woman being murdered, but that the police had arrested someone and he'd confessed. Later, she told me about the trial and him being found guilty.

'I've been back in England for over five years and until I saw this in the papers, I always thought that the Daniel Weaver fellow who had murdered that Lucy woman that night was the man in the red car. It's only now seeing his photo that I realised he's the man who argued with her that night and then walked away. And that you made a mistake about who killed her. Am I right? Do you think it's the man who I saw dragging her into the red car who killed her?'

Dawn nodded. 'I think you may have seen who killed Lucy. It's a shame you didn't recognise him.'

'I didn't know him but I heard his name if that's any help.'

Dawn's face lit up. 'You heard his name?'

'Well, not his full name, but when the guy was trying to get her into the car, I heard her shout at him, "Just let go of me, Peter, will you?"'

'She definitely said the name Peter?'

'Definitely.'

'It just has to be Lucy's husband,' said Dawn Leggate, roaming around the office. She fixed her gaze on Michael Robshaw, standing by the incident boards. 'I mean, which other Peter has featured in our investigation?'

'I agree,' Robshaw said. 'Did you ask Lisa Aldridge if she would be able to give us an e-fit? It's a long shot, and Peter Blake-Hall will have changed considerably, but maybe we can do a comparison with old photographs Lucy's parents have of him.'

'I considered it, but I didn't ask because of the time lapse. We need to determine if Peter owned a red Mercedes back in 1983. We know he was shipping them in from Germany during the early 80s, and that would certainly tie in with the foreign number plate Lisa recognised.'

Robshaw leant against Lucy Blake-Hall's board. 'I've already passed out this information to Tony and Mike who have been trying to locate Ronnie Fisher and track down the black four-by-four registered to him. They're parked up near to Peter Blake-Hall's club, and I've asked them to update me if either of them turn up there. So far, the pair have gone off the radar. I'm guessing Alan Darbyshire's arrest has spooked them.' Robshaw turned to Hunter. 'Can I ask you to update everyone regarding your interview with Darbyshire?'

From his desk, Hunter addressed the group. 'It went well at the start. He was unaware of the contemporaneous notes we found in Jeffery Howson's safe. Unfortunately, once we showed our hand, he clammed up. He's refused to comment on the photos which Guy Armstrong took of him arguing with Peter Blake-Hall and Ronnie Fisher. And I didn't want to push him about Jodie's murder just yet. We've given him enough to think about for now.'

'So you and Grace will have another crack at him tomorrow morning?' said Robshaw.

'Yeah. His face was a picture when I told him that. I think he thought we were going to bail him. We'll see what a night in the cells will do.'

'Good, let's hope that'll loosen him up.' Robshaw turned back to Dawn. 'And I gather the search of Alan's home hasn't turned up anything?'

She shook her head. 'I'm afraid not. Though, if truth be known, I wasn't expecting us to find anything. He's had enough time to get rid of anything incriminating. Even his mobile has disappeared, so we can't track who he's phoned or where he's been. And, not surprisingly, his wife has given him an alibi for the night of Jeffery's murder.'

50 yards from Peter Blake-Hall's club, in the driver's seat of the unmarked car, Mike Sampson switched on the wipers and swept the back of his hand across the inside of the windscreen. It wasn't just the foul weather outside, a mixture of drizzle and sleet, which was fogging his view, but a thin film of moisture had also collected on the inside of the screen. He switched on the demister and cracked the driver's side window a fraction to clear his view. He badly needed the toilet. He had felt it creep up on him half an hour ago but had tried to will it away, but it hadn't worked. He powered the window shut.

After a few seconds the screen began to clear, and in an attempt to divert his mind away from the uncomfortable feeling in his groin, he focused on what he was there to do. He now had a good view of the front aspect of 'Le Chambre Rose' and was waiting for his targets to make an appearance.

In the dimness of the car's interior, he took a look at his watch. He struggled to see the time at first, but eventually managed to make out that it was just after 10 p.m. He and Tony had parked up two hours ago. Mike sighed. There was still over an hour before they could call off the observations.

Initially, the pair had been directed to find the black Mitsubishi Shogun and since early that morning they had driven around every location frequented by Peter Blake-Hall and Ronnie Fisher. Unfortunately, they had found neither the 4x4 nor its owner. It had been a tedious and frustrating day. To compound their frustration, as they were about to head back in for evening de-brief, they had been given new orders to drive straight over to Peter Blake-Hall's club, park nearby, and report on any sightings of Peter or Ronnie. If either of them appeared, they were to call it in and await back-up.

More rain and sleet splattered the windscreen, once more blurring Mike's view of the street. He cleared the screen again and took another glance at his watch. *Bully's been gone a long time,* he said to himself.

15 minutes earlier, Tony had offered to get them both fish and chips from a shop he'd spotted a couple of streets away. Mike stared out across the street. In the past two hours they had only counted half a dozen punters going inside the club. Going for a piss would only take a couple of minutes, he told himself — he wouldn't miss anything, and he'd hear if a car pulled up.

He eased open the door, activating the car's interior light. Quickly, he switched it off and climbed out of the car. 'Fucking freezing,' he muttered under his breath, pulling his jacket tighter.

For a few seconds, he stood by the car, watching and listening. The only sounds he picked up were those of the rain and sleet peppering the roof. He quietly closed the door. There was an unlit alleyway to his left and he strode towards it.

For a good 20 seconds, he stood in the dark, listening to his stream of piss cascading against the crumbling brickwork, sighing with relief as the pain in his bladder eased. Then the sloshing sounds of tyres splashing through puddles fractured the silence. He heard a vehicle stop nearby, followed by the opening of a car door.

He tried to finish his piss but he was still in full flow. *Fuck!*

It took another ten seconds for him to stop. Thankfully, he could still hear the purring of an engine as he zipped up his fly.

He edged towards the entrance of the alleyway. It sounded as if the vehicle wasn't too far away. He wanted to see who it was, but he didn't want to reveal himself.

Craning his neck around the entrance of the alleyway, he scanned the street. Parked immediately in front of their car was the black Mitsubishi Shogun they had been looking for. A dark figure was crouched down by the front of their car. It looked as though he was letting air out of their tyres. Mike stepped into the street, shouting, 'Oi!'

A face partially covered by a dark woollen hat glanced his way. Mike darted out of the shadows.

In the couple of seconds it took Mike to get from the alleyway to his car, the squat man had straightened. As Mike steamed towards him, balling his fists into a punch, the man took up a defensive posture, his eyes bulging and menacing.

Mike swung an arcing punch, but the man ducked away and he found himself hitting thin air. The momentum spun him sideways and he banged against the side of the car just as a retaliatory thump found his unguarded ribs, knocking the wind clean out of him. A second punch found Mike's head and his vision exploded into a thousand stars. His legs buckled and he threw out an arm to protect himself.

Suddenly, everything became a blur. He felt a searing sting in his groin and stumbled onto his knees. Then he felt a thump to the middle of his back. Then another and another. A sudden weakness overcame him. There was a sensation of a cold trickle of fluid washing around the sides of his waist and he realised he was having difficulty breathing. A veil of clouds swilled into his brain.

The last thing he heard as his face hit the wet tarmac was Tony calling out his name.

Tucked up in bed, Hunter's eyes were closed but he wasn't asleep. For the past half an hour, he had been mentally rehearsing the questions he was going to put to Alan Darbyshire the following morning. The ringing of the bedside telephone made him jump. Beside him, he felt Beth stir. He snatched up the phone and propped himself up on one elbow.

'Hello.'

'Hunter, sorry to disturb you.'

It was Dawn Leggate. He raised himself against the headboard.

'This is just a courtesy call, Hunter. I'm currently down at the District General.' There was a pause, then she continued, 'Mike's been stabbed.'

It took a couple of seconds for what she had said to sink in. Once it had, he said, 'Mike? Mike Sampson?'

'Aye.'

'When? Who?'

'About three-quarters of an hour ago. As you know, he and Tony were carrying out obs on Peter Blake-Hall's club. Well, it happened there. We think it was Ronnie Fisher, but we aren't sure.'

'And what about Bully? Is he okay?'

'Tony's fine.' There was a little hesitation before she replied, 'He found him.'

'Found him?'

'Long story, Hunter. I'll explain tomorrow.'

'Tomorrow?'

'Yeah. As I said, this is a courtesy call because he's on your team. I've called out Mark Gamble and his team to process the scene, and Tony and I are here at the hospital with Mike. Uniform and CID are searching for Ronnie, and we're bringing the job forward on Peter Blake-Hall. We're doing it in the next couple of hours.'

'Give me 20 minutes, boss, and I'll join you.'

'No, Hunter. Everything's sorted.' There was another pause down the line before she said, 'It's not that I don't want you here, or need your help, but you've got Alan Darbyshire to sort out tomorrow and I want you interviewing him with a clear head. I want him to get what's coming to him, okay?'

Frustrated though he was at not being able to do anything, Hunter knew that what Dawn was saying made sense. He nodded in the dark, then asked, 'How is he?'

'To be honest, Hunter, I don't know. He's lost a lot of blood, though the ambulance crew stabilised him at the scene. He's in theatre and we'll not know anything for the next couple of hours at least.'

Hunter heard her sigh. With a heavy heart, he said, 'So you want me and Grace in at the normal time?'

'Aye. There's no morning briefing. I'll leave an update for you when you get in. DS Robshaw will more than likely be around to bring you up to speed anyway.' There was another long pause and then she finished with, 'Hunter, I'm sure everything is going to be fine. You know Mike. He's made of good old Yorkshire grit.' Then the line went dead.

DAY FIFTEEN

Grace was already at her desk when Hunter got in at 7.30 a.m. He hadn't even closed the door before she exclaimed, 'You could have rung me!'

He slipped off his coat. 'It was late, Grace, I didn't want to disturb you.'

'But it's Mike.'

Hunter held up his hands in surrender. 'Sorry, Grace. I know it's Mike. But I couldn't afford for both of us to be worried and knackered this morning. We've got a big job ahead of us today and I wanted one of us functioning properly.' He rummaged over his desk, searching for a note. He turned his attention to his in-tray. There was nothing. 'Has anyone said anything about Mike? Do we know how he is?'

'Apparently Bully and Dawn are still at the hospital. He was in theatre for four hours. They're saying he should pull through.'

'I'll make us a drink before we get started on Alan Darbyshire.' Hunter checked the kettle for water. 'Has anyone said anything else about the attack?'

'Isobel got me first thing. She said that Bully nipped off for fish and chips for them both and that when he got back he found Mike like that and Ronnie Fisher's car fleeing the scene.'

'Did he see Ronnie carrying out the attack?'

Grace shrugged. 'I don't think so. Bully found Mike unconscious and he still hasn't come around. Isobel says they're keeping him sedated for at least 24-hours to help his recovery.'

'Have they got Ronnie?'

'No, not yet. Apparently, they turned out everyone and their grandmother last night, but it looks as though Ronnie's done a runner. They've got Blake-Hall though. They knocked him up in the early hours. He's downstairs in the trap.'

'Have they locked him up for the stabbing as well?'

'No, for the murder of Lucy. Apparently, Swansea emailed back Peter's vehicle records. He owned a red Mercedes at the time of Lucy's disappearance and it still had the foreign plates on it until it was re-registered in October 1983. How good is that?'

'Not good enough for a conviction.'

'Oh, you pessimist. It's a start though.'

Hunter switched on the kettle, and arranged his and Grace's mugs, putting a teabag in his and a heaped spoonful of coffee in hers. 'Do we know the state of Mike's injuries?'

'Isobel said that he'd been stabbed four times. Once in the back and three times in his right side. Thankfully, none of them penetrated any major organs.'

'So he should make a full recovery?'

'Finger's crossed, yes.'

Hunter swept a finger around the room. 'I'm guessing everyone else is out?'

'Yeah, Mark and his team are at Blake-Hall's place with forensics and Robshaw is at District HQ in the Intelligence office, running the op from there. I think CID are helping with the search of Ronnie's place, and he and his vehicle have been circulated.'

Hunter pressed the entrance bell to the custody suite and he and Grace were let in. As they passed through the second security door into the detention area they were greeted by pandemonium.

The custody sergeant was on the telephone, his back towards them. Another two phones were ringing behind the reception point. From the cell area, Hunter could hear metal doors being repeatedly banged and a medley of raised voices. He tried to work out what was going on.

The custody sergeant spun to face them, mouthing the words 'two minutes', and returned to his phone call. He looked stressed.

Hunter turned to Grace. He nodded towards the cell corridor and gave her a 'wonder what's going on?' look.

She shrugged.

It was well over two minutes before the custody sergeant slammed down the phone. The other two phones were still ringing but he chose to ignore them. 'Ha, the dynamic duo!' he said. 'You two have caused me some right grief.'

Hunter raised his eyebrows and pointed in the direction of the noise. 'Am I missing something here? Are the prisoners a tad unhappy this morning?'

'Alan Darbyshire's collapsed.'

'What?'

The sergeant nodded. 'The custody officer found him unconscious in his cell half an hour ago. The paramedics are down there with him now. They think he's had a heart attack. They're just getting him ready to take him to the hospital.'

'He's bullshitting. He's pulling a fast one.'

The custody sergeant shook his head. 'Sorry, Hunter, it's genuine. They've put monitors on him. You won't be interviewing him today.'

An agitated Hunter stomped back to the office, leaving Grace to catch up. He slammed his folder down on his desk and snatched up the phone. A female voice answered at the other end. He asked curtly, 'Is DS Robshaw or DI Scaife there?'

'Just a second,' the girl replied and then he heard the phone being put aside.

Hunter listened to a distant humming down the line and then he heard the phone being picked up. Gerald's voice came on.

Hunter explained what had happened to Alan Darbyshire. 'We're not going to get to him today, boss. We don't even know how bad he is until he's checked out up at the hospital. They're bound to keep him in him for a couple of days, at the least.'

Gerald told Hunter to wait a minute and went off the line. For the best part of a minute Hunter listened to distant voices, trying to pick out what was being said, but it sounded as if the DI had covered the mouthpiece with his hand.

Then the line opened and Gerald was back on. 'Hunter, the boss is still co-ordinating the search for Ronnie Fisher, who's done a disappearing act. We're turning over his house now. Some of his clothes have gone and there's no sign of his passport. We're currently trying to find where his relatives and associates live. His four-by-four's been found burned out on wasteland near the canal. We're in the thick of it here, so he's suggesting you speak with Superintendent Leggate. She's left the hospital and is overseeing the search of Peter Blake-Hall's place.' With that, he hung up.

Hunter punched in Dawn's mobile number. She answered on the third ring. He repeated what he had told the DI. When he had finished, he heard the word 'Shit' explode down the line.

'My feelings exactly, boss.'

There were a few seconds of silence. Hunter knew she would be running through a back-up plan inside her head.

'Okay, Hunter, all is not lost. Peter's in the cell down there. You and Grace can have an interim chat with him. We haven't found anything here, I'm afraid. SOCO are still going through the house, but they're not hopeful. And with regards to Mike's stabbing, we don't think Peter was involved. When we got to him in the early hours he was in bed with a woman and she's said they both stayed there last night. You're going to have to run with what we've got from Lisa Aldridge's statement for now. I'm going to be here for another couple of hours and then I'll join you back at the station and we'll see what we've got, okay?'

'Okay, boss.'

By the time Hunter and Grace returned to the custody suite the excitement had subsided. The ambulance taking Alan Darbyshire to hospital had left and Hunter could see that normality — if one could call it that — had returned. The custody sergeant certainly looked less stressed.

Peter Blake-Hall had requested the services of a solicitor and Hunter wasn't surprised when he heard it was Thomas Wilkinson, a partner with a firm who frequently represented clients who had grievances against the police.

As he entered the interview room, Hunter rolled his neck, just like he did before climbing into the boxing-ring. He felt wired.

'Mr Blake-Hall, we meet again,' he said, dragging out a chair and sitting down. He placed his folder down on the table. Shifting his gaze to the solicitor, he asked, 'And you are?' even though, he knew who it was. He was in no mood to acknowledge his celebrity status.

'Mr Thomas Wilkinson, of Grant, Harding and Wilkinson.'

Hunter said, 'I presume you have fully briefed your client and he understands why he's here?'

'Two o'clock this fucking morning when I was banged up,' Peter interrupted. 'For the murder of my wife, they said. You have to be kidding.'

Hunter edged forward slightly, pointing at his face. 'Does it look like I'm kidding?'

The solicitor made an exaggerated attempt at clearing his throat. 'No need for sarcasm, DS Kerr.'

Grace quickly intervened. 'Peter, we're going to tape record an interview with you.' She switched on the equipment and began the open preamble and formally cautioned him.

Hunter reached across the table, interlaced his fingers and fixed Peter Blake-Hall with a determined look. He took a deep breath and composed himself, before saying, 'You have been arrested on suspicion of the murder of your wife, Lucy, back in 1983. Although we never found your wife's body, someone else was charged, tried and convicted of her murder, but new evidence has come to light which throws that conviction into doubt. We have begun a new investigation into her murder and as a result of our enquiries you have been put into the frame for her disappearance.'

Peter's arms remained locked in a folded position and he stared back at Hunter, straight-faced.

Hunter opened his folder, slipped out a photocopy of a witness statement and carefully placed it on the table. 'Peter, I have here a photocopy of the original statement you made to Detective Sergeant Alan Darbyshire and Detective Constable Jeffery Howson, who came to see you after you had reported Lucy missing, on the morning of Saturday 27th August, 1983. Can you recall making that statement to those detectives?'

'Yeah, though I can't remember what I put in it. It was so long ago.'

'That's understandable, but don't worry because I'm going to take you through it.' Hunter picked up the first page. 'According to this, you told those detectives that you last saw Lucy at about seven p.m. on Friday, the 26th of August, when she left the house, telling you that she was meeting up with a couple of friends.'

'Yeah, Amanda Smith was one of them. I think she's called Rawlinson now. I can't remember the others though.'

'No problem, Peter. And you say in this statement that you believe she caught the bus into town?'

Peter nodded. 'Yeah. She did, because I can remember they tracked down the bus driver who dropped her off near the marketplace.'

'Did she tell you what her arrangements were that night?'

'You mean regarding her meeting up with Danny?'

'Well, I'm after what she said to you.'

'She didn't mention that slime-ball, if that's what you're getting at. She said she was just meeting up with a few friends and she'd be back about ten. I was looking after Jessica and she knew I normally went to the club about that time. When she didn't come back, I rang round some of her mates, Amanda first, and that's when I realised she hadn't gone out to meet them. I waited till midnight and then, when she still hadn't come in, I rang the police. I told you the rest the other day.'

'Yes, you did.' Hunter roved his eyes through the statement. 'You've put in this statement a description of the clothing she was wearing when she went out. Can you remember that still?'

Peter stared up to the ceiling. He appeared to be deep in thought. Then he replied, 'She had on a yellow dress and a fawn cardigan that had some kind of design around the neck and cuffs. She had her handbag with her as well. The one you lot found in Danny Weaver's shed.'

'The one Alan Darbyshire and Jeffery Howson found, you mean?'

'Yeah.'

'They showed you that bag on the Sunday, according to your statement?'

'Yeah, that's right. They brought it to my house. Asked me if I recognised it. I told them it was Lucy's and that's when they told me they had Danny locked up. And that's when they also told me she'd been carrying on with him for six months.'

'So, until Alan and Jeffery told you Lucy was having an affair with Danny Weaver, you had no idea.'

'None at all. It was a complete shock.'

'Can I just take you back to that Friday night when Lucy went out?'

Peter tipped his head.

'You said, both in your statement and just now on tape, that when Lucy had not come home, you first phoned around her friends and then just after midnight you rang the police?'

'Yeah.'

'Did you go out looking for her?' Hunter thought he caught a flicker of unease in Peter's eyes. The man tightened the lock in his folded arms.

'No.' A split-second later, he added, 'I was looking after Jessica, wasn't I? How could I go out?'

'Yes, of course you were.' Hunter looked down at the last page of Peter's statement. He moved his head to make it look as though he was reading what was recorded, then he raised his eyes. 'Peter, just one thing. Can you remember what car you were driving at that time?'

Peter frowned. 'What's the relevance of that?'

'It's cropped up in our enquiries.'

Peter shrugged. 'No idea.'

'What if I give you a bit of a help?' Hunter leafed through his folder again and picked out the recent witness statement supplied by Lisa Aldridge. 'What about a red Mercedes Benz on German plates? I am right in thinking that around that time you were importing cars from Germany — Mercedes and BMWs?'

'No secret. They were cheaper from there. You didn't have to pay VAT on them. I wasn't doing anything illegal.'

'I'm not accusing you of anything. I'm just trying to help you recall if you owned a red Mercedes saloon on the night of Lucy's disappearance.'

'Can't remember. Might have done. I've owned one in the past.'

'What if I help you out further by telling you that we have checked your records at the DVLA and they show that in 1983 you owned a red Mercedes-Benz 380SL on German plates, which you re-registered in October of that year.'

Before Peter had time to reply, his solicitor intervened. 'Detective Sergeant, what is the relevance of this line of questioning?'

Although Hunter was replying to the solicitor, he looked squarely into the eyes of Peter. 'The relevance is that this statement here —' Hunter began shaking Lisa's witness statement — 'puts your client in Barnwell marketplace at around 10.45 p.m. on Friday the 26th of August, 1983. He was seen driving his red Mercedes into the marketplace, pulling up in front of his wife, and then dragging Lucy into the front passenger seat, before driving away. According to this statement, your client is the last person to have seen Lucy alive, and in my book that puts him clearly in the frame as a murder suspect.'

Hunter watched Peter Blake-Hall's face turn ashen. He was waiting for him to respond when the solicitor laid a hand on Peter's tightly folded arms.

'In the light of this recent evidence, I would like to confer with my client.'

Following the solicitor's request, Hunter and Grace had no option but to bring the interview to an end. Hunter grinned at Peter Blake-Hall as they formally wrapped up the session. He knew he had him rattled. He also knew that because of the solicitor's intervention there was the likelihood of him engaging in a 'no comment' interview to any future questions.

20 minutes later, when he and Grace returned to the interview room that was precisely the case as they tried a second bout of questioning.

Peter sat back in his chair, arms folded, as Hunter read out the statement from Amanda Rawlinson. He deliberately broke off at the end of every paragraph, to check back with a question, but Peter continuously replied with, 'No comment.' 35 minutes into the second interview, Hunter called it a day and handed Peter over to the custody sergeant to be returned to his cell.

Hunter trudged his way up the stairs with a head full of dark thoughts. He shouldered the doors into the office. The sight of Dawn Leggate, sitting at his desk, took him by surprise. 'Oh, hello boss, I wasn't expecting to see you.'

'I've just called the custody suite and they said you were on your way up here. How did it go?'

Hunter dropped down into Grace's empty chair and outlined the interview they had just had. When he finished, Dawn said, 'Bollocks.'

It drew a smile from Hunter. 'Couldn't have put it any finer, boss. Anyway, how's it gone at Peter's place?'

'The house is spotless.'

'We tried to draw him out about Ronnie but he was having none of it. Said he wasn't saying anything until his solicitor was present. I've seized his phone though — if he's had it a while, it'll give us some info. One of the team has whisked that across to Headquarters and the techies have promised to fast-track it.'

'Good.' Dawn rang her hands together. 'You didn't show him the photographs taken by Guy Armstrong, did you?'

Hunter shook his head.

'And you didn't drop out what Chicken George saw?'

'For what that evidence is worth, no.'

'I know it's not worth much, but we have to put it to him and see what reaction he gives to it.'

'You want me and Grace to do another interview with him?'

'Not today, Hunter, no. We'll let Mark's team and SOCO finish off at his house and have another go at him tomorrow. We'll bed him down for the night and start afresh. I'll authorise the extension to his detention. We can't have him disappearing like his mate Ronnie. In the meantime, check on how Alan Darbyshire is getting on. The last I was told was that it definitely was a heart-attack, and that he's now comfortable on a ward, but they're not going to release him for a couple of days at least. I've already given instructions for them to release his guard. He's not going anywhere.' She yawned, clamping a hand across her mouth. 'Mr Robshaw's going to give a de-briefing at seven tonight. I'm going to call it a day before I collapse. Is there anything you and Grace can pick up?'

Her question triggered a thought from Hunter. 'There is something I'd like to run past you.'

'Go on then.'

'No one's talked to Jessica. We've spoken with Lucy's parents but we've not spoken with her daughter. Her grandparents said she'd seen a psychiatrist in the past because of nightmares and problems she had suffered as a child, but we never asked if their sessions had revealed anything. Why don't we speak to her? It's not going to harm anything, is it? She was five when her mum disappeared, and it's surprising just how much kids are aware of at that age.'

'I agree, Hunter. You and Grace see if you can fix it up and feed it back in at briefing.' With that, Dawn levered herself out of Hunter's chair and headed for the door. She waved a hand without looking back. 'See you in the morning.'

When Grace returned to the office, Hunter updated her about his conversation with Dawn and she searched for a contact number for Jessica. They hadn't a direct phone number for her but they had Lucy's parents' telephone number on file.

Grace's call to them was picked up within seconds and the first minute of the conversation were a barrage of questions about the latest developments in the investigation. Grace happily provided the answers, then moved on to the real purpose of her call. She explained that they had Peter in custody and needed to speak with Jessica. Margaret Hall was anxious but Grace managed to convince her that it was necessary, assuring her that they would tread sensitively. She invited Margaret to come along with her granddaughter and arranged to meet them the next day.

As expected, evening briefing was short. Nothing incriminating had been found at Peter Blake-Hall's home and the search teams were going to start on his club the next day. Ronnie Fisher had gone to ground. Task Force and CID had turned over a number of homes belonging to family members and close associates but they hadn't been able to find him. A nationwide manhunt was now in place.

Robshaw concluded the session by telling everyone that he wanted them all in for 7 a.m. the following morning.

Hunter decided to call in and see Mike on his way home. He rode the lift up to the third floor of the District General hospital. Mike was on the surgical ward. Following the signs, Hunter strode down the corridor, entered the ward and found the unit where Mike was sitting up in bed. There was a dark-haired woman sitting at his bedside. Her face was in side profile and the sight of her took Hunter by surprise. He had only ever seen Chief Inspector Janet Dobson in uniform. He knew from his visits to Headquarters that she was in charge of the Prosecutions Department. But here, she was in civvies, leaning across Mike's bed, holding his hand and chatting to him.

Hunter smirked. *Well, you crafty old bugger. All that time, I thought you were alone, but you've been knocking off a Chief Inspector.* Hunter retraced his steps. *You don't need me tonight for company, Mike Sampson.*

Hunter was about to get in the lift when he felt a tap on his shoulder. He turned to see Pauline Darbyshire. She looked drained.

'I thought it was you,' she said.

He picked out a note of nervousness in her voice. 'Have you just been visiting Alan?' he asked. This felt awkward.

'Yes. Have you come to check on how he's doing?'

'No, I've just called in to see a colleague.'

'Oh, I hope it's nothing serious. I'm glad I've caught you, DS Kerr. Alan said he'd like to talk to you.'

Hunter threw her a quizzical look. 'What do you mean?'

575

'He's finally told me what's happened. He's in a right state. He knows it's pretty serious but he wants to get it sorted out.' She touched Hunter's arm. 'I think he trusts you. Go and have a word with him, will you? He's only just down the corridor.'

'But I can't speak to him, Mrs Darbyshire. I can only do that in a proper interview. I can't do it here in hospital.'

She gripped his coat. 'Please, DS Kerr, he sounds desperate.'

Hunter sighed.

'Please,' she repeated.

He was about to politely refuse once more and then curiosity kicked in. Hunter patted Pauline's hand. 'Of course I'll have a chat with Alan.'

He followed her back along the corridor to the admissions ward.

Pauline pointed out where her husband was and left Hunter at the door.

Alan Darbyshire was propped up in his bed, hooked up to a beeping monitor. Hunter thought he looked surprisingly well, given that he'd had a heart attack only 12 hours earlier.

'Gave us quite a scare there, Alan,' he opened, dragging a chair over.

'They've said it was a warning. Got to change my lifestyle, blah, blah, blah. You know, the usual routine. A couple of days and I'll be out of here and back in your cell.' Darbyshire gave a reluctant smile.

'Pauline told me you wanted a word?'

'If you wouldn't mind.'

Hunter sank into the chair. 'What can I do for you?'

'Look, I know from yesterday's interview that you've got enough on me for perverting the course of justice and perjury, but I think I should explain things so you understand how I got into this mess.'

'You can do that when we interview you once you get out of here.'

'Oh, come off it, Hunter. You'll get the version I want to give you in interview. Don't you really want to know what went off?'

Hunter eyed him curiously for a few seconds. Then he said, 'I'm listening.'

Darbyshire's mouth tightened. 'I'm not as bad as you think, you know. Sure, I've strayed a little, but that's what we all did back in the 70s and 80s. Dodging and weaving with a job ran with the territory. I include Jeff in that as well. It was just how we worked as a team.' His look hardened. 'But Jeff didn't deserve this. This has gone beyond what I thought would happen.'

'I'm listening.'

'I was never into Peter Blake-Hall for anything, neither was Jeff. We were not on the take, like you're thinking. True, Jeff and I got a new car and a holiday at Peter's place in Benidorm, but we paid for those. You probably know that Peter was my snout. I came across him as a young man, when he was just setting up his own mechanic's business. He knew who was into ringing motors and doing bits of handling and he helped me put a few villains away. It was a good little number I had going with him. It helped me get promoted and in return I helped him out when he got that club. I advised him how to run it, and how not to get caught out, especially with it being a strip-club. I mean, he wasn't doing any harm, was he?' Darbyshire chewed his bottom lip and said, 'Getting round to Lucy. When Peter rang me that day and told me she was missing, Jeff and I went to see him and we really did believe what he told us. We did all those enquiries that are on the file and from what the witnesses said, we genuinely thought we'd find her at Daniel Weaver's house. So when we went there and saw those scratches to his face and no sign of Lucy, we thought he'd harmed her. Finding Lucy's bag in his shed sealed it for us.'

'You really found that bag in the shed then?'

'On my honour, yes, I promise. Jeff and I firmly believed Daniel had done something to Lucy. We found out he'd been having an affair with her and that she was pregnant with his child. We assumed he'd flipped that Friday night and killed her. As you know, he didn't confess, but we were absolutely convinced he'd done it and so that's why we did those extra notes.' Darbyshire shook his head. 'When he was found guilty, we still believed we'd got our man. Jeff and I visited him in prison with the aim of finding out where he'd buried Lucy, and even when he continued with the innocent act, we thought it was just a show.'

'When did everything change?'

'When we started to hear a few whispers about Peter and Ronnie bringing in drugs. And then there was that accident where the undercover officer got killed in that reporter's car. Which, as you know, was covered up by crime squad. I saw him, you know, at Peter's club, but I didn't know he was an undercover cop. I was with Peter on the night he got killed, so I knew he wasn't involved in that.'

'And Ronnie?'

'Ronnie is a nasty piece of work. I believe it was Ronnie who did Jeff, and it wouldn't surprise me if he'd been involved in running that reporter's car off the road. Nothing would surprise me about that man.'

'What makes you say that?'

'I've got to know him these past dozen or so years. I've seen what he's done to a few who've upset him at the club. Ronnie is a psycho.'

'So what happened before Jeff got killed? Did he tell you about the notes he'd kept of Daniel's interview?'

'He didn't say he had the notes. I actually thought those were long gone. I watched him burn them, or at least I thought so. I never knew he'd kept them all these years.'

'So what happened?'

'A couple of weeks before he was killed, he rang me. He said it had been preying on his mind about what we'd done to Danny Weaver, and that maybe Peter had really killed Lucy. I told him he was just feeling low. He told me about his cancer and that he'd not got long to live and that he wanted to make amends. He said he was just letting me know he'd kept some evidence to help Danny get his conviction overturned. I told him to think about what he was doing — meaning the consequences for me, but he just repeated he'd thought about it a long time. He thought Peter was responsible for Lucy's death and maybe a new investigation would prove it. Then he hung up on me.'

'And you told Peter.'

Darbyshire slunk low on his pillow, looking defeated. 'Yes, that's what those photos are about. I'd phoned Peter and told him that I needed to see him urgently. I went to his club and told him what Jeff had said to me. And I asked him straight out if he'd killed Lucy.'

'And what did he say?'

'He denied it, of course. But I've been a detective a long time and I could tell when I looked him in the face that he knew something about it. And by that, I'm thinking Ronnie. Ronnie was the one who kept saying I needed to do something about it. Make sure the evidence disappeared. I'll never forget what his face was like when he told me that either I sort it or he'd sort it for me. I'm telling you, Ronnie killed Jeff.'

Hunter wasn't about to tell Darbyshire that post-mortem findings indicated that the likelihood was that two people had been involved in

Howson's murder. He said, 'And what about the girl, Jodie Marie Jenkinson?'

'I didn't know about that. It was Peter who rang me and told me that a reporter was bugging him and asked me if I'd said anything to anyone. I told him I wasn't that stupid. Then he told me that this Guy Armstrong knew an awful lot, and that if it wasn't me then someone had to have overheard our conversation. The only two people in the club that morning besides me, Peter and Ronnie, were the bar manager and a girl stocking up the bar. I told him not to do anything stupid.'

'You know the girl was found murdered in the old Barnwell Inn, don't you?'

'Yeah, I saw it on the local news. But I swear that is nothing to do with me. That's down to Peter and Ronnie.'

Hunter leaned forward and scrutinised Darbyshire's face. Then he asked, 'What are you after, Alan? Telling me all this?'

'Look, I know you've got enough on me. I'm not stupid. Those notes Jeff kept have sunk me, but at least I can broker a deal.'

'A deal?'

'Yes.' Darbyshire grabbed Hunter's sleeve. 'I wish I could turn the clock back. I really do. And believe me, recently I've not been able to sleep over it, but I can honestly say that at the time I believed Danny Weaver had murdered Lucy.'

'But he didn't, did he?'

Darbyshire looked shamefaced. 'That's why I need to make amends. I'll stand up in court and give evidence against Peter and Ronnie about those photographs you have of us. I'll tell the court what that meeting was about, just before Jeff and that girl's murder. It'll be enough to swing a jury. And in return I want a reduced sentence in an open prison. That's the deal.'

DAY SIXTEEN

'He doesn't deserve it, but I think CPS will go for it,' Robshaw said, having listened to Hunter's version of the previous evening's chat with Alan Darbyshire. 'Evidence in a murder, or in this case four murders, outweighs a 25-year-old perjury charge. And don't forget the press coverage on this one. I'll speak with CPS first thing this morning and run it past them.'

Robshaw rubbed his hands together and then gave them a loud clap. 'Okay everyone, we pick up where we left off yesterday.' He pointed at Hunter. 'You and Grace re-interview Peter. The clock on him runs out at two p.m. today. Hit him with the photographs Guy Armstrong took and Kerri-Ann Bairstow's statement. Let's see what he says about those. I've asked the techies at Headquarters to examine the memory of his phone today to see if we can put him anywhere near our murder sites and also check if he has any incriminating texts. If I get that information back in the next couple of hours, then we can hopefully squeeze in another interview before the end of his detention. Given what Alan Darbyshire has said, together with Lisa Aldridge's statement, I'm going to see if CPS are happy with what we've got so far and get them to agree to a holding charge for the murder of his wife Lucy.'

He turned to Tony Bullars. 'Tony, I want you and Carol to take Jessica out to her father's house and see if anything comes of it. It's a long shot, but I know of cases where it has worked. The psychologists call it recovered memory therapy.' Pausing, Robshaw cast his eyes around the incident room, breaking into a smile. 'Good news, everyone. Mike came around yesterday afternoon and, except for a few war wounds, he's none the worse for wear. He's identified his attacker as Ronnie Fisher. We've got him bang to rights on one thing at least. Let's make today count. Good hunting, everyone.'

Peter Blake-Hall, now sporting a fresh shirt and pair of jeans, looked relaxed as Hunter and Grace entered the interview room and sat down.

His solicitor sat beside him, legal pad and pen at the ready.

'Found Ronnie yet?' Peter asked smugly.

Hunter slowly opened his folder and took a deep breath. 'This interview is about you, Mr Blake-Hall. It does not concern Ronnie Fisher.'

'I take it, then, that you haven't found him,' Peter said with a wide grin.

Hunter felt himself tense.

Grace toe-tapped one of his ankles, her reminder to him to stay in control. Then she started the tape machine and went through the opening procedures before the interview could commence.

When she had finished, Hunter said, 'Peter, this morning I want to talk to you about an incident which went on at the front of your club on the morning of the of the tenth of November, just over a month ago. You and Ronnie Fisher had a meeting with a man called Alan Darbyshire, a retired police officer.' He watched the smirk disappear from Peter's face. 'Or rather, I should say disagreement. Do you remember that?'

'No.'

'Well, let me help you remember.' Hunter opened his folder and slid out the A4 photographs Guy Armstrong had taken. He dabbed at the one that showed Peter stabbing Alan Darbyshire in the chest with his finger. 'Take a look at these carefully, Peter. You'll see they are timed and dated. Do these help your memory?'

Peter's head was down, his eyes on the photographs, but Hunter could see the colour draining from his face. He mumbled, 'No comment.'

'Now I've shown you these photographs, can you recall what was said during your meeting?'

'No comment.'

'I can help you there as well, because I've been chatting with Alan Darbyshire, and he says he came to see you that morning because he'd had a phone call from Jeffery Howson saying he had evidence, which he had kept hidden for 25 years, which would exonerate Daniel Weaver and blow Lucy's murder case wide open again. And I understand you were not too happy about that and threats were made against Jeffery, together with suggestions that the evidence should be made to disappear.'

Peter raised his head. He looked livid.

'And a couple of weeks after that meeting, Jeffery Howson was found murdered at his home. Do you know anything about that?'

Peter chewed on his lip.

'I would appreciate an answer. In your own time, of course.' Hunter sized his prisoner up across the table.

Through clenched teeth, Peter replied, 'No comment.'

Hunter leaned back in the seat. 'Did you expect Alan Darbyshire to keep quiet about this, Peter? Well, unfortunately for you, he's in the process of making a deal with CPS. He's not too happy about his friend being killed.'

'Detective Sergeant Kerr!' the solicitor intervened. He tapped his pen sharply on the table. 'Kindly stick to the proper methods of interviewing, if you wouldn't mind.'

'Sorry, Mr Wilkinson, I thought I was.'

The solicitor scowled.

Hunter put on a false smile and returned his gaze to Peter. 'Have you ever been to Jeffery Howson's house or near Woodland View where he lived?'

'No.'

'You're absolutely sure of that?' Hunter studied his face.

'I would know if I'd been to his house, wouldn't I? No, I haven't.'

'Okay, thank you.' Hunter played with the photographs, straightening them along the table. 'I just want to take you back to these photos. I've already mentioned Alan Darbyshire's take on this meeting. What if I also tell you that your conversation was overheard by a girl who was working that morning in your bar. What if I tell you that she told a friend of hers that she overheard you talking about the murder of your wife Lucy, and that person has made a statement about your conversation between yourself, Ronnie Fisher and Alan Darbyshire.'

'Is there a question there, officer?' the solicitor asked.

Hunter fixed him with a hard stare. 'There is, if you'd let me finish.' He looked at Peter. 'Did you know that a girl called Jodie Marie Jenkinson, who worked for you behind your bar, overheard your conversation that morning?'

'No comment.'

'And that she then contacted a reporter called Guy Armstrong and that she told him of the conversation. Were you aware of that?'

'No comment.'

'Was that why he was at your house that morning when we came? He wanted a comment from you regarding the conversation Jodie had overheard. That was why we caught you arguing and pushing him away, wasn't it, Peter?'

'No comment.'

'Jodie was found dead three weeks ago in a pub called the Barnwell Inn and we're treating that death as murder. Have you been to that pub in recent weeks?'

'No.'

'Sure about that, Peter?'

'Definitely.'

'Peter, we seem to be going nowhere here. I've explained that several people have either given statements against you, or are about to give a statement, which puts you in the frame for the murder of your wife, Lucy. Would you like to say something in your defence, other than to answer no comment?'

'No comment.'

'What about the murder of Jeffery Howson?'

'No comment.'

'Do you want to say anything in relation to the murder of Jodie Marie Jenkinson?'

'No comment.'

Hunter shuffled the photographs together, stacked them one on top of the other and slipped them back into his folder. He said, 'This interview is over.'

Hunter picked up his folder. As he got to the door, Peter Blake-Hall called out, 'How is your colleague, Detective?'

Hunter swivelled to see Peter targeting him with a menacing stare. Hunter spat out, 'Sorry?'

'Your colleague? The one who was stabbed outside my club?'

'Why — do you know something about that?'

The edges of Peter's mouth curled upwards. 'It's a dangerous place out there, Detective. Be careful.'

Reading the underlying threat in what Peter had just said, Hunter stared back. He wanted to smash that smug grin right off his face. Instead, he replied, 'Thank you for your concern, but I'm a big boy, Peter, I think I can look after myself.'

Jessica and her grandmother arrived at reception ten minutes before their appointed time. Carol Ragen nipped downstairs to meet them, taking them through to the car park where Tony Bullars was waiting in an unmarked car.

Carol hopped into the passenger seat and Jessica and Margaret slid into the back.

As they belted up, Tony thanked them for coming. He couldn't help but notice how much Jessica looked like her mother. She had the same blonde hair, though in Jessica's case, it was slightly longer. It was swept back from her face, cascading down the back of her coat.

He said. 'Your grandmother's explained the purpose of your visit today?'

Jessica nodded. She glanced at Margaret and grasped her hand.

'And you're okay with everything?'

'I think so, yes.'

'Before we take you to your father's house…'

Jessica interrupted, 'He's not there, is he?'

'No, he isn't.'

She breathed a sigh of relief. 'Good.'

'Before we go there, I just want to ask you a few questions, Jessica. If you are uncomfortable at any time with what I'm asking, you just tell me, okay?'

She nodded.

'When we spoke with your grandmother the other day, she happened to mention that you had seen a psychiatrist —'

'Only until I was 15. I didn't think there was any point after that.'

'Okay, fine. And you had been seeing him because of the dreams you were having?'

'Nightmares. And I still have them, but I can cope with them a lot better now. They're just part of my life.'

'Jessica, I just want to ask you what you see in these nightmares. We haven't spoken with your psychiatrist, and I appreciate this is confidential and personal to you, but it might just be of help to us.'

'I don't see how it can.'

'Well, you never know. We've completed a lot more enquiries now that were overlooked in the original case when your mother went missing and we've learned a bit more. It might link in with something. After all, something in your past is responsible for triggering them. Don't you agree?'

She shrugged.

'Can you tell us what happens in them?'

Jessica squeezed her grandmother's hand tighter. 'They always seem to start off with either a scream or a moan. Sometimes it's both. And then I'm in this long corridor and then suddenly I'm standing in a doorway and when I look down...' She paused and stared blankly through the windscreen, before continuing. 'It's like an out of body experience, you know? Weird like. Well, then I'm looking down at my feet and blood's coming up through my toes.' For a couple of seconds, she remained transfixed, staring. Then her focus was back and she said, 'That's it. Almost the same thing, every time.'

'So you don't see anyone in these nightmares?'

Jessica lapsed into a thoughtful silence for a few seconds and then replied, 'No, I don't think so. Though I do see shadows.'

'Shadows?'

'Just shadows. That's it, I'm afraid.'

'Okay, thank you.' Tony started the car. 'Right, let's get you over to your dad's place.'

They had only travelled a mile before Jessica piped up from the back, 'Where are we going?'

'To your dad's house,' said Tony.

'But you're going the wrong way.'

'No, this is the way to Hooton Roberts.'

'Hooton Roberts?'

'Yes! Where your dad lives.'

'No, we didn't live there. Me and Mum. We used to live outside Wortley.'

Tony slowed the car and pulled into the kerb. A car behind blared its horn. Turning around, he said, 'You're saying there's another house?'

'Another house? No, I'm saying the house that I know, and where I was brought up, was a cottage between Wortley and Birdwell. Dad was doing it up when Mum disappeared.'

Glancing sideways, Tony's surprised look mirrored his colleague's. He turned back to Jessica. 'We've been searching the wrong house. We thought Peter's current home was where he lived when your mum disappeared.'

'No, I've never been to that house. He got that house about 18 months after Daniel's trial.'

Tony slammed into first gear, wrenched hard on the steering and spun the car around onto the opposite carriageway. He managed a U-turn in one manoeuvre. 'Right, Jessica, you point the way to the house.'

Shooting up the Dearne Parkway, Tony picked up the Stocksbridge bypass and then took the minor road to Wortley.

Passing the church, Margaret pointed out Constable Row, where she and her husband used to live. Then 100 yards further on she called out again, 'Turn right, just ahead, that's where the house is.'

Tony turned and found himself driving along a narrow road. Skeletal trees lined the first 200 yards of the route and as he left them behind the view opened out to farmland either side. The only cottages he could make out seemed to be those on the hillsides, miles away. As he came out of a left-hand bend, Jessica called from the back, 'It's just along here.'

Tony spotted the cottage up ahead, slightly set back from the road. It was larger than he had imagined; a solid Yorkshire stone farmhouse. He had to mount the grassy verge at the front to park, otherwise he would have blocked the carriageway.

Turning in his seat, he said, 'Just give me a couple of minutes. I'll see if there's anyone in.' He turned off the engine.

Five minutes later he returned to the car and stuck his head inside. 'There's a woman in. Her husband's at work. Not surprisingly, she was taken aback when I told her why I'd come, but she's kindly agreed to let us in to have a look round.' He set his gaze upon Jessica. 'Are you still okay with this?'

'I think so, yes.'

Tony opened the door to let out Jessica and Margaret.

For a few seconds Jessica stood and stared. Her grandmother wound a protective arm around her. She said softly, 'Are you okay, love?'

'Yes thanks, Gran,' Jessica answered.

Tony led the way and the others followed him down the path, skirting around the side of the house to the rear. At the back door a well-made lady in her early 50s was waiting. She looked perplexed and Tony wasn't surprised, given the strange request he had made.

As they stepped into the kitchen, Tony turned to Jessica. 'Anything?' He watched as Jessica's gaze darted around the room.

She said, 'Most of its how I remember. The units look familiar, though there wasn't a table and chairs here.' Pointing to the far wall, she added, 'And that dresser wasn't here.' She stepped into the middle of the floor and slowly turned her head. She looked at the woman who owned the house. 'Do you mind?' she asked, pointing at a door which connected with the hallway.

'Be my guest,' the woman replied. She still wore a bewildered expression.

Jessica walked to the doorway, spent a few seconds looking around the hallway, and then pirouetted on her heels and faced the kitchen. Suddenly, she clamped a hand over her mouth. 'Oh my God!' Her face paled. Then she started to sway.

Tony got to her just as her legs buckled. He caught her under the arms and then half-dragged, half-carried her to a chair Carol pulled from beneath the table. He lowered her into the seat and supported her.

Jessica's face was waxen and a band of sweat had gathered on her forehead. She took a deep breath. 'I saw my mother!' she gasped. 'She was lying just there!'

A Welsh dresser, shelves laden with blue and white decorative pottery, stood on the spot where she was pointing.

'Bingo!' Hunter called, as he read what was on his computer screen for the second time. Behind him, the printer whirred into action and he picked out each page as it fell into the feed tray. He fanned out five sheets of paper like a winning poker hand and checked everything had been printed out. Satisfied, he picked them up, patted them together and rang the custody suite. It was answered by the custody officer.

Hunter said, 'Can you rouse Peter Blake-Hall's solicitor for me, please? You can tell him I've got some good news for his client.' As he hung up, he slid the papers across his desk to Grace. 'Just feast your eyes upon those goodies, Grace,' he said, checking his watch. 'Good timing. We've got another hour before his clock runs out. Can you help me knock some charges together? I'm going to give Peter Blake-Hall an early Christmas present.'

Clasping a handful of rolled up papers, Hunter skipped across the rear yard to the custody suite like a child released from class at the end of the day.

Grace was on his coat-tails. As they entered the charging area, Hunter saw Peter Blake-Hall standing next to his solicitor.

The solicitor tapped the face of his watch. 'DS Kerr, in 20 minutes, my client's time is up and you will have to either release him or charge him.'

'Thank you for pointing that out to me, Mr Wilkinson, I am fully aware of that. This will be short and sweet.'

'Then you will be bailing Mr Blake-Hall?'

'On this occasion, no.' Hunter slowly unfolded his paperwork. 'You remember we seized your mobile phone, Peter?' He searched his face for a reaction. 'Well, I don't know if you are aware, but those things hold such a vast amount of information. It logs every call you make and every text, even if you delete them —'

'Is there a point to these deliberations, Detective?' asked the solicitor.

'There is, if you'd kindly give me a moment.' Hunter rocked and flexed his neck. 'There is also a magical thing called cell-site analysis. We can pick out every location you have ever been to with your phone. Not only can we accurately map where you have been, we can also time and date those visits.' Hunter saw Peter Blake-Hall's face drain of colour. 'And I can tell you, Peter, that from your mobile, we have been able to log you as being on Jeffery Howson's street at 10.52 pm on the night of Saturday the 22nd of November, which was the night he was murdered. But then, of course you would know that.'

Hunter paused for a couple of seconds, hoping for a response. When there was none, he continued, 'We also have you logged at the site of the old Barnwell Inn on the afternoon of the fifth of November. That is the location where we found Jodie Marie Jenkinson's body. Finally, we have you logged at various locations between Wentworth and Harley on the night of the first of December, which is when Guy Armstrong was run off the road and his car set on fire, killing him.'

Hunter watched Peter's jaw drop. 'Peter Blake-Hall, I am charging you with the murders of Jeffery Howson, Jodie Marie Jenkinson and Guy Armstrong.' As he cautioned him, Hunter thought, *There's just one more murder now to resolve — the one that had triggered this whole dramatic chain of events — that of Peter's wife, Lucy.*

DAY SEVENTEEN

The Incident Room was packed. Task Force Officers had been drafted in to search for Lucy's body. There were bums on seats and on desks, and uniform and plain clothed officers stood shoulder to shoulder in the aisles for the morning briefing.

The previous afternoon, the Scenes of Crime Team had visited the cottage where the Blake-Halls once lived. In an area behind the present owner's Welsh dresser, traces of blood were found in the gap between the floor and the skirting board. That sample had been transported by a police motor cyclist earlier the previous evening, together with a comparison DNA sample from Jessica. If it was Lucy's blood, they would soon know.

The house had been sealed off as a crime scene and the shocked owners had been shipped out to stay with relatives. A Forensics team had been working through the night examining the kitchen; floor tiles and part of the skirting board had been removed and additional dried blood patches had been found — every indication that they had found the spot where Lucy was murdered.

The focus of this morning's briefing was to find Lucy's burial site. A police expert in body search techniques was leading the briefing. He said, 'I visited the farmhouse yesterday afternoon and the woodland below the house is the most probable location where Lucy's body is buried.'

Directly behind him, taped to Lucy's incident board, was a large-scale ordnance map of the Wortley area. He placed a hand over part of it. 'I have identified three key sites in the woods.' He prodded three areas of the map. Each of the sections had been marked by oblong shapes. He pointed to one of the boxes. 'This will be our first search quadrant this morning. If we get an indication that it is a burial site, then we will fix the area and call in forensics.

'The weather forecast over the next few days is in our favour and the winter terrain on the ground is thin at this time of the year, so that is also an advantage. However, what is against us is the length of time Lucy has been in the ground, so everyone has to move extra slow within the search grids and keep their eyes peeled.' He wound up by saying, 'If you find something, call me.'

While most of MIT were out searching for Ronnie Fisher, Hunter and Grace's assignment for that day was to prepare the remand file for Peter Blake-Hall. His first court appearance was that afternoon and they already knew that his solicitor was not going to be contesting the remand. Nevertheless, the file they presented before the magistrates still had to contain all the relevant evidence from the major witnesses, together with the forensic information which had sealed Blake-Hall's fate.

Grace's desk phone started ringing. She let it go for a few seconds before picking up. The voice at the other end caused her head to jolt. She grabbed Hunter's attention by pointing excitedly at the handset. Snatching up a piece of scrap paper, Grace began scribbling as she listened.

Hunter tried to make sense of the one-sided conversation. He could tell from Grace's reaction and wild note-taking that it had to be important.

Finally, after ten minutes, she slammed down the phone. 'You'll never guess who that was.'

Hunter opened his hands and shrugged.

'Kerri-Ann Bairstow. And guess what?'

'Grace!'

'Okay, okay, I'll tell you. She thinks she knows where Ronnie Fisher is, or at least where he's going to be later today.'

'Bloody hell, Grace.'

'Exactly. She says the info's come from a mate of hers who used to buy their smack from Ronnie. He's got his head down in a flat at Lundwood, but he's booked on board a ship tonight to Amsterdam. He's sailing from Hull at midnight. But before that he's got to collect some cash stashed in the safe at Peter Blake-Hall's club. He's going there some time later today before it opens.' She took another look at her notes. 'A guy called Scott Riley is picking him up and running him out there.'

Scott Riley wasn't hard to find; he'd got plenty of form. And they had found a red Vauxhall Corsa registered to him behind his flat. Now all they had to do was wait for it to move.

To help with the capture of Ronnie Fisher, the Force Surveillance Team had been brought in and they were currently parked up in various streets around Scott Riley's address. They had every road and side-street around his home covered. The moment he drove away, someone would be tailing him.

At Peter Blake-Hall's club, the police were waiting. A four-man Task Force Firearms team, together with a dog-handler, were hidden behind garages three streets away, and Hunter and Grace, with Dawn Leggate, were in an unmarked car, parked behind a derelict warehouse on waste ground at the rear of the club.

Hunter was in the driver's seat, shuffling uncomfortably, his fingers rapping away gently at the steering wheel. They had been parked for almost an hour and a trickle of nervous excitement ran through him. As he checked his watch for the umpteenth time, Hunter's personal radio crackled into life. The Surveillance Team were breaking their silence. The crew in the 'eyeball' vehicle announced that two men had just got into Scott Riley's red Corsa, but they were unable to identify the occupants.

A woman's voice announced, 'Target vehicle is off, off, off.'

Hunter gripped the steering wheel — the waiting was over. If it was Ronnie Fisher in the car, then in another 20 minutes, he would be here and within his grasp.

Within five minutes the commentator's voice had changed — the first car had fallen back and a new lead car was now on the Corsa's tail. Hunter could make out that the target vehicle was indeed heading their way. For a couple of seconds, he could hear the blood rushing inside his ears and felt the muscles in his legs and forearms beginning to tighten. The adrenaline had kicked in.

Ten minutes into the unwavering commentary, Hunter heard the sentence he had been waiting for — Ronnie Fisher was the front seat passenger in the Corsa. He turned on the ignition and revved the engine.

The next ten minutes seemed to fly. From the radio chatter, Hunter determined that the Corsa hadn't deviated — it was still heading their way. As the red car entered the final section of side-streets that led to the club, the chatter over the airwaves increased. Hunter knew that several of the tail-end cars from the surveillance convoy would now be peeling away, increasing their speed, ready to block off any escape attempt by the driver of the Corsa. In a few minutes he would be boxed in and going nowhere.

'It's a stop outside the Le Chambre Rose,' came the cry over the radio, quickly followed by, 'Target is out of the vehicle and heading for the front doors.'

Dawn Leggate issued the order, 'Strike, strike, strike!'

Hunter gunned the engine. The car's wheels spun and slid momentarily, churning up loose gravel. Then they gripped and Hunter tore towards the back entrance of the club.

100 yards from the rear of the premises, the call of, 'He's doing a runner,' blared over the airwaves. Hunter saw the emergency double-doors explode open as he entered the rear car park. Ronnie Fisher came out of them so fast he almost fell over. He caught himself, then spun away sideways and picked up his sprint.

Hunter yanked the steering wheel hard, hitting the brakes, and the car skewed. Before it had even jerked to a halt, Hunter had his door open and was launching himself out.

Ronnie was 20 metres ahead but Hunter quickly made ground, snapping close to his heels within seconds. He barked out, 'Police, stop.' It had the desired effect — Ronnie skidded to a halt.

Before Hunter could get within striking distance, Ronnie had turned and dropped into a rugby-squat. Hunter didn't have time to stop and threw himself side-on, catching Ronnie full in the chest with his shoulder. They hit the ground together, Hunter's momentum rolling him away. As he leapt to his feet, Ronnie was mirroring his actions, stretching out his arms to do battle.

In the blink of an eye, Ronnie reached down snatched something out of his right boot. 'I'll fucking kill you,' he growled.

Behind him, Hunter heard Grace scream, 'He's got a knife.' He jerked back. And only just in time, as a glint of metal flashed before him. The blade had missed him by a few inches.

Ronnie slashed forward with the knife again. This time Hunter was ready. He swung his left arm across to deflect the blow. Ronnie wheeled to one side, exposing his ribs. Hunter hooked in his right fist, putting his whole weight behind the punch. A bone-jarring crack resounded and Ronnie screamed in pain as the air exploded from his chest. He toppled, instinctively flinging out an arm to prevent himself from hitting the ground. Hunter brought his elbow crashing down onto the top of his skull like an executioner's axe.

Ronnie hit the ground with a thud.

Hunter jumped away from him, forming a boxing stance just in case Ronnie got up. When he saw that he was well out of it, he clawed in a long gulp of air.

Dawn and Grace approached. Hunter could hear other detectives spilling through the emergency doors, scrambling towards them.

Everyone stopped and encircled the dazed and confused Ronnie Fisher. Blood was trickling from his mouth and nose.

Hunter raised himself up to his full height and took in another deep breath. He was beginning to shake. The first thing he saw was the bemused look upon Dawn's face as she viewed their bloodied target.

Straight-faced, he said, 'Reasonable force, boss!'

DAY EIGHTEEN

After being treated for two broken ribs, a busted nose and a split lip, Ronnie Fisher was released from hospital at 3.30 a.m. and transported across to Barnwell Custody Suite, where he was bedded down for the night.

Back home, Hunter awoke just before 5.30 a.m., and after half an hour of tossing and turning, gave up and climbed into the shower. He drove into work in the dark, his thoughts drifting towards the day ahead.

When he arrived at the office he almost collided with Grace coming out of the toilets. Catching his balance, he said, 'You're in early.'

'Couldn't sleep. Been putting on my face for the day.'

Not surprisingly, they were the first ones in the office, and while Hunter made the hot drinks, Grace put bread into the toaster. They had polished the toast off and replenished their drinks before the first of the other team members arrived.

As they savoured a second round of drinks, they checked and doubled-checked their evidence and made a start on the drafting of preparatory notes for their first interview with Ronnie Fisher. They had Mike's statement identifying Ronnie as the person who had stabbed him, and they had recovered the knife which he had attempted to use on Hunter. They were confident Mike's DNA would be on it.

Ronnie was already looking at charges of attempted murder against Mike and the attempted murder of Hunter. The weight of those two charges would be enough to hold him, giving them sufficient time to collate the evidence relating to the murders of Jeffery Howson, Jodie Marie Jenkinson and Guy Armstrong. And they were very hopeful of getting a result from those as well — like Peter Blake-Hall, Ronnie had kept his mobile phone and that had been seized for examination.

The morning briefing was led by Dawn Leggate. She congratulated everyone on the previous evening's success, and followed up by announcing that as of today she was running everything — Robshaw had been called across to the Force Headquarters in Sheffield to discuss his promotion and new role with the Assistant Chief Constable, and to organise a full press conference to hail the success of their investigation. She then moved on to the real purpose of the briefing — the collating and preservation of evidence against Ronnie Fisher. A search of the red Corsa had turned up several bags of clothing, shoes and trainers, and in Scott Riley's wheelie bin they had found a pair of woollen gloves, smelling strongly of petrol.

She reminded everyone that woollen fibres had been found on Guy Armstrong's petrol cap, at the homes of Jeffery Howson and Jodie Marie Jenkinson, and at the Barnwell Inn. 'If these are the same gloves, then we've really got him bang to rights,' she said proudly, and after a slight pause, continued, 'It doesn't end there, guys. I got another phone call late yesterday — forensics have come up trumps as well. The DNA sample provided by Jessica has helped us identify that the dried bloodstains in the kitchen belong to her mother. It appears we have found where Lucy was murdered. SOCO and the forensic team at the farmhouse are currently extending their examination into other rooms. We are almost there, everyone. All we have to do now is find Lucy's body.'

A solicitor from the firm of Grant, Harding and Wilkinson was representing Ronnie Fisher, and as Hunter stepped into the interview room he had already prepared his thoughts for a challenging interrogation, most likely a battle of wills between himself and a 'pain in the arse' defence solicitor.

Seeing the legal representative, Hunter took in a deep breath and let it out slowly. This one had an appearance even smoother than Peter Blake-Hall's solicitor. He looked to be in his mid-50s with a good head of neatly trimmed silver-grey hair and wore a dark blue pinstriped suit, which appeared handmade. A white Oxford, button-down shirt was teamed with a dark blue monogrammed tie. This man was no legal clerk, thought Hunter, as he dragged out a chair. His appearance shouted senior partner.

Hunter dropped his folder onto the table and lowered himself slowly into the chair. Grace took the seat beside him, next to the tape-recording machine.

Hunter made the introductions and flipped open his folder of notes.

'Mr James Harding,' the solicitor replied.

Guessed right.

Ronnie Fisher was silent. He didn't acknowledge them. Hunter couldn't help but notice the ugly red graze across his forehead and his badly swollen nose and mouth. He fought back the urge to smirk. He waited for the tape machine to kick in and then cautioned Ronnie Fisher. 'Do you understand what I have just said, Mr Fisher?'

Silence.

'I first want to talk to you about the attack on me last night, when you tried to stab me.'

Silence.

For almost 45 minutes, Hunter fired round after round of questions, firstly regarding the attack upon himself and then the stabbing of Mike Sampson. Ronnie Fisher refused to speak.

As the first tape came to an end, Hunter closed his folder and rose from his chair. Leaning across the table, he announced in a formal voice, 'Ronnie Fisher, I am charging you with the attempted murder of Detective Constable Michael Sampson and the attempted murder of myself. Would you like to say anything about that?'

Ronnie Fisher raised his head, gave Hunter a hate-filled stare and growled, 'Fuck you.'

After charging Ronnie Fisher, Hunter and Grace made their way back to the office. They were greeted by Dawn Leggate as they entered.

'Drop what you're doing. You two are coming with me,' she ordered. She told them that the search team thought they may have found where Lucy had been buried. They piled into a spare car and raced up to the scene.

Hunter drove at break-neck speed. At one stage, coming out of a bend, close to the public entrance into the woods, he had to brake sharply to avoid hitting a photographer dashing from between the trees.

'It hasn't taken the press long,' Dawn said, as a posse of them swarmed towards their slowing car. As Hunter weaved a course through, he saw a couple of uniformed officers were doing their level best to corral them back.

Hunter jockeyed the unmarked car between the ruts of a thin winding path for another few hundred yards, until he spotted a caravan of parked and marked Task Force vans and Scenes of Crime vehicles lining the narrow track. There, he stopped.

Quickly suiting themselves into protective coveralls, the three left their car, and tramped the small distance, over damp and springy ground, to where a white forensic tent had been erected. Uniformed officers were putting the finishing touches to the setting up of a sterile perimeter of blue and white crime scene tape.

The team had worked fast, thought Hunter, as he ducked beneath the plastic tape and headed towards the tent. Outside of it, two members of the Forensic Team were sifting loose soil onto a small pile. Inside, three forensic specialists were on their knees, using hand trowels to scrape away lumps of soil. Duncan Wroe, clipboard in hand, was supervising things. They had already removed a good couple of inches of topsoil.

Duncan levelled his gaze at Dawn. 'You've already been updated, ma'am?'

She nodded. 'The task force inspector rang the office half an hour ago. He said that they think they've found a body.'

'It's certainly looking like that, unless someone's buried their pet here.'

Another hour later, soil scraping resulted in a six-inch dip in the earth. The loose dirt had been emptied into plastic containers and carried outside to be sifted for evidence — a slow but necessary job.

Hunter was just checking the time on his watch — his stomach was telling him it was long past lunch-time, when he heard a rustling from the ground. He glanced down, just as a member of the digging team pushed themselves back from the hole.

A young woman's voice announced excitedly, 'I've found something!'

It took the forensic team another two hours to fully unearth the remains of the body, wrapped inside opaque, extra-strong plastic sheeting, the type used by builders.

It took another half an hour of careful handling before they loaded it into a private ambulance so that it could be safely transported to the Medico Legal Centre for a post-mortem.

Professor McCormack had been called out to carry out the examination of the human remains, and by 3.30 p.m., she and her technician, together with Hunter, Dawn and Duncan, had assembled inside the autopsy room at the centre.

The pathologist sliced open the heavy-duty plastic sheeting which contained the cadaver. As she worked, she talked; the in-built microphones picking up everything she said, relaying her words back to state-of-the-art digital voice recording machine.

Duncan was capturing it all on camera.

As Hunter watched and listened, he tensed. He had waited for this moment for so long. He hoped it was Lucy's body.

Carefully, Professor McCormack peeled back the first membrane. There was another layer beneath, and she cut through this and repeated the process. Slowly, the plastic was peeled away and the body revealed. Its flesh was gone and only a dirty brown skeleton remained. A stained, dirty, blue satin, knee-length nightdress covered the torso.

'Definitely female,' announced Professor McCormack. 'And I think this goes a good way to help identify her.' She reached down and hooked a finger around a thin metal chain encircling the corpse's neck, raising it slightly. It was a silver necklace with interlinked lettering. There was no mistaking what the lettering spelled — 'Lucy'.

'Bingo,' said Dawn through gritted teeth.

Professor McCormack smiled. She rested the necklace back onto the bones and then moved a hand down towards the pelvic area, lifted her head and peered over the top of her spectacles. 'And this definitely proves it!' She pointed into the pelvic area and drew a circle in the air. 'This young lady was with child. Not full term, but there's enough bone and cartilage to determine it was over the 24 weeks' stage.' She pursed her lips. 'And I can see straight away the cause of this young lady's death.' She lifted her hand from the pelvis, up towards the skeleton's skull and pointed to the right temple.

Duncan leaned in with his camera.

Hunter stepped to one side to get better sight of what Professor McCormack was pointing to. He got a good view over Duncan's dipped shoulder. An irregular-shaped hole, the size of a two pence piece, had been smashed into the head.

'Fracture of the skull,' Professor McCormack continued, 'and looking at the area of damage, and its position, that would have caused death within a few seconds, or at least would have rendered her immediately unconscious and she would have died within a very short period of time. A lot of force has caused that injury and the object would have had a sharp edge.'

'Like a knife, for instance?' Hunter said.

'Oh no. Something far more substantial than that. A hammer is more likely.'

Hunter was just about to ask another question when the lightbulb went off inside his head. He hadn't spotted its significance at first. His eyes met Dawn's. 'When Peter Blake-Hall made his original statement the day he reported Lucy missing, he described her as going out wearing a yellow smock dress and a fawn cardigan. And the witness Lisa Aldridge, states in her statement that she saw Lucy being dragged into her husband's car and the yellow dress stood out in her description of Lucy. If that's the case, how do we account for this body here wearing a nightdress? The only way that could have happened is if she went home and got changed into it.'

Dawn nodded in agreement. 'And that would fit in with why we found blood at the farmhouse and Jessica's recollections from her nightmares. Peter dragged her into his car that night and brought her back home.'

'She got changed out of her clothes and into her nightie.'

'And they had an argument over her meeting with Daniel Weaver. Remember, he had asked her to run away with him?'

They finished the last sentence together. 'And that's when he struck her and killed her!'

Turning away from the bar, clutching the round of drinks he had just bought, Hunter felt a hand on his shoulder.

'Are we friends?'

He met Dawn's questioning look. 'We were never enemies.'

She removed her hand. 'No, but we didn't get off to a good start, did we? You're in my team now and I just want to know that things between us are good for the future?'

'Things are good, boss.'

She smiled. 'Good. I feel like a drink now.' She pointed to the three drinks he was holding. 'I see you've got yours already.'

He laughed. 'Not all for me. One's for Barry Newstead and the other's for Grace.'

'And I'll stand the next round when those have gone. Everyone's earned this. That was a good result, Hunter. Finding Lucy's body was the icing on the cake.'

'Yes. And it's especially good for Mr and Mrs Hall, and for Jessica. They can finally have closure after all this time.'

Their conversation was interrupted by a shout of 'Mike's here' from Grace.

Hunter looked towards the door. Mike Sampson was being helped through by Tony Bullars. He stepped in gingerly, his right arm clamped to his side, shielding the area where he had been stabbed. Mike raised his free hand in a gesture of thanks and then headed off towards Grace and Barry, who were in the process of dragging seats around a table. Tony followed behind like his minder.

Dawn spoke into Hunter's ear. 'I'll get their drinks.'

Hunter acknowledged her with a nod and then edged his way to his crew. He slid the drinks onto the table, pushed a pint towards Barry and handed Grace a white wine. 'The gaffer's treating you two,' he said to Mike and Tony. Mike seemed be having difficulty getting himself settled in his seat. Hunter turned to him. 'I've told her to get you an orange, you're on antibiotics.'

Mike wagged a finger at him and they all chuckled.

'I came to see you the other night,' Hunter told Mike.

'Oh yeah? I can't remember. Was I sedated?'

'No, you were otherwise engaged.'

Grace piped up, 'What's this then?'

Hunter nodded at Mike. 'Are you going to tell them, or do I let the cat out of the bag?'

Sheepishly, Mike replied, 'You mean me and Janet Dobson.'

Grace's jaw dropped. 'You mean Janet Dobson, as in *Chief Inspector* Janet Dobson?'

Mike affirmed with a quick dip of his head; his face flushed.

'Well, you've kept that a bloody secret. When did that start?' Grace asked.

'Just over a year ago.'

'And you've kept it to yourself all this time?'

'We wanted to keep it to ourselves for a while longer. I've no bloody chance of that now, have I?'

Everyone laughed.

'How did this come about then?' asked Barry.

'I knew her husband. I used to go match-fishing with him. He collapsed and died of a heart attack three years ago while we were out. Nothing I could do to help him. I used to go around and keep her company and we just hit it off.'

With a sardonic grin Barry added, 'You ought to be ashamed of yourself, taking advantage of a vulnerable widow.'

Grace gave Barry a friendly punch to the arm. 'You leave him alone. I think it's wonderful.' She raised her glass. 'I hope you'll be very happy.'

Hunter flopped back against his seat. The warm atmosphere, the relaxing effects of the beer and lack of sleep over the past few weeks had suddenly all taken their toll. As his team's banter drifted into the background, he was thinking about home.

He finished his beer and checked the time, reaching into his pocket for his car keys. He'd spend a couple of hours with Beth and the boys, have a warm bath and then he'd collapse in his bed.

It was always the same at the end of an investigation.

A NOTE TO THE READER

Dear Reader,

I am a plotter and planner when it comes to writing, and generally have a beginning, middle and end drafted before making a start. The ending of this book, however, changed dramatically after bumping into a former colleague in the pub. The colleague in question was attached to Task Force and during our chat he revealed that he and his team had been involved in the search for a doctor who had been missing for three weeks and it was suspected he had been murdered and buried in woodland. As he unveiled how his body had been discovered that day, it not only changed my ending, but gave me my prologue as well. I have former PC, Steve Cook, to thank for this.

I also have former Detective Sergeant Ian Harding, who ran South Yorkshire's Cold Case Unit, to thank as well. I contacted Ian prior to beginning the book, telling him the storyline I had planned and seeking his guidance. Without hesitation, he invited me to the cold case office for a cuppa and to talk it through. As he introduced me to his unit, I immediately discovered I had worked with over half the detective's based there and knew the others from previous investigations. Not only did I get the background to this case but he provided me with their working practices and also gave me some great quotes that I just had to use.

Finally, I also want to give special mention to CSI Supervisor, Stuart Sosnowski. Stuart is a good friend and a great asset to me as a writer. No matter how busy he is he never lets me down, no matter how many crime scenes I conjure up in my imagination for him to process.

I'd love to think that readers will embrace Hunter Kerr and his casework and one of the ways you can let me know that is by placing a review on **Amazon** or **Goodreads**. And, if you want to contact me, then please do so via **my website**.

Thank you for reading.
Michael Fowler

www.mjfowler.co.uk

Sapere Books is an exciting new publisher of brilliant fiction and popular history.

To find out more about our latest releases and our monthly bargain books visit our website:
saperebooks.com

Printed in Great Britain
by Amazon